D1576313

SPECIAL MESSAGE TO READERS

This book is published by

THE ULVERSCROFT FOUNDATION,

a registered charity in the U.K., No. 264873

The Foundation was established in 1974 to provide funds to help towards research, diagnosis and treatment of eye diseases. Below are a few examples of contributions made by THE ULVERSCROFT FOUNDATION:

★ A new Children's Assessment Unit at Moorfield's Hospital, London.

★ Twin operating theatres at the Western Ophthalmic Hospital, London.

★ The Frederick Thorpe Ulverscroft Chair of Ophthalmology at the University of Leicester.

★ Eye Laser equipment to various eye hospitals.

If you would like to help further the work of the Foundation by making a donation or leaving a legacy, every contribution, no matter how small, is received with gratitude. Please write for details to:

THE ULVERSCROFT FOUNDATION,
The Green, Bradgate Road, Anstey,
Leicestershire, LE7 7FU. England.
Telephone: (0533) 364325

I've travelled the world twice over,
Met the famous: saints and sinners,
Poets and artists, kings and queens,
Old stars and hopeful beginners,
I've been where no-one's been before,
Learned secrets from writers and cooks
All with one library ticket
To the wonderful world of books.

© JANICE JAMES.

GONE WITH THE WIND
(Book I)

This drama of the American Civil War portrays the soul of a people mortally divided, living through the events of a cataclysmic era. But although the Civil War and its aftermath provides the background, the story concerns the lives and loves of many unforgettable characters—above all the beautiful, ruthless Scarlet O'Hara and her tumultuous love affair with Rhett Butler.

Margaret Mitchell was born in Atlanta, Georgia, in 1902 and died there after a car accident in 1949. GONE WITH THE WIND, her only book, took her nearly eight years to write.

MARGARET MITCHELL

GONE WITH THE WIND

Book I

Complete and Unabridged

CHARNWOOD
Leicester

First Charnwood Edition
published June 1990
by arrangement with
Macmillan London Ltd.

Copyright © 1936 by Margaret Mitchell
All rights reserved

British Library CIP Data

Mitchell, Margaret, *1900–1949*
Gone with the wind.—Large print ed.—
1
Charnwood library series
I. Title
8134'.52[F]

ISBN 0-7089-8547-5

Published by
F. A. Thorpe (Publishing) Ltd.
Anstey, Leicestershire
Set by Rowland Phototypesetting Ltd.
Bury St. Edmunds, Suffolk
Printed and bound in Great Britain by
T. J. Press (Padstow) Ltd., Padstow, Cornwall

To

J.R.M.

Part One

Part One

1

SCARLETT O'HARA was not beautiful, but men seldom realized it when caught by her charm as the Tarleton twins were. In her face were too sharply blended the delicate features of her mother, a Coast aristocrat of French descent, and the heavy ones of her florid Irish father. But it was an arresting face, pointed of chin, square of jaw. Her eyes were pale green without a touch of hazel, starred with bristly black lashes and slightly tilted at the ends. Above them, her thick black brows slanted upward, cutting a startling oblique line in her magnolia-white skin—that skin so prized by Southern women and so carefully guarded with bonnets, veils and mittens against hot Georgia suns.

Seated with Stuart and Brent Tarleton in the cool shade of the porch of Tara, her father's plantation, that bright April afternoon of 1861, she made a pretty picture. Her new green flowered-muslin dress spread its twelve yards of billowing material over her hoops and exactly matched the flat-heeled green morocco slippers her father had recently brought her from Atlanta. The dress set off to perfection the seventeen-inch waist, the smallest in three counties, and the tightly fitting basque showed breasts well matured for her sixteen years. But for all the modesty of her spreading skirts, the demureness of hair netted smoothly into a chignon and the quietness of

3

small white hands folded in her lap, her true self was poorly concealed. The green eyes in the carefully sweet face were turbulent, wilful, lusty with life, distinctly at variance with her decorous demeanour. Her manners had been imposed upon her by her mother's gentle admonitions and the sterner discipline of her mammy; her eyes were her own.

On either side of her, the twins lounged easily in their chairs, squinting at the sunlight through tall mint-garnished glasses as they laughed and talked, their long legs, booted to the knee and thick with saddle muscles, crossed negligently. Nineteen years old, six feet two inches tall, long of bone and hard of muscle, with sunburned faces and deep auburn hair, their eyes merry and arrogant, their bodies clothed in identical blue coats and mustard-coloured breeches, they were as much alike as two bolls of cotton.

Outside, the late afternoon sun slanted down in the yard, throwing into gleaming brightness the dogwood trees that were solid masses of white blossoms against the background of new green. The twins' horses were hitched in the driveway, big animals, red as their masters' hair; and around the horses' legs quarrelled the pack of lean, nervous possum hounds that accompanied Stuart and Brent wherever they went. A little aloof, as became an aristocrat, lay a black-spotted carriage dog, muzzle on paws, patiently waiting for the boys to go home to supper.

Between the hounds and the horses and the twins there was a kinship deeper than that of their constant companionship. They were all healthy,

4

thoughtless young animals, sleek, graceful, high-spirited, the boys as mettlesome as the horses they rode, mettlesome and dangerous but, withal, sweet-tempered to those who knew how to handle them.

Although born to the ease of plantation life, waited on hand and foot since infancy, the faces of the three on the porch were neither slack nor soft. They had the vigour and alertness of country people who have spent all their lives in the open and troubled their heads very little with dull things in books. Life in the north Georgia county of Clayton was still new and, according to the standards of Augusta, Savannah and Charleston, a little crude. The more sedate and older sections of the South looked down their noses at the up-country Georgians, but here in north Georgia, a lack of the niceties of classical education carried no shame, provided a man was smart in the things that mattered. And raising good cotton, riding well, shooting straight, dancing lightly, squiring the ladies with elegance and carrying one's liquor like a gentleman were the things that mattered.

In these accomplishments the twins excelled, and they were equally outstanding in their notorious inability to learn anything contained between the covers of books. Their family had more money, more horses, more slaves than anyone else in the County, but the boys had less grammar than most of their poor Cracker neighbours.

It was for this precise reason that Stuart and Brent were idling on the porch of Tara this April afternoon. They had just been expelled from the

5

University of Georgia, the fourth university that had thrown them out in two years; and their older brothers, Tom and Boyd, had come home with them, because they refused to remain at an institution where the twins were not welcome. Stuart and Brent considered their latest expulsion a fine joke, and Scarlett, who had not willingly opened a book since leaving the Fayetteville Female Academy the year before, thought it just as amusing as they did.

"I know you two don't care about being expelled, or Tom either," she said. "But what about Boyd? He's kind of set on getting an education, and you two have pulled him out of the University of Virginia and Alabama and South Carolina and now Georgia. He'll never get finished at this rate."

"Oh, he can read law in Judge Parmalee's office over in Fayetteville," answered Brent carelessly. "Besides, it don't matter much. We'd have had to come home before the term was out anyway."

"Why?"

"The war, goose! The war's going to start any day, and you don't suppose any of us would stay in college with a war going on, do you?"

"You know there isn't going to be any war," said Scarlett, bored. "It's all just talk. Why, Ashley Wilkes and his father told Pa just last week that our commissioners in Washington would come to—to—an—amicable agreement with Mr. Lincoln about the Confederacy. And anyway, the Yankees are too scared of us to fight. There won't be any war, and I'm tired of hearing about it."

"Not going to be any war!" cried the twins indignantly, as though they had been defrauded.

"Why, honey, of course there's going to be a war," said Stuart. "The Yankees may be scared of us, but after the way General Beauregard shelled them out of Fort Sumter day before yesterday, they'll have to fight or stand branded as cowards before the whole world. Why, the Confederacy—"

Scarlett made a mouth of bored impatience.

"If you say 'war' just once more, I'll go in the house and shut the door. I've never gotten so tired of any one word in my life as 'war', unless it's 'secession'. Pa talks war morning, noon and night, and all the gentlemen who come to see him shout about Fort Sumter and States' Rights and Abe Lincoln till I get so bored I could scream! And that's all the boys talk about, too, that and their old Troop. There hasn't been any fun at any party this spring because the boys can't talk about anything else. I'm mighty glad Georgia waited till after Christmas before it seceded or it would have ruined the Christmas parties, too. If you say 'war' again, I'll go in the house."

She meant what she said, for she could never long endure any conversation of which she was not the chief subject. But she smiled when she spoke, consciously deepening her dimple and fluttering her bristly black lashes as swiftly as butterflies' wings. The boys were enchanted, as she had intended them to be, and they hastened to apologize for boring her. They thought none the less of her for her lack of interest. Indeed, they thought more. War was men's business, not

7

ladies', and they took her attitude as evidence of her femininity.

Having manoeuvred them away from the boring subject of war, she went back with interest to their immediate situation.

"What did your mother say about you two being expelled again?"

The boys looked uncomfortable, recalling their mother's conduct three months ago when they had come home, by request, from the University of Virginia.

"Well," said Stuart, "she hasn't had a chance to say anything yet. Tom and us left home early this morning before she got up, and Tom's laying out over at the Fontaines' while we came over here."

"Didn't she say anything when you got home last night?"

"We were in luck last night. Just before we got home that new stallion Ma got in Kentucky last month was brought in, and the place was in a stew. The big brute—he's a grand horse, Scarlett; you must tell your pa to come over and see him right away—he'd already bitten a hunk out of his groom on the way down here and he'd trampled two of Ma's darkies who met the train at Jonesboro. And just before we got home, he'd about kicked the stable down and half-killed Strawberry, Ma's old stallion. When we got home, Ma was out in the stable with a sackful of sugar smoothing him down and doing it mighty well, too. The darkies were hanging from the rafters, popeyed, they were so scared, but Ma was talking to the horse like he was folks and he was eating out of her hand. There ain't nobody like Ma with a horse. And when she saw us she said: 'In Heaven's name, what are you four doing home again? You're worse than the plagues of Egypt!' And then the horse began snorting and rearing and she said: 'Get out of here! Can't you see he's nervous, the big darling? I'll tend to you four in the morning!' So we went to bed, and this morning we got away before she could catch us and left Boyd to handle her."

"Do you suppose she'll hit Boyd?" Scarlett, like the rest of the County, could never get used to the way small Mrs. Tarleton bullied her grown sons and laid her riding-crop on their backs if the occasion seemed to warrant it.

Beatrice Tarleton was a busy woman, having on her hands not only a large cotton plantation, a hundred negroes and eight children, but the largest horse-breeding farm in the state as well. She was hot-tempered and easily plagued by the frequent scrapes of her four sons, and while no one was permitted to whip a horse or a slave, she felt that a lick now and then didn't do the boys any harm.

"Of course she won't hit Boyd. She never did beat Boyd much because he's the oldest and besides he's the runt of the litter," said Stuart, proud of his six feet two. "That's why we left him at home to explain things to her. God'lmighty, Ma ought to stop licking us! We're nineteen and Tom's twenty-one, and she acts like we're six years old."

"Will your mother ride the new horse to the Wilkes barbecue to-morrow?"

"She wants to, but Pa says he's too dangerous. And, anyway, the girls won't let her. They said they were going to have her go to one party at least like a lady, riding in the carriage."

"I hope it doesn't rain to-morrow," said Scarlett. "It's rained nearly every day for a week. There's nothing worse than a barbecue turned into an indoor picnic."

"Oh, it'll be clear to-morrow and hot as June," said Stuart. "Look at that sunset. I never saw one redder. You can always tell weather by sunsets."

They looked out across the endless acres of Gerald O'Hara's newly ploughed cotton fields toward the red horizon. Now that the sun was setting in a welter of crimson behind the hills across the Flint River, the warmth of the April day was ebbing into a faint but balmy chill.

Spring had come early that year, with warm quick rains and sudden frothing of pink peach blossoms and dogwood dappling with white stars the dark river swamp and far-off hills. Already the ploughing was nearly finished, and the bloody glory of the sunset coloured the fresh-cut furrows of red Georgia clay to even redder hues. The moist hungry earth, waiting upturned for the cotton seeds, showed pinkish on the sandy tops of furrows, vermilion and scarlet and maroon where shadows lay along the sides of the trenches. The whitewashed brick plantation house seemed an island set in a wild red sea, a sea of spiralling, curving, crescent billows petrified suddenly at the moment when the pink-tipped waves were breaking into surf. For here were no long, straight furrows, such as could be seen in the yellow clay fields of the flat middle Georgia country or in the lush black earth of the coastal plantations. The rolling foothill country of north Georgia was ploughed in a million curves to keep the rich earth from washing down into the river bottoms.

It was a savagely red land, blood-coloured after rains, brick-dust in droughts, the best cotton land in the world. It was a pleasant land of white houses, peaceful ploughed fields and sluggish yellow rivers, but a land of contrasts, of brightest sun-glare and densest shade. The plantation clearings and miles of cotton fields smiled up to a warm sun, placid, complacent. At their edges rose the virgin forests, dark and cool even in the hottest noons, mysterious, a little sinister, the soughing pines seeming to wait with an age-old patience, to threaten with soft sighs: "Be careful! Be careful! We had you once. We can take you back again."

To the ears of the three on the porch came the sounds of hooves, the jingling of harness chains and the shrill careless laughter of negro voices, as the field hands and mules came in from the fields. From within the house floated the soft voice of Scarlett's mother, Ellen O'Hara, as she called to the little black girl who carried her basket of keys. The high-pitched childish voice answered "Yas'm," and there were sounds of footsteps going out the back way toward the smokehouse where Ellen would ration out the food to the home-coming hands. There was the click of china and the rattle of silver as Pork, the valet-butler of Tara, laid the table for supper.

At these last sounds, the twins realized it was time they were starting home. But they were loath to face their mother and they lingered on the porch of Tara, momentarily expecting Scarlett to give them an invitation to supper.

"Look, Scarlett. About tomorrow," said Brent. "Just because we've been away and didn't know about the barbecue and the ball, that's no reason why we shouldn't get plenty of dances to-morrow night. You haven't promised them all, have you?"

"Well, I have! How did I know you all would be home? I couldn't risk being a wallflower just waiting on you two."

"You a wallflower!" The boys laughed uproariously.

"Look, honey. You've got to give me the first waltz and Stu the last one and you've got to eat supper with us. We'll sit on the stair landing like we did at the last ball and get Mammy Jincy to come tell our fortunes again."

"I don't like Mammy Jincy's fortunes. You know she said I was going to marry a gentleman with jet-black hair and a long black moustache, and I don't like black-haired gentlemen."

"You like 'em red-headed, don't you, honey?" grinned Brent. "Now, come on, promise us all the waltzes and the supper."

"If you'll promise, we'll tell you a secret," said Stuart.

"What?" cried Scarlett, alert as a child at the word.

"Is it what we heard yesterday in Atlanta, Stu? If it is, you know we promised not to tell."

"Well, Miss Pitty told us."

"Miss Who?"

"You know, Ashley Wilkes' cousin who lives in Atlanta, Miss Pittypat Hamilton—Charles and Melanie Hamilton's aunt."

"I do, and a sillier old lady I never met in all my life."

"Well, when we were in Atlanta yesterday, waiting for the home train, her carriage went by the depot and she stopped and talked to us, and she told us there was going to be an engagement announced to-morrow night at the Wilkes ball."

"Oh, I know about that," said Scarlett in disappointment. "That silly nephew of hers, Charlie Hamilton, and Honey Wilkes. Everybody's known for years that they'd get married some time, even if he did seem kind of lukewarm about it."

"Do you think he's silly?" questioned Brent. "Last Christmas you sure let him buzz round you plenty."

"I couldn't help him buzzing," Scarlett shrugged negligently. "I think he's an awful sissy."

"Besides, it isn't his engagement that's going to be announced," said Stuart triumphantly. "It's Ashley's to Charlie's sister, Miss Melanie!"

Scarlett's face did not change but her lips went white—like a person who has received a stunning blow without warning and who, in the first moments of shock, does not realize what has happened. So still was her face as she stared at Stuart that he, never analytic, took it for granted that she was merely surprised and very interested.

"Miss Pitty told us they hadn't intended

13

announcing it till next year, because Miss Melly hasn't been very well; but with all the war talk going around, everybody in both families thought it would be better to get married real soon. So it's to be announced to-morrow night at the supper intermission. Now, Scarlett, we've told you the secret, so you've got to promise to eat supper with us."

"Of course I will," Scarlett said automatically.

"And all the waltzes?"

"All."

"You're sweet! I'll bet the other boys will be hopping mad."

"Let 'em be mad," said Brent. "We two can handle 'em. Look, Scarlett. Sit with us at the barbecue in the morning."

"What?"

Stuart repeated his request.

"Of course."

The twins looked at each other jubilantly but with some surprise. Although they considered themselves Scarlett's favoured suitors, they had never before gained tokens of this favour so easily. Usually she made them beg and plead, while she put them off, refusing to give a Yes or No answer, laughing if they sulked, growing cool if they became angry. And here she had practically promised them the whole of to-morrow— seats by her at the barbecue, all the waltzes (and they'd see to it that the dances were all waltzes!) and the supper intermission. That was worth getting expelled from the university.

Filled with new enthusiasm by their success, they lingered on, talking about the barbecue and the ball and Ashley Wilkes and Melanie Hamilton, interrupting each other, making jokes and laughing at them, hinting broadly for invitations to supper. Some time had passed before they realized that Scarlett was having very little to say. The atmosphere had somehow changed. Just how, the twins did not know, but the fine glow had gone out of the afternoon. Scarlett seemed to be paying little attention to what they said, although she made the correct answers. Sensing something they could not understand, baffled and annoyed by it, the twins struggled along for a while, and then rose reluctantly, looking at their watches.

The sun was low across the new-ploughed fields and the tall woods across the river were looming blackly in silhouette. Chimney swallows were darting swiftly across the yard, and chickens, ducks and turkeys were waddling and strutting and straggling in from the fields.

Stuart bellowed: "Jeems!" And after an interval a tall black boy of their own age ran breathlessly around the house and out toward the tethered horses. Jeems was their body-servant and, like the dogs, accompanied them everywhere. He had been their childhood playmate and had been given to the twins for their own on their tenth birthday. At the sight of him, the Tarleton hounds rose up out of the red dust and stood waiting expectantly for their masters. The boys bowed, shook hands and told Scarlett they'd be over at the Wilkeses' early in the morning, waiting for her. Then they were off down the walk at a rush, mounted their horses and,

15

followed by Jeems, went down the avenue of cedars at a gallop, waving their hats and yelling back to her.

When they had rounded the curve of the dusty road that hid them from Tara, Brent drew his horse to a stop under a clump of dogwood. Stuart halted, too, and the darky boy pulled up a few paces behind them. The horses, feeling slack reins, stretched down their necks to crop the tender spring grass, and the patient hounds lay down again in the soft red dust and looked up longingly at the chimney swallows circling in the gathering dusk. Brent's wide ingenuous face was puzzled and mildly indignant.

"Look," he said. "Don't it look to you like she would of asked us to stay for supper?"

"I thought she would," said Stuart. "I kept waiting for her to do it, but she didn't. What do you make of it?"

"I don't make anything of it. But it just looks to me like she might of. After all, it's our first day home and she hasn't seen us in quite a spell. And we had lots more things to tell her."

"It looked to me like she was mighty glad to see us when we came."

"I thought so, too."

"And then, about a half-hour ago, she got kind of quiet, like she had a headache."

"I noticed that but I didn't pay it any mind then. What do you suppose ailed her?"

"I dunno. Do you suppose we said something that made her mad?"

They both thought for a minute.

"I can't think of anything. Besides, when

16

Scarlett gets mad, everybody knows it. She don't hold herself in like some girls do."

"Yes, that's what I like about her. She don't go around being cold and hateful when she's mad —she tells you about it. But it was something we did or said that made her shut up talking and look sort of sick. I could swear she was glad to see us when we came and was aiming to ask us to supper."

"You don't suppose it's because we got expelled?"

"Hell, no! Don't be a fool. She laughed like everything when we told her about it. And besides Scarlett don't set any more store by book learning than we do."

Brent turned in the saddle and called to the negro groom.

"Jeems!"

"Suh?"

"You heard what we were talking to Miss Scarlett about?"

"Nawsuh, Mist' Brent! Huccome you think Ah be spyin' on w'ite folks?"

"Spying, my God! You darkies know everything that goes on. Why, you liar, I saw you with my own eyes sidle round the corner of the porch and squat in the cape jessamine bush by the wall. Now, did you hear us say anything that might have made Miss Scarlett mad—or hurt her feelings?"

Thus appealed to, Jeems gave up further pretence of not having overheard the conversation and furrowed his black brow.

"Nawsuh, Ah din' notice y'all say anything ter

mek her mad. Look ter me lak she sho glad ter see you an' sho had missed you, an' she cheep along happy as a bird, tell 'bout de time y'all got ter talkin' 'bout Mist' Ashley an' Miss Melly Hamilton gittin' mah'ied. Den she quiet down lak a bird w'en de hawk fly ober."

The twins looked at each other and nodded, but without comprehension.

"Jeems is right. But I don't see why," said Stuart. "My Lord! Ashley don't mean anything to her, 'cept a friend. She's not crazy about him. It's us she's crazy about."

Brent nodded an agreement.

"But do you suppose," he said, "that maybe Ashley hadn't told her he was going to announce it to-morrow night and she was mad at him for not telling her, an old friend, before he told everybody else? Girls set a big store on knowing such things first."

"Well, maybe. But what if he hadn't told her it was to-morrow? It was supposed to be a secret and a surprise, and a man's got a right to keep his own engagement quiet, hasn't he? We wouldn't have known it if Miss Melly's aunt hadn't let it out. But Scarlett must have known he was going to marry Miss Melly some time. Why, we've known it for years. The Wilkes and Hamiltons always marry their own cousins. Everybody knew he'd probably marry her some day, just like Honey Wilkes is going to marry Miss Melly's brother, Charles."

"Well, I give it up. But I'm sorry she didn't ask us to supper. I swear I don't want to go home and listen to Ma take on about us being expelled. It isn't as if this was the first time."

"Maybe Boyd will have smoothed her down by now. You know what a slick talker that little varmint is. You know he always can smooth her down."

"Yes, he can do it, but it takes Boyd time. He has to talk around in circles till Ma gets so confused that she gives up and tells him to save his voice for his law practice. But he ain't had time to get good started yet. Why, I'll bet you Ma is still so excited about the new horse that she'll never even realize we're home again till she sits down to supper to-night and sees Boyd. And before supper is over she'll be going strong and breathing fire. And it'll be ten o'clock before Boyd gets a chance to tell her that it wouldn't have been honourable for any of us to stay in college after the way the Chancellor talked to you and me. And it'll be midnight before he gets her turned around to where she's so mad at the Chancellor she'll be asking Boyd why he didn't shoot him. No, we can't go home till after midnight."

The twins looked at each other glumly. They were completely fearless of wild horses, shooting affrays and the indignation of their neighbours, but they had a wholesome fear of their red-haired mother's outspoken remarks and the riding-crop that she did not scruple to lay across their breeches.

"Well, look," said Brent. "Let's go over to the Wilkes. Ashley and the girls'll be glad to have us for supper."

Stuart looked a little discomforted.

19

"No, don't let's go there. They'll be in a stew getting ready for the barbecue to-morrow and besides—"

"Oh, I forgot about that," said Brent hastily. "No, don't let's go there."

They clucked to their horses and rode along in silence for a while, a flush of embarrassment on Stuart's brown cheeks. Until the previous summer, Stuart had courted India Wilkes with the approbation of both families and the entire County. The County felt that perhaps the cool and contained India Wilkes would have a quieting effect on him. They fervently hoped so, at any rate. And Stuart might have made the match, but Brent had not been satisfied. Brent liked India but he thought her mighty plain and tame, and he simply could not fall in love with her himself to keep Stuart company. That was the first time the twins' interests had ever diverged, and Brent was resentful of his brother's attentions to a girl who seemed to him not at all remarkable.

Then, last summer at a political speaking in a grove of oak trees at Jonesboro, they both suddenly became aware of Scarlett O'Hara. They had known her for years, and, since their childhood, she had been a favourite playmate, for she could ride horses and climb trees almost as well as they. But now to their amazement she had become a grown-up young lady and quite the most charming one in all the world.

They noticed for the first time how her green eyes danced, how deep her dimples were when she laughed, how tiny her hands and feet and what a small waist she had. Their clever remarks sent her into merry peals of laughter and, inspired by the thought that she considered them a remarkable pair, they fairly outdid themselves.

It was a memorable day in the life of the twins. Thereafter, when they talked it over, they always wondered just why they had failed to notice Scarlett's charms before. They never arrived at the correct answer, which was that Scarlett on that day had decided to make them notice. She was constitutionally unable to endure any man being in love with any woman not herself, and the sight of India Wilkes and Stuart at the speaking had been too much for her predatory nature. Not content with Stuart alone, she had set her cap for Brent as well, and with a thoroughness that overwhelmed the two of them.

Now they were both in love with her, and India Wilkes and Letty Munroe, from Lovejoy, whom Brent had been half-heartedly courting, were far in the back of their minds. Just what the loser would do, should Scarlett accept either one of them, the twins did not ask. They would cross that bridge when they came to it. For the present they were quite satisfied to be in accord again about one girl, for they had no jealousies between them. It was a situation which interested the neighbours and annoyed their mother, who had no liking for Scarlett.

"It will serve you right if that sly piece does accept one of you," she said. "Or maybe she'll accept both of you, and then you'll have to move to Utah, if the Mormons'll have you—which I doubt. . . . All that bothers me is that some one of these days you're both going to get lickered up

21

and jealous of each other about that two-faced, little, green-eyed baggage, and you'll shoot each other. But that might not be a bad idea either."

Since the day of the speaking, Stuart had been uncomfortable in India's presence. Not that India ever reproached him or even indicated by look or gesture that she was aware of his abruptly changed allegiance. She was too much of a lady. But Stuart felt guilty and ill at ease with her. He knew he had made India love him and he knew that she still loved him and, deep in his heart, he had the feeling that he had not played the gentleman. He still liked her tremendously and respected her for her cool good breeding, her book learning and all the sterling qualities she possessed. But, damn it, she was just so pallid and uninteresting and always the same, beside Scarlett's bright and changeable charm. You always knew where you stood with India and you never had the slightest notion with Scarlett. That was enough to drive a man to distraction, but it had its charm.

"Well, let's go over to Cade Calvert's and have supper. Scarlett said Cathleen was home from Charleston. Maybe she'll have some news about Fort Sumter that we haven't heard."

"Not Cathleen. I'll lay you two to one she didn't even know the fort was out there in the harbour, much less that it was full of Yankees until we shelled them out. All she'll know about is the balls she went to and the beaux she collected."

"Well, it's fun to hear her gabble. And it'll be somewhere to hide out till Ma has gone to bed."

"Well, hell! I like Cathleen and she is fun and I'd like to hear about Caro Rhett and the rest of the Charleston folks; but I'm damned if I can stand sitting through another meal with that Yankee stepmother of hers."

"Don't be too hard on her, Stuart. She means well."

"I'm not being hard on her. I feel sorry for her, but I don't like people I've got to feel sorry for. And she fusses around so much, trying to do the right thing and make you feel at home, that she always manages to say and do just exactly the wrong thing. She gives me the fidgets! And she thinks Southerners are wild barbarians. She even told Ma so. She's afraid of Southerners. Whenever we're there she always looks scared to death. She reminds me of a skinny hen perched on a chair, her eyes kind of bright and blank and scared, all ready to flap and squawk at the slightest move anybody makes."

"Well, you can't blame her. You did shoot Cade in the leg."

"Well, I was lickered up or I wouldn't have done it," said Stuart. "And Cade never had any hard feelings. Neither did Cathleen or Raiford or Mr. Calvert. It was just that Yankee stepmother who squalled and said I was a wild barbarian and decent people weren't safe around uncivilized Southerners."

"Well, you can't blame her. She's a Yankee and ain't got very good manners; and, after all, you did shoot him and he is her stepson."

"Well, hell! That's no excuse for insulting me! You are Ma's own blood son, but did she take on

23

that time Tony Fontaine shot you in the leg? No, she just sent for old Doc Fontaine to dress it and asked the doctor what ailed Tony's aim. Said she guessed licker was spoiling his marksmanship. Remember how mad that made Tony?"

Both boys yelled with laughter.

"Ma's a card!" said Brent with loving approval. "You can always count on her to do the right thing and not embarrass you in front of folks."

"Yes, but she's mighty liable to talk embarrassing in front of Father and the girls when we get home to-night," said Stuart gloomily. "Look, Brent, I guess this means we don't go to Europe. You know Mother said if we got expelled from another college we couldn't have our Grand Tour."

"Well, hell! We don't care, do we? What is there to see in Europe? I'll bet those foreigners can't show us a thing we haven't got right here in Georgia. I'll bet their horses aren't as fast or their girls as pretty, and I know damn well they haven't got any rye whisky that can touch Father's."

"Ashley Wilkes said they had an awful lot of scenery and music. Ashley liked Europe. He's always talking about it."

"Well—you know how the Wilkes are. They are kind of queer about music and books and scenery. Mother says it's because their grandfather came from Virginia. She says Virginians set quite a store by such things."

"They can have 'em. Give me a good horse to ride and some good licker to drink and a good girl to court and a bad girl to have fun with and

24

anybody can have their Europe. . . . What do we care about missing the Tour? Suppose we were in Europe now, with the war coming on? We couldn't get home soon enough. I'd heap rather go to a war than go to Europe."

"So would I, any day. . . . Look, Brent! I know where we can go for supper. Let's ride across the swamp to Able Wynder's place and tell him we're all four home again and ready for drill."

"That's an idea!" cried Brent with enthusiasm. "And we can hear all the news of the Troop and find out what colour they finally decided on for the uniforms."

"If it's Zouave, I'm damned if I'll go in the Troop. I'd feel like a sissy in those baggy red pants. They look like ladies' red flannel drawers to me."

"Is y'all aimin' ter go ter Mist' Wynder's? 'Cause ef you is, you ain' gwine git much supper," said Jeems. "Dey cook done died, an' dey ain' bought a new one. Dey got a fe'el han' cookin', an' de niggers tells me she is de wustest cook in de state."

"Good God! Why don't they buy another cook?"

"Huccome po' w'ite trash buy any niggers? Dey ain' never owned mo'n fo' at de mostes'."

There was frank contempt in Jeems' voice. His own social status was assured because the Tarletons owned a hundred negroes and, like all slaves of large planters, he looked down on small farmers whose slaves were few.

"I'm going to beat your hide off for that," cried

Stuart fiercely. "Don't you call Able Wynder 'po' white. Sure he's poor, but he ain't trash; and I'm damned if I'll have any man, darky or white throwing off on him. There ain't a better man in this County, or why else did the Troop elect him lieutenant?"

"Ah ain' never figgered dat out, mahseff," replied Jeems, undisturbed by his master's scowl. "Look ter me lak dey'd 'lect all de awficers frum rich gempmum, 'stead of swamp trash."

"He ain't trash! Do you mean to compare him with real white trash like the Slatterys? Able just ain't rich. He's a small farmer, not a big planter, and if the boys thought enough of him to elect him lieutenant, then it's not for any darky to talk impudent about him. The Troop knows what it's doing."

The troop of cavalry had been organized three months before, the very day that Georgia seceded from the Union, and since then the recruits had been whistling for war. The outfit was as yet unnamed, though not for want of suggestions. Everyone had his own idea on that subject and was loath to relinquish it, just as everyone had ideas about the colour and cut of the uniforms. "Clayton Wild Cats", "Fire Eaters", "North Georgia Hussars", "Zouaves", "The Inland Rifles" (although the Troop was to be armed with pistols, sabres and bowie knives, and not with rifles), "The Clayton Grays", "The Blood and Thunderers", "The Rough and Readys", all had their adherents. Until matters were settled, everyone referred to the organization as the Troop and, despite the high-sounding name finally

26

adopted, they were known to the end of their usefulness simply as "The Troop".

The officers were elected by the members, for no one in the County had had any military experience except a few veterans of the Mexican and Seminole wars and, besides, the Troop would have scorned a veteran as a leader if they had not personally liked him and trusted him. Everyone liked the four Tarleton boys and the three Fontaines, but regretfully refused to elect them, because the Tarletons got lickered up too quickly and liked to skylark, and the Fontaines had such quick, murderous tempers. Ashley Wilkes was elected captain, because he was the best rider in the County and because his cool head was counted on to keep some semblance of order. Raiford Calvert was made first lieutenant, because everybody liked Raif, and Able Wynder, son of a swamp trapper, himself a small farmer, was elected second lieutenant.

Able was a shrewd, grave giant, illiterate, kind of heart, older than the other boys and with as good or better manners in the presence of ladies. There was little snobbery in the Troop. Too many of their fathers and grandfathers had come up to wealth from the small farmer class for that. Moreover, Able was the best shot in the Troop, a real sharpshooter who could pick out the eye of a squirrel at seventy-five yards, and, too, he knew all about living outdoors, building fires in the rain, tracking animals and finding water. The Troop bowed to real worth and moreover, because they liked him, they made him an officer. He bore the honour gravely and with no untoward conceit, as though it were only his due. But the planters' ladies and the planters' slaves could not overlook the fact that he was not born a gentleman, even if their men folks could.

In the beginning, the Troop had been recruited exclusively from the sons of planters, a gentleman's outfit, each man supplying his own horse, arms, equipment, uniform and body-servant. But rich planters were few in the young county of Clayton, and, in order to muster a full-strength troop, it had been necessary to raise more recruits among the sons of small farmers, hunters in the backwoods, swamp trappers, Crackers and, in a very few cases, even poor whites, if they were above the average of their class.

These latter young men were as anxious to fight the Yankees, should war come, as were their richer neighbours; but the delicate question of money arose. Few small farmers owned horses. They carried on their farm operations with mules and they had no surplus of these, seldom more than four. The mules could not be spared to go off to war, even if they had been acceptable for the Troop, which they emphatically were not. As for the poor whites, they considered themselves well off if they owned one mule. The backwoods folks and the swamp dwellers owned neither horses nor mules. They lived entirely off the produce of their lands and the game in the swamp, conducting their business generally by the barter system and seldom seeing five dollars in cash a year, and horses and uniforms were out of their reach. But they were as fiercely proud in their poverty as the planters were in their wealth, and they would accept nothing that smacked of charity from their rich neighbours. So, to save the feelings of all and to bring the Troop up to full strength, Scarlett's father, John Wilkes, Buck Munroe, Jim Tarleton, Hugh Calvert, in fact every large planter in the County with the one exception of Angus MacIntosh, had contributed money to completely outfit the Troop, horse and man. The upshot of the matter was that every planter agreed to pay for equipping his own sons and a certain number of the others, but the manner of handling the arrangements was such that the less wealthy members of the outfit could accept horses and uniforms without offence to their honour.

The Troop met twice a week in Jonesboro to drill and to pray for the war to begin. Arrangements had not yet been completed for obtaining the full quota of horses, but those who had horses performed what they imagined to be cavalry manoeuvres in the field behind the courthouse, kicked up a great deal of dust, yelled themselves hoarse and waved the Revolutionary-war swords that had been taken down from parlour walls. Those who, as yet, had no horses sat on the kerb in front of Bullard's store and watched their mounted comrades, chewed tobacco and told yarns. Or else engaged in shooting matches. There was no need to teach any of the men to shoot. Most Southerners were born with guns in their hands, and lives spent in hunting had made marksmen of them all.

From planters' homes and swamp cabins, a

varied array of firearms came to each muster. There were long squirrel guns that had been new when first the Alleghenies were crossed, old muzzle-loaders that had claimed many an Indian when Georgia was new, horse pistols that had seen service in 1812, in the Seminole wars and in Mexico, silver-mounted duelling pistols, pocket derringers, double-barrelled hunting pieces and handsome new rifles of English make with shining stocks of fine wood.

Drill always ended in the saloons of Jonesboro, and by nightfall so many fights had broken out that the officers were hard put to ward off casualties until the Yankees could inflict them. It was during one of these brawls that Stuart Tarleton had shot Cade Calvert and Tony Fontaine had shot Brent. The twins had been at home, freshly expelled from the University of Virginia, at the time the Troop was organized and they had joined enthusiastically; but after the shooting episode, two months ago, their mother had packed them off to the state university, with orders to stay there. They had sorely missed the excitement of the drills while away, and they counted education well lost if only they could ride and yell and shoot off rifles in the company of their friends.

"Well, let's cut across country to Able's," suggested Brent. "We can go through Mr. O'Hara's river bottom and the Fontaines' pasture and get there in no time."

"We ain' gwine git nothin' ter eat 'cept possum an' greens," argued Jeems.

"You ain't going to get anything," grinned

30

Stuart. "Because you are going home and tell Ma that we won't be home for supper."

"No, Ah ain'!" cried Jeems in alarm. "No, Ah ain'! Ah doan git no mo' fun outer havin' Miss Beetriss lay me out dan y'all does. Fust place she'll ast me huccome Ah let y'all git expelled agin. An' nex thing, huccome Ah din' bring y'all home ternight so she could lay you out. An' den she'll light on me lak a duck on a June bug, an' fust thing Ah know Ah'll be ter blame fer it all. Ef y'all doan tek me ter Mist' Wynder's, Ah'll lay out in de woods all night an' maybe de patterollers git me, 'cause Ah heap ruther de patterollers git me dan Miss Beetriss when she in a state."

The twins looked at the determined black boy in perplexity and indignation.

"He'd be just fool enough to let the patterollers get him and that would give Ma something else to talk about for weeks. I swear, darkies are more trouble. Sometimes I think the Abolitionists have got the right idea."

"Well, it wouldn't be right to make Jeems face what we don't want to face. We'll have to take him. But, look, you impudent black fool, if you put on any airs in front of the Wynder darkies and hint that we all the time have fried chicken and ham, while they don't have nothing but rabbit and possum, I'll—I'll tell Ma. And we won't let you go to the war with us, either."

"Airs? Me put on airs fo' dem cheap niggers? Nawsuh, Ah got better manners. Ain' Miss Beetriss taught me manners same as she taught y'all?"

"She didn't do a very good job on any of the

three of us," said Stuart. "Come on, let's get going."

He backed his big red horse and then, putting spurs to his side, lifted him easily over the split-rail fence into the soft field of Gerald O'Hara's plantation. Brent's horse followed and then Jeems', with Jeems clinging to pommel and mane. Jeems did not like to jump fences, but he had jumped higher ones than this in order to keep up with his masters.

As they picked their way across the red furrows and down the hill to the river bottom in the deepening dusk, Brent yelled to his brother:

"Look, Stu! Don't it seem like to you that Scarlett *would* have asked us to supper?"

"I kept thinking she would," yelled Stuart. "Why do you suppose. . . ."

2

WHEN the twins left Scarlett standing on the porch of Tara and the last sound of flying hooves had died away, she went back to her chair like a sleepwalker. Her face felt stiff as from pain and her mouth actually hurt from having stretched it, unwillingly, in smiles to prevent the twins from learning her secret. She sat down wearily, tucking one foot under her, and her heart swelled up with misery, until it felt too large for her bosom. It beat with odd little jerks; her hands were cold, and a feeling of disaster oppressed her. There were pain and bewilderment in her face, the bewilderment of a pampered child who has always had her own way for the asking and who now, for the first time, was in contact with the unpleasantness of life.

Ashley to marry Melanie Hamilton!

Oh, it couldn't be true! The twins were mistaken. They were playing one of their jokes on her. Ashley couldn't, couldn't be in love with her. Nobody could, not with a mousy little person like Melanie. Scarlett recalled with contempt Melanie's thin childish figure, her serious heart-shaped face that was plain almost to homeliness. And Ashley couldn't have seen her in months. He hadn't been in Atlanta more than twice since the house party he gave last year at Twelve Oaks. No, Ashley couldn't be in love with Melanie, because—oh, she couldn't be mistaken!—because he was in love with her! She, Scarlett, was the one he loved—she knew it!

Scarlett heard Mammy's lumbering tread shaking the floor of the hall and she hastily untucked her foot and tried to rearrange her face in more placid lines. It would never do for Mammy to suspect that anything was wrong. Mammy felt that she owned the O'Haras, body and soul, that their secrets were her secrets; and even a hint of a mystery was enough to set her upon the trail as relentlessly as a bloodhound. Scarlett knew from experience that, if Mammy's curiosity were not immediately satisfied, she would take up the matter with Ellen, and then Scarlett would be forced to reveal everything to her mother, or think up some plausible lie.

Mammy emerged from the hall, a huge old woman with the small, shrewd eyes of an elephant. She was shining black, pure African, devoted to her last drop of blood to the O'Haras, Ellen's mainstay, the despair of her three daughters, the terror of the other house servants. Mammy was black, but her code of conduct and her sense of pride were as high as or higher than those of her owners. She had been raised in the bedroom of Solange Robillard, Ellen O'Hara's mother, a dainty, cold, high-nosed French-woman, who spared neither her children nor her servants their just punishment for any infringement of decorum. She had been Ellen's mammy and had come with her from Savannah to the up-country when she married. Whom Mammy loved, she chastened. And, as her love for Scarlett and

34

her pride in her were enormous, the chastening process was practically continuous.

"Is de gempmum gone? Huccome you din' ast dem ter stay fer supper, Miss Scarlett? Ah done tole Poke ter lay two extry plates fer dem. Whar's yo' manners?"

"Oh, I was so tired of hearing them talk about the war that I couldn't have endured it through supper, especially with Pa joining in and shouting about Mr. Lincoln."

"You ain' got no mo' manners dan a fe'el han', an' affer Miss Ellen an' me done laboured wid you. An' hyah you is widout yo' shawl! An' de night air fixin' ter set in! Ah done tole you an' tole you 'bout gittin' fever frum settin' in de night air wid nuthin' on yo' shoulders. Come on in de house, Miss Scarlett."

Scarlett turned away from Mammy with studied nonchalance, thankful that her face had been unnoticed in Mammy's preoccupation with the matter of the shawl.

"No, I want to sit here and watch the sunset. It's so pretty. You run get my shawl. Please, Mammy, and I'll sit here till Pa comes home."

"Yo' voice soun' lak you catchin' a cole," said Mammy suspiciously.

"Well, I'm not," said Scarlett impatiently. "You fetch me my shawl."

Mammy waddled back into the hall and Scarlett heard her call softly up the stairwell to the upstairs maid.

"You, Rosa! Drap me Miss Scarlett's shawl." Then, more loudly: "Wuthless nigger! She ain' never whar she does nobody no good. Now, Ah got ter climb up an' git it mahseff."

Scarlett heard the stairs groan and she got softly to her feet. When Mammy returned she would resume her lecture on Scarlett's breach of hospitality, and Scarlett felt that she could not endure prating about such a trivial matter when her heart was breaking. As she stood, hesitant, wondering where she could hide until the ache in her breast subsided a little, a thought came to her, bringing a small ray of hope. Her father had ridden over to Twelve Oaks, the Wilkes plantation, that afternoon to offer to buy Dilcey, the broad wife of his valet, Pork. Dilcey was head woman and midwife at Twelve Oaks, and, since the marriage six months ago, Pork had devilled his master night and day to buy Dilcey, so the two could live on the same plantation. That afternoon, Gerald, his resistance worn thin, had set out to make an offer for Dilcey.

Surely, thought Scarlett, Pa will know whether this awful story is true. Even if he hasn't actually heard anything this afternoon, perhaps he's noticed something, sensed some excitement in the Wilkes family. If I can just see him privately before supper, perhaps I'll find out the truth—that it's just one of the twins' nasty practical jokes.

It was time for Gerald's return and, if she expected to see him alone, there was nothing for her to do except meet him where the driveway entered the road. She went quietly down the front steps, looking carefully over her shoulder to make sure Mammy was not observing her from the

36

upstairs windows. Seeing no broad black face, turbaned in snowy white, peering disapprovingly from between fluttering curtains, she boldly snatched up her green flowered skirts and sped down the path toward the driveway as fast as her small ribbon-laced slippers would carry her.

The dark cedars on either side of the gravelled drive met in an arch overhead, turning the long avenue into a dim tunnel. As soon as she was beneath the gnarled arms of the cedars, she knew she was safe from observation from the house and she slowed her swift pace. She was panting, for her stays were laced too tightly to permit much running, but she walked on as rapidly as she could. Soon she was at the end of the driveway and out on the main road, but she did not stop until she had rounded a curve that put a large clump of trees between her and the house.

Flushed and breathing hard, she sat down on a stump to wait for her father. It was past time for him to come home, but she was glad that he was late. The delay would give her time to quiet her breathing and calm her face so that his suspicions would not be aroused. Every moment she expected to hear the pounding of his horse's hooves and see him come charging up the hill at his usual breakneck speed. But the minutes slipped by and Gerald did not come. She looked down the road for him, the pain in her heart swelling up again.

"Oh, it can't be true!" she thought. "Why doesn't he come?"

Her eyes followed the winding road, blood-red now after the morning rain. In her thought she traced its course as it ran down the hill to the sluggish Flint River, through the tangled swampy bottoms and up the next hill to Twelve Oaks where Ashley lived. That was all the road meant now—a road to Ashley and the beautiful white columned house that crowned the hill like a Greek temple.

"Oh, Ashley! Ashley!" she thought, and her heart beat faster.

Some of the cold sense of bewilderment and disaster that had weighted her down since the Tarleton boys told her their gossip was pushed into the background of her mind, and in its place crept the fever that had possessed her for two years.

It seemed strange now that when she was growing up Ashley had never seemed so very attractive to her. In childhood days, she had seen him come and go and never given him a thought. But since that day two years ago when Ashley, newly home from his three years' Grand Tour in Europe, had called to pay his respects, she had loved him. It was as simple as that.

She had been on the front porch and he had ridden up the long avenue, dressed in grey broadcloth with a wide black cravat setting off his frilled shirt to perfection. Even now, she could recall each detail of his dress, how brightly his boots shone, the head of a Medusa in cameo on his cravat pin, the wide Panama hat that was instantly in his hand when he saw her. He had alighted and tossed his bridle reins to a piccaninny and stood looking up at her, his drowsy grey eyes wide with a smile and the sun so bright on his blond hair that it seemed like a cap of shining silver. And he said, "So you've grown up, Scarlett." And, coming lightly up the steps, he had kissed her hand. And his voice! She would never forget the leap of her heart as she heard it, as if for the first time, drawling, resonant, musical.

She had wanted him, in that first instant, wanted him as simply and unreasoningly as she wanted food to eat, horses to ride and a soft bed on which to lay herself.

For two years he had squired her about the County, to balls, fish-fries, picnics and court days, never so often as the Tarleton twins or Cade Calvert, never so importunate as the younger Fontaine boys, but, still, never the week went by that Ashley did not come calling at Tara.

True, he never made love to her, not did the clear grey eyes ever glow with that hot light Scarlett knew so well in other men. And yet—and yet—she knew he loved her. She could not be mistaken about it. Instinct stronger than reason and knowledge born of experience told her that he loved her. Too often she had surprised him when his eyes were neither drowsy nor remote, when he looked at her with a yearning and a sadness which puzzled her. She *knew* he loved her. Why did he not tell her so? That she could not understand. But there were so many things about him that she did not understand.

He was courteous always, but aloof, remote. No one could ever tell what he was thinking about, Scarlett least of all. In a neighbourhood where everyone said exactly what he thought as soon as he thought it, Ashley's quality of reserve was exasperating. He was as proficient as any of the other young men in the usual County diversions, hunting, gambling, dancing and politics, and was the best rider of them all; but he differed from all the rest in that these pleasant activities were not the end and aim of life to him. And he stood alone in his interest in books and music and his fondness for writing poetry.

Oh, why was he so handsomely blond, so courteously aloof, so maddeningly boring with his talk about Europe and books and music and poetry and things that interested her not at all—and yet so desirable? Night after night, when Scarlett went to bed after sitting on the front porch in the semi-darkness with him, she tossed restlessly for hours and comforted herself only with the thought that the very next time he saw her he certainly would propose. But the next time came and went, and the result was nothing—nothing except that the fever possessing her rose higher and hotter.

She loved him and she wanted him and she did not understand him. She was as forthright and simple as the winds that blew over Tara and the yellow river that wound about it, and to the end of her days she would never be able to understand a complexity. And now, for the first time in her life, she was facing a complex nature.

For Ashley was born of a line of men who used their leisure for thinking, not doing, for spinning brightly coloured dreams that had in them no touch of reality. He moved in an inner world that was more beautiful than Georgia and came back to reality with reluctance. He looked on people, and he neither liked nor disliked them. He looked on life and was neither heartened nor saddened. He accepted the universe and his place in it for what they were and, shrugging, turned to his music and books and his better world.

Why he should have captivated Scarlett when his mind was a stranger to hers she did not know. The very mystery of him excited her curiosity like a door that had neither lock nor key. The things about him which she could not understand only made her love him more, and his odd, restrained courtship only served to increase her determination to have him for her own. That he would propose some day she had never doubted, for she was too young and too spoiled ever to have known defeat. And now, like a thunderclap, had come this horrible news. Ashley to marry Melanie! It couldn't be true!

Why, only last week, when they were riding home at twilight from Fairhill, he had said: "Scarlett, I have something so important to tell you that I hardly know how to say it."

She had cast down her eyes demurely, her heart beating with wild pleasure, thinking the happy moment had come. Then he had said: "Not now! We're nearly home and there isn't time. Oh, Scarlett, what a coward I am!" And putting spurs to his horse, he had raced her up the hill to Tara.

Scarlett, sitting on the stump, thought of those words which had made her so happy, and suddenly they took on another meaning, a hideous meaning. Suppose it was the news of his engagement he had intended to tell her!

GWTW BK(1)4

Oh, if Pa would only come home! She could not endure the suspense another moment. She looked impatiently down the road again, and again she was disappointed.

The sun was now below the horizon and the red glow at the rim of the world faded into pink. The sky above turned slowly from azure to the delicate blue-green of a robin's egg, and the unearthly stillness of rural twilight came stealthily down about her. Shadowy dimness crept over the countryside. The red furrows and the gashed red road lost their magical blood colour and became plain brown earth. Across the road, in the pasture, the horses, mules and cows stood quietly with heads over the split-rail fence, waiting to be driven to the stables and supper. They did not like the dark shade of the thickets hedging the pasture creek, and they twitched their ears at Scarlett as if appreciative of human companionship.

In the strange half-light, the tall pines of the river swamp, so warmly green in the sunshine, were black against the pastel sky, an impenetrable row of black giants hiding the slow yellow water at their feet. On the hill across the river, the tall white chimneys of the Wilkes home faded gradually into the darkness of the thick oaks surrounding them, and only far-off pin points of supper lamps showed that a house was here. The warm damp balminess of spring encompassed her sweetly with the moist smells of new-ploughed earth and all the fresh green things pushing up to the air.

Sunset and spring and new-fledged greenery

were no miracle to Scarlett. Their beauty she accepted as casually as the air she breathed and the water she drank, for she had never consciously seen beauty in anything but women's faces, horses, silk dresses and like tangible things. Yet the serene half-light over Tara's well-kept acres brought a measure of quiet to her disturbed mind. She loved this land so much, without even knowing she loved it, loved it as she loved her mother's face under the lamp at prayer time.

Still there was no sign of Gerald on the quiet winding road. If she had to wait much longer, Mammy would certainly come in search of her and bully her into the house. But even as she strained her eyes down the darkening road, she heard a pounding of hooves at the bottom of the pasture hill and saw the horses and cows scatter in fright. Gerald O'Hara was coming home across country and at top speed.

He came up the hill at a gallop on his thick-barrelled, long-legged hunter, appearing in the distance like a boy on a too large horse. His long white hair standing out behind him, he urged the horse forward with crop and loud cries.

Filled with her own anxieties, she nevertheless watched him with affectionate pride, for Gerald was an excellent horseman.

"I wonder why he always wants to jump fences when he's had a few drinks," she thought. "And after that fall he had right here last year when he broke his knee. You'd think he'd learn. Especially when he promised Mother on oath he'd never jump again."

Scarlett had no awe of her father and felt him

more her contemporary than her sisters, for jumping fences and keeping it a secret from his wife gave him a boyish pride and guilty glee that matched her own pleasure in outwitting Mammy. She rose from her seat to watch him.

The big horse reached the fence, gathered himself and soared over as effortlessly as a bird, his rider yelling enthusiastically, his crop beating the air, his white curls jerking out behind him. Gerald did not see his daughter in the shadow of the trees, and he drew rein in the road, patting his horse's neck with approbation.

"There's none in the County can touch you, nor in the state," he informed his mount, with pride, the brogue of County Meath still heavy on his tongue in spite of thirty-nine years in America. Then he hastily set about smoothing his hair and settling his ruffled shirt and his cravat which had slipped awry behind one ear. Scarlett knew these hurried preenings were being made with an eye toward meeting his wife with the appearance of a gentleman who had ridden sedately home from a call on a neighbour. She knew also that he was presenting her with just the opportunity she wanted for opening the conversation without revealing her true purpose.

She laughed aloud. As she had intended, Gerald was startled by the sound; then he recognized her, and a look both sheepish and defiant came over his florid face. He dismounted with difficulty, because his knee was stiff, and, slipping the reins over his arm, stumped toward her.

"Well, Missy," he said, pinching her cheek, "so, you've been spying on me and, like your

44

sister Suellen last week, you'll be telling your mother on me?"

There was indignation in his hoarse bass voice but also a wheedling note, and Scarlett teasingly clicked her tongue against her teeth as she reached out to pull his cravat into place. His breath in her face was strong with Bourbon whisky mingled with a faint fragrance of mint. Accompanying him also were the smells of chewing tobacco, well-oiled leather and horses— a combination of odours that she always associated with her father and instinctively liked in other men.

"No, Pa, I'm no tattletale like Suellen," she assured him, standing off to view his rearranged attire with a judicious air.

Gerald was a small man, little more than five feet tall, but so heavy of barrel and thick of neck that his appearance, when seated, led strangers to think him a larger man. His thickset torso was supported by short sturdy legs, always encased in the finest leather boots procurable and always planted wide apart like a swaggering small boy's. Most small people who take themselves seriously are a little ridiculous; but the bantam cock is respected in the barnyard, and so it was with Gerald. No one would ever have the temerity to think of Gerald O'Hara as a ridiculous little figure.

He was sixty years old and his crisp curly hair was silver-white, but his shrewd face was unlined and his hard little blue eyes were young with the unworried youthfulness of one who has never taxed his brain with problems more abstract than how many cards to draw in a poker game. His was as Irish a face as could be found in the length and breadth of the homeland he had left so long ago—round, high-coloured, short-nosed, wide-mouthed and belligerent.

Beneath his choleric exterior Gerald O'Hara had the tenderest of hearts. He could not bear to see a slave pouting under a reprimand, no matter how well deserved, or hear a kitten mewing or a child crying; but he had a horror of having this weakness discovered. That everyone who met him did discover his kindly heart within five minutes was unkown to him; and his vanity would have suffered tremendously if he had found it out, for he liked to think that when he bawled orders at the top of his voice everyone trembled and obeyed. It had never occurred to him that only one voice was obeyed on the plantation—the soft voice of his wife Ellen. It was a secret he would never learn, for everyone from Ellen down to the stupidest field hand was in a tacit and kindly conspiracy to keep him believing that his word was law.

Scarlett was impressed less than anyone else by his tempers and his roarings. She was his oldest child and, now that Gerald knew there would be no more sons to follow the three who lay in the family burying-ground, he had drifted into a habit of treating her in a man-to-man manner which she found most pleasant. She was more like her father than her younger sisters, for Carreen, who had been born Caroline Irene, was delicate and dreamy, and Suellen, christened Susan Elinor, prided herself on her elegance and ladylike deportment.

Moreover, Scarlett and her father were bound together by a mutual suppression agreement. If Gerald caught her climbing a fence instead of walking half a mile to a gate, or sitting too late on the front steps with a beau, he castigated her personally and with vehemence, but he did not mention the fact to Ellen or to Mammy. And when Scarlett discovered him jumping fences after his solemn promise to his wife, or learned the exact amount of his losses at poker, as she always did from County gossip, she refrained from mentioning the fact at the supper table in the artfully artless manner Suellen had. Scarlett and her father each assured the other solemnly that to bring such matters to the ears of Ellen would only hurt her, and nothing would induce them to wound her gentleness.

Scarlett looked at her father in the fading light, and, without knowing why, she found it comforting to be in his presence. There was something vital and earthy and coarse about him that appealed to her. Being the least analytic of people, she did not realize that this was because she possessed in some degree these same qualities, despite sixteen years of effort on the part of Ellen and Mammy to obliterate them.

"You look very presentable now," she said, "and I don't think anyone will suspect you've been up to your tricks unless you brag about them. But it does seem to me that after you broke your knee last year, jumping that same fence—"

"Well, may I be damned if I'll have me own

daughter telling me what I shall jump and not jump," he shouted, giving her cheek another pinch. "It's me own neck, so it is. And besides, Missy, what are you doing out here without your shawl?"

Seeing that he was employing familiar manoeuvres to extricate himself from unpleasant conversation, she slipped her arm through his and said: "I was waiting for you. I didn't know you would be so late. I just wondered if you had bought Dilcey."

"Bought her I did, and the price has ruined me. Bought her and her little wench, Prissy. John Wilkes was for almost giving them away, but never will I have it said that Gerald O'Hara used friendship in a trade. I made him take three thousand for the two of them."

"In the name of Heaven, Pa, three thousand! And you didn't need to buy Prissy!"

"Has the time come when me own daughters sit in judgment on me?" shouted Gerald rhetorically. "Prissy is a likely little wench and so—"

"I know her. She's a sly, stupid creature," Scarlett rejoined calmly, unimpressed by his uproar. "And the only reason you bought her was because Dilcey asked you to buy her."

Gerald looked crestfallen and embarrassed, as always when caught in a kind deed, and Scarlett laughed outright at his transparency.

"Well, what if I did? Was there any use buying Dilcey if she was going to mope about the child? Well, never again will I let a darky on this place marry off it. It's too expensive. Well, come on, Puss, let's go in to supper."

The shadows were falling thicker now, the last greenish tinge had left the sky and a slight chill was displacing the balminess of spring. But Scarlett loitered, wondering how to bring up the subject of Ashley without permitting Gerald to suspect her motive. This was difficult, for Scarlett had not a subtle bone in her body; and Gerald was so much like her he never failed to penetrate her weak subterfuges, even as she penetrated his. And he was seldom tactful in doing it.

"How are they all over at Twelve Oaks?"

"About as usual. Cade Calvert was there and, after I settled about Dilcey, we all set on the gallery and had several toddies. Cade has just come from Atlanta, and it's all upset they are there and talking war and—"

Scarlett sighed. If Gerald once got on the subject of war and secession, it would be hours before he relinquished it. She broke in with another line.

"Did they say anything about the barbecue tomorrow?"

"Now that I think of it they did. Miss—what's-her-name—the sweet little thing who was here last year, you know, Ashley's cousin—oh, yes, Miss Melanie Hamilton, that's the name—she and her brother Charles have already come from Atlanta and—"

"Oh, so she did come?"

"She did, and a sweet quiet thing she is, with never a word to say for herself, like a woman should be. Come now, daughter, don't lag. Your mother will be hunting for us."

Scarlett's heart sank at the news. She had

49

hoped against hope that something would keep Melanie Hamilton in Atlanta where she belonged, and the knowledge that even her father approved of her sweet quiet nature, so different from her own, forced her into the open.

"Was Ashley there, too?"

"He was." Gerald let go of his daughter's arm and turned, peering sharply into her face. "And if that's why you came out here to wait for me, why didn't you say so without beating around the bush?"

Scarlett could think of nothing to say, and she felt her face growing red with annoyance.

"Well, speak up."

Still she said nothing, wishing that it was permissible to shake one's father and tell him to hush his mouth.

"He was there and he asked most kindly after you, as did his sisters, and said they hoped nothing would keep you from the barbecue tomorrow. I'll warrant nothing will," he said shrewdly. "And now, daughter, what's all this about you and Ashley?"

"There is nothing," she said shortly, tugging at his arm. "Let's go in, Pa."

"So now 'tis you wanting to go in," he observed. "But here I'm going to stand till I'm understanding you. Now that I think of it, 'tis strange you've been recently. Has he been trifling with you? Has he asked to marry you?"

"No," she said shortly.

"Nor will he," said Gerald.

Fury flamed in her, but Gerald waved her quiet with a hand.

"Hold your tongue, Miss! I had it from John Wilkes this afternoon in the strictest confidence that Ashley's to marry Miss Melanie. It's to be announced to-morrow."

Scarlett's hand fell from his arm. So it was true!

A pain slashed at her heart as savagely as a wild animal's fangs. Through it all, she felt her father's eyes on her, a little pitying, a little annoyed at being faced with a problem for which he knew no answer. He loved Scarlett, but it made him uncomfortable to have her forcing her childish problems on him for a solution. Ellen knew all the answers. Scarlett should have taken her troubles to her.

"Is it a spectacle you've been making of yourself—of all of us?" he bawled, his voice rising as always in moments of excitement. "Have you been running after a man who's not in love with you, when you could have any of the bucks in the County?"

Anger and hurt pride drove out some of the pain.

"I haven't been running after him. It—it just surprised me."

"It's lying you are!" said Gerald, and then, peering at her stricken face, he added in a burst of kindliness: "I'm sorry, daughter. But after all, you are nothing but a child and there's lots of other beaux."

"Mother was only fifteen when she married you, and I'm sixteen," said Scarlett, her voice muffled.

"Your mother was different," said Gerald. "She was never flighty like you. Now come, daughter, cheer up, and I'll take you to Charleston next week to visit your Aunt Eulalie and, what with all the hullabaloo they are having over there about Fort Sumter, you'll be forgetting about Ashley in a week."

"He thinks I'm a child," thought Scarlett, grief and rage choking utterance, "and he's only got to dangle a new toy and I'll forget my bumps."

"Now, don't be jerking your chin at me," warned Gerald. "If you had any sense you'd have married Stuart or Brent Tarleton long ago. Think it over, daughter. Marry one of the twins and then the plantations will run together and Jim Tarleton and I will build you a fine house, right where they join, in that big pine grove and—"

"Will you stop treating me like a child!" cried Scarlett. "I don't want to go to Charleston or have a house or marry the twins. I only want—" She caught herself but not in time.

Gerald's voice was strangely quiet and he spoke slowly as if drawing his words from a store of thought seldom used.

"It's only Ashley you're wanting, and you'll not be having him. And if he wanted to marry you, 'twould be with misgivings that I'd say Yes, for all the fine friendship that's between me and John Wilkes." And, seeing her startled look, he continued: "I want my girl to be happy and you wouldn't be happy with him."

"Oh, I would! I would!"

"That you would not, daughter. Only when like marries like can there be any happiness."

Scarlett had a sudden treacherous desire to cry out, "But you've been happy, and you and

Mother aren't alike," but she repressed it, fearing that he would box her ears for her impertinence.

"Our people and the Wilkes are different," he went on slowly, fumbling for words. "The Wilkes are different from any of our neighbours—different from any family I ever knew. They are queer folk, and it's best that they marry their cousins and keep their queerness to themselves."

"Why, Pa, Ashley is not—"

"Hold your whist, puss! I said nothing against the lad, for I like him. And when I say queer, it's not crazy I'm meaning. He's not queer like the Calverts who'd gamble everything they have on a horse, or the Tarletons who turn out a drunkard or two in every litter, or the Fontaines who are hot-headed little brutes and after murdering a man for a fancied slight. That kind of queerness is easy to understand, for sure, and but for the grace of God Gerald O'Hara would be having all those faults! And I don't mean that Ashley would run off with another woman, if you were his wife, or beat you. You'd be happier if he did, for at least you'd be understanding that. But he's queer in other ways, and there's no understanding him at all. I like him, but it's neither heads nor tails I can make of most he says. Now, Puss, tell me true, do you understand his folderol about books and poetry and music and oil paintings and such foolishness?"

"Oh, Pa," cried Scarlett impatiently, "if I married him, I'd change all that!"

"Oh, you would, would you now?" said Gerald testily, shooting a sharp look at her. "Then it's little enough you are knowing of any man living, let alone Ashley. No wife has ever changed a husband one whit, and don't you be forgetting that. And as for changing a Wilkes—God's nightgown, daughter! The whole family is that way, and they've always been that way. And probably always will. I tell you they're born queer. Look at the way they go tearing up to New York and Boston to hear operas and see oil paintings. And ordering French and German books by the crate from the Yankees! And there they sit reading and dreaming the dear God knows what, when they'd be better spending their time hunting and playing poker as proper men should."

"There's nobody in the County sits a horse better than Ashley," said Scarlett, furious at the slur of effeminacy flung on Ashley, "nobody except maybe his father. And as for poker, didn't Ashley take two hundred dollars away from you just last week in Jonesboro?"

"The Calvert boys have been blabbing again," Gerald said resignedly, "else you'd not be knowing the amount. Ashley can ride with the best and play poker with the best—that's me, Puss! And I'm not denying that when he sets out to drink he can put even the Tarletons under the table. He can do all those things, but his heart's not in it. That's why I say he's queer."

Scarlett was silent and her heart sank. She could think of no defence for this last, for she knew Gerald was right. Ashley's heart was in none of the pleasant things he did so well. He was never more than politely interested in any of the things that vitally interested everyone else.

Rightly interpreting her silence, Gerald patted

her arm and said triumphantly: "There now, Scarlett! You admit 'tis true. What would you be doing with a husband like Ashley? 'Tis moonstruck they all are, all the Wilkes." And then, in a wheedling tone: "When I was mentioning the Tarletons the while ago, I wasn't pushing them. They're fine lads, but if it's Cade Calvert you're setting your cap after, why, 'tis the same with me. The Calverts are good folk, all of them, for all the old man marrying a Yankee. And when I'm gone—Whist, darlin', listen to me! I'll leave Tara to you and Cade—"

"I wouldn't have Cade on a silver tray," cried Scarlett in fury. "And I wish you'd quit pushing him at me! I don't want Tara or any old plantation. Plantations don't amount to anything when—"

She was going to say "when you haven't the man you want", but Gerald, incensed by the cavalier way in which she treated his proffered gift, the thing which, next to Ellen, he loved best in the whole world, uttered a roar.

"Do you stand there, Scarlett O'Hara, and tell me that Tara—that land—doesn't amount to anything?"

Scarlett nodded obstinately. Her heart was too sore to care whether or not she put her father in a temper.

"Land is the only thing in the world that amounts to anything," he shouted, his thick, short arms making wide gestures of indignation, "for 'tis the only thing in this world that lasts, and don't you be forgetting it! 'Tis the only thing worth working for, worth fighting for—worth dying for."

"Oh, Pa," she said disgustedly, "you talk like an Irishman!"

"Have I ever been ashamed of it? No, 'tis proud I am. And don't be forgetting that you are half Irish, Miss! And to anyone with a drop of Irish blood in them the land they live on is like their mother. 'Tis ashamed of you I am this minute. I offer you the most beautiful land in the world—saving County Meath in the Old Country—and what do you do? You sniff!"

Gerald had begun to work himself up into a pleasurable shouting rage when something in Scarlett's woebegone face stopped him.

"But there, you're young. 'Twill come to you, this love of land. There's no getting away from it, if you're Irish. You're just a child and bothered about your beaux. When you're older, you'll be seeing how 'tis. . . . Now, do you be making up your mind about Cade or the twins or one of Evan Munroe's young bucks, and see how fine I turn you out!"

"Oh, Pa!"

By this time, Gerald was thoroughly tired of the conversation and thoroughly annoyed that the problem should be upon his shoulders. He felt aggrieved, moreover, that Scarlett should still look desolate after being offered the best of the County boys and Tara, too. Gerald liked his gifts to be received with clapping of hands and kisses.

"Now, none of your pouts, Miss. It doesn't matter who you marry, as long as he thinks like you and is a gentleman and a Southerner and prideful. For a woman, love comes after marriage."

"Oh, Pa, that's such an Old Country notion!"

"And a good notion it is! All this American business of running around marrying for love, like servants, like Yankees! The best marriages are when the parents choose for the girl. For how can a silly piece like yourself tell a good man from a scoundrel? Now, look at the Wilkes. What's kept them prideful and strong all these generations? Why, marrying the likes of themselves, marrying the cousins their family always expects them to marry."

"Oh," cried Scarlett, fresh pain striking her as Gerald's words brought home the terrible inevitability of the truth. Gerald looked at her bowed head and shuffled his feet uneasily.

"It's not crying you are?" he questioned, fumbling clumsily at her chin, trying to turn her face upward, his own face furrowed with pity.

"No," she cried vehemently, jerking away.

"It's lying you are, and I'm proud of it. I'm glad there's pride in you, Puss. And I want to see pride in you to-morrow at the barbecue. I'll not be having the County gossiping and laughing at you for mooning your heart out about a man who never gave you a thought beyond friendship."

"He did give me a thought," thought Scarlett, sorrowfully in her heart. "Oh, a lot of thoughts! I know he did. I could tell. If I'd just had a little longer, I know I could have made him say—Oh, if it only wasn't that the Wilkes always feel that they have to marry their cousins!"

Gerald took her arm and passed it through his.

"We'll be going in to supper now, and all this is between us. I'll not be worrying your mother with this—nor do you do it, either. Blow your nose, daughter."

Scarlett blew her nose on her torn handkerchief, and they started up the dark drive arm in arm, the horse following slowly. Near the house, Scarlett was at the point of speaking again when she saw her mother in the dim shadows of the porch. She had on her bonnet, shawl and mittens, and behind her was Mammy, her face like a thundercloud, holding in her hand the black leather bag in which Ellen O'Hara always carried the bandages and medicines she used in doctoring the slaves. Mammy's lips were large and pendulous and, when indignant, she could push out her lower one to twice its normal length. It was pushed out now, and Scarlett knew that Mammy was seething over something of which she did not approve.

"Mr. O'Hara," called Ellen as she saw the two coming up the driveway—Ellen belonged to a generation that was formal even after seventeen years of wedlock and the bearing of six children —"Mr. O'Hara, there is illness at the Slattery house. Emmie's baby has been born and is dying and must be baptized. I am going there with Mammy to see what I can do."

Her voice was raised questioningly, as though she hung on Gerald's assent to her plan, a mere formality but one dear to the heart of Gerald.

"In the name of God!" blustered Gerald. "Why should those white trash take you away just at your supper hour and just when I'm wanting to tell you about the war talk that's going on in Atlanta! Go, Mrs. O'Hara. You'd not rest easy on your pillow the night if there was trouble abroad and you not there to help."

"She doan never git no res' on her piller fer hoppin' up at night time nursin' niggers an' po' w'ite trash dat could ten' to deyseff," grumbled Mammy in a monotone as she went down the stairs toward the carriage which was waiting in the side drive.

"Take my place at the table, dear," said Ellen, patting Scarlett's cheek softly with a mittened hand.

In spite of her choked-back tears, Scarlett thrilled to the never-failing magic of her mother's touch, to the faint fragrance of lemon verbena sachet that came from her rustling silk dress. To Scarlett, there was something breath-taking about Ellen O'Hara, a miracle that lived in the house with her and awed her and charmed and soothed her.

Gerald helped his wife into the carriage and gave orders to the coachman to drive carefully. Toby, who had handled Gerald's horses for twenty years, pushed out his lips in mute indignation at being told how to conduct his own business. Driving off, with Mammy beside him, each was a perfect picture of pouting African disapproval.

"If I didn't do so much for those trashy Slatterys that they'd have to pay money for elsewhere," fumed Gerald, "they'd be willing to sell me their miserable few acres of swamp bottom, and the County would be well rid of them."

Then, brightening, in anticipation of one of his practical jokes: "Come, daughter, let's go tell Pork that instead of buying Dilcey, I've sold him to John Wilkes."

He tossed the reins of his horse to a small piccaninny standing near and started up the steps. He had already forgotten Scarlett's heartbreak and his mind was only on plaguing his valet. Scarlett slowly climbed the steps after him, her feet leaden. She thought that, after all, a mating between herself and Ashley could be no queerer than that of her father and Ellen Robillard O'Hara. As always, she wondered how her loud, insensitive father had managed to marry a woman like her mother, for never were two people farther apart in birth, breeding and habits of mind.

3

ELLEN O'HARA was thirty-two years old, and, according to the standards of her day, she was a middle-aged woman, one who had borne six children and buried three. She was a tall woman, standing a head higher than her fiery little husband, but she moved with such quiet grace in her swaying hoops that her height attracted no attention to itself. Her neck, rising from the black taffeta sheath of her basque, was creamy-skinned, rounded and slender, and it seemed always tilted slightly backward by the weight of her luxuriant hair in its net at the back of her head. From her French mother, whose parents had fled Haiti in the Revolution of 1791, had come her slanting dark eyes, shadowed by inky lashes, and her black hair; and from her father, a soldier of Napoleon, she had her long straight nose and her square-cut jaw that was softened by the gentle curving of her cheeks. But only from life could Ellen's face have acquired its look of pride that had no haughtiness, its graciousness, its melancholy and its utter lack of humour.

She would have been a strikingly beautiful woman had there been any glow in her eyes, any responsive warmth in her smile or any spontaneity in her voice that fell with gentle melody on the ears of her family and her servants. She spoke in the soft slurring voice of the coastal Georgian, liquid of vowels, kind to consonants and with the barest trace of French accent. It was a voice never raised in command to a servant or reproof to a child but a voice that was obeyed instantly at Tara, where her husband's blustering and roaring were quietly disregarded.

As far back as Scarlett could remember, her mother had always been the same, her voice soft and sweet whether in praising or in reproving, her manner efficient and unruffled despite the daily emergencies of Gerald's turbulent household, her spirit always calm and her back unbowed, even in the deaths of her three baby sons. Scarlett had never seen her mother's back touch the back of any chair on which she sat. Nor had she ever seen her sit down without a bit of needlework in her hands, except at mealtime, while attending the sick or while working at the bookkeeping of the plantation. It was delicate embroidery if company were present, but at other times her hands were occupied with Gerald's ruffled shirts, the girls' dresses or garments for the slaves. Scarlett could not imagine her mother's hands without her gold thimble or her rustling figure unaccompanied by the small negro girl whose sole function in life was to remove basting threads and carry the rosewood sewing-box from room to room, as Ellen moved about the house superintending the cooking, the cleaning and the wholesale clothes-making for the plantation.

She had never seen her mother stirred from her austere placidity, nor her personal appointments anything but perfect, no matter what the hour of day or night. When Ellen was dressing for a ball or for guests or even to go to Jonesboro for Court Day, it frequently required two hours, two maids and Mammy to turn her out to her own satisfaction; but her swift toilets in times of emergency were amazing.

Scarlett, whose room lay across the hall from her mother's, knew from babyhood the soft sound of scurrying bare black feet on the hardwood floor in the hours of dawn, the urgent tappings on her mother's door, and the muffled, frightened negro voices that whispered of sickness and birth and death in the long row of whitewashed cabins in the quarters. As a child, she often had crept to the door and, peeping through the tiniest crack, had seen Ellen emerge from the dark room, where Gerald's snores were rhythmic and untroubled, into the flickering light of an upheld candle, her medicine-case under her arm, her hair smoothed neatly into place, and no button on her basque unlooped.

It had always been so soothing to Scarlett to hear her mother whisper, firmly but compassionately, as she tiptoed down the hall: "Hush, not so loudly. You will wake Mr. O'Hara. They are not sick enough to die."

Yes, it was good to creep back into bed and know that Ellen was abroad in the night and everything was right.

In the mornings, after all-night sessions at births and deaths, when old Dr. Fontaine and young Dr. Fontaine were both out on calls and could not be found to help her, Ellen presided at the breakfast table as usual, her dark eyes circled with weariness but her voice and manner revealing none of the strain. There was a steely quality under her stately gentleness that awed the whole household, Gerald as well as the girls, though he would have died rather than admit it.

Sometimes when Scarlett tiptoed at night to kiss her tall mother's cheek, she looked up at the mouth with its too short, too tender upper lip, a mouth too easily hurt by the world, and wondered if it had ever curved in silly girlish giggling or whispered secrets through long nights to intimate girl friends. But no, that wasn't possible. Mother had always been just as she was, a pillar of strength, a fount of wisdom, the one person who knew the answers to everything.

But Scarlett was wrong, for, years before, Ellen Robillard of Savannah had giggled as inexplicably as any fifteen-year-old in that charming coastal city and whispered the long nights through with friends, exchanging confidences, telling all secrets but one. That was the year when Gerald O'Hara, twenty-eight years older than she, came into her life—the year, too, when youth and her black-eyed cousin, Philippe Robillard, went out of it. For when Philippe, with his snapping eyes and his wild ways, left Savannah forever, he took with him all the glow that was in Ellen's heart and left for the bandy-legged little Irishman who married her only a gentle shell.

But that was enough for Gerald, overwhelmed at his unbelievable luck in actually marrying her. And if anything was gone from her, he never missed it. Shrewd man that he was, he knew that it was no less than a miracle that he, an Irishman with nothing of family and wealth to recommend him, should win the daughter of one of the wealthiest and proudest families on the Coast. For Gerald was a self-made man.

Gerald had come to America from Ireland when he was twenty-one. He had come hastily, as many a better and worse Irishman before and since, with the clothes he had on his back, two shillings above his passage money and a price on his head that he felt was larger than his misdeed warranted. There was no Orangeman this side of hell worth a hundred pounds to the British government or to the devil himself; but if the government felt so strongly about the death of an English absentee landlord's rent agent, it was time for Gerald O'Hara to be leaving and leaving suddenly. True, he had called the rent agent "a bastard of an Orangeman", but that, according to Gerald's way of looking at it, did not give the man any right to insult him by whistling the opening bars of "The Boyne Water".

The Battle of the Boyne had been fought more than a hundred years before, but, to the O'Haras and their neighbours, it might have been yesterday when their hopes and their dreams, as well as their lands and wealth, went off in the same cloud of dust that enveloped a frightened and fleeing Stuart prince, leaving William of Orange and his hated troops with their orange cockades to cut down the Irish adherents of the Stuarts.

For this and other reasons, Gerald's family was not inclined to view the fatal outcome of his quarrel as anything very serious, except for the fact that it was charged with serious consequences. For years, the O'Haras had been in bad odour with the English constabulary on account of suspected activities against the government, and Gerald was not the first O'Hara to take his foot in his hand and quit Ireland between dawn and morning. His two oldest brothers, James and Andrew, he hardly remembered, save as close-lipped youths who came and went at odd hours of the night on mysterious errands or disappeared for weeks at a time, to their mother's gnawing anxiety. They had come to America years before, after the discovery of a small arsenal of rifles buried under the O'Hara pigsty. Now they were successful merchants in Savannah, "though the dear God alone knows where that may be," as their mother always interpolated when mentioning the two oldest of her male brood, and it was to them that young Gerald was sent.

He left home with his mother's hasty kiss on his cheek and her fervent Catholic blessing in his ears, and his father's parting admonition, "Remember who ye are and don't be taking nothing off no man." His five tall brothers gave him good-bye with admiring but slightly patronizing smiles, for Gerald was the baby and the little one of a brawny family.

His five brothers and their father stood six feet and over and broad in proportion, but little Gerald, at twenty-one, knew that five feet four and a half inches was as much as the Lord in His wisdom was going to allow him. It was like Gerald that he never wasted regrets on his lack of height and never found it an obstacle to his acquisition of anything he wanted. Rather, it was Gerald's compact smallness that made him what he was, for he had learned early that little people must be hardy to survive among large ones. And Gerald was hardy.

His tall brothers were a grim, quiet lot, in whom the family tradition of past glories, lost forever, rankled in unspoken hate and crackled out in bitter humour. Had Gerald been brawny he would have gone the way of the other O'Haras and moved quietly and darkly among the rebels against the government. But Gerald was "loud-mouthed and bullheaded", as his mother fondly phrased it, hair-trigger of temper, quick with his fists and possessed of a chip on his shoulder so large as to be almost visible to the naked eye. He swaggered among the tall O'Haras like a strutting bantam in a barnyard of giant Cochin roosters, and they loved him, baited him affectionately to hear him roar and hammered on him with their large fists no more than was necessary to keep a baby brother in his proper place.

If the educational equipment which Gerald brought to America was scant, he did not even know it. Nor would he have cared if he had been told. His mother had taught him to read and to write a clear hand. He was adept at ciphering. And there his book knowledge stopped. The only Latin he knew was the responses of the Mass and the only history the manifold wrongs of Ireland. He knew no poetry save that of Moore and no music except the songs of Ireland that had come down through the years. While he entertained the liveliest respect for those who had more book learning than he, he never felt his own lack. And what need had he of these things in a new country where the most ignorant of bogtrotters had made great fortunes? in this country which asked only that a man be strong and unafraid of work?

Nor did James and Andrew, who took him into their store in Savannah, regret his lack of education. His clear hand, his accurate figures and his shrewd ability in bargaining won their respect, where a knowledge of literature and a fine appreciation of music, had young Gerald possessed them, would have moved them to snorts of contempt. America, in the early years of the century, had been kind to the Irish. James and Andrew, who had begun by hauling goods in covered wagons from Savannah to Georgia's inland towns, had prospered into a store of their own, and Gerald prospered with them.

He liked the South, and he soon became, in his own opinion, a Southerner. There was much about the South—and Southerners—that he would never comprehend; but, with the whole-heartedness that was his nature, he adopted its ideas and customs, as he understood them, for his own—poker and horse racing, red-hot politics and the code duello, States' Rights and damnation to all Yankees, slavery and King Cotton, contempt for white trash and exaggerated courtesy to women. He even learned to chew tobacco. There was no need for him to acquire a good head for whisky, he had been born with one.

But Gerald remained Gerald. His habits of living and his ideas changed, but his manners he would not change, even had he been able to change them. He admired the drawling elegance of the wealthy rice and cotton planters, who rode into Savannah from their moss-hung kingdoms, mounted on thoroughbred horses and followed by the carriages of their equally elegant ladies and the wagons of their slaves. But Gerald could never attain elegance. Their lazy, blurred voices fell pleasantly on his ears, but his own brisk brogue clung to his tongue. He liked the casual grace with which they conducted affairs of importance, risking a fortune, a plantation or a slave on the turn of a card and writing off their losses with careless good humour and no more ado than when they scattered pennies to piccaninnies. But Gerald had known poverty, and he could never learn to lose money with good humour or good grace. They were a pleasant race, these coastal Georgians, with their soft-voiced, quick rages and their charming inconsistencies, and Gerald liked them. But there was a brisk and restless vitality about the young Irishman, fresh from a country where winds blew wet and chill, where misty swamps held no fevers, that set him apart from these indolent gentlefolk of semi-tropical weather and malarial marshes.

From them he learned what he found useful, and the rest he dismissed. He found poker the most useful of all Southern customs, poker and a steady head for whisky; and it was his natural aptitude for cards and amber liquor that brought to Gerald two of his three most prized possessions, his valet and his plantation. The other was his wife, and he could only attribute her to the mysterious kindness of God.

The valet, Pork by name, shining black, dignified and trained in all the arts of sartorial elegance, was the result of an all-night poker game with a planter from St. Simon's Island, whose courage in a bluff equalled Gerald's but whose head for New Orleans rum did not. Though Pork's former owner later offered to buy him back at twice his value, Gerald obstinately refused, for the possession of his first slave, and that slave the "best damn valet on the Coast", was the first step upward toward his heart's desire. Gerald wanted to be a slave-owner and a landed gentleman.

His mind was made up that he was not going to spend all of his days, like James and Andrew, in bargaining, or all his nights, by candlelight, over long columns of figures. He felt keenly, as his brothers did not, the social stigma attached to those "in trade". Gerald wanted to be a planter. With the deep hunger of an Irishman who has been a tenant on the lands his people once had owned and hunted, he wanted to see his own acres stretching green before his eyes. With a ruthless singleness of purpose, he desired his own house, his own plantation, his own horses, his own slaves. And here in this new country, safe from the twin perils of the land he had left—taxation that ate up crops and barns and the ever-present threat of sudden confiscation—he intended to have them. But having that ambition and bringing it to realization were two different matters, he discovered as time went by. Coastal Georgia was too firmly held by an entrenched aristocracy for him ever to hope to win the place he intended to have.

Then the hand of Fate and a hand of poker combined to give him the plantation which he afterwards called Tara, and at the same time moved him out of the Coast into the upland country of north Georgia.

It was in a saloon in Savannah, on a hot night in spring, when the chance conversation of a stranger sitting near-by made Gerald prick up his ears. The stranger, a native of Savannah, had just returned after twelve years in the inland country. He had been one of the winners in the land lottery conducted by the State to divide up the vast area in middle Georgia, ceded by the Indians the year before Gerald came to America. He had gone up there and established a plantation; but, now the house had burned down, he was tired of the "accursed place" and would be most happy to get it off his hands.

Gerald, his mind never free of the thought of owning a plantation of his own, arranged an introduction, and his interest grew as the stranger told how the northern section of the state was filling up with newcomers from the Carolinas and Virginia. Gerald had lived in Savannah long enough to acquire the viewpoint of the Coast— that all of the rest of the state was backwoods, with an Indian lurking in every thicket. In transacting business for O'Hara Brothers, he had visited Augusta, a hundred miles up the Savannah River, and he had travelled inland far enough to visit the old towns westward from that city. He knew that section to be as well settled as the

71

Coast, but from the stranger's description, his plantation was more than two hundred and fifty miles inland from Savannah to the north and west, and not many miles south of the Chattahoochee River. Gerald knew that northward beyond that stream the land was still held by the Cherokees, so it was with amazement that he heard the stranger jeer at suggestions of trouble with the Indians and narrate how thriving towns were growing up and plantations prospering in the new country.

An hour later when the conversation began to lag, Gerald, with a guile that belied the wide innocence of his bright blue eyes, proposed a game. As the night wore on and the drinks went round, there came a time when all the others in the game laid down their hands and Gerald and the stranger were battling alone. The stranger shoved in all his chips and·followed with the deed to his plantation. Gerald shoved in all his chips and laid on top of them his wallet. If the money it contained happened to belong to the firm of O'Hara Brothers, Gerald's conscience was not sufficiently troubled to confess it before Mass the following morning. He knew what he wanted, and when Gerald wanted something he gained it by taking the most direct route. Moreover, such was his faith in his destiny and four deuces that he never for a moment wondered just how the money would be paid back should a higher hand be laid down across the table.

"It's no bargain you're getting and I am glad not to have to pay more taxes on the place," sighed the possessor of an "ace full", as he called for pen and ink. "The big house burned a year ago and the fields are growing up in brush and seedling pine. But it's yours."

"Never mix cards and whisky unless you were weaned on Irish poteen," Gerald told Pork gravely the same evening, as Pork assisted him to bed. And the valet, who had begun to attempt a brogue out of admiration for his new master, made requisite answer in a combination of Geechee and County Meath that would have puzzled anyone except those two alone.

The muddy Flint River, running silently between walls of pine and water oak covered with tangled vines, wrapped about Gerald's new land like a curving arm and embraced it on two sides. To Gerald standing on the small knoll where the house had been, this tall barrier of green was as visible and pleasing an evidence of ownership as though it were a fence that he himself had built to mark his own. He stood on the blackened foundation stones of the burned building, looked down the long avenue of trees leading toward the road and swore lustily, with a joy too deep for thankful prayer. These twin lines of sombre trees were his, his the abandoned lawn, waist-high in weeds under white-starred young magnolia trees. The uncultivated fields, studded with tiny pines and underbrush, that stretched their rolling red-clay surface away into the distance on four sides belonged to Gerald O'Hara—were all his because he had an unbefuddled Irish head and the courage to stake everything on a hand of cards.

Gerald closed his eyes and, in the stillness of the unworked acres, he felt that he had come home. Here under his feet would rise a house of whitewashed brick. Across the road would be new rail fences, enclosing fat cattle and blooded horses, and the red earth that rolled down the hillside to the rich river bottom land would gleam white as eiderdown in the sun—cotton, acres and acres of cotton! The fortunes of the O'Haras would rise again.

With his own small stake, what he could borrow from his unenthusiastic brothers and a neat sum from mortgaging the land, Gerald bought his first field hands and came to Tara to live in bachelor solitude in the four-room overseer's house, till such a time as the white walls of Tara should rise.

He cleared the fields and planted cotton and borrowed more money from James and Andrew to buy more slaves. The O'Haras were a clannish tribe, clinging to one another in prosperity as well as in adversity, not for any overweening family affection but because they had learned through grim years that to survive a family must present an unbroken front to the world. They lent Gerald the money and, in the years that followed, the money came back to them with interest. Gradually the plantation widened out, as Gerald bought more acres lying near him, and in time the white house became a reality instead of a dream.

It was built by slave labour, a clumsy sprawling building that crowned the rise of ground overlooking the green incline of pasture land running down to the river; and it pleased Gerald greatly, for, even when new, it wore a look of mellowed years. The old oaks, which had seen Indians pass under their limbs, hugged the house closely with their great trunks and towered their branches over the roof in dense shade. The lawn, reclaimed from weeds, grew thick with clover and Bermuda grass, and Gerald saw to it that it was well kept. From the avenue of cedars to the row of white cabins in the slave quarters, there was an air of solidness, of stability and permanence about Tara; and whenever Gerald galloped around the bend in the road and saw his own roof rising through green branches, his heart swelled with pride as though each sight of it were the first sight.

He had done it all, little, hard-headed, blustering Gerald.

Gerald was on excellent terms with all his neighbours in the County, except the MacIntoshes whose land adjoined his on the left and the Slatterys whose meagre three acres stretched on his right along the swamp bottoms between the river and John Wilkes' plantation.

The MacIntoshes were Scotch-Irish and Orangemen and, had they possessed all the saintly qualities of the Catholic calendar, this ancestry would have damned them forever in Gerald's eyes. True, they had lived in Georgia for seventy years and, before that, had spent a generation in the Carolinas; but the first of the family who set foot on American shores had come from Ulster, and that was enough for Gerald.

They were a close-mouthed and stiff-necked family, who kept strictly to themselves and intermarried with their Carolina relatives, and Gerald was not alone in disliking them, for the County people were neighbourly and sociable and none too tolerant of anyone lacking in those same qualities. Rumours of Abolitionist sympathies did not enhance the popularity of the MacIntoshes. Old Angus had never manumitted a single slave and had committed the unpardonable social breach of selling some of his negroes to passing slave-traders en route to the cane fields of Louisiana, but the rumours persisted.

"He's an Abolitionist, no doubt," observed Gerald to John Wilkes. "But, in an Orangeman, when a principle comes up against Scotch tightness, the principle fares ill."

The Slatterys were another affair. Being poor white, they were not even accorded the grudging respect that Angus MacIntosh's dour independence wrung from neighbouring families. Old Slattery, who clung persistently to his few acres, in spite of repeated offers from Gerald and John Wilkes, was shiftless and whining. His wife was a snarly-haired woman, sickly and washed-out of appearance, the mother of a brood of sullen and rabbity-looking children—a brood which was increased regularly every year. Tom Slattery owned no slaves, and he and his two oldest boys spasmodically worked their few acres of cotton, while the wife and younger children tended what was supposed to be a vegetable garden. But, somehow, the cotton always failed, and the garden, due to Mrs. Slattery's constant childbearing, seldom furnished enough to feed her flock.

The sight of Tom Slattery dawdling on his neighbours' porches, begging cotton seed for planting or a side of bacon to "tide him over", was a familiar one. Slattery hated his neighbours with what little energy he possessed, sensing their contempt beneath their courtesy, and especially did he hate "rich folks' uppity niggers". The house negroes of the County considered themselves superior to white trash, and their unconcealed scorn stung him, while their more secure position in life stirred his envy. By contrast with his own miserable existence, they were well-fed, well-clothed and looked after in sickness and old age. They were proud of the good names of their owners and, for the most part, proud to belong to people who were quality, while he was despised by all.

Tom Slattery could have sold his farm for three times its value to any of the planters in the County. They would have considered it money well spent to rid the community of an eyesore, but he was well satisfied to remain and to subsist miserably on the proceeds of a bale of cotton a year and the charity of his neighbours.

With all the rest of the County, Gerald was on terms of amity and some intimacy. The Wilkeses, the Calverts, the Tarletons, the Fontaines, all smiled when the small figure on the big white horse galloped up their driveways, smiled and signalled for tall glasses in which a pony of Bourbon had been poured over a teaspoon of sugar and a sprig of crushed mint. Gerald was likeable, and the neighbours learned in time what the children, negroes and dogs discovered at first sight, that a kind heart, a ready and sympathetic ear and an open pocketbook lurked just behind his bawling voice and his truculent manner.

His arrival was always amid a bedlam of hounds barking and small black children shouting as they raced to meet him, quarrelling for the privilege of holding his horse and squirming and grinning under his good-natured insults. The white children clamoured to sit on his knee and be trotted, while he denounced to their elders the infamy of Yankee politicians; the daughters of his friends took him into their confidence about their love affairs; and the youths of the neighbourhood, fearful of confessing debts of honour upon the carpets of their fathers, found him a friend in need.

"So, you've been owing this for a month, you young rascal!" he would shout. "And, in God's name, why haven't you been asking me for the money before this?"

His rough manner of speech was too well known to give offence, and it only made the young men grin sheepishly and reply: "Well, sir, I hated to trouble you, and my father—"

"Your father's a good man, and no denying it, but strict, and so take this and let's be hearing no more of it."

The planters' ladies were the last to capitulate. But, when Mrs. Wilkes, "a great lady and with a rare gift for silence", as Gerald characterized her, told her husband one evening, after Gerald's horse had pounded down the driveway, "He has a rough tongue, but he is a gentleman," Gerald had definitely arrived.

He did not know that he had taken nearly ten years to arrive, for it never occurred to him that his neighbours had eyed him askance at first. In his own mind, there had never been any doubt that he belonged, from the moment he first set foot on Tara.

When Gerald was forty-three, so thickset of body and florid of face that he looked like a hunting squire out of a sporting print, it came to him that Tara, dear though it was, and the County folk, with their open hearts and open houses, were not enough. He wanted a wife.

Tara cried out for a mistress. The fat cook, a yard negro elevated by necessity to the kitchen, never had the meals on time, and the chamber-maid, formerly a field hand, let dust accumulate on the furniture and never seemed to have clean linen on hand, so that the arrival of guests was always the occasion of much stirring and to-do. Pork, the only trained house negro on the place, had general supervision over the other servants, but even he had grown slack and careless after several years of exposure to Gerald's happy-go-lucky mode of living. As valet, he kept Gerald's bedroom in order, and, as butler, he served the meals with dignity and style but otherwise he pretty well let matters follow their own course.

With unerring African instinct, the negroes had all discovered that Gerald had a loud bark and no bite at all, and they took shameless advantage of him. The air was always thick with threats of selling slaves south and of direful whippings, but there never had been a slave sold from Tara and only one whipping, and that administered for not grooming down Gerald's pet horse after a long day's hunting.

Gerald's sharp blue eyes noticed how efficiently

his neighbours' houses were run and with what ease the smooth-haired wives in rustling skirts managed their servants. He had no knowledge of the dawn-till-midnight activities of these women, chained to supervision of cooking, nursing, sewing and laundering. He only saw the outward results, and those results impressed him.

The urgent need of a wife became clear to him one morning when he was dressing to ride to town for Court Day. Pork brought forth his favourite ruffled shirt, so inexpertly mended by the chambermaid as to be unwearable by anyone except his valet.

"Mist' Gerald," said Pork, gratefully rolling up the shirt as Gerald fumed, "whut you needs is a wife, and a wife whut has got plen'y of house niggers."

Gerald upbraided Pork for his impertinence, but he knew that he was right. He wanted a wife and he wanted children and, if he did not acquire them soon, it would be too late. But he was not going to marry just anyone, as Mr. Calvert had done, taking to wife the Yankee governess of his motherless children. His wife must be a lady and a lady of blood, with as many airs and graces as Mrs. Wilkes and the ability to manage Tara as well as Mrs. Wilkes ordered her own domain.

But there were two difficulties in the way of marriage into the County families. The first was the scarcity of girls of marriageable age. The second, and more serious one, was that Gerald was a "new man", despite his nearly ten years' residence, and a foreigner. No one knew anything about his family. While the society of up-country

Georgia was not so impregnable as that of the Coast aristocrats, no family wanted a daughter to wed a man about whose grandfather nothing was known.

Gerald knew that despite the genuine liking of the County men with whom he hunted, drank and talked politics there was hardly one whose daughter he could marry. And he did not intend to have it gossiped about over supper tables that this, that or the other father had regretfully refused to let Gerald O'Hara pay court to his daughter. This knowledge did not make Gerald feel inferior to his neighbours. Nothing could ever make Gerald feel that he was inferior in any way to anyone. It was merely a quaint custom of the County that daughters only married into families who had lived in the South much longer than twenty-two years, had owned land and slaves and been addicted only to the fashionable vices during that time.

"Pack up. We're going to Savannah," he told Pork. "And if I hear you say 'Whist!' or 'Faith!' but once, it's selling you I'll be doing, for they are words I seldom say meself."

James and Andrew might have some advice to offer on this subject of marriage, and there might be daughters among their old friends who would both meet his requirements and find him acceptable as a husband. James and Andrew listened to his story patiently but they gave him little encouragement. They had no Savannah relatives to whom they might look for assistance, for they had been married when they came to America. And the daughters of their old friends had long since married and were raising small children of their own.

"You're not a rich man and you haven't a great family," said James.

"I've made me money and I can make a great family. And I won't be marrying just anyone."

"You fly high," observed Andrew, dryly.

But they did their best for Gerald. James and Andrew were old men and they stood well in Savannah. They had many friends, and for a month they carried Gerald from home to home, to suppers, dances and picnics.

"There's only one who takes me eye," Gerald said finally. "And she not even born when I landed here."

"And who is it takes your eye?"

"Miss Ellen Robillard," said Gerald, trying to speak casually, for the slightly tilting dark eyes of Ellen Robillard had taken more than his eye. Despite a mystifying listlessness of manner, so strange in a girl of fifteen, she charmed him. Moreover, there was a haunting look of despair about her that went to his heart and made him more gentle with her than he had ever been with any person in all the world.

"And you old enough to be her father!"

"And me in me prime!" cried Gerald, stung.

James spoke quietly.

"Jerry, there's no girl in Savannah you'd have less chance of marrying. Her father is a Robillard, and those French are proud as Lucifer. And her mother—God rest her soul—was a very great lady."

"I care not," said Gerald heatedly. "Besides,

her mother is dead, and old man Robillard likes me."

"As a man, yes, but as a son-in-law, no."

"The girl wouldn't have you anyway," interposed Andrew. "She's been in love with that wild buck of a cousin of hers, Philippe Robillard, for a year now, despite her family being at her morning and night to give him up."

"He's been gone to Louisiana this month now," said Gerald.

"And how do you know?"

"I know," answered Gerald, who did not care to disclose that Pork had supplied this valuable bit of information, or that Philippe had departed for the West at the express desire of his family. "And I do not think she's been so much in love with him that she won't forget him. Fifteen is too young to know much about love."

"They'd rather have that breakneck cousin for her than you."

So, James and Andrew were as startled as anyone when the news came out that the daughter of Pierre Robillard was to marry the little Irishman from up the country. Savannah buzzed behind its doors and speculated about Philippe Robillard, who had gone West, but the gossiping brought no answer. Why the loveliest of the Robillard daughters should marry a loud-voiced, red-faced little man who came hardly up to her ears remained a mystery to all.

Gerald himself never quite knew how it all came about. He only knew that a miracle had happened. And, for once in his life, he was utterly humble when Ellen, very white but very calm,

83

put a light hand on his arm and said: "I will marry you, Mr. O'Hara."

The thunderstruck Robillards knew the answer in part, but only Ellen and her mammy ever knew the whole story of the night when the girl sobbed till the dawn like a broken-hearted child and rose up in the morning a woman with her mind made up.

With foreboding, Mammy had brought her young mistress a small package, addressed in a strange hand from New Orleans, a package containing a miniature of Ellen, which she flung to the floor with a cry, four letters in her own handwriting to Philippe Robillard, and a brief letter from a New Orleans priest, announcing the death of her cousin in a barroom brawl.

"They drove him away, Father and Pauline and Eulalie. They drove him away. I hate them. I hate them all. I never want to see them again. I want to get away. I will go away where I'll never see them again, or this town, or anyone who reminds me of—of—him."

And when the night was nearly spent, Mammy, who had cried herself out over her mistress' dark head, protested, "But, honey, you kain do dat!"

"I will do it. He is a kind man. I will do it or go into the convent at Charleston."

It was the threat of the convent that finally won the assent of bewildered and heartstricken Pierre Robillard. He was staunchly Presbyterian, even though his family were Catholic, and the thought of his daughter becoming a nun was even worse than that of her marrying Gerald O'Hara. After

84

all, the man had nothing against him but a lack of family.

So, Ellen, no longer Robillard, turned her back on Savannah, never to see it again, and with a middle-aged husband, Mammy, and twenty "house niggers" journeyed toward Tara.

The next year, their first child was born and they named her Katie Scarlett, after Gerald's mother. Gerald was disappointed, for he had wanted a son, but he nevertheless was pleased enough over his small black-haired daughter to serve rum to every slave at Tara and to get roaringly, happily drunk himself.

If Ellen had ever regretted her sudden decision to marry him, no one ever knew it, certainly not Gerald, who almost burst with pride whenever he looked at her. She had put Savannah and its memories behind her when she left that gently mannered city by the sea, and, from the moment of her arrival in the County, north Georgia was her home.

When she departed from her father's house forever, she had left a home whose lines were as beautiful and flowing as a woman's body, as a ship in full sail; a pale-pink stucco house built in the French colonial style, set high from the ground in a dainty manner, approached by swirling stairs, banistered with wrought iron as delicate as lace; a dim, rich house, gracious but aloof.

She had left not only that graceful dwelling but also the entire civilization that was behind the building of it, and she found herself in a world that was as strange and different as if she had crossed a continent.

Here in north Georgia was a rugged section held by a hardy people. High up on the plateau at the foot of the Blue Ridge Mountains, she saw rolling red hills wherever she looked, with huge outcroppings of the underlying granite and gaunt pines towering sombrely everywhere. It all seemed wild and untamed to her coast-bred eyes accustomed to the quiet jungle beauty of the sea islands draped in their grey moss and tangled green, the white stretches of beach hot beneath a semi-tropic sun, the long flat vistas of sandy land studded with palmetto and palm.

This was a section that knew the chill of winter, as well as the heat of summer, and there was a vigour and energy in the people that was strange to her. They were a kindly people, courteous, generous, filled with abounding good nature, but sturdy, virile, easy to anger. The people of the Coast which she had left might pride themselves on taking all of their affairs, even their duels and their feuds, with a careless air; but these north Georgia people had a streak of violence in them. On the Coast, life had mellowed—here it was young and lusty and new.

All the people Ellen had known in Savannah might have been cast from the same mould, so similar were their viewpoints and traditions, but here was a variety of people. North Georgia's settlers were coming in from many different places, from other parts of Georgia, from the Carolinas and Virginia, from Europe and the North. Some of them, like Gerald, were new people seeking their fortunes. Some, like Ellen, were members of old families who had found life intolerable in their former homes and sought haven in a distant land. Many had moved for no reason at all, except that the restless blood of pioneering fathers quickened in their veins.

These people, drawn from many different places and with many different backgrounds, gave the whole life of the County an informality that was new to Ellen, an informality to which she never quite accustomed herself. She instinctively knew how Coast people would act in any circumstance. There was never any telling what north Georgians would do.

And, quickening all of the affairs of the section, was the high tide of prosperity then rolling over the South. All of the world was crying out for cotton, and the new land of the County, unworn and fertile, produced it abundantly. Cotton was the heartbeat of the section, the planting and the picking were the diastole and systole of the red earth. Wealth came out of the curving furrows, and arrogance came too—arrogance built on green bushes and the acres of fleecy white. If cotton could make them rich in one generation, how much richer they would be in the next!

This certainty of the morrow gave zest and enthusiasm to life, and the County people enjoyed life with a heartiness that Ellen could never understand. They had money enough and slaves enough to give them time to play, and they liked to play. They seemed never too busy to drop work for a fish-fry, a hunt or a horse race, and scarcely a week went by without its barbecue or ball.

Ellen never would, or could, quite become one of them—she had left too much of herself in Savannah—but she respected them and, in time, learned to admire the frankness and forthrightness of these people, who had few reticences and who valued a man for what he was.

She became the best-loved neighbour in the County. She was a thrifty and kind mistress, a good mother and a devoted wife. The heartbreak and selflessness that she would have dedicated to the Church were devoted instead to the service of her child, her household and the man who had taken her out of Savannah and its memories and had never asked any questions.

When Scarlett was a year old, and more healthy and vigorous than a girl baby had any right to be, in Mammy's opinion, Ellen's second child, named Susan Elinor, but always called Suellen, was born, and in due time came Carreen, listed in the family Bible as Caroline Irene. Then followed three little boys, each of whom died before he had learned to walk—three little boys who now lay under the twisted cedars in the burying-ground a hundred yards from the house, beneath three stones, each bearing the name of "Gerald O'Hara, Jr.".

From the day when Ellen first came to Tara, the place had been transformed. If she was only fifteen years old, she was nevertheless ready for the responsibilities of the mistress of a plantation. Before marriage, young girls must be, above all other things, sweet, gentle, beautiful and ornamental, but, after marriage, they were expected to manage households that numbered a hundred people or more, white and black, and they were trained with that in view.

Ellen had been given this preparation for marriage which any well-brought-up young lady received, and she also had Mammy, who could galvanize the most shiftless negro into energy. She quickly brought order, dignity and grace into Gerald's household, and she gave to Tara a beauty it had never had before.

The house had been built according to no architectural plan whatever, with extra rooms added where and when it seemed convenient, but, with Ellen's care and attention, it gained a charm that made up for its lack of design. The avenue of cedars leading from the main road to the house —that avenue of cedars without which no Georgia planter's home could be complete—had a cool dark shadiness that gave a brighter tinge, by contrast, to the green of the other trees. The wisteria tumbling over the verandas showed bright against the whitewashed brick, and it joined with the pink crêpe myrtle bushes by the door and the white-blossomed magnolias in the yard to disguise some of the awkward lines of the house.

In springtime and summer, the Bermuda grass and clover on the lawn became emerald, so enticing an emerald that it presented an irresistible temptation to the flocks of turkeys and white geese that were supposed to roam only the regions in the rear of the house. The elders of the flocks continually led stealthy advances into the front yard, lured on by the green of the grass and the luscious promise of the cape jessamine buds and the zinnia beds. Against their depredations, a small black sentinel was stationed on the front porch. Armed with a ragged towel, the little negro boy sitting on the steps was part of the picture of Tara—and an unhappy one, for he was forbidden to chunk the fowls and could only flap the towel at them and shoo them.

Ellen set dozens of little black boys to this task, the first position of responsibility a male slave had at Tara. After they had passed their tenth year, they were sent to old Daddy the plantation cobbler to learn his trade, or to Amos the wheel-wright and carpenter, or Phillip the cow man, or Cuffee the mule boy. If they showed no aptitude for any of these trades, they became field hands and, in the opinion of the negroes, they had lost their claim to any social standing at all.

Ellen's life was not easy, nor was it happy, but she did not expect life to be easy, and, if it was not happy, that was woman's lot. It was a man's world, and she accepted it as such. The man owned the property, and the woman managed it. The man took the credit for the management, and the woman praised his cleverness The man roared like a bull when a splinter was in his finger, and the woman muffled the moans of childbirth, lest she disturb him. Men were rough of speech and often drunk. Women ignored the lapses of speech and put the drunkards to bed without bitter words. Men were rude and outspoken; women were always kind, gracious and forgiving.

She had been reared in the tradition of great

ladies, which had taught her how to carry her burden and still retain her charm, and she intended that her three daughters should be great ladies also. With her younger daughters, she had success, for Suellen was so anxious to be attractive she lent an attentive and obedient ear to her mother's teachings, and Carreen was shy and easily led. But Scarlett, child of Gerald, found the road to ladyhood hard.

To Mammy's indignation, her preferred playmates were not her demure sisters or the well-brought-up Wilkes girls but the negro children on the plantation and the boys of the neighbourhood, and she could climb a tree or throw a rock as well as any of them. Mammy was greatly perturbed that Ellen's daughter should display such traits and frequently adjured her to "ack lak a lil lady". But Ellen took a more tolerant and long-sighted view of the matter. She knew that from childhood playmates grew beaux in later years, and the first duty of a girl was to get married. She told herself that the child was merely full of life and there was still time in which to teach her the arts and graces of being attractive to men.

To this end, Ellen and Mammy bent their efforts, and as Scarlett grew older she became an apt pupil in this subject, even though she learned little else. Despite a succession of governesses and two years at the near-by Fayetteville Female Academy, her education was sketchy, but no girl in the County danced more gracefully than she. She knew how to smile so that her dimples leaped, how to walk pigeon-toed so that her wide hoop skirts swayed entrancingly, how to look up into a man's face and then drop her eyes and bat the lids rapidly so that she seemed a-tremble with gentle emotion. Most of all she learned how to conceal from men a sharp intelligence beneath a face as sweet and bland as a baby's.

Ellen, by soft-voiced admonition, and Mammy, by constant carping, laboured to inculcate in her the qualities that would make her truly desirable as a wife.

"You must be more gentle, dear, more sedate," Ellen told her daughter. "You must not interrupt gentlemen when they are speaking, even if you do think you know more about matters than they do. Gentlemen do not like forward girls."

"Young misses whut frowns an' pushes out dey chins an' says 'Ah will' an' 'Ah woan' mos' gener 'ly doan ketch husbands," prophesied Mammy gloomily. "Young misses should cas' down dey eyes an' say, 'Well, suh, Ah mout' an' 'Jes' as you say, suh.'"

Between them, they taught her all that a gentle-woman should know, but she learned only the outward signs of gentility. The inner grace from which these signs should spring, she never learned nor did she see any reason for learning it. Appearances were enough, for the appearances of ladyhood won her popularity and that was all she wanted. Gerald bragged that she was the belle of five counties, and with some truth, for she had received proposals from nearly all the young men in the neighbourhood and many from places as far away as Atlanta and Savannah.

At sixteen, thanks to Mammy and Ellen, she looked sweet, charming and giddy, but she was, in reality, self-willed, vain and obstinate. She had the easily stirred passions of her Irish father and nothing except the thinnest veneer of her mother's unselfish and forbearing nature. Ellen never fully realized that it was only a veneer, for Scarlett always showed her best face to her mother, concealing her escapades, curbing her temper and appearing as sweet-natured as she could in Ellen's presence, for her mother could shame her to tears with a reproachful glance.

But Mammy was under no illusions about her and was constantly alert for breaks in the veneer. Mammy's eyes were sharper than Ellen's, and Scarlett could never recall in all her life having fooled Mammy for long.

It was not that these two loving mentors deplored Scarlett's high spirits, vivacity and charm. These were traits of which Southern women were proud. It was Gerald's headstrong and impetuous nature in her that gave them concern, and they sometimes feared they would not be able to conceal her damaging qualities until she had made a good match. But Scarlett intended to marry—and marry Ashley—and she was willing to appear demure, pliable and scatter-brained, if those were the qualities that attracted men. Just why men should be this way, she did not know. She only knew that such methods worked. It never interested her enough to try to think out the reason for it, for she knew nothing of the inner workings of any human being's mind, not even her own. She knew only that if she did or said thus-and-so, men would unerringly respond with the complementary thus-and-so. It was like a mathematical formula and no more difficult, for mathematics was the one subject that had come easy to Scarlett in her schooldays.

If she knew little about men's minds, she knew even less about the minds of women, for they interested her less. She had never had a girl friend, and she never felt any lack on that account. To her, all women, including her two sisters, were natural enemies in pursuit of the same prey—man.

All women with the one exception of her mother.

Ellen O'Hara was different, and Scarlett regarded her as something holy and apart from all the rest of humankind. When Scarlett was a child, she had confused her mother with the Virgin Mary, and now that she was older she saw no reason for changing her opinion. To her, Ellen represented the utter security that only Heaven or a mother can give. She knew that her mother was the embodiment of justice, truth, loving tenderness and profound wisdom—a great lady.

Scarlett wanted very much to be like her mother. The only difficulty was that by being just and truthful and tender and unselfish, one missed most of the joys of life, and certainly many beaux. And life was too short to miss such pleasant things. Some day when she was married to Ashley and old, some day when she had time for it, she intended to be like Ellen. But, until then . . .

4

THAT night at supper, Scarlett went through the motions of presiding over the table in her mother's absence, but her mind was in a ferment over the dreadful news she had heard about Ashley and Melanie. Desperately she longed for her mother's return from the Slatterys', for, without her, she felt lost and alone. What right had the Slatterys and their everlasting sickness to take Ellen away from home just at this time when she, Scarlett, needed her so much?

Throughout the dismal meal, Gerald's booming voice battered against her ears until she thought she could endure it no longer. He had forgotten completely about his conversation with her that afternoon and was carrying on a monologue about the latest news from Fort Sumter, which he punctuated by hammering his fist on the table and waving his arms in the air. Gerald made a habit of dominating the conversation at mealtimes, and usually Scarlett, occupied with her own thoughts, scarcely heard him; but to-night she could not shut out his voice, no matter how much she strained to listen for the sound of carriage wheels that would herald Ellen's return.

Of course, she did not intend to tell her mother what was so heavy on her heart, for Ellen would be shocked and grieved to know that a daughter of hers wanted a man who was engaged to another girl. But, in the depths of the first tragedy she

95

had ever known, she wanted the very comfort of her mother's presence. She always felt secure when Ellen was by her, for there was nothing so bad that Ellen could not better it, simply by being there.

She rose suddenly from her chair at the sound of creaking wheels in the driveway and then sank down again as they went on around the house to the back yard. It could not be Ellen, for she would alight at the front steps. Then there was an excited babble of negro voices in the darkness of the yard and high-pitched negro laughter. Looking out the window, Scarlett saw Pork, who had left the room a moment before, holding high a flaring pine knot, while indistinguishable figures descended from a wagon. The laughter and talking rose and fell in the dark night air, pleasant, homely, carefree sounds, gutturally soft, musically shrill. Then feet shuffled up the back-porch stairs and into the passageway leading to the main house, stopping in the hall just outside the dining-room. There was a brief interval of whispering, and Pork entered, his usual dignity gone, his eyes rolling and his white teeth a-gleam.

"Mist' Gerald," he announced, breathing hard, the pride of a bridegroom all over his shining face, "yo' new 'oman done come."

"New woman? I didn't buy any new woman," declared Gerald, pretending to glare.

"Yassah, you did, Mist' Gerald! Yassah! An' she out hyah now wantin' ter speak wid you," answered Pork, giggling and twisting his hands in excitement.

"Well, bring in the bride," said Gerald, and

Pork, turning, beckoned into the hall to his wife, newly arrived from the Wilkes plantation to become a part of the household of Tara. She entered, and behind her, almost hidden by her voluminous calico skirts, came her twelve-year-old daughter, squirming against her mother's legs.

Dilcey was tall and bore herself erectly. She might have been any age from thirty to sixty, so unlined was her immobile bronze face. Indian blood was plain in her features, overbalancing the negroid characteristics. The red colour of her skin, narrow high forehead, prominent cheekbones and the hawk-bridged nose which flattened at the end above thick negro lips, all showed the mixture of two races. She was self-possessed and walked with a dignity that surpassed even Mammy's, for Mammy had acquired her dignity and Dilcey's was in her blood.

When she spoke, her voice was not so slurred as most negroes' and she chose her words more carefully.

"Good evenin', young Misses. Mist' Gerald, I is sorry to 'sturb you, but I wanted to come here and thank you agin fo' buyin' me and my chile. Lots of gentlemens might a' bought me but they wouldn't a' bought my Prissy, too, jes' to keep me frum grievin' and I thanks you. I'm gwine do my bes' fo' you and show you I ain't forgettin'."

"Hum—hurrump," said Gerald, clearing his throat in embarrassment at being caught openly in an act of kindness.

Dilcey turned to Scarlett and something like a smile wrinkled the corners of her eyes. "Miss

97

Scarlett, Poke done tole me how you ast Mist' Gerald to buy me. And so I'm gwine give you my Prissy fo' yo' own maid."

She reached behind her and jerked the little girl forward. She was a brown little creature, with skinny legs like a bird and a myriad of pigtails carefully wrapped with twine sticking stiffly out from her head. She had sharp, knowing eyes that missed nothing and a studiedly stupid look on her face.

"Thank you, Dilcey," Scarlett replied, "but I'm afraid Mammy will have something to say about that. She's been my maid ever since I was born."

"Mammy gettin' ole," said Dilcey, with a calmness that would have enraged Mammy. "She a good mammy, but you a young lady now and needs a good maid, and my Prissy been maidin' fo' Miss India fo' a year now. She kin sew and fix hair good as a grown pusson."

Prodded by her mother, Prissy bobbed a sudden curtsy and grinned at Scarlett, who could not help grinning back.

"A sharp little wench," she thought, and said aloud: "Thank you, Dilcey, we'll see about it when Mother comes home."

"Thank'ee, Ma'm. I gives you good night," said Dilcey, and, turning, left the room with her child, Pork dancing attendance.

The supper things cleared away, Gerald resumed his oration, but with little satisfaction to himself and none at all to his audience. His thunderous predictions of immediate war and his rhetorical questions as to whether the South would stand for further insults from the Yankees only produced faintly bored, "Yes, Papas" and "No, Pas." Carreen, sitting on a hassock under the big lamp, was deep in the romance of a girl who had taken the veil after her lover's death and, with silent tears of enjoyment oozing from her eyes, was pleasurably picturing herself in a white coif. Suellen, embroidering on what she gigglingly called her "hope chest", was wondering if she could possibly detach Stuart Tarleton from her sister's side at the barbecue to-morrow and fascinate him with the sweet womanly qualities which she possessed and Scarlett did not. And Scarlett was in a tumult about Ashley.

How could Pa talk on and on about Fort Sumter and the Yankees when he knew her heart was breaking? As usual in the very young, she marvelled that people could be so selfishly oblivious to her pain and the world rock along just the same, in spite of her heartbreak.

Her mind was as if a cyclone had gone through it, and it seemed strange that the dining-room where they sat should be so placid, so unchanged from what it had always been. The heavy mahogany table and sideboards, the massive silver, the bright rag rugs on the shining floor were all in their accustomed places, just as if nothing had happened. It was a friendly and comfortable room and, ordinarily, Scarlett loved the quiet hours which the family spent there after supper; but to-night she hated the sight of it and, if she had not feared her father's loudly bawled questions, she would have slipped away, down the dark hall to Ellen's little office and cried out her sorrow on the old sofa.

That was the room that Scarlett liked best in all the house. There, Ellen sat before her tall secretary each morning, keeping the accounts of the plantation and listening to the reports of Jonas Wilkerson, the overseer. There also the family idled while Ellen's quill scratched across her ledgers, Gerald in the old rocker, the girls on the sagging cushions of the sofa that was too battered and worn for the front of the house. Scarlett longed to be there now, alone with Ellen, so she could put her head in her mother's lap and cry in peace. Wouldn't Mother ever come home?

Then, wheels ground sharply on the gravelled driveway, and the soft murmur of Ellen's voice dismissing the coachman floated into the room. The whole group looked up eagerly as she entered rapidly, her hoops swaying, her face tired and sad. There entered with her the faint fragrance of lemon verbena sachet, which seemed always to creep from the folds of her dresses, a fragrance that was always linked in Scarlett's mind with her mother. Mammy followed at a few paces, the leather bag in her hand, her underlip pushed out and her brow lowering. Mammy muttered darkly to herself as she waddled, taking care that her remarks were pitched too low to be understood but loud enough to register her unqualified disapproval.

"I am sorry I am so late," said Ellen, slipping her plaid shawl from drooping shoulders and handing it to Scarlett, whose cheek she patted in passing.

Gerald's face had brightened as if by magic at her entrance.

"Is the brat baptized?" he questioned.

"Yes, and dead, poor thing," said Ellen. "I feared Emmie would die too, but I think she will live."

The girls' faces turned to her, startled and questioning, and Gerald wagged his head philosophically.

"Well, 'tis better so that the brat is dead, no doubt, poor fatherle—"

"It is late. We had better have prayers now," interrupted Ellen so smoothly that, if Scarlett had not known her mother well, the interruption would have passed unnoticed.

It would be interesting to know who was the father of Emmie Slattery's baby, but Scarlett knew she would never learn the truth of the matter if she waited to hear it from her mother. Scarlett suspected Jonas Wilkerson, for she had frequently seen him walking down the road with Emmie at nightfall. Jonas was a Yankee and a bachelor, and the fact that he was an overseer forever barred him from any contact with the County social life. There was no family of any standing into which he could marry, no people with whom he could associate except the Slatterys and riff-raff like them. As he was several cuts above the Slatterys in education, it was only natural that he should not want to marry Emmie, no matter how often he might walk with her in the twilight.

Scarlett sighed, for her curiosity was sharp. Things were always happening under her mother's eyes which she noticed no more than if they had not happened at all. Ellen ignored all things contrary to her ideas of propriety and tried to teach Scarlett to do the same, but with poor success.

Ellen had stepped to the mantel to take her rosary beads from the small inlaid casket in which they always reposed when Mammy spoke up with firmness.

"Miss Ellen, you gwine eat some supper befo' you does any prayin'."

"Thank you, Mammy, but I am not hungry."

"Ah gwine fix yo' supper mahseff an' you eats it," said Mammy, her brow furrowed with indignation as she started down the hall for the kitchen. "Poke!" she called, "tell Cookie stir up de fiah. Miss Ellen home."

As the boards shuddered under her weight, the soliloquy she had been muttering in the front hall grew louder and louder, coming clearly to the ears of the family in the dining-room.

"Ah has said time an' agin, it doan do no good doin' nuthin' fer w'ite trash. Dey is de shiflesses', mos' ungrateful passel of no-counts livin'. An' Miss Ellen got no bizness weahin' herseff out waitin' on folks dat did dey be wuth shootin' dey'd have niggers ter wait on dem. An' Ah has said—"

Her voice trailed off as she went down the long open passageway, covered only by a roof, that led into the kitchen. Mammy had her own method of letting her owners know exactly where she stood on all matters. She knew it was beneath the dignity of quality white folks to pay the slightest attention to what a darky said when she was just grumbling to herself. She knew that to uphold this dignity, they must ignore what she said, even if she stood in the next room and almost shouted. It protected her from reproof, and it left no doubt in anyone's mind as to her exact views on any subject.

Pork entered the room, bearing a plate, silver and a napkin. He was followed closely by Jack, a black little boy of ten, hastily buttoning a white linen jacket with one hand and bearing in the other a fly-swisher, made of thin strips of newspaper tied to a reed longer than he was. Ellen had a beautiful peacock-feather fly-brusher, but it was used only on very special occasions and then only after domestic struggle, due to the obstinate conviction of Pork, Cookie and Mammy that peacock feathers were bad luck.

Ellen sat down in the chair which Gerald pulled out for her and four voices attacked her.

"Mother, the lace is loose on my new ball dress and I want to wear it to-morrow night at Twelve Oaks. Won't you please fix it?"

"Mother, Scarlett's new dress is prettier than mine and I look like a fright in pink. Why can't she wear my pink and let me wear her green? She looks all right in pink."

"Mother, can I stay up for the ball to-morrow night? I'm thirteen now—"

"Mrs. O'Hara, would you believe it—Hush, you girls, before I take me crop to you! Cade Calvert was in Atlanta this morning and he says —Will you be quiet and let me be hearing me own voice?—and he says it's all upset they are there and talking nothing but war, militia drilling, troops forming. And he says the news from Charleston is that they will be putting up with no more Yankee insults."

Ellen's tired mouth smiled into the tumult as she addressed herself first to her husband, as a wife should.

"If the nice people of Charleston feel that way, I'm sure we will all feel the same way soon," she said, for she had a deeply rooted belief that, excepting only Savannah, most of the gentle blood of the whole continent could be found in that small seaport city, a belief shared largely by Charlestonians.

"No, Carreen, next year, dear. Then you can stay up for balls and wear grown-up dresses, and what a good time my little pink cheeks will have! Don't pout, dear. You can go to the barbecue, remember that, and stay up through supper, but no balls till you are fourteen.

"Give me your gown, Scarlett. I will whip the lace for you after prayers.

"Suellen, I do not like your tone, dear. Your pink gown is lovely and suitable to your complexion, as Scarlett's is to hers. But you may wear my garnet necklace to-morrow night."

Suellen, behind her mother's back, wrinkled her nose triumphantly at Scarlett, who had been planning to beg the necklace for herself. Scarlett put out her tongue at her. Suellen was an annoying sister with her whining and selfishness, and had it not been for Ellen's restraining hand, Scarlett would frequently have boxed her ears.

"Now, Mr. O'Hara, tell me more about what Mr. Calvert said about Charleston," said Ellen.

Scarlett knew her mother cared nothing at all about war and politics and thought them masculine matters about which no lady could intelligently concern herself. But it gave Gerald pleasure to air his views, and Ellen was unfailingly thoughtful of her husband's pleasure.

While Gerald launched forth on his news, Mammy set the plates before her mistress, golden-topped biscuits, breast of fried chicken and a yellow yam open and steaming, with melted butter dripping from it. Mammy pinched small Jack, and he hastened to his business of slowly swishing the paper ribbons back and forth behind Ellen. Mammy stood beside the table, watching every forkful that travelled from plate to mouth, as though she intended to force the food down Ellen's throat should she see signs of flagging. Ellen ate diligently, but Scarlett could see that she was too tired to know what she was eating. Only Mammy's implacable face forced her to it.

When the dish was empty and Gerald only midway in his remarks on the thievishness of Yankees who wanted to free darkies and yet offered no penny to pay for their freedom, Ellen rose.

"We'll be having prayers?" he questioned, reluctantly.

"Yes. It is so late—why, it is actually ten o'clock," as the clock with coughing and tinny thumps marked the hour. "Carreen should have been asleep long ago. The lamp, please, Pork, and my prayer-book, Mammy."

Prompted by Mammy's hoarse whisper, Jack set his fly-brush in the corner and removed the dishes, while Mammy fumbled in the sideboard drawer for Ellen's worn prayer-book. Pork, tiptoeing, reached the ring in the chain and drew the lamp slowly down until the table top was brightly bathed in light and the ceiling receded into shadows. Ellen arranged her skirts and sank to the floor on her knees, laying the open prayer-book on the table before her and clasping her hands upon it. Gerald knelt beside her, and Scarlett and Suellen took their accustomed places on the opposite side of the table, folding their voluminous petticoats in pads under their knees, so they would ache less from contact with the hard floor. Carreen, who was small for her age, could not kneel comfortably at the table and so knelt facing a chair, her elbows on the seat. She liked this position, for she seldom failed to go to sleep during prayers and, in this posture, it escaped her mother's notice.

The house servants shuffled and rustled in the hall to kneel by the doorway, Mammy groaning aloud as she sank down, Pork straight as a ramrod, Rosa and Teena, the maids, graceful in their spreading bright calicoes, Cookie gaunt and yellow beneath her snowy head-rag, and Jack, stupid with sleep, as far away from Mammy's pinching fingers as possible. Their dark eyes gleamed expectantly, for praying with their white folks was one of the events of the day. The old and colourful phrases of the litany with its Oriental imagery meant little to them but it satisfied something in their hearts, and they always swayed when they chanted the responses: "Lord, have mercy on us," "Christ, have mercy on us."

Ellen closed her eyes and began praying, her voice rising and falling, lulling and soothing. Heads bowed in the circle of yellow light as Ellen thanked God for the health and happiness of her home, her family and her negroes.

When she had finished her prayers for those beneath the roof of Tara, her father, mother, sisters, three dead babies and "all the poor souls in Purgatory", she clasped her white beads between long fingers and began the Rosary. Like the rushing of a soft wind, the responses from black throats and white throats rolled back:

"Holy Mary, Mother of God, pray for us sinners, now, and at the hour of our death."

Despite her heartache and the pain of unshed tears, a deep sense of quiet and peace fell upon Scarlett as it always did at this hour. Some of the disappointment of the day and the dread of the morrow departed from her, leaving a feeling of hope. It was not the lifting up of her heart to God that brought this balm, for religion went no more than lip-deep with her. It was the sight of her mother's serene face upturned to the throne of God and His saints and angels, praying for blessings on those whom she loved. When Ellen intervened with Heaven, Scarlett felt certain that Heaven heard.

Ellen finished and Gerald, who could never find his beads at prayer time, began furtively counting his decade on his fingers. As his voice droned on, Scarlett's thoughts strayed, in spite of herself. She knew she should be examining her conscience.

Ellen had taught her that at the end of each day it was her duty to examine her conscience thoroughly, to admit her numerous faults and pray to God for forgiveness and strength never to repeat them. But Scarlett was examining her heart.

She dropped her head upon her folded hands so that her mother could not see her face, and her thoughts went sadly back to Ashley. How could he be planning to marry Melanie when he really loved her, Scarlett? And when he knew how much she loved him? How could he deliberately break her heart?

Then, suddenly, an idea, shining and new, flashed like a comet through her brain.

"Why, Ashley hasn't an idea that I'm in love with him!"

She almost gasped aloud in the shock of its unexpectedness. Her mind stood still as if paralysed for a long, breathless instant, and then raced forward.

"How could he know? I've always acted so prissy and ladylike and touch-me-not around him he probably thinks I don't care a thing about him except as a friend. Yes, that's why he's never spoken! He thinks his love is hopeless. And that's why he's looked so—"

Her mind went swiftly back to those times when she had caught him looking at her in that strange manner, when the grey eyes that were such perfect curtains for his thoughts had been wide and naked and had in them a look of torment and despair.

"He's been broken-hearted because he thinks

I'm in love with Brent or Stuart or Cade. And probably he thinks that if he can't have me, he might as well please his family and marry Melanie. But if he knew I did love him—"

Her volatile spirits shot up from deepest depression to excited happiness. This was the answer to Ashley's reticence, to his strange conduct. He didn't know! Her vanity leaped to the aid of her desire to believe, making belief a certainty. If he knew she loved him, he would hasten to her side. She had only to—

"Oh!" she thought rapturously, digging her fingers into her lowered brow. "What a fool I've been not to think of this till now! I must think of some way to let him know. He wouldn't marry her if he knew I loved him! How could he?"

With a start, she realized that Gerald had finished and her mother's eyes were on her. Hastily she began her decade, telling off the beads automatically but with a depth of emotion in her voice that caused Mammy to open her eyes and shoot a searching glance at her. As she finished her prayers and Suellen, then Carreen, began their decades, her mind was still speeding onward with her entrancing new thought.

Even now, it wasn't too late! Too often the County had been scandalized by elopements when one or the other of the participating parties was practically at the altar with a third. And Ashley's engagement had not even been announced yet! Yes, there was plenty of time!

If no love lay between Ashley and Melanie but only a promise given long ago, then why wasn't it possible for him to break that promise and marry her? Surely he would do it, if he knew that she, Scarlett, loved him. She must find some way to let him know. She would find some way! And then—

Scarlett came abruptly out of her dream of delight, for she had neglected to make the responses and her mother was looking at her reprovingly. As she resumed the ritual, she opened her eyes briefly and cast a quick glance around the room. The kneeling figures, the soft glow of the lamp, the dim shadows where the negroes swayed, even the familiar objects that had been so hateful to her sight an hour ago, in an instant took on the colour of her own emotions, and the room seemed once more a lovely place. She would never forget this moment or this scene!

"Virgin most faithful," her mother intoned. The Litany of the Virgin was beginning, and obediently Scarlett responded: "Pray for us," as Ellen praised in soft contralto the attributes of the Mother of God.

As always since childhood, this was, for Scarlett, a moment for adoration of Ellen, rather than the Virgin. Sacrilegious though it might be, Scarlett always saw, through her closed eyes, the upturned face of Ellen and not the Blessed Virgin, as the ancient phrases were repeated. "Health of the Sick", "Seat of Wisdom", "Refuge of Sinners", "Mystical Rose"—they were beautiful words because they were the attributes of Ellen. But to-night, because of the exaltation of her own spirit, Scarlett found in the whole ceremonial, the softly spoken words, the murmur of the responses, a surpassing beauty beyond any that she had ever experienced before. And her heart went up to God in sincere thankfulness that a pathway for her feet had been opened—out of her misery and straight to the arms of Ashley.

When the last "Amen" sounded, they all rose, somewhat stiffly, Mammy being hauled to her feet by the combined efforts of Teena and Rosa. Pork took a long spiller from the mantelpiece, lit it from the lamp-flame and went into the hall. Opposite the winding stair stood a walnut sideboard, too large for use in the dining-room, bearing on its wide top several lamps and a long row of candles in candlesticks. Pork lit one lamp and three candles and, with the pompous dignity of a first chamberlain of the royal bedchamber lighting a king and queen to their rooms, he led the procession up the stairs, holding the light high above his head. Ellen, on Gerald's arm, followed him, and the girls, each taking her own candlestick, mounted after them.

Scarlett entered her room, set the candle on the tall chest of drawers and fumbled in the dark closet for the dancing dress that needed stitching. Throwing it across her arm, she crossed the hall quietly. The door of her parents' bedroom was slightly ajar and, before she could knock, Ellen's voice, low but stern, came to her ears.

"Mr. O'Hara, you must dismiss Jonas Wilkerson."

Gerald exploded, "And where will I be getting another overseer who wouldn't be cheating me out of me eyeteeth?"

"He must be dismissed, immediately, tomorrow morning. Big Sam is a good foreman and

111

he can take over the duties until you can hire another overseer."

"Ah, ha!" came Gerald's voice. "So, I understand! Then the worthy Jonas sired the—"

"He must be dismissed."

"So, he is the father of Emmie Slattery's baby," thought Scarlett. "Oh, well. What else can you expect from a Yankee man and a white-trash girl?"

Then, after a discreet pause which gave Gerald's splutterings time to die away, she knocked on the door and handed the dress to her mother.

By the time Scarlett had undressed and blown out the candle, her plan for to-morrow had worked itself out in every detail. It was a simple plan, for, with Gerald's single-mindedness of purpose, her eyes were centred on the goal and she thought only of the most direct steps by which to reach it.

First, she would be "prideful", as Gerald had commanded. From the moment she arrived at Twelve Oaks, she would be her gayest, most spirited self. No one would suspect that she had ever been downhearted because of Ashley and Melanie. And she would flirt with every man there. That would be cruel to Ashley, but it would make him yearn for her all the more. She wouldn't overlook a man of marriageable age, from ginger-whiskered old Frank Kennedy, who was Suellen's beau, on down to shy, quiet, blushing Charles Hamilton, Melanie's brother. They would swarm around her like bees around a hive, and certainly Ashley would be drawn from

Melanie to join the circle of her admirers. Then somehow she would manoeuvre to get a few minutes alone with him, away from the crowd. She hoped everything would work out that way, because it would be more difficult otherwise. But if Ashley didn't make the first move, she would simply have to do it herself.

When they were finally alone, he would have fresh in his mind the picture of the other men thronging about her, he would be newly impressed with the fact that every one of them wanted her, and that look of sadness and despair would be in his eyes. Then she would make him happy again by letting him discover that, popular though she was, she preferred him above any other man in all the world. And when she admitted it, modestly and sweetly, she would look a thousand things more. Of course, she would do it all in a ladylike way. She wouldn't even dream of saying to him boldly that she loved him—that would never do. But the manner of telling him was a detail that troubled her not at all. She had managed such situations before and she could do it again.

Lying in the bed with the moonlight streaming dimly over her, she pictured the whole scene in her mind. She saw the look of surprise and happiness that would come over his face when he realized that she really loved him, and she heard the words he would say asking her to be his wife.

Naturally, she would have to say then that she simply couldn't think of marrying a man when he was engaged to another girl, but he would insist and finally she would let herself be persuaded.

Then they would decide to run off to Jonesboro that very afternoon and—

Why, by this time to-morrow night, she might be Mrs. Ashley Wilkes!

She sat up in bed, hugging her knees, and for a long happy moment she *was* Mrs. Ashley Wilkes—Ashley's bride! Then a slight chill entered her heart. Suppose it didn't work out this way? Suppose Ashley didn't beg her to run away with him? Resolutely she pushed the thought from her mind.

"I won't think of that now," she said firmly. "If I think of it now, it will upset me. There's no reason why things won't come out the way I want them—if he loves me. And I know he does!"

She raised her chin and her pale, black-fringed eyes sparkled in the moonlight. Ellen had never told her that desire and attainment were two different matters; life had not taught her that the race was not to the swift. She lay in the silvery shadows with courage rising and made the plans that a sixteen-year-old makes when life has been so pleasant that defeat is an impossibility and a pretty dress and a clear complexion are weapons to vanquish fate.

5

IT was ten o'clock in the morning. The day was warm for April and the golden sunlight streamed brilliantly into Scarlett's room through the blue curtains of the wide windows. The cream-coloured walls glowed with light and the depths of the mahogany furniture gleamed deep red like wine, while the floor glistened as if it were glass, except where the rag rugs covered it and they were spots of gay colour.

Already summer was in the air, the first hint of Georgia summer when the high tide of spring gives way reluctantly before a fiercer heat. A balmy, soft warmth poured into the room, heavy with velvety smells, redolent of many blossoms, of newly fledged trees and of the moist, freshly turned red earth. Through the window Scarlett could see the bright riot of the twin lines of daffodils bordering the gravelled driveway and the golden masses of yellow jessamine spreading flowery sprangles modestly to the earth like crinolines. The mocking-birds and the jays, engaged in their old feud for possession of the magnolia tree beneath her window, were bickering, the jays strident, acrimonious, the mockers sweet-voiced and plaintive.

Such a glowing morning usually called Scarlett to the window, to lean arms on the broad sill and drink in the scents and sounds of Tara. But today she had no eye for sun or azure sky beyond

115

a hasty thought, "Thank God, it isn't raining." On the bed lay the apple-green, watered-silk ball dress with its festoons of ecru lace, neatly packed in a large cardboard box. It was ready to be carried to Twelve Oaks to be donned before the dancing began, but Scarlett shrugged at the sight of it. If her plans were successful, she would not wear that dress to-night. Long before the ball began, she and Ashley would be on their way to Jonesboro to be married. The troublesome question was—what dress should she wear to the barbecue?

What dress would best set off her charms and make her most irresistible to Ashley? Since eight o'clock she had been trying on and rejecting dresses, and now she stood dejected and irritable in lace pantalets, linen corset cover and three billowing lace and linen petticoats. Discarded garments lay about her on the floor, the bed, the chairs, in bright heaps of colour and straying ribbons.

The rose organdie with long pink sash was becoming, but she had worn it last summer when Melanie visited Twelve Oaks and she'd be sure to remember it. And might be catty enough to mention it. The black bombazine, with its puffed sleeves and princess lace collar, set off her white skin superbly, but it did make her look a trifle elderly. Scarlett peered anxiously in the mirror at her sixteen-year-old face as if expecting to see wrinkles and sagging chin muscles. It would never do to appear sedate and elderly before Melanie's sweet youthfulness. The lavender-barred muslin was beautiful with those wide insets of lace and net about the hem, but it had never suited her type. It would suit Carreen's delicate profile and wishy-washy expression perfectly, but Scarlett felt that it made her look like a schoolgirl. It would never do to appear schoolgirlish beside Melanie's poised self. The green plaid taffeta, frothing with flounces and each flounce edged in green velvet ribbon, was most becoming, in fact her favourite dress, for it darkened her eyes to emerald. But there was unmistakably a grease spot on the front of the basque. Of course, her brooch could be pinned over the spot, but perhaps Melanie had sharp eyes. There remained varicoloured cotton dresses which Scarlett felt were not festive enough for the occasion, ball dresses and the green sprigged muslin she had worn yesterday. But it was an afternoon dress. It was not suitable for a barbecue, for it had only tiny puffed sleeves and the neck was low enough for a dancing dress. But there was nothing else to do but wear it. After all, she was not ashamed of her neck and arms and bosom, even if it was not correct to show them in the morning.

As she stood before the mirror and twisted herself about to get a side view, she thought that there was absolutely nothing about her figure to cause her shame. Her neck was short but rounded and her arms plump and enticing. Her breasts, pushed high by her stays, were very nice breasts. She had never had to sew tiny rows of silk ruffles in the lining of her basques, as most sixteen-year-old girls did, to give their figures the desired curves and fullness. She was glad she had inherited Ellen's slender white hands and tiny feet, and she wished she had Ellen's height, too, but her own height pleased her very well. What a pity legs could not be shown, she thought, pulling up her petticoats and regretfully viewing them, plump and neat under pantalets. She had such nice legs. Even the girls at the Fayetteville Academy had admitted as much. And as for her waist—there was no one in Fayetteville, Jonesboro or in three counties, for that matter, who had so small a waist.

The thought of her waist brought her back to practical matters. The green muslin measured seventeen inches about the waist, and Mammy had laced her for the eighteen-inch bombazine. Mammy would have to lace her tighter. She pushed open the door, listened and heard Mammy's heavy tread in the downstairs hall. She shouted for her impatiently, knowing she could raise her voice with impunity, as Ellen was in the smokehouse, measuring out the day's food to Cookie.

"Some folks thinks as how Ah kin fly," grumbled Mammy, shuffling up the stairs. She entered puffing, with the expression of one who expects battle and welcomes it. In her large black hands was a tray upon which food smoked, two large yams covered with butter, a pile of buckwheat cakes dripping syrup, and a large slice of ham swimming in gravy. Catching sight of Mammy's burden, Scarlett's expression changed from one of minor irritation to obstinate belligerency. In the excitement of trying on dresses she had forgotten Mammy's ironclad rule that, before going to any party, the O'Hara girls must be crammed so full of food at home they would be unable to eat any refreshments at the party.

"It's no use. I won't eat it. You can just take it back to the kitchen."

Mammy set the tray on the table and squared herself, hands on hips.

"Yas'm, you is! Ah ain' figgerin' on havin' happen whut happen at dat las' barbecue w'en Ah wuz too sick frum dem chittlins Ah et ter fetch you no tray befo' you went. You is gwine eat eve'y bite of dis."

"I am not! Now, come here and lace me tighter because we are late already. I heard the carriage come round to the front of the house."

Mammy's tone became wheedling.

"Now, Miss Scarlett, you be good an' come eat jes' a lil. Miss Carreen an' Miss Suellen done eat all dey'n."

"They would," said Scarlett contemptuously. "They haven't any more spirit than a rabbit. But I won't! I'm through with trays. I'm not forgetting the time I ate a whole tray and went to the Calverts' and they had ice-cream out of ice they'd brought all the way from Savannah, and I couldn't eat but a spoonful. I'm going to have a good time to-day and eat as much as I please."

At this defiant heresy, Mammy's brow lowered with indignation. What a young miss could do and what she could not do were as different as black and white in Mammy's mind; there was no middle ground of deportment between. Suellen and Carreen were clay in her powerful hands and harkened respectfully to her warnings. But it had

119

always been a struggle to teach Scarlett that most of her natural impulses were unladylike. Mammy's victories over Scarlett were hard-won and represented guile unknown to the white mind.

"Ef you doan care 'bout how folks talks 'bout dis fambly, Ah does," she rumbled. "Ah ain' gwine stand by an' have eve'ybody at de pahty sayin' how you ain' fotched up right. Ah has tole you an' tole you dat you kin allus tell a lady by dat she eat lak a bird. An' Ah ain' aimin' ter have you go ter Mist' Wilkes' an' eat lak a fe'el han' an' gobble lak a hawg."

"Mother is a lady and she eats," countered Scarlett.

"W'en you is mahied, you kin eat, too," retorted Mammy. "W'en Miss Ellen yo' age, she never et nuthin' w'en she went out, an' needer yo' Aunt Pauline nor yo' Aunt Eulalie. An' dey all done mahied. Young misses whut eats heavy mos' gener'ly doan never ketch husbands."

"I don't believe it. At that barbecue when you were sick and I didn't eat beforehand, Ashley Wilkes told me he *liked* to see a girl with a healthy appetite."

Mammy shook her head ominously.

"Whut gempmums says an' whut dey thinks is two diffunt things. An' Ah ain' noticed Mist' Ashley axing fer ter mahy you."

Scarlett scowled, started to speak sharply and then caught herself. Mammy had her there and there was no argument. Seeing the obdurate look on Scarlett's face, Mammy picked up the tray and, with the bland guile of her race, changed her tactics. As she started for the door, she sighed.

"Well'm, awright. Ah wuz tellin' Cookie w'ile she wuz a-fixin' dis tray, 'You kin sho tell a lady by whut she *doan* eat,' an' Ah say ter Cookie, 'Ah ain' never seed no w'ite lady who et less'n Miss Melly Hamilton did las' time she wuz visitin' Mist' Ashley'—Ah means, visitin' Miss India."

Scarlett shot a look of sharp suspicion at her, but Mammy's broad face carried only a look of innocence and of regret that Scarlett was not the lady Melanie Hamilton was.

"Put down that tray and come lace me tighter," said Scarlett irritably. "And I'll try to eat a little afterwards. If I ate now I couldn't lace tight enough."

Cloaking her triumph, Mammy set down the tray.

"Whut mah lamb gwine wear?"

"That," answered Scarlett, pointing at the fluffy mass of green flowered muslin. Instantly Mammy was in arms.

"No, you ain'. It ain' fittin' fer mawnin'. You kain show yo' buzzum befo' three o'clock an' dat dress ain' got no neck an' no sleeves. An' you'll git freckled sho as you born, an' Ah ain' figgerin' on you gittin' freckled affer all de buttermilk Ah been puttin' on you all dis winter, bleachin' dem freckles you got at Savannah settin' on de beach. Ah sho gwine speak ter yo' Ma 'bout you."

"If you say one word to her before I'm dressed I won't eat a bite," said Scarlett coolly. "Mother won't have time to send me back to change once I'm dressed."

Mammy sighed resignedly, beholding herself outguessed. Between the two evils, it was better to have Scarlett wear an afternoon dress at a morning barbecue than to have her gobble like a hog.

"Hole onter sumpin' an' suck in yo' breaf," she commanded.

Scarlett obeyed, bracing herself and catching firm hold of one of the bedposts. Mammy pulled and jerked vigorously and, as the tiny circumference of whalebone-girdled waist grew smaller, a proud, fond look came into her eyes.

"Ain' nobody got a wais' lak mah lamb," she said approvingly. "Eve'y time Ah pulls Miss Suellen littler dan twenty inches, she up an' faint."

"Pooh!" gasped Scarlett, speaking with difficulty. "I never fainted in my life."

"Well, 'twouldn' do no hahm ef you wuz ter faint now an' den," advised Mammy. "You is so brash sometimes, Miss Scarlett. Ah been aimin' ter tell you, it jes' doan look good de way you doan faint 'bout snakes an' mouses an' sech. Ah doan mean round home but w'en you is out in comp'ny. An' Ah has tole you an'—"

"Oh, hurry! Don't talk so much. I'll catch a husband. See if I don't, even if I don't scream and faint. Goodness, but my stays are tight! Put on the dress."

Mammy carefully dropped the twelve yards of green sprigged muslin over the mountainous petticoats and hooked up the back of the tight, low-cut basque.

"You keep yo' shawl on yo' shoulders w'en you is in de sun, an' doan you go takin' off yo' hat w'en you is wahm," she commanded. "Elsewise you be comin' home lookin' brown lak Ole Miz Slattery. Now, you come eat, honey, but doan eat too fas'. No use havin' it come right back up agin."

Scarlett obediently sat down before the tray, wondering if she would be able to get any food into her stomach and still have room to breathe. Mammy plucked a large towel from the washstand and carefully tied it around Scarlett's neck, spreading the white folds over her lap. Scarlett began on the ham, because she liked ham, and forced it down.

"I wish to Heaven I was married," she said resentfully as she attacked the yams with loathing. "I'm tired of everlastingly being unnatural and never doing anything I want to do. I'm tired of acting like I don't eat more than a bird, and walking when I want to run and saying I feel faint after a waltz, when I could dance for two days and never get tired. I'm tired of saying, 'How wonderful you are!' to fool men who haven't got one-half the sense I've got, and I'm tired of pretending I don't know anything, so men can tell me things and feel important while they're doing it. . . . I can't eat another bite."

"Try a hot cake," said Mammy inexorably.

"Why is it a girl has to be so silly to catch a husband?"

"Ah specs it's kase gempmums doan know

whut dey wants. Dey jes' knows whut dey thinks dey wants. An' givin' dem whut dey thinks dey wants saves a pile of mizry an' bein' a ole maid. An' dey thinks dey wants mousy lil gals wid bird's tastes an' no sense at all. It doan make a gempmum feel lak mahyin' a lady ef he suspicions she got mo' sense dan he has."

"Don't you suppose men get surprised after they're married to find that their wives do have sense?"

"Well, it's too late den. Dey's already mahied. 'Sides, gempmums specs dey wives ter have sense."

"Some day I'm going to do and say everything I want to do and say, and if people don't like it I don't care."

"No, you ain'," said Mammy grimly. "Not while Ah got breaf. You eat dem cakes. Sop dem in de gravy, honey."

"I don't think Yankee girls have to act like such fools. When we were at Saratoga last year, I noticed plenty of them acting like they had right good sense and in front of men, too."

Mammy snorted.

"Yankee gals! Yas'm, Ah guess dey speaks dey minds awright, but Ah ain' noticed many of dem gittin' proposed ter at Saratoga."

"But Yankees must get married," argued Scarlett. "They don't just grow. They must get married and have children. There's too many of them."

"Men mahys dem fer dey money," said Mammy firmly.

Scarlett sopped the wheat cake in the gravy and

put it in her mouth. Perhaps there was something in what Mammy said. There must be something in it, for Ellen said the same things, in different and more delicate words. In fact, the mothers of all her girl friends impressed on their daughters the necessity of being helpless, clinging, doe-eyed creatures. Really, it took a lot of sense to cultivate and hold such a pose. Perhaps she had been too brash. Occasionally she had argued with Ashley and frankly aired her opinions. Perhaps this and her healthy enjoyment of walking and riding had turned him from her to the frail Melanie. Perhaps if she changed her tactics—But she felt that if Ashley succumbed to premeditated feminine tricks, she could never respect him as she now did. Any man who was fool enough to fall for a simper, a faint and an "Oh, how wonderful you are!" wasn't worth having. But they all seemed to like it.

If she had used the wrong tactics with Ashley in the past—well, that was the past and done with. To-day she would use different ones, the right ones. She wanted him and she had only a few hours in which to get him. If fainting, or pretending to faint, would do the trick, then she would faint. If simpering, coquetry or empty-headedness would attract him, she would gladly play the flirt and be more empty-headed than even Cathleen Calvert. And if bolder measures were necessary, she would take them. To-day was the day!

There was no one to tell Scarlett that her own personality, frighteningly vital though it was, was more attractive than any masquerade she might adopt. Had she been told, she would have been pleased but unbelieving. And the civilization of which she was a part would have been unbelieving too, for at no time, before or since, had so low a premium been placed on feminine naturalness.

As the carriage bore her down the red road toward the Wilkes plantation, Scarlett had a feeling of guilty pleasure that neither her mother nor Mammy was with the party. There would be no one at the barbecue who, by delicately lifted brows or out-thrust underlip, could interfere with her plan of action. Of course, Suellen would be certain to tell tales to-morrow, but if all went as Scarlett hoped, the excitement of the family over her engagement to Ashley or her elopement would more than overbalance their displeasure. Yes, she was very glad Ellen had been forced to stay at home.

Gerald, primed with brandy, had given Jonas Wilkerson his dismissal that morning, and Ellen had remained at Tara to go over the accounts of the plantation before he took his departure. Scarlett had kissed her mother good-bye in the little office where she sat before the tall secretary with its paper-stuffed pigeonholes. Jonas Wilkerson, hat in hand, stood beside her, his sallow tight-skinned face hardly concealing the fury of hate that possessed him at being so unceremoniously turned out of the best overseer's job in the County. And all because of a bit of minor philandering. He had told Gerald over and over that Emmie Slattery's baby might have been fathered by any one of a dozen men as easily as himself—an idea in which Gerald concurred—but that had not altered his case so far as Ellen was concerned. Jonas hated all Southerners. He hated their cool courtesy to him and their contempt for his social status, so inadequately covered by their courtesy. He hated Ellen O'Hara above anyone else, for she was the epitome of all that he hated in Southerners.

Mammy, as head woman of the plantation, had remained to help Ellen, and it was Dilcey who rode on the driver's seat beside Toby, the girls' dancing dresses in a long box across her lap. Gerald rode beside the carriage on his big hunter, warm with brandy and pleased with himself for having gotten through with the unpleasant business of Wilkerson so speedily. He had shoved the responsibility on to Ellen, and her disappointment at missing the barbecue and the gathering of her friends did not enter his mind; for it was a fine spring day and his fields were beautiful and the birds were singing and he felt too young and frolicsome to think of anyone else. Occasionally he burst out with "Peg in a Low-backed Car" and other Irish ditties or the more lugubrious lament for Robert Emmet, "She is far from the land where her young hero sleeps".

He was happy, pleasantly excited over the prospect of spending the day shouting about the Yankees and the war, and proud of his three pretty daughters in their bright spreading hoop skirts beneath foolish little lace parasols. He gave no thought to his conversation of the day before with Scarlett, for it had completely slipped his mind. He only thought that she was pretty and a great credit to him and that, to-day, her eyes were as green as the hills of Ireland. The last thought made him think better of himself, for it had a certain poetic ring to it, and so he favoured the girls with a loud and slightly off-key rendition of "The Wearin' o' the Green".

Scarlett, looking at him with the affectionate contempt that mothers feel for small swaggering sons, knew that he would be very drunk by sundown. Coming home in the dark, he would try, as usual, to jump every fence between Twelve Oaks and Tara and, she hoped, by the mercy of Providence and the good sense of his horse, would escape breaking his neck. He would disdain the bridge and swim his horse through the river and come home roaring, to be put to bed on the sofa in the office by Pork, who always waited up with a lamp in the front hall on such occasions.

He would ruin his new grey broadcloth suit, which would cause him to swear horribly in the morning and tell Ellen at great length how his horse fell off the bridge in the darkness—a palpable lie which would fool no one but which would be accepted by all and make him feel very clever.

"Pa is a sweet, selfish, irresponsible darling," Scarlett thought, with a surge of affection for him. She felt so excited and happy this morning that she included the whole world, as well as Gerald, in her affection. She was pretty and she knew it; she would have Ashley for her own before the day was over; the sun was warm and tender and the glory of the Georgia spring was spread before her eyes. Along the roadside the blackberry brambles were concealing with softest green the savage red gulches cut by the winter's rains, and the bare granite boulders pushing up through the red earth were being draped with sprangles of Cherokee roses and compassed about by wild violets of palest purple hue. Upon the wooded hills above the river, the dogwood blossoms lay glistening and white, as if snow still lingered among the greenery. The flowering crab trees were bursting their buds and rioting from delicate white to deepest pink and, beneath the trees where the sunshine dappled the pine straw, the wild honeysuckle made a varicoloured carpet of scarlet and orange and rose. There was a faint wild fragrance of sweet shrub on the breeze and the world smelled good enough to eat.

"I'll remember how beautiful this day is till I die," thought Scarlett. "Perhaps it will be my wedding day!"

And she thought with a tingling in her heart how she and Ashley might ride swiftly through this beauty of blossom and greenery this very afternoon, or to-night by moonlight, toward Jonesboro and a preacher. Of course, she would have to be remarried by a priest from Atlanta, but that would be something for Ellen and Gerald to worry about. She quailed a little as she thought how white with mortification Ellen would be at hearing that her daughter had eloped with another girl's fiancé, but she knew Ellen would forgive her when she saw her happiness. And Gerald would scold and bawl but, for all his remarks of yesterday about not wanting her to marry Ashley, he would be pleased beyond words at an alliance between his family and the Wilkes.

"But that'll be something to worry about after I'm married," she thought, tossing the worry from her.

It was impossible to feel anything but palpitating joy in this warm sun, in this spring, with the chimneys of Twelve Oaks just beginning to show on the hill across the river.

"I'll live there all my life and I'll see fifty springs like this and maybe more, and I'll tell my children and my grandchildren how beautiful this spring was, lovelier than any they'll ever see." She was so happy at this last thought that she joined in the last chorus of "The Wearin' o' the Green" and won Gerald's shouted approval.

"I don't know why you're so happy this morning," said Suellen crossly, for the thought still rankled in her mind that she would look far better in Scarlett's green silk dancing frock than its rightful owner would. And why was Scarlett always so selfish about lending her clothes and bonnets? And why did Mother always back her up, declaring green was not Suellen's colour? "You know as well as I do that Ashley's engagement is going to be announced to-night. Pa said so this morning. And I know you've been sweet on him for months."

"That's all you know," said Scarlett, putting out her tongue and refusing to lose her good humour. How surprised Miss Sue would be by this time to-morrow morning!

"Susie, you know that's not so," protested

Carreen, shocked. "It's Brent that Scarlett cares about."

Scarlett turned smiling green eyes upon her younger sister, wondering how anyone could be so sweet. The whole family knew that Carreen's thirteen-year-old heart was set upon Brent Tarleton, who never gave her a thought except as Scarlett's baby sister. When Ellen was not present, the O'Haras teased her to tears about him.

"Darling, I don't care a thing about Brent," declared Scarlett, happy enough to be generous. "And he doesn't care a thing about me. Why, he's waiting for you to grow up!"

Carreen's round little face became pink, as pleasure struggled with incredulity.

"Oh, Scarlett, really?"

"Scarlett, you know Mother said Carreen was too young to think about beaux yet, and there you go putting ideas in her head."

"Well, go and tattle and see if I care," replied Scarlett. "You want to hold Sissy back, because you know she's going to be prettier than you in a year or so."

"You'll be keeping civil tongues in your heads this day, or I'll be taking me crop to you," warned Gerald. "Now whist! Is it wheels I'm hearing? That'll be the Tarletons or the Fontaines."

As they neared the intersecting road that came down the thickly wooded hill from Mimosa and Fairhill, the sound of hooves and carriage wheels became plainer and clamorous feminine voices raised in pleasant dispute sounded from behind the screen of trees. Gerald, riding ahead, pulled up his horse and signed to Toby to stop the carriage where the two roads met.

"'Tis the Tarleton ladies," he announced to his daughters, his florid face abeam, for excepting Ellen there was no lady in the County he liked more than the red-haired Mrs. Tarleton. "And 'tis herself at the reins. Ah, there's a woman with fine hands for a horse! Feather light and strong as rawhide, and pretty enough to kiss for all that. More's the pity none of you have such hands," he added, casting fond but reproving glances at his girls. "With Carreen afraid of the poor beasts and Sue with hands like sad-irons when it comes to reins and you, Puss—"

"Well, at any rate I've never been thrown," cried Scarlett indignantly. "And Mrs. Tarleton takes a toss at every hunt."

"And breaks a collar-bone like a man," said Gerald. "No fainting, no fussing. Now, no more of it, for here she comes."

He stood up in his stirrups and took off his hat with a sweep, as the Tarleton carriage, overflowing with girls in bright dresses and parasols and fluttering veils, came into view, with Mrs. Tarleton on the box as Gerald had said. With her four daughters, their mammy and their ball dresses in long cardboard boxes crowding the carriage, there was no room for the coachman. And, besides, Beatrice Tarleton never willingly permitted anyone, black or white, to hold reins when her arms were out of slings. Frail, fine-boned, so white of skin that her flaming hair seemed to have drawn all the colour from her face into its vital burnished mass, she was nevertheless possessed of exuberant health and untiring energy. She had borne eight children, as red of hair and as full of life as she, and had raised them most successfully, so the County said, because she gave them all the loving neglect and the stern discipline she gave the colts she bred. "Curb them but don't break their spirits," was Mrs. Tarleton's motto.

She loved horses and talked horses constantly. She understood them and handled them better than any man in the County. Colts overflowed the paddock on to the front lawn, even as her eight children overflowed the rambling house on the hill, and colts and sons and daughters and hunting dogs tagged after her as she went about the plantation. She credited her horses, especially her red mare, Nellie, with human intelligence; and if the cares of the house kept her busy beyond the time when she expected to take her daily ride, she put the sugar-bowl in the hands of some small piccaninny and said: "Give Nellie a handful and tell her I'll be out terrectly."

Except on rare occasions she always wore her riding habit, for whether she rode or not she always expected to ride and in that expectation put on her habit upon arising. Each morning, rain or shine, Nellie was saddled and walked up and down in front of the house, waiting for the time when Mrs. Tarleton could spare an hour away from her duties. But Fairhill was a difficult plantation to manage and spare time hard to get, and more often than not Nellie walked up and down riderless hour after hour, while Beatrice Tarleton went through the day with the skirt of her habit absently looped up over her arm and six inches of shining boot showing below it.

To-day, dressed in dull black silk over unfashionably narrow hoops, she still looked as though in her habit, for the dress was as severely tailored as her riding costume and the small black hat with its long black plume perched over one warm, twinkling, brown eye was a replica of the battered old hat she used for hunting.

She waved her whip when she saw Gerald and drew her dancing pair of red horses to a halt, and the four girls in the back of the carriage leaned out and gave such vociferous cries of greeting that the team pranced in alarm. To a casual observer it would seem that years had passed since the Tarletons had seen the O'Haras, instead of only two days. But they were a sociable family and liked their neighbours, especially the O'Hara girls. That is, they liked Suellen and Carreen. No girl in the County, with the possible exception of the empty-headed Cathleen Calvert, really liked Scarlett.

In summers, the County averaged a barbecue and ball nearly every week, but to the red-haired Tarletons with their enormous capacity for enjoying themselves, each barbecue and each ball was as exciting as if it were the first they had ever attended. They were a pretty, buxom quartette, so crammed into the carriage that their hoops and flounces overlapped and their parasols nudged and bumped together above their wide leghorn sun hats, crowned with roses and dangling with black velvet chin ribbons. All shades of red hair were represented beneath these hats, Hetty's plain red hair, Camilla's strawberry blonde, Randa's coppery auburn and small Betsy's carrot top.

"That's a fine bevy, Ma'm," said Gerald gallantly, reining his horse alongside the carriage. "But it's far they'll go to beat their mother."

Mrs. Tarleton rolled her red-brown eyes and sucked in her lower lip in burlesqued appreciation, and the girls cried, "Ma, stop making eyes or we'll tell Pa!" "I vow, Mr. O'Hara, she never gives us a chance when there's a handsome man like you around!"

Scarlett laughed with the rest at these sallies but, as always, the freedom with which the Tarletons treated their mother came as a shock. They acted as if she were one of themselves and not a day over sixteen. To Scarlett, the very idea of saying such things to her own mother was almost sacrilegious. And yet—and yet—there was something very pleasant about the Tarleton girls' relations with their mother, and they adored her for all that they criticized and scolded and teased her. Not, Scarlett loyally hastened to tell herself, that she would prefer a mother like Mrs. Tarleton to Ellen, but still it would be fun to romp with a mother. She knew that even that thought was disrespectful to Ellen and felt ashamed of it. She knew no such troublesome thoughts ever disturbed the brains under the four flaming thatches in the carriage and, as always when she felt herself different from her neighbours, an irritated confusion fell upon her.

Quick though her brain was, it was not made for analysis, but she half-consciously realized that, for all the Tarleton girls were as unruly as colts and wild as March hares, there was an unworried single-mindedness about them that was part of their inheritance. On both their mother's and their father's side they were Georgians, north Georgians, only a generation away from pioneers. They were sure of themselves and of their environment. They knew instinctively what they were about, as did the Wilkeses, though in widely divergent ways, and in them there was no such conflict as frequently raged in Scarlett's bosom where the blood of a soft-voiced, overbred Coast aristocrat mingled with the shrewd, earthy blood of an Irish peasant. Scarlett wanted to respect and adore her mother like an idol and to rumple her hair and tease her too. And she knew she should be altogether one way or the other. It was the same conflicting emotion that made her desire to appear a delicate and high-bred lady with boys and to be, as well, a hoyden who was not above a few kisses.

"Where's Ellen this morning?" asked Mrs. Tarleton.

"She's after discharging our overseer and stayed home to go over the accounts with him. Where's himself and the lads?"

"Oh, they rode over to Twelve Oaks hours ago —to sample the punch and see if it was strong enough, I dare say, as if they wouldn't have from now till to-morrow morning to do it! I'm going to ask John Wilkes to keep them overnight, even if he has to bed them down in the stable. Five men in their cups are just too much for me. Up to three, I do very well but—"

Gerald hastily interrupted to change the subject. He could feel his own daughters snickering behind his back as they remembered in what condition he had come home from the Wilkeses' last barbecue the autumn before.

"And why aren't you riding to-day, Mrs. Tarleton? Sure, you don't look yourself at all without Nellie. It's a stentor, you are."

"A stentor, me ignorant broth of a boy!" cried Mrs. Tarleton, aping his brogue. "You mean a centaur. Stentor was a man with a voice like a brass gong."

"Stentor or centaur, 'tis no matter," answered Gerald, unruffled by his error. "And 'tis a voice like brass you have, Ma'm, when you're urging on the hounds, so it is."

"That's one on you, Ma," said Hetty. "I told you you yelled like a Comanche whenever you saw a fox."

"But not as loud as you yell when Mammy washes your ears," returned Mrs. Tarleton. "And you sixteen! Well, as to why I'm not riding to-day, Nellie foaled early this morning."

"Did she now!" cried Gerald with real interest, his Irishman's passion for horses shining in his eyes, and Scarlett again felt the sense of shock in comparing her mother with Mrs. Tarleton. To Ellen, mares never foaled nor cows calved. In fact, hens almost didn't lay eggs. Ellen ignored these matters completely. But Mrs. Tarleton had no such reticences.

"A little filly, was it?"

"No, a fine little stallion with legs two yards long. You must ride over and see him, Mr.

O'Hara. He's a real Tarleton horse. He's as red as Hetty's curls."

"And looks a lot like Hetty, too," said Camilla, and then disappeared shrieking amid a welter of skirts and pantalets and bobbing hats, as Hetty, who did have a long face, began pinching her.

"My fillies are feeling their oats this morning," said Mrs. Tarleton. "They've been kicking up their heels ever since we heard the news this morning about Ashley and that little cousin of his from Atlanta. What's her name? Melanie? Bless the child, she's a sweet little thing, but I can never remember either her name or her face. Our cook is the broad wife of the Wilkes butler, and he was over last night with the news that the engagement would be announced to-night and Cookie told us this morning. The girls are all excited about it, though I can't see why. Everybody's known for years that Ashley would marry her, that is, if he didn't marry one of his Burr cousins from Macon. Just like Honey Wilkes is going to marry Melanie's brother, Charles. Now, tell me, Mr. O'Hara, is it illegal for the Wilkes to marry outside of their family? Because if—"

Scarlett did not hear the rest of the laughing words. For one short instant, it was as though the sun had ducked behind a cool cloud, leaving the world in shadow, taking the colour out of things. The freshly green foliage looked sickly, the dogwood pallid, and the flowering crab, so beautifully pink a moment ago, faded and dreary. Scarlett dug her fingers into the upholstery of the carriage and for a moment her parasol wavered. It was one thing to know that Ashley was engaged

138

but it was another to hear people talk about it so casually. Then her courage flowed strongly back and the sun came out again and the landscape glowed anew. She knew Ashley loved her. That was certain. And she smiled as she thought how surprised Mrs. Tarleton would be when no engagement was announced that night—how surprised if there were an elopement. And she'd tell neighbours what a slyboots Scarlett was to sit there and listen to her talk about Melanie when all the time she and Ashley—She dimpled at her own thoughts and Hetty, who had been watching sharply the effect of her mother's words, sank back with a small puzzled frown.

"I don't care what you say, Mr. O'Hara," Mrs. Tarleton was saying emphatically. "It's all wrong, this marrying of cousins. It's bad enough for Ashley to be marrying the Hamilton child, but for Honey to be marrying that pale-looking Charles Hamilton—"

"Honey'll never catch anybody else if she doesn't marry Charlie," said Randa, cruel and secure in her own popularity. "She's never had another beau except him. And he's never acted very sweet on her, for all that they're engaged. Scarlett, you remember how he ran after you last Christmas—"

"Don't be a cat, Miss," said her mother. "Cousins shouldn't marry, even second cousins. It weakens the strain. It isn't like horses. You can breed a mare to a brother or a sire to a daughter and get good results if you know your blood strains, but in people it just doesn't work. You get good lines, perhaps, but no stamina. You—"

"Now, Ma'm, I'm taking issue with you on that! Can you name me better people than the Wilkes? And they've been intermarrying since Brian Boru was a boy."

"And high time they stopped it, for it's beginning to show. Oh, not Ashley so much, for he's a good-looking devil, though even he—But look at those two washed-out-looking Wilkes girls, poor things! Nice girls, of course, but washed out. And look at little Miss Melanie. Thin as a rail and delicate enough for the wind to blow away and no spirit at all. Not a notion of her own. 'No, Ma'm!' 'Yes, Ma'm!' That's all she has to say. You see what I mean? That family needs new blood, fine vigorous blood like my red-heads or your Scarlett. Now, don't misunderstand me. The Wilkes are fine folks in their way, and you know I'm fond of them all, but be frank! They are overbred and inbred too, aren't they? They'll do fine on a dry track, a fast track, but mark my words, I don't believe the Wilkes can run on a mud track. I believe the stamina has been bred out of them, and when the emergency arises I don't believe they can run against odds. Dry-weather stock. Give me a big horse who can run in any weather! And their intermarrying has made them different from other folks around here. Always fiddling with the piano or sticking their heads in a book. I do believe Ashley would rather read than hunt! Yes, I honestly believe that, Mr. O'Hara! And just look at the bones of them. Too slender. They need dams and sires with strength—"

"Ah-ah-hum," said Gerald, suddenly and

140

guiltily aware that the conversation, a most interesting and entirely proper one to him, would seem quite otherwise to Ellen. In fact, he knew she would never recover should she learn that her daughters had been exposed to so frank a conversation. But Mrs. Tarleton was, as usual, deaf to all other ideas when pursuing her favourite topic, breeding, whether it be horses or humans.

"I know what I'm talking about because I had some cousins who married each other and I give you my word their children all turned out as popeyed as bullfrogs, poor things. And when my family wanted me to marry a second cousin, I bucked like a colt. I said, 'No, Ma. Not for me. My children will all have spavins and heaves.' Well, Ma fainted when I said that about spavins, but I stood firm and Grandma backed me up. She knew a lot about horse breeding too, you see, and said I was right. And she helped me run away with Mr. Tarleton. And look at my children! Big and healthy and not a sickly one or a runt among them, though Boyd is only five feet ten. Now, the Wilkes—"

"Not meaning to change the subject, Ma'm," broke in Gerald hurriedly, for he had noticed Carreen's bewildered look and the avid curiosity on Suellen's face and feared lest they might ask Ellen embarrassing questions which would reveal how inadequate a chaperon he was. Puss, he was glad to notice, appeared to be thinking of other matters as a lady should.

Hetty Tarleton rescued him from his predicament.

"Good Heavens, Ma, do let's get on!" she cried

impatiently. "This sun is broiling me and I can just hear freckles popping out on my neck."

"Just a minute, Ma'm, before you go," said Gerald. "But what have you decided to do about selling us the horses for the Troop? War may break any day now and the boys want the matter settled. It's a Clayton County troop and it's Clayton County horses we want for them. But you, obstinate creature that you are, are still refusing to sell us your fine beasts."

"Maybe there won't be any war," Mrs. Tarleton temporized, her mind diverted completely from the Wilkeses' odd marriage habits.

"Why, Ma'm, you can't—"

"Ma," Hetty interrupted again, "can't you and Mr. O'Hara talk about the horses at Twelve Oaks as well as here?"

"That's just it, Miss Hetty," said Gerald, "and I won't be keeping you but one minute by the clock. We'll be getting to Twelve Oaks in a little bit, and every man there, old and young, wanting to know about the horses. Ah, but it's breaking me heart to see such a fine pretty lady as your mother so stingy with her beasts! Now, where's your patriotism, Mrs. Tarleton? Does the Confederacy mean nothing to you at all?"

"Ma," cried small Betsy, "Randa's sitting on my dress and I'm getting all wrinkled."

"Well, push Randa off you, Betsy, and hush. Now, listen to me, Gerald O'Hara," she retorted, her eyes beginning to snap. "Don't you go throwing the Confederacy in my face! I reckon the Confederacy means as much to me as it does to you, me with four boys in the Troop and you with none. But my boys can take care of themselves and my horses can't. I'd gladly give the horses free of charge if I knew they were going to be ridden by boys I know, gentlemen used to thoroughbreds. No, I wouldn't hesitate a minute. But let my beauties be at the mercy of backwoodsmen and Crackers who are used to riding mules! No, sir! I'd have nightmares thinking they were being ridden with saddle-galls and not groomed properly. Do you think I'd let ignorant fools ride my tender-mouthed darlings and saw their mouths to pieces and beat them till their spirits were broken? Why, I've got gooseflesh this minute, just thinking about it! No, Mr. O'Hara, you're mighty nice to want my horses, but you'd better go to Atlanta and buy some old plugs for your clodhoppers. They'll never know the difference."

"Ma, can't we please go on?" asked Camilla, joining the impatient chorus. "You know mighty well you're going to end up giving them your darlings anyhow. When Pa and the boys get through talking about the Confederacy needing them and so on, you'll cry and let them go."

Mrs. Tarleton grinned and shook the lines.

"I'll do no such thing," she said, touching the horses lightly with the whip. The carriage went off swiftly.

"That's a fine woman," said Gerald, putting on his hat and taking his place beside his own carriage. "Drive on, Toby. We'll wear her down and get the horses yet. Of course, she's right. She's right. If a man's not a gentleman, he's no

143

business on a horse. The infantry is the place for him. But more's the pity, there's not enough planters' sons in this County to make up a full troop. What did you say, Puss?"

"Pa, please ride behind us or in front of us. You kick up such a heap of dust that we're choking," said Scarlett, who felt that she could endure conversation no longer. It distracted her from her thoughts and she was very anxious to arrange both her thoughts and her face in attractive lines before reaching Twelve Oaks. Gerald obediently put spurs to his horse and was off in a red cloud after the Tarleton carriage where he could continue his horsy conversation.

6

THEY crossed the river and the carriage mounted the hill. Even before Twelve Oaks came into view Scarlett saw a haze of smoke hanging lazily in the tops of the tall trees and smelled the mingled savoury odours of burning hickory logs and roasting pork and mutton.

The barbecue pits, which had been slowly burning since last night, would now be long troughs of rose-red embers, with the meats turning on spits above them and the juices trickling down and hissing into the coals. Scarlett knew that the fragrance carried on the faint breeze came from the grove of great oaks in the rear of the big house. John Wilkes always held his barbecues there, on the gentle slope leading down to the rose garden, a pleasant shady place and a far pleasanter place, for instance, than that used by the Calverts. Mrs. Calvert did not like barbecue food and declared that the smells remained in the house for days, so her guests always sweltered on a flat unshaded spot a quarter of a mile from the house. But John Wilkes, famed throughout the state for his hospitality, really knew how to give a barbecue.

The long trestled picnic tables, covered with the finest of the Wilkes' linen, always stood under the thickest shade, with backless benches on either side; and chairs, hassocks and cushions from the house were scattered about the glade for those who did not fancy the benches. At a distance great enough to keep the smoke away from the guests were the long pits where the meats cooked and the huge iron wash-pots from which the succulent odours of barbecue sauce and Brunswick stew floated. Mr. Wilkes always had at least a dozen darkies busy running back and forth with trays to serve the guests. Over behind the barns there was always another barbecue pit, where the house servants and the coachmen and maids of the guests had their own feast of hoecakes and yams and chitterlings, that dish of hog entrails so dear to negro hearts, and, in season, watermelons enough to satiate.

As the smell of crisp fresh pork came to her, Scarlett wrinkled her nose appreciatively, hoping that by the time it was cooked she would feel some appetite. As it was, she was so full of food and so tightly laced that she feared every moment she was going to belch. That would be fatal, as only old men and very old ladies could belch without fear of social disapproval.

They topped the rise and the white house reared its perfect symmetry before her, tall of columns, wide of verandas, flat of roof, beautiful as a woman is beautiful who is so sure of her charm that she can be generous and gracious to all. Scarlett loved Twelve Oaks even more than Tara, for it had a stately beauty, a mellowed dignity that Gerald's house did not possess.

The wide curving driveway was full of saddle horses and carriages and guests alighting and calling greetings to friends. Grinning negroes, excited as always at a party, were leading the animals to the barnyard to be unharnessed and unsaddled for the day. Swarms of children, black and white, ran yelling about the newly green lawn, playing hopscotch and tag and boasting how much they were going to eat. The wide hall which ran from front to back of the house was swarming with people, and as the O'Hara carriage drew up at the front steps, Scarlett saw girls in crinolines, bright as butterflies, going up and coming down the stairs from the second floor, arms about each other's waists, stopping to lean over the delicate handrail of the banisters, laughing and calling to young men in the hall below them.

Through the open french windows, she caught glimpses of the older women seated in the drawing-room, sedate in dark silks as they sat fanning themselves and talking of babies and sicknesses and who had married whom and why. The Wilkes butler, Tom, was hurrying through the halls, a silver tray in his hands, bowing and grinning, as he offered tall glasses to young men in fawn and grey trousers and fine ruffled linen shirts.

The sunny front veranda was thronged with guests. Yes, the whole County was here, thought Scarlett. The four Tarleton boys and their father leaned against the tall columns, the twins, Stuart and Brent, side by side, inseparable as usual, Boyd and Tom with their father, James Tarleton. Mr. Calvert was standing close by the side of his Yankee wife, who even after fifteen years in Georgia never seemed to quite belong anywhere. Everyone was very polite and kind to her because they felt sorry for her, but no one could forget that she had compounded her initial error of birth by being the governess of Mr. Calvert's children. The two Calvert boys, Raiford and Cade, were there with their dashing blonde sister, Cathleen, teasing the dark-faced Joe Fontaine and Sally Munroe, his pretty bride-to-be. Alex and Tony Fontaine were whispering in the ears of Dimity Munroe and sending her into gales of giggles. There were families from as far as Lovejoy, ten miles away, and from Fayetteville and Jonesboro, a few even from Atlanta and Macon. The house seemed bursting with the crowd, and a ceaseless babble of talking and laughter and giggles and shrill feminine squeaks and screams rose and fell.

On the porch steps stood John Wilkes, silver-haired, erect, radiating the quiet charm and hospitality that was as warm and never-failing as the sun of Georgia summer. Beside him Honey Wilkes, so called because she indiscriminately addressed everyone from her father to the field hands by that endearment, fidgeted and giggled as she called greetings to the arriving guests.

Honey's nervously obvious desire to be attractive to every man in sight contrasted sharply with her father's poise, and Scarlett had the thought that perhaps there was something in what Mrs. Tarleton said, after all. Certainly the Wilkes men got the family looks. The thick deep-gold lashes that set off the grey eyes of John Wilkes and Ashley were sparse and colourless in the faces of Honey and her sister India. Honey had the odd lashless look of a rabbit, and India could be described by no other word than plain.

India was nowhere to be seen, but Scarlett knew she probably was in the kitchen giving final instructions to the servants. "Poor India," thought Scarlett, "she's had so much trouble keeping house since her mother died that she's never had the chance to catch any beau except Stuart Tarleton, and it certainly wasn't my fault if he thought I was prettier than she."

John Wilkes came down the steps to offer his arm to Scarlett. As she descended from the carriage, she saw Suellen smirk and knew that she must have picked out Frank Kennedy in the crowd.

"If I couldn't catch a better beau than that old maid in britches!" she thought contemptuously, as she stepped to the ground and smiled her thanks to John Wilkes.

Frank Kennedy was hurrying to the carriage to assist Suellen, and Suellen was bridling in a way that made Scarlett want to slap her. Frank Kennedy might own more land than anyone in the County and he might have a very kind heart, but these things counted for nothing against the fact that he was forty, slight and nervous, and had a thin ginger-coloured beard and an old-maidish, fussy way about him. However, remembering her plan, Scarlett smothered her contempt and cast such a flashing smile of greeting at him that he stopped short, his arm outheld to Suellen, and goggled at Scarlett in pleased bewilderment.

Scarlett's eyes searched the crowd for Ashley, even while she made pleasant small talk with John Wilkes, but he was not on the porch. There were cries of greeting from a dozen voices and Stuart and Brent Tarleton moved toward her. The Munroe girls rushed up to exclaim over her dress, and she was speedily the centre of a circle of voices that rose higher and higher in efforts to be heard above the din. But where was Ashley? And Melanie and Charles? She tried not to be obvious as she looked about and peered down the hall into the laughing group inside.

As she chattered and laughed and cast quick glances into the house and the yard, her eyes fell on a stranger, standing alone in the hall, staring at her in a cool impertinent way that brought her up sharply with a mingled feeling of feminine pleasure that she had attracted a man and an embarrassed sensation that her dress was too low in the bosom. He looked quite old, at least thirty-five. He was a tall man and powerfully built. Scarlett thought she had never seen a man with such wide shoulders, so heavy with muscles, almost too heavy for gentility. When her eye caught his, he smiled, showing animal-white teeth below a close-clipped black moustache. He was dark of face, swarthy as a pirate, and his eyes were as bold and black as any pirate's appraising a galleon to be scuttled or a maiden to be ravished. There was a cool recklessness in his face and a cynical humour in his mouth as he smiled at her, and Scarlett caught her breath. She felt that she should be insulted by such a look and was annoyed with herself because she did not feel insulted. She did not know who he could be, but there was undeniably a look of good blood in his dark face. It showed in the thin hawk nose over the full red lips, the high forehead and the wide-set eyes.

She dragged her eyes away from his without

smiling back, and he turned as someone called: "Rhett! Rhett Butler! Come here! I want you to meet the most hard-hearted girl in Georgia."

Rhett Butler? The name had a familiar sound, somehow connected with something pleasantly scandalous, but her mind was on Ashley and she dismissed the thought.

"I must run upstairs and smooth my hair," she told Stuart and Brent, who were trying to get her cornered from the crowd. "You boys wait for me and don't run off with any other girl or I'll be furious."

She could see that Stuart was going to be difficult to handle to-day if she flirted with anyone else. He had been drinking and wore the arrogant looking-for-a-fight expression that she knew from experience meant trouble. She paused in the hall to speak to friends and to greet India who was emerging from the back of the house, her hair untidy and tiny beads of perspiration on her forehead. Poor India! It would be bad enough to have pale hair and eyelashes and a jutting chin that meant a stubborn disposition, without being twenty years old and an old maid in the bargain. She wondered if India resented very much her taking Stuart away from her. Lots of people said she was still in love with him, but then you could never tell what a Wilkes was thinking about. If she did resent it, she never gave any sign of it, treating Scarlett with the same slightly aloof, kindly courtesy she had always shown her.

Scarlett spoke pleasantly to her and started up the wide stairs. As she did, a shy voice behind her called her name and, turning, she saw Charles

Hamilton. He was a nice-looking boy with a riot of soft brown curls on his white forehead and eyes as deep brown, as clean and as gentle as a collie dog's. He was well turned out in mustard-coloured trousers and black coat and his pleated shirt was topped by the widest and most fashionable of black cravats. A faint blush was creeping over his face as she turned, for he was timid with girls. Like most shy men he greatly admired airy, vivacious, always-at-ease girls like Scarlett. She had never given him more than perfunctory courtesy before, and so the beaming smile of pleasure with which she greeted him and the two hands outstretched to his almost took his breath away.

"Why, Charles Hamilton, you handsome old thing, you! I'll bet you came all the way down here from Atlanta just to break my poor heart!"

Charles almost stuttered with excitement, holding her warm little hands in his and looking into the dancing green eyes. This was the way girls talked to other boys but never to him. He never knew why, but girls always treated him like a younger brother and were very kind, but never bothered to tease him. He had always wanted girls to flirt and frolic with him as they did with boys much less handsome and less endowed with this world's goods than he. But on the few occasions when this had happened he could never think of anything to say and he suffered agonies of embarrassment at his dumbness. Then he lay awake at night thinking of all the charming gallantries he might have employed; but he rarely got a second chance, for the girls left him alone after a trial or two.

Even with Honey, with whom he had an unspoken understanding of marriage when he came into his property next fall, he was diffident and silent. At times, he had an ungallant feeling that Honey's coquetries and proprietary airs were no credit to him, for she was so boy-crazy he imagined she would use them on any man who gave her the opportunity. Charles was not excited over the prospect of marrying her, for she stirred in him none of the emotions of wild romance that his beloved books had assured him were proper for a lover. He had always yearned to be loved by some beautiful, dashing creature full of fire and mischief.

And here was Scarlett O'Hara teasing him about breaking her heart!

He tried to think of something to say and couldn't and silently he blessed her because she kept up a steady chatter which relieved him of any necessity for conversation. It was too good to be true.

"Now, you wait right here till I come back, for I want to eat barbecue with you. And don't you go off philandering with those other girls, because I'm mighty jealous," came the incredible words from red lips with a dimple on each side; and bristly black lashes swept demurely over green eyes.

"I won't," he finally managed to breathe, never dreaming that she was thinking he looked like a calf waiting for the butcher.

Tapping him lightly on the arm with her folded fan, she turned to start up the stairs and her eyes again fell on the man called Rhett Butler, who stood alone a few feet away from Charles. Evidently he had overheard the whole conversation, for he grinned up at her as maliciously as a tomcat, and again his eyes went over her, in a gaze totally devoid of the deference she was accustomed to.

"God's nightgown!" said Scarlett to herself in indignation, using Gerald's favourite oath. "He looks as if—as if he knew what I looked like without my shimmy," and, tossing her head, she went up the steps.

In the bedroom where the wraps were laid, she found Cathleen Calvert preening before the mirror and biting her lips to make them look redder. There were fresh roses in her sash that matched her cheeks, and her cornflower-blue eyes were dancing with excitement.

"Cathleen," said Scarlett, trying to pull the corsage of her dress higher, "who is that nasty man downstairs named Butler?"

"My dear, don't you know?" whispered Cathleen excitedly, a weather eye on the next room where Dilcey and the Wilkes girls' mammy were gossiping. "I can't imagine how Mr. Wilkes must feel having him here, but he was visiting Mr. Kennedy in Jonesboro—something about buying cotton—and, of course, Mr. Kennedy had to bring him along with him. He couldn't just go off and leave him."

"What is the matter with him?"

"My dear, he isn't received!"

"Not really!"

"No."

Scarlett digested this in silence, for she had

154

never before been under the same roof with anyone who was not received. It was very exciting.

"What did he do?"

"Oh, Scarlett, he has the most terrible reputation. His name is Rhett Butler and he's from Charleston and his folks are some of the nicest people there, but they won't even speak to him. Caro Rhett told me about him last summer. He isn't any kin to her family, but she knows all about him, everybody does. He was expelled from West Point. Imagine! And for things too bad for Caro to know. And then there was that business about the girl he didn't marry."

"Do tell me!"

"Darling, don't you know anything? Caro told me all about it last summer and her mama would die if she thought Caro even knew about it. Well, this Mr. Butler took a Charleston girl out buggy riding. I never did know who she was, but I've got my suspicions. She couldn't have been very nice or she wouldn't have gone out with him in the late afternoon without a chaperon. And, my dear, they stayed out nearly all night and walked home finally, saying the horse had run away and smashed the buggy and they had gotten lost in the woods. And guess what—"

"I can't guess. Tell me," said Scarlett enthusiastically, hoping for the worst.

"He refused to marry her the next day!"

"Oh," said Scarlett, her hopes dashed.

"He said he hadn't—er—done anything to her and he didn't see why he should marry her. And, of course, her brother called him out, and Mr.

155

Butler said he'd rather be shot than marry a stupid fool. And so they fought a duel and Mr. Butler shot the girl's brother and he died, and Mr. Butler had to leave Charleston and now nobody receives him," finished Cathleen triumphantly, and just in time, for Dilcey came back into the room to oversee the toilet of her charge.

"Did she have a baby?" whispered Scarlett in Cathleen's ear.

Cathleen shook her head violently. "But she was ruined just the same," she hissed back.

"I wish I had gotten Ashley to compromise me," thought Scarlett suddenly. "He'd be too much of a gentleman not to marry me." But somehow, unbidden, she had a feeling of respect for Rhett Butler for refusing to marry a girl who was a fool.

Scarlett sat on a high rosewood ottoman, under the shade of a huge oak in the rear of the house, her flounces and ruffles billowing about her and two inches of green morocco slippers—all that a lady could show and still remain a lady—peeping from beneath them. She had a scarcely touched plate in her hands and seven cavaliers about her. The barbecue had reached its peak and the warm air was full of laughter and talk, the click of silver on porcelain and the rich heavy smells of roasting meats and redolent gravies. Occasionally when the slight breeze veered, puffs of smoke from the long barbecue pits floated over the crowd and were greeted with squeals of mock dismay from the ladies and violent flappings of palmetto fans.

Most of the young ladies were seated with partners on the long benches that faced the tables, but Scarlett, realizing that a girl has only two sides and only one man can sit on each of these sides, had elected to sit apart so she could gather about her as many men as possible.

Under the arbour sat the married women, their dark dresses decorous notes in the surrounding colour and gaiety. Matrons, regardless of their ages, always grouped together apart from the bright-eyed girls, beaux and laughter, for there were no married belles in the South. From Grandma Fontaine, who was belching frankly with the privilege of her age, to seventeen-year-old Alice Munroe, struggling against the nausea of a first pregnancy, they had their heads together in the endless genealogical and obstetrical discussions that made such gatherings very pleasant and instructive affairs.

Casting contemptuous glances at them, Scarlett thought that they looked like a clump of fat crows. Married women never had any fun. It did not occur to her that if she married Ashley she would automatically be relegated to arbours and front parlours with staid matrons in dull silks, as staid and dull as they and not a part of the fun and frolicking. Like most girls, her imagination carried her just as far as the altar and no further. Besides, she was too unhappy now to pursue an abstraction.

She dropped her eyes to her plate and nibbled daintily on a beaten biscuit with an elegance and an utter lack of appetite that would have won Mammy's approval. For all that she had a superfluity of beaux, she had never been more miserable in her life. In some way that she could not understand, her plans of last night had failed utterly so far as Ashley was concerned. She had attracted other beaux by the dozens, but not Ashley, and all the fears of yesterday afternoon were sweeping back upon her, making her heart beat fast and then slow, and colour flame and whiten in her cheeks.

Ashley had made no attempt to join the circle about her, in fact she had not had a word alone with him since arriving, or even spoken to him since their first greeting. He had come forward to welcome her when she came into the back garden, but Melanie had been on his arm then, Melanie who hardly came up to his shoulder.

She was a tiny, fraily built girl, who gave the appearance of a child masquerading in her mother's enormous hoop skirts—an illusion that was heightened by the shy, almost frightened look in her too large brown eyes. She had a cloud of curly dark hair which was so sternly repressed beneath its net that no vagrant tendrils escaped, and this dark mass, with its long widow's peak, accentuated the heart shape of her face. Too wide across the cheek-bones, too pointed at the chin, it was a sweet, timid face but a plain face, and she had no feminine tricks of allure to make observers forget its plainness. She looked—and was—as simple as earth, as good as bread, as transparent as spring water. But for all her plainness of feature and smallness of stature, there was a sedate dignity about her movements that was oddly touching and far older than her seventeen years.

Her grey organdie dress, with its cherry-coloured satin sash, disguised with its billows and ruffles how childishly undeveloped her body was, and the yellow hat with long cherry streamers made her creamy skin glow. Her heavy earbobs with their long gold fringe hung down from loops of tidily netted hair, swinging close to her brown eyes, eyes that had the still gleam of a forest pool in winter when brown leaves shine up through quiet water.

She had smiled with timid liking when she greeted Scarlett and told her how pretty her green dress was, and Scarlett had been hard put to be even civil in reply, so violently did she want to speak alone with Ashley. Since then, Ashley had sat on a stool at Melanie's feet, apart from the other guests and talked quietly with her, smiling the slow drowsy smile that Scarlett loved. What made matters worse was that under his smile a little sparkle had come into Melanie's eyes, so that even Scarlett had to admit that she looked almost pretty. As Melanie looked at Ashley, her plain face lit up as with an inner fire, for if ever a loving heart showcd itself upon a face, it was showing now on Melanie Hamilton's.

Scarlett tried to keep her eyes from these two but could not, and after each glance she redoubled her gaiety with her cavaliers, laughing, saying daring things, teasing, tossing her head at their compliments until her earrings danced. She said "Fiddle-dee-dee!" many times, declared that the truth wasn't in any of them, and vowed that she'd never believe anything any man told her. But Ashley did not seem to notice her at all. He only looked up at Melanie and talked on, and Melanie looked down at him with an expression that radiated the fact that she belonged to him.

So, Scarlett was miserable.

To the outward eye, never had a girl less cause to be miserable. She was undoubtedly the belle of the barbecue, the centre of attention. The furore she was causing among the men, coupled with the heart-burnings of the other girls, would have pleased her enormously at any other time.

Charles Hamilton, emboldened by her notice, was firmly planted on her right, refusing to be dislodged by the combined efforts of the Tarleton twins. He held her fan in one hand and his untouched plate of barbecue in the other and stubbornly refused to meet the eyes of Honey, who seemed on the verge of an outburst of tears. Cade lounged gracefully on her left, plucking at her skirt to attract her attention and staring up with smouldering eyes at Stuart. Already the air was electric between him and the twins and rude words had passed. Frank Kennedy fussed about like a hen with one chick, running back and forth from the shade of the oak to the tables to fetch dainties to tempt Scarlett, as if there were not a dozen servants there for that purpose. As a result, Suellen's sullen resentment had passed beyond the point of ladylike concealment and she glowered at Scarlett. Small Carreen could have cried because, for all Scarlett's encouraging words that morning, Brent had done no more than say "Hello, Sis" and jerk her hair-ribbon before turning his full attention to Scarlett. Usually he was so kind and treated her with a careless deference that made her feel grown up, and Carreen secretly dreamed of the day when she would put her hair up and her skirts down and receive him as a real beau. And now it seemed that Scarlett had him. The Munroe girls were concealing their chagrin at the defection of the swarthy Fontaine boys, but they were annoyed at the way Tony and Alex stood about the circle, jockeying for a position near Scarlett should any of the others arise from their places.

They telegraphed their disapproval of Scarlett's conduct to Hetty Tarleton by delicately raised eyebrows. "Fast" was the only word for Scarlett. Simultaneously, the three young ladies raised lacy parasols, said they had had quite enough to eat, thank you, and, laying light fingers on the arms of the men nearest them, clamoured sweetly to see the rose garden, the spring and the summer-house. This strategic retreat in good order was not lost on a woman present or observed by a man.

Scarlett giggled as she saw three men dragged out of the line of her charms to investigate landmarks familiar to the girls from childhood, and cut her eye sharply to see if Ashley had taken note. But he was playing with the ends of Melanie's sash and smiling up at her. Pain twisted Scarlett's heart. She felt that she could claw Melanie's ivory skin till the blood ran and take pleasure in doing it.

As her eyes wandered from Melanie, she caught the gaze of Rhett Butler, who was not mixing with the crowd but standing apart talking to John Wilkes. He had been watching her and when she looked at him he laughed outright. Scarlett had an uneasy feeling that this man who was not received was the only one present who knew what lay behind her wild gaiety and that it was affording him sardonic amusement. She could have clawed him with pleasure too.

"If I can just live through this barbecue till this afternoon," she thought, "all the girls will go upstairs to take naps to be fresh for to-night and I'll stay downstairs and get to talk to Ashley. Surely he must have noticed how popular I am." She soothed her heart with another hope: "Of course, he has to be attentive to Melanie because, after all, she is his cousin and she isn't popular at all, and if he didn't look out for her she'd just be a wallflower."

She took new courage at this thought and redoubled her efforts in the direction of Charles, whose brown eyes glowed down eagerly at her. It was a wonderful day for Charles, a dream day, and he had fallen in love with Scarlett with no effort at all. Before this new emotion, Honey receded into a dim haze. Honey was a shrill-voiced sparrow and Scarlett a gleaming humming-bird. She teased him and favoured him and asked him questions and answered them herself, so that he appeared very clever without having to say a word. The other boys were puzzled and annoyed by her obvious interest in him, for they knew Charles was too shy to hitch two consecutive words together, and politeness was being severely strained to conceal their growing rage. Everyone was smouldering, and it would have been a positive triumph for Scarlett, except for Ashley.

When the last forkful of pork and chicken and mutton had been eaten, Scarlett hoped the time had come when India would rise and suggest that the ladies retire to the house. It was two o'clock and the sun was warm overhead, but India, wearied with the three-day preparations for the barbecue, was only too glad to remain sitting beneath the arbour, shouting remarks to a deaf old gentleman from Fayetteville.

A lazy somnolence descended on the crowd. The negroes idled about, clearing the long tables on which the food had been laid. The laughter and talking became less animated and groups here and there fell silent. All were waiting for their hostess to signal the end of the morning festivities. Palmetto fans were wagging more slowly, and several old gentlemen were nodding from the heat and overloaded stomachs. The barbecue was over and all were content to take their ease while the sun was at its height.

In this interval between the morning party and the evening's ball, they seemed a placid, peaceful lot. Only the young men retained the restless energy which had filled the whole throng a short while before. Moving from group to group, drawling in their soft voices, they were as handsome as blooded stallions and as dangerous. The languor of midday had taken hold of the gathering, but underneath lurked tempers that could rise to killing heights in a second and flare out as quickly. Men and women, they were beautiful and wild, all a little violent under their pleasant ways and only a little tamed.

Some time dragged by while the sun grew hotter, and Scarlett and others looked again toward India. Conversation was dying out when, in the lull, everyone in the grove heard Gerald's voice raised in furious accents. Standing some little distance away from the barbecue tables, he was at the peak of an argument with John Wilkes.

"God's nightgown, man! Pray for a peaceable settlement with the Yankees? After we've fired on the rascals at Fort Sumter? Peaceable? The South should show by arms that she cannot be insulted and that she is not leaving the Union by the Union's kindness but by her own strength!"

"Oh, my God!" thought Scarlett. "He's done it! Now, we'll all sit here till midnight."

In an instant, the somnolence had fled from the lounging throng and something electric went snapping through the air. The men sprang from benches and chairs, arms in wide gestures, voices clashing for the right to be heard above other voices. There had been no talk of politics or impending war all during the morning, because of Mr. Wilkes' request that the ladies should not be bored. But now Gerald had bawled the words "Fort Sumter", and every man present forgot his host's admonition.

"Of course we'll fight—" "Yankee thieves—" "We could lick them in a month—" "Why, one Southerner can lick twenty Yankees—" "Teach them a lesson they won't soon forget—" "Peaceably? They won't let us go in peace—" "No, look how Mr. Lincoln insulted our Commissioners!"

"Yes, kept them hanging around for weeks—swearing he'd have Sumter evacuated!" "They want war; we'll make them sick of war—" And above all the voices, Gerald's boomed. All Scarlett could hear was "States' rights, by God!" shouted over and over. Gerald was having an excellent time, but not his daughter.

Secession, war—these words long since had become acutely boring to Scarlett from much repetition, but now she hated the sound of them, for they meant that the men would stand there for hours haranguing one another and she would have no chance to corner Ashley. Of course there would be no war and the men all knew it. They just loved to talk and hear themselves talk.

Charles Hamilton had not risen with the others and, finding himself comparatively alone with Scarlett, he leaned closer and, with the daring born of new love, whispered a confession.

"Miss O'Hara—I—I had already decided that if we did fight, I'd go over to South Carolina and join a troop there. It's said that Mr. Wade Hampton is organizing a cavalry troop, and of course I would want to go with him. He's a splendid person and was my father's best friend."

Scarlett thought, "What am I supposed to do —give three cheers?" for Charles' expression showed that he was baring his heart's secrets to her. She could think of nothing to say and so merely looked at him wondering why men were such fools as to think women interested in such matters. He took her expression to mean stunned approbation and went on rapidly, daringly—

165

"If I went—would—would you be sorry, Miss O'Hara?"

"I should cry into my pillow every night," said Scarlett, meaning to be flippant, but he took the statement at face value and went red with pleasure. Her hand was concealed in the folds of her dress and he cautiously wormed his hand to it and squeezed it, overwhelmed at his own boldness and at her acquiescence.

"Would you pray for me?"

"What a fool!" thought Scarlett bitterly, casting a surreptitious glance about her in the hope of being rescued from the conversation.

"Would you?"

"Oh—yes, indeed, Mr. Hamilton. Three Rosaries a night, at least!"

Charles gave a swift look about him, drew in his breath, stiffened the muscles of his stomach. They were practically alone and he might never get another such opportunity. And, even given another such Godsent occasion, his courage might fail him.

"Miss O'Hara—I must tell you something. I— I love you!"

"Um?" said Scarlett absently, trying to peer through the crowd of arguing men to where Ashley still sat talking at Melanie's feet.

"Yes!" whispered Charles, in a rapture that she had neither laughed, screamed nor fainted, as he had always imagined young girls did under such circumstances. "I love you! You are the most— the most—" and he found his tongue for the first time in his life. "The most beautiful girl I've ever known and the sweetest and the kindest, and you have the dearest ways and I love you with all my heart. I cannot hope that you could love anyone like me but, my dear Miss O'Hara, if you can give me any encouragement, I will do anything in the world to make you love me. I will—"

Charles stopped, for he couldn't think of anything difficult enough of accomplishment to really prove to Scarlett the depth of his feeling, so he said simply: "I want to marry you."

Scarlett came back to earth with a jerk, at the sound of the word "marry". She had been thinking of marriage and of Ashley, and she looked at Charles with poorly concealed irritation. Why must this calf-like fool intrude his feelings on this particular day when she was so worried she was about to lose her mind? She looked into the pleading brown eyes and she saw none of the beauty of a shy boy's first love, of the adoration of an ideal come true or the wild happiness and tenderness that were sweeping through him like a flame. Scarlett was used to men asking her to marry them, men much more attractive than Charles Hamilton, and men who had more finesse than to propose at a barbecue when she had more important matters on her mind. She only saw a boy of twenty, red as a beet and looking very silly. She wished that she could tell him how silly he looked. But automatically, the words Ellen had taught her to say in such emergencies rose to her lips and, casting down her eyes, from force of long habit, she murmured: "Mr. Hamilton, I am not unaware of the honour you have bestowed on me in wanting me to become your wife, but this is all so sudden that I do not know what to say."

That was a neat way of smoothing a man's vanity and yet keeping him on the string, and Charles rose to it as though such bait were new and he the first to swallow it.

"I would wait forever! I wouldn't want you unless you were quite sure. Please, Miss O'Hara, tell me that I may hope!"

"Um," said Scarlett, her sharp eyes noting that Ashley, who had not risen to take part in the war talk, was smiling up at Melanie. If this fool who was grappling for her hand would only keep quiet for a moment, perhaps she could hear what they were saying. She must hear what they said. What did Melanie say to him that brought that look of interest to his eyes?

Charles' words blurred the voices she strained to hear.

"Oh, hush!" she hissed at him, pinching his hand and not even looking at him.

Startled, at first abashed, Charles blushed at the rebuff and then, seeing how her eyes were fastened on his sister, he smiled. Scarlett was afraid someone might hear his words. She was naturally embarrassed and shy, and in agony lest they be overheard. Charles felt a surge of masculinity such as he had never experienced, for this was the first time in his life that he had ever embarrassed any girl. The thrill was intoxicating. He arranged his face in what he fancied was an expression of careless unconcern and cautiously returned Scarlett's pinch to show that he was man of the world enough to understand and accept her reproof.

She did not even feel his pinch, for she could

hear clearly the sweet voice that was Melanie's chief charm: "I fear I cannot agree with you about Mr. Thackeray's works. He is a cynic. I fear he is not the gentleman Mr. Dickens is."

What a silly thing to say to a man, thought Scarlett, ready to giggle with relief. Why, she's no more than a bluestocking and everyone knows what men think of bluestockings. . . . The way to get a man interested and to hold his interest was to talk about him, and then gradually lead the conversation around to yourself—and keep it there. Scarlett would have felt some cause for alarm if Melanie had been saying: "How wonderful you are!" or "How do you ever think of such things? My little ole brain would bust if I even tried to think about them!" But here she was, with a man at her feet, talking as seriously as if she were in church. The prospect looked brighter to Scarlett, so bright in fact that she turned beaming eyes on Charles and smiled from pure joy. Enraptured at this evidence of her affection, he grabbed up her fan and plied it so enthusiastically her hair began to blow about untidily.

"Ashley, you have not favoured us with your opinion," said Jim Tarleton, turning from the group of shouting men, and with an apology Ashley excused himself and rose. There was no one there so handsome, thought Scarlett, as she marked how graceful was his negligent pose and how the sun gleamed on his gold hair and moustache. Even the older men stopped to listen to his words.

"Why, gentlemen, if Georgia fights, I'll go with

her. Why else would I have joined the Troop?"
he said. His grey eyes opened wide and their
drowsiness disappeared in an intensity that
Scarlett had never seen before. "But, like
Father, I hope the Yankees will let us go in peace
and that there will be no fighting—" He held up
his hand with a smile, as a babel of voices from
the Fontaine and Tarleton boys began. "Yes, yes,
I know we've been insulted and lied to—but if
we'd been in the Yankees' shoes and they were
trying to leave the Union, how would we have
acted? Pretty much the same. We wouldn't have
liked it."

"There he goes again," thought Scarlett.
"Always putting himself in the other fellow's
shoes." To her, there was never but one fair side
to an argument. Sometimes, there was no understanding Ashley.

"Let's don't be too hot-headed and let's don't
have any war. Most of the misery of the world
has been caused by wars. And when the wars
were over, no one ever knew what they were all
about."

Scarlett sniffed. Lucky for Ashley that he had
an unassailable reputation for courage, or else
there'd be trouble. As she thought this, the
clamour of dissenting voices rose up about
Ashley, indignant, fiery.

Under the arbour, the deaf old gentleman from
Fayetteville punched India.

"What's it all about? What are they saying?"

"War!" shouted India, cupping her hand to his
ear. "They want to fight the Yankees!"

"War, is it?" he cried, fumbling about him for

his cane and heaving himself out of his chair with more energy than he had shown in years. "I'll tell 'um about war. I've been there." It was not often that Mr. McRae had the opportunity to talk about war, the way his women folks shushed him.

He stumped rapidly to the group, waving his cane and shouting and, because he could not hear the voices about him, he soon had undisputed possession of the field.

"You fire-eating young bucks, listen to me. You don't want to fight. I fought and I know. Went out in the Seminole War and was a big enough fool to go to the Mexican War, too. You all don't know what war is. You think it's riding a pretty horse and having the girls throw flowers at you and coming home a hero. Well, it ain't. No, sir! It's going hungry, and getting the measles and pneumonia from sleeping in the wet. And if it ain't measles and pneumonia, it's your bowels. Yes, sir, what war does to a man's bowels —dysentery and things like that—"

The ladies were pink with blushes. Mr. McRae was a reminder of a cruder era, like Grandma Fontaine and her embarrassingly loud belches, an era everyone would like to forget.

"Run get your grandpa," hissed one of the old gentleman's daughters to a young girl standing near by. "I declare," she whispered to the fluttering matrons about her, "he gets worse every day. Would you believe it, this very morning he said to Mary—and she's only sixteen: 'Now, Missy . . .'" and the voice went off into a whisper as the granddaughter slipped out to try to induce Mr. McRae to return to his seat in the shade.

Of all the group that milled about under the trees, girls smiling excitedly, men talking impassionedly, there was only one who seemed calm. Scarlett's eyes turned to Rhett Butler, who leaned against a tree, his hands shoved deep in his trouser pockets. He stood alone, since Mr. Wilkes had left his side, and had uttered no word as the conversation grew hotter. The red lips under the close-clipped black moustache curled down and there was a glint of amused contempt in his black eyes—contempt, as if he listened to the braggings of children. A very disagreeable smile, Scarlett thought. He listened quietly until Stuart Tarleton, his red hair tousled and his eyes gleaming, repeated: "Why, we could lick them in a month! Gentlemen always fight better than rabble. A month—why, one battle—"

"Gentlemen," said Rhett Butler, in a flat drawl that bespoke his Charleston birth, not moving from his position against the tree or taking his hands from his pockets, "may I say a word?"

There was contempt in his manner as in his eyes, contempt overlaid with an air of courtesy that somehow burlesqued their own manners.

The group turned toward him and accorded him the politeness always due an outsider.

"Has any one of you gentlemen ever thought that there's not a cannon factory south of the Mason-Dixon Line? Or how few iron foundries there are in the South? Or woollen mills or cotton factories or tanneries? Have you thought that we would not have a single warship and that the Yankee fleet could bottle up our harbours in a week, so that we could not sell our cotton abroad?

But—of course—you gentlemen have thought of these things."

"Why, he means the boys are a passel of fools!" thought Scarlett indignantly, the hot blood coming to her cheeks.

Evidently, she was not the only one to whom this idea occurred, for several of the boys were beginning to stick out their chins. John Wilkes casually but swiftly came back to his place beside the speaker, as if to impress on all present that this man was his guest and that, moreover, there were ladies present.

"The trouble with most of us Southerners," continued Rhett Butler, "is that we either don't travel enough or we don't profit enough by our travels. Now, of course, all you gentlemen are well travelled. But what have you seen? Europe and New York and Philadelphia and, of course, the ladies have been to Saratoga" (he bowed slightly to the group under the arbour). "You've seen the hotels and the museums and the balls and the gambling houses. And you've come home believing that there's no place like the South. As for me, I was Charleston born, but I have spent the last few years in the North." His white teeth showed in a grin, as though he realized that everyone present knew just why he no longer lived in Charleston, and cared not at all if they did know. "I have seen many things that you all have not seen. The thousands of immigrants who'd be glad to fight for the Yankees for food and a few dollars, the factories, the foundries, the shipyards, the iron and coal mines—all the things we haven't got. Why, all we have is cotton and slaves and arrogance. They'd lick us in a month."

For a tense moment, there was silence. Rhett Butler removed a fine linen handkerchief from his coat pocket and idly flicked dust from his sleeve. Then an ominous murmuring arose in the crowd and from under the arbour came a humming as unmistakable as that of a hive of newly disturbed bees. Even while she felt the hot blood of wrath still in her cheeks, something in Scarlett's practical mind prompted the thought that what this man said was right, and it sounded like common sense. Why, she'd never even seen a factory, or known anyone who had seen a factory. But, even if it were true, he was no gentleman to make such a statement—and at a party, too, where everyone was having a good time.

Stuart Tarleton, brows lowering, came forward with Brent close at his heels. Of course, the Tarleton twins had nice manners and they wouldn't make a scene at a barbecue, even though tremendously provoked. Just the same, all the ladies felt pleasantly excited, for it was so seldom that they actually saw a scene or a quarrel. Usually they had to hear of it third-hand.

"Sir," said Stuart heavily, "what do you mean?"

Rhett looked at him with polite but mocking eyes.

"I mean," he answered, "what Napoleon—perhaps you've heard of him?—remarked once, 'God is on the side of the strongest battalion!'" and, turning to John Wilkes, he said with courtesy that was unfeigned: "You promised to show

174

me your library, sir. Would it be too great a favour to ask to see it now? I fear I must go back to Jonesboro early this afternoon where a bit of business calls me."

He swung about, facing the crowd, clicked his heels together and bowed like a dancing master, a bow that was graceful for so powerful a man, and as full of impertinence as a slap in the face. Then he walked across the lawn with John Wilkes, his black head in the air, and the sound of his discomforting laughter floated back to the group about the tables.

There was a startled silence and then the buzzing broke out again. India rose tiredly from her seat beneath the arbour and went toward the angry Stuart Tarleton. Scarlett could not hear what she said, but the look in her eyes as she gazed up into his lowering face gave Scarlett something like a twinge of conscience. It was the same look of belonging that Melanie wore when she looked at Ashley, only Stuart did not see it. So India did love him. Scarlett thought for an instant that if she had not flirted so blatantly with Stuart at that political speaking a year ago, he might have married India long ere this. But then the twinge passed with the comforting thought that it wasn't her fault if other girls couldn't keep their men.

Finally Stuart smiled down at India, an unwilling smile, and nodded his head. Probably India had been pleading with him not to follow Mr. Butler and make trouble. A polite tumult broke out under the trees as the guests arose, shaking crumbs from laps. The married women called to nurses and small children and gathered their broods together to take their departure, and groups of girls started off, laughing and talking, toward the house to exchange gossip in the upstairs bedrooms and to take their naps.

All the ladies except Mrs. Tarleton moved out of the back yard, leaving the shade of oaks and arbour to the men. She was detained by Gerald, Mr. Calvert and the others who wanted an answer from her about the horses for the Troop.

Ashley strolled over to where Scarlett and Charles sat, a thoughtful and amused smile on his face.

"Arrogant devil, isn't he?" he observed, looking after Butler. "He looks like one of the Borgias."

Scarlett thought quickly but could remember no family in the County or Atlanta or Savannah by that name.

"I don't know them. Is he kin to them? Who are they?"

An odd look came over Charles' face, incredulity and shame struggling with love. Love triumphed as he realized that it was enough for a girl to be sweet and gentle and beautiful, without having an education to hamper her charms, and he made swift answer: "The Borgias were Italians."

"Oh," said Scarlett, losing interest, "foreigners."

She turned her prettiest smile on Ashley, but for some reason he was not looking at her. He was looking at Charles, and there was understanding in his face and a little pity.

Scarlett stood on the landing and peered cautiously over the banisters into the hall below. It was empty. From the bedrooms on the floor above came an unending hum of low voices, rising and falling, punctuated with squeaks of laughter and, "Now, you didn't, really!" and "What did he say then?" On the beds and couches of the six great bedrooms, the girls were resting, their dresses off, their stays loosed, their hair flowing down their backs. Afternoon naps were a custom of the country and never were they so necessary as on the all-day parties, beginning early in the morning and culminating in a ball. For half an hour, the girls would chatter and laugh, and then servants would pull in the shutters, and in the warm half-gloom the talk would die to whispers and finally expire in silence broken only by soft regular breathing.

Scarlett had made certain that Melanie was lying down on the bed with Honey and Hetty Tarleton before she slipped into the hall and started down the stairs. From the window on the landing, she could see the group of men sitting under the arbour, drinking from tall glasses, and she knew they would remain there until late afternoon. Her eyes searched the group but Ashley was not among them. Then she listened and she heard his voice. As she had hoped, he was still in the front driveway bidding good-bye to departing matrons and children.

Her heart in her throat, she went swiftly down

the stairs. What if she should meet Mr. Wilkes? What excuse could she give for prowling about the house when all the other girls were getting their beauty naps? Well, that had to be risked.

As she reached the bottom step, she heard the servants moving about in the dining-room under the butler's orders, lifting out the table and the chairs in preparation for the dancing. Across the wide hall was the open door of the library and she sped into it noiselessly. She could wait there until Ashley finished his adieux and then call to him when he came into the house.

The library was in semi-darkness, for the blinds had been drawn against the sun. The dim room with towering walls completely filled with dark books depressed her. It was not the place which she would have chosen for a tryst such as she hoped this one would be. Large numbers of books always depressed her, as did people who liked to read large numbers of books. That is—all people except Ashley. The heavy furniture rose up at her in the half-light: high-backed chairs with deep seats and wide arms, made for the tall Wilkes men, squatty soft chairs of velvet with velvet hass-ocks before them for the girls. Far across the long room before the hearth, the seven-foot sofa, Ashley's favourite seat, reared its high back, like some huge sleeping animal.

She closed the door except for a crack and tried to make her heart beat more slowly. She tried to remember just exactly what she had planned last night to say to Ashley, but she couldn't recall anything. Had she thought up something and forgotten it—or had she only planned that Ashley

178

should say something to her? She couldn't remember, and a sudden cold fright fell upon her. If her heart would only stop pounding in her ears, perhaps she could think of what to say. But the quick thudding only increased as she heard him call a final farewell and walk into the front hall.

All she could think of was that she loved him —everything about him, from the proud lift of his gold head to his slender dark boots, loved his laughter even when it mystified her, loved his bewildering silences. Oh, if only he would walk in on her now and take her in his arms, so she would be spared the need of saying anything. He must love her—"Perhaps if I prayed—" She squeezed her eyes tightly and began gabbling to herself, "Hail Mary, fullofgrace—"

"Why, Scarlett!" said Ashley's voice, breaking in through the roaring in her ears and throwing her into utter confusion. He stood in the hall peering at her through the partly opened door, a quizzical smile on his face.

"Who are you hiding from—Charles or the Tarletons?"

She gulped. So he had noticed how the men had swarmed about her! How unutterably dear he was standing there with his eyes twinkling, all unaware of her excitement. She could not speak, but she put out a hand and drew him into the room. He entered, puzzled but interested. There was a tenseness about her, a glow in her eyes that he had never seen before, and even in the dim light he could see the rosy flush on her cheeks. Automatically he closed the door behind him and took her hand.

"What is it?" he said, almost in a whisper.

At the touch of his hand, she began to tremble. It was going to happen now, just as she had dreamed it. A thousand incoherent thoughts shot through her mind, and she could not catch a single one to mould into a word. She could only shake and look up into his face. Why didn't he speak?

"What is it?" he repeated. "A secret to tell me?"

Suddenly she found her tongue and just as suddenly all the years of Ellen's teachings fell away, and the forthright Irish blood of Gerald spoke from his daughter's lips.

"Yes—a secret. I love you."

For an instant there was a silence so acute it seemed that neither of them even breathed. Then the trembling fell away from her, as happiness and pride surged through her. Why hadn't she done this before? How much simpler than all the ladylike manoeuvrings she had been taught. And then her eyes sought his.

There was a look of consternation in them, of incredulity and something more—what was it? Yes, Gerald had looked that way the day his pet hunter had broken his leg and he had had to shoot him. Why did she have to think of that now? Such a silly thought. And why did Ashley look so oddly and say nothing? Then something like a well-trained mask came down over his face and he smiled gallantly.

"Isn't it enough that you've collected every other man's heart here to-day?" he said, with the old, teasing caressing note in his voice. "Do you want to make it unanimous? Well, you've always had my heart, you know. You cut your teeth on it."

Something was wrong—all wrong! This was not the way she had planned it. Through the mad tearing of ideas round and round in her brain, one was beginning to take form. Somehow—for some reason—Ashley was acting as if he thought she was just flirting with him. But he knew differently. She knew he did.

"Ashley—Ashley—tell me—you must—oh, don't tease me now! Have I your heart? Oh, my dear, I lo—"

His hand went across her lips, swiftly. The mask was gone.

"You must not say these things, Scarlett! You mustn't. You don't mean them. You'll hate yourself for saying them, and you'll hate me for hearing them!"

She jerked her head away. A hot swift current was running through her.

"I couldn't ever hate you. I tell you I love you and I know you must care about me because—" She stopped. Never before had she seen so much misery in anyone's face. "Ashley, do you care—you do, don't you?"

"Yes," he said dully. "I care."

If he had said he loathed her, she could not have been more frightened. She plucked at his sleeve, speechless.

"Scarlett," he said, "can't we go away and forget that we have ever said these things?"

"No," she whispered. "I can't. What do you mean? Don't you want to—to marry me?"

He replied, "I'm going to marry Melanie."

Somehow she found that she was sitting on the low velvet chair and Ashley, on the hassock at her feet, was holding both her hands in his, in a hard grip. He was saying things—things that made no sense. Her mind was quite blank, quite empty of all the thoughts that had surged through it only a moment before, and his words made no more impression than rain on glass. They fell on unhearing ears, words that were swift and tender and full of pity, like a father speaking to a hurt child.

The sound of Melanie's name caught in her consciousness and she looked into his crystal-grey eyes. She saw in them the old remoteness that had always baffled her—and a look of self-hatred.

"Father is to announce the engagement to-night. We are to be married soon. I should have told you, but I thought you knew. I thought everyone knew—had known for years. I never dreamed that you—You've so many beaux. I thought Stuart—"

Life and feeling and comprehension were beginning to flow back into her.

"But you just said you cared for me."

His warm hands hurt hers.

"My dear, must you make me say things that will hurt you?"

Her silence pressed him on.

"How can I make you see these things, my dear? You who are so young and unthinking that you do not know what marriage means."

"I know I love you."

"Love isn't enough to make a successful

marriage when two people are as different as we are. You would want all of a man, Scarlett, his body, his heart, his soul, his thoughts. And if you did not have them, you would be miserable. And I couldn't give you all of me. I couldn't give all of me to anyone. And I would not want all of your mind and your soul. And you would be hurt, and then you would come to hate me—how bitterly! You would hate the books I read and the music I loved, because they took me away from you even for a moment. And I—perhaps I—"

"Do you love her?"

"She is like me, part of my blood, and we understand each other. Scarlett! Scarlett! Can't I make you see that a marriage can't go on in any sort of peace unless the two people are alike?"

Someone else had said that: "Like must marry like or there'll be no happiness." Who was it? It seemed a million years since she had heard that, but it still did not make sense.

"But you said you cared."

"I shouldn't have said it."

Somewhere in her brain, a slow fire rose and rage began to blot out everything else.

"Well, having been cad enough to say it—"

His face went white.

"I was a cad to say it, as I'm going to marry Melanie. I did you a wrong and Melanie a greater one. I should not have said it, for I knew you wouldn't understand. How could I help caring for you—you who have all the passion for life that I have not? You who can love and hate with a violence impossible to me? Why, you are as elemental as fire and wind and wild things and I—"

She thought of Melanie and saw suddenly her quiet brown eyes with their far-off look, her placid little hands in their black lace mitts, her gentle silences. And then her rage broke, the same rage that drove Gerald to murder and other Irish ancestors to misdeeds that cost them their necks. There was nothing in her now of the well-bred Robillards who could bear with white silence anything the world might cast.

"Why don't you say it, you coward! You're afraid to marry me! You'd rather live with that stupid little fool who can't open her mouth except to say 'Yes' or 'No' and raise a passel of mealy-mouthed brats just like her! Why—"

"You must not say these things about Melanie!"

"'I mustn't' be damned to you! Who are you to tell me I mustn't? You coward, you cad, you —You made me believe you were going to marry me—"

"Be fair," his voice pleaded. "Did I ever—"

She did not want to be fair, although she knew what he said was true. He had never once crossed the borders of friendliness with her and, when she thought of this, fresh anger rose, the anger of hurt pride and feminine vanity. She had run after him and he would have none of her. He preferred a whey-faced little fool like Melanie to her. Oh, far better that she had followed Ellen and Mammy's precepts and never, never revealed that she even liked him—better anything than to be faced with this scorching shame!

She sprang to her feet, her hands clenched, and he rose towering over her, his face full of the mute misery of one forced to face realities when realities are agonies.

"I shall hate you till I die, you cad—you lowdown—lowdown—" What was the word she wanted? She could not think of any word bad enough.

"Scarlett—please—"

He put out his hand toward her and, as he did, she slapped him across the face with all the strength she had. The noise cracked like a whip in the still room and suddenly her rage was gone, and there was desolation in her heart.

The red mark of her hand showed plainly on his white tired face. He said nothing, but lifted her limp hand to his lips and kissed it. Then he was gone before she could speak again, closing the door softly behind him.

She sat down again very suddenly, the reaction from her rage making her knees feel weak. He was gone and the memory of his stricken face would haunt her till she died.

She heard the soft muffled sound of his footsteps dying away down the long hall, and the complete enormity of her actions came over her. She had lost him forever. Now he would hate her and every time he looked at her he would remember how she threw herself at him when he had given her no encouragement at all.

"I'm as bad as Honey Wilkes," she thought suddenly, and remembered how everyone, and she more than anyone else, had laughed contemptuously at Honey's forward conduct. She saw Honey's awkward wigglings and heard her silly titters as she hung on to boys' arms, and the thought stung her to new rage, rage at herself, at Ashley, at the world. Because she hated herself, she hated them all with the fury of the thwarted and humiliated love of sixteen. Only a little true tenderness had been mixed into her love. Mostly it had been compounded out of vanity and complacent confidence in her own charms. Now she had lost, and greater than her sense of loss was the fear that she had made a public spectacle of herself. Had she been as obvious as Honey? Was everyone laughing at her? She began to shake at the thought.

Her hand dropped to a little table beside her, fingering a tiny china rose-bowl on which two china cherubs smirked. The room was so still she almost screamed to break the silence. She must do something or go mad. She picked up the bowl and hurled it viciously across the room toward the fireplace. It barely cleared the tall back of the sofa and splintered with a little crash against the marble mantelpiece.

"This," said a voice from the depths of the sofa, "is too much."

Nothing had ever startled or frightened her so much, and her mouth went too dry for her to utter a sound. She caught hold of the back of the chair, her knees going weak under her, as Rhett Butler rose from the sofa where he had been lying and made her a bow of exaggerated politeness.

"It is bad enough to have an afternoon nap disturbed by such a passage as I've been forced to hear, but why should my life be endangered?"

He was real. He wasn't a ghost. But, saints

186

preserve us, he had heard everything! She rallied her forces into a semblance of dignity.

"Sir, you should have made known your presence."

"Indeed?" His white teeth gleamed and his bold dark eyes laughed at her. "But you were the intruder. I was forced to wait for Mr. Kennedy, and feeling that I was perhaps persona non grata in the back yard, I was thoughtful enough to remove my unwelcome presence here where I thought I would be undisturbed. But, alas!" He shrugged and laughed softly.

Her temper was beginning to rise again at the thought that this rude and impertinent man had heard everything—heard things she now wished she had died before she ever uttered.

"Eavesdroppers—" she began furiously.

"Eavesdroppers often hear highly entertaining and instructive things," he grinned. "From a long experience in eavesdropping, I—"

"Sir," she said, "you are no gentleman!"

"An apt observation," he answered airily. "And you, Miss, are no lady." He seemed to find her very amusing, for he laughed softly again. "No one can remain a lady after saying and doing what I have just overheard. However, ladies have seldom held any charms for me. I know what they are thinking, but they never have the courage or lack of breeding to say what they think. And that, in time, becomes a bore. But you, my dear Miss O'Hara, are a girl of rare spirit, very admirable spirit, and I take off my hat to you. I fail to understand what charms the elegant Mr. Wilkes can hold for a girl of your tempestuous nature.

He should thank God on bended knee for a girl with your—how did he put it?—'passion for living', but being a poor-spirited wretch—"

"You aren't fit to wipe his boots!" she shouted in rage.

"And you were going to hate him all your life!" He sank down on the sofa and she heard him laughing.

If she could have killed him, she would have done it. Instead, she walked out of the room with such dignity as she could summon and banged the heavy door behind her.

She went up the stairs so swiftly that, when she reached the landing, she thought she was going to faint. She stopped, clutching the banisters, her heart hammering so hard from anger, insult and exertion that it seemed about to burst through her basque. She tried to draw deep breaths but Mammy's lacings were too tight. If she should faint and they should find her here on the landing, what would they think? Oh, they'd think everything, Ashley and that vile Butler man and those nasty girls who were so jealous! For once in her life, she wished that she carried smelling salts, like the other girls, but she had never owned a vinaigrette. She had always been so proud of never feeling giddy. She simply could not let herself faint now!

Gradually the sickening feeling began to depart. In a minute, she'd feel all right and then she'd slip quietly into the little dressing-room adjoining India's room, unloose her stays and creep in and lay herself on one of the beds beside the sleeping girls. She tried to quiet her heart and fix her face into more composed lines, for she knew she must look like a crazy woman. If any of the girls were awake, they'd know something was wrong. And no one must ever, ever know that anything had happened.

Through the wide bay window on the landing, she could see the men still lounging in their chairs under the trees and in the shade of the arbour. How she envied them! How wonderful to be a man and never have to undergo miseries such as she had just passed through! As she stood watching them, hot-eyed and dizzy, she heard the rapid pounding of a horse's hooves on the front drive, the scattering of gravel and the sound of an excited voice calling a question to one of the negroes. The gravel flew again and across her vision a man on horseback galloped over the green lawn toward the lazy group under the trees.

Some late-come guest; but why did he ride his horse across the turf that was India's pride? She could not recognize him, but as he flung himself from the saddle and clutched John Wilkes' arm, she could see that there was excitement in every line of him. The crowd swarmed about him, tall glasses and palmetto fans abandoned on tables and on the ground. In spite of the distance, she could hear the hubbub of voices, questioning, calling, feel the fever-pitch tenseness of the men. Then above the confused sounds Stuart Tarleton's voice rose, in an exultant shout, "Yee-aay-ee!" as if he were on the hunting field. And she heard for the first time, without knowing it, the Rebel yell.

As she watched, the four Tarletons followed by the Fontaine boys broke from the group and began hurrying toward the stable, yelling as they ran, "Jeems! You, Jeems! Saddle the horses!"

"Somebody's house must have caught fire," Scarlett thought. But fire or no fire, her job was to get herself back into the bedroom before she was discovered.

Her heart was quieter now and she tiptoed up the steps into the silent hall. A heavy warm somnolence lay over the house, as if it slept at ease like the girls, until night when it would burst into its full beauty with music and candle-flames. Carefully, she eased open the door of the dressing-room and slipped in. Her hand was behind her, still holding the knob, when Honey Wilkes' voice, low pitched, almost in a whisper, came to her through the crack of the opposite door leading into the bedroom.

"I think Scarlett acted as fast as a girl could act to-day."

Scarlett felt her heart begin its mad racing again and she clutched her hand against it unconsciously, as if she would squeeze it into submission. "Eavesdroppers often hear highly instructive things," jibed a memory. Should she slip out again? Or make herself known and embarrass Honey as she deserved? But the next voice made her pause. A team of mules could not have dragged her away when she heard Melanie's voice.

"Oh, Honey, no! Don't be unkind. She's just high-spirited and vivacious. I thought her most charming."

"Oh," thought Scarlett, clawing her nails into her basque. "To have that mealy-mouthed little mess take up for me!"

It was harder to bear than Honey's out-and-out cattiness. Scarlett had never trusted any woman and had never credited any woman except her mother with motives other than selfish ones. Melanie knew she had Ashley securely, so she could well afford to show such a Christian spirit. Scarlett felt it was just Melanie's way of parading her conquest and getting credit for being sweet at the same time. Scarlett had frequently used the same trick herself when discussing other girls with men, and it had never failed to convince foolish males of her sweetness and unselfishness.

"Well, Miss," said Honey tartly, her voice rising, "you must be blind."

"Hush, Honey," hissed the voice of Sally Munroe. "They'll hear you all over the house!"

Honey lowered her voice, but went on.

"Well, you saw how she was carrying on with every man she could get hold of—even Mr. Kennedy and he's her own sister's beau. I never saw the like! And she certainly was going after Charles." Honey giggled self-consciously. "And you know, Charles and I—"

"Are you really?" whispered voices excitedly.

"Well, don't tell anybody, girls—not yet!"

There were more gigglings and the bed-springs creaked as someone squeezed Honey. Melanie murmured something about how happy she was that Honey would be her sister.

"Well, I won't be happy to have Scarlett for my sister, because she's a fast piece if ever I saw one," came the aggrieved voice of Hetty Tarleton. "But she's as good as engaged to Stuart. Brent says she doesn't give a rap about him, but, of course, Brent's crazy about her, too."

"If you should ask me," said Honey with mysterious importance, "there's only one person she does give a rap about. And that's Ashley!"

As the whisperings merged together violently, questioning, interrupting, Scarlett felt herself go cold with fear and humiliation. Honey was a fool, a silly, a simpleton about men, but she had a feminine instinct about other women that Scarlett had under-estimated. The mortification and hurt pride that she had suffered in the library with Ashley and with Rhett Butler were pin-pricks to this. Men could be trusted to keep their mouths shut, even men like Mr. Butler, but with Honey Wilkes giving tongue like a hound in the field, the entire County would know about it before six o'clock. And Gerald had said only last night that he wouldn't be having the County laughing at his daughter. And how they would all laugh now! Clammy perspiration, starting under her armpits, began to creep down her ribs.

Melanie's voice, measured and peaceful, a little reproving, rose above the others.

"Honey, you know that isn't so. And it's so unkind."

"It is too, Melly, and if you weren't always so busy looking for the good in people that haven't got any good in them, you'd see it. And I'm glad it's so. It serves her right. All Scarlett O'Hara has ever done has been to stir up trouble and try to get other girls' beaux. You know mighty well she took Stuart from India and she didn't want him. And to-day she tried to take Mr. Kennedy and Ashley and Charles—"

"I must get home!" thought Scarlett. "I must get home!"

If she could only be transferred by magic to Tara and to safety. If she could only be with Ellen, just to see her, to hold on to her skirt, to cry and pour out the whole story in her lap. If she had to listen to another word, she'd rush in and pull out Honey's straggly pale hair in big handfuls and spit on Melanie Hamilton to show her just what she thought of her charity. But she'd already acted common enough to-day, enough like white trash—that was where all her trouble lay.

She pressed her hands hard against her skirts, so they would not rustle, and backed out as stealthily as an animal. "Home," she thought, as she sped down the hall, past the closed doors and still rooms, "I must go home."

She was already on the front porch when a new thought brought her up sharply—she couldn't go home! She couldn't run away! She would have to see it through, bear all the malice of the girls and her own humiliation and heartbreak. To run away would only give them more ammunition.

She pounded her clenched fist against the tall white pillar beside her, and she wished that she were Samson, so that she could pull down all of Twelve Oaks and destroy every person in it. She'd make them sorry. She'd show them. She didn't quite see how she'd show them, but she'd do it all the same. She'd hurt them worse than they hurt her.

For the moment, Ashley as Ashley was forgotten. He was not the tall drowsy boy she loved but part and parcel of the Wilkeses, Twelve Oaks, the County—and she hated them all because they laughed. Vanity was stronger than love at sixteen and there was no room in her hot heart now for anything but hate.

"I won't go home," she thought. "I'll stay here and I'll make them sorry. And I'll never tell Mother. No, I'll never tell anybody." She braced herself to go back into the house, to reclimb the stairs and go into another bedroom.

As she turned, she saw Charles coming into the house from the other end of the long hall. When he saw her, he hurried toward her. His hair was tousled and his face near geranium with excitement.

"Do you know what's happened?" he cried, even before he reached her. "Have you heard? Paul Wilson just rode over from Jonesboro with the news!"

He paused, breathless, as he came up to her. She said nothing and only stared at him.

"Mr. Lincoln has called for men, soldiers— I mean volunteers—seventy-five thousand of them!"

Mr. Lincoln again! Didn't men ever think about anything that really mattered? Here was this fool expecting her to be excited about Mr. Lincoln's didoes when her heart was broken and her reputation as good as ruined.

Charles stared at her. Her face was paper white

194

and her narrow eyes blazing like emeralds. He had never seen such fire in any girl's face, such a glow in anyone's eyes.

"I'm so clumsy," he said. "I should have told you more gently. I forgot how delicate ladies are. I'm sorry I've upset you so. You don't feel faint, do you? Can I get you a glass of water?"

"No," she said, and managed a crooked smile.

"Shall we go sit on the bench?" he asked, taking her arm.

She nodded and he carefully handed her down the front steps and led her across the grass to the iron bench beneath the largest oak in the front yard. "How fragile and tender women are," he thought; "the mere mention of war and harshness makes them faint." The idea made him feel very masculine and he was doubly gentle as he seated her. She looked so strangely, and there was a wild beauty about her white face that set his heart leaping. Could it be that she was distressed by the thought that he might go to the war? No, that was too conceited for belief. But why did she look at him so oddly? And why did her hands shake as they fingered her lace handkerchief? And her thick sooty lashes—they were fluttering just like the eyes of girls in romances he had read, fluttering with timidity and love.

He cleared his throat three times to speak and failed each time. He dropped his eyes because her own green ones met his so piercingly, almost as if she were not seeing him.

"He has a lot of money," she was thinking swiftly, as a thought and a plan went through her brain. "And he hasn't any parents to bother me

195

and he lives in Atlanta. And if I married him right away, it would show Ashley that I didn't care a rap—that I was only flirting with him. And it would just kill Honey. She'd never, never catch another beau and everybody'd laugh fit to die at her. And it would hurt Melanie, because she loves Charles so much. And it would hurt Stu and Brent—" She didn't quite know why she wanted to hurt them, except that they had catty sisters. "And they'd all be sorry when I came back here to visit in a fine carriage and with lots of pretty clothes and a house of my own. And they would never, never laugh at me."

"Of course, it will mean fighting," said Charles, after several more embarrassed attempts. "But don't you fret, Miss Scarlett, it'll be over in a month and we'll have them howling. Yes, sir! Howling! I wouldn't miss it for anything. I'm afraid there won't be much of a ball to-night, because the Troop is going to meet at Jonesboro. The Tarleton boys have gone to spread the news. I know the ladies will be sorry."

She said, "Oh," for want of anything better, but it sufficed.

Coolness was beginning to come back to her and her mind was collecting itself. A frost lay over all her emotions and she thought that she would never feel anything warmly again. Why not take this pretty, flushed boy? He was as good as anyone else and she didn't care. No, she could never care about anything again, not if she lived to be ninety.

"I can't decide now whether to go with Mr.

Wade Hampton's South Carolina Legion or with the Atlanta Gate City Guard."

She said, "Oh," again and their eyes met and the fluttering lashes were his undoing.

"Will you wait for me, Miss Scarlett? It—it would be Heaven just knowing that you were waiting for me until after we licked them!" He hung breathless on her words, watching the way her lips curled up at the corners, noting for the first time the shadows about these corners and thinking what it would mean to kiss them. Her hand, with palm clammy with perspiration, slid into his.

"I wouldn't want to wait," she said, and her eyes were veiled.

He sat clutching her hand, his mouth wide open. Watching him from under her lashes, Scarlett thought detachedly that he looked like a gigged frog. He stuttered several times, closed his mouth and opened it again, and again became geranium-coloured.

"Can you possibly love me?"

She said nothing but looked down into her lap, and Charles was thrown into new states of ecstasy and embarrassment. Perhaps a man should not ask a girl such a question. Perhaps it would be unmaidenly for her to answer it. Having never possessed the courage to get himself into such a situation before, Charles was at a loss as to how to act. He wanted to shout and to sing and to kiss her and to caper about the lawn and then run tell everyone, black and white, that she loved him. But he only squeezed her hand until he drove her rings into the flesh.

"You will marry me soon, Miss Scarlett?"

"Um," she said, fingering a fold of her dress.

"Shall we make it a double wedding with Mel—"

"No," she said quickly, her eyes glinting up at him ominously. Charles knew again that he had made an error. Of course, a girl wanted her own wedding—not shared glory. How kind she was to overlook his blunderings! If it were only dark and he had the courage of shadows and could kiss her hand and say the things he longed to say.

"When may I speak to your father?"

"The sooner the better," she said, hoping that perhaps he would release the crushing pressure on her rings before she had to ask him to do it.

He leaped up and for a moment she thought he was going to cut a caper, before dignity claimed him. He looked down at her radiantly, his whole clean simple heart in his eyes. She had never had anyone look at her thus before and would never have it from any other man, but in her queer detachment she only thought that he looked like a calf.

"I'll go now and find your father," he said, smiling all over his face. "I can't wait. Will you excuse me—dear?" The endearment came hard but having said it once, he repeated it again with pleasure.

"Yes," she said, "I'll wait here. It's so cool and nice here."

He went off across the lawn and disappeared around the house, and she was alone under the rustling oak. From the stables, men were streaming out on horseback, negro servants riding hard behind their masters. The Munroe boys tore past waving their hats, and the Fontaines and Calverts went down the road yelling. The four Tarletons charged across the lawn by her and Brent shouted: "Mother's going to give us the horses! Yee-aay-ee!" Turf flew and they were gone, leaving her alone again.

The white house reared its tall columns before her, seeming to withdraw with dignified aloofness from her. It would never be her house now. Ashley would never carry her over the threshold as his bride. Oh, Ashley, Ashley! What have I done? Deep in her, under layers of hurt pride and cold practicality, something stirred hurtingly. An adult emotion was being born, stronger than her vanity or her wilful selfishness. She loved Ashley and she knew she loved him, and she had never cared so much as in that instant when she saw Charles disappearing around the curved gravelled walk.

7

WITHIN two weeks Scarlett had become a wife, and within two months more she was a widow. She was soon released from the bonds she had assumed with so much haste and so little thought, but she was never again to know the careless freedom of her unmarried days. Widowhood had crowded closely on the heels of marriage but, to her dismay, motherhood soon followed.

In after years when she thought of those last days of April, 1861, Scarlett could never quite remember details. Time and events were telescoped, jumbled together like a nightmare that had no reality or reason. Till the day she died there would be blank spots in her memories of those days. Especially vague were her recollections of the time between her acceptance of Charles and her wedding. Two weeks! So short an engagement would have been impossible in times of peace. Then there would have been a decorous interval of a year or at least six months. But the South was aflame with war, events roared along as swiftly as if carried by a mighty wind and the slow tempo of the old days was gone. Ellen had wrung her hands and counselled delay, in order that Scarlett might think the matter over at greater length. But to her pleadings, Scarlett turned a sullen face and a deaf ear. Marry she would! And quickly too. Within two weeks.

Learning that Ashley's wedding had been moved up from the autumn to the first of May, so he could leave with the Troop as soon as it was called into service, Scarlett set the date of her wedding for the day before his. Ellen protested but Charles pleaded with new-found eloquence, for he was impatient to be off to South Carolina to join Wade Hampton's Legion, and Gerald sided with the two young people. He was excited by the war fever and pleased that Scarlett had made so good a match, and who was he to stand in the way of young love when there was a war? Ellen, distracted, finally gave in as other mothers throughout the South were doing. Their leisured world had been turned topsy-turvy, and their pleadings, prayers and advice availed nothing against the powerful forces sweeping them along.

The South was intoxicated with enthusiasm and excitement. Everyone knew that one battle would end the war and every young man hastened to enlist before the war should end—hastened to marry his sweetheart before he rushed off to Virginia to strike a blow at the Yankees. There were dozens of war weddings in the County and there was little time for the sorrow of parting, for everyone was too busy and excited for either solemn thoughts or tears. The ladies were making uniforms, knitting socks and rolling bandages, and the men were drilling and shooting. Train-loads of troops passed through Jonesboro daily on their way north to Atlanta and Virginia. Some detachments were gaily uniformed in the scarlets and light blues and greens of select social-militia companies; some small groups were in homespun and coonskin caps; others, ununiformed, were in broadcloth and fine linen; all were half-drilled, half-armed, wild with excitement and shouting as though en route to a picnic. The sight of these men threw the County boys into a panic for fear the war would be over before they could reach Virginia, and preparations for the Troop's departure were speeded.

In the midst of the turmoil, preparations went forward for Scarlett's wedding and, almost before she knew it, she was clad in Ellen's wedding dress and veil, coming down the wide stairs of Tara on her father's arm, to face a house packed full with guests. Afterward she remembered, as from a dream, the hundreds of candles flaring on the walls, her mother's face, loving, a little bewildered, her lips moving in a silent prayer for her daughter's happiness, Gerald flushed with brandy and pride that his daughter was marrying both money, a fine name and an old one—and Ashley, standing at the bottom of the steps with Melanie's arm through his.

When she saw the look on his face, she thought: "This can't be real. It can't be. It's a nightmare. I'll wake up and find it's all been a nightmare. I mustn't think of it now, or I'll begin screaming in front of all these people. I can't think now. I'll think later, when I can stand it— when I can't see his eyes."

It was all very dreamlike, the passage through the aisle of smiling people, Charles' scarlet face and stammering voice and her own replies, so startlingly clear, so cold. And the congratulations afterward and the kissing and the toasts and the dancing—all, all like a dream. Even the feel of Ashley's kiss upon her cheek, even Melanie's soft whisper, "Now, we're really and truly sisters," were unreal. Even the excitement caused by the swooning spell that overtook Charles' plump emotional aunt, Miss Pittypat Hamilton, had the quality of a nightmare.

But when the dancing and toasting were finally ended and the dawn was coming, when all the Atlanta guests who could be crowded into Tara and the overseer's house had gone to sleep on beds, sofas and pallets on the floor, and all the neighbours had gone home to rest in preparation for the wedding at Twelve Oaks the next day, then the dreamlike trance shattered like crystal before reality. The reality was the blushing Charles, emerging from her dressing-room in his nightshirt, avoiding the startled look she gave him over the high-pulled sheet.

Of course, she knew that married people occupied the same bed but she had never given the matter a thought before. It seemed very natural in the case of her mother and father, but she had never applied it to herself. Now for the first time since the barbecue she realized just what she had brought on herself. The thought of this strange boy whom she hadn't really wanted to marry getting into bed with her, when her heart was breaking with an agony of regret at her hasty action and the anguish of losing Ashley forever, was too much to be borne. As he hesitatingly approached the bed she spoke in a hoarse whisper.

"I'll scream out loud if you come near me. I

will! I will—at the top of my voice! Get away from me! Don't you dare touch me!"

So Charles Hamilton spent his wedding night in an armchair in the corner, not too unhappily, for he understood, or thought he understood, the modesty and delicacy of his bride. He was willing to wait until her fears subsided, only—only—He sighed as he twisted about seeking a comfortable position, for he was going away to the war so very soon.

Nightmarish as her own wedding had been, Ashley's wedding was even worse. Scarlett stood in her apple-green "second-day" dress in the parlour of Twelve Oaks amid the blaze of hundreds of candles, jostled by the same throng as the night before, and saw the plain little face of Melanie Hamilton glow into beauty as she became Melanie Wilkes. Now, Ashley was gone forever. Her Ashley. No, not her Ashley now. Had he ever been hers? It was all so mixed up in her mind and her mind was so tired, so bewildered. He had said he loved her, but what was it that had separated them? If she could only remember. She had stilled the County's gossiping tongue by marrying Charles, but what did that matter now? It had seemed so important once, but now it didn't seem important at all. All that mattered was Ashley. Now he was gone and she was married to a man she not only did not love but for whom she had an active contempt.

Oh, how she regretted it all. She had often heard of people cutting off their noses to spite their faces but heretofore it had been only a figure of speech. Now she knew just what it meant. And

204

mingled with her frenzied desire to be free of Charles and safely back at Tara, an unmarried girl again, ran the knowledge that she had only herself to blame. Ellen had tried to stop her and she would not listen.

So she danced through the night of Ashley's wedding in a daze and said things mechanically and smiled and irrelevantly wondered at the stupidity of people who thought her a happy bride and could not see that her heart was broken. Well, thank God, they couldn't see!

That night after Mammy had helped her undress and had departed and Charles had emerged shyly from the dressing-room, wondering if he was to spend a second night in the horsehair chair, she burst into tears. She cried until Charles climbed into bed beside her and tried to comfort her, cried without words until no more tears would come and at last she lay sobbing quietly on his shoulder.

If there had not been a war, there would have been a week of visiting about the County, with balls and barbecues in honour of the two newly married couples before they set off to Saratoga or White Sulphur for wedding trips. If there had not been a war, Scarlett would have had third-day and fourth-day and fifth-day dresses to wear to the Fontaine and Calvert and Tarleton parties in her honour. But there were no parties now and no wedding trips. A week after the wedding Charles left to join Colonel Wade Hampton, and two weeks later Ashley and the Troop departed, leaving the whole County bereft.

In those two weeks, Scarlett never saw Ashley

alone, never had a private word with him. Not even at the terrible moment of parting, when he stopped by Tara on his way to the train, did she have a private talk. Melanie, bonneted and shawled, sedate in newly acquired matronly dignity, hung on his arm and the entire personnel of Tara, black and white, turned out to see Ashley off to the war.

Melanie said: "You must kiss Scarlett, Ashley. She's my sister now," and Ashley bent and touched her cheek with cold lips, his face drawn and taut. Scarlett could hardly take any joy from that kiss, so sullen was her heart at Melly's prompting it. Melanie smothered her with an embrace at parting.

"You will come to Atlanta and visit me and Aunt Pittypat, won't you? Oh, darling, we want to have you so much! We want to know Charlie's wife better."

Five weeks passed during which letters, shy, ecstatic, loving, came from Charles in South Carolina telling of his love, his plans for the future when the war was over, his desire to become a hero for her sake and his worship of his commander, Wade Hampton. In the seventh week, there came a telegram from Colonel Hampton himself, and then a letter, a kind, dignified letter of condolence. Charles was dead. The colonel would have wired earlier, but Charles, thinking his illness a trifling one, did not wish to have his family worried. The unfortunate boy had not only been cheated of the love he thought he had won but also of his high hopes of honour and glory on the field of battle. He had died ignominiously and swiftly of pneumonia, following measles, without ever having gotten any closer to the Yankees than the camp in South Carolina.

In due time, Charles' son was born and, because it was fashionable to name boys after their fathers' commanding officers, he was called Wade Hampton Hamilton. Scarlett had wept with despair at the knowledge that she was pregnant and wished that she were dead. But she carried the child through its time with a minimum of discomfort, bore him with little distress and recovered so quickly that Mammy told her privately it was downright common—ladies should suffer more. She felt little affection for the child, hide the fact though she might. She had not wanted him and she resented his coming and, now that he was here, it did not seem possible that he was hers, a part of her.

Though she recovered physically from Wade's birth in a disgracefully short time, mentally she was dazed and sick. Her spirits drooped, despite the efforts of the whole plantation to revive them. Ellen went about with a puckered, worried forehead and Gerald swore more frequently than usual and brought her useless gifts from Jonesboro. Even old Dr. Fontaine admitted that he was puzzled, after his tonic of sulphur, molasses and herbs failed to perk her up. He told Ellen privately that it was a broken heart that made Scarlett so irritable and listless by turns. But Scarlett, had she wished to speak, could have told them that it was a far different and more complex trouble. She did not tell them that it was utter boredom, bewilderment at actually being a mother and, most of all, the absence of Ashley that made her look so woebegone.

Her boredom was acute and ever present. The County had been devoid of any entertainment or social life ever since the Troop had gone away to war. All of the interesting young men were gone —the four Tarletons, the two Calverts, the Fontaines, the Munroes and everyone from Jonesboro, Fayetteville and Lovejoy who was young and attractive. Only the older men, the cripples and the women were left, and they spent their time knitting and sewing, growing more cotton and corn, raising more hogs and sheep and cows for the army. There was never a sight of a real man except when the commissary troop under Suellen's middle-aged beau, Frank Kennedy, rode by every month to collect supplies. The men in the commissary were not very exciting, and the sight of Frank's timid courting annoyed her until she found it difficult to be polite to him. If he and Suellen would only get it over with!

Even if the commissary troop had been more interesting, it would not have helped her situation any. She was a widow and her heart was in the grave. At least, everyone thought it was in the grave and expected her to act accordingly. This irritated her for, try as she could, she could recall nothing about Charles except the dying-calf look on his face when she told him she would marry him. And even that picture was fading. But she was a widow and she had to watch her behaviour. Not for her the pleasures of unmarried girls. She had to be grave and aloof. Ellen had stressed this at great length after catching Frank's lieutenant swinging Scarlett in the garden swing and making her squeal with laughter. Deeply distressed, Ellen had told her how easily a widow might get herself talked about. The conduct of a widow must be twice as circumspect as that of a matron.

"And God only knows," thought Scarlett, listening obediently to her mother's soft voice, "matrons never have any fun at all. So widows might as well be dead."

A widow had to wear hideous black dresses without even a touch of braid to enliven them, no flower or ribbon or lace or even jewellery, except onyx mourning brooches or necklaces made from the deceased's hair. And the black crêpe veil on her bonnet had to reach to her knees, and only after three years of widowhood could it be shortened to shoulder length. Widows could never chatter vivaciously or laugh aloud. Even when they smiled, it must be a sad, tragic smile. And, most dreadful of all, they could in no way indicate an interest in the company of gentlemen. And should a gentleman be so ill-bred as to indicate an interest in her, she must freeze him with a dignified but well-chosen reference to her dead husband. "Oh, yes," thought Scarlett, drearily, "some widows do remarry eventually, when they are old and stringy. Though Heaven knows how they manage it, with their neighbours watching. And then it's generally to some desperate old widower with a large plantation and a dozen children."

Marriage was bad enough, but to be widowed —oh, then life was over forever! How stupid people were when they talked about what a comfort little Wade Hampton must be to her, now that Charles was gone! How stupid of them to say that now she had something to live for! Everyone talked about how sweet it was that she had this posthumous token of her love and she naturally did not disabuse their minds. But that thought was farthest from her mind. She had very little interest in Wade and sometimes it was difficult to remember that he was actually hers.

Every morning she woke up and for a drowsy moment she was Scarlett O'Hara again and the sun was bright in the magnolia outside her window and the mockers were singing and the sweet smell of frying bacon was stealing to her nostrils. She was carefree and young again. Then she heard the fretful hungry wail and always— always there was a startled moment when she thought: "Why, there's a baby in the house!" Then she remembered that it was her baby. It was all very bewildering.

And Ashley! Oh, most of all Ashley! For the first time in her life, she hated Tara, hated the long red road that led down the hill to the river, hated the red fields with springing green cotton. Every foot of ground, every tree and brook, every lane and bridle path reminded her of him. He belonged to another woman and he had gone to the war, but his ghost still haunted the roads in the twilight, still smiled at her from drowsy grey eyes in the shadows of the porch. She never heard the sound of hooves coming up the river road from Twelve Oaks that for a sweet moment she did not think—Ashley!

She hated Twelve Oaks now and once she had

loved it. She hated it but she was drawn there, so she could hear John Wilkes and the girls talk about him—hear them read his letters from Virginia. They hurt her but she had to hear them. She disliked the stiff-necked India and the foolish prattling Honey and knew they disliked her equally, but she could not stay away from them. And every time she came home from Twelve Oaks, she lay down on her bed morosely and refused to get up for supper.

It was this refusal of food that worried Ellen and Mammy more than anything else. Mammy brought up tempting trays, insinuating that now she was a widow she might eat as much as she pleased, but Scarlett had no appetite.

When Dr. Fontaine told Ellen gravely that heartbreak frequently led to a decline and women pined away into the grave, Ellen went white, for that fear was what she had carried in her heart.

"Isn't there anything to be done, Doctor?"

"A change of scene will be the best thing in the world for her," said the doctor, only too anxious to be rid of an unsatisfactory patient.

So Scarlett, unenthusiastic, went off with her child, first to visit her O'Hara and Robillard relatives in Savannah and then to Ellen's sisters, Pauline and Eulalie, in Charleston. But she was back at Tara a month before Ellen expected her, with no explanation of her return. They had been kind in Savannah, but James and Andrew and their wives were old and content to sit quietly and talk of a past in which Scarlett had no interest. It was the same with the Robillards, and Charleston was terrible, Scarlett thought.

Aunt Pauline and her husband, a little old man, with a formal, brittle courtesy and the absent air of one living in an older age, lived on a plantation on the river, far more isolated than Tara. Their nearest neighbour was twenty miles away by dark roads through still jungles of cypress swamp and oak. The live oaks with their waving curtains of grey moss gave Scarlett the creeps and always brought to her mind Gerald's stories of Irish ghosts roaming in shimmering grey mists. There was nothing to do but knit all day and at night listen to Uncle Carey read aloud from the improving works of Mr. Bulwer-Lytton.

Eulalie, hidden behind a high-walled garden in a great house on the Battery in Charleston, was no more entertaining. Scarlett, accustomed to wide vistas of rolling red hills, felt that she was in prison. There was more social life here than at Aunt Pauline's, but Scarlett did not like the people who called, with their airs and their traditions and their emphasis on family. She knew very well they all thought she was a child of a mésalliance and wondered how a Robillard ever married a newly come Irishman. Scarlett felt that Aunt Eulalie apologized for her behind her back. This aroused her temper, for she cared no more about family than her father. She was proud of Gerald and what he had accomplished unaided except by his shrewd Irish brain.

And the Charlestonians took so much upon themselves about Fort Sumter! Good Heavens, didn't they realize that if they hadn't been silly enough to fire the shot that started the war some other fools would have done it? Accustomed to the brisk voices of upland Georgia, the drawling flat voices of the low country seemed affected to her. She thought if she ever again heard voices that said "paams" for "palms" and "hoose" for "house" and "woon't" for "won't" and "Maa and Paa" for "Ma and Pa", she would scream. It irritated her so much that during one formal call she aped Gerald's brogue to her aunt's distress. Then she went back to Tara. Better to be tormented with memories of Ashley than Charleston accents.

Ellen, busy night and day, doubling the productiveness of Tara to aid the Confederacy, was terrified when her eldest daughter came home from Charleston thin, white and sharp-tongued. She had known heartbreak herself, and night after night she lay beside the snoring Gerald trying to think of some way to lessen Scarlett's distress. Charles' aunt, Miss Pittypat Hamilton, had written her several times, urging her to permit Scarlett to come to Atlanta for a long visit, and now for the first time Ellen considered it seriously.

She and Melanie were alone in a big house "and without male protection," wrote Miss Pittypat, "now that dear Charlie has gone. Of course, there is my brother Henry but he does not make his home with us. But perhaps Scarlett has told you of Henry. Delicacy forbids my putting more concerning him on paper. Melly and I would feel so much easier and safer if Scarlett were with us. Three lonely women are better than two. And perhaps dear Scarlett could find some ease for her sorrow, as Melly is doing, by nursing our brave boys in the hospitals here—and, of course, Melly and I are longing to see the dear baby. . . ."

So Scarlett's trunk was packed again with her mourning clothes and off she went to Atlanta with Wade Hampton and his nurse Prissy, a headful of admonitions as to her conduct from Ellen and Mammy and a hundred dollars in Confederate bills from Gerald. She did not especially want to go to Atlanta. She thought Aunt Pitty the silliest of old ladies and the very idea of living under the same roof with Ashley's wife was abhorrent. But the County with its memories was impossible now, and any change was welcome.

Part Two

1

AS the train carried Scarlett northward that May morning in 1862, she thought that Atlanta couldn't possibly be so boring as Charleston and Savannah had been, and, in spite of her distaste for Miss Pittypat and Melanie, she looked forward with some curiosity toward seeing how the town had fared since her last visit, in the winter before the war began.

Atlanta had always interested her more than any other town because when she was a child Gerald had told her that she and Atlanta were exactly the same age. She discovered when she grew older that Gerald had stretched the truth somewhat, as was his habit when a little stretching would improve a story; but Atlanta was only nine years older than she was, and that still left the place amazingly young by comparison with any other town she had ever heard of. Savannah and Charleston had the dignity of their years, one being well along in its second century and the other entering its third, and in her young eyes they had always seemed like aged grandmothers fanning themselves placidly in the sun. But Atlanta was of her own generation, crude with the crudities of youth and as headstrong and impetuous as herself.

The story Gerald had told her was based on the fact that she and Atlanta were christened in the same year. In the nine years before Scarlett was born, the town had been called, first, Terminus and then Marthasville, and not until the year of Scarlett's birth had it become Atlanta.

When Gerald first moved to north Georgia, there had been no Atlanta at all, not even the semblance of a village, and wilderness rolled over the site. But the next year, in 1836, the State had authorized the building of a railroad north-westward through the territory which the Cherokees had recently ceded. The destination of the proposed railroad, Tennessee and the West, was clear and definite, but its beginning point in Georgia was somewhat uncertain until, a year later, an engineer drove a stake in the red clay to mark the southern end of the line, and Atlanta, born Terminus, had begun.

There were no railroads then in north Georgia, and very few anywhere else. But during the years before Gerald married Ellen, the tiny settlement, twenty-five miles north of Tara, slowly grew into a village and the tracks slowly pushed northward. Then the railroad-building era really began. From the old city of Augusta, a second railroad was extended westward across the state to connect with the new road to Tennessee. From the old city of Savannah, a third railroad was built first to Macon, in the heart of Georgia, and then north through Gerald's own county to Atlanta, to link up with the other two roads and give Savannah's harbour a highway to the West. From the same junction point, the young Atlanta, a fourth railroad was constructed south-westward to Montgomery and Mobile.

Born of a railroad, Atlanta grew as its railroads

grew. With the completion of the four lines, Atlanta was now connected with the West, with the South, with the Coast and, through Augusta, with the North and East. It had become the crossroads of travel north and south and east and west, and the little village leaped to life.

In a space of time but little longer than Scarlett's seventeen years, Atlanta had grown from a single stake driven in the ground into a thriving small city of ten thousand that was the centre of attention for the whole state. The older, quieter cities were wont to look upon the bustling new town with the sensations of a hen which has hatched a duckling. Why was the place so different from the other Georgia towns? Why did it grow so fast? After all, they thought, it had nothing whatever to recommend it—only its railroads and a bunch of mighty pushy people.

The people who settled in the town called successively Terminus, Marthasville and Atlanta were a pushy people. Restless, energetic people from the older sections of Georgia and from more distant states were drawn to this town that sprawled itself around the junction of the railroads in its centre. They came with enthusiasm. They built their stores around the five muddy red roads that crossed near the depot. They built their fine homes on Whitehall and Washington streets and along the high ridge of land on which countless generations of moccasined Indian feet had beaten a path called the Peachtree Trail. They were proud of the place, proud of its growth, proud of themselves for making it grow. Let the older towns call Atlanta anything they pleased. Atlanta did not care.

Scarlett had always liked Atlanta for the very same reasons that made Savannah, Augusta and Macon condemn it. Like herself, the town was a mixture of the old and new in Georgia, in which the old often came off second best in its conflicts with the self-willed and vigorous new. Moreover, there was something personal, exciting about a town that was born—or at least christened—the same year she was christened.

The night before had been wild and wet with rain, but when Scarlett arrived in Atlanta a warm sun was at work, bravely attempting to dry the streets that were winding rivers of red mud. In the open space around the depot, the soft ground had been cut and churned by the constant flow of traffic in and out until it resembled an enormous hog wallow, and here and there vehicles were mired to the hubs in the ruts. A never-ceasing line of army wagons and ambulances, loading and unloading supplies and wounded from the trains, made the mud and confusion worse as they toiled in and struggled out, drivers swearing, mules plunging and mud spattering for yards.

Scarlett stood on the lower step of the train, a pale pretty figure in her black mourning dress, her crêpe veil fluttering almost to her heels. She hestitated, unwilling to soil her slippers and hems, and looked about in the shouting tangle of wagons, buggies and carriages for Miss Pittypat. There was no sign of that chubby pink-cheeked lady, but as Scarlett searched anxiously a spare old negro, with grizzled kinks and an air of dignified authority, came toward her through the mud, his hat in his hand.

"Dis Miss Scarlett, ain' it? Dis hyah Peter, Miss Pitty's coachman. Doan step down in dat mud," he ordered severely, as Scarlett gathered up her skirts preparatory to descending. "You is as bad as Miss Pitty an' she lak a chile 'bout gittin' her feets wet. Lemme cahy you."

He picked Scarlett up with ease despite his apparent frailness and age and, observing Prissy standing on the platform of the train, the baby in her arms, he paused: "Is dat air chile yo' nuss? Miss Scarlett, she too young ter be handlin' Mist' Charles' onlies' baby! But we ten' to dat later. You gal, foller me, an' doan you go drappin' dat baby."

Scarlett submitted meekly to being carried toward the carriage and also to the peremptory manner in which Uncle Peter criticized her and Prissy. As they went through the mud with Prissy sloshing, pouting, after them, she recalled what Charles had said about Uncle Peter.

"He went through all the Mexican campaigns with Father, nursed him when he was wounded —in fact, he saved his life. Uncle Peter practically raised Melanie and me, for we were very young when Father and Mother died. Aunt Pitty had a falling-out with her brother, Uncle Henry, about that time, so she came to live with us and take care of us. She is the most helpless soul—just like a sweet grown-up child, and Uncle Peter treats her that way. To save her life, she couldn't make

221

up her mind about anything, so Peter makes it up for her. He was the one who decided I should have a larger allowance when I was fifteen, and he insisted that I should go to Harvard for my senior year, when Uncle Henry wanted me to take my degree at the University. And he decided when Melly was old enough to put up her hair and go to parties. He tells Aunt Pitty when it's too cold or too wet for her to go calling and when she should wear a shawl. . . . He's the smartest old darky I've ever seen and about the most devoted. The only trouble with him is that he owns the three of us, body and soul, and he knows it."

Charles' words were confirmed as Peter climbed on to the box and took the whip.

"Miss Pitty in a state bekase she din' come ter meet you. She's feared you mout not unnerstan' but Ah tole her she an' Miss Melly jes' git splashed wid mud an' ruin dey new dresses an' Ah'd 'splain ter you. Miss Scarlett, you better tek dat chile. Dat lil piccaninny gwine let it drap."

Scarlett looked at Prissy and sighed. Prissy was not the most adequate of nurses. Her recent graduation from a skinny piccaninny with brief skirts and stiffly wrapped braids into the dignity of a long calico dress and starched white turban was an intoxicating affair. She would never have arrived at this eminence so early in life had not the exigencies of war and the demands of the commissary department on Tara made it impossible for Ellen to spare Mammy or Dilcey or even Rosa or Teena. Prissy had never been more than a mile away from Twelve Oaks or Tara before, and the trip on the train plus her elevation to nurse was almost more than the brain in her little black skull could bear. The twenty-mile journey from Jonesboro to Atlanta had so excited her that Scarlett had been forced to hold the baby all the way. Now, the sight of so many buildings and people completed Prissy's demoralization. She twisted from side to side, pointed, bounced about and so jounced the baby that he wailed miserably.

Scarlett longed for the fat old arms of Mammy. Mammy had only to lay hands on a child and it hushed crying. But Mammy was at Tara and there was nothing Scarlett could do. It was useless for her to take little Wade from Prissy. He yelled just as loudly when she held him as when Prissy did. Besides, he would tug at the ribbons of her bonnet and, no doubt, rumple her dress. So she pretended she had not heard Uncle Peter's suggestion.

"Maybe I'll learn about babies some time," she thought irritably, as the carriage jolted and swayed out of the morass surrounding the station, "but I'm never going to like fooling with them." And as Wade's face went purple with his squalling, she snapped crossly: "Give him that sugartit in your pocket, Priss. Anything to make him hush. I know he's hungry, but I can't do anything about that now."

Prissy produced the sugar-tit, given her that morning by Mammy, and the baby's wails subsided. With quiet restored and with the new sights that met her eyes, Scarlett's spirits began to rise a little. When Uncle Peter finally manoeuvred the carriage out of the mudholes and on to Peachtree Street, she felt the first surge of interest she had known in months. How the town had grown! It was not much more than a year since she had last been here, and it did not seem possible that the little Atlanta she knew could have changed so much.

For the past year, she had been so engrossed in her own woes, so bored by any mention of war, she did not know that from the minute the fighting first began, Atlanta had been transformed. The same railroads which had made the town the crossroads of commerce in time of peace were now of vital strategic importance in time of war. Far from the battle-lines, the town and its railroads provided the connecting link between the two armies of the Confederacy, the army in Virginia and the army in Tennessee and the West. And Atlanta likewise linked both of the armies with the deeper South from which they drew their supplies. Now, in response to the needs of war, Atlanta had become a manufacturing centre, a hospital base and one of the South's chief depots for the collecting of food and supplies for the armies in the field.

Scarlett looked about her for the little town she remembered so well. It was gone. The town she was now seeing was like a baby grown overnight into a busy, sprawling giant.

Atlanta was humming like a beehive, proudly conscious of its importance to the Confederacy, and work was going forward night and day toward turning an agricultural section into an industrial one. Before the war there had been few cotton factories, woollen mills, arsenals and machine shops south of Maryland—a fact of which all Southerners were proud. The South produced statesmen and soldiers, planters and doctors, lawyers and poets, but certainly not engineers or mechanics. Let the Yankees adopt such low callings. But now the Confederate ports were stoppered with Yankee gunboats, only a trickle of blockade-run goods was slipping in from Europe, and the South was desperately trying to manufacture her own war materials. The North could call on the whole world for supplies and for soldiers, and thousands of Irish and Germans were pouring into the Union Army, lured by the bounty money offered by the North. The South could only turn in upon itself.

In Atlanta, there were machine factories tediously turning out machinery to manufacture war materials—tediously, because there were few machines in the South from which they could model and nearly every wheel and cog had to be made from drawings that came through the blockade from England. There were strange faces on the streets of Atlanta now, and citizens who a year ago would have pricked up their ears at the sound of even a Western accent paid no heed to the foreign tongues of Europeans who had run the blockade to build machines and turn out Confederate munitions. Skilled men these, without whom the Confederacy would have been hard put to make pistols, rifles, cannon and powder.

Almost the pulsing of the town's heart could be felt as the work went forward night and day, pumping the materials of war up the railway arteries to the two battle fronts. Trains roared in and out of the town at all hours. Soot from the newly erected factories fell in showers on the white houses. By night, the furnaces glowed and the hammers clanged long after townsfolk were abed. Where vacant lots had been a year before, there were now factories turning out harness, saddles and shoes, ordnance-supply plants making rifles and cannon, rolling mills and foundries producing iron rails and freight cars to replace those destroyed by the Yankees, and a variety of industries manufacturing spurs, bridle bits, buckles, tents, buttons, pistols and swords. Already the foundries were beginning to feel the lack of iron, for little or none came through the blockade, and the mines in Alabama were standing almost idle while the miners were at the front. There were no iron picket fences, iron summerhouses, iron gates or even iron statuary on the lawns of Atlanta now, for they had early found their way into the melting-pots of the rolling mills.

Here along Peachtree Street and near-by streets were the headquarters of the various army departments, each office swarming with uniformed men, the commissary, the signal corps, the mail service, the railway transport, the provost marshal. On the outskirts of town were the remount depots where horses and mules milled about in large corrals, and along side streets were the hospitals. As Uncle Peter told her about them, Scarlett felt that Atlanta must be a city of the wounded, for there were general hospitals, contagious hospitals, convalescent hospitals without number. And every day the trains just below Five Points disgorged more sick and more wounded.

The little town was gone and the face of the rapidly growing city was animated with never-ceasing energy and bustle. The sight of so much hurrying made Scarlett, fresh from rural leisure and quiet, almost breathless, but she liked it. There was an exciting atmosphere about the place that uplifted her. It was as if she could actually feel the accelerated steady pulse of the town's heart beating in time with her own.

As they slowly made their way through the mudholes of the town's chief street, she noted with interest all the new buildings and the new faces. The sidewalks were crowded with men in uniform, bearing the insignia of all ranks and all service branches; the narrow street was jammed with vehicles—carriages, buggies, ambulances, covered army wagons with profane drivers swearing as the mules struggled through the ruts; grey-clad couriers dashed spattering through the streets from one headquarters to another, bearing orders and telegraphic dispatches; convalescents limped about on crutches, usually with a solicitous lady at either elbow; bugle and drum and barked orders sounded from the drill fields where the recruits were being turned into soldiers; and with her heart in her throat, Scarlett had her first sight of Yankee uniforms, as Uncle Peter pointed with his whip to a detachment of dejected-looking bluecoats being shepherded toward the depot by a squad of Confederates with fixed bayonets, to entrain for the prison camp.

"Oh," thought Scarlett, with the first feeling of real pleasure she had experienced since the day of the barbecue, "I'm going to like it here! It's so alive and exciting!"

The town was even more alive than she realized, for there were new bar-rooms by the dozens; prostitutes, following the army, swarmed the town and bawdy houses were blossoming with women to the consternation of the Church people. Every hotel, boarding house and private residence was crammed with visitors who had come to be near wounded relatives in the big Atlanta hospitals. There were parties and balls and bazaars every week and war weddings without number, with the grooms on furlough in bright grey and gold braid and the brides in blockade-run finery, aisles of crossed swords, toasts drunk in blockaded champagne and tearful farewells. Nightly the dark tree-lined streets resounded with dancing feet, and from parlours tinkled pianos where soprano voices blended with those of soldier guests in the pleasing melancholy of "The Bugles Sang Truce" and "Your Letter Came, but Came Too Late"—plaintive ballads that brought exciting tears to soft eyes which had never known the tears of real grief.

As they progressed down the street, through the sucking mud, Scarlett bubbled over with questions and Peter answered them, pointing here and there with his whip, proud to display his knowledge.

"Dat air de arsenal. Yas'm, dey keeps guns an' sech lak dar. No'm, dem air ain' sto's, dey's blockade awfisses. Law, Miss Scarlett, doan you know whut blockade awfisses is? Dey's awfisses whar furriners stays dat buys us Confedruts' cotton an' ship it outer Cha'ston and Wilmin'ton an' ship us back gunpowder. No'm, Ah ain' sho whut kine of furriners dey is. Miss Pitty, she say dey is Inlish but kain nobody unnerstan' a wud dey says. Yas'm, 'tis pow'ful smoky an' de soot jes' ruinin' Miss Pitty's silk cuttins. It's frum de foun'ry an' de rollin' mills. An' de noise dey meks at night! Kain nobody sleep. No'm, Ah kain stop fer you ter look around. Ah done promise Miss Pitty Ah bring you straight home. . . . Miss Scarlett, mek yo' cu'tsy. Dar's Miss Merriwether an' Miss Elsing a-bowin' to you."

Scarlett vaguely remembered two ladies of those names who came from Atlanta to Tara to attend her wedding and she remembered that they were Miss Pittypat's best friends. So she turned quickly where Uncle Peter pointed and bowed. The two were sitting in a carriage outside a drygoods store. The proprietor and two clerks stood on the sidewalk with armfuls of bolts of cotton cloth they had been displaying. Mrs. Merriwether was a tall, stout woman and so tightly corseted that her bust jutted forward like the prow of a ship. Her iron-grey hair was eked out by a curled false fringe that was proudly brown and disdained to match the rest of her hair. She had a round, highly coloured face in which were combined good-natured shrewdness and the habit of command. Mrs. Elsing was younger, a thin frail woman, who had been a beauty, and about her there still clung a faded freshness, a dainty imperious air.

These two ladies with a third, Mrs. Whiting, were the pillars of Atlanta. They ran the three churches to which they belonged, the clergy, the choirs and the parishioners. They organized bazaars and presided over sewing circles, they chaperoned balls and picnics, they knew who made good matches and who did not, who drank secretly, who were to have babies and when. They were authorities on the genealogies of everyone who was anyone in Georgia, South Carolina and Virginia and did not bother their heads about the other states, because they believed that no one who was anybody ever came from states other than these three. They knew what was decorous behaviour and what was not and they never failed to make their opinions known—Mrs. Merriwether at the top of her voice, Mrs. Elsing in an elegant die-away drawl and Mrs. Whiting in a distressed whisper which showed how much she hated to speak of such things. These three ladies disliked and distrusted one another as heartily as the First Triumvirate of Rome, and their close alliance was probably for the same reason.

"I told Pitty I had to have you in my hospital," called Mrs. Merriwether, smiling. "Don't you go promising Mrs. Meade or Mrs. Whiting!"

"I won't," said Scarlett, having no idea what Mrs. Merriwether was talking about but feeling a glow of warmth at being welcomed and wanted. "I hope to see you again soon."

The carriage ploughed its way farther and halted for a moment to permit two ladies with baskets of bandages on their arms to pick precarious passages across the sloppy street on stepping-stones. At the same moment, Scarlett's eye was caught by a figure on the sidewalk in a brightly coloured dress—too bright for street wear—covered by a Paisley shawl with fringes to the heels. Turning, she saw a tall handsome woman with a bold face and a mass of red hair, too red to be true. It was the first time she had ever seen any woman who she knew for certain had "done something to her hair" and she watched her, fascinated.

"Uncle Peter, who is that?" she whispered.

"Ah doan know."

"You do, too. I can tell. Who is she?"

"Her name Belle Watling," said Uncle Peter, his lower lip beginning to protrude.

Scarlett was quick to catch the fact that he had not preceded the name with "Miss" or "Mrs.".

"Who is she?"

"Miss Scarlett," said Peter darkly, laying the whip on the startled horse, "Miss Pitty ain' gwine ter lak it you astin' questions dat ain' none of yo' bizness. Dey's a passel of no-count folks in dis town now dat it ain' no use talkin' about."

"Good Heavens!" thought Scarlett, reproved into silence. "That must be a bad woman!"

She had never seen a bad woman before and she twisted her head and stared after her until she was lost in the crowd.

The stores and the new war buildings were farther apart now, with vacant lots between. Finally the business section fell behind and the residences came into view. Scarlett picked them out as old friends: the Leyden house, dignified and stately; the Bonnells', with little white columns and green blinds; the close-lipped red-brick Georgian home of the McLure family, behind its low box hedges. Their progress was slower now, for from porches and gardens and sidewalks ladies called to her. Some she knew slightly, others she vaguely remembered, but most of them she knew not at all. Pittypat had certainly broadcast her arrival. Little Wade had to be held up time and again, so that ladies who ventured as far through the ooze as their carriage blocks could exclaim over him. They all cried to her that she must join their knitting and sewing circles and their hospital committees, and no one else's, and she promised recklessly to right and left.

As they passed a rambling green clapboard house, a little black girl posted on the front steps cried, "Hyah she come," and Dr. Meade and his wife and little thirteen-year-old Phil emerged, calling greetings. Scarlett recalled that they too had been at her wedding. Mrs. Meade mounted her carriage block and craned her neck for a view of the baby, but the doctor, disregarding the mud, ploughed through to the side of the carriage. He was tall and gaunt and wore a pointed beard of iron grey, and his clothes hung on his spare figure as though blown there by a hurricane. Atlanta considered him the root of all strength and all wisdom and it was not strange that he had absorbed something of their belief. But for all his habit of making oracular statements and his slightly pompous manner, he was as kindly a man as the town possessed.

232

After shaking her hand and prodding Wade in the stomach and complimenting him, the doctor announced that Aunt Pittypat had promised on oath that Scarlett should be on no other hospital and bandage-rolling committee save Mrs. Meade's.

"Oh, dear, but I've promised a thousand ladies already!" said Scarlett.

"Mrs. Merriwether, I'll be bound!" cried Mrs. Meade indignantly. "Drat the woman! I believe she meets every train!"

"I promised because I hadn't a notion what it was all about," Scarlett confessed. "What are hospital committees anyway?"

Both the doctor and his wife looked slightly shocked at her ignorance.

"But, of course, you've been buried in the country and couldn't know," Mrs. Meade apologized for her. "We have nursing committees for different hospitals and for different days. We nurse the men and help the doctors and make bandages and clothes and when the men are well enough to leave the hospitals we take them into our homes to convalesce till they are able to go back in the army. And we look after the wives and families of some of the wounded who are destitute—yes, worse than destitute. Dr. Meade is at the Institute hospital where my committee works, and everyone says he's marvellous and—"

"There, there, Mrs. Meade," said the doctor fondly. "Don't go bragging on me in front of folks. It's little enough I can do, since you wouldn't let me go in the army."

"'Wouldn't let!'" she cried indignantly. "Me?

The town wouldn't let you and you know it. Why, Scarlett, when folks heard he was intending to go to Virginia as an army surgeon, all the ladies signed a petition begging him to stay here. Of course, the town couldn't do without you."

"There, there, Mrs. Meade," said the doctor, basking obviously in the praise. "Perhaps with one boy at the front, that's enough for the time being."

"And I'm going next year!" cried little Phil, hopping about excitedly. "As a drummer boy. I'm learning how to drum now. Do you want to hear me? I'll run get my drum."

"No, not now," said Mrs. Meade, drawing him closer to her, a sudden look of strain coming over her face. "Not next year, darling. Maybe the year after."

"But the war will be over then!" he cried petulantly, pulling away from her. "And you promised!"

Over his head the eyes of the parents met and Scarlett saw the look. Darcy Meade was in Virginia and they were clinging closer to the little boy that was left.

Uncle Peter cleared his throat.

"Miss Pitty were in a state when Ah lef' home an' ef Ah doan git dar soon, she'll done swooned."

"Good-bye. I'll be over this afternoon," called Mrs. Meade. "And you tell Pitty for me that if you aren't on my committee, she's going to be in a worse state."

The carriage slipped and slid down the muddy road and Scarlett leaned back on the cushions and

234

smiled. She felt better now than she had felt in months. Atlanta, with its crowds and its hurry and its undercurrent of driving excitement, was very pleasant, very exhilarating, so very much nicer than the lonely plantation out from Charleston, where the bellow of alligators broke the night stillness; better than Charleston itself, dreaming in its gardens behind its high walls; better than Savannah with its wide streets lined with palmetto and the muddy river beside it. Yes, and temporarily even better than Tara, dear though Tara was.

There was something exciting about this town with its narrow muddy streets, lying among rolling red hills, something raw and crude that appealed to the rawness and crudeness underlying the fine veneer that Ellen and Mammy had given her. She suddenly felt that this was where she belonged, not in serene and quiet old cities, flat beside yellow waters.

The houses were farther and farther apart now, and leaning out Scarlett saw the red-brick and slate roof of Miss Pittypat's house. It was almost the last house on the north side of town. Beyond it, Peachtree road narrowed and twisted under great trees out of sight into thick quiet woods. The neat wooden-panelled fence had been newly painted white and the front yard it enclosed was yellow-starred with the last jonquils of the season. On the front steps stood two women in black and behind them a large yellow woman with her hands under her apron and her white teeth showing in a wide smile. Plump Miss Pittypat was teetering excitedly on tiny feet, one hand pressed to her copious bosom to still her fluttering heart. Scarlett saw Melanie standing by her and, with a surge of dislike, she realized that the fly in the ointment of Atlanta would be this slight little person in black mourning dress, her riotous dark curls subdued to matronly smoothness and a loving smile of welcome and happiness on her heart-shaped face.

When a Southerner took the trouble to pack a trunk and travel twenty miles for a visit, the visit was seldom of shorter duration than a month, usually much longer. Southerners were as enthusiastic visitors as they were hosts, and there was nothing unusual in relatives coming to spend the Christmas holidays and remaining until July. Often when newly married couples went on the usual round of honeymoon visits, they lingered in some pleasant home until the birth of their second child. Frequently elderly aunts and uncles came to Sunday dinner and remained until they were buried years later. Visitors presented no problem, for houses were large, servants numerous and the feeling of several extra mouths a minor matter in that land of plenty. All ages and sexes went visiting: honeymooners, young mothers showing off new babies, convalescents, the bereaved, girls whose parents were anxious to remove them from the dangers of unwise matches, girls who had reached the danger age without becoming engaged and who, it was hoped, would make suitable matches under the guidance of relatives in other places. Visitors added excitement and variety to the slow-moving Southern life and they were always welcome.

So Scarlett had come to Atlanta with no idea as to how long she would remain. If her visit proved as dull as those in Savannah and Charleston, she would return home in a month. If her stay was pleasant, she would remain indefinitely. But no sooner had she arrived than Aunt Pitty and Melanie began a campaign to induce her to make her home permanently with them. They brought up every possible argument. They wanted her for her own self because they loved her. They were lonely and often frightened at night in the big house, and she was so brave she gave them courage. She was so charming that she cheered them in their sorrow. Now that Charles was dead, her place and her son's place were with his kindred. Besides, half the house now belonged to her, through Charles' will. Last, the Confederacy needed every pair of hands for sewing, knitting, bandage rolling and nursing the wounded.

Charles' Uncle Henry Hamilton, who lived in bachelor state at the Atlanta Hotel near the depot, also talked seriously to her on this subject. Uncle Henry was a short, pot-bellied, irascible old gentleman with a pink face, a shock of long silver hair and an utter lack of patience with feminine timidities and vapourings. It was for the latter reason that he was barely on speaking terms with his sister, Miss Pittypat. From childhood, they had been exact opposites in temperament and they had been further estranged by his objections to the manner in which she had reared Charles— "Making a damn sissy out of a soldier's son!"

Years before, he had so insulted her that now Miss Pitty never spoke of him except in guarded whispers and with so great reticence that a stranger would have thought the honest old lawyer a murderer, at the least. The insult had occurred on a day when Pitty wished to draw five hundred dollars from her estate, of which he was trustee, to invest in a non-existent gold mine. He had refused to permit it and stated heatedly that she had no more sense than a June bug and furthermore it gave him the fidgets to be around her longer than five minutes. Since that day, she only saw him formally, once a month, when Uncle Peter drove her to his office to get the housekeeping money. After these brief visits, Pitty always took to her bed for the rest of the day with tears and smelling salts. Melanie and Charles, who were on excellent terms with their uncle, had frequently offered to relieve her of this ordeal, but Pitty always set her babyish mouth firmly and refused. Henry was her cross and she must bear him. From this, Charles and Melanie could only infer that she took a profound pleasure in this occasional excitement, the only excitement in her sheltered life.

Uncle Henry liked Scarlett immediately because, he said, he could see that for all her silly affectations she had a few grains of sense. He was trustee, not only of Pitty's and Melanie's estates, but also of that left Scarlett by Charles. It came to Scarlett as a pleasant surprise that she was now a well-to-do young woman, for Charles had not only left her half of Aunt Pitty's house but farm lands and town property as well. And the stores and warehouses along the railroad track near the depot, which were part of her inheritance, had tripled in value since the war began. It was when Uncle Henry was giving her an account of her property that he broached the matter of her permanent residence in Atlanta.

"When Wade Hampton comes of age, he's going to be a rich young man," he said. "The way Atlanta is growing his property will be ten times more valuable in twenty years, and it's only right that the boy should be raised where his property is, so he can learn to take care of it—yes, and of Pitty's and Melanie's, too. He'll be the only man of the Hamilton name left before long, for I won't be here forever."

As for Uncle Peter, he took it for granted that Scarlett had come to stay. It was inconceivable to him that Charles' only son should be reared where he could not supervise the rearing. To all these arguments, Scarlett smiled but said nothing, unwilling to commit herself before learning how she would like Atlanta and constant association with her in-laws. She knew, too, that Gerald and Ellen would have to be won over. Moreover, now that she was away from Tara, she missed it dreadfully, missed the red fields and the springing green cotton and the sweet twilight silences. For the first time, she realized dimly what Gerald had meant when he said that the love of the land was in her blood.

So she gracefully evaded, for the time being, a definite answer as to the duration of her visit and slipped easily into the life of the red-brick house at the quiet end of Peachtree Street.

Living with Charles' blood kin, seeing the home from which he came, Scarlett could now understand a little better the boy who had made her wife, widow and mother in such rapid succession. It was easy to see why he had been so shy, so unsophisticated, so idealistic. If Charles had inherited any of the qualities of the stern, fearless, hot-tempered soldier who had been his father, they had been obliterated in childhood by the ladylike atmosphere in which he had been reared. He had been devoted to the childlike Pitty and closer than brothers usually are to Melanie, and two more sweet, unworldly women could not be found.

Aunt Pittypat had been christened Sarah Jane Hamilton sixty years before, but since the long-past day when her doting father had fastened this nickname upon her, because of her airy, restless, pattering little feet, no one had called her anything else. In the years that followed that second christening, many changes had taken place in her that made the pet name incongruous. Of the swiftly scampering child, all that now remained were two tiny feet, inadequate to her weight, and a tendency to prattle happily and aimlessly. She was stout, pink-cheeked and silver-haired and always a little breathless from too tightly laced stays. She was unable to walk more than a block on the tiny feet which she crammed into too small slippers. She had a heart which fluttered at any excitement and she pampered it shamelessly, fainting at any provocation. Everyone knew that her swoons were generally mere ladylike pretences but they loved her enough to refrain from saying so. Everyone loved her, spoiled her like a child and refused to take her seriously—everyone except her brother Henry.

She liked gossip better than anything else in the world, even more than she liked the pleasures of the table, and she prattled on for hours about other people's affairs in a harmless kindly way. She had no memory for names, dates or places and frequently confused the actors in one Atlanta drama with the actors in another, which misled no one for no one was foolish enough to take seriously anything she said. No one ever told her anything really shocking or scandalous, for her spinster state must be protected even if she was sixty years old, and her friends were in a kindly conspiracy to keep her a sheltered and petted old child.

Melanie was like her aunt in many ways. She had her shyness, her sudden blushes, her modesty, but she did have common sense—"Of a sort, I'll admit that," Scarlett thought grudgingly. Like Aunt Pitty, Melanie had the face of a sheltered child who had never known anything but simplicity and kindness, truth and love, a child who had never looked upon harshness or evil and would not recognize them if she saw them. Because she had always been happy, she wanted everyone about her to be happy or, at least, pleased with themselves. To this end, she always saw the best in everyone and remarked kindly upon it. There was no servant so stupid that she did not find some redeeming trait of loyalty and kind-heartedness, no girl so ugly and disagreeable that she could not discover grace of form or nobility of character in her, and no man so worthless or so boring that she did not view him in the light of his possibilities rather than his actualities.

Because of these qualities that came sincerely and spontaneously from a generous heart, everyone flocked about her, for who can resist the charm of one who discovers in others admirable qualities undreamed of even by themselves? She had more girl friends than anyone in town and more men friends too, though she had few beaux for she lacked the wilfulness and selfishness that go far toward trapping men's hearts.

What Melanie did was no more than all Southern girls were taught to do—to make those about them feel at ease and pleased with themselves. It was this happy feminine conspiracy which made Southern society so pleasant. Women knew that a land where men were contented, uncontradicted and safe in possession of unpunctured vanity was likely to be a very pleasant place for women to live. So, from the cradle to the grave, women strove to make men pleased with themselves, and the satisfied men repaid lavishly with gallantry and adoration. In fact, men willingly gave the ladies everything in the world except credit for having intelligence. Scarlett exercised the same charms as Melanie but with a studied artistry and consummate skill. The difference between the two girls lay in the fact that Melanie spoke kind and flattering words from a desire to make people happy, if only temporarily, and Scarlett never did it except to further her own aims.

From the two he loved best, Charles had received no toughening influences, learned nothing of harshness or reality, and the home in which he grew to manhood was as soft as a bird's nest. It was such a quiet, old-fashioned, gentle home compared with Tara. To Scarlett, this house cried out for the masculine smells of brandy, tobacco and Macassar oil, for hoarse voices and occasional curses, for guns, for whiskers, for saddles and bridles and for hounds underfoot. She missed the sounds of quarrelling voices that were always heard at Tara when Ellen's back was turned—Mammy quarrelling with Pork, Rosa and Teena bickering, her own acrimonious arguments with Suellen, Gerald's bawling threats. No wonder Charles had been a sissy, coming from a home like this. Here, excitement never entered in, voices were never raised, everyone deferred gently to the opinions of others, and, in the end, the black grizzled autocrat in the kitchen had his way. Scarlett, who had hoped for a freer rein when she escaped Mammy's supervision, discovered to her sorrow that Uncle Peter's standards of ladylike conduct, especially for Mist' Charles' widow, were even stricter than Mammy's.

In such a household, Scarlett came back to herself, and almost before she realized it her spirits rose to normal. She was only seventeen, she had superb health and energy, and Charles' people did their best to make her happy. If they fell a little short of this, it was not their fault, for no one could take out of her heart the ache that throbbed whenever Ashley's name was

243

mentioned. And Melanie mentioned it so often! But Melanie and Pitty were tireless in planning ways to soothe the sorrow under which they thought she laboured. They put their own grief into the background in order to divert her. They fussed about her food and her hours for taking afternoon naps and for taking carriage rides. They not only admired her extravagantly, her high-spiritedness, her figure, her tiny hands and feet, her white skin, but they said so frequently, petting, hugging and kissing her to emphasize their loving words.

Scarlett did not care for the caresses, but she basked in the compliments. No one at Tara had ever said so many charming things about her. In fact, Mammy had spent her time deflating her conceit. Little Wade was no longer an annoyance, for the family, black and white, and the neighbours idolized him and there was a never-ceasing rivalry as to whose lap he should occupy. Melanie especially doted on him. Even in his worst screaming spells, Melanie thought him adorable and said so, adding, "Oh, you precious darling! I just wish you were mine!"

Sometimes Scarlett found it hard to dissemble her feelings, for she still thought Aunt Pitty the silliest of old ladies and her vagueness and vapourings irritated her unendurably. She disliked Melanie with a jealous dislike that grew as the days went by, and sometimes she had to leave the room abruptly when Melanie, beaming with loving pride, spoke of Ashley or read his letters aloud. But, all in all, life went on as happily as was possible under the circumstances. Atlanta was more interesting than Savannah or Charleston or Tara and it offered so many strange war-time occupations she had little time to think or mope. But, sometimes, when she blew out the candle and burrowed her head into the pillow, she sighed and thought: "If only Ashley wasn't married! If only I didn't have to nurse in that plagued hospital! Oh, if only I could have some beaux!"

She had immediately loathed nursing but she could not escape this duty because she was on both Mrs. Meade's and Mrs. Merriwether's committees. That meant four mornings a week in the sweltering, stinking hospital with her hair tied up in a towel and a hot apron covering her from neck to feet. Every matron, old or young, in Atlanta nursed and did it with an enthusiasm that seemed to Scarlett little short of fanatic. They took it for granted that she was imbued with their own patriotic fervour and would have been shocked to know how slight an interest in the war she had. Except for the ever-present torment that Ashley might be killed, the war interested her not at all, and nursing was something she did simply because she didn't know how to get out of it.

Certainly there was nothing romantic about nursing. To her, it meant groans, delirium, death and smells. The hospitals were filled with dirty, bewhiskered, verminous men who smelled terribly and bore on their bodies wounds hideous enough to turn a Christian's stomach. The hospitals stank of gangrene, the odour assaulting her nostrils long before the doors were reached, a sickish sweet smell that clung to her hands and hair and haunted her in her dreams. Flies, mosquitoes and gnats hovered in droning, singing swarms over the wards, tormenting the men to curses and weak sobs; and Scarlett, scratching her own mosquito bites, swung palmetto fans until her shoulders ached and she wished that all the men were dead.

Melanie, however, did not seem to mind the smells, the wounds or the nakedness, which Scarlett thought strange in one who was the most timorous and modest of women. Sometimes when holding basins and instruments while Dr. Meade cut out gangrened flesh, Melanie looked very white. And once, after such an operation, Scarlett found her in the linen closet vomiting quietly into a towel. But as long as she was where the wounded could see her, she was gentle, sympathetic and cheerful, and the men in the hospitals called her an angel of mercy. Scarlett would have liked that title too, but it involved touching men crawling with lice, running fingers down throats of unconscious patients to see if they were choking on swallowed tobacco quids, bandaging stumps and picking maggots out of festering flesh. No, she did not like nursing!

Perhaps it might have been endurable if she had been permitted to use her charms on the convalescent men, for many of them were attractive and well born, but this she could not do in her widowed state. The young ladies of the town, who were not permitted to nurse for fear they would see sights unfit for virgin eyes, had the convalescent wards in their charge. Unhampered by matrimony or widowhood, they made vast inroads on the convalescents, and even the least attractive girls, Scarlett observed gloomily, had no difficulty in getting engaged.

With the exception of desperately ill and severely wounded men, Scarlett's was a completely feminized world and this irked her, for she neither liked nor trusted her own sex and, worse still, was always bored by it. But on three afternoons a week she had to attend sewing circles and bandage-rolling committees of Melanie's friends. The girls, who had all known Charles, were very kind and attentive to her at these gatherings, especially Fanny Elsing and Maybelle Merriwether, the daughters of the town dowagers. But they treated her deferentially, as if she were old and finished, and their constant chatter of dances and beaux made her both envious of their pleasures and resentful that her widowhood barred her from such activities. Why, she was three times as attractive as Fanny and Maybelle! Oh, how unfair life was! How unfair that everyone should think her heart was in the grave when it wasn't at all! It was in Virginia with Ashley!

But in spite of these discomforts, Atlanta pleased her very well. And her visit lengthened as the weeks slipped by.

2

SCARLETT sat in the window of her bedroom that midsummer morning and disconsolately watched the wagons and carriages full of girls, soldiers and chaperons ride gaily out Peachtree road in search of woodland decorations for the bazaar which was to be held that evening for the benefit of the hospitals. The red road lay chequered in shade and sun-glare beneath the over-arching trees and the many hooves kicked up little red clouds of dust. One wagon, ahead of the others, bore four stout negroes with axes to cut evergreens and drag down the vines, and the back of this wagon was piled high with napkin-covered hampers, split-oak baskets of lunch and a dozen watermelons. Two of the black bucks were equipped with banjo and harmonica and they were rendering a spirited version of "If You Want to Have a Good Time, Jine the Cavalry". Behind them streamed the merry cavalcade: girls cool in flowered cotton dresses, with light shawls, bonnets and mitts to protect their skins and little parasols held over their heads; elderly ladies placid and smiling amid the laughter and carriage-to-carriage calls and jokes; convalescents from the hospitals wedged in between stout chaperons and slender girls who made great fuss and to-do over them; officers on horseback idling at snail's pace beside the carriages—wheels creaking, spurs jingling, gold braid gleaming, parasols bobbing, fans swishing, negroes singing. Everybody was riding out Peachtree road to gather greenery and have a picnic and melon cutting. "Everybody," thought Scarlett, morosely, "except me."

They all waved and called to her as they went by and she tried to respond with a good grace, but it was difficult. A hard little pain had started in her heart and was travelling slowly up toward her throat where it would become a lump and the lump would soon become tears. Everybody was going to the picnic except her. And everybody was going to the bazaar and the ball to-night except her. That is everybody except her and Pittypat and Melly and the other unfortunates in town who were in mourning. But Melly and Pittypat did not seem to mind. It had not even occurred to them to want to go. It had occurred to Scarlett. And she did want to go, tremendously.

It simply wasn't fair. She had worked twice as hard as any girl in town, getting things ready for the bazaar. She had knitted socks and baby caps and afghans and mufflers and tatted yards of lace and painted china hair-receivers and moustache cups. And she had embroidered half a dozen sofa-pillow cases with the Confederate flag on them. (The stars were a bit lopsided, to be sure, some of them being almost round and others having six or even seven points, but the effect was good.) Yesterday she had worked until she was worn out in the dusty old barn of an Armoury draping yellow and pink and green cheesecloth on the booths that lined the walls. Under the supervision of the Ladies' Hospital Committee, this was plain hard work and no fun at all. It was never fun to be around Mrs. Merriwether and Mrs. Elsing and Mrs. Whiting and have them boss you like you were one of the darkies. And have to listen to them brag about how popular their daughters were. And, worst of all, she had burned two blisters on her fingers helping Pittypat and Cookie make layer cakes for raffling.

And now, having worked like a field hand, she had to retire decorously when the fun was just beginning. Oh, it wasn't fair that she should have a dead husband and a baby yelling in the next room and be out of everything that was pleasant. Just a little over a year ago, she was dancing and wearing bright clothes instead of this dark mourning and was practically engaged to three boys. She was only seventeen now and there was still a lot of dancing left in her feet. Oh, it wasn't fair! Life was going past her, down a hot shady summer road—life with grey uniforms and jingling spurs and flowered organdie dresses and banjos playing. She tried not to smile and wave too enthusiastically to the men she knew best, the ones she'd nursed in the hospital, but it was hard to subdue her dimples, hard to look as though her heart were in the grave—when it wasn't.

Her bowing and waving were abruptly halted when Pittypat entered the room, panting as usual from climbing the stairs, and jerked her away from the window unceremoniously.

"Have you lost your mind, honey, waving at men out of your bedroom window? I declare, Scarlett, I'm shocked! What would your mother say?"

"Well, they didn't know it was my bedroom."

"But they'd suspect it was your bedroom and that's just as bad. Honey, you mustn't do things like that. Everybody will be talking about you and saying you are fast—and anyway, Mrs. Merriwether knew it was your bedroom."

"And I suppose she'll tell all the boys, the old cat."

"Honey, hush! Dolly Merriwether's my best friend."

"Well, she's a cat just the same—oh, I'm sorry, Auntie, don't cry! I forgot it was my bedroom window. I won't do it again—I—I just wanted to see them go by. I wish I was going."

"Honey!"

"Well, I do. I'm so tired of sitting at home."

"Scarlett, promise me you won't say things like that. People would talk so. They'd say you didn't have the proper respect for poor Charlie—"

"Oh, Auntie, don't cry!"

"Oh, now I've made you cry, too," sobbed Pittypat, in a pleased way, fumbling in her skirt pocket for her handkerchief.

The hard little pain had at last reached Scarlett's throat and she wailed out loud—not, as Pittypat thought, for poor Charlie but because the last sounds of the wheels and the laughter were dying away. Melanie rustled in from her room, a worried frown puckering her forehead, a brush in her hands, her usually tidy black hair, freed of its net, fluffing about her face in a mass of tiny curls and waves.

"Darlings! What is the matter?"

"Charlie!" sobbed Pittypat, surrendering

251

utterly to the pleasure of her grief and burying her head on Melly's shoulder.

"Oh," said Melly, her lip quivering at the mention of her brother's name. "Be brave, dear. Don't cry. Oh, Scarlett!"

Scarlett had thrown herself on the bed and was sobbing at the top of her voice, sobbing for her lost youth and the pleasures of youth that were denied her, sobbing with the indignation and despair of a child who once could get anything she wanted by sobbing and now knows that sobbing can no longer help her. She burrowed her head in the pillow and cried and kicked with her feet at the tufted counterpane.

"I might as well be dead!" she sobbed passionately. Before such an exhibition of grief, Pittypat's easy tears ceased and Melly flew to the bedside to comfort her sister-in-law.

"Dear, don't cry! Try to think how much Charlie loved you and let that comfort you! Try to think of your darling baby."

Indignation at being misunderstood mingled with Scarlett's forlorn feeling of being out of everything and strangled all utterance. That was fortunate, for if she could have spoken she would have cried out truths couched in Gerald's forthright words. Melanie patted her shoulder and Pittypat tiptoed heavily about the room pulling down the shades.

"Don't do that!" shouted Scarlett, raising a red and swollen face from the pillow. "I'm not dead enough for you to pull down the shades—though I might as well be. Oh, do go away and leave me alone!"

She sank her face into the pillow again and, after a whispered conference, the two standing over her tiptoed out. She heard Melanie say to Pittypat in a low voice as they went down the stairs:

"Aunt Pitty, I wish you wouldn't speak of Charles to her. You know how it always affects her. Poor thing, she gets that queer look and I know she's trying not to cry. We mustn't make it harder for her."

Scarlett kicked the coverlet in impotent rage, trying to think of something bad enough to say.

"God's nightgown!" she cried at last, and felt somewhat relieved. How could Melanie be content to stay at home and never have any fun and wear crêpe for her brother when she was only eighteen years old? Melanie did not seem to know, or care, that life was riding by with jingling spurs.

"But she's such a stick," thought Scarlett, pounding the pillow. "And she never was popular like me, so she doesn't miss the things I miss. And—and besides she's got Ashley and I—I haven't got anybody!" And at this fresh woe, she broke into renewed outcries.

She remained gloomily in her room until afternoon and then the sight of the returning picnickers with wagons piled high with pine boughs, vines and ferns did not cheer her. Everyone looked happily tired as they waved to her again and she returned their greetings drearily. Life was a hopeless affair and certainly not worth living.

Deliverance came in the form she least

expected when, during the after-dinner-nap period, Mrs. Merriwether and Mrs. Elsing drove up. Startled at having callers at such an hour, Melanie, Scarlett and Aunt Pittypat roused themselves, hastily hooked their basques, smoothed their hair and descended to the parlour.

"Mrs. Bonnell's children have the measles," said Mrs. Merriwether abruptly, showing plainly that she held Mrs. Bonnell personally responsible for permitting such a thing to happen.

"And the McLure girls have been called to Virginia," said Mrs. Elsing in her die-away voice, fanning herself languidly as if neither this nor anything else mattered very much. "Dallas McLure is wounded."

"How dreadful!" chorused their hostesses. "Is poor Dallas—"

"No. Just through the shoulder," said Mrs. Merriwether briskly. "But it couldn't possibly have happened at a worse time. The girls are going North to bring him home. But, skies above, we haven't time to sit here talking. We must hurry back to the Armoury and get the decorating done. Pitty, we need you and Melly to-night to take Mrs. Bonnell's and the McLure girls' places."

"Oh, but, Dolly, we can't go."

"Don't say 'can't' to me, Pittypat Hamilton," said Mrs. Merriwether vigorously. "We need you to watch the darkies with the refreshments. That was what Mrs. Bonnell was to do. And Melly, you must take the McLure girls' booth."

"Oh, we just couldn't—with poor Charlie dead only a—"

"I know how you feel but there isn't any sacrifice too great for the Cause," broke in Mrs. Elsing in a soft voice that settled matters.

"Oh, we'd love to help but—why can't you get some sweet pretty girls to take the booths?"

Mrs. Merriwether snorted a trumpeting snort.

"I don't know what's come over the young people these days. They have no sense of responsibility. All the girls who haven't already taken booths have more excuses than you could shake a stick at. Oh, they don't fool me! They just don't want to be hampered in making up to the officers, that's all. And they're afraid their new dresses won't show off behind booth counters. I wish to goodness that blockade runner —what's his name?"

"Captain Butler," supplied Mrs. Elsing.

"I wish he'd bring in more hospital supplies and less hoop skirts and lace. If I've had to look at one dress to-day I've had to look at twenty dresses that he ran in. Captain Butler—I'm sick of the name. Now, Pitty, I haven't time to argue. You must come. Everybody will understand. Nobody will see you in the back room anyway, and Melly won't be conspicuous. The poor McLure girls' booth is way down at the end and not very pretty so nobody will notice you."

"I think we should go," said Scarlett, trying to curb her eagerness and to keep her face earnest and simple. "It is the least we can do for the hospital."

Neither of the visiting ladies had even mentioned her name, and they turned and looked sharply at her. Even in their extremity, they had not considered asking a widow of scarcely a year to appear at a social function. Scarlett bore their gaze with a wide-eyed childlike expression.

"I think we should go and help to make it a success, all of us. I think I should go in the booth with Melly because—well, I think it would look better for us both to be there instead of just one. Don't you think so, Melly?"

"Well," began Melly helplessly. The idea of appearing publicly at a social gathering while in mourning was so unheard-of she was bewildered.

"Scarlett's right," said Mrs. Merriwether, observing signs of weakening. She rose and jerked her hoops into place. "Both of you—all of you must come. Now, Pitty, don't start your excuses again. Just think how much the hospital needs money for new beds and drugs. And I know Charlie would like you to help the Cause he died for."

"Well," said Pittypat, helpless as always in the presence of a stronger personality, "if you think people will understand."

"Too good to be true! Too good to be true!" sang Scarlett's joyful heart as she slipped unobtrusively into the pink- and yellow-draped booth that was to have been the McLure girls'. Actually she was at a party! After a year's seclusion, after crêpe and hushed voices and nearly going crazy with boredom, she was actually at a party, the biggest party Atlanta had ever seen. And she could see people and many lights and hear music and view for herself the lovely laces and frocks and frills

256

that the famous Captain Butler had run through the blockade on his last trip.

She sank down on one of the little stools behind the counter of the booth and looked up and down the long hall which, until this afternoon, had been a bare and ugly drill-room. How the ladies must have worked to-day to bring it to its present beauty! It looked lovely. Every candle and candlestick in Atlanta must be in this hall to-night, she thought, silver ones with a dozen sprangling arms, china ones with charming figurines clustering their bases, old brass stands, erect and dignified, laden with candles of all sizes and colours, smelling fragrantly of bayberries, standing on the gun-racks that ran the length of the hall, on the long flower-decked tables, on booth counters, even on the sills of the open windows where the draughts of warm summer air were just strong enough to make them flare.

In the centre of the hall the huge ugly lamp, hanging from the ceiling by rusty chains, was completely transformed by twining ivy and wild grapevines that were already withering from the heat. The walls were banked with pine branches that gave out a spicy smell, making the corners of the room into pretty bowers where the chaperons and old ladies would sit. Long graceful ropes of ivy and grapevine and smilax were hung everywhere, in looping festoons on the walls, draped above the windows, twined in scallops all over the brightly coloured cheesecloth booths. And everywhere amid the greenery, on flags and bunting, blazed the bright stars of the Confederacy on their background of red and blue.

The raised platform for the musicians was especially artistic. It was completely hidden from view by the banked greenery and starry bunting, and Scarlett knew that every potted and tubbed plant in town was there: coleus, geranium, hydrangea, oleander, elephant ear—even Mrs. Elsing's four treasured rubber plants, which were given posts of honour at the four corners.

At the other end of the hall from the platform, the ladies had eclipsed themselves. On this wall hung large pictures of President Davis and Georgia's own "Little Alec" Stephens, Vice-President of the Confederacy. Above them was an enormous flag and, beneath, on long tables was the loot of the gardens of the town: ferns, banks of roses, crimson and yellow and white, proud sheaths of golden gladioli, masses of varicoloured nasturtiums, tall stiff hollyhocks rearing deep maroon and creamy heads above the other flowers. Among them, candles burned serenely like altar fires. The two faces looked down on the scene, two faces as different as could be possible in two men at the helm of so momentous an undertaking: Davis with the flat cheeks and cold eyes of an ascetic, his thin proud lips set firmly; Stephens with dark burning eyes deep-socketed in a face that had known nothing but sickness and pain and had triumphed over them with humour and with fire—two faces that were greatly loved.

The elderly ladies of the committee in whose hands rested the responsibility for the whole bazaar rustled in as importantly as full-rigged ships, hurried the belated young matrons and giggling girls into their booths, and then swept through the doors into the back rooms where the refreshments were being laid out. Aunt Pitty panted after them.

The musicians clambered upon their platform, black, grinning, their fat cheeks already shining with perspiration, and began tuning their fiddles and sawing and whanging with their bows in anticipatory importance. Old Levi, Mrs. Merriwether's coachman, who had led the orchestras for every bazaar, ball and wedding since Atlanta was named Marthasville, rapped with his bow for attention. Few except the ladies who were conducting the bazaar had arrived yet, but all eyes turned toward him. Then the fiddles, bull fiddles, accordions, banjos and knuckle-bones broke into a slow rendition of "Lorena"—too slow for dancing, the dancing would come later when the booths were emptied of their wares. Scarlett felt her heart beat faster as the sweet melancholy of the waltz came to her:

"The years creep slowly by, Lorena!
The snow is on the grass again.
The sun's far down the sky, Lorena . . .

One-two-three, one-two-three, dip-sway—three, turn—two-three. What a beautiful waltz! She extended her hands slightly, closed her eyes and swayed with the sad haunting rhythm. There was something about the tragic melody and Lorena's lost love that mingled with her own excitement and brought a lump into her throat.

Then, as if brought into being by the waltz

music, sounds floated in from the shadowy moonlit street below, the trample of horses' hooves and the sound of carriage wheels, laughter on the warm sweet air and the soft acrimony of negro voices raised in argument over hitching-places for the horses. There was confusion on the stairs and light-hearted merriment, the mingling of girls' fresh voices with the bass notes of their escorts, airy cries of greeting and squeals of joy as girls recognized friends from whom they had parted only that afternoon.

Suddenly the hall burst into life. It was full of girls—girls who floated in butterfly bright dresses, hooped out enormously, lace pantalets peeping from beneath; round little white shoulders bare, and faintest traces of soft little bosoms showing above lace flounces; lace shawls carelessly hanging from arms; fans spangled and painted, fans of swansdown and peacock feathers, dangling at wrists by tiny velvet ribbons; girls with dark hair smoothed sleekly from ears into chignons so heavy that their heads were tilted back with saucy pride; girls with masses of golden curls about their necks and fringed gold earbobs that tossed and danced with their dancing curls. Laces and silks and braid and ribbons, all blockade-run, all the more precious and more proudly worn because of it, finery flaunted with an added pride as an extra affront to the Yankees.

Not all the flowers of the town were standing in tribute to the leaders of the Confederacy. The smallest, the most fragrant blossoms bedecked the girls. Tea roses tucked behind pink ears, cape jessamine and bud roses in round little garlands over cascades of sidecurls, blossoms thrust demurely into satin sashes, flowers that before the night was over would find their way into the breast pockets of grey uniforms as treasured souvenirs.

There were so many uniforms in the crowd— so many uniforms on so many men whom Scarlett knew, men she had met on hospital cots, on the streets, at the drill-ground. They were such resplendent uniforms, brave with shining buttons and dazzling with twined gold braid on cuffs and collars, the red and yellow and blue stripes on the trousers, for the different branches of the service, setting off the grey to perfection. Scarlet and gold sashes swung to and fro, sabres glittered and banged against shining boots, spurs rattled and jingled.

Such handsome men, thought Scarlett, with a swell of pride in her heart, as the men called greetings, waved to friends, bent low over the hands of elderly ladies. All of them were so young-looking, even with their sweeping yellow moustaches and full black and brown beards, so handsome, so reckless, with their arms in slings, with head bandages startlingly white across sun-browned faces. Some of them were on crutches, and how proud were the girls who solicitously slowed their steps to their escorts' hopping pace! There was one gaudy splash of colour among the uniforms that put the girls' bright finery to shame and stood out in the crowd like a tropical bird— a Louisiana Zouave, with baggy blue and white striped pants, cream gaiters and tight little red jacket, a dark, grinning little monkey of a man, with his arm in a black silk sling. He was Maybelle Merriwether's especial beau, René Picard. The whole hospital must have turned out, at least everybody who could walk, and all the men on furlough and sick leave and all the railroad and mail service and hospital and commissary departments between here and Macon. How pleased the ladies would be! The hospital should make a mint of money to-night.

There was a ruffle of drums from the street below, the tramp of feet, the admiring cries of coachmen. A bugle blared and a bass voice shouted the command to break ranks. In a moment, the Home Guard and the militia unit in their bright uniforms shook the narrow stairs and crowded into the room, bowing, saluting, shaking hands. There were boys in the Home Guard, proud to be playing at war, promising themselves they would be in Virginia this time next year, if the war would just last that long; old men with white beards, wishing they were younger, proud to march in uniform in the reflected glory of sons at the front. In the militia, there were many middle-aged men and some older men but there was a fair sprinkling of men of military age who did not carry themselves quite so jauntily as their elders or their juniors. Already people were beginning to whisper, asking why they were not with Lee.

How would they all get into the hall! It had seemed such a large place a few minutes before, and now it was packed, warm with summer-night odours of sachet and cologne water and hair pomade and burning bayberry candles, fragrant with flowers, faintly dusty as many feet trod the old drill floors. The din and hubbub of voices made it almost impossible to hear anything and, as if feeling the joy and excitement of the occasion, old Levi choked off "Lorena" in mid-bar, rapped sharply with his bow and, sawing away for dear life, the orchestra burst into "Bonnie Blue Flag".

A hundred voices took it up, sang it, shouted it like a cheer. The Home Guard bugler, climbing on to the platform, caught up with the music just as the chorus began, and the high silver notes soared out thrillingly above the massed singing, causing goose-bumps to break out on bare arms and cold chills of deeply felt emotion to fly down spines:

"Hurrah! Hurrah! For the Southern Rights, hurrah!
Hurrah for the Bonnie Blue Flag
That bears a single star!"

They crashed into the second verse and Scarlett, singing with the rest, heard the high sweet soprano of Melanie mounting behind her, clear and true and thrilling as the bugle notes. Turning, she saw that Melly was standing with her hands clasped to her breast, her eyes closed, and tiny tears oozing from the corners. She smiled at Scarlett, whimsically, as the music ended, making a little moue of apology as she dabbed with her handkerchief.

"I'm so happy," she whispered, "and so proud

of the soldiers that I just can't help crying about it."

There was a deep, almost fanatic glow in her eyes that for a moment lit up her plain little face and made it beautiful.

The same look was on the faces of all the women as the song ended, tears of pride on cheeks, pink or wrinkled, smiles on lips, a deep hot glow in eyes, as they turned to their men, sweetheart to lover, mother to son, wife to husband. They were all beautiful with the blinding beauty that transfigures even the plainest woman when she is utterly protected and utterly loved and is giving back that love a thousandfold.

They loved their men, they believed in them, they trusted them to the last breaths of their bodies. How could disaster ever come to women such as they when their stalwart grey line stood between them and the Yankees? Had there ever been such men as these since the first dawn of the world, so heroic, so reckless, so gallant, so tender? How could anything but overwhelming victory come to a Cause as just and right as theirs? A Cause they loved as much as they loved their men, a Cause they served with their hands and their hearts, a Cause they talked about, thought about, dreamed about—a Cause to which they would sacrifice these men if need be, and bear their loss as proudly as the men bore their battle flags.

It was high tide of devotion and pride in their hearts, high tide of the Confederacy, for final victory was at hand. Stonewall Jackson's triumphs in the Valley and the defeat of the Yankees in the

264

Seven Days' Battle around Richmond showed that clearly. How could it be otherwise with such leaders as Lee and Jackson? One more victory and the Yankees would be on their knees yelling for peace and the men would be riding home and there would be kissing and laughter. One more victory and the war was over!

Of course, there were empty chairs and babies who would never see their fathers' faces and unmarked graves by lonely Virginia creeks and in the still mountains of Tennessee, but was that too great a price to pay for such a Cause? Silks for the ladies and tea and sugar were hard to get, but that was something to joke about. Besides, the dashing blockade runners were bringing in these very things under the Yankees' disgruntled noses, and that made the possession of them many times more thrilling. Soon Raphael Semmes and the Confederate Navy would tend to those Yankee gunboats and the ports would be wide open. And England was coming in to help the Confederacy win the war, because the English mills were standing idle for want of Southern cotton. And naturally the British aristocracy sympathized with the Confederacy, as one aristocrat with another, against a race of dollar-lovers like the Yankees.

So the women swished their silks and laughed and, looking on their men with hearts bursting with pride, they knew that love snatched in the face of danger and death was doubly sweet for the strange excitement that went with it.

When first she looked at the crowd, Scarlett's heart had thump-thumped with the unaccustomed excitement of being at a party, but as she halfcomprehendingly saw the high-hearted look on the faces about her, her joy began to evaporate. Every woman present was blazing with an emotion she did not feel. It bewildered and depressed her. Somehow, the hall did not seem so pretty nor the girls so dashing, and the white heat of devotion to the Cause that was still shining on every face seemed—why, it just seemed silly!

In a sudden flash of self-knowledge that made her mouth pop open with astonishment, she realized that she did not share with these women their fierce pride, their desire to sacrifice themselves and everything they had for the Cause. Before horror made her think, "No—no! I mustn't think such things! They're wrong—sinful," she knew the Cause meant nothing at all to her and that she was bored with hearing other people talk about it with that fanatic look in their eyes. The Cause didn't seem sacred to her. The war didn't seem to be a holy affair, but a nuisance that killed men senselessly and cost money and made luxuries hard to get. She saw that she was tired of the endless knitting and the endless bandage-rolling and lint-picking that roughened the cuticle of her nails. And oh, she was so tired of the hospital! Tired and bored and nauseated with the sickening gangrene smells and the endless moaning, frightened by the look that coming death gave to sunken faces.

She looked furtively around her, as the treacherous, blasphemous thoughts rushed through her mind, fearful that someone might find them written clearly upon her face. Oh, why couldn't she feel like these other women! They were whole-hearted and sincere in their devotion to the Cause. They really meant everything they said and did. And if anyone should ever suspect that she—No, no one must ever know! She must go on making a pretence of enthusiasm and pride in the Cause which she could not feel, acting out her part of the widow of a Confederate officer who bears her grief bravely, whose heart is in the grave, who feels that her husband's death meant nothing if it aided the Cause to triumph.

Oh, why was she different, apart from these loving women? She could never love anything or anyone so selflessly as they did. What a lonely feeling it was—and she had never been lonely either in body or spirit before. At first she tried to stifle the thoughts, but the hard self-honesty that lay at the base of her nature would not permit it. And so, while the bazaar went on, while she and Melanie waited on the customers who came to their booth, her mind was busily working, trying to justify herself to herself—a task which she seldom found difficult.

The other women were simply silly and hysterical with their talk of patriotism and the Cause, and the men were almost as bad with their talk of vital issues and States' Rights. She, Scarlett O'Hara Hamilton, alone had good hard-headed Irish sense. She wasn't going to make a fool out of herself about the Cause, but neither was she going to make a fool out of herself by admitting her true feelings. She was hard-headed enough to be practical about the situation, and no one would ever know how she felt. How surprised the bazaar would be if they knew what she really was thinking! How shocked if she suddenly climbed on the bandstand and declared that she thought the war ought to stop, so everybody could go home and tend to their cotton and there could be parties and beaux again and plenty of pale-green dresses!

For a moment, her self-justification buoyed her up but still she looked about the hall with distaste. The McLure girls' booth was inconspicuous, as Mrs. Merriwether had said, and there were long intervals when no one came to their corner and Scarlett had nothing to do but look enviously on the happy throng. Melanie sensed her moodiness but, crediting it to longing for Charlie, did not try to engage her in conversation. She busied herself arranging the articles in the booth in more attractive display, while Scarlett sat and looked glumly around the room. Even the banked flowers below the pictures of Mr. Davis and Mr. Stephens displeased her.

"It looks like an altar," she sniffed. "And the way they all carry on about those two, they might as well be the Father and the Son!" Then smitten with sudden fright at her irreverence she began hastily to cross herself by way of apology but caught herself in time.

"Well, it's true," she argued with her conscience. "Everybody carries on like they were holy and they aren't anything but men, and mighty unattractive-looking ones at that."

Of course, Mr. Stephens couldn't help how he looked for he had been an invalid all his life, but Mr. Davis—She looked up at the cameo-clean, proud face. It was his goatee that annoyed her the most. Men should either be clean-shaven, moustached or wear full beards.

"That little wisp looks like it was just the best he could do," she thought, not seeing in his face the cold hard intelligence that was carrying the weight of a new nation.

No, she was not happy now, and at first she had been radiant with the pleasure of being in a crowd. Now just being present was not enough. She was at the bazaar but not a part of it. No one paid her any attention and she was the only young unmarried woman present who did not have a beau. And all her life she had enjoyed the centre of the stage. It wasn't fair! She was seventeen years old and her feet were patting the floor, wanting to skip and dance. She was seventeen years old and she had a husband lying at Oakland Cemetery and a baby in his cradle at Aunt Pittypat's, and everyone thought she should be content with her lot. She had a whiter bosom and a smaller waist and a tinier foot than any girl present, but for all they mattered she might just as well be lying beside Charles with "Beloved Wife of" carved over her.

She wasn't a girl who could dance and flirt and she wasn't a wife who could sit with other wives and criticize the dancing and flirting girls. And she wasn't old enough to be a widow. Widows should be old—so terribly old they didn't want to dance and flirt and be admired. Oh, it wasn't fair that she should have to sit here primly and be the acme of widowed dignity and propriety when she was only seventeen. It wasn't fair that she must keep her voice low and her eyes cast modestly down when men, attractive ones, too, came to their booth.

Every girl in Atlanta was three deep in men. Even the plainest girls were carrying on like belles—and, oh, worst of all, they were carrying on in such lovely, lovely dresses!

Here she sat like a crow with hot black taffeta to her wrists and buttoned up to her chin, with not even a hint of lace or braid, not a jewel except Ellen's onyx mourning brooch, watching tacky-looking girls hanging on the arms of good-looking men. All because Charles Hamilton had had the measles. He didn't even die in a fine glow of gallantry in battle, so she could brag about him.

Rebelliously she leaned her elbows on the counter and looked at the crowd, flouting Mammy's oft-repeated admonition against leaning on elbows and making them ugly and wrinkled. What did it matter if they did get ugly? She'd probably never get a chance to show them again. She looked hungrily at the frocks floating by: butter-yellow watered silks with garlands of rose-buds; pink satins with eighteen flounces edged with tiny black velvet ribbons; baby blue taffeta, ten yards in the skirt and foamy with cascading lace; exposed bosoms; seductive flowers. Maybelle Merriwether went toward the next booth on the arm of the Zouave, in an apple-green tarlatan so wide that it reduced her waist to nothingness. It was showered and flounced with cream-coloured Chantilly lace that had come from Charleston on the last blockader, and Maybelle was flaunting it as saucily as if she and not the famous Captain Butler had run the blockade.

"How sweet I'd look in that dress!" thought Scarlett, a savage envy in her heart. "Her waist is as big as a cow's. That green is just my colour and it would make my eyes look—Why will blondes try to wear that colour? Her skin looks as green as an old cheese. And to think I'll never wear that colour again, not even when I do get out of mourning. No, not even if I do manage to get married again. Then I'll have to wear tacky old greys and tans and lilacs."

For a brief moment she considered the unfairness of it all. How short was the time for fun, for pretty clothes, for dancing, for coquetting! Only a few, too few years! Then you married and wore dull-coloured dresses and had babies that ruined your waist-line and sat in corners at dances with other sober matrons and only emerged to dance with your husband or with old gentlemen who stepped on your feet. If you didn't do these things, the other matrons talked about you and then your reputation was ruined and your family disgraced. It seemed such a terrible waste to spend all your little girlhood learning how to be attractive and how to catch men and then only use the knowledge for a year or two. When she considered her training at the hands of Ellen and Mammy, she knew it had been thorough and good because it had always reaped results. There were set rules to be followed, and if you followed them success crowned your efforts.

With old ladies you were sweet and guileless and appeared as simple-minded as possible, for old ladies were sharp and they watched girls as jealously as cats, ready to pounce on any indiscretion of tongue or eye. With old gentlemen, a girl was pert and saucy and almost, but not quite, flirtatious, so that the old fools' vanities would be tickled. It made them feel devilish and young and they pinched your cheek and declared you were a minx. And, of course, you always blushed on such occasions, otherwise they would pinch you with more pleasure than was proper and then tell their sons that you were fast.

With young girls and young married women, you slopped over with sugar and kissed them every time you met them, even if it was ten times a day. And you put your arms about their waists and suffered them to do the same to you, no matter how much you disliked it. You admired their frocks or their babies indiscriminately and teased about beaux and complimented husbands and giggled modestly and denied that you had any charms at all compared with theirs. And, above all, you never said what you really thought about anything, any more than they said what they really thought.

Other women's husbands you let severely alone, even if they were your own discarded beaux, and no matter how temptingly attractive they were. If you were too nice to young husbands, their wives said you were fast and you got a bad reputation and never caught any beaux of your own.

But with young bachelors—ah, that was a different matter! You could laugh softly at them and when they came flying to see why you laughed, you could refuse to tell them and laugh harder and keep them around indefinitely trying to find out. You could promise, with your eyes, any number of exciting things that would make a man manoeuvre to get you alone. And, having gotten you alone, you could be very, very hurt or very, very angry when he tried to kiss you. You could make him apologize for being a cur and forgive him so sweetly that he would hang around trying to kiss you a second time. Sometimes, but not often, you did let him kiss you. (Ellen and Mammy had not taught her that but she learned it was effective.) Then you cried and declared you didn't know what had come over you and that he couldn't ever respect you again. Then he had to dry your eyes and usually he proposed, to show just how much he did respect you. And then there were—Oh, there were so many things to do to bachelors and she knew them all, the nuance of the sidelong glance, the half-smile behind the fan, the swaying of the hips so that skirts swung like a bell, the tears, the laughter, the flattery, the sweet sympathy. Oh, all the tricks that never failed to work—except with Ashley.

No, it didn't seem right to learn all these smart tricks, use them so briefly and then put them away forever. How wonderful it would be never to marry but to go on being lovely in pale-green dresses and forever courted by handsome men! But, if you went on too long, you got to be an old maid like India Wilkes and everyone said "poor thing" in that smug hateful way. No, after all it was better to marry and keep your self-respect even if you never had any more fun.

Oh, what a mess life was! Why had she been

such an idiot as to marry Charles of all people and have her life end at sixteen?

Her indignant and hopeless reverie was broken when the crowd began pushing back against the walls, the ladies carefully holding their hoops so that no careless contact should turn them up against their bodies and show more pantalets than was proper. Scarlett tiptoed above the crowd and saw the captain of the militia mounting the orchestra platform. He shouted orders and half of the Company fell into line. For a few minutes they went through a brisk drill that brought perspiration to their foreheads and cheers and applause from the audience. Scarlett clapped her hands dutifully with the rest and, as the soldiers pushed forward toward the punch and lemonade booths after they were dismissed, she turned to Melanie, feeling that she had better begin her deception about the Cause as soon as possible.

"They looked fine, didn't they?" she said.

Melanie was fussing about with the knitted things on the counter.

"Most of them would look a lot finer in grey uniforms and in Virginia," she said, and she did not trouble to lower her voice.

Several of the proud mothers of members of the militia were standing close by and overheard the remark. Mrs. Guinan turned scarlet and then white, for her twenty-five-year-old Willie was in the Company.

Scarlett was aghast at such words coming from Melly of all people.

"Why, Melly!"

"You know it's true, Scarlett. I don't mean the

little boys and the old gentlemen. But a lot of the militia are perfectly able to tote a rifle and that's what they ought to be doing this minute."

"But—but—" began Scarlett, who had never considered the matter before. "Somebody's got to stay home to—" What was it Willie Guinan had told her by way of excusing his presence in Atlanta? "Somebody's got to stay home to protect the state from invasion."

"Nobody's invading us and nobody's going to," said Melly coolly, looking toward a group of the militia. "And the best way to keep out invaders is to go to Virginia and beat the Yankees there. And as for all this talk about the militia staying here to keep the darkies from rising—why, it's the silliest thing I ever heard of. Why should our people rise? It's just a good excuse for cowards. I'll bet we could lick the Yankees in a month if all the militia of all the states went to Virginia. So there!"

"Why, Melly!" cried Scarlett again, staring.

Melly's soft dark eyes were flashing angrily. "My husband wasn't afraid to go and neither was yours. And I'd rather they'd both be dead than here at home—Oh, darling, I'm sorry. How thoughtless and cruel of me!"

She stroked Scarlett's arm appealingly and Scarlett stared at her. But it was not of dead Charles she was thinking. It was of Ashley. Suppose he too were to die? She turned quickly and smiled automatically as Dr. Meade walked up to their booth.

"Well, girls," he greeted them, "it was nice of you to come. I know what a sacrifice it must have been for you to come out to-night. But it's all for the Cause. And I'm going to tell you a secret. I've a surprise way for making some more money to-night for the hospital, but I'm afraid some of the ladies are going to be shocked about it."

He stopped and chuckled as he tugged at his grey goatee.

"Oh, what? Do tell!"

"On second thought I believe I'll keep you guessing, too. But you girls must stand up for me if the Church members want to run me out of town for doing it. However, it's for the hospital. You'll see. Nothing like this has ever been done before."

He went off pompously toward a group of chaperons in one corner, and just as the two girls had turned to each other to discuss the possibilities of the secret, two old gentlemen bore down on the booth, declaring in loud voices that they wanted ten miles of tatting. Well, after all, old gentlemen were better than no gentlemen at all, thought Scarlett, measuring out the tatting and submitting demurely to being chucked under the chin. The old blades charged off toward the lemonade booth and others took their places at the counter. Their booth did not have so many customers as did the other booths where the tootling laugh of Maybelle Merriwether sounded and Fanny Elsing's giggles and the Whiting girls' repartee made merriment. Melly sold useless stuff to men who could have no possible use for it as quietly and serenely as a shopkeeper, and Scarlett patterned her conduct on Melly's.

There were crowds in front of every other

counter but theirs, girls chattering, men buying. The few who came to them talked about how they went to the university with Ashley and what a fine soldier he was or spoke in respectful tones of Charles and how great a loss to Atlanta his death had been.

Then the music broke into the rollicking strains of "Johnny Booker, he'p dis Nigger!" and Scarlett thought she would scream. She wanted to dance. She wanted to dance. She looked across the floor and tapped her foot to the music and her green eyes blazed so eagerly that they fairly snapped. All the way across the floor, a man, newly come and standing in the doorway, saw them, started in recognition and watched closely the slanting eyes in the sulky, rebellious face. Then he grinned to himself as he recognized the invitation that any male could read.

He was dressed in black broadcloth, a tall man, towering over the officers who stood near him, bulky in the shoulders but tapering to a small waist and absurdly small feet in varnished boots. His severe black suit, with fine ruffled shirt and trousers smartly strapped beneath high insteps, was oddly at variance with his physique and face, for he was foppishly groomed, the clothes of a dandy on a body that was powerful and latently dangerous in its lazy grace. His hair was jet black, and his black moustache was small and closely clipped, almost foreign-looking compared with the dashing, swooping moustaches of the cavalrymen near by. He looked, and was, a man of lusty and unashamed appetites. He had an air of utter assurance, of displeasing insolence about him, and there was a twinkle of malice in his bold eyes as he stared at Scarlett, until finally, feeling his gaze, she looked toward him.

Somewhere in her mind, the bell of recognition rang, but for the moment she could not recall who he was. But he was the first man in months who had displayed an interest in her, and she threw him a gay smile. She made a little curtsy as he bowed, and then, as he straightened and started toward her with a peculiarly lithe Indian-like gait, her hand went to her mouth in horror, for she knew who he was.

Thunderstruck, she stood as if paralysed while he made his way through the crowd. Then she turned blindly, bent on flight into the refreshment rooms, but her skirt caught on a nail of the booth. She jerked furiously at it, tearing it and, in an instant, he was beside her.

"Permit me," he said, bending over and disentangling the flounce. "I hardly hoped that you would recall me, Miss O'Hara."

His voice was oddly pleasant to the ear, the well-modulated voice of a gentleman, resonant and overlaid with the flat slow drawl of the Charlestonian.

She looked up at him imploringly, her face crimson with the shame of their last meeting, and met two of the blackest eyes she had ever seen, dancing in merciless merriment. Of all the people in the world to turn up here, this terrible person who had witnessed that scene with Ashley which still gave her nightmares; this odious wretch who ruined girls and was not received by nice people;

this despicable man who had said, and with good cause, that she was not a lady.

At the sound of his voice, Melanie turned and for the first time in her life Scarlett thanked God for the existence of her sister-in-law.

"Why—it's—it's Mr. Rhett Butler, isn't it?" said Melanie with a little smile, putting out her hand. "I met you—"

"On the happy occasion of the announcement of your betrothal," he finished, bending over her hand. "It is kind of you to recall me."

"And what are you doing so far from Charleston, Mr. Butler?"

"A boring matter of business, Mrs. Wilkes. I will be in and out of your town from now on. I find I must not only bring in goods but see to the disposal of them."

"Bring in—" began Melly, her brow wrinkling, and then she broke into a delighted smile. "Why, you—you must be the famous Captain Butler we've been hearing so much about—the blockade runner. Why, every girl here is wearing dresses you brought in. Scarlett, aren't you thrilled— what's the matter, dear? Are you faint? Do sit down."

Scarlett sank to the stool, her breath coming so rapidly she feared the lacings of her stays would burst. Oh, what a terrible thing to happen! She had never thought to meet this man again. He picked up her black fan from the counter and began fanning her solicitously, too solicitously, his face grave but his eyes still dancing.

"It is quite warm in here," he said. "No

wonder Miss O'Hara is faint. May I lead you to a window?"

"No," said Scarlett, so rudely that Melly stared.

"She is not Miss O'Hara any longer," said Melly. "She is Mrs. Hamilton. She is my sister now," and Melly bestowed one of her fond little glances on her. Scarlett felt that she would strangle at the expression on Captain Butler's swarthy piratical face.

"I am sure that is a great gain to two charming ladies," said he, making a slight bow. That was the kind of remark all men made, but when he said it it seemed to her that he meant just the opposite.

"Your husbands are here to-night, I trust, on this happy occasion? It would be a pleasure to renew acquaintances."

"My husband is in Virginia," said Melly with a proud lift of her head. "But Charles—" Her voice broke.

"He died in camp," said Scarlett flatly. She almost snapped the words. Would this creature never go away? Melly looked at her, startled, and the Captain made a gesture of self-reproach

"My dear ladies—how could I! You must forgive me. But permit a stranger to offer the comfort of saying that to die for one's country is to live forever."

Melanie smiled at him through sparkling tears while Scarlett felt the fox of wrath and impotent hate gnaw at her vitals. Again he had made a graceful remark, the kind of compliment any gentleman would pay under such circumstances, but he did not mean a word of it. He was jeering at her. He knew she hadn't loved Charles. And Melly was just a big enough fool not to see through him. Oh, please God, don't let anybody else see through him, she thought with a start of terror. Would he tell what he knew? Of course he wasn't a gentleman and there was no telling what men would do when they weren't gentlemen. There was no standard to judge them by. She looked up at him and saw that his mouth was pulled down at the corners in mock sympathy, even while he swished the fan. Something in his look challenged her spirit and brought her strength back in a surge of dislike. Abruptly she snatched the fan from his hand.

"I'm quite all right," she said tartly. "There's no need to blow my hair out of place."

"Scarlett, darling! Captain Butler, you must forgive her. She—she isn't herself when she hears poor Charlie's name spoken—and perhaps, after all, we shouldn't have come here to-night. We're still in mourning, you see, and it's quite a strain on her—all this gaiety and music, poor child."

"I quite understand," he said with elaborate gravity, but as he turned and gave Melanie a searching look that went to the bottom of her sweet worried eyes, his expression changed, reluctant respect and gentleness coming over his dark face. "I think you're a courageous little lady, Mrs. Wilkes."

"Not a word about me!" thought Scarlett indignantly, as Melly smiled in confusion and answered:

"Dear me, no, Captain Butler! The hospital

committee just had to have us for this booth because at the last minute—A pillowcase? Here's a lovely one with a flag on it."

She turned to three cavalrymen who appeared at her counter. For a moment, Melanie thought how nice Captain Butler was. Then she wished that something more substantial than cheesecloth was between her skirt and the spittoon that stood just outside the booth, for the aim of the horsemen with amber streams of tobacco juice was not so unerring as with their long horse pistols. Then she forgot about the Captain, Scarlett and the spittoons as more customers crowded to her.

Scarlett sat quietly on the stool fanning herself, not daring to look up, wishing Captain Butler back on the deck of his ship where he belonged.

"Your husband has been dead long?"

"Oh, yes, a long time. Almost a year."

"An aeon, I'm sure."

Scarlett was not sure what an aeon was, but there was no mistaking the baiting quality of his voice, so she said nothing.

"Had you been married long? Forgive my questions but I have been away from this section for so long."

"Two months," said Scarlett, unwillingly.

"A tragedy, no less," his easy voice continued.

"Oh, damn him," she thought violently. "If he was any other man in the world I could simply freeze up and order him off. But he knows about Ashley and he knows I didn't love Charlie. And my hands are tied." She said nothing, still looking down at her fan.

"And this is your first social appearance?"

"I know it looks quite odd," she explained rapidly. "But the McLure girls who were to take this booth were called away and there was no one else, so Melanie and I—"

"No sacrifice is too great for the Cause."

Why, that was what Mrs. Elsing had said, but when she said it it didn't sound the same way. Hot words started to her lips but she choked them back. After all, she was here, not for the Cause, but because she was tired of sitting at home.

"I have always thought," he said reflectively, "that the system of mourning, of immuring women in crêpe for the rest of their lives and forbidding them normal enjoyment, is just as barbarous as the Hindu suttee."

"Settee?"

He laughed and she blushed for her ignorance. She hated people who used words unknown to her.

"In India, when a man dies he is burned, instead of buried, and his wife always climbs on the funeral pyre and is burned with him."

"How dreadful! Why do they do it? Don't the police do anything about it?"

"Of course not. A wife who didn't burn herself would be a social outcast. All the worthy Hindu matrons would talk about her for not behaving as a well-bred lady should—precisely as those worthy matrons in the corner would talk about you, should you appear to-night in a red dress and lead a reel. Personally, I think suttee much more merciful than our charming Southern custom of burying widows alive."

"How dare you say I'm buried alive!"

"How closely women clutch the very chains that bind them! You think the Hindu custom barbarous—but would you have had the courage to appear here to-night if the Confederacy hadn't needed you?"

Arguments of this character were always confusing to Scarlett. His were doubly confusing because she had a vague idea there was truth in them. But now was the time to squelch him.

"Of course, I wouldn't have come. It would have been—well, disrespectful to—it would have seemed as if I hadn't lov—"

His eyes waited on her words, cynical amusement in them, and she could not go on. He knew she hadn't loved Charlie and he wouldn't let her pretend to the nice polite sentiments that she should express. What a terrible, terrible thing it was to have to do with a man who wasn't a gentleman. A gentleman always appeared to believe a lady even when he knew she was lying. That was Southern chivalry. A gentleman always obeyed the rules and said the correct things and made life easier for a lady. But this man seemed not to care for rules and evidently enjoyed talking of things no one ever talked about.

"I am waiting breathlessly."

"I think you are horrid," she said, helplessly, dropping her eyes.

He leaned down across the counter until his mouth was near her ear and hissed, in a very creditable imitation of the stage villains who appeared infrequently at the Athenaeum Hall:

"Fear not, fair lady! Your guilty secret is safe with me!"

"Oh," she whispered, feverishly, "how can you say such things!"

"I only thought to ease your mind. What would you have me say? 'Be mine, beautiful female, or I will reveal all'?"

She met his eyes unwillingly and saw they were as teasing as a small boy's. Suddenly she laughed. It was such a silly situation, after all. He laughed too, and so loudly that several of the chaperons in the corner looked their way. Observing how good a time Charles Hamilton's widow appeared to be having with a perfect stranger, they put their heads together disapprovingly.

There was a roll of drums and many voices cried "Sh!" as Dr. Meade mounted the platform and spread out his arms for quiet.

"We must all give grateful thanks to the charming ladies whose indefatigable and patriotic efforts have made this bazaar not only a pecuniary success," he began, "but have transformed this rough hall into a bower of loveliness, a fit garden for the charming rosebuds I see about me."

Everyone clapped approvingly.

"The ladies have given their best, not only of their time but of the labour of their hands, and these beautiful objects in the booths are doubly beautiful, made as they are by the fair hands of our charming Southern women."

There were more shouts of approval, and Rhett Butler, who had been lounging negligently against the counter at Scarlett's side, whispered: "Pompous goat, isn't he?"

Startled, at first horrified, at this lèse-majesty toward Atlanta's most beloved citizen, she stared reprovingly at him. But the doctor did look like a goat with his grey chin-whiskers wagging away at a great rate, and with difficulty she stifled a giggle:

"But these things are not enough. The good ladies of the hospital committee, whose cool hands have soothed many a suffering brow and brought back from the jaws of death our brave men wounded in the bravest of all Causes, know our needs. I will not enumerate them. We must have more money to buy medical supplies from England, and we have with us to-night the intrepid captain who has so successfully run the blockade for a year and who will run it again to bring us the drugs we need. Captain Rhett Butler!"

Though caught unawares, the blockader made a graceful bow—too graceful, thought Scarlett, trying to analyse it. It was almost as if he overdid his courtesy because his contempt for everybody present was so great. There was a loud burst of applause as he bowed and a craning of necks from the ladies in the corner. So that was who poor Charles Hamilton's widow was carrying on with! And Charlie hardly dead a year!

"We need more gold and I am asking you for it," the doctor continued. "I am asking a sacrifice but a sacrifice so small compared with the sacrifices our gallant men in grey are making that it will seem laughably small. Ladies, I want your jewellery. *I* want your jewellery? No, the Confederacy wants your jewellery, the Confederacy calls for it and I know no one will hold back. How fair a gem gleams on a lovely wrist! How beautifully gold brooches glitter on the bosoms of our patriotic women! But how much more beautiful is sacrifice than all the gold and gems of the Ind! The gold will be melted and the stones sold and the money used to buy drugs and other medical supplies. Ladies, there will pass among you two of our gallant wounded, with baskets and—" But the rest of his speech was lost in the storm and tumult of clapping hands and cheering voices.

Scarlett's first thought was one of deep thankfulness that mourning forbade her wearing her precious earbobs and the heavy gold chain that had been Grandma Robillard's and the gold and black enamelled bracelets and the garnet brooch. She saw the little Zouave, a split-oak basket over his unwounded arm, making the rounds of the crowd on her side of the hall and saw women, old and young, laughing, eager, tugging at bracelets, squealing in pretended pain as earrings came from pierced flesh, helping each other undo stiff necklace clasps, unpinning brooches from bosoms. There was a steady little clink-clink of metal on metal and cries of "Wait—wait! I've got it unfastened now. There!" Maybelle Merriwether was pulling off her lovely twin bracelets from above and below her elbows. Fanny Elsing, crying "Mamma, may I?" was tearing from her curls the seed-pearl ornament set in heavy gold which had been in the family for generations. As each offering went into the basket, there was applause and cheering.

The grinning little man was coming to their booth now, his basket heavy on his arm, and as he passed Rhett Butler a handsome gold cigar-case was thrown carelessly into the basket. When he came to Scarlett and rested his basket on the counter, she shook her head, throwing wide her hands to show that she had nothing to give. It was embarrassing to be the only person present who was giving nothing. And then she saw the bright gleam of her wide gold wedding ring.

For a confused moment she tried to remember Charles' face—how he had looked when he slipped it on her finger. But the memory was blurred, blurred by the sudden feeling of irritation that memory of him always brought to her. Charles—he was the reason why life was over for her, why she was an old woman.

With a sudden wrench she seized the ring but it stuck. The Zouave was moving toward Melanie.

"Wait!" cried Scarlett. "I have something for you!" The ring came off and, as she started to throw it into the basket, heaped up with chains, watches, rings, pins and bracelets, she caught Rhett Butler's eye. His lips were twisted in a slight smile. Defiantly, she tossed the ring on to the top of the pile.

"Oh, my darling!" whispered Melly, clutching her arm, her eyes blazing with love and pride. "You brave, brave girl! Wait—please, wait, Lieutenant Picard! I have something for you, too!"

She was tugging at her own wedding ring, the

ring Scarlett knew had never once left that finger since Ashley put it there. Scarlett knew, as no one did, how much it meant to her. It came off with difficulty and for a brief instant was clutched tightly in the small palm. Then it was laid gently on the pile of jewellery. The two girls stood looking after the Zouave who was moving toward the group of elderly ladies in the corner, Scarlett defiant, Melanie with a look more pitiful than tears. And neither expression was lost on the man who stood beside them.

"If you hadn't been brave enough to do it, I would never have been, either," said Melly, putting her arm about Scarlett's waist and giving her a gentle squeeze. For a moment Scarlett wanted to shake her off and cry "Name of God!" at the top of her lungs, as Gerald did when he was irritated, but she caught Rhett Butler's eye and managed a very sour smile. It was annoying the way Melly always misconstrued her motives —but perhaps that was far preferable to having her suspect the truth.

"What a beautiful gesture!" said Rhett Butler softly. "It is such sacrifices as yours that hearten our brave lads in grey."

Hot words bubbled to her lips and it was with difficulty that she checked them. There was mockery in everything he said. She disliked him heartily, lounging there against the booth. But there was something stimulating about him, something warm and vital and electric. All that was Irish in her rose to the challenge of his black eyes. She decided she was going to take this man down a notch or two. His knowledge of her secret

289

gave him an advantage over her that was exasperating, so she would have to change that by putting him at a disadvantage somehow. She stifled her impulse to tell him exactly what she thought of him. Sugar always caught more flies than vinegar, as Mammy often said, and she was going to catch and subdue this fly, so he could never again have her at his mercy.

"Thank you," she said sweetly, deliberately misunderstanding his jibe. "A compliment like that coming from so famous a man as Captain Butler is appreciated."

He threw back his head and laughed freely—yelped, was what Scarlett thought fiercely, her face becoming pink again.

"Why don't you say what you really think?" he demanded, lowering his voice so that in the clatter and excitement of the collection it came only to her ears. "Why don't you say I'm a damned rascal and no gentleman and that I must take myself off or you'll have one of these gallant boys in grey call me out?"

It was on the tip of her tongue to answer tartly, but she managed by heroic control to say: "Why, Captain Butler! How you do run on! As if everybody didn't know how famous you are and how brave and what a—what a—"

"I am disappointed in you," he said.

"Disappointed?"

"Yes. On the occasion of our first eventful meeting I thought to myself that I had at last met a girl who was not only beautiful but who had courage. And now I see that you are only beautiful."

"Do you mean to call me a coward?" She was ruffling like a hen.

"Exactly. You lack the courage to say what you really think. When I first met you, I thought: There is a girl in a million. She isn't like these other silly little fools who believe everything their mammas tell them and act on it, no matter how they feel. And conceal all their feelings and desires and little heartbreaks behind a lot of sweet words. I thought: Miss O'Hara is a girl of rare spirit. She knows what she wants and she doesn't mind speaking her mind—or throwing vases."

"Oh," she said, rage breaking through. "Then I'll speak my mind right this minute. If you'd had any raising at all you'd never have come over here and talked to me. You'd have known I never wanted to lay eyes on you again! But you aren't a gentleman! You are just a nasty ill-bred creature! And you think that because your rotten little boats can outrun the Yankees, you've the right to come here and jeer at men who are brave and women who are sacrificing everything for the Cause—"

"Stop, stop—" he begged with a grin. "You started off very nicely and said what you thought, but don't begin talking to me about the Cause. I'm tired of hearing about it and I'll bet you are, too—"

"Why, how did—" she began, caught off her balance, and then checked herself hastily, boiling with anger at herself for falling into his trap.

"I stood there in the doorway before you saw me and I watched you," he said. "And I watched the other girls. And they all looked as though

291

their faces came out of one mould. Yours didn't. You have an easy face to read. You didn't have your mind on your business and I'll wager you weren't thinking about our Cause or the hospital. It was all over your face that you wanted to dance and have a good time and you couldn't. So you were mad clean through. Tell the truth. Am I not right?"

"I have nothing more to say to you, Captain Butler," she said as formally as she could, trying to draw the rags of her dignity about her. "Just because you're conceited at being the 'great blockader' doesn't give you the right to insult women."

"The great blockader! That's a joke. Pray give me only one moment more of your precious time before you cast me into darkness. I wouldn't want so charming a little patriot to be left under a misapprehension about my contribution to the Confederate Cause."

"I don't care to listen to your brags."

"Blockading is a business with me and I'm making money out of it. When I stop making money out of it, I'll quit. What do you think of that?"

"I think you're a mercenary rascal—just like the Yankees."

"Exactly," he grinned. "And the Yankees help me make my money. Why, last month I sailed my boat right into New York harbour and took on a cargo."

"What!" cried Scarlett, interested and excited in spite of herself. "Didn't they shell you?"

"My poor innocent! Of course not. There are

plenty of sturdy Union patriots who are not averse to picking up money selling goods to the Confederacy. I run my boat into New York, buy from Yankee firms, sub rosa, of course, and away I go. And when that gets a bit dangerous, I go to Nassau where these same Union patriots have brought powder and shells and hoop skirts for me. It's more convenient than going to England. Sometimes it's a bit difficult running it into Charleston or Wilmington—but you'd be surprised how far a little gold goes."

"Oh, I knew Yankees were vile but I didn't know—"

"Why quibble about the Yankees earning an honest penny selling out the Union? It won't matter in a hundred years. The result will be the same. They know the Confederacy will be licked eventually, so why shouldn't they cash in on it?"

"Licked—us?"

"Of course."

"Will you please leave me—or will it be necessary for me to call my carriage and go home to get rid of you?"

"A red-hot little Rebel," he said, with another sudden grin. He bowed and sauntered off, leaving her with her bosom heaving with impotent rage and indignation. There was disappointment burning in her that she could not quite analyse, the disappointment of a child seeing illusions crumble. How dared he take the glamour from the blockaders! And how dared he say the Confederacy would be licked! He should be shot for that—shot like a traitor. She looked about the hall at the familiar faces, so assured of success,

293

so brave, so devoted, and somehow a cold little chill set in at her heart. Licked? These people— why, of course not! The very idea was impossible, disloyal.

"What were you two whispering about?" asked Melanie, turning to Scarlett as her customers drifted off. "I couldn't help seeing that Mrs. Merriwether had her eye on you all the time and, dear, you know how she talks."

"Oh, the man's impossible—an ill-bred boor," said Scarlett. "And as for old lady Merriwether, let her talk. I'm sick of acting like a ninny, just for her benefit."

"Why, Scarlett!" cried Melanie, scandalized.

"Sh-sh," said Scarlett. "Dr. Meade is going to make another announcement."

The gathering quieted again as the doctor raised his voice, at first in thanks to the ladies who had so willingly given their jewellery.

"And now, ladies and gentlemen, I am going to propose a surprise—an innovation that may shock some of you, but I ask you to remember that all this is done for the hospital and for the benefit of our boys lying there."

Everyone edged forward, in anticipation, trying to imagine what the sedate doctor could propose that would be shocking.

"The dancing is about to begin and the first number will, of course, be a reel, followed by a waltz. The dances following, the polkas, the schottisches, the mazurkas, will be preceded by short reels. I know the gentle rivalry to lead the reels very well and so—" The doctor mopped his brow and cast a quizzical glance at the corner, where his wife sat among the chaperons. "Gentlemen, if you wish to lead a reel with the lady of your choice, you must bargain for her. I will be auctioneer and the proceeds will go to the hospital."

Fans stopped in mid-swish and a ripple of excited murmuring ran through the hall. The chaperons' corner was in tumult and Mrs. Meade, anxious to support her husband in an action of which she heartily disapproved, was at a disadvantage. Mrs. Elsing, Mrs. Merriwether and Mrs. Whiting were red with indignation. But suddenly the Home Guard gave a cheer and it was taken up by the other uniformed guests. The young girls clapped their hands and jumped excitedly.

"Don't you think it's—it's just—just a little like a slave auction?" whispered Melanie, staring uncertainly at the embattled doctor who heretofore had been perfect in her eyes.

Scarlett said nothing but her eyes glittered and her heart contracted with a little pain. If only she were not a widow. If only she were Scarlett O'Hara again, out there on the floor in an apple-green dress with dark-green velvet ribbons dangling from her bosom and tuberoses in her black hair—she'd lead that reel. Yes, indeed. There'd be a dozen men battling for her and paying over money to the doctor. Oh, to have to sit here, a wallflower against her will, and see Fanny or Maybelle lead the first reel as the belle of Atlanta!

Above the tumult sounded the voice of the little Zouave, his Creole accent very obvious: "Eef

I may—twenty dollars for Mees Maybelle Merriwether."

Maybelle collapsed with blushes against Fanny's shoulder and the two girls hid their faces in each other's necks and giggled, as other voices began calling other names, other amounts of money. Dr. Meade had begun to smile again, ignoring completely the indignant whispers that came from the Ladies' Hospital Committee in the corner.

At first, Mrs. Merriwether had stated flatly and loudly that her Maybelle would never take part in such a proceeding; but as Maybelle's name was called most often and the amount went up to seventy-five dollars, her protests began to dwindle. Scarlett leaned her elbows on the counter and almost glared at the excited laughing crowd surging about the platform, their hands full of Confederate paper money.

Now they would all dance—except her and the old ladies. Now everyone would have a good time, except her. She saw Rhett Butler standing just below the doctor and, before she could change the expression of her face, he saw her and one corner of his mouth went down and one eyebrow went up. She jerked her chin up and turned away from him and suddenly she heard her own name called—called in an unmistakable Charleston voice that rang out above the hubbub of other names.

"Mrs. Charles Hamilton—one hundred and fifty dollars—in gold."

A sudden hush fell on the crowd both at the mention of the sum and at the name. Scarlett was so startled she could not even move. She remained sitting with her chin in her hands, her eyes wide with astonishment. Everybody turned to look at her. She saw the doctor lean down from the platform and whisper something to Rhett Butler. Probably telling him she was in mourning and it was impossible for her to appear on the floor. She saw Rhett's shoulders shrug lazily.

"Another one of our belles, perhaps?" questioned the doctor.

"No," said Rhett clearly, his eyes sweeping the crowd carelessly, "Mrs. Hamilton."

"I tell you it is impossible," said the doctor testily. "Mrs. Hamilton will not—"

Scarlett heard a voice which, at first, she did not recognize as her own.

"Yes, I will!"

She leaped to her feet, her heart hammering so wildly she feared she could not stand, hammering with the thrill of being the centre of attention again, of being the most highly desired girl present and oh, best of all, at the prospect of dancing again.

"Oh, I don't care! I don't care what they say!" she whispered, as a sweet madness swept over her. She tossed her head and sped out of the booth, tapping her heels like castanets, snapping open her black silk fan to its widest. For a fleeting instant she saw Melanie's incredulous face, the look on the chaperons' faces, the petulant girls, the enthusiastic approval of the soldiers.

Then she was on the floor and Rhett Butler was advancing toward her through the aisle of the crowd, that nasty mocking smile on his face. But she didn't care—didn't care if he were Abe Lincoln himself! She was going to dance again. She was going to lead the reel. She swept him a low curtsy and a dazzling smile and he bowed, one hand on his frilled bosom. Levi, horrified, was quick to cover the situation and bawled: "Choose yo' padners fo' de Ferginny reel!"

And the orchestra crashed into that best of all reel tunes, "Dixie".

"How dare you make me so conspicuous, Captain Butler?"

"But, my dear Mrs. Hamilton, you so obviously wanted to be conspicuous!"

"How could you call my name out in front of everybody?"

"You could have refused."

"But—I owe it to the Cause—I—I couldn't think of myself when you were offering so much in gold. Stop laughing, everyone is looking at us."

"They will look at us anyway. Don't try to palm off that twaddle about the Cause to me. You wanted to dance and I gave you the opportunity. This march is the last figure of the reel, isn't it?"

"Yes—really, I must stop and sit down now."

"Why? Have I stepped on your feet?"

"No—but they'll talk about me."

"Do you really care—down in your heart?"

"Well—"

"You aren't committing any crime, are you? Why not dance the waltz with me?"

"But if Mother ever—"

"Still tied to mamma's apron-strings."

298

"Oh, you have the nastiest way of making virtues sound so stupid."

"But virtues are stupid. Do you care if people talk?"

"No—but—well, let's don't talk about it. Thank goodness the waltz is beginning. Reels always leave me breathless."

"Don't dodge my questions. Has what other women said ever mattered to you?"

"Oh, if you're going to pin me down—no! But a girl is supposed to mind. To-night, though, I don't care."

"Bravo! Now you are beginning to think for yourself instead of letting others think for you. That's the beginning of wisdom."

"Oh, but—"

"When you've been talked about as much as I have, you'll realize how little it matters. Just think, there's not a home in Charleston where I am received. Not even my contribution to our just and holy Cause lifts the ban."

"How dreadful!"

"Oh, not at all. Until you've lost your reputation, you never realize what a burden it was or what freedom really is."

"You do talk scandalous!"

"Scandalously and truly. Always providing you have enough courage—or money—you can do without a reputation."

"Money can't buy everything."

"Someone must have told you that. You'd never think of such a platitude all by yourself. What can't it buy?"

"Oh, well, I don't know—not happiness or love, anyway."

"Generally it can. And when it can't, it can buy some of the most remarkable substitutes."

"And have you so much money, Captain Butler?"

"What an ill-bred question, Mrs. Hamilton! I'm surprised. But, yes. For a young man cut off without a shilling in early youth, I've done very well. And I'm sure I'll clean up a million on the blockade."

"Oh, no!"

"Oh, yes! What most people don't seem to realize is that there is just as much money to be made out of the wreckage of a civilization as from the upbuilding of one."

"And what does all that mean?"

"Your family and my family and everyone here to-night made their money out of changing a wilderness into a civilization. That's empire building. There's good money in empire building. But, there's more in empire wrecking."

"What empire are you talking about?"

"This empire we're living in—the South— the Confederacy—the Cotton Kingdom—it's breaking up right under our feet. Only most fools won't see it and take advantage of the situation created by the collapse. I'm making my fortune out of the wreckage."

"Then you really think we're going to get licked?"

"Yes. Why be an ostrich?"

"Oh, dear, it bores me to talk about such like.

Don't you ever say pretty things, Captain Butler?"

"Would it please you if I said your eyes were twin goldfish bowls filled to the brim with the clearest green water and that when the fish swim to the top, as they are doing now, you are devilishly charming?"

"Oh, I don't like that. . . . Isn't the music gorgeous? Oh, I could waltz forever! I didn't know I had missed it so!"

"You are the most beautiful dancer I've ever held in my arms."

"Captain Butler, you must not hold me so tightly. Everybody is looking."

"If no one were looking, would you care?"

"Captain Butler, you forget yourself."

"Not for a minute. How could I, with you in my arms?. . . What is that tune? Isn't it new?"

"Yes. Isn't it divine? It's something we captured from the Yankees."

"What's the name of it?"

"'When This Cruel War Is Over'."

"What are the words? Sing them to me."

"Dearest one, do you remember
   When we last did meet?
When you told me how you loved me,
   Kneeling at my feet?
Oh, how proud you stood before me
   In your suit of grey,
When you vowed from me and country
   Ne'er to go astray.
Weeping sad and lonely,
   Sighs and tears how vain!

301

When this cruel war is over
Pray that we meet again!"

"Of course, it was 'suit of blue' but we changed it to 'grey'. . . . Oh, you waltz so well, Captain Butler. Most big men don't, you know. And to think it will be years and years before I'll dance again."

"It will only be a few minutes. I'm going to bid you in for the next reel—and the next and the next."

"Oh, no, I couldn't! You mustn't! My reputation will be ruined."

"It's in shreds already, so what does another dance matter? Maybe I'll give the other boys a chance after I've had five or six, but I must have the last one."

"Oh, all right. I know I'm crazy but I don't care. I don't care a bit what anybody says. I'm so tired of sitting at home. I'm going to dance and dance. . . ."

"And not wear black? I loathe funeral crêpe."

"Oh, I couldn't take off mourning—Captain Butler, you must not hold me so tightly. I'll be mad at you if you do."

"And you look gorgeous when you are mad. I'll squeeze you again—there—just to see if you will really get mad. You have no idea how charming you were that day at Twelve Oaks when you were mad and throwing things."

"Oh, please—won't you forget that?"

"No, it is one of my most priceless memories —a delicately nurtured Southern belle with her Irish up—You are very Irish, you know."

"Oh, dear, there's the end of the music and there's Aunt Pittypat coming out of the back room. I know Mrs. Merriwether must have told her. Oh, for goodness' sake, let's walk over and look out the window. I don't want her to catch me now. Her eyes are as big as saucers."

3

OVER the waffles next morning, Pittypat was lachrymose, Melanie was silent and Scarlett defiant.

"I don't care if they do talk. I'll bet I made more money for the hospital than any girl there —more than all the messy old stuff we sold, too."

"Oh, dear, what does the money matter?" wailed Pittypat, wringing her hands. "I just couldn't believe my eyes, and poor Charlie hardly dead a year. . . . And that awful Captain Butler, making you so conspicuous, and he's a terrible, terrible person, Scarlett. Mrs. Whiting's cousin, Mrs. Coleman, whose husband came from Charleston, told me about him. He's the black sheep of a lovely family—oh, how could any of the Butlers ever turn out anything like him? He isn't received in Charleston and he has the fastest reputation and there was something about a girl—something so bad Mrs. Coleman didn't even know what it was—"

"Oh, I can't believe he's that bad," said Melly gently. "He seemed a perfect gentleman and when you think how brave he's been, running the blockade—"

"He isn't brave," said Scarlett perversely, pouring half a pitcher of syrup over her waffles. "He just does it for money. He told me so. He doesn't care anything about the Confederacy and he says we're going to get licked. But he dances divinely."

Her audience was speechless with horror.

"I'm tired of sitting at home and I'm not going to do it any longer. If they all talked about me about last night, then my reputation is already gone and it won't matter what else they say."

It did not occur to her that the idea was Rhett Butler's. It came so patly and fitted so well with what she was thinking.

"Oh! What will your mother say when she hears? What will she think of me?"

A cold qualm of guilt assailed Scarlett at the thought of Ellen's consternation, should she ever learn of her daughter's scandalous conduct. But she took heart at the thought of the twenty-five miles between Atlanta and Tara. Miss Pitty certainly wouldn't tell Ellen. It would put her in such a bad light as a chaperon. And if Pitty didn't tattle, she was safe.

"I think—" said Pitty, "yes, I think I'd better write Henry a letter about it—much as I hate it —but he's our only male relative, and make him go speak reprovingly to Captain Butler—Oh, dear, if Charlie were only alive—You must never, never speak to that man again, Scarlett."

Melanie had been sitting quietly, her hands in her lap, her waffles cooling on her plate. She arose and, coming behind Scarlett, put her arms about her neck.

"Darling," she said, "don't you get upset. I understand and it was a brave thing you did last night and it's going to help the hospital a lot. And if anybody dares say one little word about you,

I'll tend to them. . . . Aunt Pitty, don't cry. It has been hard on Scarlett, not going anywhere. She's just a baby." Her fingers played in Scarlett's black hair. "And maybe we'd all be better off if we went out occasionally to parties. Maybe we've been very selfish, staying here with our grief. War times aren't like other times. When I think of all the soldiers in town who are far from home and haven't any friends to call on at night—and the ones in the hospital who are well enough to be out of bed and not well enough to go back in the army—Why, we have been selfish. We ought to have three convalescents in our house this minute, like everybody else, and some of the soldiers out to dinner every Sunday. There, Scarlett, don't you fret. People won't talk when they understand. We know you loved Charlie."

Scarlett was far from fretting and Melanie's soft hands in her hair were irritating. She wanted to jerk her head away and say "Oh, fiddle-dee-dee!" for the warming memory was still on her of how the Home Guard and the militia and the soldiers from the hospital had fought for her dances last night. Of all the people in the world, she didn't want Melly for a defender. She could defend herself, thank you, and if the old cats wanted to squall—well, she could get along without the old cats. There were too many nice officers in the world for her to bother about what old women said.

Pittypat was dabbing at her eyes under Melanie's soothing words when Prissy entered with a bulky letter.

306

"Fer you, Miss Melly. A lil nigger boy brung it."

"For me?" said Melly, wondering, as she ripped open the envelope.

Scarlett was making headway with her waffles and so noticed nothing until she heard a burst of tears from Melly and, looking up, saw Aunt Pittypat's hand go to her heart.

"Ashley's dead!" screamed Pittypat, throwing her head back and letting her arms go limp.

"Oh, my God!" cried Scarlett, her blood turning to ice water.

"No! No!" cried Melanie. "Quick! Her smelling salts, Scarlett! There, there, honey, do you feel better? Breathe deep. No, it's not Ashley. I'm so sorry I scared you. I was crying because I'm so happy," and suddenly she opened her clenched palm and pressed some object that was in it to her lips. "I'm so happy," and burst into tears again.

Scarlett caught a fleeting glimpse and saw that it was a broad gold ring.

"Read it," said Melly, pointing to the letter on the floor. "Oh, how sweet, how kind, he is!"

Scarlett, bewildered, picked up the single sheet and saw written in a black, bold hand: "The Confederacy may need the lifeblood of its men but not yet does it demand the heart's blood of its women. Accept, dear Madam, this token of my reverence for your courage and do not think that your sacrifice has been in vain, for this ring has been redeemed at ten times its value. Captain Rhett Butler."

Melanie slipped the ring on her finger and looked at it lovingly.

"I told you he was a gentleman, didn't I?" she said, turning to Pittypat, her smile bright through the teardrops on her face. "No one but a gentleman of refinement and thoughtfulness would ever have thought how it broke my heart to—I'll send my gold chain instead. Aunt Pittypat, you must write him a note and invite him to Sunday dinner so I can thank him."

In the excitement, neither of the others seemed to have thought that Captain Butler had not returned Scarlett's ring, too. But she thought of it, annoyed. And she knew it had not been Captain Butler's refinement that had prompted so gallant a gesture. It was that he intended to be asked into Pittypat's house and knew unerringly how to get the invitation.

"I was greatly disturbed to hear of your recent conduct," ran Ellen's letter, and Scarlett, who was reading it at the table, scowled. Bad news certainly travelled swiftly. She had often heard in Charleston and Savannah that Atlanta people gossiped more and meddled in other people's business more than any other people in the South, and now she believed it. The bazaar had taken place Monday night and to-day was only Thursday. Which of the old cats had taken it upon herself to write Ellen? For a moment she suspected Pittypat but immediately abandoned that thought. Poor Pittypat had been quaking in her number-three shoes for fear of being blamed for Scarlett's forward conduct and would be the last to notify Ellen of her own inadequate chaperonage. Probably it was Mrs. Merriwether.

"It is difficult for me to believe that you could so forget yourself and your rearing. I will pass over the impropriety of your appearing publicly while in mourning, realizing your warm desire to be of assistance to the hospital. But to dance, and with such a man as Captain Butler! I have heard much of him (as who has not?) and Pauline wrote me only last week that he is a man of bad repute and not even received by his own family in Charleston, except of course by his heart-broken mother. He is a thoroughly bad character who would take advantage of your youth and innocence to make you conspicuous and publicly disgrace you and your family. How could Miss Pittypat have so neglected her duty to you?"

Scarlett looked across the table at her aunt. The old lady had recognized Ellen's handwriting and her fat little mouth was pursed in a frightened way, like a baby who fears a scolding and hopes to ward it off by tears.

"I am heartbroken to think that you could so soon forget your rearing. I have thought of calling you home immediately but will leave that to your father's discretion. He will be in Atlanta Friday to speak with Captain Butler and to escort you home. I fear he will be severe with you despite my pleadings. I hope and pray it was only youth and thoughtlessness that prompted such forward conduct. No one can wish to serve our Cause more than I, and I wish my daughters to feel the same way, but to disgrace—"

There was more in the same vein but Scarlett did not finish it. For once, she was thoroughly frightened. She did not feel reckless and defiant now. She felt as young and guilty as when she was ten and had thrown a buttered biscuit at Suellen at the table. To think of her gentle mother reproving her so harshly and her father coming to town to talk to Captain Butler. The real seriousness of the matter grew on her. Gerald was going to be severe. This was one time when she knew she couldn't wriggle out of her punishment by sitting on his knee and being sweet and pert.

"Not—not bad news?" quavered Pittypat.

"Pa is coming to-morrow and he's going to land on me like a duck on a June bug," answered Scarlett dolorously.

"Prissy, find my salts," fluttered Pittypat, pushing back her chair from her half-eaten meal. "I—I feel faint."

"Dey's in yo' skirt pocket," said Prissy, who had been hovering behind Scarlett, enjoying the sensational drama. Mist' Gerald in a temper was always exciting, providing his temper was not directed at her kinky head. Pitty fumbled at her skirt and held the vial to her nose.

"You all must stand by me and not leave me alone with him for one minute," cried Scarlett. "He's so fond of you both, and if you are with me he can't fuss at me."

"I couldn't," said Pittypat weakly, rising to her feet. "I—I feel ill. I must go lie down. I shall lie down all day to-morrow. You must give him my excuses."

"Coward!" thought Scarlett, glowering at her.

Melly rallied to the defence, though white and frightened at the prospect of facing the fire-eating Mr. O'Hara. "I'll—I'll help you explain how you did it for the hospital. Surely he'll understand."

"No, he won't," said Scarlett. "And oh, I shall die if I have to go back to Tara in disgrace, like Mother threatens!"

"Oh, you can't go home," cried Pittypat, bursting into tears. "If you did I should be forced —yes, forced to ask Henry to come live with us, and you know I just couldn't live with Henry. I'm so nervous with just Melly in the house at night, with so many strange men in town. You're so brave I don't mind being here without a man!"

"Oh, he couldn't take you to Tara!" said Melly, looking as if she too would cry in a moment. "This is your home now. What would we ever do without you?"

"You'd be glad to do without me if you knew what I really think of you," thought Scarlett sourly, wishing there were some other person than Melanie to help ward off Gerald's wrath. It was sickening to be defended by someone you disliked so much.

"Perhaps we should recall our invitation to Captain Butler—" began Pittypat.

"Oh, we couldn't! It would be the height of rudeness!" cried Melly, distressed.

"Help me to bed. I'm going to be ill," moaned Pittypat. "Oh, Scarlett, how could you have brought this on me?"

Pittypat was ill and in her bed when Gerald arrived the next afternoon. She sent many messages of regret to him from behind her closed door and left the two frightened girls to preside over the supper table. Gerald was ominously silent although he kissed Scarlett and pinched Melanie's cheek approvingly and called her "Cousin Melly". Scarlett would have infinitely preferred bellowing oaths and accusations. True to her promise, Melanie clung to Scarlett's skirts like a small rustling shadow and Gerald was too much of a gentleman to upbraid his daughter in front of her. Scarlett had to admit that Melanie carried off things very well, acting as if she knew nothing was amiss, and she actually succeeded in engaging Gerald in conversation, once the supper had been served.

"I want to know all about the County," she said, beaming upon him. "India and Honey are such poor correspondents, and I know you know everything that goes on down there. Do tell us about Joe Fontaine's wedding."

Gerald warmed to the flattery and said that the wedding had been a quiet affair, "not like you girls had," for Joe had only a few days' furlough. Sally, the little Munroe chit, looked very pretty. No, he couldn't recall what she wore but he did hear that she didn't have "second-day" dress.

"She didn't!" exclaimed the girls, scandalized.

"Sure, because she didn't have a second day," Gerald explained and bawled with laughter before recalling that perhaps such remarks were not fit for female ears. Scarlett's spirits soared at his laugh and she blessed Melanie's tact.

"Back Joe went to Virginia the next day," Gerald added hastily. "There was no visiting about and dancing afterwards. The Tarleton twins are home."

"We heard that. Have they recovered?"

"They weren't badly wounded. Stuart had it in the knee and a minie ball went through Brent's shoulder. You had it, too, that they were mentioned in dispatches for bravery?"

"No! Tell us!"

"Hare-brained—both of them. I'm believing there's Irish in them," said Gerald complacently. "I forget what they did, but Brent is a lieutenant now."

Scarlett felt pleased at hearing of their exploits, pleased in a proprietary manner. Once a man had been her beau, she never lost the conviction that he belonged to her, and all his good deeds redounded to her credit.

"And I've news that'll be holding the both of you," said Gerald. "They're saying Stu is courting at Twelve Oaks again."

"Honey or India?" questioned Melly excitedly, while Scarlett stared almost indignantly.

"Oh, Miss India, to be sure. Didn't she have him fast till this baggage of mine winked at him?"

"Oh," said Melly, somewhat embarrassed at Gerald's outspokenness.

"And more than that, young Brent has taken to hanging about Tara. Now!"

Scarlett could not speak. The defection of her beaux was almost insulting. Expecially when she recalled how wildly both the twins had acted when she told them she was going to marry

313

Charles. Stuart had even threatened to shoot Charles, or Scarlett, or himself, or all three. It had been most exciting.

"Suellen?" questioned Melly, breaking into a pleased smile. "But I thought Mr. Kennedy—"

"Oh, him?" said Gerald. "Frank Kennedy still pussyfoots about, afraid of his shadow, and I'll be asking him his intentions soon if he doesn't speak up. No, 'tis me baby."

"Carreen?"

"She's nothing but a child!" said Scarlett sharply, finding her tongue.

"She's little more than a year younger than you were, Miss, when you married," retorted Gerald. "Is it you're grudging your old beau to your sister?"

Melly blushed, unaccustomed to such frankness, and signalled Peter to bring in the sweet potato pie. Frantically she cast about in her mind for some other topic of conversation which would not be so personal but which would divert Mr. O'Hara from the purpose of his trip. She could think of nothing but, once started, Gerald needed no stimulus other than an audience. He talked on about the thievery of the commissary department which every month increased its demands, the knavish stupidity of Jefferson Davis and the blackguardery of the Irish who were being enticed into the Yankee army by bounty money.

When the wine was on the table and the two girls rose to leave him, Gerald cocked a severe eye at his daughter from under frowning brows and commanded her presence alone for a few minutes. Scarlett cast a despairing glance at

Melly, who twisted her handkerchief helplessly and went out, softly pulling the sliding doors together.

"How now, Missy!" bawled Gerald, pouring himself a glass of port. "'Tis a fine way to act! Is it another husband you're trying to catch and you so fresh a widow?"

"Not so loud, Pa, the servants—"

"They know already, to be sure, and everybody knows of our disgrace. And your poor mother taking to her bed with it and me not able to hold up me head. 'Tis shameful. No, Puss, you need not think to get around me with tears this time," he said hastily and with some panic in his voice as Scarlett's lids began to bat and her mouth to screw up. "I know you. You'd be flirting at the wake of your own husband. Don't cry. There, I'll be saying no more to-night, for I'm going to see this fine Captain Butler who makes so light of me daughter's reputation. But in the morning— There now, don't cry. 'Twill do you no good at all, at all. 'Tis firm that I am and back to Tara you'll be going to-morrow before you're disgracing the lot of us again. Don't cry, pet. Look what I've brought you! Isn't that a pretty present? See, look! How could you be putting so much trouble on me, bringing me all the way up here when 'tis a busy man I am? Don't cry!"

Melanie and Pittypat had gone to sleep hours before, but Scarlett lay awake in the warm darkness, her heart heavy and frightened in her breast. To leave Atlanta when life had just begun again and go home and face Ellen! She would rather die than face her mother. She wished she were dead, this very minute, then everyone would be sorry they had been so hateful. She turned and tossed on the hot pillow until a noise far up the quiet street reached her ears. It was an oddly familiar noise, blurred and indistinct though it was. She slipped out of bed and went to the window. The street with its over-arching trees was softly, deeply black under a dim star-studded sky. The noise came closer, the sound of wheels, the plod of a horse's hooves and voices. And suddenly she grinned for, as a voice thick with brogue and whisky came to her, raised in "Peg in a Low-backed Car", she knew. This might not be Jonesboro on Court Day, but Gerald was coming home in the same condition.

She saw the dark bulk of a buggy stop in front of the house and indistinct figures alight. Someone was with him. Two figures paused at the gate and she heard the click of the latch and Gerald's voice came plain.

"Now I'll be giving you the 'Lament for Robert Emmet'. 'Tis a song you should be knowing, me lad. I'll teach it to you."

"I'd like to learn it," replied his companion, a hint of buried laughter in his flat drawling voice. "But not now, Mr. O'Hara."

"Oh, my God, it's that hateful Butler man!" thought Scarlett, at first annoyed. Then she took heart. At least they hadn't shot each other. And they must be on amicable terms to be coming home together at this hour and in this condition.

"Sing it I will and listen you will or I'll be shooting you for the Orangeman you are."

"Not Orangeman—Charlestonian."

"'Tis no better. 'Tis worse. I have two sister-in-laws in Charleston and I know."

"Is he going to tell the whole neighbourhood?" thought Scarlett, panic-stricken, reaching for her wrapper. But what could she do? She couldn't go downstairs at this hour of the night and drag her father in from the street.

With no further warning, Gerald, who was hanging on the gate, threw back his head and began the "Lament", in a roaring bass. Scarlett rested her elbows on the window-sill and listened, grinning unwillingly. It would be a beautiful song, if only her father could carry a tune. It was one of her favourite songs and, for a moment, she followed the fine melancholy of those verses beginning:

"She is far from the land where her young
   hero sleeps
And lovers are round her sighing."

The song went on and she heard stirrings in Pittypat's and Melly's rooms. Poor things, they'd certainly be upset. They were not used to full-blooded males like Gerald. When the song had finished, two forms merged into one, came up the walk and mounted the steps. A discreet knock sounded at the door.

"I suppose I must go down," thought Scarlett. "After all he's my father and poor Pitty would die before she'd go." Besides, she didn't want the servants to see Gerald in his present condition. And if Peter tried to put him to bed, he might

317

get unruly. Pork was the only one who knew how to handle him.

She pinned the wrapper close about her throat, lit her bedside candle and hurried down the dark stairs into the front hall. Setting the candle on the stand, she unlocked the door and in the wavering light she saw Rhett Butler, not a ruffle disarranged, supporting her small, thickset father. The "Lament" had evidently been Gerald's swansong, for he was frankly hanging on to his companion's arm. His hat was gone, his crisp long hair was tumbled in a white mane, his cravat was under one ear, and there were liquor stains down his shirt bosom.

"Your father, I believe?" said Captain Butler, his eyes amused in his swarthy face. He took in her dishabille in one glance that seemed to penetrate through her wrapper.

"Bring him in," she said shortly, embarrassed at her attire, infuriated at Gerald for putting her in a position where this man could laugh at her.

Rhett propelled Gerald forward. "Shall I help you take him upstairs? You cannot manage him. He's quite heavy."

Her mouth fell open with horror at the audacity of his proposal. Just imagine what Pittypat and Melly cowering in their beds would think, should Captain Butler come upstairs!

"Mother of God, no! In here, in the parlour on that settee."

"The suttee, did you say?"

"I'll thank you to keep a civil tongue in your head. Here. Now lay him down."

"Shall I take off his boots?"

318

"No. He's slept in them before."

She could have bitten off her tongue for that slip, for he laughed softly as he crossed Gerald's legs.

"Please go, now."

He walked out into the dim hall and picked up the hat he had dropped on the doorsill.

"I will be seeing you Sunday at dinner," he said and went out, closing the door noiselessly behind him.

Scarlett arose at five-thirty, before the servants had come in from the back yard to start breakfast, and slipped down the steps to the quiet lower floor. Gerald was awake, sitting on the sofa, his hands gripping his bullet head as if he wished to crush it between his palms. He looked up furtively as she entered. The pain of moving his eyes was too excruciating to be borne and he groaned.

"Wurra the day!"

"It's a fine way you've acted, Pa," she began in a furious whisper. "Coming home at such an hour and waking all the neighbours with your singing."

"I sang?"

"Sang! You woke the echoes singing the 'Lament'."

"'Tis nothing I'm remembering."

"The neighbours will remember it till their dying day and so will Miss Pittypat and Melanie."

"Mother of Sorrows," moaned Gerald, moving a thickly furred tongue around parched lips. "'Tis little I'm remembering after the game started."

"Game?"

"That laddybuck Butler bragged that he was the best poker player in—"

"How much did you lose?"

"Why, I won, naturally. A drink or two helps me game."

"Look in your wallet."

As if every movement was agony, Gerald removed his wallet from his coat and opened it. It was empty and he looked at it in forlorn bewilderment.

"Five hundred dollars," he said. "And 'twas to buy things from the blockaders for Mrs. O'Hara, and now not even fare left to Tara."

As she looked indignantly at the empty purse, an idea took form in Scarlett's mind and grew swiftly.

"I'll not be holding up my head in this town," she began. "You've disgraced us all."

"Hold your tongue, Puss. Can you not see me head is bursting?"

"Coming home drunk with a man like Captain Butler, and singing at the top of your lungs for everyone to hear and losing all that money."

"The man is too clever with cards to be a gentleman. He—"

"What will Mother say when she hears?"

He looked up in sudden anguished apprehension.

"You wouldn't be telling your mother a word and upsetting her, now would you?"

Scarlett said nothing but pursed her lips.

"Think now how 'twould hurt her and her so gentle."

"And to think, Pa, that you said only last night I had disgraced the family! Me, with my poor little dance to make money for the soldiers. Oh, I could cry."

"Well, don't," pleaded Gerald. "'Twould be more than me poor head could stand and sure 'tis bursting now."

"And you said that I—"

"Now, Puss, now, Puss, don't you be hurt at what your poor old father said and him not meaning a thing and not understanding a thing! Sure, you're a fine well-meaning girl, I'm sure."

"And wanting to take me home in disgrace."

"Ah, darling, I wouldn't be doing that.'Twas to tease you. You won't be mentioning the money to your mother and her in a flutter about expenses already?"

"No," said Scarlett frankly, "I won't, if you'll let me stay here and if you'll tell Mother that 'twas nothing but a lot of gossip from old cats."

Gerald looked mournfully at his daughter.

"'Tis blackmail, no less."

"And last night was a scandal, no less."

"Well," he began wheedlingly, "we'll be forgetting all that. And do you think a fine pretty lady like Miss Pittypat would be having any brandy in the house? The hair of the dog—"

Scarlett turned and tiptoed through the silent hall into the dining-room to get the brandy bottle that she and Melly privately called the "swoon bottle" because Pittypat always took a sip from it when her fluttering heart made her faint—or seem to faint. Triumph was written on her face and no trace of shame for her unfilial treatment of Gerald. Now Ellen would be soothed with lies if any other busybody wrote her. Now she could stay in Atlanta. Now she could do almost as she pleased, Pittypat being the weak vessel that she was. She unlocked the cellaret and stood for a moment with the bottle and glass pressed to her bosom.

She saw a long vista of picnics by the bubbling waters of Peachtree Creek and barbecues at Stone Mountain, receptions and balls, afternoon dance-ables, buggy rides and Sunday-night buffet suppers. She would be there, right in the heart of things, right in the centre of a crowd of men. And men fell in love so easily, after you did little things for them at the hospital. She wouldn't mind the hospital so much now. Men were so easily stirred when they had been ill. They fell into a clever girl's hand, just like the ripe peaches at Tara when the trees were gently shaken.

She went back toward her father with the reviving liquor, thanking Heaven that the famous O'Hara head had not been able to survive last night's bout and wondering suddenly if Rhett Butler had had anything to do with that.

4

ON an afternoon of the following week, Scarlett came home from the hospital weary and indignant. She was tired from standing on her feet all morning and irritable because Mrs. Merriwether had scolded her sharply for sitting on a soldier's bed while she dressed his wounded arm. Aunt Pitty and Melanie, bonneted in their best, were on the porch with Wade and Prissy, ready for their weekly round of calls. Scarlett asked to be excused from accompanying them and went upstairs to her room.

When the last sound of carriage wheels had died away and she knew the family was safely out of sight, she slipped quietly into Melanie's room and turned the key in the lock. It was a prim, virginal little room and it lay still and warm in the slanting rays of the four-o'clock sun. The floors were glistening and bare except for a few bright rag rugs, and the white walls unornamented save for one corner which Melanie had fitted up as a shrine.

Here, under a draped Confederate flag, hung the gold-hilted sabre that Melanie's father had carried in the Mexican War, the same sabre Charles had worn away to war. Charles' sash and pistol-belt hung there too, with his revolver in the holster. Between the sabre and the pistol was a daguerreotype of Charles himself, very stiff and proud in his grey uniform, his great brown eyes shining out of the frame and a shy smile on his lips.

Scarlett did not even glance at the picture but went unhesitatingly across the room to the square rosewood writing-box that stood on the table beside the narrow bed. From it she took a pack of letters tied together with a blue ribbon, addressed in Ashley's hand to Melanie. On the top was the letter which had come that morning and this one she opened.

When Scarlett first began secretly reading these letters, she had been so stricken of conscience and so fearful of discovery she could hardly open the envelopes for trembling. Now, her never-too-scrupulous sense of honour was dulled by repetition of the offence and even fear of discovery had subsided. Occasionally, she thought with a sinking heart, "What would Mother say if she knew?" She knew Ellen would rather see her dead than know her guilty of such dishonour. This had worried Scarlett at first, for she still wanted to be like her mother in every respect. But the temptation to read the letters was too great and she put the thought of Ellen out of her mind. She had become adept at putting unpleasant thoughts out of her mind these days. She had learned to say, "I won't think of this or that bothersome thought now. I'll think about it to-morrow." Generally when to-morrow came, the thought either did not occur at all or it was so attenuated by the delay it was not very troublesome. So the matter of Ashley's letters did not lie very heavily on her conscience.

Melanie was always generous with the letters, reading parts of them aloud to Aunt Pitty and Scarlett. But it was the part she did not read that tormented Scarlett, that drove her to surreptitious reading of her sister-in-law's mail. She had to know if Ashley had come to love his wife since marrying her. She had to know if he even pretended to love her. Did he address tender endearments to her? What sentiments did he express and with what warmth?

She carefully smoothed out the letter.

Ashley's small even writing leaped up at her as she read, "My dear wife", and she breathed in relief. He wasn't calling Melanie "Darling" or "Sweetheart" yet. *Ashley's Letter.*

"My dear wife: You write me saying you are alarmed lest I be concealing my real thoughts from you and you ask me what is occupying my mind these days—"

"Mother of God!" thought Scarlett, in a panic of guilt. "'Concealing his real thoughts'. Can Melly have read his mind? Or my mind? Does she suspect that he and I—"

Her hands trembled with fright as she held the letter closer, but as she read the next paragraph she relaxed.

"Dear Wife, if I have concealed aught from you it is because I did not wish to lay a burden on your shoulders, to add to your worries for my physical safety with those of my mental turmoil. But I can keep nothing from you, for you know me too well. Do not be alarmed. I have no wound. I have not been ill. I have enough to eat and occasionally a bed to sleep in. A soldier can ask for no more. But, Melanie, heavy thoughts lie on my heart and I will open my heart to you.

"These summer nights I lie awake, long after the camp is sleeping, and I look up at the stars and, over and over, I wonder, 'Why are you here. Ashley Wilkes? What are you fighting for?'

"Not for honour and glory, certainly. War is a dirty business and I do not like dirt. I am not a soldier and I have no desire to seek the bubble reputation even in the cannon's mouth. Yet, here I am at the wars—whom God never intended to be other than a studious country gentleman. For, Melanie, bugles do not stir my blood nor drums entice my feet and I see too clearly that we have been betrayed, betrayed by our arrogant Southern selves, believing that one of us could whip a dozen Yankees, believing that King Cotton could rule the world. Betrayed, too, by words and catch-phrases, prejudices and hatreds coming from the mouths of those highly placed, those men whom we respected and revered—'King Cotton, Slavery, States' Rights, Damn' Yankees'.

"And so when I lie on my blanket and look up at the stars and say 'What are you fighting for?' I think of States' Rights and cotton and the darkies and the Yankees whom we have been bred up to hate, and I know that none of these is the reason why I am fighting. Instead, I see Twelve Oaks and remember how the moonlight slants across the white columns, and the unearthly way the magnolias look, opening under the moon, and how the climbing roses make the side porch shady even at hottest noon. And I see Mother, sewing there, as she did when I was a little boy. And I hear the darkies coming home across the fields at dusk, tired and singing and ready for supper, and the sound of the windlass as the bucket goes down into the cool well. And there's the long view down the road to the river, across the cotton fields, and the mist rising from the bottom lands in the twilight. And that is why I'm here who have no love of death or misery or glory and no hatred for anyone. Perhaps that is what is called patriotism, love of home and country. But, Melanie, it goes deeper than that. For, Melanie, these things I have named are but the symbols of the thing for which I risk my life, symbols of the kind of life I love. For I am fighting for the old days, the old ways I love so much but which, I fear, are now gone forever, no matter how the die may fall. For, win or lose, we lose just the same.

"If we win this war and have the Cotton Kingdom of our dreams, we still have lost, for we will become a different people and the old quiet ways will go. The world will be at our doors clamouring for cotton and we can command our own price. Then, I fear, we will become like the Yankees, at whose money-making activities, acquisitiveness and commercialism we now sneer. And if we lose, Melanie, if we lose!

"I am not afraid of danger or capture or wounds or even death, if death must come, but I do fear that once this war is over, we will never get back to the old times. And I belong in those old times. I do not belong in this mad present of killing and I fear I will not fit into any future, try though I may. Nor will you, my dear, for you and I are of the same blood. I do not know what the future will bring, but it cannot be as beautiful or as satisfying as the past.

"I lie and look at the boys sleeping near me and I wonder if the twins or Alex or Cade think these same thoughts. I wonder if they know they are fighting for a Cause that was lost the minute the first shot was fired, for our Cause is really our own way of living and that is gone already. But I do not think they think these things and they are lucky.

"I had not thought of this for us when I asked you to marry me. I had thought of life going on at Twelve Oaks as it had always done, peacefully, easily, unchanging. We are alike, Melanie, loving the same quiet things, and I saw before us a long stretch of uneventful years in which to read, hear music and dream. But not this! Never this! That this could happen to us all, this wrecking of old ways, this bloody slaughter and hate! Melanie, nothing is worth it—States' Rights, nor slaves, nor cotton. Nothing is worth what is happening to us now and what may happen, for if the Yankees whip us the future will be one of incredible horror. And, my dear, they may yet whip us.

"I should not write those words. I should not even think them. But you have asked me what was in my heart, and the fear of defeat is there. Do you remember at the barbecue, the day our engagement was announced, that a man named Butler, a Charlestonian by his accent, nearly caused a fight by his remarks about the ignorance of Southerners? Do you recall how the twins wanted to shoot him because he said we had few foundries and factories, mills and ships, arsenals and machine shops? Do you recall how he said the Yankee fleet could bottle us up so tightly we could not ship out our cotton? He was right. We are fighting the Yankees' new rifles with Revolutionary War muskets, and soon the blockade will be too tight for even medical supplies to slip in. We should have paid heed to cynics like Butler who knew, instead of statesmen who felt —and talked. He said, in effect, that the South had nothing with which to wage war but cotton and arrogance. Our cotton is worthless and what he called arrogance is all that is left. But I call that arrogance matchless courage. If—"

But Scarlett folded up the letter without finishing it and thrust it back into the envelope, too bored to read farther. Besides, the tone of the letter vaguely depressed her with its foolish talk of defeat. After all, she wasn't reading Melanie's mail to learn Ashley's puzzling and uninteresting ideas. She had had to listen to enough of them when he sat on the porch at Tara in days gone by.

All she wanted to know was whether he wrote impassioned letters to his wife. So far he had not. She had read every letter in the writing-box and there was nothing in any one of them that a brother might not have written to a sister. They were affectionate, humorous, discursive, but not the letters of a lover. Scarlett had received too many ardent love letters herself not to recognize the authentic note of passion when she saw it. And that note was missing. As always after her secret readings, a feeling of smug satisfaction enveloped her, for she felt certain that Ashley still loved her. And always she wondered sneeringly why Melanie did not realize that Ashley only loved her as a friend. Melanie evidently found nothing lacking in her husband's messages, but Melanie had had no other man's love letters with which to compare Ashley's.

"He writes such crazy letters," Scarlett thought. "If ever any husband of mine wrote me such twaddle-twaddle, he'd certainly hear from me! Why, even Charlie wrote better letters than these."

She flipped back the edges of the letters, looking at the dates, remembering their contents. In them there were no fine descriptive passages of bivouacs and charges such as Darcy Meade wrote his parents or poor Dallas McLure had written his old-maid sisters, Misses Faith and Hope. The Meades and the McLures proudly read these letters all over the neighbourhood, and Scarlett had frequently felt a secret shame that Melanie had no such letters from Ashley to read aloud at sewing circles.

It was as though when writing to Melanie, Ashley tried to ignore the war altogether, and sought to draw about the two of them a magic circle of timelessness, shutting out everything that had happened since Fort Sumter was the news of the day. It was almost as if he were trying to believe there wasn't any war. He wrote of books which he and Melanie had read and songs they had sung, of old friends they knew and places he had visited on his Grand Tour. Through the letters ran a wistful yearning to be back home at Twelve Oaks, and for pages he wrote of the hunting and the long rides through the still forest paths under frosty autumn stars, the barbecues, the fish-fries, the quiet of moonlight nights and the serene charm of the old house.

She thought of his words in the letter she had just read: "Not this! Never this!" and they seemed the cry of a tormented soul facing something he could not face, yet must face. It puzzled her for, if he was not afraid of wounds and death, what was it he feared? Unanalytical, she struggled with the complex thought.

"The war disturbs him and he—he doesn't like things that disturb him. . . . Me, for instance. . . . He loved me but he was afraid to marry me because—for fear I'd upset his way of thinking and living. No, it wasn't exactly that he was afraid. Ashley isn't a coward. He couldn't be when he's been mentioned in dispatches and when Colonel Sloan wrote that letter to Melly all about his gallant conduct in leading the charge. Once he's made up his mind to something, no one could be braver or more determined but— He lives inside his head instead of outside in the world and he hates to come out into the world and—Oh, I don't know what it is! If I'd just understood this one thing about him years ago, I know he'd have married me."

She stood for a moment holding the letters to her breast, thinking longingly of Ashley. Her emotions toward him had not changed since the day when she first fell in love with him. They were the same emotions that struck her speechless that day when she was fourteen years old and she had stood on the porch of Tara and seen Ashley ride up smiling, his hair shining silver in the morning sun. Her love was still a young girl's adoration for a man she could not understand, a man who possessed all the qualities she did not own but which she admired. He was still a young girl's dream of the Perfect Knight and her dream asked no more than acknowledgment of his love, went no further than hopes of a kiss.

After reading the letters, she felt certain he did love her, Scarlett, even though he had married Melanie, and that certainty was almost all that she desired. She was still that young and untouched. Had Charles with his fumbling awkwardness and his embarrassed intimacies tapped any of the deep vein of passionate feeling within her, her dreams of Ashley would not be ending with a kiss. But those few moonlight nights alone with Charles had not touched her emotions or ripened her to maturity. Charles had awakened no idea of what passion might be or tenderness or true intimacy of body or spirit.

All that passion meant to her was servitude to inexplicable male madness, unshared by females, a painful and embarrassing process that led inevitably to the still more painful process of childbirth. That marriage should be like this was no surprise to her. Ellen had hinted before the wedding that marriage was something women must bear with dignity and fortitude, and the whispered comments of other matrons since her widowhood had confirmed this. Scarlett was glad to be done with passion and marriage.

She was done with marriage but not with love,

for her love for Ashley was something different, having nothing to do with passion or marriage, something sacred and breath-takingly beautiful, an emotion that grew stealthily through the long days of her enforced silence, feeding on oft-thumbed memories and hopes.

She sighed as she carefully tied the ribbon about the packet, wondering for the thousandth time just what it was in Ashley that eluded her understanding. She tried to think the matter to some satisfactory conclusion but, as always, the conclusion evaded her uncomplex mind. She put the letters back in the lap secretary and closed the lid. Then she frowned, for her mind went back to the last part of the letter she had just read, to his mention of Captain Butler. How strange that Ashley should be impressed by something that scamp had said a year ago! Undeniably Captain Butler was a scamp, for all that he danced divinely. No one but a scamp would say the things about the Confederacy that he had said at the bazaar.

She crossed the room to the mirror and patted her smooth hair approvingly. Her spirits rose, as always at the sight of her white skin and slanting green eyes, and she smiled to bring out her dimples. Then she dismissed Captain Butler from her mind as she happily viewed her reflection, remembering how Ashley had always liked her dimples. No pang of conscience at loving another woman's husband or reading that woman's mail disturbed her pleasure in her youth and charm and her renewed assurance of Ashley's love.

She unlocked the door and went down the dim winding stair with a light heart. Half-way down she began singing "When This Cruel War Is Over".

5

THE war went on, successfully for the most part, but people had stopped saying "One more victory and the war is over," just as they had stopped saying the Yankees were cowards. It was obvious to all now that the Yankees were far from cowardly and that it would take more than one victory to conquer them. However, there were the Confederate victories in Tennessee scored by General Morgan and General Forrest and the triumph at the Second Battle of Bull Run hung up like visible Yankee scalps to gloat over. But there was a heavy price on these scalps. The hospitals and homes of Atlanta were overflowing with sick and wounded, and more and more women were appearing in black. The monotonous rows of soldiers' graves at Oakland Cemetery stretched longer every day.

Confederate money had dropped alarmingly and the price of food and clothing had risen accordingly. The commissary was laying such heavy levies on foodstuffs that the tables of Atlanta were beginning to suffer. White flour was scarce and so expensive that corn bread was universal instead of biscuits, rolls and waffles. The butcher shops carried almost no beef and very little mutton, and that mutton cost so much only the rich could afford it. However, there was still plenty of hog meat, as well as chickens and vegetables.

The Yankee blockade about the Confederate ports had tightened, and luxuries such as tea, coffee, silks, whalebone stays, colognes, fashion magazines and books were scarce and dear. Even the cheapest cotton goods had skyrocketed in price and ladies were regretfully making their old dresses do another season. Looms that had gathered dust for years had been brought down from attics, and there were webs of homespun to be found in nearly every parlour. Everyone, soldiers, civilians, women, children and negroes, began to wear homespun. Grey, as the colour of the Confederate uniform, practically disappeared and homespun of a butternut shade took its place.

Already the hospitals were worrying about the scarcity of quinine, calomel, opium, chloroform and iodine. Linen and cotton bandages were too precious now to be thrown away when used, and every lady who nursed at the hospitals brought home baskets of bloody strips to be washed and ironed and returned for use on other sufferers.

But to Scarlett, newly emerged from the chrysalis of widowhood, all the war meant was a time of gaiety and excitement. Even the small privations of clothing and food did not annoy her, so happy was she to be in the world again.

When she thought of the dull times of the past year, with the days going by one very much like another, life seemed to have quickened to an incredible speed. Every day dawned as an exciting adventure, a day in which she would meet new men who would ask to call on her, tell her how pretty she was, and how it was a privilege to fight and, perhaps, to die for her. She could and did love Ashley with the last breath in her body, but that did not prevent her from inveigling other men into asking to marry her.

The ever-present war in the background lent a pleasant informality to social relations, an informality which older people viewed with alarm. Mothers found strange men calling on their daughters, men who came without letters of introduction and whose antecedents were unknown. To their horror, mothers found their daughters holding hands with these men. Mrs. Merriwether, who had never kissed her husband until after the wedding ceremony, could scarcely believe her eyes when she caught Maybelle kissing the little Zouave, René Picard, and her consternation was even greater when Maybelle refused to be ashamed. Even the fact that René immediately asked for her hand did not improve matters. Mrs. Merriwether felt that the South was heading for a complete moral collapse and frequently said so. Other mothers concurred heartily with her and blamed it on the war.

But men who expected to die within a week or a month could not wait a year before they begged to call a girl by her first name, with "Miss", of course, preceding it. Nor would they go through the formal and protracted courtships which good manners had prescribed before the war. They were likely to propose in three or four months. And girls who knew very well that a lady always refused a gentleman the first three times he proposed rushed headlong to accept the first time.

This informality made the war a lot of fun for Scarlett. Except for the messy business of nursing and the bore of bandage rolling, she did not care if the war lasted forever. In fact, she could endure the hospital with equanimity now because it was a perfect happy hunting-ground. The helpless wounded succumbed to her charms without a struggle. Renew their bandages, wash their faces, pat up their pillows and fan them, and they fell in love. Oh, it was Heaven after the last dreary year!

Scarlett was back again where she had been before she married Charles and it was as if she had never married him, never felt the shock of his death, never borne Wade. War and marriage and childbirth had passed over her without touching any deep chord within her and she was unchanged. She had a child but he was cared for so well by the others in the red-brick house she could almost forget him. In her mind and heart, she was Scarlett O'Hara again, the belle of the County. Her thoughts and activities were the same as they had been in the old days, but the field of her activities had widened immensely. Careless of the disapproval of Aunt Pitty's friends, she behaved as she had behaved before her marriage—went to parties, danced, went riding with soldiers, flirted, did everything she had done as a girl, except stop wearing mourning. This she knew would be a straw that would break the backs of Pittypat and Melanie. She was as charming a widow as she had been a girl, pleasant when she had her own way, obliging as long as it did not discommode her, vain of her looks and her popularity.

She was happy now where a few weeks before

she had been miserable, happy with her beaux and their reassurances of her charm, as happy as she could be with Ashley married to Melanie and in danger. But somehow it was easier to bear the thought of Ashley belonging to someone else when he was far away. With the hundreds of miles stretching between Atlanta and Virginia, he sometimes seemed as much hers as Melanie's.

So the autumn months of 1862 went swiftly by with nursing, dancing, driving and bandage rolling taking up all the time she did not spend on brief visits to Tara. These visits were disappointing, for she had little opportunity for the long quiet talks with her mother to which she looked forward while in Atlanta, no time to sit by Ellen while she sewed, smelling the faint fragrance of lemon verbena sachet as her skirts rustled, feeling her soft hands on her cheek in a gentle caress.

Ellen was thin and preoccupied now and on her feet from morning until long after the plantation was asleep. The demands of the Confederate commissary were growing heavier by the month, and hers was the task of making Tara produce. Even Gerald was busy, for the first time in many years, for he could get no overseer to take Jonas Wilkerson's place and he was riding his own acres. With Ellen too busy for more than a goodnight kiss and Gerald in the fields all day, Scarlett found Tara boring. Even her sisters were taken up with their own concerns. Suellen had now come to an "understanding" with Frank Kennedy and sang "When This Cruel War Is Over" with an arch meaning that Scarlett found wellnigh unendurable, and Carreen was too wrapped up in dreams of Brent Tarleton to be interesting company.

Though Scarlett always went home to Tara with a happy heart, she was never sorry when the inevitable letters came from Pitty and Melanie, begging her to return. Ellen always sighed at these times, saddened by the thought of her oldest daughter and her only grandchild leaving her.

"But I mustn't be selfish and keep you here when you are needed to nurse in Atlanta," she said. "Only—only, my darling, it seems that I never get the time to talk to you and to feel that you are my own little girl again before you are gone from me."

"I'm always your little girl," Scarlett would say and bury her head upon Ellen's breast, her guilt rising up to accuse her. She did not tell her mother that it was the dancing and the beaux which drew her back to Atlanta and not the service of the Confederacy. There were many things she kept from her mother these days. But, most of all, she kept secret the fact that Rhett Butler called frequently at Aunt Pittypat's house.

During the months that followed the bazaar, Rhett called whenever he was in town, taking Scarlett riding in his carriage, escorting her to danceables and bazaars and waiting outside the hospital to drive her home. She lost her fear of his betraying her secret, but there always lurked in the back of her mind the disquieting memory that he had seen her at her worst and knew the truth about Ashley. It was this knowledge that checked her tongue when he annoyed her. And he annoyed her frequently.

He was in his mid-thirties, older than any beau she had ever had, and she was as helpless as a child to control and handle him as she had handled beaux nearer her own age. He always looked as if nothing had ever surprised him and much had amused him and, when he had gotten her into a speechless temper, she felt that she amused him more than anything in the world. Frequently she flared into open wrath under his expert baiting, for she had Gerald's Irish temper along with the deceptive sweetness of face she had inherited from Ellen. Heretofore she had never bothered to control her temper except in Ellen's presence. Now it was painful to have to choke back words for fear of his amused grin. If only he would ever lose his temper too, then she would not feel at such a disadvantage.

After tilts with him from which she seldom emerged the victor, she vowed he was impossible, ill-bred and no gentleman and she would have nothing more to do with him. But sooner or later, he returned to Atlanta, called, presumably on Aunt Pitty, and presented Scarlett, with overdone gallantry, a box of bonbons he had brought her from Nassau. Or pre-empted a seat by her at a musicale or claimed her at a dance, and she was usually so amused by his bland impudence that she laughed and overlooked his past misdeeds until the next occurred.

For all his exasperating qualities, she grew to look forward to his calls. There was something exciting about him that she could not analyse, something different from any man she had ever known. There was something breath-taking in the grace of his big body which made his very entrance into a room like an abrupt physical impact, something in the impertinence and bland mockery of his dark eyes that challenged her spirit to subdue him.

"It's almost like I was in love with him!" she thought, bewildered. "But I'm not and I just can't understand it."

But the exciting feeling persisted. When he came to call, his complete masculinity made Aunt Pitty's well-bred and ladylike house seem small, pale and a trifle fusty. Scarlett was not the only member of the household who reacted strangely and unwillingly to his presence, for he kept Aunt Pitty in a flutter and a ferment.

While Pitty knew Ellen would disapprove of his calls on her daughter, and knew also that the edict of Charleston banning him from polite society was not one to be lightly disregarded, she could no more resist his elaborate compliments and hand-kissing than a fly can resist a honey-pot. Moreover, he usually brought her some little gift from Nassau which he assured her he had purchased especially for her and blockaded in at risk of his life—papers of pins and needles, buttons, spools of silk thread and hairpins. It was almost impossible to obtain these small luxuries now—ladies were wearing hand-whittled wooden hairpins and covering acorns with cloth for buttons—and Pitty lacked the moral stamina to refuse them. Besides, she had a childish love of surprise packages and could not resist opening his gifts. And, having once opened them, she did not feel that she could refuse them. Then, having accepted his gifts, she could not summon courage enough to tell him his reputation made it improper for him to call on three lone women who had no male protector. Aunt Pitty always felt that she needed a male protector when Rhett Butler was in the house.

"I don't know what it is about him," she would sigh helplessly. "But—well, I do think he'd be a nice, attractive man if I could just feel that—well, that deep down in his heart he respected women."

Since the return of her wedding ring, Melanie had felt that Rhett was a gentleman of rare refinement and delicacy and she was shocked at this remark. He was unfailingly courteous to her, but she was a little timid with him, largely because she was shy with any man she had not known from childhood. Secretly she was very sorry for him, a feeling which would have amused him had he been aware of it. She was certain that some romantic sorrow had blighted his life and made him hard and bitter, and she felt that what he needed was the love of a good woman. In all her sheltered life she had never seen evil and could scarcely credit its existence, and when gossip whispered things about Rhett and the girl in Charleston she was shocked and unbelieving. And, instead of turning her against him, it only made her more timidly gracious toward him because of her indignation at what she fancied was a gross injustice done him.

Scarlett silently agreed with Aunt Pitty. She, too, felt that he had no respect for any woman, unless perhaps for Melanie. She still felt unclothed every time his eyes ran up and down her figure. It was not that he ever said anything. Then she could have scorched him with hot words. It was the bold way his eyes looked out of his swarthy face with a displeasing air of insolence, as if all women were his property to be enjoyed in his own good time. Only with Melanie was this look absent. There was never that cool look of appraisal, never mockery in his eyes, when he looked at Melanie; and there was an especial note in his voice when he spoke to her, courteous, respectful, anxious to be of service.

"I don't see why you're so much nicer to her than to me," said Scarlett petulantly, one afternoon when Melanie and Pitty had retired to take their naps and she was alone with him.

For an hour she had watched Rhett hold the yarn Melanie was winding for knitting, had noted the blank inscrutable expression when Melanie talked at length and with pride of Ashley and his promotion. Scarlett knew Rhett had no exalted opinion of Ashley and cared nothing at all about the fact that he had been made a major. Yet he made polite replies and murmured the correct things about Ashley's gallantry.

"And if I so much as mention Ashley's name," she had thought irritably, "he cocks his eyebrow up and smiles that nasty, knowing smile!"

"I'm much prettier than she is," she continued, "and I don't see why you're nicer to her."

"Dare I hope that you are jealous?"

"Oh, don't presume!"

"Another hope crushed. If I am 'nicer' to Mrs. Wilkes, it is because she deserves it. She is one of the very few kind, sincere and unselfish persons I have ever known. But perhaps you have failed to note these qualities. And moreover, for all her youth, she is one of the few great ladies I have ever been privileged to know."

"Do you mean to say you don't think I'm a great lady, too?"

"I think we agreed on the occasion of our first meeting that you were no lady at all."

"Oh, if you are going to be hateful and rude enough to bring that up again! How can you hold that bit of childish temper against me? That was so long ago and I've grown up since then and I'd forget all about it if you weren't always harping and hinting about it."

"I don't think it was childish temper and I don't believe you've changed. You are just as capable now as then of throwing vases if you don't get your own way. But you usually get your way now. And so there's no necessity for broken bric-a-brac."

"Oh, you are—I wish I was a man! I'd call you out and—"

"And get killed for your pains. I can drill a dime at fifty yards. Better stick to your own weapons—dimples, vases and the like."

"You are just a rascal."

"Do you expect me to fly into a rage at that? I am sorry to disappoint you. You can't make me mad by calling me names that are true. Certainly I'm a rascal, and why not? It's a free country and a man may be a rascal if he chooses. It's only hypocrites like you, my dear lady, just as black at heart but trying to hide it, who become enraged when called by their right names."

She was helpless before his calm smile and his drawling remarks, for she had never before met anyone who was so completely impregnable. Her weapons of scorn, coldness and abuse blunted in her hands, for nothing she could say would shame him. It had been her experience that the liar was the hottest to defend his veracity, the coward his courage, the ill-bred his gentlemanliness, and the cad his honour. But not Rhett. He admitted everything and laughed and dared her to say more.

He came and went during these months, arriving unheralded and leaving without saying good-bye. Scarlett never discovered just what business brought him to Atlanta, for few other blockaders found it necessary to come so far away from the coast. They landed their cargoes at Wilmington or Charleston, where they were met by swarms of merchants and speculators from all over the South who assembled to buy blockaded goods at auction. It would have pleased her to think that he made these trips to see her, but even her abnormal vanity refused to believe this. If he had ever once made love to her, seemed jealous of the other men who crowded about her, even tried to hold her hand or begged for a picture or a handkerchief to cherish, she would have thought triumphantly he had been caught by her charms. But he remained annoyingly unloverlike and, worst of all, seemed to see through all her manoeuvrings to bring him to his knees.

Whenever he came to town, there was a feminine fluttering. Not only did the romantic aura of the dashing blockader hang about him but there was also the titillating element of the wicked and the forbidden. He had such a bad reputation! And every time the matrons of Atlanta gathered together to gossip, his reputation grew worse, which only made him all the more glamorous to the young girls. As most of them were quite innocent, they had heard little more than that he was "quite loose with women"—and exactly how a man went about the business of being "loose" they did not know. They also heard whispers that no girl was safe with him. With such a reputation, it was strange that he had never so much as kissed the hand of an unmarried girl since he first appeared in Atlanta. But that only served to make him more mysterious and more exciting.

Outside of the army heroes, he was the most talked-about man in Atlanta. Everyone knew in detail how he had been expelled from West Point for drunkenness and "something about women". That terrific scandal concerning the Charleston girl he had compromised and the brother he had killed was public property. Correspondence with Charleston friends elicited the further information that his father, a charming old gentleman with an iron will and a ramrod for a backbone, had cast him out without a penny when he was twenty and even stricken his name from the family Bible. After that he had wandered to California in the gold rush of 1849 and thence to South America and Cuba, and the reports of his activities in these parts were none too savoury. Scrapes about women, several shootings, gun running to the revolutionists in Central America and, worst of all, professional gambling were included in his career, as Atlanta heard it.

There was hardly a family in Georgia who could not own to their sorrow at least one male member or relative who gambled, losing money, houses, land and slaves. But that was different. A man could gamble himself to poverty and still be a gentleman, but a professional gambler could never be anything but an outcast.

Had it not been for the upset conditions due to the war and his own services to the Confederate government, Rhett Butler would never have been received in Atlanta. But now, even the most strait-laced felt that patriotism called upon them to be more broad-minded. The more sentimental were inclined to the view that the black sheep of the Butler family had repented of his evil ways and was making an attempt to atone for his sins. So the ladies felt in duty bound to stretch a point, especially in the case of so intrepid a blockader. Everyone knew now that the fate of the Confederacy rested as much upon the skill of the blockade boats in eluding the Yankee fleet as it did upon the soldiers at the front.

Rumour had it that Captain Butler was one of the best pilots in the South and that he was reckless and utterly without nerves. Reared in Charleston, he knew every inlet, creek, shoal and rock of the Carolina coast near that port, and he was equally at home in the waters around Wilmington. He had never lost a boat or even been forced to dump a cargo. At the onset of the war, he had emerged from obscurity with enough money to buy a small swift boat and now, when blockaded goods realized two thousand per cent. on each cargo, he owned four boats. He had good pilots and paid them well, and they slid out of Charleston and Wilmington on dark nights, bearing cotton for Nassau, England and Canada. The cotton mills of England were standing idle and the workers were starving, and any blockader who could outwit the Yankee fleet could command his own price in Liverpool. Rhett's boats were singularly lucky both in taking out cotton for the Confederacy and bringing in the war materials for which the South was desperate. Yes, the ladies felt they could forgive and forget a great many things for such a brave man.

He was a dashing figure and one that people turned to look at. He spent money freely, rode a wild black stallion, and wore clothes which were always the height of style and tailoring. The latter in itself was enough to attract attention to him, for the uniforms of the soldiers were dingy and worn now and the civilians, even when turned out in their best, showed skilful patching and darning. Scarlett thought she had never seen such elegant pants as he wore, fawn-coloured, shepherd's plaid, and checked. As for his waist-coats, they were indescribably handsome, especially the white watered-silk one with tiny pink rosebuds embroidered on it. And he wore these garments with a still more elegant air as though unaware of their glory.

There were few ladies who could resist his charms when he chose to exert them, and finally even Mrs. Merriwether unbent and invited him to Sunday dinner.

Maybelle Merriwether was to marry her little Zouave when he got his next furlough, and she cried every time she thought of it, for she had set her heart on marrying in a white satin dress and there was no white satin in the Confederacy. Nor could she borrow a dress, for the satin wedding dresses of years past had all gone into the making of battle flags. Useless for the patriotic Mrs. Merriwether to upbraid her daughter and point out that homespun was the proper bridal attire for a Confederate bride. Maybelle wanted satin. She was willing, even proud, to go without hair-pins and buttons and nice shoes and candy and tea for the sake of the Cause, but she wanted a satin wedding dress.

Rhett, hearing of this from Melanie, brought in from England yards and yards of gleaming white satin and a lace veil and presented them to her as a wedding gift. He did it in such a way that it was unthinkable to even mention paying him for them, and Maybelle was so delighted she almost kissed him. Mrs. Merriwether knew that so expensive a gift—and a gift of clothing at that—was highly improper, but she could think of no way of refusing when Rhett told her in the most florid language that nothing was too good to deck the bride of one of our brave heroes. So Mrs. Merriwether invited him to dinner, feeling that this concession more than paid for the gift.

He not only brought Maybelle the satin but he was able to give excellent hints on the making of the wedding dress. Hoops in Paris were wider this season and skirts were shorter. They were no longer ruffled but were gathered up in scalloped festoons, showing braided petticoats beneath. He said, too, that he had seen no pantalets on the streets, so he imagined they were "out". Afterwards, Mrs. Merriwether told Mrs. Elsing she feared that if she had given him any encouragement at all, he would have told her exactly what kind of drawers were being worn by Parisiennes.

Had he been less obviously masculine, his ability to recall details of dresses, bonnets and coiffures would have been put down as the rankest effeminacy. The ladies always felt a little odd when they besieged him with questions about styles, but they did it nevertheless. They were as isolated from the world of fashion as shipwrecked mariners, for few books of fashion came through the blockade. For all they knew the ladies of France might be shaving their heads and wearing coonskin caps, so Rhett's memory for furbelows was an excellent substitute for *Godey's Lady's Book*. He could and did notice details so dear to feminine hearts, and after each trip abroad he could be found in the centre of a group of ladies, telling that bonnets were smaller this year and perched higher, covering most of the top of the head, that plumes and not flowers were being used to trim them, that the Empress of France had abandoned the chignon for evening wear and had her hair piled almost on the top of her head, showing all of her ears, and that evening frocks were shockingly low again.

For some months, he was the most popular and

romantic figure the town knew, despite his previous reputation, despite the faint rumours that he was engaged not only in blockading but in speculating on foodstuffs, too. People who did not like him said that after every trip he made to Atlanta, prices jumped five dollars. But even with this under-cover gossip seeping about, he could have retained his popularity had he considered it worth retaining. Instead, it seemed as though, after trying the company of the staid and patriotic citizens and winning their respect and grudging liking, something perverse in him made him go out of his way to affront them and show them that his conduct had been only a masquerade and one which no longer amused him.

It was as though he bore an impersonal contempt for everyone and everything in the South, the Confederacy in particular, and took no pains to conceal it. It was his remarks about the Confederacy that made Atlanta look at him first in bewilderment, then coolly and then with hot rage. Even before 1862 passed into 1863, men were bowing to him with studied frigidity and women beginning to draw their daughters to their sides when he appeared at a gathering.

He seemed to take pleasure not only in affronting the sincere and red-hot loyalties of Atlanta but in presenting himself in the worst possible light. When well-meaning people compli-mented him on his bravery in running the blockade, he blandly replied that he was always frightened when in danger, as frightened as were the brave boys at the front. Everyone knew there had never been a cowardly Confederate soldier and they found this statement peculiarly irritating. He always referred to the soldiers as "our brave boys" or "our heroes in grey" and did it in such a way as to convey the utmost in insult. When daring young ladies, hoping for a flirtation, thanked him for being one of the heroes who fought for them, he bowed and declared that such was not the case, for he would do the same thing for Yankee women if the same amount of money were involved.

Since Scarlett's first meeting with him in Atlanta on the night of the bazaar, he had talked with her in this manner, but now there was a thinly veiled note of mockery in his conversations with everyone. When praised for his services to the Confederacy, he unfailingly replied that blockading was a business with him. If he could make as much money out of government contracts, he would say, picking out with his eyes those who had government contracts, then he would certainly abandon the hazards of blockading and take to selling shoddy cloth, sanded sugar, spoiled flour and rotten leather to the Confederacy.

Most of his remarks were unanswerable, which made them all the worse. There had already been minor scandals about those holding government contracts. Letters from men at the front complained constantly of shoes that wore out in a week, gunpowder that would not ignite, harness that snapped at any strain, meat that was rotten and flour that was full of weevils. Atlanta people tried to think that the men who sold such stuff to the government must be contract-holders from

Alabama or Virginia or Tennessee, and not Georgians. For did not the Georgia contract-holders include men from the very best families? Were they not the first to contribute to hospital funds and to the aid of soldiers' orphans? Were they not the first to cheer at "Dixie" and the most rampant seekers, in oratory at least, for Yankee blood? The full tide of fury against those profiteering on government contracts had not yet risen, and Rhett's words were taken merely as evidence of his own bad breeding.

He not only affronted the town with insinuations of venality on the part of men in high places and slurs on the courage of the men in the field, but he took pleasure in tricking the dignified citizenry into embarrassing situations. He could no more resist pricking the conceits, the hypocrisies and the flamboyant patriotism of those about him than a small boy can resist putting a pin into a balloon. He neatly deflated the pompous and exposed the ignorant and the bigoted, and he did it in such subtle ways, drawing his victims out by his seemingly courteous interest, that they never were quite certain what had happened until they stood exposed as windy, high-flown and slightly ridiculous.

During the months when the town accepted him, Scarlett had been under no illusions about him. She knew that his elaborate gallantries and his florid speeches were all done with his tongue in his cheek. She knew that he was acting the part of the dashing and patriotic blockade runner simply because it amused him. Sometimes he seemed to her like the County boys with whom she had grown up: the wild Tarleton twins with their obsession for practical jokes; the devil-inspired Fontaines, teasing, mischievous; the Calverts who would sit up all night planning hoaxes. But there was a difference, for beneath Rhett's seeming lightness there was something malicious, almost sinister in its suave brutality.

Though she was thoroughly aware of his insincerity, she much preferred him in the rôle of the romantic blockader. For one thing, it made her own situation in associating with him so much easier than it had been at first. So, she was intensely annoyed when he dropped his masquerade and set out apparently upon a deliberate campaign to alienate Atlanta's good will. It annoyed her because it seemed foolish and also because some of the harsh criticism directed at him fell on her.

It was at Mrs. Elsing's silver musicale for the benefit of the convalescents that Rhett signed his final warrant of ostracism. That afternoon the Elsing home was crowded with soldiers on leave and men from the hospitals, members of the Home Guard and the militia unit, and matrons, widows and young girls. Every chair in the house was occupied, and even the long winding stair was packed with guests. The large cut-glass bowl held at the door by the Elsings' butler had been emptied twice of its burden of silver coins. That in itself was enough to make the affair a success, for now a dollar in silver was worth sixty dollars in Confederate paper money.

Every girl with any pretence to accomplishments had sung or played the piano, and the tableaux vivants had been greeted with flattering applause. Scarlett was much pleased with herself, for not only had she and Melanie rendered a touching duet, "When the Dew Is on the Blossom", followed as an encore by the more sprightly "Oh, Lawd, Ladies, Don't Mind Stephen!" but she had also been chosen to represent the Spirit of the Confederacy in the last tableau.

She had looked most fetching, wearing a modestly draped Greek robe of white cheesecloth girdled with red and blue and holding the Stars and Bars in one hand, while with the other she stretched out to the kneeling Captain Carey Ashburn, of Alabama, the gold-hilted sabre which had belonged to Charles and his father.

When her tableau was over, she could not help seeking Rhett's eyes to see if he had appreciated the pretty picture she made. With a feeling of exasperation, she saw that he was in an argument and probably had not even noticed her. Scarlett could see by the faces of the group surrounding him that they were infuriated by what he was saying.

She made her way toward them and, in one of those odd silences which sometimes fall on a gathering, she heard Willie Guinan, of the militia outfit, say plainly: "Do I understand, sir, that you mean the Cause for which our heroes have died is not sacred?"

"If you were run over by a railroad train, your death wouldn't sanctify the railroad company, would it?" asked Rhett, and his voice sounded as if he were humbly seeking information.

"Sir," said Willie, his voice shaking, "if we were not under this roof—"

"I tremble to think what would happen," said Rhett. "For, of course, your bravery is too well known."

Willie went scarlet and all conversation ceased. Everyone was embarrassed. Willie was strong and healthy and of military age and yet he wasn't at the front. Of course, he was the only boy his mother had and, after all, somebody had to be in the militia to protect the state. But there were a few irreverent snickers from convalescent officers when Rhett spoke of bravery.

"Oh, why doesn't he keep his mouth shut!" thought Scarlett indignantly. "He's simply spoiling the whole party!"

Dr. Meade's brows were thunderous.

"Nothing may be sacred to you, young man," he said, in the voice he always used when making speeches. "But there are many things sacred to the patriotic men and ladies of the South. And the freedom of our land from the usurper is one and States' Rights is another and—"

Rhett looked lazy and his voice had a silky, almost bored, note.

"All wars are sacred," he said. "To those who have to fight them. If the people who started wars didn't make them sacred, who would be foolish enough to fight? But, no matter what rallying cries the orators give to the idiots who fight, no matter what noble purposes they assign to wars, there is never but one reason for a war. And that is money. All wars are in reality money squabbles. But so few people ever realize it. Their ears are too full of bugles and drums and fine words from stay-at-home orators. Sometimes the rallying cry is 'Save the Tomb of Christ from the Heathen!' Sometimes it's 'Down With Popery!' and sometimes 'Liberty!' and sometimes 'Cotton, Slavery and States' Rights!'"

"What on earth has the Pope to do with it?" thought Scarlett. "Or Christ's tomb, either?"

But as she hurried toward the incensed group, she saw Rhett bow jauntily and start toward the doorway through the crowd. She started after him but Mrs. Elsing caught her skirt and held her.

"Let him go," she said in a clear voice that carried throughout the tensely quiet room. "Let him go. He is a traitor, a speculator! He is a viper that we have nursed to our bosoms!"

Rhett, standing in the hall, his hat in his hand, heard as he was intended to hear and, turning, surveyed the room for a moment. He looked pointedly at Mrs. Elsing's flat bosom, grinned suddenly and, bowing, made his exit.

Mrs. Merriwether rode home in Aunt Pitty's carriage, and scarcely had the four ladies seated themselves when she exploded.

"There now, Pittypat Hamilton! I hope you are satisfied!"

"With what?" cried Pitty, apprehensively.

"With the conduct of that wretched Butler man you've been harbouring."

Pittypat fluttered, too upset by the accusation to recall that Mrs. Merriwether had also been Rhett Butler's hostess on several occasions. Scarlett and Melanie thought of this, but bred to politeness to their elders, refrained from remarking on the matter. Instead they studiously looked down at their mittened hands.

"He insulted us all and the Confederacy too," said Mrs. Merriwether, and her stout bust heaved violently beneath its glittering passementerie trimmings. "Saying that we were fighting for money! Saying that our leaders had lied to us! He should be put in jail. Yes, he should. I shall speak to Dr. Meade about it. If Mr. Merriwether were only alive, he'd tend to him! Now, Pitty Hamilton, you listen to me. You mustn't ever let that scamp come into your house again!"

"Oh," mumbled Pitty, helplessly, looking as if she wished she were dead. She looked appealingly at the two girls who kept their eyes cast down and then hopefully toward Uncle Peter's erect back. She knew he was listening attentively to every word and she hoped he would turn and take a hand in the conversation, as he frequently did. She hoped he would say, "Now, Miss Dolly, you let Miss Pitty be," but Peter made no move. He disapproved heartily of Rhett Butler and poor Pitty knew it. She sighed and said: "Well, Dolly, if you think—"

"I do think," returned Mrs. Merriwether firmly. "I can't imagine what possessed you to receive him in the first place. After this afternoon, there won't be a decent home in town that he'll be welcome in. Do get up some gumption and forbid him your house."

She turned a sharp eye on the girls. "I hope you two are marking my words," she continued, "for it's partly your fault, being so pleasant to

359

him. Just tell him politely but firmly that his presence and his disloyal talk are distinctly unwelcome at your house."

By this time Scarlett was boiling, ready to rear like a horse at the touch of a strange rough hand on its bridle. But she was afraid to speak. She could not risk Mrs. Merriwether writing another letter to her mother.

"You old buffalo!" she thought, her face crimson with suppressed fury. "How heavenly it would be to tell you just what I think of you and your bossy ways!"

"I never thought to live long enough to hear such disloyal words spoken of our Cause," went on Mrs. Merriwether, by this time in a ferment of righteous anger. "Any man who does not think our Cause is just and holy should be hanged! I don't want to hear of you two girls ever even speaking to him again—For Heaven's sake, Melly, what ails you?"

Melanie was white and her eyes were enormous.

"I will speak to him again," she said in a low voice. "I will not be rude to him. I will not forbid him the house."

Mrs. Merriwether's breath went out of her lungs as explosively as though she had been punched. Aunt Pitty's fat mouth popped open and Uncle Peter turned to stare.

"Now, why didn't I have the gumption to say that?" thought Scarlett, jealousy mixing with admiration. "How did that little rabbit ever get up spunk enough to stand up to old lady Merriwether?"

Melanie's hands were shaking but she went on hurriedly, as though fearing her courage would fail her if she delayed.

"I won't be rude to him because of what he said, because—It was rude of him to say it out loud—most ill-advised—but it's—it's what Ashley thinks. And I can't forbid the house to a man who thinks what my husband thinks. It would be unjust."

Mrs. Merriwether's breath had come back and she charged.

"Melly Hamilton, I never heard such a lie in all my life! There was never a Wilkes who was a coward—"

"I never said Ashley was a coward," said Melanie, her eyes beginning to flash. "I said he thinks what Captain Butler thinks, only he expresses it in different words. And he doesn't go around saying it at musicales, I hope. But he has written it to me."

Scarlett's guilty conscience stirred as she tried to recall what Ashley might have written that would lead Melanie to make such a statement, but most of the letters she had read had gone out of her head as soon as she finished reading them. She believed Melanie had simply taken leave of her senses.

"Ashley wrote me that we should not be fighting the Yankees. And that we have been betrayed into it by statesmen and orators mouthing catchwords and prejudices," said Melly rapidly. "He said nothing in the world was worth what this war was going to do to us. He said there wasn't anything at all to glory—it was just misery and dirt."

"Oh! That letter," thought Scarlett. "Was that what he meant?"

"I don't believe it," said Mrs. Merriwether firmly. "You misunderstood his meaning."

"I never misunderstand Ashley," Melanie replied quietly, though her lips were trembling. "I understand him perfectly. He meant exactly what Captain Butler meant, only he didn't say it in a rude way."

"You should be ashamed of yourself, comparing a fine man like Ashley Wilkes to a scoundrel like Captain Butler! I suppose you, too, think the Cause is nothing!"

"I—I don't know what I think," Melanie began uncertainly, her fire deserting her and panic at her outspokenness taking hold of her. "I —I'd die for the Cause, like Ashley would. But —I mean—I mean, I'll let the men folks do the thinking, because they are so much smarter."

"I never heard the like," snorted Mrs. Merriwether. "Stop, Uncle Peter, you're driving past my house!"

Uncle Peter, preoccupied with the conversation behind him, had driven past the Merriwether carriage block and he backed up the horse. Mrs. Merriwether alighted, her bonnet ribbons shaking like sails in a storm.

"You'll be sorry," she said.

Uncle Peter whipped up the horse.

"You young misses ought ter tek shame, gittin' Miss Pitty in a state," he scolded.

"I'm not in a state," replied Pitty, surprisingly,

for less strain than this had frequently brought on fainting fits. "Melly, honey, I knew you were doing it just to take up for me and, really, I was glad to see somebody take Dolly down a peg. She's so bossy. How did you have the courage? But do you think you should have said that about Ashley?"

"But it's true," answered Melanie, and she began to cry softly. "And I'm not ashamed that he thinks that way. He thinks the war is all wrong but he's willing to fight and die anyway, and that takes lots more courage than fighting for something you think is right."

"Lawd, Miss Melly, doan cry hyah on Peachtree Street," groaned Uncle Peter, hastening his horse's pace. "Folks'll talk sumpin' scan'lous. Wait till us gits home."

Scarlett said nothing. She did not even squeeze the hand that Melanie had inserted into her palm for comfort. She had read Ashley's letters for only one purpose—to assure herself that he still loved her. Now Melanie had given a new meaning to passages in the letters which Scarlett's eyes had barely seen. It shocked her to realize that anyone as absolutely perfect as Ashley could have any thought in common with such a reprobate as Rhett Butler. She thought: "They both see the truth of this war, but Ashley is willing to die about it and Rhett isn't. I think that shows Rhett's good sense." She paused a moment, horror-struck that she could have such a thought about Ashley. "They both see the same unpleasant truth, but Rhett likes to look it in the face and enrage people by talking about it—and Ashley can hardly bear to face it."

It was very bewildering.

6

UNDER Mrs. Merriwether's goading, Dr. Meade took action, in the form of a letter to the newspaper wherein he did not mention Rhett by name, though his meaning was obvious. The editor, sensing the social drama of the letter, put it on the second page of the paper, in itself a startling innovation, as the first two pages of the paper were always devoted to advertisements of slaves, mules, ploughs, coffins, houses for sale or rent, cures for private diseases, abortifacients and restoratives for lost manhood.

The doctor's letter was the first of a chorus of indignation that was beginning to be heard all over the South against speculators, profiteers and holders of government contracts. Conditions in Wilmington, the chief blockade port, now that Charleston's port was practically sealed by the Yankee gunboats, had reached the proportions of an open scandal. Speculators swarmed Wilmington and, having the ready cash, bought up boatloads of goods and held them for a rise in prices. The rise always came, for with the increasing scarcity of necessities, prices leaped higher by the month. The civilian population had either to do without or buy at the speculators' prices, and the poor and those in moderate circumstances were suffering increasing hardships. With the rise in prices, Confederate money sank, and with its rapid fall there rose a wild passion for luxuries. Blockaders were commissioned to bring in necessities and were permitted to trade in luxuries only as a side line, but now it was the higher-priced luxuries that filled their boats to the exclusion of the things the Confederacy vitally needed. People frenziedly bought these luxuries with the money they had to-day, fearing that to-morrow's prices would be higher and the money worth less.

To make matters worse, there was only one railroad line from Wilmington to Richmond and, while thousands of barrels of flour and boxes of bacon spoiled and rotted in wayside stations for want of transportation, speculators with wines, taffetas and coffee to sell seemed always able to get their goods to Richmond two days after they were landed at Wilmington.

The rumour which had been creeping about underground was now being openly discussed, that Rhett Butler not only ran his own four boats and sold the cargoes at unheard-of prices, but bought up the cargoes of other boats and held them for rises in prices. It was said that he was at the head of a combine worth more than a million dollars, with Wilmington as its headquarters for the purpose of buying blockade goods on the docks. They had dozens of warehouses in that city and in Richmond, so the story ran, and the warehouses were crammed with food and clothing that were being held for higher prices. Already soldiers and civilians alike were feeling the pinch, and the muttering against him and his fellow speculators was bitter.

"There are many brave and patriotic men in

the blockade arm of the Confederacy's naval service," ran the last of the doctor's letter, "unselfish men who are risking their lives and all their wealth that the Confederacy may survive. They are enshrined in the hearts of all loyal Southerners, and no one begrudges them the scant monetary returns they make for their risks. They are unselfish gentlemen, and we honour them. Of these men, I do not speak.

"But there are others, scoundrels, who masquerade under the cloak of the blockader for their own selfish gains, and I call down the just wrath and vengeance of an embattled people, fighting in the justest of Causes, on these human vultures who bring in satins and laces when our men are dying for want of quinine, who load their boats with tea and wines when our heroes are writhing for lack of morphia. I execrate these vampires who are sucking the lifeblood of the men who follow Robert Lee—these men who are making the very name of blockader a stench in the nostrils of all patriotic men. How can we endure these scavengers in our midst with their varnished boots when our boys are tramping bare-foot into battle? How can we tolerate them with their champagnes and their pâtés of Strasbourg when our soldiers are shivering about their camp-fires and gnawing mouldy bacon? I call upon every loyal Confederate to cast them out."

Atlanta read, knew the oracle had spoken, and, as loyal Confederates, they hastened to cast Rhett out.

Of all the homes which had received him in the fall of 1862, Miss Pittypat's was almost the only

367

one into which he could enter in 1863. And, except for Melanie, he probably would not have been received there. Aunt Pitty was in a state whenever he was in town. She knew very well what her friends were saying when she permitted him to call but she still lacked the courage to tell him he was unwelcome. Each time he arrived in Atlanta, she set her fat mouth and told the girls that she would meet him at the door and forbid him to enter. And each time he came, a little package in his hand and a compliment for her charm and beauty on his lips, she wilted.

"I just don't know what to do," she would moan. "He just looks at me and I—I'm scared to death of what he would do if I told him. He's got such a bad reputation. Do you suppose he would strike me—or—or—Oh, dear, if Charlie were only alive! Scarlett, *you* must tell him not to call again—tell him in a nice way. Oh, me! I do believe you encourage him, and the whole town is talking and, if your mother ever finds out, what will she say to me? Melly, you must not be so nice to him. Be cool and distant and he will understand. Oh, Melly, do you think I'd better write Henry a note and ask him to speak to Captain Butler?"

"No, I don't," said Melanie. "And I won't be rude to him, either. I think people are acting like chickens with their heads off about Captain Butler. I'm sure he can't be all the bad things Dr. Meade and Mrs. Merriwether say he is. He wouldn't hold food from starving people. Why, he even gave me a hundred dollars for the orphans. I'm sure he's just as loyal and patriotic as any of us and he's just too proud to defend himself. You know how obstinate men are when they get their backs up."

Aunt Pitty knew nothing about men, either with their backs up or otherwise, and she could only wave her fat little hands helplessly. As for Scarlett, she had long ago become resigned to Melanie's habit of seeing good in everyone. Melanie was a fool, but there was nothing anybody could do about it.

Scarlett knew that Rhett was not being patriotic and, though she would have died rather than confess it, she did not care. The little presents he brought her from Nassau, little oddments that a lady could accept with propriety, were what mattered most to her. With prices as high as they were, where on earth could she get needles and bonbons and hairpins, if she forbade the house to him? No, it was easier to shift the responsibility to Aunt Pitty, who after all was the head of the house, the chaperon and the arbiter of morals. Scarlett knew the town gossiped about Rhett's calls, and about her too; but she also knew that in the eyes of Atlanta Melanie Wilkes could do no wrong, and if Melanie defended Rhett his calls were still tinged with respectability.

However, life would be pleasanter if Rhett would recant his heresies. She wouldn't have to suffer the embarrassment of seeing him cut openly when she walked down Peachtree Street with him.

"Even if you think such things, why do you say them?" she scolded. "If you'd just think what you please but keep your mouth shut, everything would be so much nicer."

"That's your system, isn't it, my green-eyed hypocrite? Scarlett, Scarlett! I hoped for more courageous conduct from you. I thought the Irish said what they thought and the Divvil take the hindermost. Tell me truthfully, don't you sometimes almost burst from keeping your mouth shut?"

"Well—yes," Scarlett confessed reluctantly. "I do get awfully bored when they talk about the Cause, morning, noon and night. But goodness, Rhett Butler, if I admitted it nobody would speak to me and none of the boys would dance with me!"

"Ah, yes, and one must be danced with, at all costs. Well, I admire your self-control but I do not find myself equal to it. Nor can I masquerade in a cloak of romance and patriotism, no matter how convenient it might be. There are enough stupid patriots who are risking every cent they have in the blockade and who are going to come out of this war paupers. They don't need me among their number, either to brighten the record of patriotism or to increase the roll of paupers. Let them have the haloes. They deserve them—for once I am being sincere—and, besides, haloes will be about all they will have in a year or so."

"I think you are very nasty to even hint such things when you know very well that England and France are coming in on our side in no time and—"

"Why, Scarlett! You must have been reading a newspaper! I'm surprised at you. Don't do it again. It addles women's brains. For your information, I was in England, not a month ago, and I'll tell you this. England will never help the Confederacy. England never bets on the underdog. That's why she's England. Besides, the fat Dutch woman who is sitting on the throne is a God-fearing soul and she doesn't approve of slavery. Let the English mill workers starve because they can't get our cotton but never, never strike a blow for slavery. And as for France, that weak imitation of Napoleon is far too busy establishing the French in Mexico to be bothered with us. In fact, he welcomes this war, because it keeps us too busy to run his troops out of Mexico. . . . No, Scarlett, the idea of assistance from abroad is just a newspaper invention to keep up the morale of the South. The Confederacy is doomed. It's living on its hump now, like the camel, and even the largest of humps aren't inexhaustible. I give myself about six months more of blockading and then I'm through. After that, it will be too risky. And I'll sell my boats to some foolish Englishman who thinks he can slip them through. But one way or the other, it's not bothering me. I've made money enough, and it's in English banks and in gold. None of this worthless paper for me."

As always when he spoke, he sounded so plausible. Other people might call his utterances treachery but, to Scarlett, they always rang with common sense and truth. And she knew that this was utterly wrong, knew she should be shocked and infuriated. Actually she was neither, but she could pretend to be. It made her feel more respectable and ladylike.

"I think what Dr. Meade wrote about you was right, Captain Butler. The only way to redeem yourself is to enlist after you sell your boats. You're a West Pointer and—"

"You talk like a Baptist preacher making a recruiting speech. Suppose I don't want to redeem myself? Why should I fight to uphold the system that cast me out? I shall take pleasure in seeing it smashed."

"I never heard of any system," she said crossly.

"No? And yet you are a part of it, like I was, and I'll wager you don't like it any more than I did. Well, why am I the black sheep of the Butler family? For this reason and no other—I didn't conform to Charleston and I couldn't. And Charleston is the South, only intensified. I wonder if you realize yet what a bore it is? So many things that one must do because they've always been done. So many things, quite harmless, that one must not do for the same reason. So many things that annoyed me by their senselessness. Not marrying the young lady, of whom you have probably heard, was merely the last straw. Why should I marry a boring fool, simply because an accident prevented me from getting her home before dark? And why permit her wild-eyed brother to shoot and kill me, when I could shoot straighter? If I had been a gentleman, of course, I would have let him kill me and that would have wiped the blot from the Butler escutcheon. But —I like to live. And so I've lived and I've had a good time. . . . When I think of my brother, living among the sacred cows of Charleston, and most reverent toward them, and remember his stodgy wife and his Saint Cecilia Balls and his everlasting rice fields—then I know the compensation for breaking with the system. Scarlett, our Southern way of living is as antiquated as the feudal system of the Middle Ages. The wonder is that it's lasted as long as it has. It had to go and it's going now. And yet you expect me to listen to orators like Dr. Meade who tell me our Cause is just and holy? And get so excited by the roll of drums that I'll grab a musket and rush off to Virginia to shed my blood for Marse Robert? What kind of a fool do you think I am? Kissing the rod that chastised me is not in my line. The South and I are even now. The South threw me out to starve once. I haven't starved, and I am making enough money out of the South's death-throes to compensate me for my lost birthright."

"I think you are vile and mercenary," said Scarlett, but her remark was automatic. Most of what he was saying went over her head, as did any conversation that was not personal. But part of it made sense. There were such a lot of foolish things about life among nice people. Having to pretend that her heart was in the grave when it wasn't. And how shocked everybody had been when she danced at the bazaar. And the infuriating way people lifted their eyebrows every time she did or said anything the least bit different from what every other young woman did and said. But still, she was jarred at hearing him attack the very traditions that irked her most. She had lived too long among people who dissembled

373

politely not to feel disturbed at hearing her own thoughts put into words.

"Mercenary? No, I'm only farsighted. Though perhaps that is merely a synonym for mercenary. At least, people who were not as farsighted as I will call it that. Any loyal Confederate who had a thousand dollars in cash in 1861 could have done what I did, but how few were mercenary enough to take advantage of their opportunities! As for instance, right after Fort Sumter fell and before the blockade was established, I bought up several thousand bales of cotton at dirt-cheap prices and ran them to England. They are still there in warehouses in Liverpool. I've never sold them. I'm holding them until the English mills have to have cotton and will give me any price I ask. I wouldn't be surprised if I got a dollar a pound."

"You'll get a dollar a pound when elephants roost in trees!"

"I believe I'll get it. Cotton is at seventy-two cents a pound already. I'm going to be a rich man when this war is over, Scarlett, because I was farsighted—pardon me, mercenary. I told you once before that there were two times for making big money, one in the upbuilding of a country and the other in its destruction. Slow money on the upbuilding, fast money in the crack-up. Remember my words. Perhaps they may be of use to you some day."

"I do appreciate good advice so much," said Scarlett, with all the sarcasm she could muster. "But I don't need your advice. Do you think Pa is a pauper? He's got all the money I'll ever need and then I have Charles' property besides."

"I imagine the French aristocrats thought practically the same thing until the very moment when they climbed into the tumbrils."

Frequently Rhett pointed out to Scarlett the inconsistency of her wearing black mourning clothes when she was participating in all social activities. He liked bright colours and Scarlett's funereal dresses and the crêpe veil that hung from her bonnet to her heels both amused him and offended him. But she clung to her dull black dresses and her veil, knowing that if she changed them for colours without waiting several more years, the town would buzz even more than it was already buzzing. And besides, how would she ever explain to her mother?

Rhett said frankly that the crêpe veil made her look like a crow and the black dresses added ten years to her age. This ungallant statement sent her flying to the mirror to see if she really did look twenty-eight instead of eighteen.

"I should think you'd have more pride than to try to look like Mrs. Merriwether," he taunted. "And better taste than to wear that veil to advertise a grief I'm sure you never felt. I'll lay a wager with you. I'll have that bonnet and veil off your head and a Paris creation on it within two months."

"Indeed, no, and don't let's discuss it any further," said Scarlett, annoyed by his reference to Charles. Rhett, who was preparing to leave for

Wilmington for another trip abroad, departed with a grin on his face.

One bright summer morning some weeks later, he reappeared with a brightly trimmed hatbox in his hand and, after finding that Scarlett was alone in the house, he opened it. Wrapped in layers of tissue was a bonnet, a creation that made her cry, "Oh, the darling thing!" as she reached for it. Starved for the sight, much less the touch, of new clothes, it seemed the loveliest bonnet she had ever seen. It was of dark-green taffeta, lined with watered silk of a pale-jade colour. The ribbons that tied under the chin were as wide as her hand and they, too, were pale green. And curled about the brim of this confection was the perkiest of green ostrich plumes.

"Put it on," said Rhett, smiling.

She flew across the room to the mirror and popped it on her head, pushing back her hair to show her earrings and tying the ribbon under her chin.

"How do I look?" she cried, pirouetting for his benefit and tossing her head so that the plume danced. But she knew she looked pretty even before she saw confirmation in his eyes. She looked attractively saucy and the green of the lining made her eyes dark emerald and sparkling.

"Oh, Rhett, whose bonnet is it? I'll buy it. I'll give you every cent I've got for it."

"It's your bonnet," he said. "Who else could wear that shade of green? Don't you think I carried the colour of your eyes well in my mind?"

"Did you really have it trimmed just for me?"

"Yes, and there's 'Rue de la Paix' on the box, if that means anything to you."

It meant nothing to her, smiling at her reflection in the mirror. Just at this moment, nothing mattered to her except that she looked utterly charming in the first pretty hat she had put on her head in two years. What she couldn't do with this hat! And then her smile faded.

"Don't you like it?"

"Oh, it's a dream but—Oh, I do hate to have to cover this lovely green with crêpe and dye the feather black."

He was beside her quickly and his deft fingers untied the wide bow under her chin. In a moment the hat was back in its box.

"What are you doing? You said it was mine."

"But not to change to a mourning bonnet. I shall find some other charming lady with green eyes who appreciates my taste."

"Oh, you shan't! I'll die if I don't have it! Oh, please, Rhett, don't be mean! Let me have it."

"And turn it into a fright like your other hats? No."

She clutched at the box. That sweet thing that made her look so young and enchanting to be given to some other girl? Oh, never! For a moment she thought of the horror of Pitty and Melanie. She thought of Ellen and what she would say, and she shivered. But vanity was stronger.

"I won't change it. I promise. Now, do let me have it."

He gave her the box with a slightly sardonic

smile and watched her while she put it on again and preened herself.

"How much is it?" she asked suddenly, her face falling. "I have only fifty dollars but next month—"

"It would cost about two thousand dollars, Confederate money," he said with a grin at her woebegone expression.

"Oh, dear—Well, suppose I give you the fifty now and then when I get—"

"I don't want any money for it," he said. "It's a gift."

Scarlett's mouth dropped open. The line was so closely, so carefully drawn where gifts from men were concerned.

"Candy and flowers, dear," Ellen had said time and again, "and perhaps a book of poetry or an album or a small bottle of Florida water are the only things a lady may accept from a gentleman. Never, never any expensive gift, even from your fiancé. And never any gift of jewellery or wearing apparel, not even gloves or handkerchiefs. Should you accept such gifts, men would know you were no lady and would try to take liberties."

"Oh, dear," thought Scarlett, looking first at herself in the mirror and then at Rhett's unreadable face. "I simply can't tell him I won't accept it. It's too darling. I'd—I'd almost rather he took a liberty, if it was a very small one." Then she was horrified at herself for having such a thought and she turned pink.

"I'll—I'll give you the fifty dollars—"

"If you do I will throw it in the gutter. Or,

better still, buy masses for your soul. I'm sure your soul could do with a few masses."

She laughed unwillingly, and the laughing reflection under the green brim decided her instantly.

"Whatever are you trying to do to me?"

"I'm tempting you with fine gifts until your girlish ideals are quite worn away and you are at my mercy," he said. "'Accept only candy and flowers from gentlemen, dearie,'" he mimicked, and she burst into a giggle.

"You are a clever, black-hearted wretch, Rhett Butler, and you know very well this bonnet's too pretty to be refused."

His eyes mocked her, even while they complimented her beauty.

"Of course, you can tell Miss Pitty that you gave me a sample of taffeta and green silk and drew a picture of the bonnet and I extorted fifty dollars from you for it."

"No. I shall say one hundred dollars and she'll tell everybody in town and everybody will be green with envy and talk about my extravagance. But, Rhett, you mustn't bring me anything else so expensive. It's awfully kind of you, but I really couldn't accept anything else."

"Indeed? Well, I shall bring you presents so long as it pleases me and so long as I see things that will enhance your charms. I shall bring you dark-green watered silk for a frock to match the bonnet. And I warn you that I am not kind. I am tempting you with bonnets and bangles and leading you into a pit. Always remember I never do anything without reason and I never give anything without expecting something in return. I always get paid."

His black eyes sought her face and travelled to her lips. Scarlett cast down her eyes, excitement filling her. Now, he was going to try to take liberties, just as Ellen predicted. He was going to kiss her, or try to kiss her, and she couldn't quite make up her flurried mind which it should be. If she refused, he might jerk the bonnet right off her head and give it to some other girl. On the other hand, if she permitted one chaste peck, he might bring her other lovely presents in the hope of getting another kiss. Men set such a store by kisses, though Heaven alone knew why. And lots of times, after one kiss they fell completely in love with a girl and made most entertaining spectacles of themselves, provided the girl was clever and withheld her kisses after the first one. It would be so exciting to have Rhett Butler in love with her and admitting it and begging for a kiss or a smile. Yes, she would let him kiss her.

But he made no move to kiss her. She gave him a sidelong glance from under her lashes and murmured encouragingly.

"So you always get paid, do you? And what do you expect to get from me?"

"That remains to be seen."

"Well, if you think I'll marry you to pay for the bonnet, I won't," she said daringly and gave her head a saucy flirt that set the plume to bobbing.

His white teeth gleamed under his little moustache.

"Madam, you flatter yourself. I do not want to

marry you or anyone else. I am not a marrying man."

"Indeed!" she cried, taken aback and now determined that he should take some liberty. "I don't even intend to kiss you, either."

"Then why is your mouth all pursed up in that ridiculous way?"

"Oh!" she cried as she caught a glimpse of herself and saw that her red lips were indeed in the proper pose for a kiss. "Oh!" she cried again, losing her temper and stamping her foot. "You are the horridest man I have ever seen and I don't care if I never lay eyes on you again!"

"If you really felt that way, you'd stamp on the bonnet. My, what a passion you are in and it's quite becoming, as you probably know. Come, Scarlett, stamp on the bonnet to show me what you think of me and my presents."

"Don't you dare touch this bonnet," she said, clutching it by the bow and retreating. He came after her, laughing softly, and took her hands in his.

"Oh, Scarlett, you are so young you wring my heart," he said. "And I shall kiss you, as you seem to expect it," and leaning down carelessly, his moustache just grazed her cheek. "Now, do you feel that you must slap me to preserve the proprieties?"

Her lips mutinous, she looked up into his eyes and saw so much amusement in their dark depths that she burst into laughter. What a tease he was and how exasperating! If he didn't want to marry her and didn't even want to kiss her, what did he want? If he wasn't in love with her, why did he call so often and bring her presents?

"That's better," he said. "Scarlett, I'm a bad influence on you and if you have any sense you will send me packing—if you can. I'm very hard to get rid of. But I'm bad for you."

"Are you?"

"Can't you see it? Ever since I met you at the bazaar, your career has been most shocking and I'm to blame for most of it. Who encouraged you to dance? Who forced you to admit that you thought our glorious Cause was neither glorious nor sacred? Who goaded you into admitting that you thought men were fools to die for high-sounding principles? Who has aided you in giving the old ladies plenty to gossip about? Who is getting you out of mourning several years too soon? And who, to end all this, has lured you into accepting a gift which no lady can accept and still remain a lady?"

"You flatter yourself, Captain Butler. I haven't done anything so scandalous and I'd have done everything you mentioned without your aid anyway."

"I doubt that," he said, and his face was suddenly quiet and sombre. "You'd still be the broken-hearted widow of Charles Hamilton and famed for your good deeds among the wounded. Eventually, however—"

But she was not listening, for she was regarding herself pleasedly in the mirror again, thinking she would wear the bonnet to the hospital this very afternoon and take flowers to the convalescent officers.

That there was truth in his last words did not occur to her. She did not see that Rhett had pried open the prison of her widowhood and set her free to queen it over unmarried girls when her days as a belle should have been long past. Nor did she see that under his influence she had come a long way from Ellen's teachings. The change had been so gradual, the flouting of one small convention seeming to have no connection with the flouting of another, and none of them any connection with Rhett. She did not realize that, with his encouragement, she had disregarded many of the sternest injunctions of her mother concerning the proprieties, forgotten the difficult lessons in being a lady.

She only saw that the bonnet was the most becoming one she ever had, that it had not cost her a penny and that Rhett must be in love with her, whether he admitted it or not. And she certainly intended to find a way to make him admit it.

The next day, Scarlett was standing in front of the mirror with a comb in her hand and her mouth full of hairpins, attempting a new coiffure which Maybelle, fresh from a visit to her husband in Richmond, had said was the rage at the Capital. It was called "Cats, Rats and Mice" and presented many difficulties. The hair was parted in the middle and arranged in three rolls of graduating size on each side of the head, the largest, nearest the part, being the "cat". The "cat" and the "rat" were easy to fix but the "mice" kept slipping out of her hairpins in an exasperating manner. However, she was determined to

383

accomplish it, for Rhett was coming to supper and he always noticed and commented upon any innovation of dress or hair.

As she struggled with her bushy, obstinate locks, perspiration beading her forehead, she heard light running feet in the downstairs hall and knew that Melanie was home from the hospital. As she heard her fly up the stairs, two at a time, she paused, hairpin in mid-air, realizing that something must be wrong, for Melanie always moved as decorously as a dowager. She went to the door and threw it open, and Melanie ran in, her face flushed and frightened, looking like a guilty child.

There were tears on her cheeks, her bonnet was hanging on her neck by the ribbons and her hoops swaying violently. She was clutching something in her hand, and the reek of heavy cheap perfume came into the room with her.

"Oh, Scarlett!" she cried, shutting the door and sinking on the bed. "Is Auntie home yet? She isn't? Oh, thank the Lord! Scarlett, I'm so mortified I could die! I nearly swooned and, Scarlett, Uncle Peter is threatening to tell Aunt Pitty!"

"Tell what?"

"That I was talking to that—to Miss—Mrs.—" Melanie fanned her hot face with her handkerchief. "That woman with red hair, named Belle Watling!"

"Why, Melly!" cried Scarlett, so shocked she could only stare.

Belle Watling was the red-haired woman she had seen on the street the first day she came to

384

Atlanta and, by now, she was easily the most notorious woman in town. Many prostitutes had flocked into Atlanta, following the soldiers, but Belle stood out above the rest, due to her flaming hair and the gaudy, overly fashionable dresses she wore. She was seldom seen on Peachtree Street or in any nice neighbourhood, but when she did appear respectable women made haste to cross the street to remove themselves from her vicinity. And Melanie had been talking with her. No wonder Uncle Peter was outraged.

"I shall die if Aunt Pitty finds out! You know she'll cry and tell everybody in town and I'll be disgraced," sobbed Melanie. "And it wasn't my fault. I—I couldn't run away from her. It would have been so rude. Scarlett, I—I felt sorry for her. Do you think I'm bad for feeling that way?"

But Scarlett was not concerned with the ethics of the matter. Like most innocent and well-bred young women, she had a devouring curiosity about prostitutes.

"What did she want? What does she talk like?"

"Oh, she used awful grammar but I could see she was trying so hard to be elegant, poor thing. I came out of the hospital and Uncle Peter and the carriage weren't waiting, so I thought I'd walk home. And when I went by the Emersons' yard, there she was hiding behind the hedge! Oh, thank Heaven, the Emersons are in Macon! And she said, 'Please, Mrs. Wilkes, do speak a minute with me.' I don't know how she knew my name. I knew I ought to run as hard as I could but— well, Scarlett, she looked so sad and—well, sort of pleading. And she had on a black dress and

385

black bonnet and no paint and really looked decent but for that red hair. And before I could answer she said, 'I know I shouldn't speak to you but I tried to talk to that old peahen, Mrs. Elsing, and she ran me away from the hospital.'"

"Did she really call her a peahen?" said Scarlett pleasedly and laughed.

"Oh, don't laugh. It isn't funny. It seems that Miss—this woman, wanted to do something for the hospital—can you imagine it? She offered to nurse every morning and, of course, Mrs. Elsing must have nearly died at the idea and ordered her out of the hospital. And then she said, 'I want to do something, too. Ain't I a Confedrut, good as you?' And, Scarlett, I was right touched at her wanting to help. You know, she can't be all bad if she wants to help the Cause. Do you think I'm bad to feel that way?"

"For Heaven's sake, Melly, who cares if you're bad? What else did she say?"

"She said she'd been watching the ladies go by to the hospital and thought I had—a—a kind face and so she stopped me. She had some money and she wanted me to take it and use it for the hospital and not tell a soul where it came from. She said Mrs. Elsing wouldn't let it be used if she knew what kind of money it was. What kind of money! That's when I thought I'd swoon! And I was so upset and anxious to get away, I just said: 'Oh, yes, indeed, how sweet of you,' or something idiotic, and she smiled and said: 'That's right Christian of you,' and shoved this dirty handkerchief into my hand. Ugh, can you smell the perfume?"

Melanie held out a man's handkerchief, soiled and highly perfumed, in which some coins were knotted.

"She was saying thank you and something about bringing me some money every week and just then Uncle Peter drove up and saw me!" Melly collapsed into tears and laid her head on the pillow. "And when he saw who was with me, he—Scarlett, he *hollered* at me! Nobody has ever hollered at me before in my whole life. And he said, 'You git in dis hyah cah'ige dis minute!' Of course, I did, and all the way home he blessed me out and wouldn't let me explain and said he was going to tell Aunt Pitty. Scarlett, do go down and beg him not to tell her. Perhaps he will listen to you. It will kill Auntie if she knows I ever even looked that woman in the face. Will you?"

"Yes, I will. But let's see how much money is in here. It feels heavy."

She untied the knot and a handful of gold coins rolled out on the bed.

"Scarlett, there's fifty dollars here! And in gold!" cried Melanie, awed, as she counted the bright pieces. "Tell me, do you think it's all right to use this kind—well, money made—er—this way for the boys? Don't you think that maybe God will understand that she wanted to help and won't care if it is tainted? When I think of how many things the hospital needs—"

But Scarlett was not listening. She was looking at the dirty handkerchief, and humiliation and fury were filling her. There was a monogram in the corner in which were the initials "R. K. B.". In her top drawer was a handkerchief just like this, one that Rhett Butler had lent her only yesterday to wrap about the stems of wild flowers they had picked. She had planned to return it to him when he came to supper to-night.

So Rhett consorted with that vile Watling creature and gave her money. That was where the contribution to the hospital came from. Blockade gold. And to think that Rhett would have the gall to look a decent woman in the face after being with that creature! And to think that she could have believed he was in love with her! This proved he couldn't be.

Bad women and all they involved were mysterious and revolting matters to her. She knew that men patronized these women for purposes which no lady should mention—or, if she did mention them, in whispers and by indirection and euphemism. She had always thought that only common vulgar men visited such women. Before this moment, it had never occurred to her that nice men—that is, men she met at nice homes and with whom she danced— could possibly do such things. It opened up an entirely new field of thought and one that was horrifying. Perhaps all men did this! It was bad enough that they forced their wives to go through such indecent performances, but to actually seek out low women and pay them for such accommodation! Oh, men were all so vile, and Rhett Butler was the worst of them all!

She would take this handkerchief and fling it in his face and show him the door and never, never speak to him again. But no, of course she couldn't do that. She could never, never let him know she even realized that bad women existed, much less that he visited them. A lady could never do that.

"Oh," she thought in fury. "If I just wasn't a lady, what wouldn't I tell that varmint!"

And, crumpling the handkerchief in her hand, she went down the stairs to the kitchen in search of Uncle Peter. As she passed the stove, she shoved the handkerchief into the flames and with impotent anger watched it burn.

7

HOPE was rolling high in every Southern heart as the summer of 1863 came in. Despite privation and hardship, despite food speculators and kindred scourges, despite death and sickness and suffering which had now left their mark on nearly every family, the South was again saying, "One more victory and the war is over," saying it with even more happy assurance than in the summer before. The Yankees were proving a hard nut to crack but they were cracking at last.

Christmas of 1862 had been a happy one for Atlanta, for the whole South. The Confederacy had scored a smashing victory at Fredericksburg and the Yankee dead and wounded were counted in the thousands. There was universal rejoicing in that holiday season, rejoicing and thankfulness that the tide was turning. The army in butternut were now seasoned fighters, their generals had proven their mettle, and everyone knew that when the campaign reopened in the spring, the Yankees would be crushed for good and all.

Spring came and the fighting recommenced. May came and the Confederacy won another great victory at Chancellorsville. The South roared with elation.

Closer at home, a Union cavalry dash into Georgia had been turned into a Confederate triumph. Folks were still laughing and slapping each other on the back and saying: "Yes, sir! When old Nathan Bedford Forrest gets after them, they better git!" Late in April, Colonel Streight and eighteen hundred Yankee cavalry had made a surprise raid into Georgia, aiming at Rome, only a little more than sixty miles north of Atlanta. They had ambitious plans to cut the vitally important railroad between Atlanta and Tennessee and then swing southward into Atlanta to destroy the factories and the war supplies concentrated there in that key city of the Confederacy.

It was a bold stroke and it would have cost the South dearly, except for Forrest. With only one-third as many men—but what men and what riders!—he had started after them, engaged them before they even reached Rome, harassed them day and night and finally captured the entire force!

The news reached Atlanta almost simultaneously with the news of the victory at Chancellorsville, and the town fairly rocked with exultation and with laughter. Chancellorsville might be a more important victory but the capture of Streight's raiders made the Yankees positively ridiculous.

"No, sir, they'd better not fool with old Forrest," Atlanta said gleefully as the story was told over and over.

The tide of the Confederacy's fortune was running strong and full now, sweeping the people jubilantly along on its flood. True, the Yankees under Grant had been besieging Vicksburg since the middle of May. True, the South had suffered a sickening loss when Stonewall Jackson had been fatally wounded at Chancellorsville. True, Georgia had lost one of her bravest and most brilliant sons when General T. R. R. Cobb had been killed at Fredericksburg. But the Yankees just couldn't stand any more defeats like Fredericksburg and Chancellorsville. They'd have to give in, and then this cruel war would be over.

The first days of July came and with them the rumour, later confirmed by dispatches, that Lee was marching into Pennsylvania. Lee in the enemy's territory! Lee forcing battle! This was the last fight of the war!

Atlanta was wild with excitement, pleasure and a hot thirst for vengeance. Now the Yankees would know what it meant to have the war carried into their own country. Now they'd know what it meant to have fertile fields stripped, horses and cattle stolen, houses burned, old men and boys dragged off to prison and women and children turned out to starve.

Everyone knew what the Yankees had done in Missouri, Kentucky, Tennessee and Virginia. Even small children could recite with hate and fear the horrors the Yankees had inflicted upon the conquered territory. Already Atlanta was full of refugees from east Tennessee, and the town had heard first-hand stories from them of what suffering they had gone through. In that section, the Confederate sympathizers were in the minority and the hand of war fell heavily upon them, as it did on all the border states, neighbour informing against neighbour and brother killing brother. These refugees cried out to see

Pennsylvania one solid sheet of flame, and even the gentlest of old ladies wore expressions of grim pleasure.

But when the news trickled back that Lee had issued orders that no private property in Pennsylvania should be touched, that looting would be punished by death and that the army would pay for every article it requisitioned—then it needed all the reverence the General had earned to save his popularity. Not turn the men loose in the rich storehouses of that prosperous state? What was General Lee thinking of? And our boys so hungry and needing shoes and clothes and horses!

A hasty note from Darcy Meade to the doctor, the only first-hand information Atlanta received during those first days of July, was passed from hand to hand, with mounting indignation.

"Pa, could you manage to get me a pair of boots? I've been barefooted for two weeks now and I don't see any prospects of getting another pair. If I didn't have such big feet I could get them off dead Yankees like the other boys, but I've never yet found a Yankee whose feet were near as big as mine. If you can get me some, don't mail them. Somebody would steal them on the way and I wouldn't blame them. Put Phil on the train and send him up with them. I'll write you soon, where we'll be. Right now I don't know, except that we're marching north. We're in Maryland now and everybody says we're going on into Pennsylvania. . . .

"Pa, I thought that we'd give the Yanks a taste of their own medicine but the General says No, and personally I don't care to get shot just for the pleasure of burning some Yank's house. Pa, today we marched through the grandest cornfields you ever saw. We don't have corn like this down home. Well, I must admit we did a bit of private looting in that corn, for we were all pretty hungry and what the General don't know won't hurt him. But that green corn didn't do us a bit of good. All the boys have got dysentery anyway, and that corn made it worse. It's easier to walk with a leg wound than with dysentery. Pa, do try to manage some boots for me. I'm a captain now, and a captain ought to have boots, even if he hasn't got a new uniform or epaulets."

But the army was in Pennsylvania—that was all that mattered. One more victory and the war would be over, and then Darcy Meade could have all the boots he wanted, and the boys would come marching home and everybody would be happy again. Mrs. Meade's eyes grew wet as she pictured her soldier son home at last, home to stay.

On the third of July, a sudden silence fell on the wires from the north, a silence that lasted till midday of the fourth when fragmentary and garbled reports began to trickle into headquarters in Atlanta. There had been hard fighting in Pennsylvania, near a little town named Gettysburg, a great battle with all Lee's army massed. The news was uncertain, slow in coming, for the battle had been fought in the enemy's territory and the reports came first through Maryland, were relayed to Richmond and then to Atlanta.

Suspense grew and the beginnings of dread

slowly crawled over the town. Nothing was so bad as not knowing what was happening. Families with sons at the front prayed fervently that their boys were not in Pennsylvania, but those who knew their relatives were in the same regiment with Darcy Meade clamped their teeth and said it was an honour for them to be in the big fight that would lick the Yankees for good and all.

In Aunt Pitty's house, the three women looked into one another's eyes with fear they could not conceal. Ashley was in Darcy's regiment.

On the fifth came evil tidings, not from the North but from the West. Vicksburg had fallen, fallen after a long and bitter siege, and practically all the Mississippi River, from St. Louis to New Orleans, was in the hands of the Yankees. The Confederacy had been cut in two. At any other time, the news of this disaster would have brought fear and lamentation to Atlanta. But now they could give little thought to Vicksburg. They were thinking of Lee in Pennsylvania, forcing battle. Vicksburg's loss would be no catastrophe if Lee won in the East. There lay Philadelphia, New York, Washington. Their capture would paralyse the North and more than cancel off the defeat on the Mississippi.

The hours dragged by and the black shadow of calamity brooded over the town, obscuring the hot sun until people looked up startled into the sky as if incredulous that it was clear and blue instead of murky and heavy with scudding clouds. Everywhere, women gathered in knots, huddled in groups on front porches, on sidewalks, even in the middle of the streets, telling each other that no news is good news, trying to comfort each other, trying to present a brave appearance. But hideous rumours that Lee was killed, the battle lost, and enormous casualty lists coming in, fled up and down the quiet streets like darting bats. Though they tried not to believe, whole neighbourhoods, swayed by panic, rushed to town, to the newspapers, to headquarters, pleading for news, any news, even bad news.

Crowds formed at the depot, hoping for news from incoming trains, at the telegraph office, in front of the harried headquarters, before the locked doors of the newspapers. They were oddly still crowds, crowds that quietly grew larger and larger. There was no talking. Occasionally an old man's treble voice begged for news, and instead of inciting the crowd to babbling it only intensified the hush as they heard the oft-repeated: "Nothing on the wires yet from the North except that there's been fighting." The fringe of women on foot and in carriages grew greater and greater, and the heat of close-packed bodies and dust rising from restless feet were suffocating. The women did not speak, but their pale set faces pleaded with a mute eloquence that was louder than wailing.

There was hardly a house in the town that had not sent away a son, a brother, a father, a lover, a husband, to this battle. They all waited to hear the news that death had come to their homes. They expected death. They did not expect defeat. That thought they dismissed. Their men might be dying, even now, on the sun-parched grass of the Pennsylvania hills. Even now the Southern

396

ranks might be falling like grain before a hailstorm, but the Cause for which they fought could never fall. They might be dying in thousands but, like the fruit of the dragon's teeth, thousands of fresh men in grey and butternut with the Rebel yell on their lips would spring up from the earth to take their places. Where these men would come from, no one knew. They only knew, as surely as they knew there was a just and jealous God in Heaven, that Lee was miraculous and the Army of Virginia invincible.

Scarlett, Melanie and Miss Pittypat sat in front of the *Daily Examiner* office in the carriage with the top back, sheltered beneath their parasols. Scarlett's hands shook so that her parasol wobbled above her head, Pitty was so excited her nose quivered in her round face like a rabbit's, but Melanie sat as though carved of stone, her dark eyes growing larger and larger as time went by. She made only one remark in two hours, as she took a vial of smelling salts from her reticule and handed it to her aunt, the only time she had ever spoken to her, in her whole life, with anything but tenderest affection.

"Take this, Auntie, and use it if you feel faint. I warn you if you do faint you'll just have to faint and let Uncle Peter take you home, for I'm not going to leave this place till I hear about—till I hear. And I'm not going to let Scarlett leave me, either."

Scarlett had no intention of leaving, no intention of placing herself where she could not have the first news of Ashley. No, even if Miss Pitty died, she wouldn't leave this spot. Somewhere, Ashley was fighting, perhaps dying, and the newspaper office was the only place where she could learn the truth.

She looked about the crowd, picking out friends and neighbours: Mrs. Meade with her bonnet askew and her arm through that of fifteen-year-old Phil; the Misses McLure trying to make their trembling upper lips cover their buck teeth; Mrs. Elsing, erect as a Spartan mother, betraying her inner turmoil only by the straggling grey locks that hung from her chignon; and Fanny Elsing white as a ghost. (Surely Fanny wouldn't be so worried about her brother Hugh. Had she a real beau at the front that no one suspected?) Mrs. Merriwether sat in her carriage patting Maybelle's hand. Maybelle looked so very pregnant it was a disgrace for her to be out in public, even if she did have her shawl carefully draped over her. Why should she be so worried? Nobody had heard that the Louisiana troops were in Pennsylvania. Probably her hairy little Zouave was safe in Richmond this very minute.

There was a movement on the outskirts of the crowd and those on foot gave way as Rhett Butler carefully edged his horse toward Aunt Pitty's carriage. Scarlett thought: "He's got courage, coming here at this time when it wouldn't take anything to make this mob tear him to pieces because he isn't in uniform." As he came nearer, she thought she might be the first to rend him. How dared he sit there on that fine horse, in shining boots and handsome white linen suit, so sleek and well fed, smoking an expensive cigar, when Ashley and all the other boys were fighting the Yankees, barefooted, sweltering in the heat, hungry, their bellies rotten with disease?

Bitter looks were thrown at him as he came slowly through the press. Old men growled in their beards, and Mrs. Merriwether, who feared nothing, rose slightly in her carriage and said clearly, "Speculator!" in a tone that made the word the foulest and most venomous of epithets. He paid no heed to anyone but raised his hat to Melly and Aunt Pitty and, riding to Scarlett's side, leaned down and whispered: "Don't you think this would be the time for Dr. Meade to give us his familiar speech about victory perching like a screaming eagle on our banners?"

Her nerves taut with suspense, she turned on him as swiftly as an angry cat, hot words bubbling to her lips, but he stopped them with a gesture.

"I came to tell you ladies," he said loudly, "that I have been to headquarters and the first casualty lists are coming in."

At these words a hum rose among those near enough to hear his remark, and the crowd surged, ready to turn and run down Whitehall Street toward headquarters.

"Don't go," he called, rising in his saddle and holding up his hand. "The lists have been sent to both newspapers and are now being printed. Stay where you are!"

"Oh, Captain Butler," cried Melly, turning to him with tears in her eyes. "How kind of you to come and tell us! When will they be posted?"

"They should be out any minute, Madam. The reports have been in the offices for half an hour now. The major in charge didn't want to let that out until the printing was done, for fear the crowd would wreck the offices trying to get news. Ah! Look!"

The side window of the newspaper office opened and a hand was extended, bearing a sheaf of long narrow galley proofs, smeared with fresh ink and thick with names closely printed. The crowd fought for them, tearing the slips in half, those obtaining them trying to back out through the crowd to read, those behind pushing forward, crying: "Let me through!"

"Hold the reins," said Rhett shortly, swinging to the ground and tossing the bridle to Uncle Peter. They saw his heavy shoulders towering above the crowd as he went through, brutally pushing and shoving. In a while he was back, with half a dozen in his hands. He tossed one to Melanie and distributed the others among the ladies in the nearest carriages, the Misses McLure, Mrs. Meade, Mrs. Merriwether, Mrs. Elsing.

"Quick, Melly," cried Scarlett, her heart in her throat, exasperation sweeping her as she saw that Melly's hands were shaking so that it was impossible for her to read.

"Take it," whispered Melly, and Scarlett snatched it from her. The Ws. Where were the Ws? Oh, there they were at the bottom and all smeared up. "White," she read and her voice shook, "Wilkins . . . Winn . . . Zebulon . . . Oh, Melly, he's not on it! He's not on it! Oh, for God's sake, Auntie! Melly, pick up the salts! Hold her up, Melly."

Melly, weeping openly with happiness, steadied Miss Pitty's rolling head and held the smelling salts under her nose. Scarlett braced the fat old lady on the other side, her heart singing with joy. Ashley was alive. He wasn't even wounded. How good God was to pass him by! How—

She heard a low moan and, turning, saw Fanny Elsing lay her head on her mother's bosom, saw the casualty list flutter to the floor of the carriage, saw Mrs. Elsing's thin lips quiver as she gathered her daughter in her arms and said quietly to the coachman: "Home. Quickly." Scarlett took a quick glance at the lists. Hugh Elsing was not listed. Fanny must have had a beau and now he was dead. The crowd made way in sympathetic silence for the Elsings' carriage, and after them followed the little wicker pony cart of the McLure girls. Miss Faith was driving, her face like a rock, and, for once, her teeth were covered by her lips. Miss Hope, death in her face, sat erect beside her, holding her sister's skirt in a tight grasp. They looked like very old women. Their young brother Dallas was their darling and the only relative the maiden ladies had in the world. Dallas was gone.

"Melly! Melly!" cried Maybelle, joy in her voice, "René is safe! And Ashley, too! Oh, thank God!" The shawl had slipped from her shoulders and her condition was most obvious but, for once, neither she nor Mrs. Merriwether cared. "Oh, Mrs. Meade! René—" Her voice changed, swiftly. "Melly, look!—Mrs. Meade, please! Darcy isn't—?"

Mrs. Meade was looking down into her lap and

she did not raise her head when her name was called, but the face of little Phil beside her was an open book that all might read.

"There, there, Mother," he said helplessly. Mrs. Meade looked up, meeting Melanie's eyes.

"He won't need those boots now," she said.

"Oh, darling!" cried Melly, beginning to sob, as she shoved Aunt Pitty on to Scarlett's shoulder and scrambled out of the carriage and toward that of the doctor's wife.

"Mother, you've still got me," said Phil, in a forlorn effort at comforting the white-faced woman beside him. "And if you'll just let me, I'll go kill all the Yank—"

Mrs. Meade clutched his arm as if she would never let it go, said "No!" in a strangled voice and seemed to choke.

"Phil Meade, you hush your mouth!" hissed Melanie, climbing in beside Mrs. Meade and taking her in her arms. "Do you think it'll help your mother to have you off getting shot too? I never heard anything so silly. Drive us home, quick!"

She turned to Scarlett as Phil picked up the reins.

"As soon as you take Auntie home, come over to Mrs. Meade's. Captain Butler, can you get word to the doctor? He's at the hospital."

The carriage moved off through the dispersing crowd. Some of the women were weeping with joy, but most looked too stunned to realize the heavy blows that had fallen upon them. Scarlett bent her head over the blurred lists, reading rapidly, to find names of friends. Now that

Ashley was safe she could think of other people. Oh, how long the list was! How heavy the toll from Atlanta, from all of Georgia!

Good Heavens! "Calvert—Raiford, Lieutenant." Raif! Suddenly she remembered the day, so long ago, when they had run away together but decided to come home at nightfall because they were hungry and afraid of the dark.

"Fontaine—Joseph K., private." Little bad-tempered Joe! And Sally hardly over having her baby!

"Munroe—LaFayette, Captain." And Lafe had been engaged to Cathleen Calvert. Poor Cathleen! Hers had been a double loss, a brother and a sweetheart. But Sally's loss was greater—a brother and a husband.

Oh, this was too terrible. She was almost afraid to read further. Aunt Pitty was heaving and sighing on her shoulder and, with small ceremony, Scarlett pushed her over into a corner of the carriage and continued her reading.

Surely, surely—there couldn't be three "Tarleton" names on that list. Perhaps—perhaps the hurried printer had repeated the name by error. But no. There they were. "Tarleton—Brenton, Lieutenant." "Tarleton—Stuart, Corporal." "Tarleton—Thomas, private." And Boyd, dead the first year of the war, was buried God knew where in Virginia. All the Tarleton boys gone. Tom and the lazy long-legged twins with their love of gossip and their absurd practical jokes and Boyd who had the grace of a dancing master and the tongue of a wasp.

She could not read any more. She could not

know if any other of those boys with whom she had grown up, danced, flirted, kissed were on that list. She wished that she could cry, do something to ease the iron fingers that were digging into her throat.

"I'm sorry, Scarlett," said Rhett. She looked up at him. She had forgotten he was still there. "Many of your friends?"

She nodded and struggled to speak: "About every family in the County—and all—all three of the Tarleton boys."

His face was quiet, almost sombre, and there was no mockery in his eyes.

"And the end is not yet," he said. "These are just the first lists and they're incomplete. There'll be a longer list to-morrow." He lowered his voice so that those in the near-by carriages could not hear. "Scarlett, General Lee must have lost the battle. I heard at headquarters that he had retreated back into Maryland."

She raised frightened eyes to his, but her fear did not spring from Lee's defeat. Longer casualty lists to-morrow! To-morrow. She had not thought of to-morrow, so happy was she at first that Ashley's name was not on that list. To-morrow. Why, right this minute he might be dead and she would not know it until to-morrow, or perhaps a week from to-morrow.

"Oh, Rhett, why do there have to be wars? It would have been so much better for the Yankees to pay for the darkies—or even for us to give them the darkies free of charge than to have this happen."

"It isn't the darkies, Scarlett. They're just the

excuse. There'll always be wars because men love wars. Women don't, but men do—yea, passing the love of women."

His mouth twisted in his old smile and the seriousness was gone from his face. He lifted his wide Panama hat.

"Good-bye. I'm going to find Dr. Meade. I imagine the irony of me being the one to tell him of his son's death will be lost on him, just now. But later, he'll probably hate to think that a speculator brought the news of a hero's death."

Scarlett put Miss Pitty to bed with a toddy, left Prissy and Cookie in attendance and went down the street to the Meade house. Mrs. Meade was upstairs with Phil, waiting her husband's return, and Melanie sat in the parlour, talking in a low voice to a group of sympathetic neighbours. She was busy with needle and scissors, altering a mourning dress that Mrs. Elsing had lent to Mrs. Meade. Already the house was full of the acrid smell of clothes boiling in home-made black dye for, in the kitchen, the sobbing cook was stirring all of Mrs. Meade's dresses in the huge wash-pot.

"How is she?" questioned Scarlett softly.

"Not a tear," said Melanie. "It's terrible when women can't cry. I don't know how men stand things without crying. I guess it's because they're stronger and braver than women. She says she's going to Pennsylvania by herself to bring him home. The doctor can't leave the hospital."

"It will be dreadful for her! Why can't Phil go?"

"She's afraid he'll join the army if he gets out

405

of her sight. You know he's so big for his age and they're taking them at sixteen now."

One by one the neighbours slipped away, reluctant to be present when the doctor came home, and Scarlett and Melanie were left alone, sewing in the parlour. Melanie looked sad but tranquil, though tears dropped down on the cloth she held in her hands. Evidently she had not thought that the battle might still be going on and Ashley perhaps dead at this very moment. With panic in her heart, Scarlett did not know whether to tell Melanie of Rhett's words and have the dubious comfort of her misery or keep it to herself. Finally she decided to remain quiet. It would never do for Melanie to think her too worried about Ashley. She thanked God that everyone, Melly and Pitty included, had been too engrossed in their own worries that morning to notice her conduct.

After an interval of silent sewing, they heard sounds outside and, peering through the curtains, they saw Dr. Meade alighting from his horse. His shoulders were sagging and his head bowed until his grey beard spread out fanlike on his chest. He came slowly into the house and, laying down his hat and bag, kissed both the girls silently. Then he went tiredly up the stairs. In a moment Phil came down, all long legs and arms and awkwardness. The two girls looked an invitation to join them, but he went on to the front porch and, seating himself on the top step, dropped his head on his cupped palm.

Melly sighed.

"He's mad because they won't let him go fight

the Yankees. Fifteen years old! Oh, Scarlett, it would be Heaven to have a son like that!"

"And have him get killed?" said Scarlett shortly, thinking of Darcy.

"It would be better to have a son even if he did get killed than to never have one," said Melanie and gulped. "You can't understand, Scarlett, because you've got little Wade, but I— Oh, Scarlett, I want a baby so bad! I know you think I'm horrid to say it right out, but it's true and only what every woman wants and you know it."

Scarlett restrained herself from sniffing.

"If God should will that Ashley should be— taken, I suppose I could bear it, though I'd rather die if he died. But God would give me strength to bear it. But I could not bear having him dead and not having—not having a child of his to comfort me. Oh, Scarlett, how lucky you are! Though you lost Charlie, you have his son. And if Ashley goes, I'll have nothing. Scarlett, forgive me, but sometimes I've been so jealous of you—"

"Jealous—of me?" cried Scarlett, stricken with guilt.

"Because you have a son and I haven't. I've even pretended sometimes that Wade was mine because it's so awful not to have a child."

"Fiddle-dee-dee!" said Scarlett in relief. She cast a quick glance at the slight figure with blushing face bent over the sewing. Melanie might want children but she certainly did not have the figure for bearing them. She was hardly taller than a twelve-year-old child, her hips were as narrow as a child's and her breasts were very flat. The very thought of Melanie having a child was repellent to Scarlett. It brought up too many thoughts she couldn't bear thinking. If Melanie should have a child of Ashley's, it would be as though something were taken from Scarlett that was her own.

"Do forgive me for saying that about Wade. You know I love him so. You aren't mad at me, are you?"

"Don't be silly," said Scarlett shortly. "And go out on the porch and do something for Phil. He's crying."

8

THE army, driven back into Virginia, went into winter quarters on the Rapidan—a tired, depleted army since the defeat at Gettysburg—and as the Christmas season approached, Ashley came home on furlough. Scarlett, seeing him for the first time in more than two years, was frightened by the violence of her feelings. When she had stood in the parlour at Twelve Oaks and seen him married to Melanie, she had thought she could never love him with a more heartbreaking intensity than she did at that moment. But now she knew her feelings of that long-past night were those of a spoiled child thwarted of a toy. Now, her emotions were sharpened by her long dreams of him, heightened by the repression she had been forced to put on her tongue.

This Ashley Wilkes in his faded, patched uniform, his blond hair bleached now by summer suns, was a different man from the easy-going, drowsy-eyed boy she had loved to desperation before the war. And he was a thousand times more thrilling. He was bronzed and lean now, where he had once been fair and slender, and the long golden moustache drooping about his mouth, cavalry style, was the last touch needed to make him the perfect picture of a soldier.

He stood with military straightness in his old uniform, his pistol in its worn holster, his battered scabbard smartly slapping his high boots, his tarnished spurs dully gleaming—Major Ashley Wilkes, CSA. The habit of command sat upon him now, a quiet air of self-reliance and authority, and grim lines were beginning to emerge about his mouth. There was something new and strange about the square set of his shoulders and the cool bright gleam of his eyes. Where he had once been lounging and indolent, he was now as alert as a prowling cat, with the tense alertness of one whose nerves are perpetually drawn as tight as the strings of a violin. In his eyes, there was a fagged, haunted look, and the sunburned skin was tight across the fine bones of his face—her same handsome Ashley, yet so very different.

Scarlett had made her plans to spend Christmas at Tara, but after Ashley's telegram came no power on earth, not even a direct command from the disappointed Ellen, could drag her away from Atlanta. Had Ashley intended going to Twelve Oaks, she would have hastened to Tara to be near him; but he had written his family to join him in Atlanta, and Mr. Wilkes and Honey and India were already in town. Go home to Tara and miss seeing him, after two long years? Miss the heart-quickening sound of his voice, miss reading in his eyes that he had not forgotten her? Never! Not for all the mothers in the world.

Ashley came home four days before Christmas, with a group of the County boys also on furlough, a sadly diminished group since Gettysburg. Cade Calvert was among them, a thin, gaunt Cade, who coughed continually, two of the Munroe boys, bubbling with the excitement of their first leave

410

since 1861, and Alex and Tony Fontaine, splen-
didly drunk, boisterous and quarrelsome. The
group had two hours to wait between trains and,
as it was taxing the diplomacy of the sober
members of the party to keep the Fontaines from
fighting each other and perfect strangers in the
depot, Ashley brought them all home to Aunt
Pittypat's.

"You'd think they'd had enough fighting in
Virginia," said Cade bitterly, as he watched the
two bristle like gamecocks over who should be
the first to kiss the fluttering and flattered Aunt
Pitty. "But no. They've been drunk and picking
fights ever since we got to Richmond. The
provost guard took them up there and if it hadn't
been for Ashley's slick tongue, they'd have spent
Christmas in jail."

But Scarlett hardly heard a word he said, so
enraptured was she at being in the same room
with Ashley again. How could she have thought
during these two years that other men were nice
or handsome or exciting? How could she have
even endured hearing them make love to her
when Ashley was in the world? He was home
again, separated from her only by the width of
the parlour rug, and it took all her strength not
to dissolve in happy tears every time she looked
at him sitting there on the sofa with Melly on one
side and India on the other and Honey hanging
over his shoulder. If only she had the right to sit
there beside him, her arm through his! If only
she could pat his sleeve every few minutes to
make sure he was really there, hold his hand and
use his handkerchief to wipe away her tears of

joy. For Melanie was doing all these things, unashamedly. Too happy to be shy and reserved, she hung on her husband's arm and adored him openly with her eyes, with her smiles, her tears. And Scarlett was too happy to resent this, too glad to be jealous. Ashley was home at last!

Now and then she put her hand up to her cheek where he had kissed her and felt again the thrill of his lips and smiled at him. He had not kissed her first, of course. Melly had hurled herself into his arms, crying incoherently, holding him as though she would never let him go. And then, India and Honey had hugged him, fairly tearing him from Melanie's arms. Then he had kissed his father, with a dignified affectionate embrace that showed the strong quiet feeling that lay between them. And then Aunt Pitty, who was jumping up and down on her inadequate little feet with excitement. Finally he turned to her, surrounded by all the boys who were claiming their kisses, and said: "Oh, Scarlett! You pretty, pretty thing!" and kissed her on the cheek.

With that kiss, everything she had intended to say in welcome took wings. Not until hours later did she recall that he had not kissed her on the lips. Then she wondered feverishly if he would have done it had she met him alone, bending his tall body over hers, pulling her up on tiptoe, holding her for a long, long time. And because it made her happy to think so, she believed that he would. But there would be time for all things, a whole week! Surely she could manoeuvre to get him alone and say: "Do you remember those rides we used to take down our secret bridle paths?"

"Do you remember how the moon looked that night when we sat on the steps at Tara and you quoted that poem?" (Good Heavens! What was the name of that poem, anyway?) "Do you remember that afternoon when I sprained my ankle and you carried me home in your arms in the twilight?"

Oh, there were so many things she would preface with "Do you remember?" So many dear memories that would bring back to him those lovely days when they roamed the County like care-free children, so many things that would call to mind the days before Melanie Hamilton entered on the scene. And while they talked she could perhaps read in his eyes some quickening of emotion, some hint that behind the barrier of husbandly affection for Melanie he still cared, cared as passionately as on that day of the barbecue when he burst forth with the truth. It did not occur to her to plan just what they would do if Ashley should declare his love for her in unmistakable words. It would be enough to know that he did care. . . . Yes, she could wait, could let Melanie have her happy hour of squeezing his arm and crying. Her time would come. After all, what did a girl like Melanie know of love?

"Darling, you look like a ragamuffin," said Melanie when the first excitement of homecoming was over. "Who did mend your uniform and why did they use blue patches?"

"I thought I looked perfectly dashing," said Ashley, considering his appearance. "Just compare me with those rag-tags over there and you'll appreciate me more. Mose mended the

413

uniform and I thought he did very well, considering that he'd never had a needle in his hand before the war. About the blue cloth, when it comes to a choice between having holes in your britches or patching them with pieces of a captured Yankee uniform—well, there just isn't any choice. And as for looking like a ragamuffin, you should thank your stars your husband didn't come home barefooted. Last week my old boots wore completely out, and I would have come home with sacks tied on my feet if we hadn't had the good luck to shoot two Yankee scouts. The boots of one of them fitted me perfectly."

He stretched out his long legs in their scarred high boots for them to admire.

"And the boots of the other scout didn't fit me," said Cade. "They're two sizes too small and they're killing me this minute. But I'm going home in style just the same."

"And the selfish swine won't give them to either of us," said Tony. "And they'd fit our small, aristocratic Fontaine feet perfectly. Hell's afire, I'm ashamed to face Mother in these brogans. Before the war she wouldn't have let one of our darkies wear them."

"Don't worry," said Alex, eyeing Cade's boots. "We'll take them off of him on the train going home. I don't mind facing Mother but I'm da— I mean, I don't intend for Dimity Munroe to see my toes sticking out."

"Why, they're my boots. I claimed them first," said Tony, beginning to scowl at his brother; and Melanie, fluttering with fear at the possibility of one of the famous Fontaine quarrels, interposed and made peace.

"I had a full beard to show you girls," said Ashley, ruefully rubbing his face where half-healed razor nicks still showed. "It was a beautiful beard and if I do say it myself, neither Jeb Stuart nor Nathan Bedford Forrest had a handsomer one. But when we got to Richmond, those two scoundrels," indicating the Fontaines, "decided that as they were shaving their beards, mine should come off too. They got me down and shaved me, and it's a wonder my head didn't come off along with the beard. It was only by the intervention of Evan and Cade that my moustache was saved."

"Snakes! Mrs. Wilkes! You ought to thank us. You'd never have recognized him and wouldn't have let him in the door," said Alex. "We did it to show our appreciation of his talking the provost guard out of putting us in jail. If you say the word, we'll take the moustache off for you, right now."

"Oh, no, thank you!" said Melanie hastily, clutching Ashley in a frightened way, for the two swarthy little men looked capable of any violence. "I think it's perfectly lovely."

"That's love," said the Fontaines, nodding gravely at each other.

When Ashley went out into the cold to see the boys off to the depot in Aunt Pitty's carriage, Melanie caught Scarlett's arm.

"Isn't his uniform dreadful? Won't my coat be a surprise? Oh, if I only had enough cloth for britches too!"

That coat for Ashley was a sore subject with Scarlett, for she wished so ardently that she and not Melanie were bestowing it as a Christmas gift. Grey wool for uniforms was now almost literally more priceless than rubies, and Ashley was wearing the familiar homespun. Even butternut was now none too plentiful, and many of the soldiers were dressed in captured Yankee uniforms which had been turned a dark-brown colour with walnut-shell dye. But Melanie, by rare luck, had come into possession of enough grey broadcloth to make a coat—a rather short coat but a coat just the same. She had nursed a Charleston boy in the hospital and when he died had clipped a lock of his hair and sent it to his mother, along with the scant contents of his pockets and a comforting account of his last hours which made no mention of the torment in which he died. A correspondence had sprung up between them and, learning that Melanie had a husband at the front, the mother had sent her the length of grey cloth and brass buttons which she had bought for her dead son. It was a beautiful piece of material, thick and warm and with a dull sheen to it, undoubtedly blockade goods and undoubtedly very expensive. It was now in the hands of the tailor and Melanie was hurrying him to have it ready by Christmas morning. Scarlett would have given anything to be able to provide the rest of the uniform, but the necessary materials were simply not to be had in Atlanta.

She had a Christmas present for Ashley, but it paled in insignificance beside the glory of Melanie's grey coat. It was a small "housewife", made of flannel, containing the whole precious pack of needles Rhett had brought her from Nassau, three of her linen handkerchiefs, obtained from the same source, two spools of thread and a small pair of scissors. But she wanted to give him something more personal, something a wife could give a husband, a shirt, a pair of gauntlets, a hat. Oh, yes, a hat by all means. That little flat-topped forage cap Ashley was wearing looked ridiculous. Scarlett had always hated them. What if Stonewall Jackson had worn one in preference to a slouch felt? That didn't make them any more dignified-looking. But the only hats obtainable in Atlanta were crudely made wool hats, and they were tackier than the monkey-hat forage caps.

When she thought of hats, she thought of Rhett Butler. He had so many hats, wide Panamas for summer, tall beavers for formal occasions, hunting hats, slouch hats of tan and black and blue. What need had he for so many when her darling Ashley rode in the rain with moisture dripping down his collar from the back of his cap?

"I'll make Rhett give me that new black felt of his," she decided. "And I'll put a grey ribbon around the brim and sew Ashley's wreath on it and it will look lovely."

She paused and thought it might be difficult to get the hat without some explanation. She simply could not tell Rhett she wanted it for Ashley. He would raise his brows in that nasty way he always had when she even mentioned Ashley's name and, like as not, would refuse to give her the hat. Well, she'd make up some pitiful story about a soldier in the hospital who needed it and Rhett need never know the truth.

All that afternoon, she manoeuvred to be alone with Ashley, even for a few minutes, but Melanie was beside him constantly, and India and Honey, their pale, lashless eyes glowing, followed him about the house. Even John Wilkes, visibly proud of his son, had no opportunity for quiet conversation with him.

It was the same at supper where they all plied him with questions about the war. The war! Who cared about the war? Scarlett didn't think Ashley cared very much for that subject either. He talked at length, laughed frequently and dominated the conversation more completely than she had ever seen him do before, but he seemed to say very little. He told them jokes and funny stories about friends, talked gaily about makeshifts, making light of hunger and long marches in the rain, and described in detail how General Lee had looked when he rode by on the retreat from Gettysburg and questioned: "Gentlemen, are you Georgia troops? Well, we can't get along without you Georgians!"

It seemed to Scarlett that he was talking feverishly to keep them from asking questions he did not want to answer. When she saw his eyes falter and drop before the long, troubled gaze of his father, a faint worry and bewilderment rose in her as to what was hidden in Ashley's heart. But it soon passed, for there was no room in her mind for anything except a radiant happiness and a driving desire to be alone with him.

That radiance lasted until everyone in the circle about the open fire began to yawn, and Mr. Wilkes and the girls took their departure for the hotel. Then as Ashley and Melanie and Pittypat and Scarlett mounted the stairs, lighted by Uncle Peter, a chill fell on her spirit. Until that moment when they stood in the upstairs hall, Ashley had been hers, only hers, even if she had not had a private word with him that whole afternoon. But now, as she said good night, she saw that Melanie's cheeks were suddenly crimson and she was trembling. Her eyes were on the carpet and, though she seemed overcome with some frightening emotion, she seemed shyly happy. Melanie did not even look up when Ashley opened the bedroom door, but sped inside. Ashley said good night abruptly, and he did not meet Scarlett's eyes either.

The door closed behind them, leaving Scarlett open-mouthed and suddenly desolate. Ashley was no longer hers. He was Melanie's. And as long as Melanie lived, she could go into rooms with Ashley and close the door—and close out the rest of the world.

Now Ashley was going away, back to Virginia, back to the long marches in the sleet, to hungry bivouacs in the snow, to pain and hardship and to the risk of all the bright beauty of his golden head and proud slender body being blotted out in an instant, like an ant beneath a careless heel. The past week with its shimmering, dreamlike beauty, its crowded hours of happiness, was gone.

The week had passed swiftly, like a dream, a

dream fragrant with the smell of pine boughs and Christmas trees, bright with little candles and home-made tinsel, a dream where minutes flew as rapidly as heartbeats. Such a breathless week when something within her drove Scarlett with mingled pain and pleasure to pack and cram every minute with incidents to remember after he was gone, happenings which she could examine at leisure in the long months ahead, extracting every morsel of comfort from them—dance, sing, laugh, fetch and carry for Ashley, anticipate his wants, smile when he smiles, be silent when he talks, follow him with your eyes so that each line of his erect body, each lift of his eyebrows, each quirk of his mouth, will be indelibly printed on your mind—for a week goes by so fast and the war goes on forever.

She sat on the divan in the parlour, holding her going-away gift for him in her lap, waiting while he said good-bye to Melanie, praying that when he did come down the stairs he would be alone and she might be granted by Heaven a few moments alone with him. Her ears strained for sounds from upstairs, but the house was oddly still, so still that even the sound of her breathing seemed loud. Aunt Pittypat was crying into her pillows in her room, for Ashley had told her good-bye half an hour before. No sounds of murmuring voices or of tears came from behind the closed door of Melanie's bedroom. It seemed to Scarlett that he had been in that room for hours, and she resented bitterly each moment that he stayed, saying good-bye to his wife, for the moments were slipping by so fast and his time was so short.

She thought of all the things she had intended to say to him during this week. But there had been no opportunity to say them, and she knew now that perhaps she would never have the chance to say them.

Such foolish little things, some of them: "Ashley, you will be careful, won't you?" "Please don't get your feet wet. You take cold so easily." "Don't forget to put a newspaper across your chest under your shirt. It keeps out the wind so well." But there were other things, more important things she had wanted to say, much more important things she had wanted to hear him say, things she had wanted to read in his eyes, even if he did not speak them.

So many things to say and now there was no time! Even the few minutes that remained might be snatched away from her if Melanie followed him to the door, to the carriage block. Why hadn't she made the opportunity during this last week? But always, Melanie was at his side, her eyes caressing him adoringly, always friends and neighbours and relatives were in the house and, from morning till night, Ashley was never alone. Then, at night, the door of the bedroom closed and he was alone with Melanie. Never once during these last days had he betrayed to Scarlett by one look, one word, anything but the affection a brother might show a sister or a friend, a life-long friend. She could not let him go away, perhaps forever, without knowing whether he still loved her. Then, even if he died, she could nurse the warm comfort of his secret love to the end of her days.

After what seemed an eternity of waiting, she heard the sound of his boots in the bedroom above and the door opening and closing. She heard him coming down the steps. Alone! Thank God for that! Melanie must be too overcome by the grief of parting to leave her room. Now she would have him for herself for a few precious minutes.

He came down the steps slowly, his spurs clinking, and she could hear the faint slap-slap of his sabre against his high boots. When he came into the parlour, his eyes were sombre. He was trying to smile but his face was as white and drawn as a man bleeding from an internal wound. She rose as he entered, thinking with proprietary pride that he was the handsomest soldier she had ever seen. His long holster and belt glistened and his silver spurs and scabbard gleamed, from the industrious polishing Uncle Peter had given them. His new coat did not fit very well, for the tailor had been hurried and some of the seams were awry. The bright new sheen of the grey coat was sadly at variance with the worn and patched butternut trousers and the scarred boots, but if he had been clothed in silver armour he could not have looked more the shining knight to her.

"Ashley," she begged abruptly, "may I go to the train with you?"

"Please don't. Father and the girls will be there. And anyway, I'd rather remember you saying good-bye to me here than shivering at the depot. There's so much to memories."

Instantly she abandoned her plan. If India and Honey who disliked her so much were to be present at the leave-taking, she would have no chance for a private word.

"Then I won't go," she said. "See, Ashley! I've another present for you."

A little shy, now that the time had come to give it to him, she unrolled the package. It was a long yellow sash, made of thick China silk and edged with heavy fringe. Rhett Butler had brought her a yellow shawl from Havana several months before, a shawl gaudily embroidered with birds and flowers in magenta and blue. During this last week, she had patiently picked out all the embroidery and cut up the square of silk and stitched it into a sash length.

"Scarlett, it's beautiful! Did you make it yourself? Then I'll value it all the more. Put it on me, my dear. The boys will be green with envy when they see me in the glory of my new coat and sash."

She wrapped the bright lengths about his slender waist, above his belt, and tied the ends in a lover's knot. Melanie might have given him his new coat but this sash was her gift, her own secret guerdon for him to wear into battle, something that would make him remember her every time he looked at it. She stood back and viewed him with pride, thinking that even Jeb Stuart with his flaunting sash and plume could not look so dashing as her cavalier.

"It's beautiful," he repeated, fingering the fringe. "But I know you've cut up a dress or a shawl to make it. You shouldn't have done it, Scarlett. Pretty things are too hard to get these days."

"Oh, Ashley, I'd—"

She had started to say: "I'd cut up my heart for you to wear if you wanted it," but she finished, "I'd do anything for you!"

"Would you?" he questioned, and some of the sombreness lifted from his face. "Then, there's something you can do for me, Scarlett, something that will make my mind easier when I'm away."

"What is it?" she asked joyfully, ready to promise prodigies.

"Scarlett, will you look after Melanie for me?"

"Look after Melly?"

Her heart sank with bitter disappointment. So this was his last request of her, when she so yearned to promise something beautiful, something spectacular! And then anger flared. This moment was her moment with Ashley, hers alone. And yet, though Melanie was absent, her pale shadow lay between them. How could he bring up her name in their moment of farewell? How could he ask such a thing of her?

He did not notice the disappointment on her face. As of old, his eyes were looking through her and beyond her, at something else, not seeing her at all.

"Yes, keep an eye on her, take care of her. She's so frail and she doesn't realize it. She'll wear herself out nursing and sewing. And she's so gentle and timid. Except for Aunt Pittypat and Uncle Henry and you, she hasn't a close relative in the world, except the Burrs in Macon and they're third cousins. And Aunt Pitty—Scarlett, you know she's like a child. And Uncle Henry is an old man. Melanie loves you so much, not just

424

because you were Charlie's wife, but because—well, because you're you and she loves you like a sister. Scarlett, I have nightmares when I think what might happen to her if I were killed and she had no one to turn to. Will you promise?"

She did not even hear his last request, so terrified was she by those ill-omened words, "if I were killed."

Every day she had read the casualty lists, read them with her heart in her throat, knowing that the world would end if anything should happen to him. But always, always, she had an inner feeling that even if the Confederate Army were entirely wiped out, Ashley would be spared. And now he had spoken the frightful words! Goosebumps came out all over her and fear swamped her, a superstitious fear she could not combat with reason. She was Irish enough to believe in second sight, especially where death premonitions were concerned, and in his wide grey eyes she saw some deep sadness which she could only interpret as that of a man who has felt the cold finger on his shoulder, has heard the wail of the Banshee.

"You mustn't say it! You mustn't even think it. It's bad luck to speak of death! Oh, say a prayer, quickly!"

"You say it for me and light some candles, too," he said, smiling at the frightened urgency in her voice.

But she could not answer, so stricken was she by the pictures her mind was drawing, Ashley lying dead in the snows of Virginia, so far away from her. He went on speaking and there was a quality in his voice, a sadness, a resignation, that increased her fear until every vestige of anger and disappointment was blotted out.

"I'm asking you for this reason, Scarlett. I cannot tell what will happen to me or what will happen to any of us. But when the end comes, I shall be far away from here, even if I am alive, too far away to look out for Melanie."

"The—the end?"

"The end of the war—and the end of the world."

"But, Ashley, surely you can't think the Yankees will beat us? All this week you've talked about how strong General Lee—"

"All this week I've talked lies, like all men talk when they're on furlough. Why should I frighten Melanie and Aunt Pitty before there's any need for them to be frightened? Yes, Scarlett, I think the Yankees have us. Gettysburg was the beginning of the end. The people back home don't know it yet. They can't realize how things stand with us, but—Scarlett, some of my men are barefooted now and the snow is deep in Virginia. And when I see their poor frozen feet, wrapped in rags and old sacks, and see the blood-prints they leave in the snow, and know that I've got a whole pair of boots—well, I feel like I should give mine away and be barefooted too."

"Oh, Ashley, promise me you won't give them away!"

"When I see things like that and then look at the Yankees—then I see the end of everything. Why, Scarlett, the Yankees are buying soldiers from Europe by the thousands! Most of the prisoners we've taken recently can't even speak English. They're Germans and Poles and wild Irishmen who talk Gaelic. But when we lose a man, he can't be replaced. When our shoes wear out, there are no more shoes. We're bottled up, Scarlett. And we can't fight the whole world."

She thought wildly: "Let the whole Confederacy crumble in the dust. Let the world end, but you must not die! I couldn't live if you were dead!"

"I hope you will not repeat what I have said, Scarlett. I do not want to alarm the others. And, my dear, I would not have alarmed you by saying these things, were it not that I had to explain why I ask you to look after Melanie. She's so frail and weak and you're so strong, Scarlett. It will be a comfort to me to know that you two are together if anything happens to me. You will promise, won't you?"

"Oh, yes!" she cried, for at that moment, seeing death at his elbow, she would have promised anything. "Ashley, Ashley! I can't let you go away! I simply can't be brave about it!"

"You must be brave," he said, and his voice changed subtly. It was resonant, deeper, and his words fell swiftly as though hurried with some inner urgency. "You must be brave. For how else can I stand it?"

Her eyes sought his face quickly and with joy, wondering if he meant that leaving her was breaking his heart, even as it was breaking hers. His face was as drawn as when he came down from bidding Melanie good-bye, but she could read nothing in his eyes. He leaned down, took

427

her face in his hands, and kissed her lightly on the forehead.

"Scarlett! Scarlett! You are so fine and strong and good. So beautiful, not just your sweet face, my dear, but all of you, your body and your mind and your soul."

"Oh, Ashley," she whispered happily, thrilling at his words and his touch on her face. "Nobody else but you ever—"

"I like to think that perhaps I know you better than most people and that I can see beautiful things buried deep in you that others are too careless and too hurried to notice."

He stopped speaking and his hands dropped from her face, but his eyes still clung to her eyes. She waited a moment, breathless for him to continue, a-tiptoe to hear him say the magic three words. But they did not come. She searched his face frantically, her lips quivering, for she saw he had finished speaking.

This second blighting of her hopes was more than heart could bear and she cried "Oh!" in a childish whisper and sat down, tears stinging her eyes. Then she heard an ominous sound in the driveway, outside the window, a sound that brought home to her even more sharply the imminence of Ashley's departure. A pagan hearing the lapping of the waters around Charon's boat could not have felt more desolate. Uncle Peter, muffled in a quilt, was bringing out the carriage to take Ashley to the train.

Ashley said "Good-bye," very softly, caught up from the table the wide felt hat she had inveigled from Rhett and walked into the dark front hall.

His hand on the door-knob, he turned and looked at her, a long, desperate look, as if he wanted to carry away with him every detail of her face and figure. Through a blinding mist of tears she saw his face and with a strangling pain in her throat she knew that he was going away, away from her care, away from the safe haven of this house, out of her life, perhaps forever, without having spoken the words she so yearned to hear. Time was going by like a mill-race, and now it was too late. She ran stumbling across the parlour and into the hall and clutched the ends of his sash.

"Kiss me," she whispered. "Kiss me good-bye."

His arms went around her gently, and he bent his head to her face. At the first touch of his lips on hers, her arms were about his neck in a strangling grip. For a fleeting immeasurable instant, he pressed her body close to his. Then she felt a sudden tensing of all his muscles. Swiftly, he dropped the hat to the floor and, reaching up, detached her arms from his neck.

"No, Scarlett, no," he said in a low voice, holding her crossed wrists in a grip that hurt.

"I love you," she said, choking. "I've always loved you. I've never loved anybody else. I just married Charlie to—to try to hurt you. Oh, Ashley, I love you so much I'd walk every step of the way to Virginia just to be near you! And I'd cook for you and polish your boots and groom your horse—Ashley, say you love me! I'll live on it for the rest of my life!"

He bent suddenly to retrieve his hat and she had one glimpse of his face. It was the unhappiest face she was ever to see, a face from which all aloofness had fled. Written on it were his love for her and joy that she loved him, but battling them both were shame and despair.

"Good-bye," he said hoarsely.

The door clicked open and a gust of cold wind swept the house, fluttering the curtains. Scarlett shivered as she watched him run down the walk to the carriage, his sabre glinting in the feeble winter sunlight, the fringe of his sash dancing jauntily.

9

JANUARY and February of 1864 passed, full of cold rains and wild winds, clouded by pervasive gloom and depression. In addition to the defeats at Gettysburg and Vicksburg, the centre of the Southern line had caved. After hard fighting, nearly all of Tennessee was now held by the Union troops. But even with this loss on the top of the others, the South's spirit was not broken. True, grim determination had taken the place of high-hearted hopes, but people could still find a silver lining in the cloud. For one thing, the Yankees had been stoutly repulsed in September when they had tried to follow up their victories in Tennessee by an advance into Georgia.

Here in the north-westernmost corner of the state, at Chickamauga, serious fighting had occurred on Georgia soil for the first time since the war began. The Yankees had taken Chattanooga and then had marched through the mountain passes into Georgia, but they had been driven back with heavy losses.

Atlanta and its railroads had played a big part in making Chickamauga a great victory for the South. Over the railroads that led down from Virginia to Atlanta and then northward to Tennessee, General Longstreet's corps had been rushed to the scene of the battle. Along the entire route of several hundred miles, the tracks had

431

been cleared and all the available rolling stock in the South-east had been assembled for the movement.

Atlanta had watched while train after train rolled through the town, hour after hour, passenger coaches, box cars, flat cars, filled with shouting men. They had come without food or sleep, without their horses, ambulances or supply trains and, without waiting for rest, they had leaped from the trains and into the battle. And the Yankees had been driven out of Georgia, back into Tennessee.

It was the greatest feat of the war, and Atlanta took pride and personal satisfaction in the thought that its railroads had made the victory possible.

But the South had needed the cheering news from Chickamauga to strengthen its morale through the winter. No one denied now that the Yankees were good fighters and, at last, they had good generals. Grant was a butcher who did not care how many men he slaughtered for a victory, but victory he would have. Sheridan was a name to bring dread to Southern hearts. And then, there was a man named Sherman who was being mentioned more and more often. He had risen to prominence in the campaigns in Tennessee and the West, and his reputation as a determined and ruthless fighter was growing.

None of them, of course, compared with General Lee. Faith in the General and the army was still strong. Confidence in ultimate victory never wavered. But the war was dragging out so long. There were so many dead, so many wounded and maimed for life, so many widowed, so many orphaned. And there was still a long hard struggle ahead, which meant more dead, more wounded, more widows and orphans.

To make matters worse, a vague distrust of those in high places had begun to creep over the civilian population. Many newspapers were outspoken in their denunciation of President Davis himself and the manner in which he prosecuted the war. There were dissensions within the Confederate cabinet, disagreements between President Davis and his generals. The currency was falling rapidly. Shoes and clothing for the army were scarce, ordnance supplies and drugs were scarcer. The railroads needed new cars to take the place of old ones and new iron rails to replace those torn up by the Yankees. The generals in the field were crying out for fresh troops, and there were fewer and fewer fresh troops to be had. Worst of all, some of the state governors, Governor Brown of Georgia among them, were refusing to send state militia troops and arms out of their borders. There were thousands of able-bodied men in the state troops for whom the army was frantic, but the government pleaded for them in vain.

With the new fall of currency, prices soared again. Beef, pork and butter cost thirty-five dollars a pound, flour fourteen hundred dollars a barrel, soda one hundred dollars a pound, tea five hundred dollars a pound. Warm clothing, when it was obtainable at all, had risen to such prohibitive prices that Atlanta ladies were lining their old dresses with rags and reinforcing them with newspapers to keep out the wind. Shoes cost from two hundred to eight hundred dollars a pair, depending on whether they were made of "cardboard" or real leather. Ladies now wore gaiters made of their old wool shawls and cut-up carpets. The soles were made of wood.

The truth was that the North was holding the South in a virtual state of siege, though many did not yet realize it. The Yankee gunboats had tightened the mesh at the ports and very few ships were now able to slip past the blockade.

The South had always lived by selling cotton and buying the things it did not produce, but now it could neither sell nor buy. Gerald O'Hara had three years' crops of cotton stored under the shed near the gin-house at Tara, but little good it did him. In Liverpool it would bring one hundred and fifty thousand dollars, but there was no hope of getting it to Liverpool. Gerald had changed from a wealthy man to a man who was wondering how he would feed his family and his negroes through the winter.

Throughout the South, most of the cotton planters were in the same fix. With the blockade closing tighter and tighter, there was no way to get the South's money crop to its market in England, no way to bring in the necessaries which cotton money had brought in years gone by. And the agricultural South, waging war with the industrial North, was needing so many things now, things it had never thought of buying in times of peace.

It was a situation made to order for speculators and profiteers, and men were not lacking to take advantage of it. As food and clothing grew scarcer and prices rose higher and higher, the public outcry against the speculators grew louder and more venomous. In those early days of 1864, no newspaper could be opened that did not carry scathing editorials denouncing the speculators as vultures and bloodsucking leeches and calling upon the government to put them down with a hard hand. The government did its best, but the efforts came to nothing, for the government was harried by many things.

Against no one was feeling more bitter than against Rhett Butler. He had sold his boats when blockading grew too hazardous, and he was now openly engaged in food speculation. The stories about him that came back to Atlanta from Richmond and Wilmington made those who had received him in other days writhe with shame.

In spite of all these trials and tribulations, Atlanta's ten thousand population had grown to double that number during the war. Even the blockade had added to Atlanta's prestige. From time immemorial, the coast cities had dominated the South, commercially and otherwise. But now with the ports closed and many of the port cities captured or besieged, the South's salvation depended upon itself. The interior section was what counted, if the South was going to win the war, and Atlanta was now the centre of things. The people of the town were suffering hardship, privation, sickness and death as severely as the rest of the Confederacy; but Atlanta, the city, had gained rather than lost as a result of the war. Atlanta, the heart of the Confederacy, was still beating full and strong, the railroads that were its arteries throbbing with the never-ending flow of men, munitions and supplies.

In other days, Scarlett would have been bitter about her shabby dresses and patched shoes but now she did not care, for the one person who mattered was not there to see her. She was happy those two months, happier than she had been in years. Had she not felt the start of Ashley's heart when her arms went round his neck, seen that despairing look on his face which was more open an avowal than any words could be? He loved her. She was sure of that now, and this conviction was so pleasant she could even be kinder to Melanie. She could be sorry for Melanie now, sorry with a faint contempt for her blindness, her stupidity.

"When the war is over!" she thought. "When it's over—then . . ."

Sometimes she thought with a small dart of fear: "What then?" But she put the thought from her mind. When the war was over, everything would be settled, somehow. If Ashley loved her, he simply couldn't go on living with Melanie.

But then, divorce was unthinkable; and Ellen and Gerald, staunch Catholics that they were, would never permit her to marry a divorced man. It would mean leaving the Church! Scarlett thought it over and decided that, in a choice between the Church and Ashley, she would choose Ashley. But, oh, it would make such a scandal! Divorced people were under the ban not only of the Church but of society. No divorced person was received. However, she would dare

436

even that for Ashley. She would sacrifice anything for Ashley.

Somehow it would come out all right, when the war was over. If Ashley loved her so much, he'd find a way. She'd make him find a way. And with every day that passed, she became more sure in her own mind of his devotion, more certain he would arrange matters satisfactorily when the Yankees were finally beaten. Of course, he had said the Yankees "had" them. Scarlett thought that was just foolishness. He had been tired and upset when he said it. But she hardly cared whether the Yankees won or not. The thing that mattered was for the war to finish quickly and for Ashley to come home.

Then, when the sleets of March were keeping everyone indoors, the hideous blow fell. Melanie, her eyes shining with joy, her head ducked with embarrassed pride, told her she was going to have a baby.

"Dr. Meade says it will be here in late August or September," she said. "I've thought—but I wasn't sure till to-day. Oh, Scarlett, isn't it wonderful? I've so envied you Wade and so wanted a baby. And I was so afraid that maybe I wasn't ever going to have one and, darling, I want a dozen!"

Scarlett had been combing her hair, preparing for bed, when Melanie spoke and she stopped, the comb in mid-air.

"Dear God!" she said and, for a moment, realization did not come. Then there suddenly leaped to her mind the closed door of Melanie's bedroom and a knifelike pain went through her, a pain as fierce as though Ashley had been her own husband and had been unfaithful to her. A baby. Ashley's baby. Oh, how could he, when he loved her and not Melanie?

"I know you're surprised," Melanie rattled on, breathlessly. "And isn't it too wonderful? Oh, Scarlett, I don't know how I shall ever write Ashley! It wouldn't be so embarrassing if I could tell him or—or—well, not say anything and just let him notice gradually, you know—"

"Dear God!" said Scarlett, almost sobbing, as she dropped the comb and caught at the marble top of the dresser for support.

"Darling, don't look like that! You know having a baby isn't so bad. You said so yourself. And you mustn't worry about me, though you are sweet to be so upset. Of course, Dr. Meade said I was—was," Melanie blushed, "quite narrow but that perhaps I shouldn't have any trouble and—Scarlett, did you write Charlie and tell him when you found out about Wade, or did your mother do it or maybe Mr. O'Hara? Oh, dear, if I only had a mother to do it! I just don't see how—"

"Hush!" said Scarlett violently. "Hush!"

"Oh, Scarlett, I'm so stupid! I'm so sorry. I guess all happy people are selfish. I forgot about Charlie, just for the moment—"

"Hush!" said Scarlett again, fighting to control her face and make her emotions quiet. Never, never must Melanie see or suspect how she felt.

Melanie, the most tactful of women, had tears in her eyes at her own cruelty. How could she have brought back to Scarlett the terrible memories of Wade being born months after poor

Charlie was dead? How could she have been so thoughtless?

"Let me help you undress, dearest," she said humbly. "And I'll rub your head for you."

"You leave me alone," said Scarlett, her face like stone. And Melanie, bursting into tears of self-condemnation, fled from the room, leaving Scarlett to a tearless bed, with wounded pride, disillusionment and jealousy for bedfellows.

She thought that she could not live any longer in the same house with the woman who was carrying Ashley's child, thought that she would go home to Tara, home, where she belonged. She did not see how she could ever look at Melanie again and not have her secret read in her face. And she arose the next morning with the fixed intention of packing her trunk immediately after breakfast. But, as they sat at the table, Scarlett silent and gloomy, Pitty bewildered and Melanie miserable, a telegram came.

It was to Melanie from Ashley's body-servant, Mose.

"I have looked everywhere and I can't find him. Must I come home?"

No one knew what it meant but the eyes of the three women went to one another, wide with terror, and Scarlett forgot all thoughts of going home. Without finishing their breakfasts they drove to town to telegraph Ashley's colonel, but even as they entered the office, there was a telegram from him.

"Regret to inform you Major Wilkes missing since scouting expedition three days ago. Will keep you informed."

It was a ghastly trip home, with Aunt Pitty crying into her handkerchief, Melanie sitting erect and white and Scarlett slumped, stunned in the corner of the carriage. Once in the house, Scarlett stumbled up the stairs to her bedroom and, clutching her Rosary from the table, dropped to her knees and tried to pray. But the prayers would not come. There only fell on her an abysmal fear, a certain knowledge that God had turned His face from her for her sin. She had loved a married man and tried to take him from his wife, and God had punished her by killing him. She wanted to pray but she could not raise her eyes to Heaven. She wanted to cry but the tears would not come. They seemed to flood her chest, and they were hot tears that burned under her bosom, but they would not flow.

Her door opened and Melanie entered. Her face was like a heart cut from white paper, framed against black hair, and her eyes were wide, like those of a frightened child lost in the dark.

"Scarlett," she said, putting out her hands. "You must forgive me for what I said yesterday, for you're—all I've got now. Oh, Scarlett, I know my darling is dead!"

Somehow, she was in Scarlett's arms, her small breasts heaving with sobs, and somehow they were lying on the bed, holding each other close, and Scarlett was crying too, crying with her face pressed close against Melanie's, the tears of one wetting the cheeks of the other. It hurt so terribly to cry, but not so much as not being able to cry. "Ashley is dead—dead," she thought, "and I have killed him by loving him!" Fresh sobs broke from her, and Melanie somehow feeling comfort in her tears tightened her arms about her neck.

"At least," she whispered, "at least—I've got his baby."

"And I," thought Scarlett, too stricken now for anything so petty as jealousy, "I've got nothing —nothing—nothing except the look on his face when he told me good-bye."

The first reports were "Missing—believed killed" and so they appeared on the casualty list. Melanie telegraphed Colonel Sloan a dozen times and finally a letter arrived, full of sympathy, explaining that Ashley and a squad had ridden out on a scouting expedition and had not returned. There had been reports of a slight skirmish within the Yankee lines and Mose, frantic with grief, had risked his own life to search for Ashley's body but had found nothing. Melanie, strangely calm now, telegraphed him money and instructions to come home.

When "Missing—believed captured" appeared on the casualty lists, joy and hope reanimated the sad household. Melanie could hardly be dragged away from the telegraph office and she met every train hoping for letters. She was sick now, her pregnancy making itself felt in many unpleasant ways, but she refused to obey Dr. Meade's commands and stay in bed. A feverish energy possessed her and would not let her be still; and at night, long after Scarlett had gone to bed, she could hear her walking the floor in the next room.

One afternoon, she came home from town, driven by the frightened Uncle Peter and supported by Rhett Butler. She had fainted at the telegraph office and Rhett, passing by and observing the excitement, had escorted her home. He carried her up the stairs to her bedroom and while the alarmed household fled hither and yon for hot bricks, blankets and whisky, he propped her on the pillows of her bed.

"Mrs. Wilkes," he questioned abruptly, "you are going to have a baby, are you not?"

Had Melanie not been so faint, so sick, so heartsore, she would have collapsed at his question. Even with women friends she was embarrassed by any mention of her condition, while visits to Dr. Meade were agonizing experiences. And for a man, especially Rhett Butler, to ask such a question was unthinkable. But lying weak and forlorn in the bed, she could only nod. After she had nodded, it did not seem so dreadful, for he looked so kind and so concerned.

"Then you must take better care of yourself. All this running about and worrying won't help you and may harm the baby. If you will permit me, Mrs. Wilkes, I will use what influence I have in Washington to learn about Mr. Wilkes' fate. If he is a prisoner, he will be on the Federal lists, and if he isn't—well, there's nothing worse than uncertainty. But I must have your promise. Take care of yourself or, before God, I won't turn a hand."

"Oh, you are so kind," cried Melanie. "How can people say such dreadful things about you?" Then overcome with the knowledge of her tactlessness and also with horror at having discussed her condition with a man, she began to cry weakly. And Scarlett, flying up the stairs with a hot brick wrapped in flannel, found Rhett patting her hand.

He was as good as his word. They never knew what wires he pulled. They feared to ask, knowing it might involve an admission of his too close affiliations with the Yankees. It was a month before he had news, news that raised them to the heights when they first heard it, but later created a gnawing anxiety in their hearts.

Ashley was not dead! He had been wounded and taken prisoner, and the records showed that he was at Rock Island, a prison camp in Illinois. In their first joy, they could think of nothing except that he was alive. But, when calmness began to return, they looked at one another and said "Rock Island!" in the same voice they would have said "In Hell!" For even as Andersonville was a name that stank in the North, so was Rock Island one to bring terror to the heart of any Southerner who had relatives imprisoned there.

When Lincoln refused to exchange prisoners, believing it would hasten the end of the war to burden the Confederacy with the feeding and guarding of Union prisoners, there were thousands of bluecoats at Andersonville, Georgia. The Confederates were on scant rations and practically without drugs or bandages for their own sick and wounded. They had little to share with the prisoners. They fed their prisoners on what the soldiers in the field were eating, fat pork and dried peas, and on this diet the Yankees died like flies, sometimes a hundred a day. Inflamed by the reports, the North resorted to harsher treatment of Confederate prisoners and at no place were conditions worse than at Rock Island. Food was scanty, one blanket did for three men, and the ravages of smallpox, pneumonia and typhoid gave the place the name of a pesthouse. Three-fourths of all the men sent there never came out alive.

And Ashley was in that horrible place! Ashley was alive but he was wounded and at Rock Island, and the snow must have been deep in Illinois when he was taken there. Had he died of his wound, since Rhett had learned his news? Had he fallen victim to smallpox? Was he delirious with pneumonia and no blanket to cover him?

"Oh, Captain Butler, isn't there some way— Can't you use your influence and have him exchanged?" cried Melanie.

"Mr. Lincoln, the merciful and just, who cries large tears over Mrs. Bixby's five boys, hasn't any tears to shed about the thousands of Yankees dying at Andersonville," said Rhett, his mouth twisting. "He doesn't care if they all die. The order is out. No exchanges. I—I hadn't told you before, Mrs. Wilkes, but your husband had a chance to get out and refused it."

"Oh, no!" cried Melanie in disbelief.

"Yes, indeed. The Yankees are recruiting men for frontier service to fight the Indians, recruiting them from among Confederate prisoners. Any prisoner who will take the oath of allegiance and enlist for Indian service for two years will be released and sent West. Mr. Wilkes refused."

"Oh, how could he?" cried Scarlett. "Why didn't he take the oath and then desert and come home as soon as he got out of jail?"

444

Melanie turned on her like a small fury.

"How can you even suggest that he would do such a thing? Betray his own Confederacy by taking that vile oath and then betray his word to the Yankees! I would rather know he was dead at Rock Island than hear he had taken that oath. I'd be proud of him if he died in prison. But if he did *that*, I would never look on his face again. Never! Of course, he refused."

When Scarlett was seeing Rhett to the door, she asked indignantly: "If it were you, wouldn't you enlist with the Yankees to keep from dying in that place and then desert?"

"Of course," said Rhett, his teeth showing beneath his moustache.

"Then why didn't Ashley do it?"

"He's a gentleman," said Rhett, and Scarlett wondered how it was possible to convey such cynicism and contempt in that one honourable word.

Part Three

1

MAY of 1864 came—a hot dry May that wilted the flowers in the buds—and the Yankees under General Sherman were in Georgia again, above Dalton, one hundred miles north-west of Atlanta. Rumour had it that there would be heavy fighting up there near the boundary between Georgia and Tennessee. The Yankees were massing for an attack on the Western and Atlantic Railroad, the line which connected Atlanta with Tennessee and the West, the same line over which the Southern troops had been rushed last fall to win the victory at Chickamauga.

But, for the most part, Atlanta was not disturbed by the prospect of fighting near Dalton. The place where the Yankees were concentrating was only a few miles south-east of the battlefield of Chickamauga. They had been driven back once when they had tried to break through the mountain passes of that region, and they would be driven back again.

Atlanta—and all of Georgia—knew that the state was far too important to the Confederacy for General Joe Johnston to let the Yankees remain inside the state's borders for long. Old Joe and his army would not let even one Yankee get south of Dalton, for too much depended on the undisturbed functioning of Georgia. The unravaged state was a vast granary, machine shop and

449

storehouse for the Confederacy. It manufactured much of the powder and arms used by the army and most of the cotton and woollen goods. Lying between Atlanta and Dalton was the city of Rome with its cannon foundry and its other industries, and Etowah and Allatoona with the largest ironworks south of Richmond. And in Atlanta were not only the factories for making pistols and saddles, tents and ammunition, but also the most extensive rolling mills in the South, the shops of the principal railroads and the enormous hospitals. And in Atlanta was the junction of the four railroads on which the very life of the Confederacy depended.

So no one worried particularly. After all, Dalton was a long way off, up near the Tennessee line. There had been fighting in Tennessee for three years and people were accustomed to the thought of that state as a far-away battlefield, almost as far away as Virginia or the Mississippi River. Moreover, Old Joe and his men were between the Yankees and Atlanta, and everyone knew that, next to General Lee himself, there was no greater general than Johnston, now that Stonewall Jackson was dead.

Dr. Meade summed up the civilian point of view on the matter, one warm May evening on the veranda of Aunt Pitty's house, when he said that Atlanta had nothing to fear, for General Johnston was standing in the mountains like an iron rampart. His audience heard him with varying emotions, for all who sat there rocking quietly in the fading twilight, watching the first fireflies of the season moving magically through the dusk, had weighty matters on their minds. Mrs. Meade, her hand upon Phil's arm, was hoping that the doctor was right. If the war came closer, she knew that Phil would have to go. He was sixteen now and in the Home Guard. Fanny Elsing, pale and hollow-eyed since Gettysburg, was trying to keep her mind from the torturing picture which had worn a groove in her tired mind these past several months—Lieutenant Dallas McLure dying in a jolting ox-cart in the rain on the long, terrible retreat into Maryland.

Captain Carey Ashburn's useless arm was hurting him again and moreover he was depressed by the thought that his courtship of Scarlett was at a standstill. That had been the situation ever since the news of Ashley Wilkes' capture, though the connection between the two events did not occur to him. Scarlett and Melanie both were thinking of Ashley, as they always did when urgent tasks or the necessity of carrying on a conversation did not divert them. Scarlett was thinking bitterly, sorrowfully: "He must be dead or else we would have heard." Melanie, stemming the tide of fear again and again, through endless hours, was telling herself: "He can't be dead. I'd know it—I'd feel it if he were dead." Rhett Butler lounged in the shadows, his long legs in their elegant boots crossed negligently, his dark face an unreadable blank. In his arms Wade slept contentedly, a cleanly picked wishbone in his small hand. Scarlett always permitted Wade to sit up late when Rhett called because the shy child was fond of him, and Rhett oddly enough seemed to be fond of Wade. Generally Scarlett was annoyed by the child's presence, but he always behaved nicely in Rhett's arms. As for Aunt Pitty, she was nervously trying to stifle a belch, for the rooster they had had for supper was a tough old bird.

That morning Aunt Pitty had reached the regretful decision that she had better kill the patriarch before he died of old age and pining for his harem which had long since been eaten. For days he had drooped about the empty chicken-run, too dispirited to crow. After Uncle Peter had wrung his neck, Aunt Pitty had been beset by conscience at the thought of enjoying him, en famille, when so many of her friends had not tasted chicken for weeks, so she suggested company for dinner. Melanie, who was now in her fifth month, had not been out in public or received guests for weeks, and she was appalled at the idea. But Aunt Pitty, for once, was firm. It would be selfish to eat the rooster alone, and if Melanie would only move her top hoop a little higher no one would notice anything and she was so flat in the bust anyway.

"Oh, but Auntie, I don't want to see people when Ashley—"

"It isn't as if Ashley were—had passed away," said Aunt Pitty, her voice quavering, for in her heart she was certain Ashley was dead. "He's just as much alive as you are and it will do you good to have company. And I'm going to ask Fanny Elsing, too. Mrs. Elsing begged me to try to do something to arouse her and make her see people—"

"Oh, but Auntie, it's cruel to force her when poor Dallas has only been dead—"

"Now, Melly, I shall cry with vexation if you argue with me. I guess I'm your auntie and I know what's what. And I want a party."

So Aunt Pitty had her party, and, at the last minute, a guest she did not expect, or desire, arrived. Just when the smell of roast rooster was filling the house, Rhett Butler, back from one of his mysterious trips, knocked at the door, with a large box of bonbons packed in paper lace under his arm and a mouthful of two-edged compliments for her. There was nothing to do but invite him to stay, although Aunt Pitty knew how the doctor and Mrs. Meade felt about him and how bitter Fanny was against any man not in uniform. Neither the Meades nor the Elsings would have spoken to him on the street, but in a friend's home they would, of course, have to be polite to him. Besides, he was now more firmly than ever under the protection of the fragile Melanie. After he had intervened for her to get the news about Ashley, she had announced publicly that her home was open to him as long as he lived and no matter what other people might say about him.

Aunt Pitty's apprehensions quieted when she saw that Rhett was on his best behaviour. He devoted himself to Fanny with such sympathetic deference she even smiled at him, and the meal went well. It was a princely feast. Carey Ashburn had brought a little tea, which he had found in the tobacco-pouch of a captured Yankee en route to Andersonville, and everyone had a cup, faintly flavoured with tobacco. There was a nibble of the tough old bird for each, an adequate amount of dressing made of corn meal and seasoned with onions, a bowl of dried peas, and plenty of rice and gravy, the latter somewhat watery, for there was no flour with which to thicken it. For dessert, there was a sweet potato pie followed by Rhett's bonbons, and when Rhett produced real Havana cigars for the gentlemen to enjoy over their glass of blackberry wine, everyone agreed it was indeed a Lucullan banquet.

When the gentlemen joined the ladies on the front porch, the talk turned to war. Talk always turned to war now, all conversations on any topic led from war or back to war—sometimes sad, often gay, but always war. War romances, war weddings, deaths in hospitals and on the field, incidents of camp and battle and march, gallantry, cowardice, humour, sadness, deprivation and hope. Always, always hope. Hope firm, unshaken despite the defeats of the summer before.

When Captain Ashburn announced he had applied for and been granted transfer from Atlanta to the army at Dalton, the ladies kissed his stiffened arm with their eyes and covered their emotions of pride by declaring he couldn't go, for then who would beau them about?

Young Carey looked confused and pleased at hearing such statements from settled matrons and spinsters like Mrs. Meade and Melanie and Aunt Pitty and Fanny, and tried to hope that Scarlett really meant it.

"Why, he'll be back in no time," said the doctor, throwing an arm over Carey's shoulder.

"There'll be just one brief skirmish and the Yankees will skedaddle back into Tennessee. And when they get there, General Forrest will take care of them. You ladies need have no alarm about the proximity of the Yankees, for General Johnston and his army stands there in the mountains like an iron rampart. Yes, an iron rampart," he repeated, relishing his phrase. "Sherman will never pass. He'll never dislodge Old Joe."

The ladies smiled approvingly, for his lightest utterance was regarded as incontrovertible truth. After all, men understood these matters much better than women, and if he said General Johnston was an iron rampart, he must be one. Only Rhett spoke. He had been silent since supper and had sat in the twilight listening to the war talk with a down-twisted mouth, holding the sleeping child against his shoulder.

"I believe that rumour has it that Sherman has over one hundred thousand men, now that his reinforcements have come up?"

The doctor answered him shortly. He had been under considerable strain ever since he first arrived and found that one of his fellow diners was this man whom he disliked so heartily. Only the respect due Miss Pittypat and his presence under her roof as a guest had restrained him from showing his feelings more obviously.

"Well, sir?" the doctor barked in reply.

"I believe Captain Ashburn said just a while ago that General Johnston had only about forty thousand, counting the deserters who were encouraged to come back to the colours by the last victory."

"Sir," said Mrs. Meade indignantly. "There are no deserters in the Confederate army."

"I beg your pardon," said Rhett with mock humility. "I meant those thousands on furlough who forgot to rejoin their regiments and those who have been over their wounds for six months but who remain at home, going about their usual business or doing the spring ploughing."

His eyes gleamed and Mrs. Meade bit her lip in a huff. Scarlett wanted to giggle at her discomfiture, for Rhett had caught her fairly. There were hundreds of men skulking in the swamps and the mountains, defying the provost guard to drag them back to the army. They were the ones who declared it was a "rich man's war and a poor man's fight", and they had had enough of it. But outnumbering these by far were men who, though carried on company rolls as deserters, had no intention of deserting permanently. They were the ones who had waited three years in vain for furloughs and while they waited received ill-spelled letters from home: "We air hungry." "There won't be no crop this year—there ain't nobody to plough. We air hungry." "The commissary took the shoats, and we ain't had no money from you in months. We air livin' on dried peas."

Always the rising chorus swelled: "We are hungry, your wife, your babies, your parents. When will it be over? When will you come home? We are hungry, hungry." When furloughs from the rapidly thinning army were denied, these soldiers went home without them, to plough their land and plant their crops, repair their houses and build up their fences. When regimental officers, understanding the situation, saw a hard fight ahead, they wrote these men, telling them to rejoin their companies and no questions would be asked. Usually the men returned when they saw that hunger at home would be held at bay for a few months longer. "Plough furloughs" were not looked upon in the same light as desertion in the face of the enemy, but they weakened the army just the same.

Dr. Meade hastily bridged over the uncomfortable pause, his voice cold: "Captain Butler, the numerical difference between our troops and those of the Yankees has never mattered. One Confederate is worth a dozen Yankees."

The ladies nodded. Everyone knew that.

"That was true at the first of the war," said Rhett. "Perhaps it's still true, provided the Confederate soldier has bullets for his gun and shoes on his feet and food in his stomach. Eh, Captain Ashburn?"

His voice was still soft and filled with specious humility. Carey Ashburn looked unhappy, for it was obvious that he, too, disliked Rhett intensely. He gladly would have sided with the doctor but he could not lie. The reason he had applied for transfer to the front, despite his useless arm, was that he realized, as the civilian population did not, the seriousness of the situation. There were many other men, stumping on wooden pegs, blind in one eye, fingers blown away, one arm gone, who were quietly transferring from the commissariat, hospital duties, mail and railroad service back to their old fighting units. They knew Old Joe needed every man.

He did not speak and Dr. Meade thundered, losing his temper: "Our men have fought without shoes before and without food and won victories. And they will fight again and win! I tell you General Johnston cannot be dislodged! The mountain fastnesses have always been the refuge and the strong forts of invaded peoples from ancient times. Think of—think of Thermopylae!"

Scarlett thought hard but Thermopylae meant nothing to her.

"They died to the last man at Thermopylae, didn't they, Doctor?" Rhett asked, and his lips twitched with suppressed laughter.

"Are you being insulting, young man?"

"Doctor! I beg of you! You misunderstand me! I merely asked for information. My memory of ancient history is poor."

"If need be, our army will die to the last man before they permit the Yankees to advance farther into Georgia," snapped the doctor. "But it will not be. They will drive them out of Georgia in one skirmish."

Aunt Pittypat rose hastily and asked Scarlett to favour them with a piano selection and a song. She saw that the conversation was rapidly getting into deep and stormy water. She had known very well there would be trouble if she invited Rhett to supper. There was always trouble when he was present. Just how he started it, she never exactly understood. Dear! Dear! What did Scarlett see in the man? And how could dear Melly defend him?

As Scarlett went obediently into the parlour, a

silence fell on the porch, a silence that pulsed with resentment toward Rhett. How could anyone not believe with heart and soul in the invincibility of General Johnston and his men? Believing was a sacred duty. And those who were so traitorous as not to believe should, at least, have the decency to keep their mouths shut.

Scarlett struck a few chords and her voice floated out to them from the parlour, sweetly, sadly, in the words of a popular song:

"Into a ward of whitewashed walls
  Where the dead and dying lay—
Wounded with bayonets, shells and balls—
  Somebody's darling was borne one day.

"Somebody's darling! so young and so brave!
  Wearing still on his pale, sweet face—
Soon to be hid by the dust of the grave—
  The lingering light of his boyhood's
    grace."

"Matted and damp are the curls of gold," mourned Scarlett's faulty soprano, and Fanny half rose and said in a faint, strangled voice: "Sing something else!"

The piano was suddenly silent as Scarlett was overtaken with surprise and embarrassment. Then she hastily blundered into the opening bars of "Jacket of Grey" and stopped with a discord as she remembered how heartrending that selection was too. The piano was silent again for she was utterly at a loss. All the songs had to do with death and parting and sorrow.

Rhett rose swiftly, deposited Wade in Fanny's lap, and went into the parlour.

"Play 'My Old Kentucky Home'," he suggested smoothly, and Scarlett gratefully plunged into it. Her voice was joined by Rhett's excellent bass, and as they went into the second verse those on the porch breathed more easily, though Heaven knew it was none too cheery a song, either.

"Just a few more days for to tote the weary load!
No matter,'twill never be light!
Just a few more days, till we totter in the road!
Then, my old Kentucky home, good night!"

Dr. Meade's prediction was right—as far as it went. Johnston did stand like an iron rampart in the mountains above Dalton, one hundred miles away. So firmly did he stand and so bitterly did he contest Sherman's desire to pass down the valley toward Atlanta that finally the Yankees drew back and took counsel with themselves. They could not break the grey lines by direct assault and so, under cover of night, they marched through the mountain passes in a semi-circle, hoping to come upon Johnston's rear and cut the railroad behind him at Resaca, fifteen miles below Dalton.

With those precious twin lines of iron in danger, the Confederates left their desperately defended rifle-pits and, under the starlight, made a forced march to Resaca by the short, direct

460

road. When the Yankees, swarming out of the hills, came upon them, the Southern troops were waiting for them, entrenched behind breastworks, batteries planted, bayonets gleaming, even as they had been at Dalton.

When the wounded from Dalton brought in garbled accounts of Old Joe's retreat to Resaca, Atlanta was surprised and a little disturbed. It was as though a small, dark cloud had appeared in the north-west, the first cloud of a summer storm. What was the General thinking about, letting the Yankees penetrate eighteen miles farther into Georgia? The mountains were natural fortresses, even as Dr. Meade had said. Why hadn't Old Joe held the Yankees there?

Johnston fought desperately at Resaca and repulsed the Yankees again, but Sherman, employing the same flanking movement, swung his vast army in another semicircle, crossed the Oostanaula River and again struck at the railroad in the Confederate rear. Again the grey lines were summoned swiftly from their red ditches to defend the railroad, and, weary for sleep, exhausted from marching and fighting, and hungry, always hungry, they made another rapid march down the valley. They reached the little town of Calhoun, six miles below Resaca, ahead of the Yankees, entrenched and were again ready for the attack when the Yankees came up. The attack came, there was fierce skirmishing and the Yankees were beaten back. Wearily the Confederates lay on their arms and prayed for respite and rest. But there was no rest. Sherman inexorably advanced, step by step, swinging his army about

461

them in a wide curve, forcing another retreat to defend the railroad at their back.

The Confederates marched in their sleep, too tired to think for the most part. But when they did think, they trusted Old Joe. They knew they were retreating but they knew they had not been beaten. They just didn't have enough men to hold their entrenchments and defeat Sherman's flanking movements, too. They could and did lick the Yankees every time the Yankees would stand and fight. What would be the end of this retreat, they did not know. But Old Joe knew what he was doing and that was enough for them. He had conducted the retreat in masterly fashion, for they had lost few men and the Yankee killed and captured ran high. They hadn't lost a single wagon and only four guns. And they hadn't lost the railroad at their back, either. Sherman hadn't laid a finger on it for all his frontal attacks, cavalry dashes and flank movements.

The railroad. It was still theirs, that slender iron line winding through the sunny valley toward Atlanta. Men lay down to sleep where they could see the rails gleaming faintly in the starlight. Men lay down to die, and the last sight that met their puzzled eyes was the rails shining in the merciless sun, heat shimmering along them.

As they fell back down the valley, an army of refugees fell back before them. Planters and Crackers, rich and poor, black and white, women and children, the old, the dying, the crippled, the wounded, the women far gone in pregnancy, crowded the road to Atlanta, on trains, afoot, on horseback, in carriages and wagons piled high with trunks and household goods. Five miles ahead of the retreating army went the refugees, halting at Resaca, at Calhoun, at Kingston, hoping at each stop to hear that the Yankees had been driven back so they could return to their homes. But there was no retracing that sunny road. The grey troops passed by empty mansions, deserted farms, lonely cabins with doors ajar. Here and there some lone woman remained with a few frightened slaves, and they came to the road to cheer the soldiers, to bring buckets of well water for the thirsty men, to bind up the wounds and bury the dead in their own family burying-grounds. But for the most part the sunny valley was abandoned and desolate and the untended crops stood in parching fields.

Flanked again at Calhoun, Johnston fell back to Adairsville, where there was sharp skirmishing, then to Cassville, then south of Cartersville. And the enemy had now advanced fifty-five miles from Dalton. At New Hope Church, fifteen miles farther along the hotly fought way, the grey ranks dug in for a determined stand. On came the blue lines, relentlessly, like a monster serpent, coiling, striking venomously, drawing its injured lengths back, but always striking again. There was desperate fighting at New Hope Church, eleven days of continuous fighting, with every Yankee assault bloodily repulsed. Then Johnston, flanked again, withdrew his thinning lines a few miles farther.

The Confederate dead and wounded at New Hope Church ran high. The wounded flooded Atlanta in trainloads and the town was appalled.

Never, even after the battle of Chickamauga, had the town seen so many wounded. The hospitals overflowed and wounded lay on the floors of empty stores and upon cotton bales in the warehouses. Every hotel, boarding-house and private residence was crowded with sufferers. Aunt Pitty had her share, although she protested that it was most unbecoming to have strange men in the house when Melanie was in a delicate condition and when gruesome sights might bring on premature birth. But Melanie reefed up her top hoop a little higher to hide her thickening figure and the wounded invaded the brick house. There was endless cooking and lifting and turning and fanning, endless hours of washing and rerolling bandages and picking lint, and endless warm nights made sleepless by the babbling delirium of men in the next room. Finally the choked town could take care of no more and the overflow of wounded was sent on to the hospitals at Macon and Augusta.

With this backwash of wounded bearing conflicting reports and the increase of frightened refugees crowding into the already crowded town, Atlanta was in an uproar. The small cloud on the horizon had blown up swiftly into a large, sullen storm-cloud and it was as though a faint, chilling wind blew from it.

No one had lost faith in the invincibility of the troops but everyone, the civilians at least, had lost faith in the General. New Hope Church was only thirty-five miles from Atlanta! The General had let the Yankees push him back sixty-five miles in three weeks! Why didn't he hold the Yankees instead of everlastingly retreating? He was a fool and worse than a fool. Greybeards in the Home Guard and members of the state militia, safe in Atlanta, insisted they could have managed the campaign better and drew maps on tablecloths to prove their contentions. As his lines grew thinner and he was forced back farther, the General called desperately on Governor Brown for these very men, but the state troops felt reasonably safe. After all, the Governor had defied Jeff Davis' demand for them. Why should he accede to General Johnston?

Fight and fall back! Fight and fall back! For seventy miles and twenty-five days the Confederates had fought almost daily. New Hope Church was behind the grey troops now, a memory in a mad haze of like memories, heat, dust, hunger, weariness, tramp-tramp on the red rutted roads, slop-slop through the red mud, retreat, entrench, fight—retreat, entrench, fight. New Hope Church was a nightmare of another life and so was Big Shanty, where they turned and fought the Yankees like demons. But, fight the Yankees till the fields were blue with dead, there were always more Yankees, fresh Yankees; there was always that sinister south-east curving of the blue lines toward the Confederate rear, toward the railroad —and toward Atlanta!

From Big Shanty, the weary sleepless lines retreated down the road to Kennesaw Mountain, near the little town of Marietta, and here they spread their lines in a ten-mile curve. On the steep sides of the mountain they dug their rifle-pits and on the towering heights they planted their batteries. Swearing, sweating men hauled the heavy guns up the precipitous slopes, for mules could not climb the hillsides. Couriers and wounded coming into Atlanta gave reassuring reports to the frightened townspeople. The heights of Kennesaw were impregnable. So were Pine Mountain and Lost Mountain near by which were also fortified. The Yankees couldn't dislodge Old Joe's men and they could hardly flank them now for the batteries on the mountain tops commanded all the roads for miles. Atlanta breathed more easily, but—

But Kennesaw Mountain was only twenty-two miles away!

On the day when the first wounded from Kennesaw Mountain were coming in, Mrs. Merriwether's carriage was at Aunt Pitty's house at the unheard-of hour of seven in the morning, and black Uncle Levi sent up word that Scarlett must dress immediately and come to the hospital. Fanny Elsing and the Bonnell girls, roused early from slumber, were yawning on the back seat and the Elsings' mammy sat grumpily on the box, a basket of freshly laundered bandages on her lap. Off Scarlett went, unwillingly, for she had danced till dawn the night before at the Home Guard's party and her feet were tired. She silently cursed the efficient and indefatigable Mrs. Merriwether, the wounded and the whole Southern Confederacy, as Prissy buttoned her in her oldest and raggedest calico frock which she used for hospital work. Gulping down the bitter brew of parched corn and dried sweet potatoes that passed for coffee, she went out to join the girls.

She was sick of all this nursing. This very day she would tell Mrs. Merriwether that Ellen had written her to come home for a visit. Much good this did her, for that worthy matron, her sleeves rolled up, her stout figure swathed in a large apron, gave her one sharp look and said: "Don't let me hear any more such foolishness, Scarlett Hamilton. I'll write your mother to-day and tell her how much we need you, and I'm sure she'll understand and let you stay. Now, put on your apron and trot over to Dr. Meade. He needs someone to help with the dressings."

"Oh, God," thought Scarlett drearily, "that's just the trouble. Mother will make me stay here and I shall die if I have to smell these stinks any longer! I wish I was an old lady so I could bully young ones, instead of getting bullied—and tell old cats like Mrs. Merriwether to go to Halifax!"

Yes, she was sick of the hospital, the foul smells, the lice, the aching, unwashed bodies. If there had ever been any novelty and romance about nursing, that had worn off a year ago. Besides, these men wounded in the retreat were not so attractive as the earlier ones had been. They didn't show the slightest interest in her and they had very little to say beyond: "How's the fightin' goin'? What's Old Joe doin' now? Mighty clever fellow, Old Joe." She didn't think Old Joe a mighty clever fellow. All he had done was let the Yankees penetrate eighty-eight miles into Georgia. No, they were not an attractive lot. Moreover, many of them were dying, dying swiftly, silently, having little strength left to combat the blood poisoning, gangrene, typhoid and pneumonia which had set in before they could reach Atlanta and a doctor.

The day was hot and the flies came in the open windows in swarms, fat lazy flies that broke the spirits of the men as pain could not. The tide of smells and pain rose and rose about her. Perspiration soaked through her freshly starched dress as she followed Dr. Meade about, a basin in her hand.

Oh, the nausea of standing by the doctor, trying not to vomit when his bright knife cut into mortifying flesh! And oh, the horror of hearing the screams from the operating ward where amputations were going on! And the sick, helpless sense of pity at the sight of tense, white faces of mangled men waiting for the doctor to get to them, men whose ears were filled with screams, men waiting for the dreadful words: "I'm sorry, my boy, but that hand will have to come off. Yes, yes, I know; but look, see those red streaks? It'll have to come off."

Chloroform was so scarce now it was used only for the worst amputations and opium was a precious thing, used only to ease the dying out of life, not the living out of pain. There was no quinine and no iodine at all. Yes, Scarlett was sick of it all, and that morning she wished that she, like Melanie, had the excuse of pregnancy to offer. That was about the only excuse that was socially acceptable for not nursing these days.

When noon came, she put off her apron and sneaked away from the hospital while Mrs. Merriwether was busy writing a letter for a gangling, illiterate mountaineer. Scarlett felt that she could stand it no longer. It was an imposition on her and she knew that when the wounded came in on the noon train there would be enough work to keep her busy until nightfall—and probably without anything to eat.

She went hastily up the two short blocks to Peachtree Street, breathing the unfouled air in as deep gulps as her tightly laced corset would permit. She was standing on the corner, uncertain as to what she would do next, ashamed to go home to Aunt Pitty's but determined not to go back to the hospital, when Rhett Butler drove by.

"You look like the ragpicker's child," he observed, his eyes taking in the mended lavender calico, streaked with perspiration and splotched here and there with water which had slopped from the basin. Scarlett was furious with embarrassment and indignation. Why did he always notice women's clothing and why was he so rude as to remark upon her present untidiness?

"I don't want to hear a word out of you. You get out and help me in and drive me somewhere where nobody will see me. I won't go back to the hospital if they hang me! My goodness, I didn't start this war and I don't see any reason why I should be worked to death and—"

"A traitor to Our Glorious Cause!"

"The pot's calling the kettle black. You help me in. I don't care where you were going. You're going to take me riding now."

He swung himself out of the carriage to the ground and she suddenly thought how nice it was to see a man who was whole, who was not minus eyes or limbs, or white with pain or yellow with malaria, and who looked well fed and healthy. He was so well dressed too. His coat and trousers were actually of the same material and they fitted him, instead of hanging in folds or being almost too tight for movement. And they were new, not ragged, with dirty bare flesh and hairy legs showing through. He looked as if he had not a care in the world and that in itself was startling these days, when other men wore such worried, preoccupied, grim looks. His brown face was bland and his mouth, red-lipped, clear-cut as a woman's, frankly sensual, smiled carelessly as he lifted her into the carriage.

The muscles of his big body rippled against his well-tailored clothes as he got in beside her, and, as always, the sense of his great physical power struck her like a blow. She watched the swell of his powerful shoulders against the cloth with a fascination that was disturbing, a little frightening. His body seemed so tough and hard, as tough and hard as his keen mind. His was such an easy, graceful strength, lazy as a panther stretching in the sun, alert as a panther to spring and strike.

"You little fraud," he said, clucking to the horse. "You dance all night with the soldiers and give them roses and ribbons and tell them how you'd die for the Cause, and when it comes to bandaging a few wounds and picking off a few lice, you decamp hastily."

"Can't you talk about something else and drive faster? It would be just my luck for Grandpa Merriwether to come out of his store and see me and tell old lady—I mean, Mrs. Merriwether."

He touched up the mare with the whip and she trotted briskly across Five Points and across the railroad tracks that cut the town in two. The train bearing the wounded had already come in and the litter-bearers were working swiftly in the hot sun, transferring wounded into ambulances and covered ordnance wagons. Scarlett had no qualm of conscience as she watched them but only a feeling of vast relief that she had made her escape.

"I'm just sick and tired of that old hospital," she said, settling her billowing skirts and tying her bonnet-bow more firmly under her chin. "And every day more and more wounded come in. It's all General Johnston's fault. If he'd just stood up to the Yankees at Dalton, they'd have—"

"But he did stand up to the Yankees, you ignorant child. And if he'd kept on standing there, Sherman would have flanked him and crushed him between the two wings of his army. And he'd have lost the railroad and the railroad is what Johnston is fighting for."

"Oh, well," said Scarlett, on whom military strategy was utterly lost. "It's his fault anyway. He ought to have done something about it and I think he ought to be removed. Why doesn't he stand and fight instead of retreating?"

"You are like everyone else, screaming 'Off with his head' because he can't do the impossible. He was Jesus the Saviour at Dalton, and now he's Judas the Betrayer at Kennesaw Mountain, all in six weeks. Yet, just let him drive the Yankees back twenty miles and he'll be Jesus again. My child, Sherman has twice as many men as

Johnston, and he can afford to lose two men for every one of our gallant laddies. And Johnston can't afford to lose a single man. He needs reinforcements badly and what is he getting? 'Joe Brown's Pets.' What a help they'll be!"

"Is the militia really going to be called out? The Home Guard, too? I hadn't heard. How do you know?"

"There's a rumour floating about to that effect. The rumour arrived on the train from Milledgeville this morning. Both the militia and the Home Guards are going to be sent in to reinforce General Johnston. Yes, Governor Brown's darlings are likely to smell powder at last, and I imagine most of them will be much surprised. Certainly they never expected to see action. The Governor as good as promised them they wouldn't. Well, that's a good joke on them. They thought they had bomb-proofs because the Governor stood up to even Jeff Davis and refused to send them to Virginia. Said they were needed for the defence of their state. Who'd have ever thought the war would come to their own back yard and they'd really have to defend their state?"

"Oh, how can you laugh, you cruel thing! Think of the old gentlemen and the little boys in the Home Guard! Why, little Phil Meade will have to go and Grandpa Merriwether and Uncle Henry Hamilton."

"I'm not talking about the little boys and the Mexican War veterans. I'm talking about brave young men like Willie Guinan who like to wear pretty uniforms and wave swords—"

"And yourself!"

"My dear, that didn't hurt a bit! I wear no uniform and wave no sword and the fortunes of the Confederacy mean nothing at all to me. Moreover, I wouldn't be caught dead in the Home Guard or in any army, for that matter. I had enough of things military at West Point to do me the rest of my life. . . . Well, I wish Old Joe luck. General Lee can't send him any help because the Yankees are keeping him busy in Virginia. So the Georgia state troops are the only reinforcements Johnston can get. He deserves better, for he's a great strategist. He always manages to get places before the Yankees do. But he'll have to keep falling back if he wants to protect the railroad; and mark my words, when they push him out of the mountains and on to the flatter land around here, he's going to be butchered."

"Around here?" cried Scarlett. "You know mighty well the Yankees will never get this far!"

"Kennesaw is only twenty-two miles away and I'll wager you—"

"Rhett, look, down the street! That crowd of men! They aren't soldiers. What on earth . . . ? Why, they're darkies!"

There was a great cloud of red dust coming up the street and from the cloud came the sound of the tramping of many feet and a hundred or more negro voices, deep-throated, careless, singing a hymn. Rhett pulled the carriage over to the kerb, and Scarlett looked curiously at the sweating black men, picks and shovels over their shoulders, shepherded along by an officer and a squad of men wearing the insignia of the engineering corps.

"What on earth . . .?" she began again.

Then her eyes lighted on a singing black buck in the front rank. He stood nearly six and a half feet tall, a giant of a man, ebony black, stepping along with the lithe grace of a powerful animal, his white teeth flashing as he led the gang in "Go Down, Moses". Surely there wasn't a negro on earth as tall and loud-voiced as this one except Big Sam, the foreman of Tara. But what was Big Sam doing here, so far away from home, especially now that there was no overseer on the plantation and he was Gerald's right-hand man?

As she half rose from her seat to look closer, the giant caught sight of her and his black face split in a grin of delighted recognition. He halted, dropped his shovel and started toward her, calling to the negroes nearest him: "Gawdlmighty! It's Miss Scarlett! You, 'Lige! 'Postle! Prophet! Dar's Miss Scarlett!"

There was confusion in the ranks. The crowd halted uncertainly, grinning, and Big Sam, followed by three other large negroes, ran across the road to the carriage, closely followed by the harried, shouting officer.

"Get back in line, you fellows! Get back, I tell you, or I'll—Why, it's Mrs. Hamilton. Good morning, Ma'm, and you, too, sir. What are you up to, inciting mutiny and insubordination? God knows, I've had trouble enough with these boys this morning."

"Oh, Captain Randall, don't scold them! They are our people. This is Big Sam, our foreman, and Elijah and Apostle and Prophet from Tara.

Of course, they had to speak to me. How are you, boys?"

She shook hands all around, her small white hand disappearing into their huge black paws, and the four capered with delight at the meeting and with pride at displaying before their comrades what a pretty Young Miss they had.

"What are you boys doing so far from Tara? You've run away, I'll be bound. Don't you know the patterollers will get you sure?"

They bellowed pleasedly at the badinage.

"Runned away?" answered Big Sam. "No'm, us ain' runned away. Dey done sont an' tuck us, kase us wuz de fo' bigges' an' stronges' han's at Tara." His white teeth showed proudly. "Dey specially sont fer me, kase Ah could sing so good. Yas'm, Mist' Frank Kennedy, he come by an' tuck us."

"But why, Big Sam?"

"Lawd, Miss Scarlett! Ain' you heerd? Us is ter dig de ditches fer de w'ite gempmums ter hide in w'en de Yankees comes."

Captain Randall and the occupants of the carriage smothered smiles at this naïve explanation of rifle-pits.

"Cose, Mist' Gerald might' nigh had a fit w'en dey tuck me, an' he say he kain run de place widout me. But Miss Ellen she say: 'Tek him, Mist' Kennedy. De Confedrutsy need Big Sam mo' dan us do.' An' she gib me a dollar an' tell me ter do jes' whut de w'ite gempmums tells me. So hyah us is."

"What does it all mean, Captain Randall?"

"Oh, it's quite simple. We have to strengthen

the fortifications of Atlanta with more miles of rifle-pits, and the General can't spare any men from the front to do it. So we've been impressing the strongest bucks in the countryside for the work."

"But—"

A cold little fear was beginning to throb in Scarlett's breast. More miles of rifle-pits! Why should they need more? Within the last year, a series of huge earth redoubts with battery emplacements had been built all around Atlanta, one mile from the centre of town. These great earthworks were connected with rifle-pits and they ran, mile after mile, completely encircling the city. More rifle-pits!

"But—why should we be fortified any more than we are already fortified? We won't need what we've got. Surely, the General won't let—"

"Our present fortifications are only a mile from town," said Captain Randall shortly. "And that's too close for comfort—or safety. These new ones are going to be farther away. You see, another retreat may bring our men into Atlanta."

Immediately he regretted his last remark, as her eyes widened with fear.

"But, of course, there won't be another retreat," he added hastily. "The lines around Kennesaw Mountain are impregnable. The batteries are planted all up the mountain sides and they command the roads, and the Yankees can't possibly get by."

But Scarlett saw him drop his eyes before the lazy, penetrating look Rhett gave him, and she was frightened. She remembered Rhett's remark:

"When the Yankees push him out of the mountains and on to the flatter land, he'll be butchered."

"Oh, Captain, do you think—"

"Why, of course not! Don't fret your mind one minute. Old Joe just believes in taking precautions. That's the only reason we're digging more entrenchments. . . . But I must be going now. It's been pleasant, talking to you. . . . Say good-bye to your mistress, boys, and let's get going."

"Good-bye, boys. Now, if you get sick or hurt or in trouble, let me know. I live right down Peachtree Street, down there in almost the last house at the end of town. Wait a minute—" She fumbled in her reticule. "Oh, dear, I haven't a cent. Rhett, give me a few shin-plasters. Here, Big Sam, buy some tobacco for yourself and the boys. And be good and do what Captain Randall tells you."

The straggling line re-formed, the dust arose again in a red cloud as they moved off and Big Sam started up the singing again.

"Go do-ow, Mos-es! Waaa-ay, do-own, in
    Eee-jup laa-an!
An' te-el O-le Faa-ro-o
Ter let mah—peee-pul go!"

"Rhett, Captain Randall was lying to me, just like all the men do—trying to keep the truth from us women for fear we'll faint. Or was he lying? Oh, Rhett, if there's no danger, why are they digging these new breastworks? Is the army so short of men they've got to use darkies?"

Rhett clucked to the mare.

"The army is damned short of men. Why else would the Home Guard be called out? And as for the entrenchments, well, fortifications are supposed to be of some value in case of a siege. The General is preparing to make his final stand here."

"A siege! Oh, turn the horse around. I'm going home, back home to Tara, right away."

"What ails you?"

"A siege! Name of God, a siege! I've heard about sieges! Pa was in one or maybe it was his Pa, and Pa told me. . . ."

"What siege?"

"The siege at Drogheda when Cromwell had the Irish, and they didn't have anything to eat and Pa said they starved and died in the streets and finally they ate all the cats and rats and even things like cockroaches. And he said they ate each other too, before they surrendered, though I never did know whether to believe that or not. And when Cromwell took the town all the women were—A siege! Mother of God!"

"You are the most barbarously ignorant young person I ever saw. Drogheda was in sixteen hundred and something and Mr. O'Hara couldn't possibly have been alive then. Besides, Sherman isn't Cromwell."

"No, but he's worse! They say—"

"And as for the exotic viands the Irish ate at the siege—personally I'd as soon eat a nice juicy rat as some of the victuals they've been serving

478

me recently at the hotel. I think I shall have to go back to Richmond. They have good food there, if you have the money to pay for it." His eyes mocked the fear in her face.

Annoyed that she had shown her trepidation, she cried: "I don't see why you've stayed here this long! All you think about is being comfortable and eating and—and things like that."

"I know no more pleasant way to pass the time than in eating and—er—things like that," he said. "And as for why I stay here—well, I've read a good deal about sieges, beleaguered cities and the like, but I've never seen one. So I think I'll stay here and watch. I won't get hurt because I'm a noncombatant and besides I want the experience. Never pass up new experiences, Scarlett. They enrich the mind."

"My mind's rich enough."

"Perhaps you know best about that, but I should say—But that would be ungallant. And perhaps, I'm staying here to rescue you when the siege does come. I've never rescued a maiden in distress. That would be a new experience, too."

She knew he was teasing her but she sensed a seriousness behind his words. She tossed her head.

"I won't need you to rescue me. I can take care of myself, thank you."

"Don't say that, Scarlett! Think it, if you like, but never, never say it to a man. That's the trouble with Yankee girls. They'd be most charming if they weren't always telling you that they can take care of themselves, thank you. Generally they are telling the truth, God help them. And so men let them take care of themselves."

"How you do run on," she said coldly, for there was no insult worse than being likened to a Yankee girl. "I believe you're lying about a siege. You know the Yankees will never get to Atlanta."

"I'll bet you they will be here within the month. I'll bet you a box of bonbons against—" His dark eyes wandered to her lips. "Against a kiss."

For a last brief moment, fear of a Yankee invasion clutched her heart but at the word "kiss", she forgot about it. This was familiar ground and far more interesting than military operations. With difficulty she restrained a smile of glee. Since the day when he gave her the green bonnet, Rhett had made no advances which could in any way be construed as those of a lover. He could never be inveigled into personal conversations, try though she might, but now with no angling on her part, he was talking about kissing.

"I don't care for such personal conversation," she said coolly and managed a frown. "Besides, I'd just as soon kiss a pig."

"There's no accounting for tastes and I've always heard the Irish were partial to pigs—kept them under their beds, in fact. But, Scarlett, you need kissing badly. That's what's wrong with you. All your beaux have respected you too much, though God knows why, or they have been too afraid of you to really do right by you. The result is that you are unendurably uppity. You should be kissed and by someone who knows how."

The conversation was not going the way she

wanted it. It never did when she was with him. Always, it was a duel in which she was worsted.

"And I suppose you think you are the proper person?" she asked with sarcasm, holding her temper in check with difficulty.

"Oh, yes, if I cared to take the trouble," he said carelessly. "They say I kiss very well."

"Oh," she began, indignant at the slight to her charms. "Why, you . . ." But her eyes fell in sudden confusion. He was smiling, but in the dark depths of his eyes a tiny light flickered for a brief moment, like a small raw flame.

"Of course, you've probably wondered why I never tried to follow up that chaste peck I gave you, the day I brought you that bonnet—"

"I have never—"

"Then you aren't a nice girl, Scarlett, and I'm sorry to hear it. All really nice girls wonder when men don't try to kiss them. They know they shouldn't want them to and they know they must act insulted if they do, but just the same, they wish the men would try. . . . Well, my dear, take heart. Some day, I will kiss you and you will like it. But not now, so I beg you not to be too impatient."

She knew he was teasing but, as always, his teasing maddened her. There was always too much truth in the things he said. Well, this finished him. If ever, ever he should be so ill-bred as to try to take any liberties with her, she would show him.

"Will you kindly turn the horse around, Captain Butler? I wish to go back to the hospital."

"Do you indeed, my ministering angel? Then lice and slops are preferable to my conversation? Well, far be it from me to keep a pair of willing hands from labouring for Our Glorious Cause." He turned the horse's head and they started back toward Five Points.

"As to why I have made no further advances," he pursued blandly, as though she had not signified that the conversation was at an end, "I'm waiting for you to grow up a little more. You see, it wouldn't be much fun for me to kiss you now and I'm quite selfish about my pleasures. I never fancied kissing children."

He smothered a grin, as from the corner of his eye he saw her bosom heave with silent wrath.

"And then, too," he continued softly, "I was waiting for the memory of the estimable Ashley Wilkes to fade."

At the mention of Ashley's name, sudden pain went through her, sudden hot tears stung her lids. Fade? The memory of Ashley would never fade, not if he were dead a thousand years. She thought of Ashley wounded, dying in a far-off Yankee prison, with no blankets over him, with no one who loved him to hold his hand, and she was filled with hate at the well-fed man who sat beside her, jeers just beneath the surface of his drawling voice.

She was too angry to speak and they rode along in silence for some while.

"I understand practically everything about you and Ashley, now," Rhett resumed. "I began with your inelegant scene at Twelve Oaks and, since then, I've picked up many things by keeping my eyes open. What things? Oh, that you still cherish a romantic schoolgirl passion for him which he reciprocates as well as his honourable nature will permit him. And that Mrs. Wilkes knows nothing and that, between the two of you, you've done her a pretty trick. I understand practically everything, except one thing and that piques my curiosity. Did the honourable Ashley ever jeopardize his immortal soul by kissing you?"

A stony silence and an averted head were his answers.

"Ah, well, so he did kiss you. I suppose it was when he was here on furlough. And now that he's probably dead you are cherishing it to your heart. But I'm sure you'll get over it and when you've forgotten his kiss, I'll—"

She turned in fury.

"You go to—Halifax," she said tensely, her green eyes slits of rage. "And let me out of this carriage before I jump over the wheels. And I don't ever want to speak to you again."

He stopped the carriage, but before he could alight and assist her she sprang down. Her hoop caught on the wheel and for a moment the crowd at Five Points had a flashing view of petticoats and pantalets. Then Rhett leaned over and swiftly released it. She flounced off without a word, without even a backward look, and he laughed softly and clicked to the horse.

2

FOR the first time since the war began, Atlanta could hear the sound of battle. In the early morning hours before the noises of the town awoke, the cannon at Kennesaw Mountain could be heard faintly, far away, a low dim booming that might have passed for summer thunder. Occasionally it was loud enough to be heard even above the rattle of traffic at noon. People tried not to listen to it, tried to talk, to laugh, to carry on their business, just as though the Yankees were not there, twenty-two miles away, but always ears were strained for the sound. The town wore a preoccupied look, for no matter what occupied their hands, all were listening, listening, their hearts leaping suddenly a hundred times a day. Was the booming louder? Or did they only think it was louder? Would General Johnston hold them this time? Would he?

Panic lay just beneath the surface. Nerves which had been stretched tighter and tighter each day of the retreat began to reach the breaking point. No one spoke of fears. That subject was taboo, but strained nerves found expression in loud criticism of the General. Public feeling was at fever heat. Sherman was at the very doors of Atlanta. Another retreat might bring the Confederates into the town.

Give us a general who won't retreat! Give us a man who will stand and fight!

With the far-off rumbling of cannon in their ears, the state militia, "Joe Brown's Pets", and the Home Guard marched out of Atlanta, to defend the bridges and ferries of the Chattahoochee River at Johnston's back. It was a grey, overcast day and, as they marched through Five Points and out the Marietta road, a fine rain began to fall. The whole town had turned out to see them off and they stood, close packed, under the wooden awnings of the stores on Peachtree Street and tried to cheer.

Scarlett and Maybelle Merriwether Picard had been given permission to leave the hospital and watch the men go out, because Uncle Henry Hamilton and Grandpa Merriwether were in the Home Guard, and they stood with Mrs. Meade, pressed in the crowd, tiptoeing to get a better view. Scarlett, though filled with the universal Southern desire to believe only the pleasantest and most reassuring things about the progress of the fighting, felt cold as she watched the motley ranks go by. Surely, things must be in a desperate pass if this rabble of bombproofers, old men and little boys were being called out! To be sure there were young and able-bodied men in the passing lines, tricked out in the bright uniforms of socially select militia units, plumes waving, sashes dancing. But there were so many old men and young boys, and the sight of them made her heart contract with pity and with fear. There were greybeards older than her father trying to step jauntily along in the needle-fine rain to the rhythm of the fife and drum corps. Grandpa Merriwether, with Mrs. Merriwether's best plaid shawl laid across

485

his shoulders to keep out the rain, was in the first rank and he saluted the girls with a grin. They waved their handkerchiefs and cried gay good-byes to him; but Maybelle, gripping Scarlett's arm, whispered: "Oh, the poor old darling! a real good rainstorm will just about finish him! His lumbago—"

Uncle Henry Hamilton marched in the rank behind Grandpa Merriwether, the collar of his long black coat turned up about his ears, two Mexican War pistols in his belt and a small carpet-bag in his hand. Beside him marched his black valet who was nearly as old as Uncle Henry, with an open umbrella held over them both. Shoulder to shoulder with their elders came the young boys, none of them looking over sixteen. Many of them had run away from school to join the army, and here and there were clumps of them in the cadet uniforms of military academies, the black cock feathers on their tight grey caps wet with rain, the clean white canvas straps crossing their chests sodden. Phil Meade was among them, proudly wearing his dead brother's sabre and horse pistols, his hat bravely pinned up on one side. Mrs. Meade managed to smile and wave until he had passed and then she leaned her head on the back of Scarlett's shoulder for a moment as though her strength had suddenly left her.

Many of the men were totally unarmed, for the Confederacy had neither rifles nor ammunition to issue to them. These men hoped to equip themselves from killed and captured Yankees. Many carried bowie-knives in their boots and bore in their hands long thick poles with iron-pointed tips known as "Joe Brown pikes". The lucky ones had old flintlock muskets slung over their shoulders and powderhorns at their belts.

Johnston had lost around ten thousand men in his retreat. He needed ten thousand more fresh troops. "And this," thought Scarlett, frightened, "is what he is getting!"

As the artillery rumbled by, splashing mud into the watching crowds, a negro on a mule, riding close to a cannon, caught her eye. He was a young, saddle-coloured negro with a serious face, and when Scarlett saw him she cried: "It's Mose! Ashley's Mose! Whatever is he doing here?" She fought her way through the crowd to the kerb and called: "Mose! Stop!"

The boy, seeing her, drew rein, smiled delightedly and started to dismount. A soaking sergeant, riding behind him, called: "Stay on that mule, boy, or I'll light a fire under you! We got to git to the mountain some time."

Uncertainly, Mose looked from the sergeant to Scarlett and she, splashing through the mud, close to the passing wheels, caught at Mose's stirrup strap.

"Oh, just a minute, Sergeant! Don't get down, Mose. What on earth are you doing here?"

"Ah's off ter de war, agin, Miss Scarlett. Dis time wid Ole Mist' John 'stead ob Mist' Ashley."

"Mr. Wilkes!" Scarlett was stunned. Mr. Wilkes was nearly seventy. "Where is he?"

"Back wid de las' cannon, Miss Scarlett. Back dar!"

"Sorry, lady. Move on, boy!"

Scarlett stood for a moment, ankle-deep in mud as the guns lurched by. "Oh, no!" she thought. "It can't be. He's too old. And he doesn't like war any more than Ashley did!" She retreated back a few paces toward the kerb and scanned each face that passed. Then, as the last cannon and limber-chest came groaning and splashing up, she saw him, slender, erect, his long silver hair wet upon his neck, riding easily upon a little strawberry mare that picked her way as daintily through the mud-holes as a lady in a satin dress. Why—that mare was Nellie! Mrs. Tarleton's Nellie! Beatrice Tarleton's treasured darling!

When he saw her standing in the mud, Mr. Wilkes drew rein with a smile of pleasure and, dismounting, came toward her.

"I had hoped to see you, Scarlett. I was charged with so many messages from your people. But there was no time. We just got in this morning and they are rushing us out immediately, as you see."

"Oh, Mr. Wilkes," she cried desperately, holding his hand. "Don't go! Why must you go?"

"Ah, so you think I'm too old!" he smiled, and it was Ashley's smile in an older face. "Perhaps I am too old to march but not to ride and to shoot. And Mrs. Tarleton so kindly lent me Nellie, so I am well mounted. I hope nothing happens to Nellie, for if something should happen to her, I could never go home and face Mrs. Tarleton. Nellie was the last horse she had left." He was laughing now, turning away her fears. "Your mother and father and the girls are well and they sent you their love. Your father nearly came up with us to-day!"

"Oh, not Pa!" cried Scarlett in terror. "Not Pa! He isn't going to the war, is he?"

"No, but he was. Of course, he can't walk far with his stiff knee, but he was all for riding away with us. Your mother agreed, providing he was able to jump the pasture fence, for, she said, there would be a lot of rough riding to be done in the army. Your father thought that easy, but—would you believe it? When his horse came to the fence, he stopped dead and over his head went your father! It's a wonder it didn't break his neck! You know how obstinate he is. He got right up and tried it again. Well, Scarlett, he came off three times before Mrs. O'Hara and Pork assisted him to bed. He was in a taking about it, swearing that your mother had 'spoken a wee word in the beast's ear'. He just isn't up to active service, Scarlett. You need have no shame about it. After all, someone must stay home and raise crops for the army."

Scarlett had no shame at all, only an active feeling of relief.

"I've sent India and Honey to Macon to stay with the Burrs and Mr. O'Hara is looking after Twelve Oaks as well as Tara. . . . I must go, my dear. Let me kiss your pretty face."

Scarlett turned up her lips and there was a choking pain in her throat. She was so fond of Mr. Wilkes. Once, long ago, she had hoped to be his daughter-in-law.

"And you must deliver this kiss to Pittypat and

this to Melanie," he said, kissing her lightly two more times. "And how is Melanie?"

"She is well."

"Ah!" His eyes looked at her but through her, past her as Ashley's had done, remote grey eyes looking on another world. "I should have liked to see my first grandchild. Good-bye, my dear."

He swung on to Nellie and cantered off, his hat in his hand, his silver hair bare to the rain. Scarlett had rejoined Maybelle and Mrs. Meade before the import of his last words broke upon her. Then in superstitious terror she crossed herself and tried to say a prayer. He had spoken of death, just as Ashley had done, and now Ashley—No one should ever speak of death! It was tempting Providence to mention death. As the three women started silently back to the hospital in the rain, Scarlett was praying: "Not him, too, God. Not him and Ashley, too!"

The retreat from Dalton to Kennesaw Mountain had taken from early May to mid-June and as the hot rainy days of June passed and Sherman failed to dislodge the Confederates from the steep slippery slopes, hope again raised its head. Everyone grew more cheerful and spoke more kindly of General Johnston. As wet June days passed into a wetter July and the Confederates, fighting desperately around the entrenched heights, still held Sherman at bay, a wild gaiety took hold of Atlanta. Hope went to their heads like champagne. Hurrah! Hurrah! We're holding them! An epidemic of parties and dances broke out. Whenever groups of men from the fighting were in town for the night, dinners were given for them and afterwards there was dancing and the girls, outnumbering the men ten to one, made much of them and fought to dance with them.

Atlanta was crowded with visitors, refugees, families of wounded men in the hospitals, wives and mothers of soldiers fighting at the mountain who wished to be near them in case of wounds. In addition, bevies of belles from the country districts, where all remaining men were under sixteen or over sixty, descended upon the town. Aunt Pitty disapproved highly of these last, for she felt they had come to Atlanta for no reason at all except to catch husbands, and the shamelessness of it made her wonder what the world was coming to. Scarlett disapproved, too. She did not care for the eager competition furnished by the sixteen-year-olds whose fresh cheeks and bright smiles made one forget their twice-turned frocks and patched shoes. Her own clothes were prettier and newer than most, thanks to the material Rhett Butler had brought her on the last boat he ran in, but, after all, she was nineteen and getting along and men had a way of chasing silly young things.

A widow with a child was at a disadvantage with these pretty minxes, she thought. But in these exciting days her widowhood and her motherhood weighed less heavily upon her than ever before. Between hospital duties in the daytime and parties at night, she hardly ever saw Wade. Sometimes she actually forgot, for long stretches, that she had a child.

In the warm wet summer nights, Atlanta's homes stood open to the soldiers, the town's defenders. The big houses from Washington Street to Peachtree Street blazed with lights, as the muddy fighters in from the rifle-pits were entertained, and the sound of banjo and fiddle and the scrape of dancing feet and light laughter carried far on the night air. Groups hung over pianos and voices sang lustily the sad words of "Your Letter Came but Came Too Late", while ragged gallants looked meaningly at girls who laughed from behind turkey-tail fans, begging them not to wait until it was too late. None of the girls waited, if they could help it. With the tide of hysterical gaiety and excitement flooding the city, they rushed into matrimony. There were so many marriages that month while Johnston was holding the enemy at Kennesaw Mountain, marriages with the bride turned out in blushing happiness and the hastily borrowed finery of a dozen friends and the groom with sabre banging at patched knees. So much excitement, so many parties, so many thrills! Hurrah! Johnston is holding the Yanks twenty-two miles away!

Yes, the lines around Kennesaw Mountain were impregnable. After twenty-five days of fighting, even General Sherman was convinced of this, for his losses were enormous. Instead of continuing the direct assault, he swung his army in a wide circle again and tried to come between the Confederates and Atlanta. Again, the strategy worked. Johnston was forced to abandon the heights he had held so well, in order to protect his rear. He had lost a third of his men in that fight and the remainder slogged tiredly through the rain across the country toward the Chatta-hoochee River. The Confederates could expect no more reinforcements, whereas the railroad, which the Yankees now held from Tennessee south to the battle-line, brought Sherman fresh troops and supplies daily. So the grey lines went back through the muddy fields, back toward Atlanta.

With the loss of the supposedly unconquerable position, a fresh wave of terror swept the town. For twenty-five wild, happy days, everyone had assured everyone else that this could not possibly happen. And now it had happened! But surely the General would hold the Yankees on the opposite bank of the river. Though God knows the river was close enough, only seven miles away!

But Sherman flanked them again, crossing the stream above them, and the weary grey files were forced to hurry across the yellow water and throw themselves again between the invaders and Atlanta. They dug in hastily in shallow pits to the north of the town in the valley of Peachtree Creek. Atlanta was in agony and panic.

Fight and fall back! Fight and fall back! And every retreat was bringing the Yankees closer to the town. Peachtree Creek was only five miles away! What was the General thinking about?

The cries of "Give us a man who will stand and fight!" penetrated even to Richmond. Richmond knew that if Atlanta was lost, the war was lost, and after the army had crossed the Chatta-hoochee, General Johnston was removed from command. General Hood, one of his corps commanders, took over the army, and the town breathed a little easier. Hood wouldn't retreat. Not that tall Kentuckian, with his flowing beard and flashing eye! He had the reputation of a bulldog. He'd drive the Yankees back from the creek, yes, back across the river and on up the road every step of the way back to Dalton. But the army cried: "Give us back Old Joe!" for they had been with Old Joe all the weary miles from Dalton and they knew, as the civilians could not know, the odds that had opposed them.

Sherman did not wait for Hood to get himself in readiness to attack. On the day after the change in command, the Yankee general struck swiftly at the little town of Decatur, six miles beyond Atlanta, captured it and cut the railroad there. This was the railroad connecting Atlanta with Augusta, with Charleston, with Wilmington and with Virginia. Sherman had dealt the Confederacy a crippling blow. The time had come for action! Atlanta screamed for action!

Then, on a July afternoon of steaming heat, Atlanta had its wish. General Hood did more than stand and fight. He assaulted the Yankees fiercely at Peachtree Creek, hurling his men from their rifle-pits against the blue lines where Sherman's men outnumbered him more than two to one.

Frightened, praying that Hood's attack would drive the Yankees back, everyone listened to the sound of booming cannon and the crackling of thousands of rifles which, though five miles away from the centre of town, were so loud as to seem almost in the next block. They could hear the rumblings of the batteries, see the smoke which rolled like low-hanging clouds above the trees, but for hours no one knew how the battle was going.

By late afternoon the first news came, but it was uncertain, contradictory, frightening, brought as it was by men wounded in the early hours of the battle. These men began straggling in, singly and in groups, the less seriously wounded supporting those who limped and staggered. Soon a steady stream of them was established, making their painful way into town toward the hospitals, their faces black as negroes' from powder stains, dust and sweat, their wounds unbandaged, blood drying, flies swarming about them.

Aunt Pitty's was one of the first houses which the wounded reached as they struggled in from the north of the town, and one after another, they tottered to the gate, sank down on the green lawn and croaked:

"Water!"

All that burning afternoon, Aunt Pitty and her family, black and white, stood in the sun with buckets of water and bandages, ladling drinks, binding wounds until the bandages gave out and even the torn sheets and towels were exhausted. Aunt Pitty completely forgot that the sight of blood always made her faint and she worked until her little feet in their too small shoes swelled and would no longer support her. Even Melanie, now great with child, forgot her modesty and worked feverishly side by side with Prissy, Cookie and Scarlett, her face as tense as any of the wounded. When at last she fainted, there was no place to lay her except on the kitchen table, as every bed, chair and sofa in the house was filled with wounded.

Forgotten in the tumult, little Wade crouched behind the banisters on the front porch, peering out on to the lawn like a caged, frightened rabbit, his eyes wide with terror, sucking his thumb and hiccoughing. Once Scarlett saw him and cried sharply: "Go play in the back yard, Wade Hampton!" but he was too terrified, too fascinated by the mad scene before him to obey.

The lawn was covered with prostrate men, too tired to walk farther, too weak from wounds to move. These Uncle Peter loaded into the carriage and drove to the hospital, making trip after trip until the old horse was lathered. Mrs. Meade and Mrs. Merriwether sent their carriages and they, too, drove off, springs sagging beneath the weight of wounded.

Later, in the long, hot summer twilight, the ambulances came rumbling down the road from the battlefield and commissary wagons, covered with muddy canvas. Then farm wagons, ox-carts and even private carriages commandeered by the medical corps. They passed Aunt Pitty's house, jolting over the bumpy road, packed with wounded and dying men, dripping blood into the red dust. At the sight of the women with buckets and dippers, the conveyances halted and the chorus went up in cries, in whispers:

"Water!"

Scarlett held wobbling heads that parched lips might drink, poured buckets of water over dusty, feverish bodies and into open wounds that the men might enjoy a brief moment's relief. She tiptoed to hand dippers to ambulance drivers and of each she questioned, her heart in her throat: "What news? What news?"

From all came back the answer: "Don't know fer sartin, lady. It's too soon to tell."

Night came and it was sultry. No air moved and the flaring pineknots the negroes held made the air hotter. Dust clogged Scarlett's nostrils and dried her lips. Her lavender calico dress, so freshly clean and starched that morning, was streaked with blood, dirt and sweat. This, then, was what Ashley had meant when he wrote that war was not glory but dirt and misery.

Fatigue gave an unreal, nightmarish cast to the whole scene. It couldn't be real—or if it was real, then the world had gone mad. If not, why should she be standing here in Aunt Pitty's peaceful front yard, amid wavering lights, pouring water over dying beaux? For so many of them were her beaux and they tried to smile when they saw her. There were so many men jolting down this dark, dusty road whom she knew so well, so many men dying here before her eyes, mosquitoes and gnats swarming their bloody faces, men with whom she had danced and laughed, for whom she had played music and sung songs, teased, comforted and loved—a little.

She found Carey Ashburn on the bottom layer of wounded in an ox-cart, barely alive from a bullet wound in his head. But she could not extricate him without disturbing six other wounded men, so she let him go on to the hospital. Later, she heard he had died before a doctor ever saw him and was buried somewhere, no one knew exactly. So many men had been buried that month, in shallow, hastily dug graves at Oakland Cemetery. Melanie felt it keenly that they had not been able to get a lock of Carey's hair to send to his mother in Alabama.

As the hot night wore on and their backs were aching and their knees buckling from weariness, Scarlett and Pitty cried to man after man: "What news? What news?"

And as the long hours dragged past, they had their answer, an answer that made them look whitely into each other's eyes.

"We're falling back." "We've got to fall back." "They outnumber us by thousands." "The Yankees have got Wheeler's cavalry cut off near Decatur. We got to reinforce them." "Our boys will all be in town soon."

Scarlett and Pitty clutched each other's arms for support.

"Are—are the Yankees coming?"

"Yes'm, they're comin' all right but they ain't goin' ter git fer, lady." "Don't fret, Miss, they can't take Atlanta." "No, M'm, we got a million miles of breastworks 'round this town." "I heard Old Joe say it myself: 'I can hold Atlanta forever.'" "But we ain't got Old Joe. We got—" "Shut up, you fool! Do you want to scare the ladies?" "The Yankees will never take this place, Ma'm." "Whyn't you ladies go ter Macon or somewheres that's safer? Ain't you got no kinfolks there?" "The Yankees ain't goin' ter take Atlanta but still it ain't goin' ter be so healthy for ladies whilst they're tryin' it." "There's goin' ter be a powerful lot of shellin'."

In a warm steaming rain the next day, the defeated army poured through Atlanta by thousands, exhausted by hunger and weariness, depleted by seventy-six days of battle and retreat, their horses starved scarecrows, their cannon and caissons harnessed with odds and ends of rope and strips of rawhide. But they did not come in as a disorderly rabble, in full rout. They marched in good order, jaunty for all their rags, their torn red battle flags flying in the rain. They had learned retreating under Old Joe, who had made it as great a feat of strategy as advancing. The bearded, shabby files swung down Peachtree Street to the tune of "Maryland! My Maryland!" and all the town turned out to cheer them. In victory or defeat, they were their boys.

The state militia who had gone out so short a time before, resplendent in new uniforms, could hardly be distinguished from the seasoned troops, so dirty and unkempt were they. There was a new look in their eyes. Three years of apologizing, of explaining why they were not at the front, was behind them now. They had traded security behind the lines for the hardships of battle. Many of their number had traded easy living for hard death. They were veterans now, veterans of brief service, but veterans just the same, and they had acquitted themselves well. They searched out the faces of friends in the crowd and stared at them proudly, defiantly. They could hold up their heads now.

The old men and boys of the Home Guard marched by, the greybeards almost too weary to lift their feet, the boys wearing the faces of tired children, confronted too early with adult problems. Scarlett caught sight of Phil Meade and hardly recognized him, so black was his face with powder and grime, so taut with strain and weariness. Uncle Henry went limping by, hatless in the rain, his head stuck through a hole in a piece of old oilcloth. Grandpa Merriwether rode in on a gun-carriage, his bare feet tied in quilt scraps. But search though she might, she saw no sign of John Wilkes.

Johnston's veterans, however, went by with the tireless, careless step which had carried them for three years, and they still had the energy to grin and wave at pretty girls and to call rude gibes to men not in uniform. They were on their way to the entrenchments that ringed the town—no shallow, hastily dug trenches, these, but earthworks, breast high, reinforced with sandbags and tipped with sharpened staves of wood. For mile after mile the trenches encircled the town, red gashes surmounted by red mounds, waiting for the men who would fill them.

The crowd cheered the troops as they would have cheered them in victory. There was fear in every heart but, now that they knew the truth, now that the worst had happened, now that the war was in their front yard, a change came over the town. There was no panic now, no hysteria. Whatever lay in hearts did not show on faces. Everyone looked cheerful even if the cheer was strained. Everyone tried to show brave, confident faces to the troops. Everyone repeated what Old Joe had said, just before he was relieved of command: "I can hold Atlanta forever."

Now that Hood had had to retreat, quite a number wished, with the soldiers, that they had Old Joe back, but they forbore saying it and took courage from Old Joe's remark.

"I can hold Atlanta forever!"

Not for Hood the cautious tactics of General Johnston. He assaulted the Yankees on the east, he assaulted them on the west. Sherman was circling the town like a wrestler seeking a fresh hold on an opponent's body, and Hood did not remain behind his rifle-pits waiting for the Yankees to attack. He went out boldly to meet them and savagely fell upon them. Within the space of a few days, the battles of Atlanta and of Ezra Church were fought, and both of them were major engagements which made Peachtree Creek seem like a skirmish.

But the Yankees kept coming back for more. They had suffered heavy losses but they could afford to lose. And all the while their batteries poured shells into Atlanta, killing people in their homes, ripping roofs off buildings, tearing huge craters in the streets. The townsfolk sheltered as best they could in cellars, in holes in the ground and in shallow tunnels dug in railroad cuts. Atlanta was under siege.

Within eleven days after he had taken command, General Hood had lost almost as many men as Johnston had lost in seventy-four days of battle and retreat, and Atlanta was hemmed in on three sides.

The railroad from Atlanta to Tennessee was now in Sherman's hands for its full length. His army was across the railroad to the east and he had cut the railroad running south-west to Alabama. Only the one railroad to the south, to Macon and Savannah, was still open. The town was crowded with soldiers, swamped with wounded, jammed with refugees, and this one line was inadequate for the crying needs of the stricken city. But as long as this railroad could be held, Atlanta could still stand.

Scarlett was terrified when she realized how important this line had become, how fiercely Sherman would fight to take it, how desperately Hood would fight to defend it. For this was the railroad which ran through the County, through Jonesboro. And Tara was only five miles from Jonesboro! Tara seemed like a haven of refuge by comparison with the screaming hell of Atlanta, but Tara was only five miles from Jonesboro!

Scarlett and many other ladies sat on the flat roofs of stores, shaded by their tiny parasols, and watched the fighting on the day of the battle of Atlanta. But when shells began falling in the streets for the first time, they fled to the cellars, and that night the exodus of women, children and old people from the city began. Macon was their destination and many of those who took the train that night had already refugeed five and six times before, as Johnston fell back from Dalton. They were travelling lighter now than when they arrived in Atlanta. Most of them carried only a carpet-bag and a scanty lunch done up in a bandana handkerchief. Here and there, frightened servants carried silver pitchers, knives and forks and a family portrait or two which had been salvaged in the first flight.

Mrs. Merriwether and Mrs. Elsing refused to leave. They were needed at the hospital and furthermore, they said proudly, they weren't afraid and no Yankees were going to run them out of their homes. But Maybelle and her baby and Fanny Elsing went to Macon. Mrs. Meade was disobedient for the first time in her married life and flatly refused to yield to the doctor's command that she take the train to safety. The doctor needed her, she said. Moreover, Phil was somewhere in the trenches and she wanted to be near by in case . . .

But Mrs. Whiting went and many other ladies of Scarlett's circle. Aunt Pitty, who had been the first to denounce Old Joe for his policy of retreat, was among the first to pack her trunks. Her nerves, she said, were delicate and she could not endure noises. She feared she might faint at an explosion and not be able to reach the cellar. No, she was not afraid. Her baby mouth tried to set in martial lines but failed. She'd go to Macon and stay with her cousin, old Mrs. Burr, and the girls should come with her.

Scarlett did not want to go to Macon. Frightened as she was of the shells, she'd rather stay in Atlanta than go to Macon, for she hated old Mrs. Burr cordially. Years ago, Mrs. Burr had said she was "fast" after catching her kissing her son Willie at one of the Wilkes' house parties. "No," she told Aunt Pitty, "I'll go home to Tara and Melly can go to Macon with you."

At this Melanie began to cry in a frightened,

heartbroken way. When Aunt Pitty fled to get Dr. Meade, Melanie caught Scarlett's hand in hers, pleading:

"Dear, don't go to Tara and leave me! I'll be so lonely without you. Oh, Scarlett, I'd just die if you weren't with me when the baby came! Yes —yes, I know I've got Aunt Pitty and she is sweet. But after all, she's never had a baby, and sometimes she makes me so nervous I could scream. Don't desert me, darling. You've been just like a sister to me, and besides," she smiled wanly, "you promised Ashley you'd take care of me. He told me he was going to ask you."

Scarlett stared down at her in wonderment. With her own dislike of this woman so strong she could barely conceal it, how could Melly love her so? How could Melly be so stupid as not to guess the secret of her love of Ashley? She had given herself away a hundred times during these months of torment, waiting for news of him. But Melanie saw nothing, Melanie who could see nothing but good in anyone she loved. . . . Yes, she had promised Ashley she would look out for Melanie. "Oh, Ashley! Ashley! you must be dead, dead these many months! And now your promise reaches out and clutches me!"

"Well," she said shortly, "I did promise him that and I don't go back on my promises. But I won't go to Macon and stay with that old Burr cat. I'd claw her eyes out in five minutes. I'm going home to Tara and you can come with me. Mother would love to have you."

"Oh, I'd like that! Your mother is so sweet. But you know Auntie would just die if she wasn't with me when the baby came, and I know she won't go to Tara. It's too close to the fighting, and Auntie wants to be safe."

Dr. Meade, who had arrived out of breath, expecting to find Melanie in premature labour at least, judging by Aunt Pitty's alarmed summoning, was indignant and said as much. And upon learning the cause of the upset, he settled the matter with words that left no room for argument.

"It's out of the question for you to go to Macon, Miss Melly. I won't answer for you if you move. The trains are crowded and uncertain and the passengers are liable to be put off in the woods at any time, if the trains are needed for the wounded or troops and supplies. In your condition—"

"But if I went to Tara with Scarlett—"

"I tell you I won't have you moved. The train to Tara is the train to Macon and the same conditions prevail. Moreover, no one knows just where the Yankees are now, but they are all over everywhere. Your train might even be captured. And even if you reached Jonesboro safely, there'd be a five-mile ride over a rough road before you ever reached Tara. It's no trip for a woman in a delicate condition. Besides, there's not a doctor in the County since old Dr. Fontaine joined the army."

"But there are midwives—"

"I said a doctor," he answered brusquely, and his eyes unconsciously went over her tiny frame. "I won't have you moved. It might be dangerous.

You don't want to have the baby on the train or in a buggy, do you?"

This medical frankness reduced the ladies to embarrassed blushes and silence.

"You've got to stay right here where I can watch you, and you must stay in bed. No running up and down stairs to cellars. No, not even if shells come right in the window. After all, there's not so much danger here. We'll have the Yankees beaten back in no time. . . . Now, Miss Pitty, you go right on to Macon and leave the young ladies here."

"Unchaperoned?" she cried, aghast.

"They are matrons," said the doctor testily. "And Mrs. Meade is just two houses away. They won't be receiving any male company anyway with Miss Melly in her condition. Good Heavens, Miss Pitty! This is war-time. We can't think of the proprieties now. We must think of Miss Melly."

He stamped out of the room and waited on the front porch until Scarlett joined him.

"I shall talk frankly to you, Miss Scarlett," he began, jerking at his grey beard. "You seem to be a young woman of common sense, so spare me your blushes. I do not want to hear any further talk about Miss Melly being moved. I doubt if she could stand the trip. She is going to have a difficult time, even in the best of circumstances —very narrow in the hips, as you know, and probably will need forceps for her delivery, so I don't want any ignorant darky midwife meddling with her. Women like her should never have children, but—Anyway, you pack Miss Pitty's trunk

506

and send her to Macon. She's so scared she'll upset Miss Melly and that won't do any good. And now, Miss," he fixed her with a piercing glance, "I don't want to hear about you going home, either. You stay with Miss Melly till the baby comes. Not afraid, are you?"

"Oh, no!" lied Scarlett stoutly.

"That's a brave girl. Mrs. Meade will give you whatever chaperonage you need and I'll send over old Betsy to cook for you, if Miss Pitty wants to take her servants with her. It won't be for long. The baby ought to be here in another five weeks, but you never can tell with first babies and all this shelling going on. It may come any day."

So Aunt Pittypat went to Macon, in floods of tears, taking Uncle Peter and Cookie with her. The carriage and horse she donated to the hospital in a burst of patriotism which she immediately regretted and that brought on more tears. And Scarlett and Melanie were left alone with Wade and Prissy in a house that was much quieter, even though the cannonading continued.

3

IN those first days of the siege, when the Yankees crashed here and there against the defences of the city, Scarlett was so frightened by the bursting shells she could only cower helplessly, her hands over her ears, expecting every moment to be blown into eternity. When she heard the whistling screams that heralded their approach, she rushed to Melanie's room and flung herself on the bed beside her, and the two clutched each other, screaming "Oh! Oh!" as they buried their heads in the pillows. Prissy and Wade scurried for the cellar and crouched in the cobwebbed darkness, Prissy squalling at the top of her voice and Wade sobbing and hiccoughing.

Suffocating under feather pillows while death screamed overhead, Scarlett silently cursed Melanie for keeping her from the safer regions below stairs. But the doctor had forbidden Melanie to walk and Scarlett had to stay with her. Added to her terror of being blown to pieces was her equally active terror that Melanie's baby might arrive at any moment. Sweat broke out on Scarlett with clammy dampness, whenever this thought entered her mind. What would she do if the baby started coming? She knew she'd rather let Melanie die than go out on the streets to hunt for the doctor when the shells were falling like April rain. And she knew Prissy could be beaten to death before she would venture forth. What would she do if the baby came?

These matters she discussed with Prissy in whispers one evening, as they prepared Melanie's supper tray, and Prissy, surprisingly enough, calmed her fears.

"Miss Scarlett, effen we kain git de doctah w'en Miss Melly's time come, doan you bodder. Ah kin manage. Ah knows all 'bout birthin'. Ain' mah ma a midwife? Ain' she raise me ter be a midwife, too? Jes' you leave it ter me."

Scarlett breathed more easily knowing that experienced hands were near, but she nevertheless yearned to have the ordeal over and done with. Mad to be away from exploding shells, desperate to get home to the quiet of Tara, she prayed every night that the baby would arrive the next day, so she would be released from her promise and could leave Atlanta. Tara seemed so safe, so far away from all this misery.

Scarlett longed for home and her mother as she had never longed for anything in all her life. If she were just near Ellen she wouldn't be afraid, no matter what happened. Every night after a day of screeching, ear-splitting shells, she went to bed determined to tell Melanie the next morning that she could not stand Atlanta another day, that she would have to go home and Melanie would have to go to Mrs. Meade's. But, as she lay on her pillow, there always rose the memory of Ashley's face as it had looked when she last saw him, drawn as with an inner pain but with a little smile on his lips: "You'll take care of Melanie, won't you? You're so strong . . . Promise me." And she had promised. Somewhere, Ashley lay dead. Wherever he was, he was watching her, holding her to that promise. Living or dead, she could not fail him, no matter what the cost. So she remained day after day.

In response to Ellen's letters, pleading with her to come home, she wrote minimizing the dangers of the siege, explaining Melanie's predicament and promising to come as soon as the baby was born. Ellen, sensitive to the bonds of kin, be they blood or marriage, wrote back reluctantly agreeing that she must stay but demanding that Wade and Prissy be sent home immediately. This suggestion met with the complete approval of Prissy, who was now reduced to teeth-chattering idiocy at every unexpected sound. She spent so much time crouching in the cellar that the girls would have fared badly but for Mrs. Meade's stolid old Betsy.

Scarlett was as anxious as her mother to have Wade out of Atlanta, not only for the child's safety, but because his constant fear irritated her. Wade was terrified to speechlessness by the shelling, and even when lulls came he clung to Scarlett's skirts, too terrified to cry. He was afraid to go to bed at night, afraid of the dark, afraid to sleep lest the Yankees should come and get him, and the sound of his soft nervous whimpering in the night grated unendurably on her nerves. Secretly she was just as frightened as he was, but it angered her to be reminded of it every minute by his tense, drawn face. Yes, Tara was the place for Wade. Prissy should take him there and return immediately to be present when the baby came.

But before Scarlett could start the two on their homeward journey, news came that the Yankees had swung to the south and were skirmishing along the railroad between Atlanta and Jonesboro. Suppose the Yankees should capture the train on which Wade and Prissy were riding—Scarlett and Melanie turned pale at the thought, for everyone knew that Yankee atrocities on helpless children were even more dreadful than on women. So she feared to send him home and he remained in Atlanta, a frightened, silent little ghost, pattering about desperately after his mother, fearing to have her skirt out of his hand for even a minute.

The siege went on through the hot days of July, thundering days following nights of sullen, ominous stillness, and the town began to adjust itself. It was as though, the worst having happened, they had nothing more to fear. They had feared a siege and now they had a siege and, after all, it wasn't so bad. Life could and did go on almost as usual. They knew they were sitting on a volcano, but until that volcano erupted there was nothing they could do. So why worry now? And probably it wouldn't erupt anyway. Just look how General Hood is holding the Yankees out of the city! And see how the cavalry is holding the railroad to Macon! Sherman will never take it!

But for all their apparent insouciance in the face of falling shells and shorter rations, for all their ignoring the Yankees, barely half a mile away, and for all their boundless confidence in the ragged line of grey men in the rifle-pits, there pulsed, just below the skin of Atlanta, a wild uncertainty over what the next day would bring. Suspense, worry, sorrow, hunger and the torment of rising, falling, rising hope was wearing that skin thin.

Gradually, Scarlett drew courage from the brave faces of her friends and from the merciful adjustment which nature makes when what cannot be cured must be endured. To be sure, she still jumped at the sound of explosions but she did not run screaming to burrow her head under Melanie's pillow. She could now gulp and say weakly: "That one was close, wasn't it?"

She was less frightened also because life had taken on the quality of a dream, a dream too terrible to be real. It wasn't possible that she, Scarlett O'Hara, should be in such a predicament, with the danger of death about her every hour, every minute. It wasn't possible that the quiet tenor of life could have changed so completely in so short a time.

It was unreal, grotesquely unreal, that morning skies which dawned so tenderly blue could be profaned with cannon smoke that hung over the town like low thunder clouds, that warm noontides filled with the piercing sweetness of massed honeysuckle and climbing roses could be so fearful, as shells screamed into the streets, bursting like the crack of doom, throwing iron splinters hundreds of yards, blowing people and animals to bits.

Quiet, drowsy afternoon siestas had ceased to be, for, though the clamour of battle might lull from time to time, Peachtree Street was alive and noisy at all hours—cannon and ambulances rumbling by, wounded stumbling in from the rifle-pits, regiments hurrying past at double-quick, ordered from the ditches on one side of town to the defence of some hard-pressed earth-works on the other, and couriers dashing head-long down the street toward headquarters as though the fate of the Confederacy hung on them.

The hot nights brought a measure of quiet but it was a sinister quiet. When the night was still, it was too still—as though the tree frogs, katydids and sleepy mocking-birds were too frightened to raise their voices in the usual summer-night chorus. Now and again, the quiet was broken sharply by the crack-cracking of musket fire in the last line of defences.

Often in the late night hours, when the lamps were out and Melanie asleep and deathly silence pressed over the town, Scarlett, lying awake, heard the latch of the front gate click and soft urgent tappings on the front door.

Always, faceless soldiers stood on the dark porch and from the darkness many different voices spoke to her. Sometimes a cultured voice came from the shadows: "Madam, my abject apologies for disturbing you, but could I have water for myself and my horse?" Sometimes it was the hard burring of a mountain voice, some-times the odd nasals of the flat Wiregrass country to the far south, occasionally the lulling drawl of the Coast that caught at her heart, reminding her of Ellen's voice.

"Missy, I got a pardner here who I wuz aimin'

ter git ter the horsepittle but looks like he ain't goin' ter last that fer. Kin you take him in?"

"Lady, I shore could do with some vittles. I'd shore relish a corn pone if it didn't deprive you none."

"Madam, forgive my intrusion but—could I spend the night on your porch? I saw the roses and smelled the honeysuckle and it was so much like home that I was emboldened—"

No, these nights were not real! They were a nightmare and the men were part of that nightmare, men without bodies or faces, only tired voices speaking to her from the warm dark. Draw water, serve food, lay pillows on the front porch, bind wounds, hold the dirty heads of the dying. No, this could not be happening to her!

Once, late in July, it was Uncle Henry Hamilton who came tapping in the night. Uncle Henry was minus his umbrella and carpet-bag now, and his fat stomach as well. The skin of his pink fat face hung down in loose folds like the dewlaps of a bulldog and his long white hair was indescribably dirty. He was almost barefoot, crawling with lice, and he was hungry, but his irascible spirit was unimpaired.

Despite his remark, "It's a foolish war when old fools like me are out toting guns," the girls received the impression that Uncle Henry was enjoying himself. He was needed, like the young men, and he was doing a young man's work. Moreover, he could keep up with the young men, which was more than Grandpa Merriwether could do, he told them gleefully. Grandpa's lumbago was troubling him greatly and the Captain wanted to discharge him. But Grandpa wouldn't go home. He said frankly that he preferred the Captain's swearing and bullying to his daughter-in-law's coddling, and her incessant demands that he give up chewing tobacco and launder his beard every day.

Uncle Henry's visit was brief, for he had only a four-hour furlough and he needed half of it for the long walk in from the breastworks and back.

"Girls, I'm not going to see you all for a while," he announced as he sat in Melanie's bedroom, luxuriously wriggling his blistered feet in the tub of cold water Scarlett had set before him. "Our company is going out in the morning."

"Where?" questioned Melanie, frightened, clutching his arm.

"Don't put your hand on me," said Uncle Henry irritably. "I'm crawling with lice. War would be a picnic if it wasn't for lice and dysentery. Where'm I going? Well, I haven't been told but I've got a good idea. We're marching south, toward Jonesboro, in the morning, unless I'm greatly in error."

"Oh, why toward Jonesboro?"

"Because there's going to be big fighting there, Missy. The Yankees are going to take that railroad if they possibly can. And if they do take it, it's good-bye, Atlanta!"

"Oh, Uncle Henry, do you think they will?"

"Shucks, girls! No! How can they when I'm there?" Uncle Henry grinned at their frightened faces and then, becoming serious again: "It's going to be a hard fight, girls. We've got to win it. You know, of course, that the Yankees have

515

got all the railroads except the one to Macon, but that isn't all they've got. Maybe you girls didn't know it, but they've got every road, too, every wagon lane and bridle path, except the McDonough road. Atlanta's in a bag and the strings of the bag are at Jonesboro. And if the Yankees can take the railroad there, they can pull up the strings and have us, just like a possum in a poke. So, we don't aim to let them get that railroad . . . I may be gone a while, girls. I just came in to tell you all good-bye and to make sure Scarlett was still with you, Melly."

"Of course, she's with me," said Melanie fondly. "Don't you worry about us, Uncle Henry, and do take care of yourself."

Uncle Henry wiped his wet feet on the rag rug and groaned as he drew on his tattered shoes.

"I got to be going," he said. "I've got five miles to walk. Scarlett, you fix me up some kind of lunch to take. Anything you've got."

After he had kissed Melanie good-bye, he went down to the kitchen where Scarlett was wrapping a corn pone and some apples in a napkin.

"Uncle Henry—is it—is it really so serious?"

"Serious? God'lmighty, yes! Don't be a goose. We're in the last ditch."

"Do you think they'll get to Tara?"

"Why—" began Uncle Henry, irritated at the feminine mind which thought only of personal things when broad issues were involved. Then, seeing her frightened, woebegone face, he softened.

"Of course they won't. Tara's five miles from the railroad and it's the railroad the Yankees want. You've got no more sense than a June bug, Missy." He broke off abruptly. "I didn't walk all this way here to-night just to tell you all good-bye. I came to bring Melly some bad news, but when I got up to it I just couldn't tell her. So I'm going to leave it to you to do."

"Ashley isn't—you haven't heard anything—that he's—dead?"

"Now, how would I be hearing about Ashley when I've been standing in rifle-pits up to the seat of my pants in mud?" the old gentleman asked testily. "No. It's about his father. John Wilkes is dead."

Scarlett sat down suddenly, the half-wrapped lunch in her hand.

"I came to tell Melly—but I couldn't. You must do it. And give her these."

He hauled from his pockets a heavy gold watch with dangling seals, a small miniature of the long dead Mrs. Wilkes and a pair of massive cuff buttons. At the sight of the watch which she had seen in John Wilkes' hands a thousand times, the full realization came over Scarlett that Ashley's father was really dead. And she was too stunned to cry or to speak. Uncle Henry fidgeted, coughed and did not look at her, lest he catch sight of a tear that would upset him.

"He was a brave man, Scarlett. Tell Melly that. Tell her to write it to his girls. And a good soldier for all his years. A shell got him. Came right down on him and his horse. Tore the horse's—I shot the horse myself, poor creature. A fine little mare she was. You'd better write Mrs. Tarleton about that, too. She set a store on that mare.

Wrap up my lunch, child. I must be going. There, dear, don't take it so hard. What better way can an old man die than doing a young man's work?"

"Oh, he shouldn't have died! He shouldn't have ever gone to the war. He should have lived and seen his grandchild grow up and died peacefully in bed. Oh, why did he go? He didn't believe in secession and he hated the war and—"

"Plenty of us think that way, but what of it?" Uncle Henry blew his nose grumpily. "Do you think I enjoy letting Yankee riflemen use me for a target at my age? But there's no other choice for a gentleman these days. Kiss me good-bye, child, and don't worry about me. I'll come through this war safely."

Scarlett kissed him and heard him go down the steps into the dark, heard the latch click on the front gate. She stood for a minute looking at the keepsakes in her hand. And then she went up the stairs to tell Melanie.

At the end of July came the unwelcome news, predicted by Uncle Henry, that the Yankees had swung around again toward Jonesboro. They had cut the railroad four miles below the town, but they had been beaten off by the Confederate cavalry; and the engineering corps, sweating in the broiling sun, had repaired the line.

Scarlett was frantic with anxiety. For three days she waited, fear growing in her heart. Then a reassuring letter came from Gerald. The enemy had not reached Tara. They had heard the sound of the fight but they had seen no Yankees.

Gerald's letter was so full of brag and bluster as to how the Yankees had been driven from the railroad that one would have thought he personally had accomplished the feat, single-handed. He wrote for three pages about the gallantry of the troops and then, at the end of his letter, mentioned briefly that Carreen was ill. The typhoid, Mrs. O'Hara said it was. She was not very ill and Scarlett was not to worry about her, but on no condition must she come home now, even if the railroad should become safe. Mrs. O'Hara was very glad now that Scarlett and Wade had not come home when the siege began. Mrs. O'Hara said Scarlett must go to church and say some Rosaries for Carreen's recovery.

Scarlett's conscience smote her at this last, for it had been months since she had been to church. Once she would have thought this omission a mortal sin but, somehow, staying away from church did not seem so sinful now as it formerly had. But she obeyed her mother and going to her room gabbled a hasty Rosary. When she rose from her knees she did not feel as comforted as she had formerly felt after prayer. For some time she had felt that God was not watching out for her, the Confederates or the South, in spite of the millions of prayers ascending to Him daily.

That night she sat on the front porch with Gerald's letter in her bosom where she could touch it occasionally and bring Tara and Ellen closer to her. The lamp in the parlour window threw odd golden shadows on to the dark vine-shrouded porch, and the matted tangle of yellow climbing roses and honeysuckle made a wall of mingled fragrance about her. The night was utterly still. Not even the crack of a rifle had sounded since sunset and the world seemed far away. Scarlett rocked back and forth, lonely, miserable since reading the news from Tara, wishing that someone, anyone, even Mrs. Merriwether, were with her. But Mrs. Merriwether was on night duty at the hospital, Mrs. Meade was at home making a feast for Phil, who was in from the front lines, and Melanie was asleep. There was not even the hope of a chance caller. Visitors had fallen off to nothing this last week, for every man who could walk was in the rifle-pits or chasing the Yankees about the countryside near Jonesboro.

It was not often that she was alone like this and she did not like it. When she was alone she had to think and, these days, thoughts were not so pleasant. Like everyone else, she had fallen into the habit of thinking of the past, the dead.

To-night when Atlanta was so quiet, she could close her eyes and imagine she was back in the rural stillness of Tara and that life was unchanged, unchanging. But she knew that life in the County would never be the same again. She thought of the four Tarletons, the red-haired twins and Tom and Boyd, and a passionate sadness caught at her throat. Why, either Stu or Brent might have been her husband. But now, when the war was over and she went back to Tara to live, she would never again hear their wild halloos as they dashed up the avenue of cedars. And Raiford Calvert, who danced so divinely, would never again choose her to be his partner.

And the Munroe boys and little Joe Fontaine and—

"Oh, Ashley!" she sobbed, dropping her head into her hands. "I'll never get used to you being gone!"

She heard the front gate click and she hastily raised her head and dashed her hand across her wet eyes. She rose and saw it was Rhett Butler coming up the walk, carrying his wide Panama hat in his hand. She had not seen him since the day when she had alighted from his carriage so precipitately at Five Points. On that occasion, she had expressed the desire never to lay eyes on him again. But she was so glad now to have someone to talk to, someone to divert her thoughts from Ashley, that she hastily put the memory from her mind. Evidently he had forgotten the contretemps, or pretended to have forgotten it, for he settled himself on the top step at her feet without mention of their late difference.

"So you didn't refugee to Macon! I heard that Miss Pitty had retreated and, of course, I thought you had gone too. So, when I saw your light I came here to investigate. Why did you stay?"

"To keep Melanie company. You see, she— well, she can't refugee just now."

"Thunderation!" he said, and in the lamplight she saw that he was frowning. "You don't mean to tell me Mrs. Wilkes is still here? I never heard of such idiocy. It's quite dangerous for her in her condition."

Scarlett was silent, embarrassed, for Melanie's condition was not a subject she could discuss with a man. She was embarrassed, too, that Rhett should know it was dangerous for Melanie. Such knowledge sat ill upon a bachelor.

"It's quite ungallant of you not to think that I might get hurt, too," she said tartly.

His eyes flickered with amusement.

"I'd back you against the Yankees any day."

"I'm not sure that that's a compliment," she said uncertainly.

"It isn't," he answered. "When will you stop looking for compliments in men's lightest utterances?"

"When I'm on my deathbed," she replied and smiled, thinking that there would always be men to compliment her, even if Rhett never did.

"Vanity, vanity," he said. "At least, you are frank about it."

He opened his cigar-case, extracted a black cigar and held it to his nose for a moment. A match flared, he leaned back against a post and, clasping his hands about his knees, smoked a while in silence. Scarlett resumed her rocking and the still darkness of the warm night closed about them. The mocking-bird, which nested in the tangle of roses and honeysuckle, roused from slumber and gave one timid, liquid note. Then, as if thinking better of the matter, it was silent again.

From the shadow of the porch, Rhett suddenly laughed, a low, soft laugh.

"So you stayed with Mrs. Wilkes! This is the strangest situation I ever encountered!"

"I see nothing strange about it," she answered uncomfortably, immediately on the alert.

"No? But then you lack the impersonal viewpoint. My impression has been for some time past that you could hardly endure Mrs. Wilkes. You think her silly and stupid and her patriotic notions bore you. You seldom pass by the opportunity to slip in some belittling remark about her, so naturally it seems strange to me that you should elect to do the unselfish thing and stay here with her during this shelling. Now, just why did you do it?"

"Because she's Charlie's sister—and like a sister to me," answered Scarlett with as much dignity as possible though her cheeks were growing hot.

"You mean because she's Ashley Wilkes' widow."

Scarlett rose quickly, struggling with her anger.

"I was almost on the point of forgiving you for your former boorish conduct but now I shan't do it. I wouldn't have ever let you come upon this porch at all, if I hadn't been feeling so blue and—"

"Sit down and smooth your ruffled fur," he said, and his voice changed. He reached up and taking her hand pulled her back into her chair. "Why are you blue?"

"Oh, I had a letter from Tara to-day. The Yankees are close to home and my little sister is ill with typhoid and—and—so now, even if I could go home, like I want to, Mother wouldn't let me for fear I'd catch it too. Oh, dear, and I do so want to go home!"

"Well, don't cry about it," he said, but his voice was kinder. "You are much safer here in Atlanta even if the Yankees do come than you'd be at Tara. The Yankees won't hurt you and typhoid would."

"The Yankees wouldn't hurt me! How can you say such a lie?"

"My dear girl, the Yankees aren't fiends. They haven't horns and hoofs, as you seem to think. They are pretty much like Southerners—except with worse manners, of course, and terrible accents."

"Why, the Yankees would—"

"Rape you? I think not. Though, of course, they'd want to."

"If you are going to talk vilely I shall go into the house," she cried, grateful that the shadows hid her crimson face.

"Be frank. Wasn't that what you were thinking?"

"Oh, certainly not!"

"Oh, but it was! No use getting mad at me for reading your thoughts. That's what all our delicately nurtured and pure-minded Southern ladies think. They have it on their minds constantly. I'll wager even dowagers like Mrs. Merriwether . . ."

Scarlett gulped in silence, remembering that wherever two or more matrons were gathered together, in these trying days, they whispered of such happenings, always in Virginia or Tennessee or Louisiana, never very close to home. The Yankees raped women and ran bayonets through children's stomachs and burned houses over the heads of old people. Everyone knew these things were true even if they didn't shout them on the street corners. And if Rhett had any decency he would realize they were true. And not talk about them. And it wasn't any laughing matter either.

She could hear him chuckling softly. Sometimes he was odious. In fact, most of the time he was odious. It was awful for a man to know what women really thought about and talked about. It made a girl feel positively undressed. And no man ever learned such things from good women either. She was indignant that he had read her mind. She liked to believe herself a thing of mystery to men, but she knew Rhett thought her as transparent as glass.

"Speaking of such matters," he continued, "have you a protector or chaperon in the house? The admirable Mrs. Merriwether or Mrs. Meade? They always look at me as if they knew I was here for no good purpose."

"Mrs. Meade usually comes over at night," answered Scarlett, glad to change the subject. "But she couldn't to-night. Phil, her boy, is home."

"What luck," he said softly, "to find you alone!"

Something in his voice made her heart beat pleasantly faster and she felt her face flush. She had heard that note in men's voices often enough to know that it presaged a declaration of love. Oh, what fun! If he would just say he loved her, how she would torment him and get even with him for all the sarcastic remarks he had flung at her these past three years. She would lead him a chase that would make up for even that awful humiliation of the day he witnessed her slapping Ashley. And then she'd tell him sweetly she could only be a sister to him and retire with the full honours of war. She laughed nervously in pleasant anticipation.

"Don't giggle," he said, and taking her hand, he turned it over and pressed his lips into the palm. Something vital, electric, leaped from him to her at the touch of his warm mouth, something that caressed her whole body thrillingly. His lips travelled to her wrist and she knew he must feel the leap of her pulse as her heart quickened and she tried to draw back her hand. She had not bargained on this—this treacherous warm tide of feeling that made her want to run her hands through his hair, to feel his lips upon her mouth.

She wasn't in love with him, she told herself confusedly. She was in love with Ashley. But how to explain this feeling that made her hands shake and the pit of her stomach grow cold?

He laughed softly.

"Don't pull away! I won't hurt you!"

"Hurt me? I'm not afraid of you, Rhett Butler, or of any man in shoe leather!" she cried, furious that her voice shook as well as her hands.

"An admirable sentiment, but do lower your voice. Mrs. Wilkes might hear you. And pray compose yourself." He sounded as though delighted at her flurry.

"Scarlett, you do like me, don't you?"

That was more like what she was expecting.

"Well, sometimes," she answered cautiously. "When you aren't acting like a varmint."

He laughed again and held the palm of her hand against his hard cheek.

"I think you like me because I am a varmint.

You've known so few dyed-in-the-wool varmints in your sheltered life that my very difference holds a quaint charm for you."

This was not the turn she had anticipated and she tried again without success to pull her hand free.

"That's not true! I like nice men—men you can depend on to always be gentlemanly."

"You mean men you can always bully. It's merely a matter of definition. But no matter."

He kissed her palm again, and again the skin on the back of her neck crawled excitingly.

"But you do like me. Could you ever love me, Scarlett?"

"Ah!" she thought, triumphantly. "Now I've got him!" and she answered with studied coolness: "Indeed, no. That is—not unless you mended your manners considerably."

"And I have no intention of mending them. So you could not love me? That is as I hoped. For while I like you immensely, I do not love you and it would be tragic indeed for you to suffer twice from unrequited love, wouldn't it, dear? May I call you 'dear', Mrs. Hamilton? I shall call you 'dear' whether you like it or not, so no matter, but the proprieties must be observed."

"You don't love me?"

"No, indeed. Did you hope that I did?"

"Don't be so presumptuous!"

"You hoped! Alas, to blight your hopes! I should love you, for you are charming and talented at many useless accomplishments. But many ladies have charm and accomplishments and are just as useless as you are. No, I don't love you. But I do like you tremendously—for the elasticity of your conscience, for the selfishness which you seldom trouble to hide, and for the shrewd practicality in you which, I fear, you get from some not too remote Irish-peasant ancestor."

Peasant! Why, he was insulting her! She began to splutter wordlessly.

"Don't interrupt," he begged, squeezing her hand. "I like you because I have those same qualities in me and like begets liking. I realize you still cherish the memory of the godlike and wooden-headed Mr. Wilkes, who's probably been in his grave these six months. But there must be room in your heart for me too. Scarlett, do stop wriggling! I am making you a declaration. I have wanted you since the first time I laid eyes on you, in the hall at Twelve Oaks, when you were bewitching poor Charlie Hamilton. I want you more than I have ever wanted any woman—and I've waited longer for you than I've ever waited for any woman."

She was breathless with surprise at his last words. In spite of all his insults, he did love her and he was just so contrary he didn't want to come out frankly and put it into words, for fear she'd laugh. Well, she'd show him and right quickly.

"Are you asking me to marry you?"

He dropped her hand and laughed so loudly she shrank back in her chair.

"Good Lord, no! Didn't I tell you I wasn't a marrying man?"

"But—but—what—"

He rose to his feet and, hand on heart, made her a burlesque bow.

"Dear," he said quietly, "I am complimenting your intelligence by asking you to be my mistress without having first seduced you."

Mistress!

Her mind shouted the word, shouted that she had been vilely insulted. But in that first startled moment she did not feel insulted. She only felt a furious surge of indignation that he should think her such a fool. He must think her a fool if he offered her a proposition like that, instead of the proposal of matrimony she had been expecting. Rage, punctured vanity and disappointment threw her mind into a turmoil and, before she even thought of the high moral grounds on which she should upbraid him, she blurted out the first words which came to her lips:

"Mistress! What would I get out of that except a passel of brats?"

And then her jaw dropped in horror as she realized what she had said. He laughed until he choked, peering at her in the shadows as she sat, stricken dumb, pressing her handkerchief to her mouth.

"That's why I like you! You are the only frank woman I know, the only woman who looks on the practical side of matters without beclouding the issue with mouthings about sin and morality. Any other woman would have swooned first and then shown me the door."

Scarlett leaped to her feet, her face red with shame. How could she have said such a thing! How could she, Ellen's daughter, with her upbringing, have sat there and listened to such debasing words and then made such a shameless reply? She should have screamed. She should have fainted. She should have turned coldly away in silence and swept from the porch. Too late now!

"I will show you the door," she shouted, not caring if Melanie or the Meades, down the street, did hear her. "Get out! How dare you say such things to me! What have I ever done to encourage you—to make you suppose . . . Get out and don't ever come back here. I mean it this time. Don't you ever come back here with any of your piddling papers of pins and ribbons, thinking I'll forgive you. I'll—I'll tell my father and he'll kill you!"

He picked up his hat and bowed, and she saw in the light of the lamp that his teeth were showing in a smile beneath his moustache. He was not ashamed, he was amused at what she had said, and he was watching her with alert interest.

Oh, he was detestable! She swung round on her heel and marched into the house. She grabbed hold of the door to shut it with a bang, but the hook which held it open was too heavy for her. She struggled with it, panting.

"May I help you?" he asked.

Feeling that she would burst a blood-vessel if she stayed another minute, she stormed up the stairs. And as she reached the upper floor, she heard him obligingly slam the door for her.

4

AS the hot noisy days of August were drawing to a close the bombardment abruptly ceased. The quiet that fell on the town was startling. Neighbours met on the streets and stared at one another, uncertain, uneasy as to what might be impending. The stillness, after the screaming days, brought no surcease to strained nerves but, if possible, made the strain even worse. No one knew why the Yankee batteries were silent; there was no news of the troops except that they had been withdrawn in large numbers from the breastworks about the town and had marched off toward the south to defend the railroad. No one knew where the fighting was, if indeed there was any fighting, or how the battle was going if there was a battle.

Nowadays the only news was that which passed from mouth to mouth. Short of paper, short of ink, short of men, the newspapers had suspended publication after the siege began, and the wildest rumours appeared from nowhere and swept through the town. Now, in the anxious quiet, crowds stormed General Hood's headquarters demanding information, crowds massed about the telegraph office and the depot hoping for tidings, good tidings, for everyone hoped that the silence of Sherman's cannon meant that the Yankees were in full retreat and the Confederates chasing them back up the road to Dalton. But no news came. The telegraph wires were still, no trains came in on the one remaining railroad from the south and the mail service was broken.

Autumn with its dusty, breathless heat was slipping in to choke the suddenly quiet town, adding its dry, panting weight to tired, anxious hearts. To Scarlett, mad to hear from Tara, yet trying to keep up a brave face, it seemed an eternity since the siege began, seemed as though she had always lived with the sound of cannon in her ears until this sinister quiet had fallen. And yet, it was only thirty days since the siege began. Thirty days of siege! The city ringed with red-clay rifle-pits, the monotonous booming of cannon that never rested, the long lines of ambulances and ox-carts dripping blood down the dusty streets toward the hospitals, the overworked burial squads dragging out men when they were hardly cold and dumping them like so many logs in endless rows of shallow ditches. Only thirty days!

And it was only four months since the Yankees moved south from Dalton! Only four months! Scarlett thought, looking back on that far day, that it had occurred in another life. Oh, no! Surely not just four months. It had been a lifetime.

Four months ago! Why, four months ago Dalton, Resaca, Kennesaw Mountain had been to her only names of places on the railroad. Now they were battles—battles desperately, vainly fought as Johnston fell back toward Atlanta. And now, Peachtree Creek, Decatur, Ezra Church and Utoy Creek were no longer pleasant names of pleasant places. Never again could she think of them as quiet villages full of welcoming friends, as green places where she picnicked with handsome officers on the soft banks of slow-moving streams. These names meant battles too, and the soft green grasses where she had sat were cut to bits by heavy cannon wheels, trampled by desperate feet when bayonet met bayonet and flattened where bodies thrashed in agonies. . . . And the lazy streams were redder now than ever Georgia clay could make them. Peachtree Creek was crimson, so they said, after the Yankees crossed it. Peachtree Creek, Decatur, Ezra Church, Utoy Creek. Never names of places any more. Names of graves where friends lay buried, names of tangled underbrush and thick woods where bodies rotted unburied, names of the four sides of Atlanta where Sherman had tried to force his army in and Hood's men had doggedly beaten him back.

At last, news came from the south to the strained town and it was alarming news, especially to Scarlett. General Sherman was trying the fourth side of the town again, striking at the railroad at Jonesboro. Yankees in large numbers were on that fourth side of the town now, no skirmishing units or cavalry detachments but the massed Yankee forces. And thousands of Confederate troops had been withdrawn from the lines close about the city to hurl themselves against them. And that explained the sudden silence.

"Why Jonesboro?" thought Scarlett, terror striking at her heart at the thought of Tara's nearness. "Why must they always hit Jonesboro? Why can't they find some other place to attack the railroad?"

For a week she had not heard from Tara and the last brief note from Gerald had added to her fears. Carreen had taken a turn for the worse and was very, very sick. Now it might be days before the mails came through, days before she heard whether Carreen was alive or dead. Oh, if she had only gone home at the beginning of the siege, Melanie or no Melanie!

There was fighting at Jonesboro—that much Atlanta knew, but how the battle went no one could tell and the most insane rumours tortured the town. Finally a courier came up from Jonesboro with the reassuring news that the Yankees had been beaten back. But they had made a sortie into Jonesboro, burned the depot, cut the telegraph wires and torn up three miles of track before they retreated. The engineering corps was working like mad, repairing the line, but it would take some time because the Yankees had torn up the crossties, made bonfires of them, laid the wrenched-up rails across them until they were red-hot and then twisted them around telegraph poles until they looked like giant corkscrews. These days it was so hard to replace iron rails, to replace anything made of iron.

No, the Yankees hadn't gotten to Tara. The same courier who brought the dispatches to General Hood assured Scarlett of that. He had met Gerald in Jonesboro after the battle, just as he was starting to Atlanta, and Gerald had begged him to bring a letter to her.

But what was Pa doing in Jonesboro? The

young courier looked ill at ease as he made answer. Gerald was hunting for an army doctor to go to Tara with him.

As she stood in the sunshine on the front porch, thanking the young man for his trouble, Scarlett felt her knees go weak. Carreen must be dying if she was so far beyond Ellen's medical skill that Gerald was hunting a doctor! As the courier went off in a small whirlwind of red dust, Scarlett tore open Gerald's letter with fingers that trembled. So great was the shortage of paper in the Confederacy now that Gerald's note was written between the lines of her last letter to him and reading it was difficult.

"Dear Daughter, Your mother and both girls have the typhoid. They are very ill but we must hope for the best. When your mother took to her bed she bade me write you that under no condition were you to come home and expose yourself and Wade to the disease. She sends her love and bids you pray for her."

"Pray for her!" Scarlett flew up the stairs to her room and, dropping on her knees by the bed, prayed as she had never prayed before. No formal Rosaries now but the same words over and over: "Mother of God, don't let her die! I'll be so good if you don't let her die! Please, don't let her die!"

For the next week Scarlett crept about the house like a stricken animal, waiting for news, starting at every sound of horses' hooves, rushing down the dark stair at night when soldiers came tapping at the door, but no news came from Tara. The width of the continent might have spread between her and home instead of twenty-five miles of dusty road.

The mails were still disrupted, no one knew where the Confederates were or what the Yankees were up to. No one knew anything except that thousands of soldiers, grey and blue, were somewhere between Atlanta and Jonesboro. Not a word from Tara in a week.

Scarlett had seen enough typhoid in the Atlanta hospitals to know what a week meant in that dread disease. Ellen was ill, perhaps dying, and here was Scarlett helpless at Atlanta with a pregnant woman on her hands and two armies between her and home. Ellen was ill—perhaps dying. But Ellen couldn't be ill! She had never been ill. The very thought was incredible and it struck at the very foundations of the security of Scarlett's life. Everyone else got sick, but never Ellen. Ellen looked after sick people and made them well again. She couldn't be sick. Scarlett wanted to be home. She wanted Tara with the desperate desire of a frightened child frantic for the only haven it had ever known.

Home! The sprawling white house with fluttering white curtains at the windows, the thick clover on the lawn with the bees busy in it, the little black boy on the front steps shooing the ducks and turkeys from the flower-beds, the serene red fields and the miles and miles of cotton turning white in the sun! Home!

If she had only gone home at the beginning of the siege, when everyone else was refugeeing! She could have taken Melanie with her in safety with weeks to spare.

"Oh, damn Melanie!" she thought a thousand times. "Why couldn't she have gone to Macon with Aunt Pitty? That's where she belongs, with her own kinsfolk, not with me. I'm not of her blood. Why does she hang on to me so hard? If she'd only gone to Macon, then I could have gone home to Mother. Even now—even now, I'd take a chance on getting home in spite of the Yankees, if it wasn't for this baby. Maybe General Hood would give me an escort. He's a nice man, General Hood, and I know I could make him give me an escort and a flag of truce to get me through the lines. But I have to wait for this baby!. . . Oh, Mother! Mother! Don't die!. . . Why don't this baby ever come? I'll see Dr. Meade to-day and ask him if there's any way to hurry babies up so I can go home—if I can get an escort. Dr. Meade said she'd have a bad time. Dear God! Suppose she should die! Melanie dead. Melanie dead. And Ashley—No, I mustn't think about that, it isn't nice. But Ashley—No, I mustn't think about that because he's probably dead, anyway. But he made me promise I'd take care of her. But—if I didn't take care of her and she died and Ashley is still alive—No, I mustn't think about that. It's sinful. And I promised God I'd be good if He would just not let Mother die. Oh, if the baby would only come. If I could only get away from here—get home—get anywhere but here."

Scarlett hated the sight of the ominously still town now and once she had loved it. Atlanta was no longer the gay, the desperately gay place she had loved. It was a hideous place like a plague-stricken city, so quiet, so dreadfully quiet after the din of the siege. There had been stimulation in the noise and the danger of the shelling. There was only horror in the quiet that followed. The town seemed haunted, haunted with fear and uncertainty and memories. People's faces looked pinched and the few soldiers Scarlett saw wore the exhausted look of racers forcing themselves on through the last lap of a race already lost.

The last day of August came and with it convincing rumours that the fiercest fighting since the battle of Atlanta was taking place. Somewhere to the south. Atlanta, waiting for news of the turn of battle, stopped even trying to laugh and joke. Everyone knew now what the soldiers had known two weeks before—that Atlanta was in the last ditch, that if the Macon railroad fell, Atlanta would fall too.

On the morning of the first of September, Scarlett awoke with a suffocating sense of dread upon her, a dread she had taken to her pillow the night before. She thought, dulled with sleep: "What was it I was worrying about when I went to bed last night? Oh, yes, the fighting. There was a battle, somewhere, yesterday! Oh, who won?" She sat up hastily, rubbing her eyes, and her worried heart took up yesterday's load again.

The air was oppressive even in the early morning hour, hot with the scorching promise of a noon of glaring blue sky and pitiless bronze sun. The road outside lay silent. No wagons creaked by. No troops raised the red dust with their tramping feet. There were no sounds of negroes' lazy voices in neighbouring kitchens, no pleasant sounds of breakfasts being prepared, for all the near neighbours except Mrs. Meade and Mrs. Merriwether had refugeed to Macon. And she could hear nothing from their houses either. Farther down the street the business section was quiet and many of the stores and offices were locked and boarded up, while their occupants were somewhere about the countryside with rifles in their hands.

The stillness that greeted her seemed even more sinister this morning than on any of the mornings of the queer quiet week preceding it. She rose hastily, without her usual preliminary burrowings and stretchings, and went to the window, hoping to see some neighbour's face, some heartening sight. But the road was empty. She noted how the leaves on the trees were still dark green but dry and heavily coated with red dust, and how withered and sad the untended flowers in the front yard looked.

As she stood, looking out of the window, there came to her ears a far-off sound, faint and sullen as the first distant thunder of an approaching storm.

"Rain," she thought in the first moment, and her country-bred mind added, "we certainly need it." But, in a split instant: "Rain? No! Not rain! Cannon!"

Her heart racing she leaned from the window, her ear cocked to the far-off roaring, trying to discover from which direction it came. But the dim thundering was so distant that, for a moment, she could not tell. "Make it from

Marietta, Lord!" she prayed. "Or Decatur. Or Peachtree Creek. But not from the south! Not from the south!" She gripped the window-sill tighter and strained her ears and the far-away booming seemed louder. And it was coming from the south.

Cannon to the south! And to the south lay Jonesboro and Tara—and Ellen.

Yankees perhaps at Tara, now, this minute! She listened again but the blood thudding in her ears all but blurred out the sound of far-off firing. No, they couldn't be at Jonesboro yet. If they were that far away, the sound would be fainter, more indistinct. But they must be at least ten miles down the road toward Jonesboro, probably near the little settlement of Rough and Ready. But Jonesboro was scarcely more than ten miles below Rough and Ready.

Cannon to the south, and they might be tolling the knell of Atlanta's fall. But to Scarlett, sick for her mother's safety, fighting to the south only meant fighting near Tara. She walked the floor and wrung her hands and for the first time the thought in all its implications came to her that the grey army might be defeated. It was the thought of Sherman's thousands so close to Tara that brought it all home to her, brought the full horror of the war to her as no sound of siege guns shattering window-panes, no privations of food and clothing and no endless rows of dying men had done. Sherman's army within a few miles of Tara! And even if the Yankees should be defeated, they might fall back down the road to

Tara. And Gerald couldn't possibly refugee out of their way with three sick women.

Oh, if she were only there now, Yankees or not. She paced the floor in her bare feet, her nightgown clinging to her legs, and the more she walked the stronger became her foreboding. She wanted to be at home. She wanted to be near Ellen.

From the kitchen below, she heard the rattle of china as Prissy prepared breakfast, but no sound of Mrs. Meade's Betsy. The shrill, melancholy minor of Prissy was raised, "Jes' a few mo' days, ter tote de wee-ry load . . ." The song grated on Scarlett, its sad implications frightening her, and slipping on a wrapper she pattered out into the hall and to the back stairs and shouted: "Shut up that singing, Prissy!"

A sullen "Yas'm" drifted up to her and she drew a deep breath, feeling suddenly ashamed of herself.

"Where's Betsy?"

"Ah doan know. She ain' came."

Scarlett walked to Melanie's door and opened it a crack, peering into the sunny room. Melanie lay in bed in her nightgown, her eyes closed and circled with black, her heart-shaped face bloated, her slender body hideous and distorted. Scarlett wished viciously that Ashley could see her now. She looked worse than any pregnant woman she had ever seen. As she looked, Melanie's eyes opened and a soft warm smile lit her face.

"Come in," she invited, turning awkwardly on her side. "I've been awake since sun-up,

541

thinking, and, Scarlett, there's something I want to ask you."

She entered the room and sat down on the bed that was glaring with harsh sunshine.

Melanie reached out and took Scarlett's hand in a gentle confiding clasp.

"Dear," she said, "I'm sorry about the cannon. It's toward Jonesboro, isn't it?"

Scarlett said "Um," her heart beginning to beat faster as the thought recurred.

"I know how worried you are. I know you'd have gone home last week when you heard about your mother, if it hadn't been for me. Wouldn't you?"

"Yes," said Scarlett ungraciously.

"Scarlett, darling. You've been so good to me. No sister could have been sweeter or braver. And I love you for it. I'm so sorry I'm in the way."

Scarlett stared. Loved her, did she? The fool!

"And, Scarlett, I've been lying here thinking and I want to ask a very great favour of you." Her clasp tightened. "If I should die, will you take my baby?"

Melanie's eyes were wide and bright with soft urgency.

"Will you?"

Scarlett jerked away her hand as fear swamped her. Fear roughened her voice as she spoke.

"Oh, don't be a goose, Melly. You aren't going to die. Every woman thinks she's going to die with her first baby. I know I did."

"No, you didn't. You've never been afraid of anything. You are just saying that to try to cheer me up. I'm not afraid to die but I'm so afraid to

542

leave the baby, if Ashley is—Scarlett, promise me that you'll take my baby if I should die. Then I won't be afraid. Aunt Pittypat is too old to raise a child and Honey and India are sweet but—I want you to have my baby. Promise me, Scarlett. And if it's a boy, bring him up like Ashley, and if it's a girl—dear, I'd like her to be like you."

"God's nightgown!" cried Scarlett, leaping from the bed. "Aren't things bad enough without you talking about dying?"

"I'm sorry, dear. But promise me. I think it'll be to-day. I'm sure it'll be to-day. Please promise me."

"Oh, all right, I promise," said Scarlett, looking down at her in bewilderment.

Was Melanie such a fool she really didn't know how she cared for Ashley? Or did she know everything and feel that because of that love, Scarlett would take good care of Ashley's child? Scarlett had a wild impulse to cry out questions, but they died on her lips as Melanie took her hand and held it for an instant against her cheek. Tranquillity had come back into her eyes.

"Why do you think it will be to-day, Melly?"

"I've been having pains since dawn—but not very bad ones."

"You have? Well, why didn't you call me? I'll send Prissy for Dr. Meade."

"No, don't do that yet, Scarlett. You know how busy he is, how busy they all are. Just send word to him that we'll need him some time to-day. Send over to Mrs. Meade's and tell her and ask her to come over and sit with me. She'll know when to really send for him."

"Oh, stop being so unselfish. You know you need a doctor as much as anybody in the hospital. I'll send for him right away."

"No, please don't. Sometimes it takes all day having a baby and I just couldn't let the doctor sit here for hours when all those poor boys need him so much. Just send for Mrs. Meade. She'll know."

"Oh, all right," said Scarlett.

5

AFTER sending up Melanie's breakfast tray, Scarlett dispatched Prissy for Mrs. Meade and sat down with Wade to eat her own breakfast. But for once she had no appetite. Between her nervous apprehension over the thought that Melanie's time was approaching and her unconscious straining to hear the sound of the cannon, she could hardly eat. Her heart acted very queerly, beating regularly for several minutes and then thumping so loudly and swiftly it almost made her sick at her stomach. The heavy hominy stuck in her throat like glue and never before had the mixture of parched corn and ground-up yams that passed for coffee been so repulsive. Without sugar or cream it was bitter as gall, for the sorghum used for "long sweetening" did little to improve the taste. After one swallow she pushed her cup away. If for no other reason she hated the Yankees because they kept her from having real coffee with sugar and thick cream in it.

Wade was quieter than usual and did not set up his every-morning complaint against the hominy that he so disliked. He ate silently the spoonfuls she pushed into his mouth and washed them down with noisily gulped water. His soft brown eyes followed her every movement, large, round as dollars, a childish bewilderment in them as though her own scarce-hidden fears had been communicated to him. When he had finished she sent him off to the back yard to play and watched him toddle across the straggling grass to his playhouse with great relief.

She arose and stood irresolutely at the foot of the stairs. She should go up and sit with Melanie and distract her mind from her coming ordeal but she did not feel equal to it. Of all days in the world, Melanie had to pick this day to have the baby! And of all days to talk about dying!

She sat down on the bottom step of the stairs and tried to compose herself, wondering again how yesterday's battle had gone, wondering how to-day's fighting was going. How strange to have a big battle going on just a few miles away and to know nothing of it! How strange the quiet of this deserted end of town in contrast with the day of the fighting at Peachtree Creek! Aunt Pitty's house was one of the last on the north side of Atlanta and with the fighting somewhere to the far south, there were no reinforcements going by at double-quick, no ambulances and staggering lines of walking wounded coming back. She wondered if such scenes were being enacted on the south side of town and thanked God she was not there. If only everyone except the Meades and the Merriwethers had not refugeed from this north end of Peachtree! It made her feel so forsaken and alone. She wished fervently that Uncle Peter were with her so he could go down to headquarters and learn the news. If it wasn't for Melanie she'd go to town this very minute and learn for herself, but she couldn't leave until Mrs. Meade arrived. Mrs. Meade. Why didn't she come on? And where was Prissy?

She rose and went out on to the front porch and looked for them impatiently, but the Meade house was around a shady bend in the street and she could see no one. After a long while Prissy came into view, alone, idling along as though she had the whole day before her, switching her skirts from side to side and looking over her shoulder to observe the effect.

"You're as slow as molasses in January," snapped Scarlett as Prissy opened the gate. "What did Mrs. Meade say? How soon will she be over here?"

"She warn't dar," said Prissy.

"Where is she? When will she be home?"

"Well'm," answered Prissy, dragging out her words pleasurably to give more weight to her message. "Dey Cookie say Miss Meade done got wud early dis mawnin' dat young Mist' Phil done been shot an' Miss Meade she tuck de cah'ige an' Ole Talbot an' Betsy an' dey done gone ter fotch him home. Cookie say he bad hurt an' Miss Meade ain' gwine ter be studyin' 'bout comin' up hyah."

Scarlett stared at her and had an impulse to shake her. Negroes were always so proud of being the bearers of evil tidings.

"Well, don't stand there like a ninny. Go down to Mrs. Merriwether's and ask her to come up or send her mammy. Now, hurry."

"Dey ain' dar, Miss Scarlett. Ah drapped in ter pass time of de day wid Mammy on mah way home. Dey's done gone. House all locked up. Spec dey's at de horsepittle."

"So that's where you were so long! Whenever

I send you somewhere you go where I tell you and don't stop to 'pass any time' with anybody. Go—"

She stopped and racked her brain. Who was left in town among their friends who would be helpful? There was Mrs. Elsing. Of course, Mrs. Elsing didn't like her at all these days but she had always been fond of Melanie.

"Go to Mrs. Elsing's, and explain everything very carefully and tell her to please come up here. And, Prissy, listen to me. Miss Melly's baby is due and she may need you any minute now. Now you hurry right straight back."

"Yas'm," said Prissy and, turning, sauntered down the walk at snail's gait.

"Hurry, you slow-poke!"

"Yas'm."

Prissy quickened her gait infinitesimally and Scarlett went back into the house. She hesitated again before going upstairs to Melanie. She would have to explain to her just why Mrs. Meade couldn't come and the knowledge that Phil Meade was badly wounded might upset her. Well, she'd tell a lie about it.

She entered Melanie's room and saw that the breakfast tray was untouched. Melanie lay on her side, her face white.

"Mrs. Meade's over at the hospital," said Scarlett. "But Mrs. Elsing is coming. Do you feel bad?"

"Not very," lied Melanie. "Scarlett, how long did it take Wade to get born?"

"Less than no time," answered Scarlett with a cheerfulness she was far from feeling. "I was out in the yard and I didn't hardly have time to get into the house. Mammy said it was scandalous—just like one of the darkies."

"I hope I'll be like one of the darkies too," said Melanie, mustering a smile which suddenly disappeared as pain contorted her face.

Scarlett looked down at Melanie's tiny hips with none too sanguine hopes but said reassuringly: "Oh, it's not really so bad."

"Oh, I know it isn't. I'm afraid I'm a little coward. Is—is Mrs. Elsing coming right away?"

"Yes, right away," said Scarlett. "I'll go down and get some fresh water and sponge you off. It's so hot to-day."

She took as long a time as possible in getting the water, running to the front door every two minutes to see if Prissy were coming. There was no sign of Prissy so she went back upstairs, sponged Melanie's perspiring body and combed out her long dark hair.

When an hour had passed she heard scuffing negro feet coming down the street, and looking out of the window, saw Prissy returning slowly, switching herself as before and tossing her head with as many airy affectations as if she had a large and interested audience.

"Some day, I'm going to take a strap to that little wench," thought Scarlett savagely, hurrying down the stairs to meet her.

"Miss Elsing ober at de horsepittle. Dey Cookie 'lows a whole lot of wounded sojers come in on de early train. Cookie fixin' soup ter tek ober dar. She say—"

"Never mind what she said," interrupted

Scarlett, her heart sinking. "Put on a clean apron because I want you to go over to the hospital. I'm going to give you a note to Dr. Meade, and if he isn't there, give it to Dr. Jones or any of the other doctors. And if you don't hurry back this time, I'll skin you alive."

"Yas'm."

"And ask any of the gentlemen for news of the fighting. If they don't know, go by the depot and ask the engineers who brought the wounded in. Ask if they are fighting at Jonesboro or near there."

"Gawdlmighty, Miss Scarlett!" and sudden fright was in Prissy's black face. "De Yankees ain' at Tara, is dey?"

"I don't know. I'm telling you to ask for news."

"Gawdlmighty, Miss Scarlett! Whut'll dey do ter Maw?"

Prissy began to bawl suddenly, loudly, the sound adding to Scarlett's own uneasiness.

"Stop bawling! Miss Melanie will hear you. Now go change your apron, quick."

Spurred to speed, Prissy hurried toward the back of the house while Scarlett scratched a hasty note on the margin of Gerald's last letter to her —the only bit of paper in the house. As she folded it, so that her note was uppermost, she caught Gerald's words, "Your mother—typhoid —under no condition—to come home—" She almost sobbed. If it wasn't for Melanie, she'd start home, right this minute, if she had to walk every step of the way.

Prissy went off at a trot, the letter gripped in

550

her hand, and Scarlett went back upstairs, trying to think of some plausible lie to explain Mrs. Elsing's failure to appear. But Melanie asked no questions. She lay upon her back, her face tranquil and sweet, and the sight of her quieted Scarlett for a while.

She sat down and tried to talk of inconsequential things, but the thoughts of Tara and a possible defeat by the Yankees prodded cruelly. She thought of Ellen dying and of the Yankees coming into Atlanta, burning everything, killing everybody. Through it all, the dull far-off thundering persisted, rolling into her ears in waves of fear. Finally, she could not talk at all and only stared out of the window at the hot still street and the dusty leaves hanging motionless on the trees. Melanie was silent too, but at intervals her quiet face was wrenched with pain.

She said, after each pain: "It wasn't very bad, really," and Scarlett knew she was lying. She would have preferred a loud scream to silent endurance. She knew she should feel sorry for Melanie, but somehow she could not muster a spark of sympathy. Her mind was too torn with her own anguish. Once she looked sharply at the pain-twisted face and wondered why it should be that she, of all people in the world, should be here with Melanie at this particular time—she who had nothing in common with her, who hated her, who would gladly have seen her dead. Well, maybe she'd have her wish, and before the day was over too. A cold superstitious fear swept her at this thought. It was bad luck to wish that someone were dead, almost as bad luck as to curse someone. Curses came home to roost, Mammy said. She hastily prayed that Melanie wouldn't die and broke into feverish small talk, hardly aware of what she said. At last, Melanie put a hot hand on her wrist.

"Don't bother about talking, dear. I know how worried you are. I'm so sorry I'm so much trouble."

Scarlett relapsed into silence but she could not sit still. What would she do if neither the doctor nor Prissy got there in time? She walked to the window and looked down the street and came back and sat down again. Then she rose and looked out of the window on the other side of the room.

An hour went by and then another. Noon came and the sun was high and hot and not a breath of air stirred the dusty leaves. Melanie's pains were harder now. Her long hair was drenched in sweat and her gown stuck in wet spots to her body. Scarlett sponged her face in silence but fear was gnawing at her. God in Heaven, suppose the baby came before the doctor arrived! What would she do? She knew less than nothing of midwifery. This was exactly the emergency she had been dreading for weeks. She had been counting on Prissy to handle the situation if no doctor should be available. Prissy knew all about midwifery. She'd said so time and again. But where was Prissy? Why didn't she come? Why didn't the doctor come? She went to the window and looked again. She listened hard and suddenly she wondered if it were only her imagination or if the sound of cannon in the distance had died away.

If it were farther away it would mean that the fighting was nearer Jonesboro and that would mean—

At last she saw Prissy coming down the street at a quick trot and she leaned out of the window. Prissy, looking up, saw her and her mouth opened to yell. Seeing the panic written on the little black face and fearing she might alarm Melanie by crying out evil tidings, Scarlett hastily put her finger to her lips and left the window.

"I'll get some cooler water," she said, looking down into Melanie's dark, deep-circled eyes and trying to smile. Then she hastily left the room, closing the door carefully behind her.

Prissy was sitting on the bottom step in the hall, panting.

"Dey's fightin' at Jonesboro, Miss Scarlett! Dey say our gempmums is gittin' beat. Oh, Gawd, Miss Scarlett! Whut'll happen ter Maw an' Poke? Oh, Gawd, Miss Scarlett! Whut'll happen ter us effen de Yankees gits hyah? Oh, Gawd—"

Scarlett clapped a hand over the blubbery mouth.

"For God's sake, hush!"

Yes, what would happen to them if the Yankees came—what would happen to Tara? She pushed the thought firmly back into her mind and grappled with the more pressing emergency. If she thought of these things, she'd begin to scream and bawl like Prissy.

"Where's Dr. Meade? When's he coming?"

"Ah ain' nebber seed him, Miss Scarlett."

"What!"

"No'm, he ain' at de horsepittle. Miss

Merriwether an' Miss Elsing ain' dar needer. A man he tole me de doctah down by de car-shed wid the wounded sojers jes' come in frum Jonesboro, but Miss Scarlett, Ah wuz sceered ter go down dar ter de shed—dey's folkses dyin' down dar. Ah's sceered of daid folkses—"

"What about the other doctors?"

"Miss Scarlett, fo' Gawd, Ah couldn' sceercely git one of dem ter read yo' note. Dey wukin' in de horsepittle lak dey all done gone crazy. One doctah he say ter me 'Dam yo' hide! Doan you come roun' hyah bodderin' me 'bout babies w'en we got a mess of men dyin' hyah. Git some woman ter he'p you.' An' den Ah went aroun' an' about an' ast fer news lak you done tole me an' dey all say 'fightin' at Jonesboro' an' Ah—"

"You say Dr. Meade's at the depot?"

"Yas'm. He—"

"Now, listen sharp to me. I'm going to get Dr. Meade and I want you to sit by Miss Melanie and do anything she says. And if you so much as breathe to her where the fighting is, I'll sell you South as sure as gun's iron. And don't you tell her that the other doctors wouldn't come either. Do you hear?"

"Yas'm."

"Wipe your eyes and get a fresh pitcher of water and go on up. Sponge her off. Tell her I've gone for Dr. Meade."

"Is her time nigh, Miss Scarlett?"

"I don't know. I'm afraid it is but I don't know. You should know. Go on up."

Scarlett caught up her wide straw bonnet from the console table and jammed it on her head. She looked in the mirror and automatically pushed up loose strands of hair but she did not see her own reflection. Cold little ripples of fear that started in the pit of her stomach were radiating outward until the fingers that touched her cheeks were cold, though the rest of her body streamed perspiration. She hurried out of the house and into the heat of the sun. It was blindingly, glaringly hot and as she hurried down Peachtree Street her temples began to throb from the heat. From far down the street she could hear the rise and fall and roar of many voices. By the time she caught sight of the Leyden house, she was beginning to pant, for her stays were tightly laced, but she did not slow her gait. The roar of noise grew louder.

From the Leyden house down to Five Points, the street seethed with activity, the activity of an anthill just destroyed. Negroes were running up and down the street, panic in their faces; and on porches, white children sat crying untended. The street was crowded with army wagons and ambulances filled with wounded and carriages piled high with valises and pieces of furniture. Men on horseback dashed out of side streets pell-mell down Peachtree toward Hood's headquarters. In front of the Bonnell house, old Amos stood holding the head of the carriage horse and he greeted Scarlett with rolling eyes.

"Ain' you gone yit, Miss Scarlett? We is goin' now. Ole Miss packin' her bag."

"Going? Where?"

"Gawd knows, Miss. Somewheres. De Yankees is comin'!"

She hurried on, not even saying good-bye. The Yankees were coming! At Wesley Chapel, she paused to catch her breath and wait for her hammering heart to subside. If she did not quiet herself she would certainly faint. As she stood clutching a lamp-post for support, she saw an officer on horseback come charging up the street from Five Points and, on an impulse, she ran out into the street and waved at him.

"Oh, stop! Please, stop!"

He reined in so suddenly the horse went back on its haunches, pawing the air. There were harsh lines of fatigue and urgency in his face but his tattered grey hat was off with a sweep.

"Madam?"

"Tell me, is it true? Are the Yankees coming?"

"I'm afraid so."

"Do you know so?"

"Yes, Ma'm. I know so. A dispatch came in to headquarters half an hour ago from the fighting at Jonesboro."

"At Jonesboro? Are you sure?"

"I'm sure. There's no use telling pretty lies, Madam. The message was from General Hardee and it said: 'I have lost the battle and am in full retreat.'"

"Oh, my God!"

The dark face of the tired man looked down without emotion. He gathered the reins again and put on his hat.

"Oh, sir, please, just a minute. What shall we do?"

"Madam, I can't say. The army is evacuating Atlanta soon."

"Going off and leaving us to the Yankees?"

"I'm afraid so."

The spurred horse went off as though on springs and Scarlett was left standing in the middle of the street with the red dust thick upon her ankles.

The Yankees were coming. The army was leaving. The Yankees were coming. What should she do? Where should she run? No, she couldn't run. There was Melanie back there in the bed expecting that baby. Oh, why did women have babies? If it wasn't for Melanie she could take Wade and Prissy and hide in the woods where the Yankees could never find them. But she couldn't take Melanie to the woods. No, not now. Oh, if she'd only had the baby sooner, yesterday even, perhaps they could get an ambulance and take her away and hide her somewhere. But now—she must find Dr. Meade and make him come home with her. Perhaps he could hurry the baby.

She gathered up her skirts and ran down the street, and the rhythm of her feet was "The Yankees are coming! The Yankees are coming!" Five Points was crowded with people who rushed here and there with unseeing eyes, jammed with wagons, ambulances, ox-carts, carriages loaded with wounded. A roaring sound like the breaking of surf rose from the crowd.

Then a strangely incongruous sight struck her eyes. Throngs of women were coming up from the direction of the railroad tracks carrying hams across their shoulders. Little children hurried by their sides, staggering under buckets of streaming molasses. Young boys dragged sacks of corn and potatoes. One old man struggled along with a small barrel of flour on a wheelbarrow. Men, women and children, black and white, hurried, hurried with straining faces, lugging packages and sacks and boxes of food—more food than she had seen in a year. The crowd suddenly gave a lane for a careering carriage and through the lane came the frail and elegant Mrs. Elsing, standing up in the front of her victoria, reins in one hand, whip in the other. She was hatless and white-faced and her long grey hair streamed down her back as she lashed the horse like a Fury. Jouncing on the back seat of the carriage was her black mammy, Melissy, clutching a greasy side of bacon to her with one hand, while with the other and both feet she attempted to hold the boxes and bags piled all about her. One bag of dried peas had burst and the peas strewed themselves into the street. Scarlett screamed to her, but the tumult of the crowd drowned her voice and the carriage rocked madly by.

For a moment she could not understand what it all meant and then, remembering that the commissary warehouses were down by the rail-road tracks, she realized that the army had thrown them open to the people to salvage what they could before the Yankees came.

She pushed her way swiftly through the crowds, past the packed, hysterical mob surging in the open space of Five Points, and hurried as fast as she could down the short block toward the depot. Through the tangle of ambulances and the clouds of dust, she could see doctors and stretcher-bearers bending, lifting, hurrying.

Thank God, she'd find Dr. Meade soon. As she rounded the corner of the Atlanta Hotel and came in full view of the depot and the tracks, she halted, appalled.

Lying in the pitiless sun, shoulder to shoulder, head to feet, were hundreds of wounded men, lining the tracks, the sidewalks, stretched out in endless rows under the car-shed. Some lay stiff and still but many writhed under the hot sun, moaning. Everywhere, swarms of flies hovered over the men, crawling and buzzing in their faces, everywhere was blood, dirty bandages, groans, screamed curses of pain as stretcher-bearers lifted men. The smell of sweat, of blood, of unwashed bodies, of excrement rose up in waves of blistering heat until the fetid stench almost nauseated her. The ambulance men hurrying here and there among the prostrate forms frequently stepped on wounded men, so thickly packed were the rows, and those trodden upon stared stolidly up, waiting their turn.

She shrank back, clapping her hand to her mouth, feeling that she was going to vomit. She couldn't go on. She had seen wounded men in the hospitals, wounded men on Aunt Pitty's lawn after the fighting at the creek, but never anything like this. Never anything like these stinking, bleeding bodies broiling under the glaring sun. This was an inferno of pain and smell and noise and hurry—hurry—hurry! The Yankees are coming! The Yankees are coming!

She braced her shoulders and went down among them, straining her eyes among the upright figures to distinguish Dr. Meade. But she discovered she could not look for him, for if she did not step carefully she would tread on some poor soldier. She raised her skirts and tried to pick her way among them toward a knot of men who were directing the stretcher-bearers.

As she walked, feverish hands plucked at her skirt and voices croaked: "Lady—water! Please, lady, water! For Christ's sake, water!"

Perspiration came down her face in streams as she pulled her skirts from clutching hands. If she stepped on one of these men, she'd scream and faint. She stepped over dead men, over men who lay dull-eyed with hands clutched to bellies where dried blood had glued torn uniforms to wounds, over men whose beards were stiff with blood and from whose broken jaws came sounds which must mean:

"Water! Water!"

If she did not find Dr. Meade soon, she would begin screaming with hysteria. She looked toward the group of men under the car-shed and cried as loudly as she could: "Dr. Meade! Is Dr. Meade there?"

From the group one man detached himself and looked toward her. It was the doctor. He was coatless and his sleeves were rolled up to his shoulders. His shirt and trousers were as red as a butcher's and even the end of his iron-grey beard was matted with blood. His face was the face of a man drunk with fatigue and impotent rage and burning pity. It was grey and dusty, and sweat had streaked long rivulets across his cheeks. But his voice was calm and decisive as he called to her.

"Thank God, you are here. I can use every pair of hands."

For a moment she stared at him bewildered, dropping her skirts in dismay. They fell over the dirty face of a wounded man who feebly tried to turn his head to escape from their smothering folds. What did the doctor mean? The dust from the ambulances came into her face with choking dryness, and the rotten smells were like a foul liquid in her nostrils.

"Hurry, child! Come here."

She picked up her skirts and went to him as fast as she could go across the rows of bodies. She put her hand on his arm and felt that it was trembling with weariness but there was no weakness in his face.

"Oh, Doctor!" she cried. "You must come. Melanie is having her baby."

He looked at her as if her words did not register on his mind. A man who lay upon the ground at her feet, his head pillowed on his canteen, grinned up companionably at her words.

"They will do it," he said cheerfully.

She did not even look down but shook the doctor's arm.

"It's Melanie. The baby. Doctor, you must come. She—the—" This was no time for delicacy but it was hard to bring out the words with the ears of hundreds of strange men listening.

"The pains are getting hard. Please, Doctor!"

"A baby? Great God!" thundered the doctor, and his face was suddenly contorted with hate and rage, a rage not directed at her or at anyone except a world wherein such things could happen.

561

"Are you crazy? I can't leave these men. They are dying, hundreds of them. I can't leave them for a damned baby. Get some woman to help you. Get my wife."

She opened her mouth to tell him why Mrs. Meade could not come and then shut it abruptly. He did not know his own son was wounded! She wondered if he would still be here if he did know, and something told her that even if Phil were dying he would still be standing on this spot, giving aid to the many instead of the one.

"No, you must come, Doctor. You know you said she'd have a hard time—" Was it really she, Scarlett, standing here saying these dreadful indelicate things at the top of her voice in this hell of heat and groans? "She'll die if you don't come!"

He shook off her hand roughly and spoke as though he hardly heard her, hardly knew what she said.

"Die? Yes, they'll all die—all these men. No bandages, no salves, no quinine, no chloroform. Oh, God, for some morphia! Just a little morphia for the worst ones. Just a little chloroform. God damn the Yankees! God damn the Yankees!"

"Give um hell, Doctor!" said the man on the ground, his teeth showing in his beard.

Scarlett began to shake and her eyes burned with tears of fright. The doctor wasn't coming with her. Melanie would die and she had wished that she would die. The doctor wasn't coming.

"Name of God, Doctor! Please!"

Dr. Meade bit his lip and his jaw hardened as his face went cool again.

"Child, I'll try. I can't promise you. But I'll try. When we get these men tended to. The Yankees are coming and the troops are moving out of town. I don't know what they'll do with the wounded. There aren't any trains. The Macon line has been captured. . . . But I'll try. Run along now. Don't bother me. There's nothing much to bringing a baby. Just tie up the cord. . . ."

He turned as an orderly touched his arm and began firing directions and pointing to this and that wounded man. The man at her feet looked up at Scarlett compassionately. She turned away, for the doctor had forgotten her.

She picked her way rapidly through the wounded and back to Peachtree Street. The doctor wasn't coming. She would have to see it through herself. Thank God, Prissy knew all about midwifery. Her head ached from the heat and she could feel her basque, soaking wet from perspiration, sticking to her. Her mind felt numb and so did her legs, numb as in a nightmare when she tried to run and could not move them. She thought of the long walk back to the house and it seemed interminable.

Then, "The Yankees are coming!" began to beat its refrain in her mind again. Her heart began to pound and new life came into her limbs. She hurried into the crowd at Five Points, now so thick there was no room on the narrow sidewalks and she was forced to walk in the street. Long lines of soldiers were passing, dust-covered, sodden with weariness. There seemed thousands of them, bearded, dirty, their guns slung over

563

their shoulders, swiftly passing at route step. Cannon rolled past, the drivers flaying the thin mules with lengths of rawhide. Commissary wagons with torn canvas covers rocked through the ruts. Cavalry raising clouds of choking dust went past endlessly. She had never seen so many soldiers together before. Retreat! Retreat! The army was moving out.

The hurrying lines pushed her back on to the packed sidewalk and she smelled the reek of cheap corn whisky. There were women in the mob near Decatur Street, garishly dressed women whose bright finery and painted faces gave a discordant note of holiday. Most of them were drunk and the soldiers on whose arms they hung were drunker. She caught a fleeting glimpse of a head of red curls and saw that creature, Belle Watling, heard her shrill drunken laughter as she clung for support to a one-armed soldier who reeled and staggered.

When she had shoved and pushed her way through the mob for a block beyond Five Points, the crowd thinned a little and, gathering up her skirts, she began to run again. When she reached Wesley Chapel, she was breathless and dizzy and sick at her stomach. Her stays were cutting her ribs in two. She sank down on the steps of the church and buried her head in her hands until she could breathe more easily. If she could only get one deep breath, way down in her abdomen. If her heart would only stop bumping and drumming and cavorting. If there were only someone in this mad place to whom she could turn.

Why, she had never had to do a thing for

herself in all her life. There had always been someone to do things for her, to look after her, shelter and protect her and spoil her. It was incredible that she could be in such a fix. Not a friend, not a neighbour to help her. There had always been friends, neighbours, the competent hands of willing slaves. And now in this hour of greatest need, there was no one. It was incredible that she could be so completely alone, and frightened, and far from home.

Home! If she were only home, Yankees or no Yankees. Home, even if Ellen was sick. She longed for the sight of Ellen's sweet face, for Mammy's strong arms around her.

She rose dizzily to her feet and started walking again. When she came in sight of the house, she saw Wade swinging on the front gate. When he saw her, his face puckered and he began to cry, holding up a grubby bruised finger.

"Hurt!" he sobbed. "Hurt!"

"Hush! Hush! Hush! Or I'll spank you. Go out in the back yard and make mud pies and don't move from there."

"Wade hungwy," he sobbed, and put the hurt finger in his mouth.

"I don't care. Go in the back yard and—"

She looked up and saw Prissy leaning out of the upstairs window, fright and worry written on her face; but in an instant they were wiped away in relief as she saw her mistress. Scarlett beckoned to her to come down and went into the house. How cool it was in the hall! She untied her bonnet and flung it on the table, drawing her forearm across her wet forehead. She heard the upstairs door open and a low wailing moan, wrenched from the depths of agony, came to her ears. Prissy came down the stairs three at a time.

"Is de doctah come?"

"No. He can't come."

"Gawd, Miss Scarlett! Miss Melly bad off!"

"The doctor can't come. Nobody can come. You've got to bring the baby and I'll help you."

Prissy's mouth fell open and her tongue wagged wordlessly. She looked at Scarlett sideways and scuffed her feet and twisted her thin body.

"Don't look so simple-minded!" cried Scarlett, infuriated at her silly expression. "What's the matter?"

Prissy edged back up the stairs.

"Fo' Gawd, Miss Scarlett—" Fright and shame were in her rolling eyes.

"Well?"

"Fo' Gawd, Miss Scarlett! We's got ter have a doctah. Ah—Ah—Miss Scarlett, Ah doan know nuthin' 'bout bringin' babies. Maw wouldn' nebber lemme be 'round folkses whut wuz havin' dem."

All the breath went out of Scarlett's lungs in one gasp of horror before rage swept her. Prissy made a lunge past her, bent on flight, but Scarlett grabbed her.

"You black liar—what do you mean? You've been saying you knew everything about birthing babies. What is the truth? Tell me!" She shook her until the kinky head rocked drunkenly.

"Ah's lyin', Miss Scarlett! Ah doan know huccome Ah tell sech a lie. Ah jes' see one baby

566

birthed, an' Maw she lak ter wo' me out fer watchin'."

Scarlett glared at her and Prissy shrank back, trying to pull loose. For a moment her mind refused to accept the truth, but when realization finally came to her that Prissy knew no more about midwifery than she did, anger went over her like a flame. She had never struck a slave in all her life, but now she slapped the black cheek with all the force in her tired arm. Prissy screamed at the top of her voice, more from fright than pain, and began to dance up and down, writhing to break Scarlett's grip.

As she screamed, the moaning from the second floor ceased and a moment later Melanie's voice, weak and trembling, called: "Scarlett? Is it you? Please come! Please!"

Scarlett dropped Prissy's arm and the wench sank whimpering to the steps. For a moment Scarlett stood still, looking up, listening to the low moaning which had begun again. As she stood there, it seemed as though a yoke descended heavily upon her neck, felt as though a heavy load were harnessed to it, a load she would feel as soon as she took a step.

She tried to think of all the things Mammy and Ellen had done for her when Wade was born but the merciful blurring of the childbirth pains obscured almost everything in mist. She did recall a few things and she spoke to Prissy rapidly, authority in her voice.

"Build a fire in the stove and keep hot water boiling in the kettle. And bring up all the towels you can find and that ball of twine. And get me the scissors. Don't come telling me you can't find them. Get them and get them quick. Now hurry."

She jerked Prissy to her feet and sent her kitchenwards with a shove. Then she squared her shoulders and started up the stairs. It was going to be difficult, telling Melanie that she and Prissy were to deliver her baby.

6

THERE would never again be an afternoon as long as this one. Or as hot. Or as full of lazy insolent flies. They swarmed on Melanie despite the fan Scarlett kept in constant motion. Her arms ached from swinging the wide palmetto leaf. All her efforts seemed futile, for while she brushed them from Melanie's moist face, they crawled on her clammy feet and legs and made her jerk them weakly and cry: "Please! On my feet!"

The room was in semi-gloom, for Scarlett had pulled down the shades to shut out the heat and brightness. Pin-points of sunlight came in through minute holes in the shades and about the edges. The room was an oven and Scarlett's sweat-drenched clothes never dried but became wetter and stickier as the hours went by. Prissy was crouched in a corner, sweating too, and smelled so abominably Scarlett would have sent her from the room had she not feared the girl would take to her heels if once out of sight. Melanie lay on the bed on a sheet dark with perspiration and splotched with dampness where Scarlett had spilled water. She twisted endlessly, to one side, to the other, to left, to right and back again.

Sometimes she tried to sit up and fell back and began twisting again. At first, she had tried to keep from crying out, biting her lips until they were raw, and Scarlett, whose nerves were as raw as the lips, said huskily: "Melly, for God's sake, don't try to be brave. Yell, if you want to. There's nobody to hear you but us."

As the afternoon wore on, Melanie moaned whether she wanted to be brave or not, and sometimes she screamed. When she did, Scarlett dropped her head into her hands and covered her ears and twisted her body and wished that she herself were dead. Anything was preferable to being a helpless witness to such pain. Anything was better than being tied here waiting for a baby that took such a long time coming. Waiting, when for all she knew the Yankees were actually at Five Points.

She fervently wished she had paid more attention to the whispered conversations of matrons on the subject of childbirth. If only she had! If only she had been more interested in such matters she'd know whether Melanie was taking a long time or not. She had a vague memory of one of Aunt Pitty's stories of a friend who was in labour for two days and died without ever having the baby. Suppose Melanie should go on like this for two days! But Melanie was so delicate. She couldn't stand two days of this pain. She'd die soon if the baby didn't hurry. And how could she ever face Ashley, if he were still alive, and tell him that Melanie had died—after she had promised to take care of her?

At first, Melanie wanted to hold Scarlett's hand when the pain was bad but she clamped down on it so hard she nearly broke the bones. After an hour of this, Scarlett's hands were so swollen and bruised she could hardly flex them. She knotted two long towels together and tied them to the foot of the bed and put the knotted end in Melanie's hands. Melanie hung on to it as though it were a life-line, straining, pulling it taut, slackening it, tearing at it. Throughout the afternoon, her voice went on like an animal dying in a trap. Occasionally she dropped the towel and rubbed her hands feebly and looked up at Scarlett with eyes enormous with pain.

"Talk to me. Please talk to me," she whispered, and Scarlett would gabble something until Melanie again gripped the knot and again began writhing.

The dim room swam with heat and pain and droning flies, and time went by on such dragging feet Scarlett could scarcely remember the morning. She felt as if she had been in this steaming, dark, sweating place all her life. She wanted very much to scream every time Melanie did, and only by biting her lips so hard it infuriated her could she restrain herself and drive off hysteria.

Once Wade came tiptoeing up the stairs and stood outside the door, wailing.

"Wade hungwy!" Scarlett started to go to him, but Melanie whispered: "Don't leave me. Please. I can stand it when you're here."

So Scarlett sent Prissy down to warm up the breakfast hominy and feed him. For herself, she felt that she could never eat again after this afternoon.

The clock on the mantel had stopped and she had no way of telling the time, but as the heat in the room lessened and the bright pin-points of light grew duller, she pulled the shade aside. She saw to her surprise that it was late afternoon and the sun, a ball of crimson, was far down the sky. Somehow, she had imagined it would remain broiling hot noon forever.

She wondered passionately what was going on downtown. Had all the troops moved out yet? Had the Yankees come? Would the Confederates march away without even a fight? Then she remembered with a sick dropping in her stomach how few Confederates there were and how many men Sherman had and how well fed they were. Sherman! The name of Satan himself did not frighten her half so much. But there was no time for thinking now, as Melanie called for water, for a cold towel on her head, to be fanned, to have the flies brushed away from her face.

When twilight came on and Prissy, scurrying like a black wraith, lit a lamp, Melanie became weaker. She began calling for Ashley, over and over, as if in a delirium, until the hideous monotony gave Scarlett a fierce desire to smother her voice with a pillow. Perhaps the doctor would come after all. If he would only come quickly! Hope raising its head, she turned to Prissy and ordered her to run quickly to the Meades' house and see if he were there or Mrs. Meade.

"And if he's not there, ask Mrs. Meade or Cookie what to do. Beg them to come!"

Prissy was off with a clatter and Scarlett watched her hurrying down the street, going faster than she had ever dreamed the worthless child could move. After a prolonged time she was back, alone.

"De doctah ain' been home all day. Sont wud he mout go off wid de sojers. Miss Scarlett, Mist' Phil's 'ceased."

"Dead?"

"Yas'm," said Prissy, expanding with importance. "Talbot, dey coachman, tole me. He wuz shot—"

"Never mind that."

"Ah din' see Miss Meade. Cookie say Miss Meade she washin' him an' fixin' ter buhy him fo' de Yankees gits hyah. Cookie say effen de pain git too bad, jes' you put a knife unner Miss Melly's bed an' it cut de pain in two."

Scarlett wanted to slap her again for this helpful information but Melanie opened wide, dilated eyes and whispered: "Dear—are the Yankees coming?"

"No," said Scarlett stoutly. "Prissy's a liar."

"Yas'm, Ah sho is," Prissy agreed fervently.

"They're coming," whispered Melanie undeceived and buried her face in the pillow. Her voice came out muffled.

"My poor baby. My poor baby." And, after a long interval: "Oh, Scarlett, you mustn't stay here. You must go and take Wade."

What Melanie said was no more than Scarlett had been thinking, but hearing it put into words infuriated her, shamed her as if her secret cowardice was written plainly in her face.

"Don't be a goose. I'm not afraid. You know I won't leave you."

"You might as well. I'm going to die." And she began moaning again.

Scarlett came down the dark stairs slowly, like an old woman, feeling her way, clinging to the banisters lest she fall. Her legs were leaden, trembling with fatigue and strain, and she shivered with cold from the clammy sweat that soaked her body. Feebly she made her way on to the front porch and sank down on the top step. She sprawled back against a pillar of the porch and with a shaking hand unbuttoned her basque halfway down her bosom. The night was drenched in warm soft darkness and she lay staring into it, dull as an ox.

It was all over. Melanie was not dead and the small baby boy who made noises like a young kitten was receiving his first bath at Prissy's hands. Melanie was asleep. How could she sleep after that nightmare of screaming pain and ignorant midwifery that hurt more than it helped? Why wasn't she dead? Scarlett knew that she herself would have died under such handling. But, when it was over, Melanie had even whispered, so weakly she had to bend over her to hear: "Thank you." And then she had gone to sleep. How could she go to sleep? Scarlett forgot that she too had gone to sleep after Wade was born. She forgot everything. Her mind was a vacuum; the world was a vacuum; there had been no life before this endless day and there would be none hereafter—only a heavily hot night, only the sound of her hoarse tired breathing, only the sweat trickling coldly from armpit to waist, from hip to knee, clammy, sticky, chilling.

She heard her own breath pass from loud evenness to spasmodic sobbing but her eyes were dry and burning as though there would never be tears in them again. Slowly, laboriously, she heaved herself over and pulled her heavy skirts up to her thighs. She was warm and cold and sticky all at the same time and the feel of the night air on her limbs was refreshing. She thought dully what Aunt Pitty would say, if she could see her sprawled here on the front porch with her skirts up and her drawers showing, but she did not care. She did not care about anything. Time had stood still. It might be just after twilight and it might be midnight. She didn't know or care.

She heard sounds of moving feet upstairs and thought, "May the Lord damn Prissy," before her eyes closed and something like sleep descended upon her. Then after an indeterminate dark interval, Prissy was beside her, chattering on in a pleased way.

"We done right good, Miss Scarlett. Ah specs Maw couldn' a did no better."

From the shadows, Scarlett glared at her, too tired to rail, too tired to upbraid, too tired to enumerate Prissy's offences—her boastful assumption of experience she didn't possess, her fright, her blundering awkwardness, her utter inefficiency when the emergency was hot, the misplacing of the scissors, the spilling of the basin of water on the bed, the dropping of the new-born baby. And now she bragged about how good she had been.

And the Yankees wanted to free the negroes! Well, the Yankees were welcome to them.

She lay back against the pillar in silence and Prissy, aware of her mood, tiptoed away into the darkness of the porch. After a long interval in which her breathing finally quieted and her mind steadied, Scarlett heard the sound of faint voices from up the road, the tramping of many feet coming from the north. Soldiers! She sat up slowly, pulling down her skirts, although she knew no one could see her in the darkness. As they came abreast the house, an indeterminate number, passing like shadows, she called to them.

"Oh, please!"

A shadow disengaged itself from the mass and came to the gate.

"Are you going? Are you leaving us?"

The shadow seemed to take off a hat and a quiet voice came from the darkness.

"Yes, Ma'm. That's what we're doing. We're the last of the men from the breastworks, 'bout a mile north from here."

"Are you—is the army really retreating?"

"Yes, Ma'm. You see, the Yankees are coming."

The Yankees are coming! She had forgotten that. Her throat suddenly contracted and she could say nothing more. The shadow moved away, merged itself with the other shadows, and the feet tramped off into the darkness. "The Yankees are coming! The Yankees are coming!" That was what the rhythm of their feet said, that was what her suddenly bumping heart thudded out with each beat. The Yankees are coming!

"De Yankees is comin'!" bawled Prissy, shrinking close to her. "Oh, Miss Scarlett, dey'll kill us all! Dey'll run dey baynits in our stummicks! Dey'll—"

"Oh, hush!" It was terrifying enough to think these things without hearing them put into trembling words. Renewed fear swept her. What could she do? How could she escape? Where could she turn for help? Every friend had failed her.

Suddenly she thought of Rhett Butler and calm dispelled her fears. Why hadn't she thought of him this morning when she had been tearing about like a chicken with its head off? She hated him, but he was strong and smart and he wasn't afraid of the Yankees. And he was still in town. Of course, she was mad at him and he had said unforgivable things the last time she'd seen him. But she could overlook such things at a time like this. And he had a horse and carriage, too. Oh, why hadn't she thought of him before! He could take them all away from this doomed place, away from the Yankees, somewhere, anywhere.

She turned to Prissy and spoke with feverish urgency.

"You know where Captain Butler lives—at the Atlanta Hotel?"

"Yas'm, but—"

"Well, go there, now, as quick as you can run and tell him I want him. I want him to come quickly and bring his horse and carriage or an ambulance if he can get one. Tell him about the baby. Tell him I want him to take us out of here. Go, now. Hurry!"

She sat upright and gave Prissy a push to speed her feet.

"Gawdlmighty, Miss Scarlett! Ah's sceered ter go runnin' roun' in de dahk by mahseff! Spose de Yankees gits me?"

"If you run fast you can catch up with those soldiers and they won't let the Yankees get you. Hurry!"

"Ah's sceered! Sposin' Cap'n Butler ain' at de hotel?"

"Then ask where he is. Haven't you any gumption? If he isn't at the hotel, go to the bar-rooms on Decatur Street and ask for him. Go to Belle Watling's house. Hunt for him. You fool, don't you see that if you don't hurry and find him the Yankees will surely get us all?"

"Miss Scarlett, Maw would weah me out wid a cotton stalk, did Ah go in a bahroom or a ho' house."

Scarlett pulled herself to her feet.

"Well, I'll wear you out if you don't. You can stand outside in the street and yell for him, can't you? Or ask somebody if he's inside. Get going."

When Prissy still lingered, shuffling her feet and mouthing, Scarlett gave her another push which nearly sent her headlong down the front steps.

"You'll go or I'll sell you down the river. You'll never see your mother again or anybody you know and I'll sell you for a field hand too. Hurry!"

"Gawdlmighty, Miss Scarlett—"

But under the determined pressure of her mistress' hand she started down the steps. The front gate clicked and Scarlett cried: "Run, you goose!"

She heard the patter of Prissy's feet as she broke into a trot, and then the sound died away on the soft earth.

7

AFTER Prissy had gone, Scarlett went wearily into the downstairs hall and lit a lamp. The house felt steamingly hot, as though it held in its walls all the heat of the noontide. Some of her dullness was passing now and her stomach was clamouring for food. She remembered she had had nothing to eat since the night before except a spoonful of hominy, and picking up the lamp she went into the kitchen. The fire in the oven had died but the room was stiflingly hot. She found half a pone of hard corn bread in the skillet and gnawed hungrily on it while she looked about for other food. There was some hominy left in the pot and she ate it with a big cooking spoon, not waiting to put it on a plate. It needed salt badly but she was too hungry to hunt for it. After four spoonfuls of it, the heat of the room was too much and, taking the lamp in one hand and a fragment of pone in the other, she went out into the hall.

She knew she should go upstairs and sit beside Melanie. If anything went wrong, Melanie would be too weak to call. But the idea of returning to that room where she had spent so many nightmare hours was repulsive to her. Even if Melanie were dying, she couldn't go back up there. She never wanted to see that room again. She set the lamp on the candle-stand by the window and returned to the front porch. It was so much cooler here, even though the night was drowned in soft warmth. She sat down on the steps in the circle of faint light thrown by the lamp and continued gnawing on the corn bread.

When she had finished it, a measure of strength came back to her and with the strength came again the pricking of fear. She could hear a humming of noise far down the street, but what it portended she did not know. She could distinguish nothing but a volume of sound that rose and fell. She strained forward trying to hear and soon she found her muscles aching from the tension. More than anything in the world she yearned to hear the sound of hooves and to see Rhett's careless, self-confident eyes laughing at her fears. Rhett would take them away, somewhere. She didn't know where. She didn't care.

As she sat straining her ears toward town, a faint glow appeared above the trees. It puzzled her. She watched it and saw it grow brighter. The dark sky became pink and then dull red and, suddenly above the trees, she saw a huge tongue of flame leap high to the heavens. She jumped to her feet, her heart beginning again its sickening thudding and bumping.

The Yankees had come! She knew they had come and they were burning the town. The flames seemed to be off to the east of the centre of town. They shot higher and higher and widened rapidly into a broad expanse of red before her terrified eyes. A whole block must be burning. A faint hot breeze that had sprung up bore the smell of smoke to her.

She fled up the stairs to her own room and

hung out the window for a better view. The sky was a hideous lurid colour and great swirls of black smoke went twisting up to hang in billowy clouds above the flames. The smell of smoke was stronger now. Her mind rushed incoherently here and there, thinking how soon the flames would spread up Peachtree Street and burn this house, how soon the Yankees would be rushing in upon her, where she would run, what she would do. All the fiends of hell seemed screaming in her ears and her brain swirled with confusion and panic so overpowering she clung to the window-sill for support.

"I must think," she told herself over and over. "I must think."

But thoughts eluded her, darting in and out of her mind like frightened humming-birds. As she stood hanging to the sill, a deafening explosion burst on her ears, louder than any cannon she had ever heard. The sky was rent with gigantic flame. Then other explosions. The earth shook and the glass in the panes above her head shivered and came down around her.

The world became an inferno of noise and flame and trembling earth as one explosion followed another in ear-splitting succession. Torrents of sparks shot to the sky and descended slowly, lazily, through blood-coloured clouds of smoke. She thought she heard a feeble call from the next room but she paid it no heed. She had no time for Melanie now. No time for anything except a fear that licked through her veins as swiftly as the flames she saw. She was a child and mad with fright and she wanted to bury her head in her mother's lap and shut out this sight. If she were only home! Home with Mother.

Through the nerve-shivering sounds, she heard another sound, that of fear-sped feet coming up the stairs three at a time, heard a voice yelping like a lost hound. Prissy broke into the room and, flying to Scarlett, clutched her arm in a grip that seemed to pinch out pieces of flesh.

"The Yankees—" cried Scarlett.

"No'm, it's our gempmums!" yelled Prissy between breaths, digging her nails deeper into Scarlett's arm. "Dey's buhnin' de foun'ry an' de ahmy supply depots an' de wa'houses an', fo' Gawd, Miss Scarlett, dey done set off dem sebenty freight cahs of cannon-balls an' gunpowder an', Jesus, we's all gwine ter buhn up!"

She began yelping again shrilly and pinched Scarlett so hard she cried out in pain and fury and shook off her hand.

The Yankees hadn't come yet! There was still time to get away! She rallied her frightened forces together.

"If I don't get a hold on myself," she thought, "I'll be squalling like a scalded cat!" and the sight of Prissy's abject terror helped steady her. She took her by the shoulders and shook her.

"Shut up that racket and talk sense. The Yankees haven't come, you fool! Did you see Captain Butler? What did he say? Is he coming?"

Prissy ceased her yelling but her teeth chattered.

"Yas'm, Ah finely foun' him. In a bahroom, lak you tole me. He—"

583

"Never mind where you found him. Is he coming? Did you tell him to bring his horse?"

"Lawd, Miss Scarlett, he say our gempmums done tuck his hawse an' cah'ige fer a amberlance."

"Dear God in Heaven!"

"But he comin'—"

"What did he say?"

Prissy had recovered her breath and a small measure of control but her eyes still rolled.

"Well'm, lak you tole me, Ah foun' him in a bahroom. Ah stood outside an' yell fer him an' he come out. An' terreckly he see me an' Ah starts ter tell him, de sojers tech off a sto' house down Decatur Street an' it flame up an' he say Come on an' he grab me an' we runs up ter Fibe Points an' he say den: What now? Talk fas'. An' Ah say you say, Cap'n Butler, come quick an' bring yo' hawse an' cah'ige. Miss Melly done had a chile an' you is bustin' ter git outer town. An' he say: Where all she studyin' 'bout goin'? An' Ah say: Ah doan know, suh, but you is boun' ter go fo' de Yankees gits hyah an' wants him ter go wid you. An' he laugh an' say dey done tuck his hawse."

Scarlett's heart went leaden as the last hope left her. Fool that she was, why hadn't she thought that the retreating army would naturally take every vehicle and animal left in the city? For a moment she was too stunned to hear what Prissy was saying but she pulled herself together to hear the rest of the story.

"An' den he say, Tell Miss Scarlett ter res' easy. Ah'll steal her a hawse outer de ahmy crall

584

effen dey's ary one lef'. An' he say, Ah done stole hawses befo' dis night. Tell her Ah git her a hawse effen Ah gits shot fer it. Den he laugh agin an' say, Cut an' run home. An' befo' Ah gits started Kerbloom! Off goes a noise an' Ah lak ter drap in mah tracks an' he tell me twarn't nuthin' but de ammernition our gempmums blowin' up so's de Yankees don't git it an'—"

"He is coming? He's going to bring a horse?"

"So he say."

She drew a long breath of relief. If there was any way of getting a horse, Rhett Butler would get one. A smart man, Rhett. She would forgive him anything if he got them out of this mess. Escape! And with Rhett she would have no fear. Rhett would protect them. Thank God for Rhett! With safety in view she turned practical.

"Wake Wade up and dress him and pack some clothes for all of us. Put them in the small trunk. And don't tell Miss Melanie we're going. Not yet. But wrap the baby in a couple of thick towels and be sure and pack his clothes."

Prissy still clung to her skirts and hardly anything showed in her eyes except the whites. Scarlett gave her a shove and loosened her grip.

"Hurry," she cried, and Prissy went off like a rabbit.

Scarlett knew she should go in and quiet Melanie's fear, knew Melanie must be frightened out of her senses by the thunderous noises that continued unabated and the glare that lighted the sky. It looked and sounded like the end of the world.

But she could not bring herself to go back into

that room just yet. She ran down the stairs with some idea of packing up Miss Pittypat's china and the little silver she had left when she refugeed to Macon. But when she reached the dining-room, her hands were shaking so badly she dropped three plates and shattered them. She ran out on to the porch to listen and back again to the dining-room and dropped the silver clattering to the floor. Everything she touched she dropped. In her hurry she slipped on the rag rug and fell to the floor with a jolt but leaped up so quickly she was not even aware of the pain. Upstairs she could hear Prissy galloping about like a wild animal and the sound maddened her, for she was galloping just as aimlessly.

For the dozenth time, she ran out on to the porch but this time she did not go back to her futile packing. She sat down. It was just impossible to pack anything. Impossible to do anything but sit with hammering heart and wait for Rhett. It seemed hours before he came. At last, far up the road, she heard the protesting screech of unoiled axles and the slow uncertain plodding of hooves. Why didn't he hurry? Why didn't he make the horse trot?

The sounds came nearer and she leaped to her feet and called Rhett's name. Then she saw him dimly as he climbed down from the seat of a small wagon, heard the clicking of the gate as he came toward her. He came into view and the light of the lamp showed him plainly. His dress was as debonair as if he were going to a ball, well-tailored white linen coat and trousers, embroidered grey watered-silk waistcoat and a

hint of ruffle on his shirt bosom. His wide
Panama hat was set dashingly on one side of his
head and in the belt of his trousers were thrust
two ivory-handled, long-barrelled duelling pistols.
The pockets of his coat sagged heavily with
ammunition.

He came up the walk with the springy stride
of a savage and his fine head was carried like a
pagan prince. The dangers of the night which had
driven Scarlett into panic had affected him like
an intoxicant. There was a carefully restrained
ferocity in his dark face, a ruthlessness which
would have frightened her had she the wits to see it.

His black eyes danced as though amused by the
whole affair, as though the earth-splitting sounds
and the horrid glare were merely things to
frighten children. She swayed toward him as he
came up the steps, her face white, her green eyes
burning.

"Good evening," he said, in his drawling voice,
as he removed his hat with a sweeping gesture.
"Fine weather we're having. I hear you're going
to take a trip."

"If you make any jokes, I shall never speak to
you again," she said with quivering voice.

"Don't tell me you are frightened!" He
pretended to be surprised and smiled in a way
that made her long to push him backwards down
the steep steps.

"Yes, I am! I'm frightened to death, and if you
had the sense God gave a goat, you'd be frightened too. But we haven't got time to talk. We
must get out of here."

"At your service, Madam. But just where were

you figuring on going? I made the trip out here for curiosity, just to see where you were intending to go. You can't go north or east or south or west. The Yankees are all around. There's just one road out of town which the Yankees haven't got yet and the army is retreating by that road. And that road won't be open long. General Steve Lee's cavalry is fighting a rearguard action at Rough and Ready to hold it open long enough for the army to get away. If you follow the army down the McDonough road, they'll take the horse away from you and, while it's not much of a horse, I did go to a lot of trouble stealing it. Just where are you going?"

She stood shaking, listening to his words, hardly hearing them. But, at his question, she suddenly knew where she was going, knew that all this miserable day she had known where she was going. The only place.

"I'm going home," she said.

"Home? You mean to Tara?"

"Yes, yes! To Tara! Oh, Rhett, we must hurry!"

He looked at her as if she had lost her mind.

"Tara? God Almighty, Scarlett! Don't you know they fought all day at Jonesboro? Fought for ten miles up and down the road from Rough and Ready even into the streets of Jonesboro? The Yankees may be all over Tara by now, all over the County. Nobody knows where they are but they're in that neighbourhood. You can't go home! You can't go right through the Yankee army!"

"I will go home!" she cried. "I will! I will!"

"You little fool," and his voice was swift and rough. "You can't go that way. Even if you didn't run into the Yankees, the woods are full of stragglers and deserters from both armies. And lots of our troops are still retreating from Jonesboro. They'd take the horse away from you as quickly as the Yankees would. Your only chance is to follow the troops down the McDonough road and pray that they won't see you in the dark. You can't go to Tara. Even if you got there, you'd probably find it burned down. I won't let you go home. It's insanity."

"I will go home!" she cried, and her voice broke and rose to a scream. "I will go home! You can't stop me! I will go home! I want my mother! I'll kill you if you try to stop me! I will go home!"

Tears of fright and hysteria streamed down her face as she finally gave way under the long strain. She beat on his chest with her fists and screamed again: "I will! I will! If I have to walk every step of the way."

Suddenly she was in his arms, her wet cheek against the starched ruffle of his shirt, her beating hands stilled against him. His hands caressed her tumbled hair gently, soothingly, and his voice was gentle too. So gentle, so quiet, so devoid of mockery, it did not seem Rhett Butler's voice at all but the voice of some kind strong stranger who smelled of brandy and tobacco and horses, comforting smells because they reminded her of Gerald.

"There, there, darling," he said softly. "Don't cry. You shall go home, my brave little girl. You shall go home. Don't cry."

She felt something brush her hair and wondered vaguely through her tumult if it were his lips. He was so tender, so infinitely soothing, she longed to stay in his arms forever. With such strong arms about her, surely nothing could harm her.

He fumbled in his pocket and produced a handkerchief and wiped her eyes.

"Now, blow your nose like a good child," he ordered, a glint of a smile in his eyes, "and tell me what to do. We must work fast."

She blew her nose obediently, still trembling, but she could not think what to tell him to do. Seeing how her lip quivered and her eyes looked up at him helplessly, he took command.

"Mrs. Wilkes has had her child? It will be dangerous to move her—dangerous to drive her twenty-five miles in that rickety wagon. We'd better leave her with Mrs. Meade."

"The Meades aren't home. I can't leave her."

"Very well. Into the wagon she goes. Where is that simple-minded little wench?"

"Upstairs packing the trunk."

"Trunk? You can't take any trunk in that wagon. It's almost too small to hold all of you and the wheels are ready to come off with no encouragement. Call her and tell her to get the smallest feather bed in the house and put it in the wagon."

Still Scarlett could not move. He took her arm in a strong grasp and some of the vitality which animated him seemed to flow into her body. If only she could be as cool and casual as he was! He propelled her into the hall but she still stood helplessly looking at him. His lip went down mockingly: "Can this be the heroic young woman who assured me she feared neither God nor man?"

He suddenly burst into laughter and dropped her arm. Stung, she glared at him, hating him.

"I'm not afraid," she said.

"Yes, you are. In another moment you'll be in a swoon and I have no smelling salts about me."

She stamped her foot impotently because she could not think of anything else to do—and without a word picked up the lamp and started up the stairs. He was close behind her and she could hear him laughing softly to himself. That sound stiffened her spine. She went into Wade's nursery and found him sitting clutched in Prissy's arms, half dressed, hiccoughing quietly. Prissy was whimpering. The feather tick on Wade's bed was small and she ordered Prissy to drag it down the stairs and into the wagon. Prissy put down the child and obeyed. Wade followed her down the stairs, his hiccoughs stilled by his interest in the proceedings.

"Come," said Scarlett, turning to Melanie's door and Rhett followed her, hat in hand.

Melanie lay quietly with the sheet up to her chin. Her face was deathly white but her eyes, sunken and black-circled, were serene. She showed no surprise at the sight of Rhett in her bedroom but seemed to take it as a matter of course. She tried to smile weakly but the smile died before it reached the corners of her mouth.

"We are going home, to Tara," Scarlett explained rapidly. "The Yankees are coming.

Rhett is going to take us. It's the only way, Melly."

Melanie tried to nod her head feebly and gestured toward the baby. Scarlett picked up the small baby and wrapped him hastily in a thick towel. Rhett stepped to the bed.

"I'll try not to hurt you," he said quietly, tucking the sheet about her. "See if you can put your arms around my neck."

Melanie tried but they fell back weakly. He bent, slipped an arm under her shoulders and another across her knees and lifted her gently. She did not cry out but Scarlett saw her bite her lip and go even whiter. Scarlett held the lamp high for Rhett to see and started toward the door when Melanie made a feeble gesture toward the wall.

"What is it?" Rhett asked softly.

"Please," Melanie whispered, trying to point. "Charles."

Rhett looked down at her as if he thought her delirious but Scarlett understood and was irritated. She knew Melanie wanted the daguerreotype of Charles which hung on the wall below his sword and pistol.

"Please," Melanie whispered again, "the sword."

"Oh, all right," said Scarlett, and, after she had lighted Rhett's careful way down the steps, she went back and unhooked the sword and pistol belts. It would be awkward, carrying them as well as the baby and the lamp. That was just like Melanie, not to be at all bothered over nearly dying and having the Yankees at her heels but to worry about Charles' things.

As she took down the daguerreotype, she caught a glimpse of Charles' face. His large brown eyes met hers and she stopped for a moment to look at the picture curiously. This man had been her husband, had lain beside her for a few nights, had given her a child with eyes as soft and brown as his. And she could hardly remember him.

The child in her arms waved small fists and mewed softly and she looked down at him. For the first time, she realized that this was Ashley's baby and suddenly wished with all the strength left in her that he were her baby, hers and Ashley's.

Prissy came bounding up the stairs and Scarlett handed the child to her. They went hastily down, the lamp throwing uncertain shadows on the wall. In the hall, Scarlett saw a bonnet and put it on hurriedly, tying the ribbons under her chin. It was Melanie's black mourning bonnet and it did not fit Scarlett's head but she could not recall where she had put her own bonnet.

She went out of the house and down the front steps, carrying the lamp and trying to keep the sabre from banging against her legs. Melanie lay full length in the back of the wagon, and beside her were Wade and the towel-swathed baby. Prissy climbed in and took the baby in her arms.

The wagon was very small and the boards about the sides very low. The wheels leaned inward as if their first revolution would make them come off. She took one look at the horse and her heart sank. He was a small emaciated animal and he stood with his head dispiritedly low, almost between his forelegs. His back was raw with sores and harness galls and he breathed as no sound horse should.

"Not much of an animal, is it?" grinned Rhett. "Looks like he'll die in the shafts. But he's the best I could do. Some day I'll tell you with embellishments just where and how I stole him and how narrowly I missed getting shot. Nothing but my devotion to you would make me, at this stage of my career, turn horse thief—and thief of such a horse. Let me help you in."

He took the lamp from her and set it on the ground. The front seat was only a narrow plank across the sides of the wagon. Rhett picked Scarlett up bodily and swung her to it. How wonderful to be a man and as strong as Rhett, she thought, tucking her wide skirts about her. With Rhett beside her, she did not fear anything, neither the fire nor the noise nor the Yankees.

He climbed on to the seat beside her and picked up the reins.

"Oh, wait!" she cried. "I forgot to lock the front door."

He burst into a roar of laughter and flapped the reins upon the horse's back.

"What are you laughing at?"

"At you—locking the Yankees out," he said, and the horse started off, slowly, reluctantly. The lamp on the sidewalk burned on, making a tiny yellow circle of light which grew smaller and smaller as they moved away.

Rhett turned the horse's slow feet westward from

594

Peachtree and the wobbling wagon jounced into the rutty lane with a violence that wrenched an abruptly stifled moan from Melanie. Dark trees interlaced above their heads, dark silent houses loomed up on either side and the white palings of fences gleamed faintly like a row of tombstones. The narrow street was a dim tunnel, but faintly through the thick leafy ceiling the hideous red glow of the sky penetrated and shadows chased one another down the dark way like mad ghosts. The smell of smoke came stronger and stronger, and on the wings of the hot breeze came a pandemonium of sound from the centre of town—yells, the dull rumbling of heavy army wagons and the steady tramp of marching feet. As Rhett jerked the horse's head and turned him into another street, another deafening explosion tore the air and a monstrous sky-rocket of flame and smoke shot up in the west.

"That must be the last of the ammunition trains," Rhett said calmly. "Why didn't they get them out this morning, the fools! There was plenty of time. Well, too bad for us. I thought by circling around the centre of town, we might avoid the fire and that drunken mob on Decatur Street and get through to the south-west part of town without any danger. But we've got to cross Marietta Street somewhere and that explosion was near Marietta Street or I miss my guess."

"Must—must we go through the fire?" Scarlett quavered.

"Not if we hurry," said Rhett and, springing from the wagon, he disappeared into the darkness of a yard. When he returned he had a small limb of a tree in his hand and he laid it mercilessly across the horse's back. The animal broke into a shambling trot, his breath panting and laboured, and the wagon swayed forward with a jolt that threw them about like popcorn in a popper. The baby wailed, and Prissy and Wade cried out as they bruised themselves against the sides of the wagon. But from Melanie there was no sound.

As they neared Marietta Street, the trees thinned out and the tall flames roaring up above the buildings threw street and houses into a glare of light brighter than day, casting monstrous shadows that twisted as wildly as torn sails flapping in a gale on a sinking ship.

Scarlett's teeth chattered but so great was her terror she was not even aware of it. She was cold and she shivered, even though the heat of the flames was already hot against their faces. This was hell and she was in it and, if she could only have conquered her shaking knees, she would have leaped from the wagon and run screaming back the dark road they had come, back to the refuge of Miss Pittypat's house. She shrank closer to Rhett, took his arm in fingers that trembled and looked up at him for words, for comfort, for something reassuring. In the unholy crimson glow that bathed them, his dark profile stood out as clearly as the head on an ancient coin, beautiful, cruel and decadent. At her touch he turned to her, his eyes gleaming with a light as frightening as the fire. To Scarlett, he seemed as exhilarated and contemptuous as if he got strong pleasure from the situation, as if he welcomed the inferno they were approaching.

"Here," he said, laying a hand on one of the long-barrelled pistols in his belt. "If anyone, black or white, comes up on your side of the wagon and tries to lay hand on the horse, shoot him and we'll ask questions later. But for God's sake, don't shoot the nag in your excitement."

"I—I have a pistol," she whispered, clutching the weapon in her lap, perfectly certain that if death stared her in the face, she would be too frightened to pull the trigger.

"You have? Where did you get it?"

"It's Charles'."

"Charles?"

"Yes, Charles—my husband."

"Did you ever really have a husband, my dear?" he whispered and laughed softly.

If he would only be serious! If he would only hurry!

"How do you suppose I got my boy?" she cried fiercely.

"Oh, there are other ways than husbands—"

"Will you hush and hurry?"

But he drew rein abruptly, almost at Marietta Street, in the shadow of a warehouse not yet touched by the flames.

"Hurry!" It was the only word in her mind. Hurry! Hurry!

"Soldiers," he said.

The detachment came down Marietta Street, between the burning buildings, walking at route step, tiredly, rifles held any way, heads down, too weary to hurry, too weary to care if timbers were crashing to right and left and smoke billowing about them. They were all ragged, so ragged that between officers and men there were no distinguishing insignia except here and there a torn hatbrim pinned up with a wreathed "CSA". Many were barefooted and here and there a dirty bandage wrapped a head or arm. They went past, looking neither to left nor right, so silent that had it not been for the steady tramp of feet they might all have been ghosts.

"Take a good look at them," came Rhett's gibing voice, "so you can tell your grandchildren you saw the rearguard of the Glorious Cause in retreat."

Suddenly she hated him, hated him with a strength that momentarily overpowered her fear, made it seem petty and small. She knew her safety and that of the others in the back of the wagon depended on him and him alone, but she hated him for his sneering at those ragged ranks. She thought of Charles who was dead and Ashley who might be dead and all the gay and gallant young men who were rotting in shallow graves and she forgot that she, too, had once thought them fools. She could not speak, but hatred and disgust burned in her eyes as she stared at him fiercely.

As the last of the soldiers were passing, a small figure in the rear rank, his rifle-butt dragging the ground, wavered, stopped and stared after the others with a dirty face so dulled by fatigue he looked like a sleepwalker. He was as small as Scarlett, so small his rifle was almost as tall as he was, and his grime-smeared face was unbearded. Sixteen at the most, thought Scarlett irrelevantly, must be one of the Home Guard or a runaway schoolboy.

As she watched, the boy's knees buckled slowly and he went down in the dust. Without a word, two men fell out of the last rank and walked back to him. One, a tall spare man with a black beard that hung to his belt, silently handed his own rifle and that of the boy to the other. Then, stooping, he jerked the boy to his shoulders with an ease that looked like sleight of hand. He started off slowly after the retreating column, his shoulders bowed under the weight, while the boy, weak, infuriated like a child teased by its elders, screamed out: "Put me down, damn you! Put me down! I can walk!"

The bearded man said nothing and plodded on out of sight around the bend of the road.

Rhett sat still, the reins lax in his hands, looking after them, a curious moody look on his swarthy face. Then there was a crash of falling timbers near by and Scarlett saw a thin tongue of flame lick up over the roof of the warehouse in whose sheltering shadow they sat. Then pennons and battle flags of flame flared triumphantly to the sky above them. Smoke burnt her nostrils and Wade and Prissy began coughing. The baby made soft sneezing sounds.

"Oh, name of God, Rhett! Are you crazy? Hurry! Hurry!"

Rhett made no reply but brought the tree-limb down on the horse's back with a cruel force that made the animal leap forward. With all the speed the horse could summon, they jolted and bounced across Marietta Street. Ahead of them was a tunnel of fire where buildings were blazing on either side of the short, narrow street that led down to the railroad tracks. They plunged into it. A glare brighter than a dozen suns dazzled their eyes, scorching heat seared their skins and the roaring, crackling and crashing beat upon their ears in painful waves. For an eternity, it seemed, they were in the midst of flaming torment and then abruptly they were in semi-darkness again.

As they dashed down the street and bumped over the railroad tracks, Rhett applied the whip automatically. His face looked set and absent, as though he had forgotten where he was. His broad shoulders were hunched forward and his chin jutted out as though the thoughts in his mind were not pleasant. The heat of the fire made sweat stream down his forehead and cheeks but he did not wipe it off.

They pulled into a side street, then another, then turned and twisted from one narrow street to another until Scarlett completely lost her bearings and the roaring of the flames died behind them. Still Rhett did not speak. He only laid on the whip with regularity. The red glow in the sky was fading now and the road became so dark, so frightening, Scarlett would have welcomed words, any words from him, even jeering, insulting words, words that cut. But he did not speak.

Silent or not, she thanked Heaven for the comfort of his presence. It was so good to have a man beside her, to lean close to him and feel the hard swell of his arm and know that he stood between her and unnameable terrors, even though he merely sat there and stared.

"Oh, Rhett," she whispered, clasping his arm, "what would we ever have done without you? I'm so glad you aren't in the army!"

He turned his head and gave her one look, a look that made her drop his arm and shrink back. There was no mockery in his eyes now. They were naked and there was anger and something like bewilderment in them. His lip curled down and he turned his head away. For a long time they jounced along in a silence unbroken except for the faint wails of the baby and sniffles from Prissy. When she was able to bear the sniffling noise no longer, Scarlett turned and pinched her viciously, causing Prissy to scream in good earnest before she relapsed into frightened silence.

Finally Rhett turned the horse at right angles and after a while they were on a wider, smoother road. The dim shapes of houses grew farther and farther apart and unbroken woods loomed wall-like on either side.

"We're out of town now," said Rhett briefly, drawing rein, "and on the main road to Rough and Ready."

"Hurry. Don't stop!"

"Let the animal breathe a bit." Then turning to her, he asked slowly: "Scarlett, are you still determined to do this crazy thing?"

"Do what?"

"Do you still want to try to get through to Tara? It's suicidal. Steve Lee's cavalry and the Yankee Army are between you and Tara."

Oh, dear God! Was he going to refuse to take

her home, after all she'd gone through this terrible day?

"Oh, yes! Yes! Please, Rhett, let's hurry. The horse isn't tired."

"Just a minute. You can't go down to Jonesboro on this road. You can't follow the train tracks. They've been fighting up and down there all day from Rough and Ready on south. Do you know any other roads, small wagon roads or lanes that don't go through Rough and Ready or Jonesboro?"

"Oh, yes," cried Scarlett in relief. "If we can just get near to Rough and Ready, I know a wagon trace that winds off from the main Jonesboro road and wanders around for miles. Pa and I used to ride it. It comes out right near the MacIntosh place and that's only a mile from Tara."

"Good. Maybe you can get past Rough and Ready all right. General Steve Lee was there during the afternoon covering the retreat. Maybe the Yankees aren't there yet. Maybe you can get through there, if Steve Lee's men don't pick up your horse."

"I—*I* can get through?"

"Yes, *you*." His voice was rough.

"But Rhett—You—Aren't you going to take us?"

"No. I'm leaving you here."

She looked around wildly, at the livid sky behind them, at the dark trees on either hand hemming them in like a prison wall, at the frightened figures in the back of the wagon—and finally at him. Had she gone crazy? Was she not hearing right?

He was grinning now. She could just see his white teeth in the faint light and the old mockery was back in his eyes.

"Leaving us? Where—where are you going?"

"I am going, dear girl, with the army."

She sighed with relief and irritation. Why did he joke at this time of all times? Rhett in the army! After all he'd said about stupid fools who were enticed into losing their lives by a roll of drums and brave words from orators—fools who killed themselves that wise men might make money!

"Oh, I could choke you for scaring me so! Let's get on."

"I'm not joking, my dear. And I am hurt, Scarlett, that you do not take my gallant sacrifice with better spirit. Where is your patriotism, your love for Our Glorious Cause? Now is your chance to tell me to return with my shield or on it. But, talk fast, for I want time to make a brave speech before departing for the wars."

His drawling voice gibed in her ears. He was jeering at her and, somehow, she knew he was jeering at himself too. What was he talking about? Patriotism, shields, brave speeches? It wasn't possible that he meant what he was saying. It just wasn't believable that he could talk so blithely of leaving her here on this dark road with a woman who might be dying, a new-born infant, a foolish black wench and a frightened child, leaving her to pilot them through miles of battlefields and stragglers and Yankees and fire and God knows what.

Once, when she was six years old, she had fallen from a tree, flat on her stomaeh. She could still recall that sickening interval before breath came back into her body. Now, as she looked at Rhett, she felt the same way she had felt then, breathless, stunned, nauseated.

"Rhett, you are joking!"

She grabbed his arm and felt her tears of fright splash down on her wrist. He raised her hand and kissed it airily.

"Selfish to the end, aren't you, my dear? Thinking only of your own precious hide and not of the gallant Confederacy. Think how our troops will be heartened by my eleventh-hour appearance." There was a malicious tenderness in his voice.

"Oh, Rhett," she wailed, "how can you do this to me? Why are you leaving me?"

"Why?" he laughed jauntily. "Because, perhaps, of the betraying sentimentality that lurks in all of us Southerners. Perhaps—perhaps because I am ashamed. Who knows?"

"Ashamed? You should die of shame. To desert us here, alone, helpless—"

"Dear Scarlett! You aren't helpless. Anyone as selfish and determined as you are is never helpless. God help the Yankees if they should get you."

He stepped abruptly down from the wagon and, as she watched him, stunned with bewilderment, he came around to her side of the wagon.

"Get out," he ordered.

She stared at him. He reached up roughly, caught her under the arms and swung her to the ground beside him. With a tight grip on her he dragged her several paces away from the wagon. She felt the dust and gravel in her slippers hurting her feet. The still hot darkness wrapped her like a dream.

"I'm not asking you to understand or forgive. I don't give a damn whether you do either, for I shall never understand or forgive myself for this idiocy. I am annoyed at myself to find that so much quixoticism still lingers in me. But our fair Southland needs every man. Didn't our brave Governor Brown say just that? No matter. I'm off to the wars." He laughed suddenly, a ringing, free laugh that startled the echoes in the dark woods.

"'I could not love thee, Dear, so much, loved I not Honour more.' That's a pat speech, isn't it? Certainly better than anything I can think up myself, at the present moment. For I do love you, Scarlett, in spite of what I said that night on the porch last month."

His drawl was caressing and his hands slid up her bare arms, warm strong hands. "I love you, Scarlett, because we are so much alike, renegades, both of us, dear, and selfish rascals. Neither of us cares a rap if the whole world goes to pot, so long as we are safe and comfortable."

His voice went on in the darkness and she heard words, but they made no sense to her. Her mind was tiredly trying to take in the harsh truth that he was leaving her here to face the Yankees alone. Her mind said: "He's leaving me. He's leaving me." But no emotion stirred.

Then his arms went around her waist and shoulders and she felt the hard muscles of his thighs against her body and the buttons of his coat pressing into her breast. A warm tide of feeling, bewildering, frightening, swept over her, carrying out of her mind the time and place and circumstances. She felt as limp as a rag doll, warm, weak and helpless, and his supporting arms were so pleasant.

"You don't want to change your mind about what I said last month? There's nothing like danger and death to give an added fillip. Be patriotic, Scarlett. Think how you would be sending a soldier to his death with beautiful memories."

He was kissing her now and his moustache tickled her mouth, kissing her with slow, hot lips that were as leisurely as though he had the whole night before him. Charles had never kissed her like this. Never had the kisses of the Tarleton and Calvert boys made her go hot and cold and shaky like this. He bent her body backward and his lips travelled down her throat to where the cameo fastened her basque.

"Sweet," he whispered. "Sweet."

She saw the wagon dimly in the dark and heard the treble piping of Wade's voice.

"Muvver! Wade fwightened!"

Into her swaying, darkened mind, cold sanity came back with a rush and she remembered what she had forgotten for the moment—that she was frightened too, and Rhett was leaving her, leaving her, the damned cad. And on top of it all, he had the consummate gall to stand here in the road and insult her with his infamous proposals. Rage and hate flowed into her and stiffened her spine and with one wrench she tore herself loose from his arms.

"Oh, you cad!" she cried, and her mind leaped about, trying to think of worse things to call him, things she had heard Gerald call Mr. Lincoln, the MacIntoshes and balky mules, but the words would not come. "You low-down, cowardly, nasty, stinking thing!" And because she could not think of anything crushing enough, she drew back her arm and slapped him across the mouth with all the force she had left. He took a step backward, his hand going to his face.

"Ah," he said quietly, and for a moment they stood facing each other in the darkness. Scarlett could hear his heavy breathing, and her own breath came in gasps as if she had been running hard.

"They were right! Everybody was right! You aren't a gentleman!"

"My dear girl," he said, "how inadequate!"

She knew he was laughing and the thought goaded her.

"Go on! Go on now! I want you to hurry. I don't want to ever see you again. I hope a cannonball lands right on you. I hope it blows you to a million pieces. I—"

"Never mind the rest. I follow your general idea. When I'm dead on the altar of my country, I hope your conscience hurts you."

She heard him laugh as he turned away and walked back toward the wagon. She saw him stand beside it, heard him speak and his voice was changed, courteous and respectful as it always was when he spoke to Melanie.

"Mrs. Wilkes?"

Prissy's frightened voice made answer from the wagon.

"Gawdlmighty, Cap'n Butler! Miss Melly done fainted way back yonder."

"She's not dead? Is she breathing?"

"Yessuh, she breathin'."

"Then she's probably better off as she is. If she were conscious, I doubt if she could live through all the pain. Take good care of her, Prissy. Here's a shin-plaster for you. Try not to be a bigger fool than you are."

"Yassuh. Thankee, suh."

"Good-bye, Scarlett."

She knew he had turned and was facing her but she did not speak. Hate choked all utterance. His feet ground on the pebbles of the road and for a moment she saw his big shoulders looming up in the dark. Then he was gone. She could hear the sound of his feet for a while and then they died away. She came slowly back to the wagon, her knees shaking.

Why had he gone, stepping off into the dark, into the war, into a Cause that was lost, into a world that was mad? Why had he gone, Rhett who loved the pleasures of women and liquor, the comfort of good food and soft beds, the feel of fine linen and good leather, who hated the South and jeered at the fools who fought for it? Now he had set his varnished boots upon a bitter road where hunger tramped with tireless stride and wounds and weariness and heartbreak ran like yelping wolves. And the end of the road was death. He need not have gone. He was safe, rich, comfortable. But he had gone, leaving her alone in a night as black as blindness, with the Yankee Army between her and home.

Now she remembered all the bad names she had wanted to call him but it was too late. She leaned her head against the bowed neck of the horse and cried.

8

THE bright glare of morning sunlight streaming through the trees overhead awakened Scarlett. For a moment, stiffened by the cramped position in which she had slept, she could not remember where she was. The sun blinded her, the hard boards of the wagon under her were harsh against her body, and a heavy weight lay across her legs. She tried to sit up and discovered that the weight was Wade, who lay sleeping with his head pillowed on her knees. Melanie's bare feet were almost in her face and, under the wagon seat, Prissy was curled up like a black cat with the small baby wedged in between her and Wade.

Then she remembered everything. She popped up to a sitting position and looked hastily all around. Thank God, no Yankees in sight! Their hiding-place had not been discovered in the night. It all came back to her now, the nightmare journey after Rhett's footsteps died away, the endless night, the black road full of ruts and boulders along which they jolted, the deep gullies on either side into which the wagon slipped, the fear-crazed strength with which she and Prissy had pushed the wheels out of the gullies. She recalled with a shudder how often she had driven the unwilling horse into fields and woods when she heard soldiers approaching, not knowing if they were friends or foes—recalled, too, her anguish lest a cough, a sneeze or Wade's hiccoughing might betray them to the marching men.

Oh, that dark road where men went by like ghosts, voices stilled, only the muffled tramping of feet on soft dirt, the faint clicking of bridles and the straining creak of leather! And, oh, that dreadful moment when the sick horse balked and cavalry and light cannon rumbled past in the darkness, past where they sat breathless, so close she could almost reach out and touch them, so close she could smell the stale sweat on the soldiers' bodies!

When, at last, they had neared Rough and Ready, a few camp-fires were gleaming where the last of Steve Lee's rearguard was awaiting orders to fall back. She had circled through a ploughed field for a mile until the light of the fires died out behind her. And then she had lost her way in the darkness and sobbed when she could not find the little wagon path she knew so well. Then finally having found it, the horse sank in the traces and refused to move, refused to rise even when she and Prissy tugged at the bridle.

So she had unharnessed him and crawled, sodden with fatigue, into the back of the wagon and stretched her aching legs. She had a faint memory of Melanie's voice before sleep clamped down her eyelids, a weak voice that apologized even as it begged: "Scarlett, can I have some water, please?"

She had said: "There isn't any," and gone to sleep before the words were out of her mouth.

Now it was morning and the world was still

and serene and green and gold with dappled sunshine. And no soldiers in sight anywhere. She was hungry and dry with thirst, aching and cramped and filled with wonder that she, Scarlett O'Hara, who could never rest well except between linen sheets and on the softest of feather beds, had slept like a field hand on hard planks.

Blinking in the sunlight, her eyes fell on Melanie and she gasped, horrified. Melanie lay so still and white Scarlett thought she must be dead. She looked dead. She looked like a dead, old woman with her ravaged face and her dark hair snarled and tangled across it. Then Scarlett saw with relief the faint rise and fall of her shallow breathing and knew that Melanie had survived the night.

Scarlett shaded her eyes with her hand and looked about her. They had evidently spent the night under the trees in someone's front yard, for a sand and gravel driveway stretched out before her, winding away under an avenue of cedars.

"Why, it's the Mallory place!" she thought, her heart leaping with gladness at the thought of friends and help.

But a stillness as of death hung over the plantation. The shrubs and grass of the lawn were cut to pieces where hooves and wheels and feet had torn frantically back and forth until the soil was churned up. She looked toward the house and instead of the old white clapboard place she knew so well, she saw there only a long rectangle of blackened granite foundation stones and two tall chimneys rearing smoke-stained bricks into the charred leaves of still trees.

She drew a deep shuddering breath. Would she find Tara like this, level with the ground, silent as the dead?

"I mustn't think about that now," she told herself hurriedly. "I mustn't let myself think about it. I'll get scared again if I think about it." But, in spite of herself, her heart quickened and each beat seemed to thunder: "Home! Hurry! Home! Hurry!"

They must be starting on toward home again. But first they must find some food and water, especially water. She prodded Prissy awake. Prissy rolled her eyes as she looked about her.

"Fo' Gawd, Miss Scarlett, Ah din' spec ter wake up agin 'cept in de Promise Lan'."

"You're a long way from there," said Scarlett, trying to smooth back her untidy hair. Her face was damp and her body was already wet with sweat. She felt dirty and messy and sticky, almost as if she smelled bad. Her clothes were crushed and wrinkled from sleeping in them and she had never felt more acutely tired and sore in all her life. Muscles she did not know she possessed ached from her unaccustomed exertions of the night before and every movement brought sharp pain.

She looked down at Melanie and saw that her dark eyes were opened. They were sick eyes, fever bright, and dark baggy circles were beneath them. She opened cracking lips and whispered appealingly: "Water."

"Get up, Prissy," ordered Scarlett. "We'll go to the well and get some water."

"But, Miss Scarlett! Dey mout be hants up dar. Sposin' somebody daid up dar?"

"I'll make a hant out of you if you don't get out of this wagon," said Scarlett, who was in no mood for argument, as she climbed lamely down to the ground.

And then she thought of the horse. Name of God! Suppose the horse had died in the night! He had seemed ready to die when she unharnessed him. She ran around the wagon and saw him lying on his side. If he were dead, she would curse God and die too. Somebody in the Bible had done just that thing. Cursed God and died. She knew just how that person felt. But the horse was alive—breathing heavily, sick eyes half closed, but alive. Well, some water would help him too.

Prissy climbed reluctantly from the wagon with many groans and timorously followed Scarlett up the avenue. Behind the ruins the row of white-washed slave quarters stood silent and deserted under the overhanging trees. Between the quarters and the smoked stone foundations they found the well, and the roof of it still stood with the bucket far down the well. Between them, they wound up the rope, and when the bucket of cool sparkling water appeared out of the dark depths, Scarlett tilted it to her lips and drank with loud sucking noises, spilling the water all over herself.

She drank until Prissy's petulant: "Well, Ah's thusty, too, Miss Scarlett," made her recall the needs of the others.

"Untie the knot and take the bucket to the wagon and give them some. And give the rest to the horse. Don't you think Miss Melanie ought to nurse the baby? He'll starve."

"Law, Miss Scarlett, Miss Melly ain' got no milk—ain' gwine have none."

"How do you know?"

"Ah's seed too many lak her."

"Don't go putting on any airs with me. A precious little you knew about babies yesterday. Hurry now. I'm going to try to find something to eat."

Scarlett's search was futile until in the orchard she found a few apples. Soldiers had been there before her and there were none on the trees. Those she found on the ground were mostly rotten. She filled her skirt with the best of them and came back across the soft earth, collecting small pebbles in her slippers. Why hadn't she thought of putting on stouter shoes last night? Why hadn't she brought her sun-hat? Why hadn't she brought something to eat? She'd acted like a fool. But, of course, she'd thought Rhett would take care of them.

Rhett! She spat on the ground, for the very name tasted bad. How she hated him! How contemptible he had been! And she had stood there in the road and let him kiss her—and almost liked it. She had been crazy last night. How despicable he was!

When she came back, she divided up the apples and threw the rest into the back of the wagon. The horse was on his feet now but the water did not seem to have refreshed him much. He looked far worse in the daylight than he had the night before. His hip-bones stood out like an old cow's, his ribs showed like a washboard and his back was a mass of sores. She shrank from touching him as she harnessed him. When she slipped the bit into his mouth, she saw that he was practically toothless. As old as the hills! While Rhett was stealing a horse, why couldn't he have stolen a good one?

She mounted the seat and brought down the hickory limb on his back. He wheezed and started, but he walked so slowly as she turned him into the road she knew she could walk faster herself with no effort whatever. Oh, if only she didn't have Melanie and Wade and the baby and Prissy to bother with! How swiftly she could walk home! Why, she would run home, run every step of the way that would bring her closer to Tara and to Mother.

They couldn't be more than fifteen miles from home, but at the rate this old nag travelled it would take all day, for she would have to stop frequently to rest him. All day! She looked down the glaring red road, cut in deep ruts where cannon wheels and ambulances had gone over it. It would be hours before she knew if Tara still stood and if Ellen were there. It would be hours before she finished her journey under the broiling September sun.

She looked back at Melanie, who lay with sick eyes closed against the sun, and jerked loose the strings of her bonnet and tossed it to Prissy.

"Put that over her face. It'll keep the sun out of her eyes." Then as the heat beat down upon her unprotected head, she thought: "I'll be as freckled as a guinea egg before this day is over."

She had never in her life been out in the sunshine without a hat or veils, never handled reins without gloves to protect the white skin of her dimpled hands. Yet here she was exposed to the sun in a broken-down wagon with a broken-down horse, dirty, sweaty, hungry, helpless to do anything but plod along at a snail's pace through a deserted land. What a few short weeks it had been since she was safe and secure! What a little while since she and everyone else had thought that Atlanta could never fall, that Georgia could never be invaded. But the small cloud which appeared in the northwest four months ago had blown up into a mighty storm and then into a screaming tornado, sweeping away her world, whirling her out of her sheltered life, and dropping her down in the midst of this still, haunted desolation.

Was Tara still standing? Or was Tara also gone with the wind which had swept through Georgia?

She laid the whip on the tired horse's back and tried to urge him on while the waggling wheels rocked them drunkenly from side to side.

There was death in the air. In the rays of the late afternoon sun, every well-remembered field and forest grove was green and still, with an unearthly quiet that struck terror to Scarlett's heart. Every empty, shell-pitted house they had passed that day, every gaunt chimney standing sentinel over smoke-blackened ruins, had frightened her more. They had not seen a living human being or animal since the night before. Dead men and dead horses, yes, and dead mules, lying by the road, swollen, covered with flies, but nothing alive. No far-off cattle lowed, no birds sang, no wind waved the trees. Only the tired plop-plop of the horse's feet and the weak wailing of Melanie's baby broke the stillness.

The countryside lay as under some dread enchantment. Or worse still, thought Scarlett with a chill, like the familiar and dear face of a mother, beautiful and quiet at last, after death agonies. She felt that the once-familiar woods were full of ghosts. Thousands had died in the fighting near Jonesboro. They were here in these haunted woods where the slanting afternoon sun gleamed eerily through unmoving leaves, friends and foes, peering at her in her rickety wagon, through eyes blinded with blood and red dust— glazed, horrible eyes.

"Mother! Mother!" she whispered. If she could only win to Ellen! If only, by a miracle of God, Tara were still standing and she could drive up the long avenue of trees and go into the house and see her mother's kind, tender face, could feel once more the soft capable hands that drove out fear, could clutch Ellen's skirts and bury her face in them. Mother would know what to do. She wouldn't let Melanie and her baby die. She would drive away all ghosts and fears with her quiet "Hush, hush". But Mother was ill, perhaps dying.

Scarlett laid the whip across the weary rump of the horse. They must go faster! They had crept along this never-ending road all the long hot day. Soon it would be night and they would be alone in this desolation that was death. She gripped the reins tighter with hands that were blistered and slapped them fiercely on the horse's back, her aching arms burning at the movement.

If she could only reach the kind arms of Tara and Ellen and lay down her burdens, far too heavy for her young shoulders—the dying woman, the fading baby, her own hungry little boy, the frightened negro, all looking to her for strength, for guidance, all reading in her straight back courage she did not possess and strength which had long since failed.

The exhausted horse did not respond to the whip or reins but shambled on, dragging his feet, stumbling on small rocks and swaying as if ready to fall to his knees. But, as twilight came, they at last entered the final lap of the long journey. They rounded the bend of the wagon path and turned into the main road. Tara was only a mile away!

Here loomed up the dark bulk of the mock-orange hedge that marked the beginning of the MacIntosh property. A little farther on, Scarlett drew rein in front of the avenue of oaks that led from the road to old Angus MacIntosh's house. She peered through the gathering dusk down the two lines of ancient trees. All was dark. Not a single light showed in the house or in the quarters. Straining her eyes in the darkness, she dimly discerned a sight which had grown familiar through that terrible day—two tall chimneys, like gigantic tombstones towering above the ruined second floor, and broken unlit windows blotching the walls like still, blind eyes.

"Hello!" she shouted, summoning all her strength. "Hello!"

Prissy clawed at her in a frenzy of fright and Scarlett, turning, saw that her eyes were rolling in her head.

"Doan holler, Miss Scarlett! Please, doan holler agin!" she whispered, her voice shaking. "Dey ain' no tellin' *whut* mout answer!"

"Dear God!" thought Scarlett, a shiver running through her. "Dear God! She's right. Anything might come out of there!"

She flapped the reins and urged the horse forward. The sight of the MacIntosh house had pricked the last bubble of hope remaining to her. It was burned, in ruins, deserted, as were all the plantations she had passed that day. Tara lay only half a mile away, on the same road, right in the path of the army. Tara was levelled, too! She would find only the blackened bricks, starlight shining through the roofless walls, Ellen and Gerald gone, the girls gone, Mammy gone, the negroes gone, God knows where, and this hideous stillness over everything.

Why had she come on this fool's errand, against all common sense, dragging Melanie and her child? Better that they had died in Atlanta than, tortured by this day of burning sun and jolting wagon, to die in the silent ruins of Tara.

But Ashley had left Melanie in her care. "Take care of her." Oh, that beautiful, heartbreaking day when he had kissed her good-bye before he went away forever! "You'll take care of her, won't you? Promise!" And she had promised. Why had she ever bound herself with such a promise,

620

doubly binding now that Ashley was gone? Even in her exhaustion she hated Melanie, hated the tiny mewing voice of her child which, fainter and fainter, pierced the stillness. But she had promised and now they belonged to her, even as Wade and Prissy belonged to her, and she must struggle and fight for them as long as she had strength or breath. She could have left them in Atlanta, dumped Melanie into the hospital and deserted her. But had she done that, she could never face Ashley, either on this earth or in the hereafter, and tell him she had left his wife and child to die among strangers.

Oh, Ashley! Where was he to-night while she toiled down this haunted road with his wife and baby? Was he alive and did he think of her as he lay behind the bars at Rock Island? Or was he dead of smallpox months ago, rotting in some long ditch with hundreds of other Confederates?

Scarlett's taut nerves almost cracked as a sudden noise sounded in the underbrush near them. Prissy screamed loudly, throwing herself to the floor of the wagon, the baby beneath her. Melanie stirred feebly, her hands seeking the baby, and Wade covered his eyes and cowered, too frightened to cry. Then the bushes beside them crashed apart under heavy hooves and a low moaning bawl assaulted their ears.

"It's only a cow," said Scarlett, her voice rough with fright. "Don't be a fool, Prissy. You've mashed the baby and frightened Miss Melly and Wade."

"It's a ghos'," moaned Prissy, writhing face down on the wagon boards.

Turning deliberately, Scarlett raised the tree-limb she had been using as a whip and brought it down across Prissy's back. She was too exhausted and weak from fright to tolerate weakness in anyone else.

"Sit up, you fool," she said, "before I wear this out on you."

Yelping, Prissy raised her head and peering over the side of the wagon saw it was, indeed, a cow, a red and white animal which stood looking at them appealingly, with large frightened eyes. Opening its mouth, it lowed again as if in pain.

"Is it hurt? That doesn't sound like an ordinary moo."

"Soun' ter me lak her bag full an' she need milkin' bad," said Prissy, regaining some measure of control. "Spec it one of Mist' MacIntosh's dat de niggers driv in de woods an' de Yankees din' git."

"We'll take it with us," Scarlett decided swiftly. "Then we can have some milk for the baby."

"How all we gwine tek a cow wid us, Miss Scarlett? We kain tek no cow wid us. Cow ain' no good nohow effen she ain' been milked lately. Dey bags swells up an' busts. Dat's why she hollerin'."

"Since you know so much about it, take off your petticoat and tear it up and tie her to the back of the wagon."

"Miss Scarlett, you knows Ah ain' had no petticoat fer a month an' did Ah have one, Ah wouldn' put it on her fer nuthin'. Ah nebber had no truck wid cows. Ah's sceered of cows."

Scarlett laid down the reins and pulled up her skirt. The lace-trimmed petticoat beneath was the last garment she possessed that was pretty—and whole. She untied the waist tape and slipped it down over her feet, crushing the soft linen folds between her hands. Rhett had brought her that linen and lace from Nassau on the last boat he slipped through the blockade and she had worked a week to make the garment. Resolutely she took it by the hem and jerked, put it in her mouth and gnawed, until finally the material gave with a rip and tore the length. She gnawed furiously, tore with both hands and the petticoat lay in strips in her hands. She knotted the ends with fingers that bled from blisters and shook from fatigue.

"Slip this over her horns," she directed. But Prissy balked.

"Ah's sceered of cows, Miss Scarlett. Ah ain' nebber had nuthin' ter do wid cows. Ah ain' no yard nigger. Ah's a house nigger."

"You're a fool nigger, and the worst day's work Pa ever did was to buy you," said Scarlett slowly, too tired for anger. "And if I ever get the use of my arm again, I'll wear this whip out on you."

"There," she thought, "I've said 'nigger' and Mother wouldn't like that at all."

Prissy rolled her eyes wildly, peeping first at the set face of her mistress and then at the cow which bawled plaintively. Scarlett seemed the less dangerous of the two, so Prissy clutched at the sides of the wagon and remained where she was.

Stiffly, Scarlett climbed down from the seat, each movement an agony of aching muscles.

623

Prissy was not the only one who was "sceered" of cows. Scarlett had always feared them, even the mildest cow seemed sinister to her, but this was no time to truckle to small fears when great ones crowded so thick upon her. Fortunately the cow was gentle. In its pain it had sought human companionship and help and it made no threatening gesture as she looped one end of the torn petticoat about its horns. She tied the other end to the back of the wagon as securely as her awkward fingers would permit. Then, as she started back toward the driver's seat, a vast weariness assailed her and she swayed dizzily. She clutched the side of the wagon to keep from falling.

Melanie opened her eyes and, seeing Scarlett standing beside her, whispered: "Dear—are we home?"

Home! Hot tears came to Scarlett's eyes at the word. Home. Melanie did not know there was no home and that they were alone in a mad and desolate world.

"Not yet," she said, as gently as the constriction of her throat would permit, "but we will be, soon. I've just found a cow and soon we'll have some milk for you and the baby."

"Poor baby," whispered Melanie, her hand creeping feebly toward her child and falling short.

Climbing back into the wagon required all the strength Scarlett could muster, but at last it was done and she picked up the lines. The horse stood with head drooping dejectedly and refused to start. Scarlett laid on the whip mercilessly. She hoped God would forgive her for hurting a tired animal. If He didn't she was sorry. After all, Tara

624

lay just ahead, and after the next quarter of a mile, the horse could drop in the shafts if he liked.

Finally he started slowly, the wagon creaking and the cow lowing mournfully at every step. The pained animal's voice rasped on Scarlett's nerves until she was tempted to stop and untie the beast. What good would the cow do them anyway if there should be no one at Tara? She couldn't milk her and, even if she could, the animal would probably kick anyone who touched her sore udders. But she had the cow and she might as well keep her. There was little else she had in this world now.

Scarlett's eyes grew misty when, at last, they reached the bottom of a gentle incline, for just over the rise lay Tara! Then her heart sank. The decrepit animal would never pull the hill. The slope had always seemed so slight, so gradual, in days when she galloped up it on her fleet-footed mare. It did not seem possible it could have grown so steep since she saw it last. The horse would never make it with the heavy load.

Wearily she dismounted and took the animal by the bridle.

"Get out, Prissy," she commanded, "and take Wade. Either carry him or make him walk. Lay the baby by Miss Melanie."

Wade broke into sobs and whimperings from which Scarlett could only distinguish: "Dark—dark—Wade fwightened!"

"Miss Scarlett, Ah kain walk. Mah feets done blistered an' dey's thoo mah shoes, an' Wade an' me doan weigh so much an'—"

"Get out! Get out before I pull you out! And if I do, I'm going to leave you right here, in the dark by yourself. Quick, now!"

Prissy moaned, peering at the dark trees that closed about them on both sides of the road—trees which might reach out and clutch her if she left the shelter of the wagon. But she laid the baby beside Melanie, scrambled to the ground and, reaching up, lifted Wade out. The little boy sobbed, shrinking close to his nurse.

"Make him hush. I can't stand it," said Scarlett, taking the horse by the bridle and pulling him to a reluctant start. "Be a little man, Wade, and stop crying or I will come over there and slap you."

Why had God invented children, she thought savagely as she turned her ankle cruelly on the dark road—useless, crying nuisances they were, always demanding care, always in the way. In her exhaustion, there was no room for compassion for the frightened child, trotting by Prissy's side, dragging at her hand and sniffling—only a weariness that she had borne him, only a tired wonder that she had ever married Charles Hamilton.

"Miss Scarlett," whispered Prissy, clutching her mistress' arm, "doan le's go ter Tara. Dey's not dar. Dey's all done gone. Maybe dey daid—Maw an' all'm."

The echo of her own thoughts infuriated her and Scarlett shook off the pinching fingers.

"Then give me Wade's hand. You can sit right down here and stay."

"No'm! No'm!"

"Then *hush!*"

How slowly the horse moved! The moisture from his slobbering mouth dripped down upon her hand. Through her mind ran a few words of the song she had once sung with Rhett—she could not recall the rest:

"Just a few more days for to tote the weary load—"

"Just a few more steps," hummed her brain, over and over, "just a few more steps for to tote the weary load."

Then they topped the rise and before them lay the oaks of Tara, a towering dark mass against the darkening sky. Scarlett looked hastily to see if there was a light anywhere. There was none.

"They are gone!" said her heart, like cold lead in her breast. "Gone!"

She turned the horse's head into the driveway, and the cedars, meeting over their heads, cast them into midnight blackness. Peering up the long tunnel of darkness, straining her eyes, she saw ahead—or did she see? Were her tired eyes playing her tricks?—the white bricks of Tara blurred and indistinct. Home! Home! The dear white walls, the windows with the fluttering curtains, the wide verandas—were they all there ahead of her, in the gloom? Or did the darkness mercifully conceal such a horror as the MacIntosh house?

The avenue seemed miles long and the horse, pulling stubbornly at her hand, plopped slower and slower. Eagerly her eyes searched the darkness. The roof seemed to be intact. Could it be

—could it be—? No, it wasn't possible. War stopped for nothing, not even Tara, built to last five hundred years. It could not have passed over Tara.

Then the shadowy outline did take form. She pulled the horse forward faster. The white walls did show there through the darkness. And untarnished by smoke. Tara had escaped! Home! She dropped the bridle and ran the last few steps, leaped forward with an urge to clutch the walls themselves in her arms. Then she saw a form, shadowy in the dimness, emerging from the blackness of the front veranda and standing at the top of the steps. Tara was not deserted. Someone was home!

A cry of joy rose to her throat and died there. The house was so dark and still and the figure did not move or call to her. What was wrong? What was wrong? Tara stood intact, yet shrouded with the same eerie quiet that hung over the whole stricken countryside. Then the figure moved. Stiffly and slowly, it came down the steps.

"Pa?" she whispered huskily, doubting almost that it was he. "It's me—Katie Scarlett. I've come home."

Gerald moved toward her, silent as a sleepwalker, his stiff leg dragging. He came close to her, looking at her in a dazed way as if he believed she was part of a dream. Putting out his hand, he laid it on her shoulder. Scarlett felt it tremble, tremble as if he had been awakened from a nightmare into a half-sense of reality.

"Daughter," he said with an effort. "Daughter."

Then he was silent.

"Why—he's an old man!" thought Scarlett.

Gerald's shoulders sagged. In the face which she could only see dimly, there was none of the virility, the restless vitality of Gerald, and the eyes that looked into hers had almost the same fear-stunned look that lay in little Wade's eyes. He was only a little old man and broken.

And now, fear of unknown things seized her, leaped swiftly out of the darkness at her, and she could only stand and stare at him, all the flood of questioning dammed up at her lips.

From the wagon the faint wailing sounded again and Gerald seemed to rouse himself with an effort.

"It's Melanie and her baby," whispered Scarlett rapidly. "She's very ill—I brought her home."

Gerald dropped his hand from her arm and straightened his shoulders. As he moved slowly to the side of the wagon, there was a ghostly semblance of the old host of Tara welcoming guests, as if Gerald spoke words from out of shadowy memory.

"Cousin Melanie!"

Melanie's voice murmured indistinctly.

"Cousin Melanie, this is your home. Twelve Oaks is burned. You must stay with us."

Thoughts of Melanie's prolonged suffering spurred Scarlett to action. The present was with her again, the necessity of laying Melanie and her child on a soft bed and doing those small things for her that could be done.

"She must be carried. She can't walk."

There was a scuffle of feet and a dark figure emerged from the cave of the front hall. Pork ran down the steps.

"Miss Scarlett! Miss Scarlett!" he cried.

Scarlett caught him by the arms. Pork, part and parcel of Tara, as dear as the bricks and the cool corridors! She felt his tears stream down on her hands as he patted her clumsily, crying: "Sho is glad you back! Sho is—"

Prissy burst into tears and incoherent mumblings: "Poke! Poke, honey!" And little Wade, encouraged by the weakness of his elders, began sniffling: "Wade thirsty!"

Scarlett caught them all in hand.

"Miss Melanie is in the wagon and her baby too. Pork, you must carry her upstairs very carefully and put her in the back company room. Prissy, take the baby and Wade inside and give Wade a drink of water. Is Mammy here, Pork? Tell her I want her."

Galvanized by the authority in her voice, Pork approached the wagon and fumbled at the backboard. A moan was wrenched from Melanie as he half-lifted, half-dragged her from the feather tick on which she had lain so many hours. And then she was in Pork's strong arms, her head drooping like a child's across his shoulder. Prissy, holding the baby and dragging Wade by the hand, followed them up the wide steps and disappeared into the blackness of the hall.

Scarlett's bleeding fingers sought her father's hand urgently.

"Did they get well, Pa?"

"The girls are recovering."

Silence fell and in the silence an idea too monstrous for words took form. She could not, could not force it to her lips. She swallowed and swallowed but a sudden dryness seemed to have stuck the sides of her throat together. Was this the answer to the frightening riddle of Tara's silence? As if answering the question in her mind Gerald spoke.

"Your mother—" he said and stopped.

"And—Mother?"

"Your mother died yesterday."

Her father's arm held tightly in her own, Scarlett felt her way down the wide dark hall which, even in its blackness, was as familiar as her own mind. She avoided the high-backed chairs, the empty gun-rack, the old sideboard with its protruding claw feet, and she felt herself drawn by instinct to the tiny office at the back of the house where Ellen always sat, keeping her endless accounts. Surely, when she entered that room, Mother would again be sitting there before the secretary and would look up, quill poised, and rise with sweet fragrance and rustling hoops to meet her tired daughter. Ellen could not be dead, not even though Pa had said it, said it over and over like a parrot that knows only one phrase: "She died yesterday—she died yesterday—she died yesterday."

Queer that she should feel nothing now, nothing except a weariness that shackled her limbs with heavy iron chains and a hunger that made her knees tremble. She would think of Mother later. She must put her mother out of her

631

mind now, else she would stumble stupidly like Gerald or sob monotonously like Wade.

Pork came down the wide dark steps toward them, hurrying to press close to Scarlett like a cold animal toward a fire.

"Lights?" she questioned. "Why is the house so dark, Pork? Bring candles."

"Dey tuck all de candles, Miss Scarlett, all 'cept one we been usin' ter fine things in de dahk wid, an' it's 'bout gone. Mammy been usin' a rag in a dish of hawg fat fer a light fer nussin' Miss Carreen an' Miss Suellen."

"Bring what's left of the candle," she ordered. "Bring it into Mother's—into the office."

Pork pattered into the dining-room and Scarlett groped her way into the inky small room and sank down on the sofa. Her father's arm still lay in the crook of hers, helpless, appealing, trusting, as only the hands of the very young and the very old can be.

"He's an old man, an old tired man," she thought again and vaguely wondered why she could not care.

Light wavered into the room as Pork entered carrying high a half-burned candle stuck in a saucer. The dark cave came to life: the sagging old sofa on which they sat, the tall secretary reaching toward the ceiling with Mother's fragile carved chair before it, the racks of pigeonholes, still stuffed with papers written in her fine hand, the worn carpet—all, all were the same, except that Ellen was not there, Ellen with the faint scent of lemon verbena sachet and the sweet look in her tip-tilted eyes. Scarlett felt a small pain in her heart as of nerves numbed by a deep wound, struggling to make themselves felt again. She must not let them come to life now; there was all the rest of her life ahead of her in which they could ache. But, not now! Please, God, not now!

She looked into Gerald's putty-coloured face and, for the first time in her life, she saw him unshaven, his once florid face covered with silvery bristles. Pork placed the candle on the candle-stand and came to her side. Scarlett felt that if he had been a dog he would have laid his muzzle in her lap and whined for a kind hand upon his head.

"Pork, how many darkies are here?"

"Miss Scarlett, dem trashy niggers done runned away an' some of dem went off wid de Yankees an'—"

"How many are left?"

"Dey's me, Miss Scarlett, an' Mammy. She been nussin' de young Misses all day. An' Dilcey, she settin' up wid de young Misses now. Us three, Miss Scarlett."

"Us three" where there had been a hundred. Scarlett with an effort lifted her head on her aching neck. She knew she must keep her voice steady. To her surprise, words came out as coolly and naturally as if there had never been a war and she could, by waving her hand, call ten house servants to her.

"Pork, I'm starving. Is there anything to eat?"

"No'm. Dey tuck it all."

"But the garden?"

"Dey tuhned dey hawses loose in it."

"Even the sweet potato hills?"

Something almost like a pleased smile broke over his thick lips.

"Miss Scarlett, Ah done fergit de yams. Ah specs dey's right dar. Dem Yankee foks ain' never seed no yams an' dey thinks dey's jes' roots an'—"

"The moon will be up soon. You go out and dig us some and roast them. There's no corn meal? No dried peas? No chickens?"

"No'm. No'm. Whut chickens dey din' eat right hyah dey cah'ied off 'cross dey saddles."

They—They—They—Was there no end to what "They" had done? Was it not enough to burn and kill? Must they also leave women and children and helpless negroes to starve in a country which they had desolated?

"Miss Scarlett, Ah got some apples Mammy buhied unner de house. We been eatin' on dem to-day."

"Bring them before you dig the potatoes. And, Pork—I—I feel so faint. Is there any wine in the cellar, even blackberry?"

"Oh, Miss Scarlett, de cellar wuz de fust place dey went."

A swimming nausea compounded of hunger, sleeplessness, exhaustion and stunning blows came on suddenly and she gripped the carved roses under her hand.

"No wine," she said dully, remembering the endless rows of bottles in the cellar. A memory stirred.

"Pork, what of the corn whisky Pa buried in the oak barrel under the scuppernong arbour?"

Another ghost of a smile lit the black face, a smile of pleasure and respect.

"Miss Scarlett, you sho is de beatenes' chile! Ah done plum fergit dat bah'l. But, Miss Scarlett, dat whisky ain' no good. Ain' been dar but 'bout a year an' whisky ain' no good fer ladies nohow."

How stupid negroes were! They never thought of anything unless they were told. And the Yankees wanted to free them.

"It'll be good enough for this lady and for Pa. Hurry, Pork, and dig it up and bring us two glasses and some mint and sugar and I'll mix a julep."

His face was reproachful.

"Miss Scarlett, you knows dey ain' been no sugar at Tara fer de longes'. An' dey hawses done et up all de mint an' dey done broke all de glasses."

"If he says 'They' once more, I'll scream. I can't help it," she thought, and then, aloud: "Well, hurry and get the whisky, quickly. We'll take it neat." And, as he turned: "Wait, Pork. There's so many things to do that I can't seem to think. . . . Oh, yes, I brought home a horse and a cow and the cow needs milking, badly, and unharness the horse and water him. Go tell Mammy to look after the cow. Tell her she's got to fix the cow up somehow. Miss Melanie's baby will die if he doesn't get something to eat and—"

"Miss Melly ain '—kain—?" Pork paused delicately.

"Miss Melanie has no milk." Dear God, but Mother would faint at that!

"Well, Miss Scarlett, mah Dilcey ten' ter Miss Melly's chile. Mah Dilcey got a new chile herseff an' she got mo'n nuff fer both."

"You've got a new baby, Pork?"

Babies, babies, babies. Why did God make so many babies? But no, God didn't make them. Stupid people made them.

"Yas'm, big fat black boy. He—"

"Go tell Dilcey to leave the girls. I'll look after them. Tell her to nurse Miss Melanie's baby and do what she can for Miss Melanie. Tell Mammy to look after the cow and put that poor horse in the stable."

"Dey ain' no stable, Miss Scarlett. Dey use it fer fiahwood."

"Don't tell me any more what 'They' did. Tell Dilcey to look after them. And you, Pork, go dig up that whisky and then some potatoes."

"But, Miss Scarlett, Ah ain' got no light ter dig by."

"You can use a stick of firewood, can't you?"

"Dey ain' no fiahwood—Dey—"

"Do something. . . . I don't care what. But dig those things and dig them fast. Now, hurry."

Pork scurried from the room as her voice roughened and Scarlett was left alone with Gerald. She patted his leg gently. She noted how shrunken were the thighs that once bulged with saddle muscles. She must do something to drag him from his apathy—but she could not ask about Mother. That must come later, when she could stand it.

"Why didn't they burn Tara?"

Gerald stared at her for a moment as if not hearing her and she repeated her question.

"Why—" he fumbled, "they used the house as a headquarters."

636

"Yankees—in this house?"

A feeling that the beloved walls had been defiled rose in her. This house, sacred because Ellen had lived in it, and those—those—in it.

"So they were, Daughter. We saw the smoke from Twelve Oaks, across the river, before they came. But Miss Honey and Miss India and some of their darkies had refugeed to Macon, so we did not worry about them. But we couldn't be going to Macon. The girls were so sick—your mother —we couldn't be going. Our darkies ran—I'm not knowing where. They stole the wagons and the mules. Mammy and Dilcey and Pork—they didn't run. The girls—your mother—we couldn't be moving them."

"Yes, yes." He mustn't talk about Mother. Anything else. Even that General Sherman himself had used this room, Mother's office, for his headquarters. Anything else.

"The Yankees were moving on Jonesboro, to cut the railroad. And they came up the road from the river—thousands and thousands—and cannon and horses—thousands. I met them on the front porch."

"Oh, gallant little Gerald!" thought Scarlett, her heart swelling—Gerald meeting the enemy on the stairs of Tara as if an army stood behind him instead of in front of him.

"They said for me to leave, that they would be burning the place. And I said that they would be burning it over my head. We could not leave— the girls—your mother—were—"

"And then?" Must he revert to Ellen always?

"I told them there was sickness in the house,

637

the typhoid, and it was death to move them. They could burn the roof over us. I did not want to leave anyway—leave Tara—"

His voice trailed off into silence as he looked absently about the walls and Scarlett understood. There were too many Irish ancestors crowding behind Gerald's shoulders, men who had died on scant acres, fighting to the end rather than leave the homes where they had lived, ploughed, loved, begotten sons.

"I said that they would be burning the house over the heads of three dying women. But we would not leave. The young officer was—was a gentleman."

"A Yankee a gentleman? Why, Pa!"

"A gentleman. He galloped away and soon he was back with a captain, a surgeon, and he looked at the girls—and your mother."

"You let a damned Yankee into their room?"

"He had opium. We had none. He saved your sisters. Suellen was haemorrhaging. He was as kind as he knew how. And when he reported that they were—ill—they did not burn the house. They moved in, some general, his staff, crowding in. They filled all the rooms except the sick-room. And the soldiers—"

He paused again, as if too tired to go on. His stubbly chin sank heavily in loose folds of flesh on his chest. With an effort he spoke again.

"They camped all round the house, everywhere, in the cotton, in the corn. The pasture was blue with them. That night there were a thousand camp-fires. They tore down the fences and burned them to cook with and the barns and the stables and the smokehouse. They killed the cows and the hogs and the chickens—even my turkeys." Gerald's precious turkeys. So they were gone. "They took things, even the pictures—some of the furniture, the china—"

"The silver?"

"Pork and Mammy did something with the silver—put it in the well—but I'm not remembering now." Gerald's voice was fretful. "Then they fought the battle from here—from Tara—there was so much noise, people galloping up and stamping about. And later the cannon at Jonesboro—it sounded like thunder—even the girls could hear it, sick as they were, and they kept saying over and over: 'Papa, make it stop thundering.'"

"And—and Mother? Did she know Yankees were in the house?"

"She—never knew anything."

"Thank God," said Scarlett. Mother was spared that. Mother never knew, never heard the enemy in the rooms below, never heard the guns at Jonesboro, never learned that the land which was part of her heart was under Yankee feet.

"I saw few of them for I stayed upstairs with the girls and your mother. I saw the young surgeon mostly. He was kind, so kind, Scarlett. After he'd worked all day with the wounded, he came and sat with them. He even left some medicine. He told me when they moved on that the girls would recover but your mother—She was so frail, he said—too frail to stand it all. He said she had undermined her strength. . . . ."

In the silence that fell, Scarlett saw her mother

639

as she must have been in those last days, a thin tower of strength in Tara, nursing, working, doing without sleep and food that the others might rest and eat.

"And then, they moved on. Then, they moved on."

He was silent for a long time and then fumbled at her hand.

"It's glad I am you are home," he said simply.

There was a scraping noise on the back porch. Poor Pork, trained for forty years to clean his shoes before entering the house, did not forget, even in a time like this. He came in, carefully carrying two gourds, and the strong smell of dripping spirits entered before him.

"Ah spilt a plen'y, Miss Scarlett. It's pow'ful hard ter po' outer a bunghole inter a go'de."

"That's quite all right, Pork, and thank you." She took the wet gourd dipper from him, her nostrils wrinkling in distaste at the reek.

"Drink this, Father," she said, pushing the whisky in its strange receptacle into his hand and taking the second gourd of water from Pork. Gerald raised it, obedient as a child, and gulped noisily. She handed the water to him but he shook his head.

As she took the whisky from him and held it to her mouth, she saw his eyes follow her, a vague stirring of disapproval in them.

"I know no lady drinks spirits," she said briefly. "But to-day I'm no lady, Pa, and there is work to do to-night."

She tilted the dipper, drew a deep breath and drank swiftly. The hot liquid burned down her throat to her stomach, choking her and bringing tears to her eyes. She drew another breath and raised it again.

"Katie Scarlett," said Gerald, the first note of authority she had heard in his voice since her return, "that is enough. You're not knowing spirits and they will be making you tipsy."

"Tipsy?" She laughed an ugly laugh. "Tipsy? I hope it makes me drunk. I would like to be drunk and forget all of this."

She drank again, a slow train of warmth lighting in her veins and stealing through her body until even her finger-tips tingled. What a blessed feeling, this kindly fire! It seemed to penetrate even her ice-locked heart and strength came coursing back into her body. Seeing Gerald's puzzled hurt face, she patted his knee again and managed an imitation of the pert smile he used to love.

"How could it make me tipsy, Pa? I'm your daughter. Haven't I inherited the steadiest head in Clayton County?"

He almost smiled into her tired face. The whisky was bracing him too. She handed it back to him.

"Now you're going to take another drink and then I am going to take you upstairs and put you to bed."

She caught herself. Why, this was the way she talked to Wade—she should not address her father like this. It was disrespectful. But he hung on her words.

"Yes, put you to bed," she added lightly, "and give you another drink—maybe all the dipper and make you go to sleep. You need sleep and Katie Scarlett is here, so you need not worry about anything. Drink."

He drank again obediently and, slipping her arm through his, she pulled him to his feet.

"Pork. . . ."

Pork took the gourd in one hand and Gerald's arm in the other. Scarlett picked up the flaring candle and the three walked slowly into the dark hall and up the winding steps toward Gerald's room.

The room where Suellen and Carreen lay mumbling and tossing on the same bed stank vilely with the smell of the twisted rag burning in a saucer of bacon fat, which provided the only light. When Scarlett first opened the door the thick atmosphere of the room, with all windows closed and the air reeking with sick-room odours, medicine smells and stinking grease, almost made her faint. Doctors might say that fresh air was fatal in a sick-room but if she were to sit here, she must have air or die. She opened the three windows, bringing in the smell of oak leaves and earth, but the fresh air could do little toward dispelling the sickening odours which had accumulated for weeks in this close room.

Carreen and Suellen, emaciated and white, slept brokenly and awoke to mumble with wide, staring eyes in the tall four-poster bed where they had whispered together in better, happier days. In the corner of the room was an empty bed, a narrow French Empire bed with curling head and foot, a bed which Ellen had brought from Savannah. This was where Ellen had lain.

Scarlett sat beside the two girls, staring at them stupidly. The whisky taken on a stomach long empty was playing tricks on her. Sometimes her sisters seemed far away and tiny and their incoherent voices came to her like the buzz of insects. And again, they loomed large, rushing at her with lightning speed. She was tired, tired to the bone. She could lie down and sleep for days.

If she could only lie down and sleep and wake to feel Ellen gently shaking her arm and saying: "It is late, Scarlett. You must not be so lazy." But she could not ever do that again. If there were only Ellen, someone older than she, wiser and unweary, to whom she could go! Someone in whose lap she could lay her head, someone on whose shoulders she could rest her burdens!

The door opened softly and Dilcey entered, Melanie's baby held to her breast, the gourd of whisky in her hand. In the smoky, uncertain light, she seemed thinner than when Scarlett last saw her and the Indian blood was more evident in her face. The high cheek-bones were more prominent, the hawk-bridged nose was sharper and her copper skin gleamed with a brighter hue. Her faded calico dress was open to the waist and her large bronze breast exposed. Held close against her, Melanie's baby pressed his pale rosebud mouth greedily to the dark nipple, sucking, gripping tiny fists against the soft flesh like a kitten in the warm fur of its mother's belly.

Scarlett rose unsteadily and put a hand on Dilcey's arm.

"It was good of you to stay, Dilcey."

"How could I go off wid them trashy niggers, Miss Scarlett, after yo' pa been so good to buy me and my little Prissy and yo' ma been so kine?"

"Sit down, Dilcey. The baby can eat all right, then? And how is Miss Melanie?"

"Nuthin' wrong wid this chile 'cept he hongry, and whut it take to feed a hongry chile I got. No'm, Miss Melanie is all right. She ain' gwine die, Miss Scarlett. Doan you fret yo'seff. I seen too many, white and black, lak her. She mighty tired and nervous like and scared fo' this baby. But I hesh her and give her some of whut was lef' in that go'de and she sleepin'."

So the corn whisky had been used by the whole family! Scarlett thought hysterically that perhaps she had better give a drink to little Wade and see if it would stop his hiccoughs—And Melanie would not die. And when Ashley came home—if he did come home . . . No, she would think of that later too. So much to think of—later! So many things to unravel—to decide. If only she could put off the hour of reckoning forever! She started suddenly as a creaking noise and a rhythmic "Ker-bunk—ker-bunk—" broke the stillness of the air outside.

"That's Mammy gettin' the water to sponge off the young Misses. They takes a heap of bathin'," explained Dilcey, propping the gourd on the table between medicine bottles and a glass.

Scarlett laughed suddenly. Her nerves must be shredded if the noise of the well windlass, bound up in her earliest memories, could frighten her. Dilcey looked at her steadily as she laughed, her face immobile in its dignity, but Scarlett felt that Dilcey understood. She sank back in her chair. If she could only be rid of her tight stays, the collar that choked her and the slippers still full of sand and gravel that blistered her feet.

The windlass creaked slowly as the rope wound up, each creak bringing the bucket nearer the top. Soon Mammy would be with her—Ellen's Mammy, her Mammy. She sat silent, intent on nothing, while the baby, already glutted with milk, whimpered because he had lost the friendly nipple. Dilcey, silent too, guided the child's mouth back, quieting him in her arms as Scarlett listened to the slow scuffing of Mammy's feet across the back yard. How still the night air was! The slightest sounds roared in her ears.

The upstairs hall seemed to shake as Mammy's ponderous weight came toward the door. Then Mammy was in the room, Mammy with shoulders dragged down by two heavy wooden buckets, her kind black face sad with the uncomprehending sadness of a monkey's face.

Her eyes lighted up at the sight of Scarlett, her white teeth gleamed as she set down the buckets, and Scarlett ran to her, laying her head on the broad, sagging breasts which had held so many heads, black and white. Here was something of stability, thought Scarlett, something of the old life that was unchanging. But Mammy's first words dispelled this illusion.

"Mammy's chile is home! Oh, Miss Scarlett, now dat Miss Ellen's in de grabe, whut is we gwine ter do? Oh, Miss Scarlett, effen Ah wuz jes' daid longside Miss Ellen! Ah kain make out

645

widout Miss Ellen. Ain' nuthin' lef' now but mizry an' trouble. Jes' weery loads, honey, jes' weery loads."

As Scarlett lay with her head hugged close to Mammy's breast, two words caught her attention, "weery loads". Those were the words which had hummed in her brain that afternoon so monotonously they had sickened her. Now she remembered the rest of the song, remembered with a sinking heart:

"Just a few more days for to tote the weary
load!
No matter, 'twill never be light!
Just a few more days till we totter in the
road—"

"No matter, 'twill never be light"—she took the words to her tired mind. Would her load never be light? Was coming home to Tara to mean, not blessed surcease, but only more loads to carry? She slipped from Mammy's arms and, reaching up, patted the wrinkled black face.

"Honey, yo' han's!" Mammy took the small hands with their blisters and blood-clots in hers and looked at them with horrified disapproval. "Miss Scarlett, Ah done tole you an' tole you dat you kin allus tell a lady by her han's an'—yo' face sunbuhnt too!"

Poor Mammy, still the martinet about such unimportant things even though war and death had just passed over her head! In another moment she would be saying that young Misses with blistered hands and freckles most generally didn't never catch husbands and Scarlett forestalled the remark.

"Mammy, I want you to tell me about Mother. I couldn't bear to hear Pa talk about her."

Tears started from Mammy's eyes as she leaned down to pick up the buckets. In silence she carried them to the bedside and, turning down the sheet, began pulling up the night clothes of Suellen and Carreen. Scarlett, peering at her sisters in the dim flaring light, saw that Carreen wore a nightgown, clean but in tatters, and Suellen lay wrapped in an old negligée, a brown linen garment heavy with tagging ends of Irish lace. Mammy cried silently as she sponged the gaunt bodies, using the remnant of an old apron as a cloth.

"Miss Scarlett, it wuz dem Slatterys, dem trashy, no-good, low-down po'-w'ite Slatterys dat kilt Miss Ellen. Ah done tole her an' tole her it doan do no good doin' things fer trashy folks, but Miss Ellen wuz so sot in her ways an' her heart so sof' she couldn' never say no ter nobody whut needed her."

"Slatterys?" questioned Scarlett, bewildered. "How do they come in?"

"Dey wuz sick wid disyere thing." Mammy gestured with her rag to the two naked girls, dripping with water on their damp sheet. "Ole Miss Slattery's gal, Emmie, come down wid it an' Miss Slattery come hotfootin' it up hyah affer Miss Ellen, lak she allus done w'en anything wrong. Why din' she nuss her own? Miss Ellen had mo'n she could tote anyways. But Miss Ellen she went down dar an' she nuss Emmie. An' Miss

Ellen wuzn' well a-tall herseff, Miss Scarlett. Yo' ma hadn' been well fer de longes'. Dey ain' been too much ter eat roun' hyah, wid de commissary stealin' eve'y thing us growed. An' Miss Ellen eat lak a bird anyways. An' Ah tole her an' tole her ter let dem w'ite trash alone, but she din' pay me no mine. Well'm, 'bout de time Emmie look lak she gittin' better, Miss Carreen come down wid it. Yas'm, de typhoy fly right up de road an' ketch Miss Carreen, an' den down come Miss Suellen. So Miss Ellen, she tuck an' nuss dem too.

"Wid all de fightin' up de road an' de Yankees 'cross de river an' us not knowin' whut wuz gwine ter happen ter us an' de fe'el han's runnin' off eve'y night, Ah's 'bout crazy. But Miss Ellen jes' as cool as a cucumber. 'Cept she wuz worried ter a ghos' 'bout de young Misses kase we couldn' git no medicines nor nuthin'. An' one night she say ter me affer we done sponge off de young Misses 'bout ten times, she say, 'Mammy, effen Ah could sell mah soul, Ah'd sell it fer some ice ter put on mah gals' haids.'

"She wouldn' let Mist' Gerald come in hyah, nor Rosa nor Teena, nobody but me, kase Ah done had de typhoy. An' den it tuck her, Miss Scarlett, an' Ah seed right off dat 'twarnt no use."

Mammy straightened up and, raising her apron, dried her streaming eyes.

"She went fas', Miss Scarlett, an' even dat nice Yankee doctah couldn' do nuthin' fer her. She din' know nuthin' a-tall. Ah call ter her an' talk

ter her but she din' even know her own
Mammy."

"Did she—did she ever mention me—call for
me?"

"No, honey. She think she a lil gal back in
Savannah. She din' call nobody by name."

Dilcey stirred and laid the sleeping baby across
her knees.

"Yes'm, she did. She did call somebody."

"You hesh yo' mouf, you Injun-nigger!"
Mammy turned with threatening violence on
Dilcey.

"Hush, Mammy! Who did she call, Dilcey?
Pa?"

"No'm. Not yo' pa. It wuz the night the cotton
buhnt—"

"Has the cotton gone—tell me quickly!"

"Yes'm, it buhnt up. The sojers rolls it out of
the shed into the back yard and hollers, 'Here the
bigges' bonfiah in Georgia' and tech it off."

Three years of stored cotton—one hundred and
fifty thousand dollars, all in one blaze!

"And the fiah light up the place lak it wuz day
—we wuz scared the house would buhn, too, and
it wuz so bright in this hyah room that you could
mos' pick a needle offen the flo'. And w'en the
light shine in the winder, it look lak it wake Miss
Ellen up and she set right up in bed and cry out
loud, time and agin: 'Feeleep! Feeleep!' I ain'
never heerd no sech name but it wuz a name and
she wuz callin' him."

Mammy stood as though turned to stone
glaring at Dilcey but Scarlett dropped her head
into her hands. Philippe—who was he and what

had he been to Mother that she died calling him?

The long road from Atlanta to Tara had ended, ended in a blank wall, the road that was to end in Ellen's arms. Never again could Scarlett lie down, as a child, secure beneath her father's roof with the protection of her mother's love wrapped about her like an eiderdown quilt. There was no security or haven to which she could turn now. No turning or twisting would avoid this dead end to which she had come. There was no one on whose shoulders she could rest her burdens. Her father was old and stunned, her sisters ill, Melanie frail and weak, the children helpless, and the negroes looking up to her with childlike faith, clinging to her skirts, knowing that Ellen's daughter would be the refuge Ellen had always been.

Through the window, in the faint light of the rising moon, Tara stretched before her, negroes gone, acres desolate, barns ruined, like a body bleeding under her eyes, like her own body, slowly bleeding. This was the end of the road, quivering old age, sickness, hungry mouths, helpless hands plucking at her skirts. And at the end of this road there was nothing—nothing but Scarlett O'Hara Hamilton, nineteen years old, a widow with a little child.

What would she do with all of this? Aunt Pitty and the Burrs in Macon could take Melanie and her baby. If the girls recovered, Ellen's family would have to take them, whether they liked it or not. And she and Gerald could turn to Uncle James and Andrew.

She looked at the thin forms tossing before her, the sheets about them moist and dark from dripping water. She did not like Suellen. She saw it now with a sudden clarity. She had never liked her. She did not especially love Carreen—she could not love anyone who was weak. But they were of her blood, part of Tara. No, she could not let them live out their lives in their aunts' homes as poor relations. An O'Hara a poor relation, living on charity bread and sufferance! Oh, never that!

Was there no escape from this dead end? Her tired brain moved so slowly. She raised her hands to her head as wearily as if the air were water against which her arms struggled. She took the gourd from between the glass and bottle and looked in it. There was some whisky left in the bottom, how much she could not tell in the uncertain light. Strange that the sharp smell did not offend her nostrils now. She drank slowly but this time the liquid did not burn, only a dull warmth followed.

She set down the empty gourd and looked about her. This was all a dream, this smoke-filled dim room, the scrawny girls, Mammy shapeless and huge crouching beside the bed, Dilcey a still bronze image with the sleeping pink morsel against her dark breast—all a dream from which she would awake, to smell bacon frying in the kitchen, hear the throaty laughter of the negroes and the creaking of wagons fieldward bound, and Ellen's gentle insistent hand upon her.

Then she discovered she was in her own room, on her own bed, faint moonlight pricking the darkness, and Mammy and Dilcey were undressing her. The torturing stays no longer pinched her waist and she could breathe deeply and quietly to the bottom of her lungs and her abdomen. She felt her stockings being stripped gently from her and heard Mammy murmuring indistinguishable comforting sounds as she bathed her blistered feet. How cool the water was, how good to lie here in softness, like a child! She sighed and relaxed and after a time which might have been a year or a second, she was alone and the room was brighter as the rays of the moon streamed in across the bed.

She did not know she was drunk, drunk with fatigue and whisky. She only knew she had left her tired body and floated somewhere above it where there was no pain and no weariness and her brain saw things with an inhuman clarity.

She was seeing things with new eyes for, somewhere along the long road to Tara, she had left her girlhood behind her. She was no longer plastic clay, yielding imprint to each new experience. The clay had hardened, some time in this indeterminate day which had lasted a thousand years. To-night was the last time she would ever be ministered to as a child. She was a woman now and youth was gone.

No, she could not, would not, turn to Gerald's or Ellen's families. The O'Haras did not take charity. The O'Haras looked after their own. Her burdens were her own and burdens were for shoulders strong enough to bear them. She thought without surprise, looking down from her height, that her shoulders were strong enough to bear anything now, having borne the worst that could ever happen to her. She could not desert Tara; she belonged to the red acres far more than they could ever belong to her. Her roots went deep into the blood-coloured soil and sucked up life, as did the cotton. She would stay at Tara and keep it, somehow, keep her father and her sisters, Melanie and Ashley's child, the negroes. To-morrow—oh, to-morrow! To-morrow she would fit the yoke about her neck. To-morrow there would be so many things to do. Go to Twelve Oaks and the MacIntosh place and see if anything was left in the deserted gardens, go to the river swamps and beat them for straying hogs and chickens, go to Jonesboro and Lovejoy with Ellen's jewellery—there must be someone left there who would sell something to eat. To-morrow—to-morrow—her brain ticked slowly and more slowly, like a clock running down, but the clarity of vision persisted.

Of a sudden, the oft-told family tales to which she had listened since babyhood, listened half-bored, impatient and but partly comprehending, were crystal clear. Gerald, penniless, had raised Tara; Ellen had risen above some mysterious sorrow; Grandfather Robillard, surviving the wreck of Napoleon's throne, had founded his fortunes anew on the fertile Georgia coast; Great-Grandfather Prudhomme had carved a small kingdom out of the dark jungles of Haiti, lost it, and lived to see his name honoured in Savannah. There were the Scarletts who had fought with the Irish Volunteers for a free Ireland and been hanged for their pains, and the O'Haras who died at the Boyne, battling to the end for what was theirs.

All had suffered crushing misfortunes and had not been crushed. They had not been broken by the crash of empires, the machetes of revolting slaves, war, rebellion, proscription, confiscation. Malign fate had broken their necks, perhaps, but never their hearts. They had not whined, they had fought. And when they died, they died spent but unquenched. All of those shadowy folks whose blood flowed in her veins seemed to move quietly in the moonlit room. And Scarlett was not surprised to see them, these kinsmen who had taken the worst that fate could send and hammered it into the best. Tara was her fate, her fight, and she must conquer it.

She turned drowsily on her side, a slow creeping blackness enveloping her mind. Were they really there, whispering wordless encouragement to her, or was this part of her dream?

"Whether you are there or not," she murmured sleepily, "good night—and thank you."

9

THE next morning Scarlett's body was so stiff and sore from the long miles of walking and jolting in the wagon that every movement was agony. Her face was crimson with sunburn and her blistered palms raw. Her tongue was furred and her throat parched as if flames had scorched it and no amount of water could assuage her thirst. Her head felt swollen and she winced even when she turned her eyes. A queasiness of the stomach reminiscent of the early days of her pregnancy made the smoking yams on the breakfast table unendurable, even to the smell. Gerald could have told her she was suffering the normal aftermath of her first experience with hard drinking but Gerald noticed nothing. He sat at the head of the table, a grey old man with absent, faded eyes fastened on the door and head cocked slightly to hear the rustle of Ellen's petticoats, to smell the lemon verbena sachet.

As Scarlett sat down, he mumbled: "We will wait for Mrs. O'Hara. She is late." She raised an aching head, looked at him with startled incredulity and met the pleading eyes of Mammy, who stood behind Gerald's chair. She rose unsteadily, her hand at her throat, and looked down at her father in the morning sunlight. He peered up at her vaguely and she saw that his hands were shaking, that his head trembled a little.

Until this moment she had not realized how

much she had counted on Gerald to take command, to tell her what she must do, and now —Why, last night he had seemed almost himself. There had been none of his usual bluster and vitality, but at least he had told a connected story, and now—now, he did not even remember Ellen was dead. The combined shock of the coming of the Yankees and her death had stunned him. She started to speak, but Mammy shook her head vehemently and raising her apron dabbed at her red eyes.

"Oh, can Pa have lost his mind?" thought Scarlett, and her throbbing head felt as if it would crack with this added strain. "No, no. He's just dazed by it all. It's like he was sick. He'll get over it. He must get over it. What will I do if he doesn't?—I won't think about it now. I won't think of him or Mother or any of these awful things now. No, not till I can stand it. There are too many other things to think about—things that can be helped—without my thinking of those I can't help."

She left the dining-room without eating, and went out on to the back porch where she found Pork, barefooted and in the ragged remains of his best livery, sitting on the steps cracking peanuts. Her head was hammering and throbbing and the bright sunlight stabbed into her eyes. Merely holding herself erect required an effort of willpower and she talked as briefly as possible, dispensing with the usual forms of courtesy her mother had always taught her to use with negroes.

She began asking questions so brusquely and giving orders so decisively Pork's eyebrows went up in mystification. Miss Ellen didn't never talk so short to nobody, not even when she caught them stealing pullets and water-melons. She asked again about the fields, the gardens, the stock, and her green eyes had a hard bright glaze which Pork had never seen in them before.

"Yas'm, dat hawse daid, layin' dar whar Ah tie him wid his nose in de water-bucket he tuhned over. No'm, de cow ain' daid. Din' you know? She done have a calf las' night. Dat why she beller so."

"A fine midwife your Prissy will make," Scarlett remarked caustically. "She said she was bellowing because she needed milking."

"Well'm, Prissy ain' fixin' ter be no cow midwife, Miss Scarlett," Pork said tactfully. "An' ain' no use quarrellin' wid blessin's,'cause dat calf gwine ter mean a full cow an' plen'y buttermilk fer de young Misses, lak dat Yankee doctah say dey'd need."

"All right, go on. Any stock left?"

"No'm. Nuthin 'cept one ole sow an' her litter. Ah driv dem inter de swamp de day de Yankees come, but de Lawd knows how we gwine git dem. She mean, dat sow."

"We'll get them all right. You and Prissy can start right now hunting for her."

Pork was amazed and indignant.

"Miss Scarlett, dat a fe'el han's bizness. Ah's allus been a house nigger."

A small fiend with a pair of hot tweezers plucked behind Scarlett's eyeballs.

"You two will catch the sow—or get out of here, like the field hands did."

Tears trembled in Pork's hurt eyes. Oh, if only Miss Ellen were here! She understood such niceties and realized the wide gap between the duties of a field hand and those of a house nigger.

"Git out, Miss Scarlett? Whar'd Ah git out to, Miss Scarlett?"

"I don't know and I don't care. But anyone at Tara who won't work can go hunt up the Yankees. You can tell the others that too."

"Yas'm."

"Now, what about the corn and the cotton, Pork?"

"De cawn? Lawd, Miss Scarlett, dey pasture dey hawses in de cawn an' cah'ied off whut de hawses din' eat or spile. An' dey driv dey cannons an' waggins 'cross de cotton till it plum ruint, 'cept a few acres over on de creek bottom dat dey din' notice. But dat cotton ain' wuth foolin' wid, 'cause ain' but 'bout three bales over dar."

Three bales. Scarlett thought of the scores of bales Tara usually yielded and her head hurt worse. Three bales. That was little more than the shiftless Slatterys raised. To make matters worse, there was the question of taxes. The Confederate government took cotton for taxes in lieu of money, but three bales wouldn't even cover the taxes. Little did it matter, though, to her or the Confederacy, now that all the field hands had run away and there was no one to pick the cotton.

"Well, I won't think of that either," she told herself. "Taxes aren't a woman's job anyway. Pa ought to look after such things, but Pa—I won't think of Pa now. The Confederacy can whistle for its taxes. What we need now is something to eat."

"Pork, have any of you been to Twelve Oaks or the MacIntosh place to see if there's anything left in the gardens there?"

"No, Ma'm! Us ain' lef' Tara. De Yankees mout git us."

"I'll send Dilcey over to MacIntosh. Perhaps she'll find something there. And I'll go to Twelve Oaks."

"Who wid, chile?"

"By myself. Mammy must stay with the girls and Mr. Gerald can't—"

Pork set up an outcry which she found infuriating. There might be Yankees or mean niggers at Twelve Oaks. She mustn't go alone.

"That will be enough, Pork. Tell Dilcey to start immediately. And you and Prissy go bring in the sow and her litter," she said briefly, turning on her heel.

Mammy's old sunbonnet, faded but clean, hung on its peg on the back porch and Scarlett put it on her head, remembering, as from another world, the bonnet with the curling green plume which Rhett had brought her from Paris. She picked up a large split-oak basket and started down the back stairs, each step jouncing her head until her spine seemed to be trying to crash through the top of her skull.

The road down to the river lay red and scorching between the ruined cotton fields. There were no trees to cast a shade and the sun beat down through Mammy's sunbonnet as if it were made of tarlatan instead of heavy quilted calico, while the dust floating upward sifted into her nose and throat until she felt the membranes would crack dryly if she spoke. Deep ruts and furrows were cut into the road where horses had dragged heavy guns along it and the red gullies on either side were deeply gashed by the wheels. The cotton was mangled and trampled where cavalry and infantry, forced off the narrow road by the artillery, had marched through the green bushes, grinding them into the earth. Here and there in road and fields lay buckles and bits of harness leather, canteens flattened by hooves and caisson wheels, buttons, blue caps, worn socks, bits of bloody rags, all the litter left by a marching army.

She passed the clump of cedars and the low brick wall which marked the family burying-ground, trying not to think of the new grave lying by the three short mounds of her little brothers. Oh, Ellen—She trudged on down the dusty hill, passing the heap of ashes and the stumpy chimney where the Slattery house had stood, and she wished savagely that the whole tribe of them had been part of the ashes. If it hadn't been for the Slatterys—if it hadn't been for that nasty Emmie, who'd had a bastard brat by their overseer—Ellen wouldn't have died.

She moaned as a sharp pebble cut into her blistered foot. What was she doing here? Why was Scarlett O'Hara, the belle of the County, the sheltered pride of Tara, tramping down this rough road almost barefoot? Her little feet were made to dance, not to limp, her tiny slippers to peep daringly from under bright silks, not to collect sharp pebbles and dust. She was born to be pampered and waited upon, and here she was, sick and ragged, driven by hunger to hunt for food in the gardens of her neighbours.

At the bottom of the long hill was the river and how cool and still were the tangled trees overhanging the water! She sank down on the low bank and, stripping off the remnants of her slippers and stockings, dabbled her burning feet in the cool water. It would be so good to sit here all day, away from the helpless eyes of Tara, here where only the rustle of leaves and the gurgle of slow water broke the stillness. But reluctantly she replaced her shoes and stockings and trudged down the bank, spongy with moss, under the shady trees. The Yankees had burned the bridge but she knew of a footlog bridge across a narrow point of the stream a hundred yards below. She crossed it cautiously and trudged uphill the hot half-mile to Twelve Oaks.

There towered the twelve oaks, as they had stood since Indian days, but with their leaves brown from fire and the branches burned and scorched. Within their circle lay the ruins of John Wilkes' house, the charred remains of that once stately home which had crowned the hill in white-columned dignity. The deep pit which had been the cellar, the blackened field-stone foundations and two mighty chimneys marked the site. One long column, half-burned, had fallen across the lawn, crushing the cape jessamine bushes.

Scarlett sat down on the column, too sick at the sight to go on. This desolation went to her heart as nothing she had ever experienced. Here was the Wilkes pride in the dust at her feet. Here was the end of the kindly, courteous house which had always welcomed her, the house where in futile dreams she had aspired to be mistress. Here she had danced and dined and flirted, and here she had watched with a jealous, hurting heart how Melanie smiled up at Ashley. Here, too, in the cool shadows of the trees, Charles Hamilton had rapturously pressed her hand when she said she would marry him.

"Oh, Ashley," she thought, "I hope you are dead! I could never bear for you to see this."

Ashley had married his bride here but his son and his son's son would never bring brides to this house. There would be no more matings and births beneath this roof which she had so loved and longed to rule. The house was dead and, to Scarlett, it was as if all the Wilkes, too, were dead in its ashes.

"I won't think of it now. I can't stand it now. I'll think of it later," she said aloud, turning her eyes away.

Seeking the garden, she limped around the ruins, by the trampled rose-beds the Wilkes girls had tended so zealously, across the back yard and through the ashes of the smokehouse, barns and chicken houses. The split-rail fence around the kitchen garden had been demolished and the once orderly rows of green plants had suffered the same treatment as those at Tara. The soft earth was scarred with hoof-prints and heavy wheels and the vegetables were mashed into the soil. There was nothing for her here.

She walked back across the yard and took the path down toward the silent row of whitewashed cabins in the quarters, calling "Hello!" as she went. But no voice answered her. Not even a dog barked. Evidently the Wilkes negroes had taken flight or followed the Yankees. She knew every slave had his own garden patch, and as she reached the quarters she hoped these little patches had been spared.

Her search was rewarded but she was too tired even to feel pleasure at the sight of turnips and cabbages, wilted for want of water but still standing, and straggling butter beans and snap beans, yellowing but edible. She sat down in the furrows and dug into the earth with hands that shook, filling her basket slowly. There would be a good meal at Tara to-night, in spite of the lack of side meat to boil with the vegetables. Perhaps some of the bacon grease Dilcey was using for illumination could be used for seasoning. She must remember to tell Dilcey to use pine-knots and save the grease for cooking.

Close to the back step of one cabin, she found a short row of radishes and hunger assaulted her suddenly. A spicy, sharp-tasting radish was exactly what her stomach craved. Hardly waiting to rub the dirt off on her skirt, she bit off half and swallowed it hastily. It was old and coarse and so peppery that tears started in her eyes. No sooner had the lump gone down than her empty outraged stomach revolted and she lay in the soft dirt and vomited tiredly.

The faint niggery smell which crept from the cabin increased her nausea and, without strength to combat it, she kept on retching miserably while the cabins and trees revolved swiftly around her. After a long time, she lay weakly on her face,

663

the earth as soft and comfortable as a feather pillow, and her mind wandered feebly here and there. She, Scarlett O'Hara, was lying behind a negro cabin, in the midst of ruins, too sick and too weak to move, and no one in the world knew or cared. No one would care if they did know, for everyone had too many troubles of their own to worry about her. And all this was happening to her, Scarlett O'Hara, who had never raised her hand even to pick up her discarded stockings from the floor or to tie the laces of her slippers —Scarlett, whose little headaches and tempers had been coddled and catered to all her life.

As she lay prostrate, too weak to fight off memories and worries, they rushed at her, circled about her like buzzards waiting for a death. No longer had she the strength to say: "I'll think of Mother and Pa and Ashley and all this ruin later —Yes, later when I can stand it." She could not stand it now, but she was thinking of them whether she willed it or not. The thoughts circled and swooped above her, dived down and drove tearing claws and sharp beaks into her mind. For a timeless time, she lay still, her face in the dirt, the sun beating hotly upon her, remembering things and people who were dead, remembering a way of living that was gone forever—and looking upon the harsh vista of the dark future.

When she arose at last and saw again the black ruins of Twelve Oaks, her head was raised high and something that was youth and beauty and potential tenderness had gone out of her face forever. What was past was past. Those who were dead were dead. The lazy luxury of the old days was gone, never to return. And, as Scarlett settled the heavy basket across her arm, she had settled her own mind and her own life.

There was no going back and she was going forward.

Throughout the South for fifty years there would be bitter-eyed women who looked backward, to dead times, to dead men, evoking memories that hurt and were futile, bearing poverty with bitter pride because they had those memories. But Scarlett was never to look back.

She gazed at the blackened stones and, for the last time, she saw Twelve Oaks rise before her eyes as it had once stood, rich and proud, symbol of a race and a way of living. Then she started down the road toward Tara, the heavy basket cutting into her flesh.

Hunger gnawed at her empty stomach again and she said aloud: "As God is my witness, as God is my witness, the Yankees aren't going to lick me. I'm going to live through this, and when it's over, I'm never going to be hungry again. No, nor any of my folks. If I have to steal or kill—as God is my witness, I'm never going to be hungry again."

In the days that followed, Tara might have been Crusoe's desert island, so still it was, so isolated from the rest of the world. The world lay only a few miles away, but a thousand miles of tumbling waves might have stretched between Tara and Jonesboro and Fayetteville and Lovejoy, even between Tara and the neighbours' plantations. With the old horse dead, their one mode of conveyance was gone, and there was neither time nor strength for walking the weary red miles.

Sometimes, in the days of backbreaking work, in the desperate struggle for food and the never-ceasing care of the three sick girls, Scarlett found herself straining her ears for familiar sounds—the shrill laughter of the piccaninnies in the quarters, the creaking of wagons home from the fields, the thunder of Gerald's stallion tearing across the pasture, the crunching of carriage wheels on the drive and the gay voices of neighbours dropping in for an afternoon of gossip. But she listened in vain. The road lay still and deserted and never a cloud of red dust proclaimed the approach of visitors. Tara was an island in a sea of rolling green hills and red fields.

Somewhere was the world and families who ate and slept safely under their own roofs. Some-where girls in thrice-turned dresses were flirting gaily and singing "When This Cruel War Is Over", as she had done only a few weeks before. Somewhere there was a war and cannon booming and burning towns and men who rotted in hospi-tals amid sickening-sweet stinks. Somewhere a barefoot army in dirty homespun was marching, fighting, sleeping, hungry and weary with the weariness that comes when hope is gone. And somewhere the hills of Georgia were blue with Yankees, well-fed Yankees on sleek corn-stuffed horses.

Beyond Tara was the war and the world. But on the plantation the war and the world did not exist except as memories which must be fought back when they rushed to mind in moments of exhaustion. The world outside receded before the demands of empty and half-empty stomachs and life resolved itself into two related thoughts, food and how to get it.

Food! Food! Why did the stomach have a longer memory than the mind? Scarlett could banish heartbreak but not hunger, and each morning as she lay half-asleep, before memory brought back to her mind war and hunger, she curled drowsily expecting the sweet smells of bacon frying and rolls baking. And each morning she sniffed so hard to really smell the food she woke herself up.

There were apples, yams, peanuts and milk on the table at Tara but never enough of even this primitive fare. At the sight of them, three times a day, her memory would rush back to the old days, the meals of the old days, the candle-lit table and the food perfuming the air.

How careless they had been of food then, what prodigal waste! Rolls, corn muffins, biscuit and waffles, dripping butter, all at one meal. Ham at one end of the table and fried chicken at the other, collards swimming richly in pot liquor iridescent with grease, snap beans in mountains on brightly flowered porcelain, fried squash, stewed okra, carrots in cream sauce thick enough to cut. And three desserts, so everyone might have his choice, chocolate layer cake, vanilla blancmange and pound cake topped with sweet whipped cream. The memory of those savoury meals had the power to bring tears to her eyes as death and war had failed to do, had the power to turn her ever-gnawing stomach from rumbling emptiness to nausea. For the appetite Mammy had always deplored, the healthy appetite of a nineteen-year-old girl, now was increased fourfold by the hard and unremitting labour she had never known before.

Hers was not the only troublesome appetite at Tara, for wherever she turned hungry faces, black and white, met her eyes. Soon Carreen and Suellen would have the insatiable hunger of typhoid convalescents. Already little Wade whined monotonously: "Wade doan like yams. Wade hungwy."

The others grumbled, too:

"Miss Scarlett, 'ness I gits mo' to eat, I kain nuss neither of these chillun."

"Miss Scarlett, ef Ah doan have mo' in mah stummick, Ah kain split no wood."

"Lamb, Ah's perishin' fer real vittles."

"Daughter, must we always have yams?"

Only Melanie did not complain, Melanie whose face grew thinner and whiter and twitched with pain even in her sleep.

"I'm not hungry, Scarlett. Give my share of the milk to Dilcey. She needs it to nurse the babies. Sick people are never hungry."

It was her gentle hardihood which irritated Scarlett more than the nagging, whining voices of the others. She could—and did—shout them down with bitter sarcasm but before Melanie's unselfishness she was helpless, helpless and resentful. Gerald, the negroes and Wade clung to Melanie now, because even in her weakness she was kind and sympathetic, and these days Scarlett was neither.

Wade especially haunted Melanie's room. There was something wrong with Wade, but just what it was Scarlett had no time to discover. She took Mammy's word that the little boy had worms and dosed him with the mixture of dried herbs and bark which Ellen always used to worm the piccaninnies. But the vermifuge only made the child look paler. These days Scarlett hardly thought of Wade as a person. He was only another worry, another mouth to feed. Some day when the present emergency was over, she would play with him, tell him stories and teach him his A B C's, but now she did not have the time or the inclination. And, because he always seemed underfoot when she was most weary and worried, she often spoke sharply to him.

It annoyed her that her quick reprimands brought such acute fright to his round eyes, for he looked so simple-minded when he was frightened. She did not realize that the little boy lived shoulder to shoulder with terror too great for an adult to comprehend. Fear lived with Wade, fear that shook his soul and made him wake screaming in the night. Any unexpected noise or sharp word set him to trembling, for in his mind noises and harsh words were inextricably mixed with Yankees and he was more afraid of Yankees than of Prissy's hants.

Until the thunders of the siege began, he had never known anything but a happy, placid, quiet life. Even though his mother paid him little attention, he had known nothing but petting and kind words until the night when he was jerked from slumber to find the sky aflame and the air deafening with explosions. In that night and the day which followed, he had been slapped by his mother for the first time and had heard her voice raised at him in harsh words. Life in the pleasant brick house on Peachtree Street, the only life he knew, had vanished that night and he would never recover from its loss. In the flight from Atlanta, he had understood nothing except that the Yankees were after him, and now he still lived in fear that the Yankees would catch him and cut him to pieces. Whenever Scarlett raised her voice in reproof, he went weak with fright as his vague childish memory brought up the horrors of the first time she had ever done it. Now, Yankees and a cross voice were linked forever in his mind and he was afraid of his mother.

Scarlett could not help noticing that the child was beginning to avoid her and, in the rare moments when her unending duties gave her time to think about it, it bothered her a great deal. It was even worse than having him at her skirts all the time, and she was offended that his refuge was Melanie's bed where he played quietly at games Melanie suggested or listened to stories she told. Wade adored "Auntee" who had a gentle voice, who always smiled and who never said: "Hush, Wade! You give me a headache," or "Stop fidgeting, Wade, for Heaven's sake!"

Scarlett had neither the time nor the impulse to pet him but it made her jealous to see Melanie do it. When she found him one day standing on his head in Melanie's bed and saw him collapse on her, she slapped him.

"Don't you know better then to jiggle Auntee

670

like that when she's sick? Now, trot right out in the yard and play, and don't come in here again."

But Melanie reached out a weak arm and drew the wailing child to her.

"There, there, Wade. You didn't mean to jiggle me, did you? He doesn't bother me, Scarlett. Do let him stay with me. Let me take care of him. It's the only thing I can do till I get well, and you've your hands full enough without having to watch him."

"Don't be a goose, Melly," said Scarlett shortly. "You aren't getting well like you should and having Wade fall on your stomach won't help you. Now, Wade, if I ever catch you on Auntee's bed again, I'll wear you out. And stop sniffling. You are always sniffling. Try to be a little man."

Wade flew sobbing to hide himself under the house. Melanie bit her lip and tears came to her eyes, and Mammy standing in the hall, a witness to the scene, scowled and breathed hard. But no one talked back to Scarlett these days. They were all afraid of her sharp tongue, all afraid of the new person who walked in her body.

Scarlett reigned supreme at Tara now and, like others suddenly elevated to authority, all the bullying instincts in her nature rose to the surface. It was not that she was basically unkind. It was because she was so frightened and unsure of herself she was harsh lest others learn her inadequacies and refuse her authority. Besides, there was some pleasure in shouting at people and knowing they were afraid. Scarlett found that it relieved her overwrought nerves. She was not blind to the fact that her personality was changing. Sometimes when her curt orders made Pork stick out his underlip and Mammy mutter: "Some folks rides mighty high dese days," she wondered where her good manners had gone. All the courtesy, all the gentleness Ellen had striven to instil in her had fallen away from her as quickly as leaves fall from trees in the first chill wind of autumn.

Time and again, Ellen had said: "Be firm but be gentle with inferiors, especially darkies." But if she was gentle the darkies would sit in the kitchen all day, talking endlessly about the good old days when a house nigger wasn't supposed to do a field hand's work.

"Love and cherish your sisters. Be kind to the afflicted," said Ellen. "Show tenderness to those in sorrow and in trouble."

She couldn't love her sisters now. They were simply a dead weight on her shoulders. And as for cherishing them, wasn't she bathing them, combing their hair and feeding them, even at the expense of walking miles every day to find vegetables? Wasn't she learning to milk the cow, even though her heart was always in her throat when that fearsome animal shook its horns at her? And as for being kind, that was a waste of time. If she was overly kind to them, they'd probably prolong their stay in bed, and she wanted them on their feet again as soon as possible, so there would be four more hands to help her.

They were convalescing slowly and lay scrawny and weak in their bed. While they had been unconscious, the world had changed. The Yankees had come, the darkies had gone and

Mother had died. Here were three unbelievable happenings and their minds could not take them in. Sometimes they believed they must still be delirious and these things had not happened at all. Certainly Scarlett was so changed she couldn't be real. When she hung over the foot of their bed and outlined the work she expected them to do when they recovered, they looked at her as if she were a hobgoblin. It was beyond their comprehension that they no longer had a hundred slaves to do the work. It was beyond their comprehension that an O'Hara lady should do manual labour.

"But, Sister," said Carreen, her sweet childish face black with consternation, "I couldn't split kindling! It would ruin my hands!"

"Look at mine," answered Scarlett with a frightening smile as she pushed blistered and calloused palms toward her.

"I think you are hateful to talk to Baby and me like this!" cried Suellen. "I think you are lying and trying to frighten us. If Mother were only here, she wouldn't let you talk to us like this! Split kindling, indeed!"

Suellen looked with weak loathing at her older sister, feeling sure Scarlett said these things just to be mean. Suellen had nearly died and she had lost her mother and she was lonely and scared and she wanted to be petted and made much of. Instead, Scarlett looked over the foot of the bed each day, appraising their improvement with a hateful new gleam in her slanting green eyes, and talked about making beds, preparing food, carrying water-buckets and splitting kindling.

And she looked as if she took a pleasure in saying such awful things.

Scarlett did take pleasure in it. She bullied the negroes and harrowed the feelings of her sisters not only because she was too worried and strained and tired to do otherwise, but because it helped her to forget her own bitterness that everything her mother had told her about life was wrong.

Nothing her mother had taught her was of any value whatsoever now and Scarlett's heart was sore and puzzled. It did not occur to her that Ellen could not have foreseen the collapse of the civilization in which she raised her daughters, could not have anticipated the disappearing of the places in society for which she trained them so well. It did not occur to her that Ellen had looked down a vista of placid future years, all like the uneventful years of her own life, when she had taught her to be gentle and gracious, honourable and kind, modest and truthful. Life treated women well when they had learned those lessons, said Ellen.

Scarlett thought in despair: "Nothing, no, nothing, she taught me is of any help to me! What good will kindness do me now? What value is gentleness? Better that I'd learned to plough or chop cotton like a darky. Oh, Mother, you were wrong!"

She did not stop to think that Ellen's ordered world was gone and a brutal world had taken its place, a world wherein every standard, every value had changed. She only saw, or thought she saw, that her mother had been wrong, and she changed swiftly to meet this new world for which she was not prepared.

Only her feeling for Tara had not changed. She never came wearily home across the fields and saw the sprawling white house that her heart did not swell with love and the joy of homecoming. She never looked out of her window at green pastures and red fields and tall tangled swamp forest that a sense of beauty did not fill her. Her love for this land with its softly rolling hills of bright-red soil, this beautiful red earth that was blood-coloured, garnet, brick-dust, vermilion, which so miraculously grew green bushes starred with white puffs, was one part of Scarlett which did not change when all else was changing. Nowhere else in the world was there land like this.

When she looked at Tara she could understand, in part, why wars were fought. Rhett was wrong when he said men fought wars for money. No, they fought for swelling acres, softly furrowed by the plough, for pastures green with stubby cropped grass, for lazy yellow rivers and white houses that were cool amid magnolias. These were the only things worth fighting for, the red earth which was theirs and would be their sons', the red earth which would bear cotton for their sons and their sons' sons.

The trampled acres of Tara were all that was left to her, now that Mother and Ashley were gone, now that Gerald was senile from shock, and money and darkies and security and position had vanished overnight. As from another world, she remembered a conversation with her father about the land and wondered how she could have been so young, so ignorant, as not to understand what he meant when he said that the land was the one thing in the world worth fighting for.

"For 'tis the only thing in the world that lasts . . . and to anyone with a drop of Irish blood in them the land they live on is like their mother. . . . 'Tis the only thing worth working for, fighting for, dying for."

Yes, Tara was worth fighting for, and she accepted simply and without question the fight. No one was going to get Tara away from her. No one was going to set her and her people adrift on the charity of relatives. She would hold Tara, if she had to break the back of every person on it.

10

SCARLETT had been at Tara two weeks since her return from Atlanta when the largest blister on her foot began to fester, swelling until it was impossible for her to put on her shoe or do more than hobble about on her heel. Desperation plucked at her when she looked at the angry sore on her toe. Suppose it should gangrene like the soldiers' wounds and she should die, far away from a doctor? Bitter as life was now, she had no desire to leave it. And who would look after Tara if she should die?

She had hoped when she first came home that Gerald's old spirit would revive and he would take command, but in these two weeks that hope had vanished. She knew now that, whether she liked it or not, she had the plantation and all its people on her two inexperienced hands, for Gerald still sat quietly, like a man in a dream, so frighteningly absent from Tara, so gentle. To her pleas for advice he gave as his only answer: "Do what you think best, Daughter." Or worse still, "Consult with your mother, Puss."

He would never be any different and now Scarlett realized the truth and accepted it without emotion—that until he died Gerald would always be waiting for Ellen, always listening for her. He was in some dim borderline country where time was standing still and Ellen was always in the next room. The mainspring of his existence was taken away when she died and with it had gone his bounding assurance, his impudence and his restless vitality. Ellen was the audience before which the blustering drama of Gerald O'Hara had been played. Now the curtain had been rung down forever, the footlights dimmed and the audience suddenly vanished, while the stunned old actor remained on his empty stage, waiting for his cues.

That morning the house was still, for everyone except Scarlett, Wade and the three sick girls was in the swamp hunting the sow. Even Gerald had aroused a little and stumped off across the furrowed fields, one hand on Pork's arm and a coil of rope in the other. Suellen and Carreen had cried themselves to sleep, as they did at least twice a day when they thought of Ellen, tears of grief and weakness oozing down their sunken cheeks. Melanie, who had been propped up on pillows for the first time that day, lay covered with a mended sheet between two babies, the downy flaxen head of one cuddled in her arm, the kinky black head of Dilcey's child held as gently in the other. Wade sat at the bottom of the bed, listening to a fairy story.

To Scarlett, the stillness at Tara was unbearable, for it reminded her too sharply of the deathlike stillness of the desolate country through which she had passed that long day on her way home from Atlanta. The cow and the calf had made no sound for hours. There were no birds twittering outside her window and even the noisy family of mockers who had lived among the harshly rustling leaves of the magnolia for generations had no song that day. She had drawn a low chair close to the open window of her bedroom, looking out on the front drive, the lawn and the empty green pasture across the road, and she sat with her skirts well above her knees and her chin resting on her arms on the window-sill. There was a bucket of well water on the floor beside her and every now and then she lowered her blistered foot into it, screwing up her face at the stinging sensation.

Fretting, she dug her chin into her arm. Just when she needed her strength most, this toe had to fester. Those fools would never catch the sow. It had taken them a week to capture the pigs, one by one, and now after two weeks the sow was still at liberty. Scarlett knew that if she were just there in the swamp with them, she could tuck up her dress to her knees and take the rope and lasso the sow before you could say Jack Robinson.

But even after the sow was caught—if she were caught? What then, after she and her litter were eaten? Life would go on and so would appetites. Winter was coming and there would be no food, not even the poor remnants of the vegetables from the neighbours' gardens. They must have dried peas and sorghum and meal and rice and—and—oh, so many things. Corn and cotton seed for next spring's planting, and new clothes too. Where was it all to come from and how would she pay for it?

She had privately gone through Gerald's pockets and his cash-box and all she could find was stacks of Confederate bonds and three thousand dollars in Confederate bills. That was about enough to buy one square meal for them all, she thought ironically, now that Confederate money was worth almost less than nothing at all. But if she did have money and could find food, how would she haul it home to Tara? Why had God let the old horse die? Even that sorry animal Rhett had stolen would make all the difference in the world to them. Oh, those fine sleek mules which used to kick up their heels in the pasture across the road, and the handsome carriage horses, her little mare, the girls' ponies and Gerald's big stallion racing about and tearing up the turf—Oh, for one of them, even the balkiest mule!

But, no matter—when her foot healed she would walk to Jonesboro. It would be the longest walk she had ever taken in her life, but walk it she would. Even if the Yankees had burned the town completely, she could certainly find someone in the neighbourhood who could tell her where to get food. Wade's pinched face rose up before her eyes. He didn't like yams, he repeated; wanted a drumstick and some rice and gravy.

The bright sunlight in the front yard suddenly clouded and the trees blurred through tears. Scarlett dropped her head on her arms and struggled not to cry. Crying was so useless now. The only time crying ever did any good was when there was a man around from whom you wished favours. As she crouched there, squeezing her eyes tightly to keep back the tears, she was startled by the sound of trotting hooves. But she did not raise her head. She had imagined that sound too often in the nights and days of these last two weeks, just as she had imagined she heard the rustle of Ellen's skirts. Her heart hammered, as it always did at such moments, before she told herself sternly: "Don't be a fool."

But the hooves slowed down in a startlingly natural way to the rhythm of a walk and there was the measured scrunch-scrunch on the gravel. It was a horse—the Tarletons, the Fontaines! She looked up quickly. It was a Yankee cavalryman.

Automatically, she dodged behind the curtain and peered fascinated at him through the dim folds of the cloth, so startled that the breath went out of her lungs with a gasp.

He sat slouched in the saddle, a thick, rough-looking man with an unkempt black beard straggling over his unbuttoned blue jacket. Little close-set eyes, squinting in the sun-glare, calmly surveyed the house from beneath the visor of his tight blue cap. As he slowly dismounted and tossed the bridle reins over the hitching-post, Scarlett's breath came back to her as suddenly and painfully as after a blow in the stomach. A Yankee, a Yankee with a long pistol on his hip! And she was alone in the house with three sick girls and the babies!

As he lounged up the walk, hand on holster, beady little eyes glancing to right and left, a kaleidoscope of jumbled pictures spun in her mind, stories Aunt Pittypat had whispered of attacks on unprotected women, throat-cuttings, houses burned over the heads of dying women, children bayoneted because they cried, all of the unspeakable horrors that lay bound up in the name of "Yankee".

Her first terrified impulse was to hide in the

closet, crawl under the bed, fly down the back stairs and run screaming to the swamp, anything to escape him. Then she heard his cautious feet on the front steps and his stealthy tread as he entered the hall and she knew that escape was cut off. Too cold with fear to move, she heard his progress from room to room downstairs, his steps growing louder and bolder as he discovered no one. Now he was in the dining-room and in a moment he would walk out into the kitchen.

At the thought of the kitchen, rage suddenly leaped up in Scarlett's breast, so sharply that it jabbed at her heart like a knife-thrust, and fear fell away before her overpowering fury. The kitchen! There, over the open kitchen fire, were two pots, one filled with apples stewing and the other with a hodge-podge of vegetables brought painfully from Twelve Oaks and the MacIntosh garden—dinner that must serve for nine hungry people and hardly enough for two. Scarlett had been restraining her appetite for hours, waiting for the return of the others, and the thought of the Yankee eating their meagre meal made her shake with anger.

God damn them all! They descended like locusts and left Tara to starve slowly and now they were back again to steal the poor leavings. Her empty stomach writhed within her. By God, this was one Yankee who would do no more stealing!

She slipped off her worn shoe and, barefooted, she pattered swiftly to the bureau, not even feeling her festered toe. She opened the top drawer soundlessly and caught up the heavy pistol

she had brought from Atlanta, the weapon
Charles had worn but never fired. She fumbled
in the leather box that hung on the wall below
his sabre and brought out a cap. She slipped it
into place with a hand that did not shake. Quickly
and noiselessly, she ran into the upper hall and
down the stairs, steadying herself on the banisters
with one hand and holding the pistol close to her
thigh in the folds of her skirt.

"Who's there?" cried a nasal voice, and she
stopped on the middle of the stairs, the blood
thudding in her ears so loudly she could hardly
hear him. "Halt or I'll shoot!" came the voice.

He stood in the door of the dining-room,
crouched tensely, his pistol in one hand and, in
the other, the small rosewood sewing-box fitted
with gold thimble, gold-handled scissors and tiny
gold-topped acorn of emery. Scarlett's legs felt
cold to the knees but rage scorched her face.
Ellen's sewing-box in his hands. She wanted to
cry: "Put it down! Put it down, you dirty—" but
words would not come. She could only stare over
the banisters at him and watch his face change
from harsh tenseness to a half-contemptuous,
half-ingratiating smile.

"So there is somebody ter home," he said, slipping his pistol back into its holster and moving
into the hall until he stood directly below her.
"All alone, little lady?"

Like lightning, she shoved her weapon over the
banisters and into the startled bearded face.
Before he could even fumble at his belt, she
pulled the trigger. The back kick of the pistol
made her reel, as the roar of the explosion filled

her ears and the acrid smoke stung her nostrils. The man crashed backwards to the floor, sprawling into the dining-room with a violence that shook the furniture. The box clattered from his hand, the contents spilling about him. Hardly aware that she was moving, Scarlett ran down the stairs and stood over him, gazing down into what was left of the face above the beard, a bloody pit where the nose had been, glazing eyes burned with powder. As she looked, two streams of blood crept across the shining floor, one from his face and one from the back of his head.

Yes, he was dead. Undoubtedly. She had killed a man.

The smoke curled slowly to the ceiling and the red streams widened about her feet. For a time-less moment she stood there and in the still hot hush of the summer morning every irrelevant sound and scent seemed magnified, the quick thudding of her heart, like a drumbeat, the slight rough rustling of the magnolia leaves, the far-off plaintive sound of a swamp bird and the sweet smell of the flowers outside the window.

She had killed a man, she who took care never to be in at the kill on a hunt, she who could not bear the squealing of a hog at slaughter or the squeak of a rabbit in a snare. Murder! she thought dully. I've done murder. Oh, this can't be happening to me! Her eyes went to the stubby hairy hand on the floor so close to the sewing-box and suddenly she was vitally alive again, vitally glad with a cool tigerish joy. She could have ground her heel into the gaping wound which had been his nose and taken sweet pleasure in the feel of his warm blood on her bare feet. She had struck a blow of revenge for Tara—and for Ellen.

There were hurried stumbling steps in the upper hall, a pause and then more steps, weak dragging steps now, punctuated by metallic clankings. A sense of time and reality coming back to her, Scarlett looked up and saw Melanie at the top of the stairs, clad only in the ragged chemise which served her as a nightgown, her weak arm weighed down with Charles' sabre. Melanie's eyes took in the scene below in its entirety—the sprawling blue-clad body in the red pool, the sewing-box beside him, Scarlett, barefooted and grey-faced, clutching the long pistol.

In silence her eyes met Scarlett's. There was a glow of grim pride in her usually gentle face, approbation and a fierce joy in her smile that equalled the fiery tumult in Scarlett's own bosom.

"Why—why—she's like me! She understands how I feel!" thought Scarlett in that long moment. "She'd have done the same thing!"

With a thrill she looked up at the frail swaying girl for whom she had never had any feelings but of dislike and contempt. Now, struggling against hatred for Ashley's wife, there surged a feeling of admiration and comradeship. She saw in a flash of clarity untouched by any petty emotion that beneath the gentle voice and the dovelike eyes of Melanie there was a thin flashing blade of unbreakable steel, felt too that there were banners and bugles of courage in Melanie's quiet blood.

"Scarlett! Scarlett!" shrilled the weak frightened voices of Suellen and Carreen, muffled by their closed door, and Wade's voice screamed,

"Auntee! Auntee!" Swiftly Melanie put her finger to her lips and, laying the sword on the top step, she painfully made her way down the upstairs hall and opened the door of the sick-room.

"Don't be scared, chickens!" came her voice with teasing gaiety. "Your big sister was trying to clean the rust off Charles' pistol and it went off and nearly scared her to death!. . . Now, Wade Hampton, Mama just shot off your dear Papa's pistol! When you are bigger, she will let you shoot it."

"What a cool liar!" thought Scarlett with admiration. "I couldn't have thought that quickly. But why lie? They've got to know I've done it."

She looked down at the body again and now revulsion came over her as her rage and fright melted away, and her knees began to quiver with the reaction. Melanie dragged herself to the top step again and started down, holding on to the banisters, her pale lower lip caught between her teeth.

"Go back to bed, silly, you'll kill yourself!" Scarlett cried, but the half-naked Melanie made her painful way down into the lower hall.

"Scarlett," she whispered, "we must get him out of here and bury him. He may not be alone and if they find him here—" She steadied herself on Scarlett's arm.

"He must be alone," said Scarlett. "I didn't see anyone else from the upstairs window. He must be a deserter."

"Even if he is alone, no one must know about it. The negroes might talk and then they'd come and get you. Scarlett, we must get him hidden before the folks come back from the swamp."

Her mind prodded to action by the feverish urgency of Melanie's voice, Scarlett thought hard.

"I could bury him in the corner of the garden under the arbour—the ground is soft there where Pork dug up the whisky barrel. But how will I get him there?"

"We'll both take a leg and drag him," said Melanie firmly.

Reluctantly, Scarlett's admiration went still higher.

"You couldn't drag a cat. I'll drag him," she said roughly. "You go back to bed. You'll kill yourself. Don't dare try to help me either or I'll carry you upstairs myself."

Melanie's white face broke into a sweet understanding smile. "You are very dear, Scarlett," she said, and softly brushed her lips against Scarlett's cheek. Before Scarlett could recover from her surprise, Melanie went on: "If you can drag him out, I'll mop up the—the mess before the folks get home, and Scarlett—"

"Yes?"

"Do you suppose it would be dishonest to go through his knapsack? He might have something to eat."

"I do not," said Scarlett, annoyed that she had not thought of this herself. "You take the knapsack and I'll go through his pockets."

Stooping over the dead man with distaste, she unbuttoned the remaining buttons of his jacket and systematically began rifling his pockets.

"Dear God," she whispered, pulling out a

bulging wallet, wrapped about with a rag. "Melanie—Melly, I think it's full of money!"

Melanie said nothing but abruptly sat down on the floor and leaned back against the wall.

"You look," she said shakily. "I'm feeling a little weak."

Scarlett tore off the rag and with trembling hands opened the leather folds.

"Look, Melly—just look!"

Melanie looked and her eyes dilated. Jumbled together was a mass of bills, United States greenbacks mingling with Confederate money and, glinting from between them, were one ten-dollar gold piece and two five-dollar gold pieces.

"Don't stop to count it now," said Melanie, as Scarlett began fingering the bills. "We haven't time—"

"Do you realize, Melanie, that this money means that we'll eat?"

"Yes, yes, dear. I know but we haven't time now. You look in his other pockets and I'll take the knapsack."

Scarlett was loath to put down the wallet. Bright vistas opened before her—real money, the Yankee's horse, food! There was a God after all, and He did provide, even if He did take very odd ways of providing. She sat on her haunches and stared at the wallet, smiling. Food! Melanie plucked it from her hands.

"Hurry!" she said.

The trouser pockets yielded nothing except a candle-end, a jack-knife, a plug of tobacco and a bit of twine. Melanie removed from the knapsack a small package of coffee which she sniffed as if it were the sweetest of perfumes, hardtack and, her face changing, a miniature of a little girl in a gold frame set with seed pearls, a garnet brooch, two broad gold bracelets with tiny dangling gold chains, a gold thimble, a small silver baby's cup, gold embroidery scissors, a diamond solitaire ring and a pair of earrings with pendent pear-shaped diamonds, which even their unpractised eyes could tell were well over a carat each.

"A thief!" whispered Melanie, recoiling from the still body. "Scarlett, he must have stolen all of this!"

"Of course," said Scarlett. "And he came here hoping to steal more from us."

"I'm glad you killed him," said Melanie, her gentle eyes hard. "Now hurry, darling, and get him out of here."

Scarlett bent over, caught the dead man by his boots and tugged. How heavy he was and how weak she suddenly felt! Suppose she shouldn't be able to move him? Turning so that she backed the corpse, she caught a heavy boot under each arm and threw her weight forward. He moved and she jerked again. Her sore foot, forgotten in the excitement, now gave a tremendous throb that made her grit her teeth and shift her weight to the heel. Tugging and straining, perspiration dripping from her forehead, she dragged him down the hall, a red stain following her path.

"If he bleeds across the yard, we can't hide it," she gasped. "Give me your shimmy, Melanie, and I'll wad it around his head."

Melanie's white face went crimson.

"Don't be silly! I won't look at you," said

Scarlett. "If I had on a petticoat or pantalets I'd use them."

Crouching back against the wall, Melanie pulled the ragged linen garment over her head and silently tossed it to Scarlett, shielding herself as best she could with her arms.

"Thank God, I'm not that modest," thought Scarlett, feeling rather than seeing Melanie's agony of embarrassment, as she wrapped the ragged cloth about the shattered face.

By a series of limping jerks, she pulled the body down the hall toward the back porch and, pausing to wipe her forehead with the back of her hand, glanced back toward Melanie, sitting against the wall hugging her thin knees to her bare breasts. How silly of Melanie to be bothering about modesty at a time like this, Scarlett thought irritably. It was just part of her nicey-nice way of acting which had always made Scarlett despise her. Then shame rose in her. After all—after all, Melanie had dragged herself from bed so soon after having a baby and had come to her aid with a weapon too heavy even for her to lift. That had taken courage, the kind of courage Scarlett honestly knew she herself did not possess, the thin-steel, spun-silk courage which had character-ized Melanie on the terrible night Atlanta fell and on the long trip home. It was the same intangible, unspectacular courage that all the Wilkeses possessed, a quality which Scarlett did not under-stand but to which she gave grudging tribute.

"Go back to bed," she threw over her shoulder. "You'll be dead if you don't. I'll clean up the mess after I've buried him."

"I'll do it with one of the rag rugs," whispered Melanie, looking at the pool of blood with a sick face.

"Well, kill yourself then and see if I care! And if any of the folks come back before I'm finished, keep them in the house and tell them the horse just walked in from nowhere."

Melanie sat shivering in the morning sunlight and covered her ears against the sickening series of thuds as the dead man's head bumped down the porch steps.

No one questioned whence the horse had come. It was so obvious he was a stray from the recent battle and they were well pleased to have him. The Yankee lay in the shallow pit Scarlett had scraped out under the scuppernong arbour. The uprights which held the thick vines were rotten, and that night Scarlett hacked at them with the kitchen knife until they fell and the tangled mass ran wild over the grave. The replacing of these posts was one bit of repair work Scarlett did not suggest and, if the negroes knew why, they kept their silence.

No ghost rose from that shallow grave to haunt her in the long nights when she lay awake, too tired to sleep. No feeling of horror or remorse assailed her at the memory. She wondered why, knowing that even a month before she could never have done the deed. Pretty young Mrs. Hamilton, with her dimple and her jingling earbobs and her helpless little ways, blowing a man's face to a pulp and then burying him in a hastily scratched-out hole! Scarlett grinned a little grimly, thinking of the consternation such an idea would bring to those who knew her.

"I won't think about it any more," she decided. "It's over and done with and I'd have been a ninny not to kill him. I reckon—I reckon I must have changed a little since coming home or else I couldn't have done it."

She did not think of it consciously but in the back of her mind, whenever she was confronted by an unpleasant and difficult task, the idea lurked, giving her strength: "I've done murder and so I can surely do this."

She had changed more than she knew and the shell of hardness which had begun to form about her heart when she lay in the slave garden at Twelve Oaks was slowly thickening.

Now that she had a horse, Scarlett could find out for herself what had happened to their neighbours. Since she came home she had wondered despairingly a thousand times: "Are we the only folks left in the County? Has everybody else been burned out? Have they all refugeed to Macon?" With the memory of the ruins of Twelve Oaks, the MacIntosh place and the Slattery shack fresh in her mind, she almost dreaded to discover the truth. But it was better to know the worst than to wonder. She decided to ride to the Fontaines' first, not because they were the nearest neighbours but because old Dr. Fontaine might be there. Melanie needed a doctor. She was not recovering as she should and Scarlett was frightened by her white weakness.

So on the first day when her foot had healed

enough to stand a slipper, she mounted the Yankee's horse. One foot in the shortened stirrup and the other leg crooked about the pommel in an approximation of a side saddle, she set out across the fields toward Mimosa, steeling herself to find it burned.

To her surprise and pleasure, she saw the faded yellow-stucco house standing amid the mimosa trees, looking as it had always looked. Warm happiness, happiness that almost brought tears, flooded her when the three Fontaine women came out of the house to welcome her with kisses and cries of joy.

But when the first exclamations of affectionate greeting were over and they all had trooped into the dining-room to sit down, Scarlett felt a chill. The Yankees had not reached Mimosa because it was far off the main road. And so the Fontaines still had their stock and their provisions, but Mimosa was held by the same strange silence that hung over Tara, over the whole countryside. All the slaves except four women house servants had run away, frightened by the approach of the Yankees. There was not a man on the place unless Sally's little boy, Joe, hardly out of diapers, could be counted as a man. Alone in the big house were Grandma Fontaine, in her seventies, her daughter-in-law, who would always be known as Young Miss, though she was in her fifties, and Sally, who had barely turned twenty. They were far away from neighbours and unprotected, but if they were afraid it did not show on their faces. Probably, thought Scarlett, because Sally and Young Miss were too afraid of the porcelain-frail but indomitable old Grandma to dare voice any qualms. Scarlett herself was afraid of the old lady, for she had sharp eyes and a sharper tongue and Scarlett had felt them both in the past.

Though unrelated by blood and far apart in age, there was a kinship of spirit and experience binding these women together. All three wore home-dyed mourning, all were worn, sad, worried, all bitter with a bitterness that did not sulk or complain but, nevertheless, peered out from behind their smiles and their words of welcome. For their slaves were gone, their money was worthless, Sally's husband, Joe, had died at Gettysburg and Young Miss was also a widow, for young Dr. Fontaine had died of dysentery at Vicksburg. The other two boys, Alex and Tony, were somewhere in Virginia and nobody knew whether they were alive or dead; and old Dr. Fontaine was off somewhere with Wheeler's cavalry.

"And the old fool is seventy-three years old though he tries to act younger and he's as full of rheumatism as a hog is of fleas," said Grandma, proud of her husband, the light in her eyes belying her sharp words.

"Have you all had any news of what's been happening in Atlanta?" asked Scarlett when they were comfortably settled. "We're completely buried at Tara."

"Law, child," said Old Miss, taking charge of the conversation, as was her habit, "we're in the same fix as you are. We don't know a thing except that Sherman finally got the town."

"So he did get it. What's he doing now? Where's the fighting now?"

"And how would three lone women out here in the country know about the war when we haven't seen a letter or a newspaper in weeks?" said the old lady tartly. "One of our darkies talked to a darky who'd seen a darky who'd been to Jonesboro, and except for that we haven't heard anything. What they said was that the Yankees were just squatting in Atlanta resting up their men and their horses, but whether it's true or not you're as good a judge as I am. Not that they wouldn't need a rest, after the fight we gave them."

"To think you've been at Tara all this time and we didn't know!" Young Miss broke in. "Oh, how I blame myself for not riding over to see! But there's been so much to do here with most all the darkies gone that I just couldn't get away. But I should have made time to go. It wasn't neighbourly of me. But, of course, we thought the Yankees had burned Tara like they did Twelve Oaks and the MacIntosh house and that your folks had gone to Macon. And we never dreamed you were home, Scarlett."

"Well, how were we to know different when Mr. O'Hara's darkies came through here so scared they were popeyed and told us the Yankees were going to burn Tara?" Grandma interrupted.

"And we could see—" Sally began.

"I'm telling this, please," said Old Miss shortly. "And they said the Yankees were camped all over Tara and you folks were fixing to go to Macon. And then that night we saw the glare of

695

fire over toward Tara and it lasted for hours and it scared our fool darkies so bad they all ran off. What burned?"

"All our cotton—a hundred and fifty thousand dollars' worth," said Scarlett bitterly.

"Be thankful it wasn't your house," said Grandma, leaning her chin on her cane. "You can always grow more cotton and you can't grow a house. By the by, had you all started picking your cotton?"

"No," said Scarlett, "and now most of it is ruined. I don't imagine there's more than three bales left standing, in the far field in the creek bottom, and what earthly good will it do? All our field hands are gone and there's nobody to pick it."

"Mercy me, 'all our field hands are gone and there's nobody to pick it'!" mimicked Grandma and bent a satiric glance on Scarlett. "What's wrong with your own pretty paws, Miss, and those of your sisters?"

"Me? Pick cotton?" cried Scarlett aghast, as if Grandma had been suggesting some repulsive crime. "Like a field hand? Like white trash? Like the Slattery women?"

"White trash, indeed! Well, isn't this generation soft and ladylike! Let me tell you, Miss, when I was a girl my father lost all his money and I wasn't above doing honest work with my hands and in the fields too, till Pa got enough money to buy some more darkies. I've hoed my row and I've picked my cotton and I can do it again if I have to. And it looks like I'll have to. White trash, indeed!"

"Oh, but Mama Fontaine," cried her daughter-in-law, casting imploring glances at the two girls, urging them to help her smooth the old lady's feathers. "That was so long ago, a different day entirely, and times have changed."

"Times never change when there's a need for honest work to be done," stated the sharp-eyed old lady, refusing to be soothed. "And I'm ashamed for your mother, Scarlett, to hear you stand there and talk as though honest work made white trash out of nice people. 'When Adam delved and Eve span—'"

To change the subject, Scarlett hastily questioned: "What about the Tarletons and the Calverts? Were they burned out? Have they refugeed to Macon?"

"The Yankees never got to the Tarletons. They're off the main road, like we are, but they did get to the Calverts and they stole all their stock and poultry and got all the darkies to run off with them—" Sally began.

Grandma interrupted.

"Hah! They promised all the black wenches silk dresses and gold earbobs—that's what they did. And Cathleen Calvert said some of the troopers went off with the black fools behind them on their saddles. Well, all they'll get will be yellow babies and I can't say that Yankee blood will improve the stock."

"Oh, Mama Fontaine!"

"Don't pull such a shocked face, Jane. We're all married, aren't we? And, God knows, we've seen mulatto babies before this."

"Why didn't they burn the Calverts' house?"

"The house was saved by the combined accents of the second Mrs. Calvert and that Yankee overseer of hers, Hilton," said Old Miss, who always referred to the ex-governess as the "second Mrs. Calvert", although the first Mrs. Calvert had been dead twenty years.

"'We are staunch Union sympathizers,'" mimicked the old lady, twanging the words through her long thin nose. "Cathleen said the two of them swore up hill and down dale that the whole passel of Calverts were Yankees. And Mr. Calvert dead in the Wilderness! And Raiford at Gettysburg and Cade in Virginia with the army! Cathleen was so mortified she said she'd rather the house had been burned. She said Cade would bust when he came home and heard about it. But then, that's what a man gets for marrying a Yankee woman—no pride, no decency, always thinking about their own skins. . . . Howcome they didn't burn Tara, Scarlett?"

For a moment Scarlett paused before answering. She knew the very next question would be: "And how are all your folks? And how is your dear mother?" She knew she could not tell them Ellen was dead. She knew that if she spoke those words or even let herself think of them in the presence of these sympathetic women, she would burst into a storm of tears and cry until she was sick. And she could not let herself cry. She had not really cried since she came home and she knew that if she once let down the floodgates, her closely husbanded courage would all be gone. But she knew, too, looking with confusion at the friendly faces about her, that if she withheld the news of Ellen's death, the Fontaines would never forgive her. Grandma in particular was devoted to Ellen and there were very few people in the County for whom the old lady gave a snap of her skinny fingers.

"Well, speak up," said Grandma, looking sharply at her. "Don't you know, Miss?"

"Well, you see, I didn't get home till the day after the battle," she answered hastily. "The Yankees were all gone then. Pa—Pa told me that —that he got them not to burn the house because Suellen and Carreen were so ill with typhoid they couldn't be moved."

"That's the first time I ever heard of a Yankee doing a decent thing," said Grandma, as if she regretted hearing anything good about the invaders. "And how are the girls now?"

"Oh, they are better, much better, almost well but quite weak," answered Scarlett. Then, seeing the question she feared hovering on the old lady's lips, she cast hastily about for some other topic of conversation.

"I—I wonder if you could lend us something to eat? The Yankees cleaned us out like a swarm of locusts. But, if you are on short rations, just tell me so plainly and—"

"Send over Pork with a wagon and you shall have half of what we've got, rice, meal, ham, some chickens," said Old Miss, giving Scarlett a sudden keen look.

"Oh, that's too much! Really, I—"

"Not a word! I won't hear it. What are neighbours for?"

"You are so kind that I can't—But I have to be going now. The folks at home will be worrying about me."

Grandma rose abruptly and took Scarlett by the arm.

"You two stay here," she commanded, pushing Scarlett toward the back porch. "I have a private word for this child. Help me down the steps, Scarlett."

Young Miss and Sally said good-bye and promised to come calling soon. They were devoured by curiosity as to what Grandma had to say to Scarlett but unless she chose to tell them, they would never know. Old ladies were so difficult, Young Miss whispered to Sally as they went back to their sewing.

Scarlett stood with her hand on the horse's bridle, a dull feeling at her heart.

"Now," said Grandma, peering into her face, "what's wrong at Tara? What are you keeping back?"

Scarlett looked up into the keen old eyes and knew she could tell the truth, without tears. No one could cry in the presence of Grandma Fontaine without her express permission.

"Mother is dead," she said flatly.

The hand on her arm tightened until it pinched and the wrinkled lids over the yellow eyes blinked.

"Did the Yankees kill her?"

"She died of typhoid. Died—the day before I came home."

"Don't think about it," said Grandma sternly and Scarlett saw her swallow. "And your Pa?"

"Pa is—Pa is not himself."

"What do you mean? Speak up. Is he ill?"

"The shock—he is so strange—he is not—"

"Don't tell me he's not himself. Do you mean his mind is unhinged?"

It was a relief to hear the truth put so baldly. How good the old lady was to offer no sympathy that would make her cry.

"Yes," she said dully, "he's lost his mind. He acts dazed and sometimes he can't seem to remember that Mother is dead. Oh, Old Miss, it's more than I can stand to see him sit by the hour, waiting for her and so patiently too, and he used to have no more patience than a child. But it's worse when he does remember that she's gone. Every now and then, after he's sat still with his ear cocked listening for her, he jumps up suddenly and stumps out of the house and down to the burying-ground. And then he comes dragging back with the tears all over his face and he says over and over till I could scream: 'Katie Scarlett, Mrs. O'Hara is dead. Your mother is dead,' and it's just like I was hearing it again for the first time. And sometimes, late at night, I hear him calling her and I get out of bed and go to him and tell him she's down at the quarters with a sick darky. And he fusses because she's always tiring herself out nursing people. And it's so hard to get him back to bed. He's like a child. Oh, I wish Dr. Fontaine was here! I know he could do something for Pa! And Melanie needs a doctor too. She isn't getting over her baby like she should—"

"Melly—a baby? And she's with you?"

"Yes."

"What's Melly doing with you? Why isn't she in Macon with her aunt and her kinfolks? I never thought you liked her any too well, Miss, for all she was Charles' sister. Now, tell me all about it."

"It's a long story, Old Miss. Don't you want to go back in the house and sit down?"

"I can stand," said Grandma shortly. "And if you told your story in front of the others, they'd be bawling and making you feel sorry for yourself. Now, let's have it."

Scarlett began haltingly with the siege and Melanie's condition, but as her story progressed beneath the sharp old eyes which never faltered in their gaze, she found words, words of power and horror. It all came back to her, the sickeningly hot day of the baby's birth, the agony of fear, the flight and Rhett's desertion. She spoke of the wild darkness of the night, the blazing camp-fires which might be friends or foes, the gaunt chimneys which met her gaze in the morning sun, the dead men and horses along the road, the hunger, the desolation, the fear that Tara had been burned.

"I thought if I could just get home to Mother, she could manage everything and I could lay down the weary load. On the way home I thought the worst had already happened to me, but when I knew she was dead I knew what the worst really was."

She dropped her eyes to the ground and waited for Grandma to speak. The silence was so prolonged she wondered if Grandma could have failed to comprehend her desperate plight. Finally the old voice spoke and her tones were kind, kinder than Scarlett had ever heard her use in addressing anyone.

"Child, it's a very bad thing for a woman to face the worst that can happen to her, because after she's faced the worst she can't ever really fear anything again. And it's very bad for a woman not to be afraid of something. You think I don't understand what you've told me—what you've been through? Well, I understand very well. When I was about your age I was in the Creek uprising, right after the Fort Mims massacre—yes," she said in a far-away voice, "just about your age for that was fifty-odd years ago. And I managed to get into the bushes and hide, and I lay there and saw our house burn and I saw the Indians scalp my brothers and sisters. And I could only lie there and pray that the light of the flames wouldn't show up my hiding-place. And they dragged Mother out and killed her about twenty feet from where I was lying. And scalped her too. And every so often one Indian would go back to her and sink his tommyhawk into her skull again. I—I was my mother's pet and I lay there and saw it all. And in the morning I set out for the nearest settlement and it was thirty miles away. It took me three days to get there, through the swamps and the Indians, and afterward they thought I'd lose my mind. . . . That's where I met Dr. Fontaine. He looked after me. . . . Ah, well, that's been fifty years ago, as I said, and since that time I've never been afraid of anything or anybody because I'd known the worst that could happen to me. And that lack of fear has gotten me into a lot of trouble and cost me a lot of happiness. God intended women to be timid frightened creatures and there's something unnatural about a woman who isn't afraid. . . . Scarlett, always save something to fear—even as you save something to love. . . ."

Her voice trailed off and she stood silent with eyes looking back over half a century to the day when she had been afraid. Scarlett moved impatiently. She had thought Grandma was going to understand and perhaps show her some way to solve her problems. But like all old people she'd gotten to talking about things that happened before anyone was born, things no one was interested in. Scarlett wished she had not confided in her.

"Well, go home, child, or they'll be worrying about you," she said suddenly. "Send Pork with the wagon this afternoon. . . . And don't think you can lay down the load, ever. Because you can't. I know."

Indian summer lingered into November that year and the warm days were bright days for those at Tara. The worst was over. They had a horse now and they could ride instead of walk. They had fried eggs for breakfast and fried ham for supper to vary the monotony of the yams, peanuts and dried apples, and on one festal occasion they even had roast chicken. The old sow had finally been captured and she and her brood rooted and grunted happily under the house where they were penned. Sometimes they squealed so loudly no one in the house could talk but it was a pleasant sound. It meant fresh pork for the white folks and chitterlings for the negroes when cold weather and hog-killing time should arrive, and it meant food for the winter for all.

Scarlett's visit to the Fontaines had heartened her more than she realized. Just the knowledge that she had neighbours, that some of the family friends and old homes had survived, drove out the terrible lost and alone feeling which had oppressed her in her first weeks at Tara. And the Fontaines and Tarletons, whose plantations had not been in the path of the army, were most generous in sharing what little they had. It was the tradition of the County that neighbour helped neighbour and they refused to accept a penny from Scarlett, telling her that she would do the same for them and she could pay them back, in kind, next year when Tara was again producing.

Scarlett now had food for her household, she had a horse, she had the money and jewellery taken from the Yankee straggler, and the greatest need was new clothing. She knew it would be risky business sending Pork south to buy clothes, when the horse might be captured by either Yankees or Confederates. But, at least, she had the money with which to buy the clothes, a horse and wagon for the trip, and perhaps Pork could make the trip without getting caught. Yes, the worst was over.

Every morning when Scarlett arose she thanked God for the pale-blue sky and the warm sun, for each day of good weather put off the inevitable time when warm clothing would be needed. And each warm day saw more and more cotton piling up in the empty slave quarters, the only storage place left on the plantation. There was more cotton in the fields than she or Pork had estimated, probably four bales, and soon the cabins would be full.

Scarlett had not intended to do any cotton picking herself, even after Grandma Fontaine's tart remark. It was unthinkable that she, an O'Hara lady, now the mistress of Tara, should work in the fields. It put her on the same level with the snarly-haired Mrs. Slattery and Emmie. She had intended that the negroes should do the field work, while she and the convalescent girls attended to the house, but here she was confronted with a caste feeling even stronger than her own. Pork, Mammy and Prissy set up outcries at the idea of working in the fields. They reiterated that they were house niggers, not field hands. Mammy, in particular, declared vehemently that she had never even been a yard nigger. She had been born in the Robillard great house, not in the quarters, and had been raised in Ole Miss' bedroom, sleeping on a pallet at the foot of the bed. Dilcey alone said nothing and she fixed her Prissy with an unwinking eye that made her squirm.

Scarlett refused to listen to the protests and drove them all into the cotton rows. But Mammy and Pork worked so slowly and with so many lamentations that Scarlett sent Mammy back to the kitchen to cook and Pork to the woods and the river with snares for rabbits and possums and lines for fish. Cotton picking was beneath Pork's dignity but hunting and fishing were not.

Scarlett next had tried her sisters and Melanie in the fields, but that had worked no better. Melanie had picked neatly, quickly and willingly for an hour in the hot sun and then fainted quietly and had to stay in bed for a week. Suellen, sullen and tearful, pretended to faint too, but came back to consciousness spitting like an angry cat when Scarlett poured a gourdful of water in her face. Finally she refused point-blank.

"I won't work in the fields like a darky! You can't make me. What if any of our friends ever heard of it? What if—if Mr. Kennedy ever knew? Oh, if Mother knew about this—"

"You just mention Mother's name once more, Suellen O'Hara, and I'll slap you flat," cried Scarlett. "Mother worked harder than any darky on this place and you know it, Miss Fine Airs!"

"She did not! At least, not in the fields. And you can't make me. I'll tell Papa on you and he won't make me work!"

"Don't you dare go bothering Pa with any of our troubles!" cried Scarlett, distracted between indignation at her sister and fear for Gerald.

"I'll help you, Sissy," interposed Carreen docilely. "I'll work for Sue and me too. She isn't well yet and she shouldn't be out in the sun."

Scarlett said gratefully: "Thank you, Sugarbaby," but looked worriedly at her younger sister. Carreen, who had always been as delicately pink and white as the orchard blossoms that are scattered by the spring wind, was no longer pink but still conveyed in her sweet thoughtful face a blossomlike quality. She had been silent, a little dazed since she came back to consciousness and found Ellen gone, Scarlett a termagant, the world changed and unceasing labour the order of the new day. It was not in Carreen's delicate nature to adjust herself to change. She simply could not comprehend what had happened and she went about Tara like a sleepwalker, doing exactly what she was told. She looked, and was, frail but she was willing, obedient and obliging. When she was not doing Scarlett's bidding, her rosary beads were always in her hands and her lips moving in prayers for her mother and for Brent Tarleton. It did not occur to Scarlett that Carreen had taken Brent's death so seriously and that her grief was unhealed. To Scarlett, Carreen was still "baby sister", far too young to have had a really serious love affair.

Scarlett, standing in the sun in the cotton rows, her back breaking from the eternal bending and her hands roughened by the dry bolls, wished she had a sister who combined Suellen's energy and strength with Carreen's sweet disposition. For Carreen picked diligently and earnestly. But after she had laboured for an hour it was obvious that she, and not Suellen, was the one not yet well enough for such work. So Scarlett sent Carreen back to the house too.

There remained with her now in the long rows only Dilcey and Prissy. Prissy picked lazily, spasmodically, complaining of her feet, her back, her internal miseries, her complete weariness, until her mother took a cotton stalk to her and whipped her until she screamed. After that she worked a little better, taking care to stay far from her mother's reach.

Dilcey worked tirelessly, silently, like a machine, and Scarlett, with her back aching and her shoulder raw from the tugging weight of the cotton-bag she carried, thought that Dilcey was worth her weight in gold.

"Dilcey," she said, "when good times come back, I'm not going to forget how you've acted. You've been mighty good."

The bronze giantess did not grin pleasedly or squirm under praise like the other negroes. She turned an immobile face to Scarlett and said with dignity: "Thankee, Ma'm. But Mist' Gerald and Miss Ellen been good to me. Mist' Gerald buy my Prissy so I wouldn' grieve and I doan forgit it. I is part Indian and Indians doan forgit them as is good to them. I is sorry 'bout my Prissy. She mighty wuthless. Look lak she all nigger lak her pa. Her pa was mighty flighty."

In spite of Scarlett's problem of getting help from the others in the picking and in spite of the weariness of doing the labour herself, her spirits lifted as the cotton slowly made its way from the fields to the cabins. There was something about cotton that was reassuring, steadying. Tara had risen to riches on cotton, even as the whole South had risen, and Scarlett was Southerner enough to believe that both Tara and the South would rise again out of the red fields.

Of course, this little cotton she had gathered was not much but it was something. It would bring a little in Confederate money and that little would help her to save the hoarded greenbacks and gold in the Yankee's wallet until they had to be spent. Next spring she would try to make the Confederate government send back Big Sam and the other field hands they had commandeered, and if the government wouldn't release them, she'd use the Yankee's money to hire field hands from the neighbours. Next spring she would plant and plant. . . . She straightened her tired back and, looking over the browning autumn fields, she saw next year's crop standing sturdy and green, acre upon acre.

Next spring! Perhaps by next spring the war would be over and good times would be back. And whether the Confederacy won or lost, times would be better. Anything was better than the constant danger of raids from both armies. When the war was over, a plantation could earn an honest living. Oh, if the war were only over! Then people could plant crops with some certainty of reaping them!

There was hope now. The war couldn't last forever. She had her little cotton, she had food, she had a horse, she had her small but treasured hoard of money. Yes, the worst was over!

11

ON a noonday in mid-November, they all sat grouped about the dinner table, eating the last of the dessert concocted by Mammy from corn meal and dried huckleberries, sweetened with sorghum. There was a chill in the air, the first chill of the year, and Pork, standing behind Scarlett's chair, rubbed his hands together in glee and questioned: "Ain' it 'bout time fer de hawg-killin', Miss Scarlett?"

"You can taste those chitlins already, can't you?" said Scarlett with a grin. "Well, I can taste fresh pork myself and if the weather holds for a few days more, we'll—"

Melanie interrupted, her spoon at her lips.

"Listen, dear! Somebody's coming!"

"Somebody hollerin'," said Pork uneasily.

On the crisp autumn air came clear the sound of horse's hooves, thudding as swiftly as a frightened heart, and a woman's voice, high pitched, screaming: "Scarlett! Scarlett!"

Eye met eye for a dreadful second around the table before chairs were pushed back and everyone leaped up. Despite the fear that made it shrill, they recognized the voice of Sally Fontaine who, only an hour before, had stopped at Tara for a brief chat on her way to Jonesboro. Now, as they all rushed pell-mell to crowd the front door, they saw her coming up the drive like the wind on a lathered horse, her hair streaming

711

behind her, her bonnet dangling by its ribbons. She did not draw rein but as she galloped madly toward them, she waved her arm back in the direction from which she had come.

"The Yankees are coming! I saw them! Down the road! The Yankees—"

She sawed savagely at the horse's mouth just in time to swerve him from leaping up the front steps. He swung around sharply, covered the side lawn in three leaps and she put him across the four-foot hedge as if she were on the hunting field. They heard the heavy pounding of his hooves as he went through the back yard and down the narrow lane between the cabins of the quarters and knew she was cutting across the fields to Mimosa.

For a moment they stood paralysed and then Suellen and Carreen began to sob and clutch each other's fingers. Little Wade stood rooted, trembling, unable to cry. What he had feared since the night he left Atlanta had happened. The Yankees were coming to get him.

"Yankees?" said Gerald vaguely. "But the Yankees have already been here."

"Mother of God!" cried Scarlett, her eyes meeting Melanie's frightened eyes. For a swift instant there went through her memory again the horrors of her last night in Atlanta, the ruined homes that dotted the countryside, all the stories of rape and torture and murder. She saw again the Yankee soldier standing in the hall with Ellen's sewing-box in his hand. She thought: "I shall die. I shall die right here. I thought we were through with all that. I shall die. I can't stand any more."

Then her eyes fell on the horse saddled and hitched and waiting for Pork to ride him to the Tarleton place on an errand. Her horse! Her only horse! The Yankees would take him and the cow and the calf. And the sow and her litter—Oh, how many tiring hours it had taken to catch that sow and her agile young! And they'd take the rooster and the setting hens and the ducks the Fontaines had given her. And the apples and the yams in the pantry bins. And the flour and rice and dried peas. And the money in the Yankee soldier's wallet. They'd take everything and leave them to starve.

"They shan't have them!" she cried aloud, and they all turned startled faces to her, fearful her mind had cracked under the tidings. "I won't go hungry! They shan't have them!"

"What is it, Scarlett? What is it?"

"The horse! The cow! The pigs! They shan't have them! I won't let them have them!"

She turned swiftly to the four negroes who huddled in the doorway, their black faces a peculiarly ashen shade.

"The swamp," she said rapidly.

"Whut swamp?"

"The river swamp, you fools! Take the pigs to the swamp. All of you. Quickly. Pork, you and Prissy crawl under the house and get the pigs out. Suellen, you and Carreen fill the baskets with as much food as you can carry and get to the woods. Mammy, put the silver in the well again. And Pork! Pork, listen to me, don't stand there like that! Take Pa with you. Don't ask me where! Anywhere! Go with Pork, Pa. That's a sweet Pa."

Even in her frenzy she thought what the sight of bluecoats might do to Gerald's wavering mind. She stopped and wrung her hands and the frightened sobbing of little Wade who was clutching Melanie's skirt added to her panic.

"What shall I do, Scarlett?" Melanie's voice was calm amid the wailing and tears and scurrying feet. Though her face was paper white and her whole body trembled, the very quietness of her voice steadied Scarlett, revealing to her that they all looked to her for commands, for guidance.

"The cow and the calf," she said quickly. "They're in the old pasture. Take the horse and drive them into the swamp and—"

Before she could finish her sentence, Melanie shook off Wade's clutches and was down the front steps and running toward the horse, pulling up her wide skirts as she ran. Scarlett caught a flashing glimpse of thin legs, a flurry of skirts and underclothing, and Melanie was in the saddle, her feet dangling far above the stirrups. She gathered up the reins and clapped her heels against the animal's sides and then abruptly pulled him in, her face twisting with horror.

"My baby!" she cried. "Oh, my baby! The Yankees will kill him! Give him to me!"

Her hand was on the pommel and she was preparing to slide off but Scarlett screamed at her.

"Go on! Go on! Get the cow! I'll look after the baby! Go on, I tell you! Do you think I'd let them get Ashley's baby? Go on!"

Melly looked despairingly backward but hammered her heels into the horse and, with a scattering of gravel, was off down the drive toward the pasture.

Scarlett thought: "I never expected to see Melly Hamilton straddling a horse!" and then she ran into the house. Wade was at her heels, sobbing, trying to catch her flying skirts. As she went up the steps, three at a bound, she saw Suellen and Carreen with split-oak baskets on their arms, running toward the pantry, and Pork tugging none too gently at Gerald's arm, dragging him toward the back porch. Gerald was mumbling querulously and pulling away like a child.

From the back yard she heard Mammy's strident voice: "You, Priss! You git unner dat house an' han' me dem shoats! You knows mighty well Ah's too big ter crawl thoo dem lattices. Dilcey, comyere an' mek dis wuthless chile—"

"And I thought it was such a good idea to keep the pigs under the house, so nobody could steal them," thought Scarlett, running into her room. "Why, oh, why didn't I build a pen for them down in the swamp?"

She tore open her top bureau drawer and scratched about in the clothing until the Yankee's wallet was in her hand. Hastily she picked up the solitaire ring and the diamond earbobs from where she had hidden them in her sewing-basket and shoved them into the wallet. But where to hide it? In the mattress? Up the chimney? Throw it in the well? Put it in her bosom? No, never there! The outlines of the wallet might show through her basque and if the Yankees saw it they would strip her naked and search her.

"I shall die if they do!" she thought wildly.

Downstairs there was a pandemonium of racing feet and sobbing voices. Even in her frenzy, Scarlett wished she had Melanie with her, Melly with her quiet voice, Melly who was so brave the day she shot the Yankee. Melly was worth three of the others. Melly—what had Melly said? Oh, yes, the baby!

Clutching the wallet to her, Scarlett ran across the hall to the room where little Beau was sleeping in the low cradle. She snatched him up into her arms and he awoke, waving small fists and slobbering sleepily.

She heard Suellen crying: "Come on, Carreen! Come on! We've got enough. Oh, Sister, hurry!" There were wild squealings, indignant gruntings in the back yard and, running to the window, Scarlett saw Mammy waddling hurriedly across the cotton field with a struggling young pig under each arm. Behind her was Pork also carrying two pigs and pushing Gerald before him. Gerald was stumping across the furrows, waving his cane.

Leaning out of the window Scarlett yelled: "Get the sow, Dilcey! Make Prissy drive her out. You can chase her across the fields."

Dilcey looked up, her bronzed face harassed. In her apron was a pile of silver tableware. She pointed under the house.

"The sow done bit Prissy and got her penned up unner the house."

"Good for the sow," thought Scarlett. She hurried back into her room and hastily gathered from their hiding-place the bracelets, brooch, miniature and cup she had found on the dead

Yankee. But where to hide them? It was awkward, carrying little Beau in one arm and the wallet and the trinkets in the other. She started to lay him on the bed.

He set up a wail at leaving her arms and a welcome thought came to her. What better hiding-place could there be than a baby's diaper? She quickly turned him over, pulled up his dress and thrust the wallet down the diaper next to his backside. He yelled louder at this treatment and she hastily tightened the triangular garment about his thrashing legs.

"Now," she thought, drawing a deep breath, "now for the swamp!"

Tucking him screaming under one arm and clutching the jewellery to her with the other, she raced into the upstairs hall. Suddenly her rapid steps paused, fright weakening her knees. How silent the house was! How dreadfully still! Had they all gone off and left her? Hadn't anyone waited for her? She hadn't meant for them to leave her here alone. These days anything could happen to a lone woman and with the Yankees coming—

She jumped as a slight noise sounded and, turning quickly, saw crouched by the banisters her forgotten son, his eyes enormous with terror. He tried to speak but his throat only worked silently.

"Get up, Wade Hampton," she commanded swiftly. "Get up and walk. Mother can't carry you now."

He ran to her, like a small frightened animal, and clutching her wide skirt, buried his face in it. She could feel his small hands groping through the folds for her legs. She started down the stairs, each step hampered by Wade's dragging hands, and she said fiercely: "Turn me loose, Wade! Turn me loose and walk!" But the child only clung the closer.

As she reached the landing, the whole lower floor leaped up at her. All the homely, well-loved articles of furniture seemed to whisper: "Good-bye! Good-bye!" A sob rose in her throat. There was the open door of the office where Ellen had laboured so diligently and she could glimpse a corner of the old secretary. There was the dining-room, with chairs pushed awry and food still on the plates. There on the floor were the rag rugs Ellen had dyed and woven herself. And there was the old portrait of Grandma Robillard, with bosoms half bared, hair piled high and nostrils cut so deeply as to give her face a perpetual well-bred sneer. Everything which had been part of her earliest memories, everything bound up with the deepest roots in her: "Good-bye! Good-bye, Scarlett O'Hara!"

The Yankees would burn it all—all!

This was her last view of home, her last view except what she might see from the cover of the woods or the swamp, the tall chimneys wrapped in smoke, the roof crashing in flame.

"I can't leave you," she thought, and her teeth chattered with fear. "I can't leave you. Pa wouldn't leave you. He told them they'd have to burn you over his head. Then, they'll burn you over my head for I can't leave you either. You're all I've got left."

With the decision, some of her fear fell away and there remained only a congealed feeling in her breast, as if all hope and fear had frozen. As she stood there, she heard from the avenue the sound of many horses' feet, the jingle of bridle-bits and sabres rattling in scabbards and a harsh voice crying a command: "Dismount!" Swiftly she bent to the child beside her and her voice was urgent but oddly gentle.

"Turn me loose, Wade, honey! You run down the stairs quick and through the back yard toward the swamp. Mammy will be there and Aunt Melly. Run quickly, darling, and don't be afraid."

At the change in her tone, the boy looked up and Scarlett was appalled at the look in his eyes, like a baby rabbit in a trap.

"Oh, Mother of God!" she prayed. "Don't let him have a convulsion! Not—not before the Yankees. They mustn't know we are afraid." And, as the child only gripped her skirt the tighter, she said clearly: "Be a little man, Wade. They're only a passel of damn Yankees!"

And she went down the steps to meet them.

Sherman was marching through Georgia, from Atlanta to the sea. Behind him lay the smoking ruins of Atlanta to which the torch had been set as the blue army tramped out. Before him lay three hundred miles of territory virtually un-defended save by a few state militia and the old men and young boys of the Home Guard.

Here lay the fertile state, dotted with plan-tations, sheltering the women and children, the very old and the negroes. In a swath eighty miles wide the Yankees were looting and burning. There were hundreds of homes in flames, hundreds of homes resounding with their footsteps. But, to Scarlett, watching the bluecoats pour into the front hall, it was not a country-wide affair. It was entirely personal, a malicious action aimed directly at her and hers.

She stood at the foot of the stairs, the baby in her arms, Wade pressed tightly against her, his head hidden in her skirts as the Yankees swarmed through the house, pushing roughly past her up the stairs, dragging furniture on to the front porch, running bayonets and knives into upholstery and digging inside for concealed valuables. Upstairs they were ripping open mattresses and feather beds until the air in the hall was thick with feathers that floated softly down on her head. Impotent rage quelled what little fear was left in her heart as she stood helpless while they plundered and stole and ruined.

The sergeant in charge was a bow-legged, grizzled little man with a large wad of tobacco in his cheek. He reached Scarlett before any of his men and, spitting freely on the floor and her skirts, said briefly:

"Lemme have what you got in yore hand, lady."

She had forgotten the trinkets she had intended to hide and, with a sneer which she hoped was as eloquent as that pictured on Grandma Robillard's face, she flung the articles to the floor and almost enjoyed the rapacious scramble that ensued.

"I'll trouble you for thet ring and them earbobs."

Scarlett tucked the baby more securely under her arm so that he hung face downward, crimson and screaming, and removed the garnet earrings which had been Gerald's wedding present to Ellen. Then she stripped off the large sapphire solitaire which Charles had given her as an engagement ring.

"Don't throw um. Hand um to me," said the sergeant, putting out his hands. "Them bastards got enough already. What else have you got?" His eyes went over her basque sharply.

For a moment Scarlett went faint, already feeling rough hands thrusting themselves into her bosom, fumbling at her garters.

"That is all, but I suppose it is customary to strip your victims?"

"Oh, I'll take your word," said the sergeant good-naturedly, spitting again as he turned away. Scarlett righted the baby and tried to soothe him, holding her hand over the place on the diaper where the wallet was hidden, thanking God that Melanie had a baby and that baby had a diaper.

Upstairs she could hear heavy boots trampling, the protesting screech of furniture pulled across the floor, the crashing of china and mirrors, the curses when nothing of value appeared. From the yard came loud cries: "Head um off! Don't let um get away!" and the despairing squawks of the hens and quacking and honking of the ducks and geese. A pang went through her as she heard an agonized squealing which was suddenly stilled by a pistol shot and she knew that the sow was dead.

Damn Prissy! She had run off and left her. If only the shoats were safe! If only the family had gotten safely to the swamp! But there was no way of knowing.

She stood quietly in the hall while the soldiers boiled about her, shouting and cursing. Wade's fingers were in her skirt in a terrified grip. She could feel his body shaking as he pressed against her but she could not bring herself to speak reassuringly to him. She could not bring herself to utter any word to the Yankees, either of pleading, protest or anger. She could only thank God that her knees still had the strength to support her, that her neck was still strong enough to hold her head high. But when a squad of bearded men came lumbering down the steps, laden with an assortment of stolen articles and she saw Charles' sword in the hands of one, she did cry out.

That sword was Wade's. It had been his father's and his grandfather's sword and Scarlett had given it to the little boy on his last birthday. They had made quite a ceremony of it and Melanie had cried, cried with tears of pride and sorrowful memory, and kissed him and said he must grow up to be a brave soldier like his father and his grandfather. Wade was very proud of it and often climbed upon the table beneath where it hung to pat it. Scarlett could endure seeing her own possessions going out of the house in hateful alien hands but not this—not her little boy's pride. Wade, peering from the protection of her skirts at the sound of her cry, found speech and courage in a mighty sob. Stretching out one hand he cried:

"Mine!"

"You can't take that!" said Scarlett swiftly, holding out her hand too.

"I can't, hey?" said the little soldier who held it, grinning impudently at her. "Well, I can! It's a Rebel sword!"

"It's—it's not. It's a Mexican War sword. You can't take it. It's my little boy's. It was his grandfather's! Oh, Captain," she cried, turning to the sergeant, "please make him give it to me!"

The sergeant, pleased at his promotion, stepped forward.

"Lemme see thet sword, Bub," he said.

Reluctantly, the little trooper handed it to him. "It's got a solid-gold hilt," he said.

The sergeant turned it in his hand, held the hilt up to the sunlight to read the engraved inscription.

"'To Colonel William R. Hamilton'," he deciphered. "'From His Staff. For Gallantry. Buena Vista. 1847.'"

"Ho, lady," he said, "I was at Buena Vista myself."

"Indeed," said Scarlett icily.

"Was I? Thet was hot fightin', lemme tell you. I ain't seen such hot fightin' in this war as we seen in thet one. So this sword was this little tyke's granddaddy's?"

"Yes."

"Well, he can have it," said the sergeant, who was satisfied enough with the jewellery and trinkets tied up in his handkerchief.

"But it's got a solid-gold hilt," insisted the little trooper.

"We'll leave her thet to remember us by," grinned the sergeant.

Scarlett took the sword, not even saying "Thank you". Why should she thank these thieves for returning her own property to her? She held the sword against her while the little cavalryman argued and wrangled with the sergeant.

"By God, I'll give these damn Rebels something to remember me by," shouted the private finally when the sergeant, losing his good-nature, told him to go to hell and not talk back. The little man went charging toward the back of the house and Scarlett breathed more easily. They had said nothing about burning the house. They hadn't told her to leave so they could fire it. Perhaps—perhaps—The men came rambling into the hall from the upstairs and the out of doors.

"Anything?" questioned the sergeant.

"One hog and a few chickens and ducks."

"Some corn and a few yams and beans. That wildcat we saw on the horse must have given the alarm, all right."

"Regular Paul Revere, eh?"

"Well, there ain't much here, Sarge. You got the pickin's. Let's move on before the whole country gets the news we're comin'."

"Didja dig under the smokehouse? They generally buries things there."

"Ain't no smokehouse."

"Didja dig in the nigger cabins?"

"Nothin' but cotton in the cabins. We set fire to it."

For a brief instant Scarlett saw the long hot

days in the cotton field, felt again the terrible ache in her back, the raw bruised flesh of her shoulders. All for nothing. The cotton was gone.

"You ain't got much, for a fac', have you, lady?"

"Your army has been here before," she said coolly.

"That's a fac'. We were in this neighbourhood in September," said one of the men, turning something in his hand. "I'd forgot."

Scarlett saw it was Ellen's gold thimble that he held. How often she had seen it gleaming in and out of Ellen's fancy work! The sight of it brought back too many hurting memories of the slender hand which had worn it. There it lay in this stranger's calloused dirty palm and soon it would find its way North and on to the finger of some Yankee woman who would be proud to wear stolen things. Ellen's thimble!

Scarlett dropped her head so the enemy could not see her cry and the tears fell slowly down on the baby's head. Through the blur, she saw the men moving toward the doorway, heard the sergeant calling commands in a loud rough voice. They were going and Tara was safe, but with the pain of Ellen's memory on her, she was hardly glad. The sound of the banging sabres and horses' hooves brought little relief and she stood, suddenly weak and nerveless, as they moved off down the avenue, every man laden with stolen goods, clothing, blankets, pictures, hens and ducks, the sow.

Then to her nostrils was borne the smell of smoke and she turned, too weak with lessening strain to care about the cotton. Through the open windows of the dining-room, she saw smoke drifting lazily out of the negro cabins. There went the cotton. There went the tax money and part of the money which was to see them through this bitter winter. There was nothing she could do about it either, except watch. She had seen fires in cotton before and she knew how difficult they were to put out, even with many men labouring at it. Thank God, the quarters were so far from the house! Thank God, there was no wind to-day to carry sparks to the roof of Tara!

Suddenly she swung about, rigid as a pointer, and stared with horror-struck eyes down the hall, down the covered passageway toward the kitchen. There was smoke coming from the kitchen!

Somewhere between the hall and the kitchen, she laid the baby down. Somewhere she flung off Wade's grip, slinging him against the wall. She burst into the smoke-filled kitchen and reeled back, coughing, her eyes streaming tears from the smoke. Again she plunged in, her skirt held over her nose.

The room was dark, lit as it was by one small window, and so thick with smoke that she was blinded, but she could hear the hiss and crackle of flames. Dashing a hand across her eyes, she peered squinting and saw thin lines of flame creeping across the kitchen floor, toward the walls. Someone had scattered the blazing logs in the open fireplace across the whole room and the tinder-dry pine floor was sucking in the flames and spewing them up like water.

Back she rushed to the dining-room and

snatched a rag rug from the floor, spilling two chairs with a crash.

"I'll never beat it out—never, never! Oh, God, if only there was someone to help! Tara is gone —gone! Oh, God! This was what that little wretch meant when he said he'd give me something to remember him by! Oh, if I'd only let him have the sword!"

In the hallway she passed her son lying in the corner with his sword. His eyes were closed and his face had a look of slack, unearthly peace.

"My God! He's dead! They've frightened him to death!" she thought in agony, but she raced by him to the bucket of drinking water which always stood in the passageway by the kitchen door.

She soused the end of the rug into the bucket and drawing a deep breath plunged again into the smoke-filled room, slamming the door behind her. For an eternity she reeled and coughed, beating the rug against the lines of fire that shot swiftly beyond her. Twice her long skirt took fire and she slapped it out with her hands. She could smell the sickening smell of her hair scorching, as it came loose from its pins and swept about her shoulders. The flames raced ever beyond her, toward the walls of the covered runway, fiery snakes that writhed and leaped and, exhaustion sweeping her, she knew that it was hopeless.

Then the door swung open and the sucking draught flung the flames higher. It closed with a bang and, in the swirling smoke, Scarlett, half blind, saw Melanie, stamping her feet on the flames, beating at them with something dark and heavy. She saw her staggering, heard her coughing, caught a lightning-flash glimpse of her set white face and eyes narrowed to slits against the smoke, saw her small body curving back and forth as she swung her rug up and down. For another eternity they fought and swayed, side by side, and Scarlett could see that the lines of fire were shortening. Then suddenly Melanie turned toward her and, with a cry, hit her across the shoulders with all her might. Scarlett went down in a whirlwind of smoke and darkness.

When she opened her eyes she was lying on the back porch, her head pillowed comfortably on Melanie's lap, and the afternoon sunlight was shining on her face. Her hands, face and shoulders smarted intolerably from burns. Smoke was still rolling from the quarters, enveloping the cabins in thick clouds, and the smell of burning cotton was strong. Scarlett saw wisps of smoke drifting from the kitchen and she stirred frantically to rise.

But she was pushed back as Melanie's calm voice said: "Lie still, dear. The fire's out."

She lay quiet for a moment, eyes closed, sighing with relief, and heard the slobbery gurgle of the baby near by and the reassuring sound of Wade's hiccoughing. So he wasn't dead, thank God! She opened her eyes and looked up into Melanie's face. Her curls were singed, her face black with smut, but her eyes were sparkling with excitement and she was smiling.

"You look like a nigger," murmured Scarlett, burrowing her head wearily into its soft pillow.

"And you look like the end man in a minstrel show," replied Melanie equably.

"Why did you have to hit me?"

"Because, my darling, your back was on fire. I didn't dream you'd faint, though the Lord knows you've had enough to-day to kill you. . . . I came back as soon as I got the stock safe in the woods. I nearly died, thinking about you and the baby alone. Did—the Yankees harm you?"

"If you mean did they rape me, no," said Scarlett, groaning as she tried to sit up. Though Melanie's lap was soft, the porch on which she was lying was far from comfortable. "But they've stolen everything, everything. We've lost everything—Well, what is there to look so happy about?"

"We haven't lost each other and our babies are all right and we have a roof over our heads," said Melanie, and there was a lilt in her voice. "And that's all anyone can hope for now. . . . Goodness, but Beau is wet! I suppose the Yankees even stole his extra diapers. He—Scarlett, what on earth is in his diaper?"

She thrust a suddenly frightened hand down the baby's back and brought up the wallet. For a moment she looked at it as if she had never seen it before and then she began to laugh, peal on peal of mirth that had in it no hint of hysteria.

"Nobody but you would ever have thought of it," she cried, and flinging her arms around Scarlett's neck she kissed her. "You are the beatenest sister I ever had!"

Scarlett permitted the embrace because she was too tired to struggle, because the words of praise brought balm to her spirit and because, in the dark smoke-filled kitchen, there had been born a greater respect for her sister-in-law, a closer feeling of comradeship.

"I'll say this for her," she thought grudgingly, "she's always there when you need her."

12

COLD weather set in abruptly with a killing frost. Chilling winds swept beneath the door-sills and rattled the loose window-panes with a monotonous tinkling sound. The last of the leaves fell from the bare trees and only the pines stood clothed, black and cold against pale skies. The rutted red roads were frozen to flintiness and hunger rode the winds through Georgia.

Scarlett recalled bitterly her conversation with Grandma Fontaine. On that afternoon two months ago, which now seemed years in the past, she had told the old lady she had already known the worst which could possibly happen to her, and she had spoken from the bottom of her heart. Now that remark sounded like schoolgirl hyperbole. Before Sherman's men came through Tara the second time, she had her small riches of food and money, she had neighbours more fortunate than she and she had the cotton which would tide her over until spring. Now the cotton was gone, the food was gone, the money was of no use to her, for there was no food to buy with it, and the neighbours were in worse plight than she. At least, she had the cow and the calf, a few shoats and the horse, and the neighbours had nothing but the little they had been able to hide in the woods and bury in the ground.

Fairhill, the Tarleton home, was burned to the foundations, and Mrs. Tarleton and the four girls were existing in the overseer's house. The Munroe house near Lovejoy was levelled too. The wooden wing of Mimosa had burned and only the thick resistant stucco of the main house and the frenzied work of the Fontaine women and their slaves with wet blankets and quilts had saved it. The Calverts' house had again been spared, due to the intercession of Hilton, the Yankee overseer, but there was not a head of livestock, not a fowl, not an ear of corn left on the place.

At Tara and throughout the County, the problem was food. Most of the families had nothing at all but the remains of their yam crops and their peanuts and such game as they could catch in the woods. What they had, each shared with less fortunate friends, as they had done in more prosperous days. But the time soon came when there was nothing to share.

At Tara, they ate rabbit and possum and catfish, if Pork was lucky. On other days a small amount of milk, hickory nuts, roasted acorns and yams. They were always hungry. To Scarlett it seemed that at every turn she met outstretched hands, pleading eyes. The sight of them drove her almost to madness, for she was as hungry as they.

She ordered the calf killed, because he drank so much of the precious milk, and that night everyone ate so much fresh veal all of them were ill. She knew that she should kill one of the shoats but she put it off from day to day, hoping to raise them to maturity. They were so small. There would be so little of them to eat if they were killed now and so much more if they could be saved a little longer. Nightly she debated with Melanie the advisability of sending Pork abroad on the horse with some greenbacks to try to buy food. But the fear that the horse might be captured and the money taken from Pork deterred them. They did not know where the Yankees were. They might be a thousand miles away or only across the river. Once, Scarlett, in desperation, started to ride out herself to search for food, but the hysterical outbursts of the whole family fearful of the Yankees made her abandon the plan.

Pork foraged far, at times not coming home all night, and Scarlett did not ask him where he went. Sometimes he returned with game, sometimes with a few ears of corn, a bag of dried peas. Once he brought home a rooster which he said he found in the woods. The family ate it with relish but a sense of guilt, knowing very well Pork had stolen it, as he had stolen the peas and corn. One night soon after this, he tapped on Scarlett's door long after the house was asleep and sheepishly exhibited a leg peppered with small shot. As she bandaged it for him, he explained awkwardly that when attempting to get into a hen-coop at Fayetteville, he had been discovered. Scarlett did not ask whose hen-coop but patted Pork's shoulder gently, tears in her eyes. Negroes were provoking sometimes and stupid and lazy, but there was loyalty in them that money couldn't buy, a feeling of oneness with their white folks which made them risk their lives to keep food on the table.

In other days Pork's pilferings would have been a serious matter, probably calling for a whipping. In other days she would have been forced at least to reprimand him severely. "Always remember, dear," Ellen had said, "you are responsible for the moral as well as the physical welfare of the darkies God has entrusted to your care. You must realize that they are like children and must be guarded from themselves like children, and you must always set them a good example."

But now, Scarlett pushed that admonition into the back of her mind. That she was encouraging theft, and perhaps theft from people worse off than she, was no longer a matter for conscience. In fact the morals of the affair weighed lightly upon her. Instead of punishment or reproof, she only regretted he had been shot.

"You must be more careful, Pork. We don't want to lose you. What would we do without you? You've been mighty good and faithful and when we get some money again, I'm going to buy you a big gold watch and engrave on it something out of the Bible, 'Well done, good and faithful servant.'"

Pork beamed under the praise and gingerly rubbed his bandaged leg.

"Dat soun' mighty fine, Miss Scarlett. W'en you speckin' ter git dat money?"

"I don't know, Pork, but I'm going to get it some time, somehow." She bent on him an unseeing glance that was so passionately bitter he stirred uneasily. "Some day, when this war is over, I'm going to have lots of money, and when I do I'll never be hungry or cold again. None of us will ever be hungry or cold. We'll all wear fine clothes and have fried chicken every day and—"

Then she stopped. The strictest rule at Tara, one which she herself had made and which she rigidly enforced, was that no one should ever talk of the fine meals they had eaten in the past or what they would eat now, if they had the opportunity.

Pork slipped from the room as she remained staring moodily into the distance. In the old days, now dead and gone, life had been so complex, so full of intricate and complicated problems. There had been the problem of trying to win Ashley's love and trying to keep a dozen other beaux dangling and unhappy. There had been small breaches of conduct to be concealed from her elders, jealous girls to be flouted or placated, styles of dresses and materials to be chosen, different coiffures to be tried and, oh, so many, many other matters to be decided! Now life was so amazingly simple. Now all that mattered was food enough to keep off starvation, clothing enough to prevent freezing and a roof overhead which did not leak too much.

It was during these days that Scarlett dreamed and dreamed again the nightmare which was to haunt her for years. It was always the same dream, the details never varied, but the terror of it mounted each time it came to her and the fear of experiencing it again troubled even her waking hours. She remembered so well the incidents of the day when she had first dreamed it.

Cold rain had fallen for days and the house was chill with draughts and dampness. The logs in the fireplace were wet and smoky and gave little heat. There had been nothing to eat except milk since breakfast, for the yams were exhausted and Pork's snares and fishlines had yielded nothing. One of the shoats would have to be killed the next day if they were to eat at all. Strained and hungry faces, black and white, were staring at her, mutely asking her to provide food. She would have to risk losing the horse and send Pork out to buy something. And to make matters worse, Wade was ill with a sore throat and a raging fever and there was neither doctor nor medicine for him.

Hungry, weary with watching her child, Scarlett left him to Melanie's care for a while and lay down on her bed to nap. Her feet icy, she twisted and turned, unable to sleep, weighed down with fear and despair. Again and again, she thought: "What shall I do? Where shall I turn? Isn't there anybody in the world who can help me?" Where had all the security of the world gone? Why wasn't there someone, some strong wise person, to take the burdens from her? She wasn't made to carry them. She did not know how to carry them. And then she fell into an uneasy doze.

She was in a wild strange country so thick with swirling mist she could not see her hand before her face. The earth beneath her feet was uneasy. It was a haunted land, still with a terrible stillness, and she was lost in it, lost and terrified as a child in the night. She was bitterly cold and hungry and so fearful of what lurked in the mists about her that she tried to scream and could not.

There were things in the fog reaching out fingers to pluck at her skirt, to drag her down into the uneasy quaking earth on which she stood, silent, relentless, spectral hands. Then, she knew that somewhere in the opaque gloom about her there was shelter, help, a haven of refuge and warmth. But where was it? Could she reach it before the hands clutched her and dragged her down into the quicksands?

Suddenly she was running, running through the mist like a mad thing, crying and screaming, throwing out her arms to clutch only empty air and wet mist. Where was the haven? It eluded her but it was there, hidden, somewhere. If she could only reach it! If she could only reach it she would be safe! But terror was weakening her legs, hunger making her faint. She gave one despairing cry and awoke to find Melanie's worried face above her and Melanie's hand shaking her to wakefulness.

The dream returned again and again, whenever she went to sleep with an empty stomach. And that was frequently enough. It so frightened her that she feared to sleep, although she feverishly told herself there was nothing in such a dream to be afraid of. There was nothing in a dream about fog to scare her so. Nothing at all—yet the thought of dropping off into that mist-filled country so terrified her she began sleeping with Melanie, who would wake her up when her moaning and twitching revealed that she was again in the clutch of the dream.

Under the strain she grew white and thin. The pretty roundness left her face, throwing her

737

cheek-bones into prominence, emphasizing her slanting green eyes and giving her the look of a prowling, hungry cat.

"Daytime is enough like a nightmare without my dreaming things," she thought desperately, and began hoarding her daily ration to eat it just before she went to sleep.

At Christmas time Frank Kennedy and a small troop from the commissary department jogged up to Tara on a futile hunt for grain and animals for the army. They were a ragged and ruffianly-appearing crew, mounted on lame and heaving horses which obviously were in too bad condition to be used for more active service. Like their animals the men had been invalided out of the front-line forces and, except for Frank, all of them had an arm missing or an eye gone or stiffened joints. Most of them wore blue overcoats of captured Yankees and, for a brief instant of horror, those at Tara thought Sherman's men had returned.

They stayed the night on the plantation, sleeping on the floor in the parlour, luxuriating as they stretched themselves on the velvet rug, for it had been weeks since they had slept under a roof or on anything softer than pine needles and hard earth. For all their dirty beards and tatters they were a well-bred crowd, full of pleasant small talk, jokes and compliments, and very glad to be spending Christmas Eve in a big house, surrounded by pretty women, as they had been accustomed to do in days long past. They refused to be serious about the war, told outrageous lies to make the girls laugh and brought to the bare and looted house the first lightness, the first hint of festivity it had known in many a day.

"It's almost like the old days when we had house parties, isn't it?" whispered Suellen happily to Scarlett. Suellen was raised to the skies by having a beau of her own in the house again and she could hardly take her eyes off Frank Kennedy. Scarlett was surprised to see that Suellen could be almost pretty, despite the thinness which had persisted since her illness. Her cheeks were flushed and there was a soft luminous look in her eyes.

"She really must care about him," thought Scarlett in contempt. "And I guess she'd be almost human if she ever had a husband of her own, even if her husband was old fuss-budget Frank."

Carreen had brightened a little too, and some of the sleep-walking look left her eyes that night. She had found that one of the men had known Brent Tarleton and had been with him the day he was killed, and she promised herself a long private talk with him after supper.

At supper Melanie surprised them all by forcing herself out of her timidity and being almost vivacious. She laughed and joked and almost but not quite coquetted with a one-eyed soldier who gladly repaid her efforts with extravagant gallantries. Scarlett knew the effort this involved both mentally and physically, for Melanie suffered torments of shyness in the presence of anything male. Moreover she was far from well. She insisted she was strong and did more work even than Dilcey, but Scarlett knew she was sick. When she lifted things her face went white and she had a way of sitting down suddenly after exertions, as if her legs would no longer support her. But to-night she, like Suellen and Carreen, was doing everything possible to make the soldiers enjoy their Christmas Eve. Scarlett alone took no pleasure in the guests.

The troop had added their ration of parched corn and side meat to the supper of dried peas, stewed dried apples and peanuts which Mammy set before them and they declared it was the best meal they had had in months. Scarlett watched them eat and she was uneasy. She not only begrudged them every mouthful they ate but she was on tenterhooks lest they discover somehow that Pork had slaughtered one of the shoats the day before. It now hung in the pantry and she had grimly promised her household that she would scratch out the eyes of anyone who mentioned the shoat to their guests or the presence of the dead pig's sisters and brothers, safe in their pen in the swamp. These hungry men could devour the whole shoat at one meal, and if they knew of the live hogs, they could commandeer them for the army. She was alarmed, too, for the cow and the horse and wished they were hidden in the swamp, instead of tied in the woods at the bottom of the pasture. If the commissary took her stock, Tara could not possibly live through the winter. There would be no way of replacing them. As to what the army would eat, she did not care. Let the army feed the army—

if it could. It was hard enough for her to feed her own.

The men added as dessert some "ramrod rolls" from their knapsacks, and this was the first time Scarlett had ever seen this Confederate article of diet about which there were almost as many jokes as about lice. They were charred spirals of what appeared to be wood. The men dared her to take a bite and, when she did, she discovered that beneath the smoke-blackened surface was un-salted corn bread. The soldiers mixed their ration of corn meal with water, and salt too when they could get it, wrapped the thick paste about their ramrods and roasted the mess over camp-fires. It was as hard as rock candy and as tasteless as sawdust, and after one bite Scarlett hastily handed it back amid roars of laughter. She met Melanie's eyes and the same thought was plain in both faces. . . . "How can they go on fighting if they have only this stuff to eat?"

The meal was gay enough and even Gerald, presiding absently at the head of the table, managed to evoke from the back of his dim mind some of the manner of a host and an uncertain smile. The men talked, the women smiled and flattered—but Scarlett, turning suddenly to Frank Kennedy to ask him news of Miss Pittypat, caught an expression on his face which made her forget what she intended to say.

His eyes had left Suellen's and were wandering about the room, to Gerald's childlike puzzled eyes, to the floor, bare of rugs, to the mantelpiece denuded of its ornaments, the sagging springs and torn upholstery into which Yankee bayonets had ripped, the cracked mirror above the sideboard, the unfaded squares on the wall where pictures had hung before the looters came, the scant table service, the decently mended but old dresses of the girls, the flour-sack which had been made into a kilt for Wade.

Frank was remembering the Tara he had known before the war and on his face was a hurt look, a look of tired impotent anger. He loved Suellen, liked her sisters, respected Gerald and had a genuine fondness for the plantation. Since Sherman had swept through Georgia, Frank had seen many appalling sights as he rode about the state trying to collect supplies, but nothing had gone to his heart as Tara did now. He wanted to do something for the O'Haras, especially Suellen, and there was nothing he could do. He was unconsciously wagging his whiskered head in pity and clicking his tongue against his teeth when Scarlett caught his eye. He saw the flame of indignant pride in hers and he dropped his gaze quickly to his plate in embarrassment.

The girls were hungry for news. There had been no mail service since Atlanta fell, now four months past, and they were in complete ignorance as to where the Yankees were, how the Confederate Army was faring, what had happened to Atlanta and to old friends. Frank, whose work took him all over the section, was as good as a newspaper, better even, for he was kin to or knew almost everyone from Macon north to Atlanta, and he could supply bits of interesting personal gossip which the papers always omitted. To cover his embarrassment at being caught by Scarlett, he plunged hastily into a recital of news. The Confederates, he told them, had retaken Atlanta after Sherman marched out, but it was a valueless prize as Sherman had burned it completely.

"But I thought Atlanta burned the night I left," cried Scarlett, bewildered. "I thought our boys burned it!"

"Oh, no, Miss Scarlett!" cried Frank, shocked. "We'd never burn one of our own towns with our own folks in it! What you saw burning was the warehouses and the supplies we didn't want the Yankees to capture and the foundries and the ammunition. But that was all. When Sherman took the town the houses and stores were standing there as pretty as you please. And he quartered his men in them."

"But what happened to the people? Did he—did he kill them?"

"He killed some—but not with bullets," said the one-eyed soldier grimly. "Soon's he marched into Atlanta he told the mayor that all the people in town would have to move out, every living soul. And there were plenty of old folks that couldn't stand the trip and sick folks that ought not to have been moved and ladies who were—well, ladies who hadn't ought to be moved either. And he moved them out in the biggest rainstorm you ever saw, hundreds and hundreds of them, and dumped them in the woods near Rough and Ready and sent word to General Hood to come and get them. And a plenty of the folks died of pneumonia and not being able to stand that sort of treatment."

"Oh, but why did he do that? They couldn't have done him any harm," cried Melanie.

"He said he wanted the town to rest his men and horses in," said Frank. "And he rested them there till the middle of November and then he lit out. And he set fire to the whole town when he left and burned everything."

"Oh, surely not everything!" cried the girls in dismay.

It was inconceivable that the bustling town they knew, so full of people, so crowded with soldiers, was gone. All the lovely homes beneath shady trees, all the big stores and the fine hotels—surely they couldn't be gone! Melanie seemed ready to burst into tears, for she had been born there and knew no other home. Scarlett's heart sank because she had come to love the place second only to Tara.

"Well, almost everything," Frank amended hastily, disturbed by the expressions on their faces. He tried to look cheerful, for he did not believe in upsetting ladies. Upset ladies always upset him and made him feel helpless. He could not bring himself to tell them the worst. Let them find out from someone else.

He could not tell them what the army saw when it marched back into Atlanta: the acres and acres of chimneys standing blackly above ashes, piles of half-burned rubbish and tumbled heaps of brick clogging the streets, old trees dying from fire, their charred limbs tumbling to the ground in the cold wind. He remembered how the sight had turned him sick, remembered the bitter curses of the Confederates when they saw the remains of the town. He hoped the ladies would never hear of the horrors of the looted cemetery, for they'd never get over that. Charlie Hamilton and Melanie's mother and father were buried there. The sight of that cemetery still gave Frank nightmares. Hoping to find jewellery buried with the dead, the Yankee soldiers had broken open vaults, dug up graves. They had robbed the bodies, stripped from the coffins gold and silver name-plates, silver trimmings and silver handles. The skeletons and corpses, flung helter-skelter among their splintered caskets, lay exposed and so pitiful.

And Frank couldn't tell them about the dogs and the cats. Ladies set such a store by pets. But the thousands of starving animals, left homeless when their masters had been so rudely evacuated, had shocked him almost as much as the cemetery, for Frank loved cats and dogs. The animals had been frightened, cold, ravenous, wild as forest creatures, the strong attacking the weak, the weak waiting for the weaker to die so they could eat them. And, above the ruined town, the buzzards splotched the wintry sky with graceful, sinister bodies.

Frank cast about in his mind for some mitigating information that would make the ladies feel better.

"There's some houses still standing," he said, "houses that set on big lots away from other houses and didn't catch fire. And the churches and the Masonic hall are left. And a few stores too. But the business section and all along the railroad tracks and at Five Points—well, ladies, that part of town is flat on the ground."

"Then," cried Scarlett bitterly, "that warehouse Charlie left me, down on the tracks, it's gone too?"

"If it was near the tracks, it's gone, but—" Suddenly he smiled. Why hadn't he thought of it before? "Cheer up, ladies! Your Aunt Pitty's house is still standing. It's kind of damaged but there it is."

"Oh, how did it escape?"

"Well, it's made of brick and it's got about the only slate roof in Atlanta and that kept the sparks from setting it afire, I guess. And then it's about the last house on the north end of town and the fire wasn't so bad over that way. Of course, the Yankees quartered there tore it up aplenty. They even burned the baseboard and the mahogany stair-rail for firewood, but shucks! It's in good shape. When I saw Miss Pitty last week in Macon—"

"You saw her? How is she?"

"Just fine. Just fine. When I told her her house was still standing, she made up her mind to come home right away. That is—if that old darky, Peter, will let her come. Lots of the Atlanta people have already come back, because they got nervous about Macon. Sherman didn't take Macon but everybody is afraid Wilson's raiders will get there soon and he's worse than Sherman."

"But how silly of them to come back if there aren't any houses! Where do they live?"

"Miss Scarlett, they're living in tents and shacks and log cabins and doubling up six and seven families in the few houses still standing. And they're trying to rebuild. Now, Miss Scarlett, don't say they are silly. You know Atlanta folks as well as I do. They are plumb set on that town, most as bad as Charlestonians are about Charleston, and it'll take more than Yankees and a burning to keep them away. Atlanta folks are—begging your pardon, Miss Melly—as stubborn as mules about Atlanta. I don't know why, for I always thought that town a mighty pushy, impudent sort of place. But then, I'm a countryman born and I don't like any town. And let me tell you, the ones who are getting back first are the smart ones. The ones who come back last won't find a stick or stone or brick of their houses, because everybody's out salvaging things all over town to rebuild their houses. Just day before yesterday, I saw Mrs. Merriwether and Miss Maybelle and their old darky woman out collecting brick in a wheelbarrow. And Mrs. Meade told me she was thinking about building a log cabin when the doctor comes back to help her. She said she lived in a log cabin when she first came to Atlanta, when it was Marthasville, and it wouldn't bother her none to do it again. 'Course, she was only joking, but that shows you how they feel about it."

"I think they've got a lot of spirit," said Melanie proudly. "Don't you, Scarlett?"

Scarlett nodded, a grim pleasure and pride in her adopted town filling her. As Frank said, it was a pushy, impudent place and that was why she liked it. It wasn't hidebound and stick-in-the-muddish like the older towns and it had a brash exuberance that matched her own. "I'm like Atlanta," she thought. "It takes more than Yankees or a burning to keep me down."

"If Aunt Pitty is going back to Atlanta, we'd better go back and stay with her, Scarlett," said Melanie, interrupting her train of thought. "She'll die of fright alone."

"Now, how can I leave here, Melly?" Scarlett asked crossly. "If you are so anxious to go, go. I won't stop you."

"Oh, I didn't mean it that way, darling," cried Melanie, flushing with distress. "How thoughtless of me! Of course, you can't leave Tara and—and I guess Uncle Peter and Cookie can take care of Auntie."

"There's nothing to keep you from going," Scarlett pointed out shortly.

"You know I wouldn't leave you," answered Melanie. "And I—I would be just frightened to death without you."

"Suit yourself. Besides, you wouldn't catch me going back to Atlanta. Just as soon as they get a few houses up, Sherman will come back and burn it again."

"He won't be back," said Frank and, despite his efforts, his face dropped. "He's gone on through the state to the coast. Savannah was captured this week and they say the Yankees are going on up into South Carolina."

"Savannah taken!"

"Yes. Why, ladies, Savannah couldn't help but fall. They didn't have enough men to hold it, though they used every man they could get— every man who could drag one foot after another.

Do you know that when the Yankees were marching on Milledgeville, they called out all the cadets from the military academies, no matter how young they were, and even opened the state penitentiary to get fresh troops? Yes, sir, they turned loose every convict who was willing to fight and promised him a pardon if he lived through the war. It kind of gave me the creeps to see those little cadets in the ranks with thieves and cut-throats."

"They turned loose the convicts on us!"

"Now, Miss Scarlett, don't you get upset. They're a long way off from here, and furthermore they're making good soldiers. I guess being a thief don't keep a man from being a good soldier, does it?"

"I think it's wonderful," said Melanie softly.

"Well, I don't," said Scarlett flatly. "There's thieves enough running around the country anyway, what with the Yankees and—" She caught herself in time but the men laughed.

"What with Yankees and our commissary department," they finished, and she flushed.

"But where's General Hood's army?" interposed Melanie hastily. "Surely he could have held Savannah."

"Why, Miss Melanie"—Frank was startled and reproachful—"General Hood hasn't been down in that section at all. He's been fighting up in Tennessee, trying to draw the Yankees out of Georgia."

"And didn't his little scheme work well!" cried Scarlett sarcastically. "He left the damn Yankees to go through us with nothing but schoolboys and convicts and Home Guards to protect us."

"Daughter," said Gerald, rousing himself, "you are profane. Your mother will be grieved."

"They are damn Yankees!" cried Scarlett passionately. "And I never expect to call them anything else."

At the mention of Ellen everyone felt queer and conversation suddenly ceased. Melanie again interposed.

"When you were in Macon did you see India and Honey Wilkes? Did they—had they heard anything of Ashley?"

"Now, Miss Melly, you know if I'd had news of Ashley, I'd have ridden up here from Macon right away to tell you," said Frank reproachfully. "No, they didn't have any news but—now, don't you fret about Ashley, Miss Melly. I know it's been a long time since you heard from him, but you can't expect to hear from a fellow when he's in prison, can you? And things aren't as bad in Yankee prisons as they are in ours. After all, the Yankees have plenty to eat and enough medicines and blankets. They aren't like we are—not having enough to feed ourselves, much less our prisoners."

"Oh, the Yankees have got plenty," cried Melanie, passionately bitter. "But they don't give things to the prisoners. You know they don't, Mr. Kennedy. You are just saying that to make me feel better. You know that our boys freeze to death up there and starve too and die without doctors and medicine, simply because the Yankees hate us so much! Oh, if we could just

750

wipe every Yankee off the face of the earth! Oh, I know that Ashley is—"

"Don't say it!" cried Scarlett, her heart in her throat. As long as no one said Ashley was dead, there persisted in her heart a faint hope that he lived, but she felt that if she heard the words pronounced, in that moment he would die.

"Now, Mrs. Wilkes, don't you bother about your husband," said the one-eyed man soothingly. "I was captured after first Manassas and exchanged later, and when I was in prison they fed me off the fat of the land, fried chicken and hot biscuits—"

"I think you are a liar," said Melanie with a faint smile and the first sign of spirit Scarlett had ever seen her display with a man. "What do you think?"

"I think so too," said the one-eyed man and slapped his leg with a laugh.

"If you'll all come into the parlour, I'll sing you some Christmas carols," said Melanie, glad to change the subject. "The piano was one thing the Yankees couldn't carry away. Is it terribly out of tune. Suellen?"

"Dreadfully," answered Suellen, happily beckoning with a smile to Frank.

But as they all passed from the room, Frank hung back, tugging at Scarlett's sleeve.

"May I speak to you alone?"

For an awful moment she feared he was going to ask about her livestock and she braced herself for a good lie.

When the room was cleared and they stood by the fire, all the false cheerfulness which had coloured Frank's face in front of the others passed and she saw that he looked like an old man. His face was as dried and brown as the leaves that were blowing about the lawn of Tara and his ginger-coloured whiskers were thin and scraggy and streaked with grey. He clawed at them absently and cleared his throat in an annoying way before he spoke.

"I'm mighty sorry about your ma, Miss Scarlett."

"Please don't talk about it."

"And your pa—Has he been this way since—?"

"Yes—he's—he's not himself, as you can see."

"He sure set a store by her."

"Oh, Mr. Kennedy, please don't let's talk—"

"I'm sorry, Miss Scarlett," and he shuffled his feet nervously. "The truth is I wanted to take up something with your pa and now I see it won't do any good."

"Perhaps I can help you, Mr. Kennedy. You see—I'm the head of the house now."

"Well, I—" began Frank and again clawed nervously at his beard. "The truth is—Well, Miss Scarlett, I was aiming to ask him for Miss Suellen."

"Do you mean to tell me," cried Scarlett in amused amazement, "that you haven't yet asked Pa for Suellen? And you've been courting her for years!"

He flushed and grinned embarrassedly and in general looked like a shy and sheepish boy.

"Well, I—I didn't know if she'd have me. I'm so much older than she is and—there were so many good-looking young bucks hanging around Tara—"

"Hump!" thought Scarlett, "they were hanging around me, not her!"

"And I don't know yet if she'll have me. I've never asked her but she must know how I feel. I —I thought I'd ask Mr. O'Hara's permission and tell him the truth. Miss Scarlett, I haven't got a cent now. I used to have a lot of money, if you'll forgive me mentioning it, but right now all I own is my horse and the clothes I've got on. You see, when I enlisted I sold most of my land and I put all my money in Confederate bonds and you know what they're worth now. Less than the paper they're printed on. And anyway, I haven't got them now, because they burned up when the Yankees burned my sister's house. I know I've got gall asking for Miss Suellen now when I haven't a cent but—well, it's this way. I got to thinking that we don't know how things are going to turn out about this war. It sure looks like the end of the world to me. There's nothing we can be sure of and—and I thought it would be a heap of comfort to me and maybe to her if we were engaged. That would be something sure. I wouldn't ask to marry her till I could take care of her, Miss Scarlett, and I don't know when that will be. But if true love carries any weight with you, you can be certain Miss Suellen will be rich in that if nothing else."

He spoke the last words with a simple dignity that touched Scarlett, even in her amusement. It was beyond her comprehension that anyone could love Suellen. Her sister seemed to her a monster

753

of selfishness, of complaints and of what she could only describe as pure cussedness.

"Why, Mr. Kennedy," she said kindly, "it's quite all right. I'm sure I can speak for Pa. He always set a store by you and he always expected Suellen to marry you."

"Did he now?" cried Frank, happiness in his face.

"Indeed yes," answered Scarlett, concealing a grin as she remembered how frequently Gerald had rudely bellowed across the supper table to Suellen: "How now, Missy! Hasn't your ardent beau popped the question yet? Shall I be asking him his intentions?"

"I shall ask her to-night," he said, his face quivering, and he clutched her hand and shook it. "You're so kind, Miss Scarlett."

"I'll send her to you," smiled Scarlett, starting for the parlour. Melanie was beginning to play. The piano was sadly out of tune but some of the chords were musical, and Melanie was raising her voice to lead the others in "Hark, the Herald Angels Sing!"

Scarlett paused. It did not seem possible that war had swept over them twice, that they were living in a ravaged country, close to the border of starvation, when this old sweet Christmas hymn was being sung. Abruptly she turned to Frank.

"What did you mean when you said it looked like the end of the world to you?"

"I'll talk frankly," he said slowly, "but I wouldn't want you to be alarming the other ladies with what I say. The war can't go on much longer. There aren't any fresh men to fill the

754

ranks and the desertions are running high—higher than the army likes to admit. You see, the men can't stand to be away from their families when they know they're starving, so they go home to try to provide for them. I can't blame them but it weakens the army. And the army can't fight without food and there isn't any food. I know because, you see, getting food is my business. I've been all up and down this section since we retook Atlanta and there isn't enough to feed a jaybird. It's the same way for three hundred miles south to Savannah. The folks are starving and the railroads are torn up and there aren't any new rifles and the ammunition is giving out and there's no leather at all for shoes. . . . So, you see, the end is almost here."

But the fading hopes of the Confederacy weighed less heavily on Scarlett than his remark about the scarcity of food. It had been her intention to send Pork out with the horse and wagon, the gold pieces and the United States money to scour the countryside for provisions and material for clothes. But if what Frank said was true—

But Macon hadn't fallen. There must be food in Macon. Just as soon as the commissary department was safely on its way, she'd start Pork for Macon and take the chance of having the precious horse picked up by the army. She'd have to risk it.

"Well, let's don't talk about unpleasant things to-night, Mr. Kennedy," she said. "You go and sit in Mother's little office and I'll send Suellen to you so you can—well, so you'll have a little privacy."

Blushing, smiling, Frank slipped out of the room and Scarlett watched him go.

"What a pity he can't marry her now!" she thought. "That would be one less mouth to feed."

13

THE following April General Johnston, who had been given back the shattered remnants of his old command, surrendered them in North Carolina and the war was over. But not until two weeks later did the news reach Tara. There was too much to do at Tara for anyone to waste time travelling abroad and hearing gossip and, as the neighbours were just as busy as they, there was little visiting and news spread slowly.

Spring ploughing was at its height and the cotton and garden seed Pork had brought from Macon were being put into the ground. Pork had been almost worthless since the trip, so proud was he of returning safely with his wagonload of dress goods, seed, fowls, hams, side meat and meal. Over and over, he told the story of his many narrow escapes, of the bypaths and country lanes he had taken on his return to Tara, the unfrequented roads, the old trails, the bridle paths. He had been five weeks on the road, agonizing weeks for Scarlett. But she did not upbraid him on his return, for she was happy that he had made the trip successfully and pleased that he brought back so much of the money she had given him. She had a shrewd suspicion that the reason he had so much money left over was that he had not bought the fowls or most of the food. Pork would have taken shame to himself had he spent her money when there were unguarded hencoops along the road and smokehouses handy.

Now that they had a little food, everyone at Tara was busy trying to restore some semblance of naturalness to life. There was work for every pair of hands, too much work, never-ending work. The withered stalks of last year's cotton had to be removed to make way for this year's seeds and the balky horse, unaccustomed to the plough, dragged unwillingly through the fields. Weeds had to be pulled from the garden and the seeds planted, firewood had to be cut, a beginning had to be made toward replacing the pens and the miles and miles of fences so casually burned by the Yankees. The snares Pork set for rabbits had to be visited twice a day and the fishlines in the river rebaited. There were beds to be made and floors to be swept, food to be cooked and dishes washed, hogs and chickens to be fed and eggs gathered. The cow had to be milked and pastured near the swamp and someone had to watch her all day for fear the Yankees or Frank Kennedy's men would return and take her. Even little Wade had his duties. Every morning he went out importantly with a basket to pick up twigs and chips to start the fires with.

It was the Fontaine boys, the first of the County men home from the war, who brought the news of the surrender. Alex, who still had boots, was walking and Tony, barefooted, was riding on the bare back of a mule. Tony always managed to get the best things in that family. They were swarthier than ever from four years' exposure to sun and storm, thinner, more wiry, and the wild black beards they brought back from the war made them seem like strangers.

On their way to Mimosa and eager for home, they only stopped a moment at Tara to kiss the girls and give them news of the surrender. It was all over, they said, all finished, and they did not seem to care much or want to talk about it. All they wanted to know was whether Mimosa had been burned. On the way south from Atlanta, they had passed chimney after chimney where the homes of friends had stood and it seemed almost too much to hope that their own house had been spared. They sighed with relief at the welcome news and laughed, slapping their thighs when Scarlett told them of Sally's wild ride and how neatly she had cleared their hedge.

"She's a spunky girl," said Tony, "and it's rotten luck for her, Joe getting killed. You all got any chewing tobacco, Scarlett?"

"Nothing but rabbit tobacco. Pa smokes it in a corn cob."

"I haven't fallen that low yet," said Tony, "but I'll probably come to it."

"Is Dimity Munroe all right?" asked Alex, eagerly but a little embarrassed, and Scarlett recalled vaguely that he had been sweet on Sally's younger sister.

"Oh, yes. She's living with her aunt over in Fayetteville now. You know their house in Lovejoy was burned. And the rest of her folks are in Macon."

"What he means is—has Dimity married some brave colonel in the Home Guard?" jeered Tony, and Alex turned furious eyes upon him.

"Of course, she isn't married," said Scarlett, amused.

"Maybe it would be better if she had," said Alex gloomily. "How the hell—I beg your pardon, Scarlett. But how can a man ask a girl to marry him when his darkies are all freed and his stock gone and he hasn't got a cent in his pockets?"

"You know that wouldn't bother Dimity," said Scarlett. She could afford to be loyal to Dimity and say nice things about her, for Alex Fontaine had never been one of her own beaux.

"Hell's afire—Well, I beg your pardon again. I'll have to quit swearing or Grandma will sure tan my hide. I'm not asking any girl to marry a pauper. It mightn't bother her but it would bother me."

While Scarlett talked to the boys on the front porch, Melanie, Suellen and Carreen slipped silently into the house as soon as they heard the news of the surrender. After the boys had gone, cutting across the back fields of Tara toward home, Scarlett went inside and heard the girls sobbing together on the sofa in Ellen's little office. It was all over, the bright beautiful dream they had loved and hoped for, the Cause which had taken their friends, lovers, husbands and beggared their families. The Cause they had thought could never fall had fallen forever.

But for Scarlett, there were no tears. In the first moment when she heard the news she thought: "Thank God! Now the cow won't be stolen. Now the horse is safe. Now we can take the silver out of the well and everybody can have a knife and fork. Now I won't be afraid to drive round the country looking for something to eat."

What a relief! Never again would she start in fear at the sound of hooves. Never again would she wake in the dark nights, holding her breath to listen, wondering if it were reality or only a dream that she heard in the yard the rattle of bits, the stamping of hooves and the harsh crying of orders by the Yankees. And, best of all, Tara was safe! Now her worst nightmare would never come true. Now she would never have to stand on the lawn and see smoke billowing from the beloved house and hear the roar of flames as the roof fell in.

Yes, the Cause was dead but war had always seemed foolish to her and peace was better. She had never stood starry-eyed when the Stars and Bars ran up a pole or felt cold chills when "Dixie" sounded. She had not been sustained through privations, the sickening duties of nursing, the fears of the siege and the hunger of the last few months by the fanatic glow which made all these things endurable to others, if only the Cause prospered. It was all over and done with and she was not going to cry about it.

All over! The war which had seemed so endless, the war which, unbidden and unwanted, had cut her life in two, had made so clean a cleavage that it was difficult to remember those other care-free days. She could look back, unmoved, at the pretty Scarlett with her fragile green morocco slippers and her flounces fragrant with lavender, but she wondered if she could be that same girl. Scarlett O'Hara, with the County at her feet, a hundred slaves to do her bidding, the wealth of Tara like a wall behind her and doting parents anxious to grant any desire of her heart. Spoiled, careless Scarlett who had never known an ungratified wish except where Ashley was concerned.

Somewhere, on the long road that wound through those four years, the girl with her sachet and dancing slippers had slipped away and there was left a woman with sharp green eyes, who counted pennies and turned her hands to many menial tasks, a woman to whom nothing was left from the wreckage except the indestructible red earth on which she stood.

As she stood in the hall, listening to the girls sobbing, her mind was busy.

"We'll plant more cotton, lots more. I'll send Pork to Macon to-morrow to buy more seed. Now the Yankees won't burn it and our troops won't need it. Good Lord! Cotton ought to go sky high this fall!"

She went into the little office and, disregarding the weeping girls on the sofa, seated herself at the secretary and picked up a quill to balance the cost of more cotton seed against her remaining cash.

"The war is over," she thought, and suddenly she dropped the quill as a wild happiness flooded her. The war was over and Ashley—if Ashley was alive he'd be coming home! She wondered if Melanie, in the midst of mourning for the lost Cause, had thought of this.

"Soon we'll get a letter—no, not a letter. We can't get letters. But soon—oh, somehow he'll let us know!"

But the days passed into weeks and there was no news from Ashley. The mail service in the South was uncertain and in the rural districts there was none at all. Occasionally a passing traveller from Atlanta brought a note from Aunt Pitty tearfully begging the girls to come back. But never news of Ashley.

After the surrender, an ever-present feud over the horse smouldered between Scarlett and Suellen. Now that there was no danger of Yankees, Suellen wanted to go calling on the neighbours. Lonely and missing the happy sociability of the old days, Suellen longed to visit friends, if for no other reason than to assure herself that the rest of the County was as bad off as Tara. But Scarlett was adamant. The horse was for work, to drag logs from the woods, to plough and for Pork to ride in search of food. On Sundays he had earned the right to graze in the pasture and rest. If Suellen wanted to go visiting she could go afoot.

Before the last year Suellen had never walked a hundred yards in her life and this prospect was anything but pleasing. So she stayed at home and nagged and cried and said, once too often: "Oh, if only Mother was here!" At that, Scarlett gave her the long-promised slap, hitting her so hard it knocked her screaming to the bed and caused great consternation throughout the house. Thereafter, Suellen whined the less, at least in Scarlett's presence.

Scarlett spoke truthfully when she said she wanted the horse to rest but that was only half of the truth. The other half was that she had paid one round of calls on the County in the first month after the surrender and the sight of old friends and old plantations had shaken her courage more than she liked to admit.

The Fontaines had fared best of any, thanks to Sally's hard ride, but it was flourishing only by comparison with the desperate situation of the other neighbours. Grandma Fontaine had never completely recovered from the heart attack she had the day she led the others in beating out the flames and saving the house. Old Dr. Fontaine was convalescing slowly from an amputated arm. Alex and Tony were turning awkward hands to ploughs and hoe handles. They leaned over the fence rail to shake hands with Scarlett when she called and they laughed at her rickety wagon, their black eyes bitter, for they were laughing at themselves as well as her. She asked to buy seed corn from them and they promised it and fell to discussing farm problems. They had twelve chickens, two cows, five hogs and the mule they brought home from the war. One of the hogs had just died and they were worried about losing the others. At hearing such serious words about hogs from these ex-dandies who had never given life a more serious thought than which cravat was most fashionable, Scarlett laughed and this time her laugh was bitter too.

They had all made her welcome at Mimosa and had insisted on giving, not selling, her the seed corn. The quick Fontaine tempers flared when she put a greenback on the table and they flatly refused payment. Scarlett took the corn and privately slipped a dollar bill into Sally's hand.

Sally looked like a different person from the girl who had greeted her eight months before when Scarlett first came home to Tara. Then she had been pale and sad but there had been a buoyancy about her. Now that buoyancy had gone, as if the surrender had taken all hope from her.

"Scarlett," she whispered as she clutched the bill, "what was the good of it all? Why did we ever fight? Oh, my poor Joe! Oh, my poor baby!"

"I don't know why we fought and I don't care," said Scarlett. "And I'm not interested. I never was interested. War is a man's business, not a woman's. All I'm interested in now is a good cotton crop. Now take this dollar and buy little Joe a dress. God knows, he needs it. I'm not going to rob you of your corn, for all Alex and Tony's politeness."

The boys followed her to the wagon and assisted her in, courtly for all their rags, gay with the volatile Fontaine gaiety, but with the picture of their destitution in her eyes, she shivered as she drove away from Mimosa. She was so tired of poverty and pinching. What a pleasure it would be to know people who were rich and not worried as to where their next meal was coming from!

Cade Calvert was at home at Pine Bloom and, as Scarlett came up the steps of the old house in which she had danced so often in happier days, she saw that death was in his face. He was emaciated and he coughed as he lay in an easy chair in the sunshine with a shawl across his knees, but his face lit up when he saw her. Just a little cold which had settled in his chest, he said, trying to rise to greet her. Got it from

765

sleeping so much in the rain. But it would be gone soon and then he'd lend a hand in the work.

Cathleen Calvert, who came out of the house at the sound of voices, met Scarlett's eyes above her brother's head and in them Scarlett read knowledge and bitter despair. Cade might not know but Cathleen knew. Pine Bloom looked straggly and overgrown with weeds, seedling pines were beginning to show in the fields and the house was sagging and untidy. Cathleen was thin and taut.

The two of them, with their Yankee stepmother, their four little half-sisters, and Hilton, the Yankee overseer, remained in the silent, oddly echoing house. Scarlett had never liked Hilton any more than she liked their own overseer, Jonas Wilkerson, and she liked him even less now, as he sauntered forward and greeted her like an equal. Formerly he had the same combination of servility and impertinence which Wilkerson possessed but now, with Mr. Calvert and Raiford dead in the war and Cade sick, he had dropped all servility. The second Mrs. Calvert had never known how to compel respect from negro servants and it was not to be expected that she could get it from a white man.

"Mr. Hilton has been so kind about staying with us through these difficult times," said Mrs. Calvert nervously, casting quick glances at her silent stepdaughter. "Very kind. I suppose you heard how he saved our house twice when Sherman was here. I'm sure I don't know how we would have managed without him, with no money and Cade—"

A flush went over Cade's white face and Cathleen's long lashes veiled her eyes as her mouth hardened. Scarlett knew their souls were writhing in helpless rage at being under obligations to their Yankee overseer. Mrs. Calvert seemed ready to weep. She had somehow made a blunder. She was always blundering. She just couldn't understand Southerners, for all that she had lived in Georgia twenty years. She never knew what not to say to her stepchildren and, no matter what she said or did, they were always so exquisitely polite to her. Silently she vowed she would go North to her own people, taking her children with her, and leave these puzzling stiff-necked strangers.

After these visits, Scarlett had no desire to see the Tarletons. Now that the four boys were gone, the house burned and the family cramped in the overseer's cottage, she could not bring herself to go. But Suellen and Carreen begged and Melanie said it would be unneighbourly not to call and welcome Mr. Tarleton back from the war, so one Sunday they went.

This was the worst of all.

As they drove up by the ruins of the house, they saw Beatrice Tarleton, dressed in a worn riding habit, a crop under her arm, sitting on the top rail of the fence about the paddock, staring moodily at nothing. Beside her perched the bow-legged little negro who had trained her horses and he looked as glum as his mistress. The paddock, once full of frolicking colts and placid brood mares, was empty now except for one mule, the mule Mr. Tarleton had ridden home from the surrender.

"I swear I don't know what to do with myself now that my darlings are gone," said Mrs. Tarleton, climbing down from the fence. A stranger might have thought she spoke of her four dead sons, but the girls from Tara knew her horses were in her mind. "All my beautiful horses dead. And oh, my poor Nellie! If I just had Nellie! And nothing but a damned mule on the place. A damned mule," she repeated, looking indignantly at the scrawny beast. "It's an insult to the memory of my blooded darlings to have a mule in their paddock. Mules are misbegotten, unnatural critters and it ought to be illegal to breed them."

Jim Tarleton, completely disguised by a bushy beard, came out of the overseer's house to welcome and kiss the girls, and his four red-haired daughters in mended dresses streamed out behind him, tripping over the dozen black and tan hounds which ran barking to the door at the sound of strange voices. There was an air of studied and determined cheerfulness about the whole family which brought a colder chill to Scarlett's bones than the bitterness of Mimosa or the deathly brooding of Pine Bloom.

The Tarletons insisted that the girls stay for dinner, saying they had so few guests these days and wanted to hear all the news. Scarlett did not want to linger, for the atmosphere oppressed her, but Melanie and her two sisters were anxious for a longer visit, so the four stayed for dinner and ate sparingly of the side meat and dried peas which were served them.

There was laughter about the skimpy fare and the Tarleton girls giggled as they told of make-shifts for clothes, as if they were telling the most amusing of jokes. Melanie met them half-way, surprising Scarlett with her unexpected vivacity as she told of trials at Tara, making light of hardships. Scarlett could hardly speak at all. The room seemed so empty without the four great Tarleton boys, lounging and smoking and teasing. And if it seemed empty to her, what must it seem to the Tarletons who were offering a smiling front to their neighbours?

Carreen had said little during the meal but when it was over she slipped over to Mrs. Tarleton's side and whispered something. Mrs. Tarleton's face changed and the brittle smile left her lips as she put her arm around Carreen's slender waist. They left the room, and Scarlett, who felt she could not endure the house another minute, followed them. They went down the path through the garden and Scarlett saw they were going toward the burying-ground. Well, she couldn't go back to the house now. It would seem too rude. But what on earth did Carreen mean dragging Mrs. Tarleton out to the boys' graves when Beatrice was trying so hard to be brave?

There were two new marble markers in the brick-enclosed lot under the funereal cedars—so new that no rain had splashed them with red dust.

"We got them last week," said Mrs. Tarleton proudly. "Mr. Tarleton went to Macon and brought them home in the wagon."

Tombstones! And what they must have cost! Suddenly Scarlett did not feel as sorry for the Tarletons as she had at first. Anybody who would waste precious money on tombstones when food was so dear, so almost unattainable, didn't deserve sympathy. And there were several lines carved on each of the stones. The more carving, the more money. The whole family must be crazy! And it had cost money, too, to bring the three boys' bodies home. They had never found Boyd or any trace of him.

Between the graves of Brent and Stuart was a stone which read: "They were lovely and pleasant in their lives, and in their death they were not divided."

On the other stone were the names of Boyd and Tom with something in Latin which began "Dulce et—", but it meant nothing to Scarlett who had managed to evade Latin at the Fayetteville Academy.

All that money for tombstones! Why, they were fools! She felt as indignant as if her own money had been squandered.

Carreen's eyes were shining oddly.

"I think it's lovely," she whispered, pointing to the first stone.

Carreen would think it lovely. Anything sentimental stirred her.

"Yes," said Mrs. Tarleton, and her voice was soft, "we thought it very fitting—they died almost at the same time, Stuart first and then Brent who caught up the flag he dropped."

As the girls drove back to Tara, Scarlett was silent for a while, thinking of what she had seen in the various homes, remembering against her will the County in its glory, with visitors at all the big houses and money plentiful, negroes crowding the quarters and the well-tended fields glorious with cotton.

"In another year, there'll be little pines all over these fields," she thought, and looking toward the encircling forest she shuddered. "Without the darkies, it will be all we can do to keep body and soul together. Nobody can run a big plantation without the darkies, and lots of the fields won't be cultivated at all and the woods will take over the fields again. Nobody can plant much cotton, and what will we do then? What'll become of country folks? Town folks can manage somehow. They've always managed. But we country folks will go back a hundred years like the pioneers who had little cabins and just scratched a few acres—and barely existed.

"No—" she thought grimly, "Tara isn't going to be like that. Not even if I have to plough myself. This whole section, this whole state can go back to woods if it wants to, but I won't let Tara go. And I don't intend to waste my money on tombstones or my time crying about the war. We can make out somehow. I know we could make out somehow if the men weren't all dead. Losing the darkies isn't the worst part about this. It's the loss of the men, the young men." She thought again of the four Tarletons and Joe Fontaine, of Raiford Calvert and the Munroe brothers and all the boys from Fayetteville and Jonesboro whose names she had read on the casualty lists. "If there were just enough men left, we could manage somehow but—"

Another thought struck her—suppose she wanted to marry again. Of course, she didn't want to marry again. Once was certainly enough. Besides, the only man she'd ever wanted was Ashley and he was married, if he was still living. But suppose she should want to marry. Who would there be to marry her? The thought was appalling.

"Melly," she said, "what's going to happen to Southern girls?"

"What do you mean?"

"Just what I say. What's going to happen to them? There's no one to marry them. Why, Melly, with all the boys dead, there'll be thousands of girls all over the South who'll die old maids."

"And never have any children," added Melanie, to whom this was the most important thing.

Evidently the thought was not new to Suellen who sat in the back of the wagon, for she suddenly began to cry. She had not heard from Frank Kennedy since Christmas. She did not know if the lack of mail service was the cause, or if he had merely trifled with her affections and then forgotten her. Or maybe he had been killed in the last days of the war! The latter would have been infinitely preferable to his forgetting her, for at least there was some dignity about a dead love, such as Carreen and India Wilkes had, but none about a deserted fiancée.

"Oh, in the name of God, hush!" said Scarlett.

"Oh, you can talk," sobbed Suellen, "because you've been married and had a baby and everybody knows some man wanted you. But look at me! And you've got to be mean and throw it up to me that I'm an old maid when I can't help myself. I think you're hateful."

"Oh, hush! You know how I hate people who bawl all the time. You know perfectly well old Ginger Whiskers isn't dead and that he'll come back and marry you. He hasn't any better sense. But personally, I'd rather be an old maid than marry him."

There was silence from the back of the wagon for a while and Carreen comforted her sister with absent-minded pats, for her mind was a long way off, riding paths three years old with Brent Tarleton beside her. There was a glow, an exaltation in her eyes.

"Ah," said Melanie sadly, "what will the South be like without all our fine boys? What would the South have been if they had lived? We could use their courage and their energy and their brains. Scarlett, all of us with little boys must raise them to take the places of the men who are gone, to be brave men like them."

"There will never again be men like them," said Carreen softly. "No one can take their places."

They drove home the rest of the way in silence.

One day not long after this, Cathleen Calvert rode up to Tara at sunset. Her sidesaddle was strapped on as sorry a mule as Scarlett had ever seen, a flop-eared lame brute, and Cathleen was almost as sorry-looking as the animal she rode. Her dress was of faded gingham of the type once worn only by house servants, and her sunbonnet was secured under her chin by a piece of twine. She rode up to the front porch but did not dismount, and Scarlett and Melanie, who had been watching the sunset, went down the steps to meet her. Cathleen was as white as Cade had been the day Scarlett called, white and hard and brittle, as if her face would shatter if she spoke. But her back was erect and her head was high as she nodded to them.

Scarlett suddenly remembered the day of the Wilkes barbecue when she and Cathleen had whispered together about Rhett Butler. How pretty and fresh Cathleen had been that day in a swirl of blue organdie with fragrant roses at her sash and little black velvet slippers laced about her small ankles. And now there was not a trace of that girl in the stiff figure sitting on the mule.

"I won't get down, thank you," she said. "I just came to tell you that I'm going to be married."

"What!"

"Who to?"

"Cathy, how grand!"

"When?"

"To-morrow," said Cathleen quietly, and there was something in her voice which took the eager smiles from their faces. "I came to tell you that I'm going to be married to-morrow, in Jonesboro —and I'm not inviting you all to come."

They digested this in silence, looking up at her, puzzled. Then Melanie spoke.

"Is it someone we know, dear?"

"Yes," said Cathleen shortly. "It's Mr. Hilton."

"Mr. Hilton?"

"Yes, Mr. Hilton, our overseer."

Scarlett could not even find voice to say "Oh!" but Cathleen, peering down suddenly at Melanie, said in a low savage voice: "If you cry, Melly, I can't stand it. I shall die!"

Melanie said nothing, but patted the foot in its awkward homemade shoe which hung from the stirrup. Her head was low.

"And don't pat me! I can't stand that either."

Melanie dropped her hand but still did not look up.

"Well, I must go. I only came to tell you." The white brittle mask was back again and she picked up the reins.

"How is Cade?" asked Scarlett, utterly at a loss but fumbling for some words to break the awkward silence.

"He is dying," said Cathleen shortly. There seemed to be no feeling in her voice. "And he is going to die in some comfort and peace if I can manage it, without worry about who will take care of me when he's gone. You see, my stepmother and the children are going North for good, tomorrow. Well, I must be going."

Melanie looked up and met Cathleen's hard eyes. There were bright tears on Melanie's lashes and understanding in her eyes, and before them, Cathleen's lips curved into the crooked smile of a brave child who tries not to cry. It was all very bewildering to Scarlett, who was still trying to grasp the idea that Cathleen Calvert was going to

775

marry an overseer—Cathleen, daughter of a rich planter, Cathleen who, next to Scarlett, had had more beaux than any girl in the County.

Cathleen bent down and Melanie tiptoed. They kissed. Then Cathleen flapped the bridle reins sharply and the old mule moved off.

Melanie looked after her, the tears streaming down her face. Scarlett stared, still dazed.

"Melly, is she crazy? You know she can't be in love with him."

"In love? Oh, Scarlett, don't even suggest such a horrid thing! Oh, poor Cathleen! Poor Cade!"

"Fiddle-dee-dee!" cried Scarlett, beginning to be irritated. It was annoying that Melanie always seemed to grasp more of situations than she herself did. Cathleen's plight seemed to her more startling than catastrophic. Of course it was no pleasant thought, marrying Yankee white trash, but after all a girl couldn't live alone on a plantation; she had to have a husband to help her run it.

"Melly, it's like I said the other day. There isn't anybody for girls to marry and they've got to marry someone."

"Oh, they don't have to marry! There's nothing shameful in being a spinster. Look at Aunt Pitty. Oh, I'd rather see Cathleen dead! I know Cade would rather see her dead! It's the end of the Calverts. Just think what her—what their children will be. Oh, Scarlett, have Pork saddle the horse quickly and you ride after her and tell her to come live with us!"

"Good Lord!" cried Scarlett, shocked at the matter-of-fact way in which Melanie was offering

Tara. Scarlett certainly had no intention of feeding another mouth. She started to say this but something in Melanie's stricken face halted the words.

"She wouldn't come, Melly," she amended. "You know she wouldn't. She's so proud and she'd think it was charity."

"That's true, that's true!" said Melanie distractedly, watching the small cloud of red dust disappear down the road.

"You've been with me for months," thought Scarlett grimly, looking at her sister-in-law, "and it's never occurred to you that it's charity you're living on. And I guess it never will. You're one of those people the war didn't change and you go right on thinking and acting just like nothing had happened—like we were still rich as Croesus and had more food than we knew what to do with and guests didn't matter. I guess I've got you on my neck for the rest of my life. But I won't have Cathleen too."

14

IN that warm summer after peace came, Tara
suddenly lost its isolation. And for months
thereafter a stream of scarecrows, bearded,
ragged, footsore and always hungry, toiled up the
red hill to Tara and came to rest on the shady
front steps, wanting food and a night's lodging.
They were Confederate soldiers walking home.
The railroad had carried the remains of Johnston's army from North Carolina to Atlanta and
dumped them there, and from Atlanta they began
their pilgrimages afoot. When the wave of Johnston's men had passed, the weary veterans from
the Army of Virginia arrived and then men from
the Western troops, beating their way south
toward homes which might not exist and families
which might be scattered or dead. Most of them
were walking; a few fortunate ones rode bony
horses and mules which the terms of the
surrender had permitted them to keep, gaunt
animals which even an untrained eye could tell
would never reach far-away Florida and south
Georgia.

Going home! Going home! That was the only
thought in the soldiers' minds. Some were sad
and silent, others gay and contemptuous of hardships, but the thought that it was all over and
they were going home was the one thing that
sustained them. Few of them were bitter. They
left bitterness to their women and their old

people. They had fought a good fight, had been licked and were willing to settle down peaceably to ploughing beneath the flag they had fought.

Going home! Going home! They could talk of nothing else, neither battles nor wounds, nor imprisonment nor the future. Later, they would refight battles and tell children and grandchildren of pranks and forays and charges, of hunger, forced marches and wounds, but not now. Some of them lacked an arm or a leg or an eye, many had scars which would ache in rainy weather if they lived for seventy years, but these seemed small matters now. Later, it would be different.

Old and young, talkative and taciturn, rich planter and sallow Cracker, they all had two things in common, lice and dysentery. The Confederate soldier was so accustomed to his verminous state he did not give it a thought and scratched unconcernedly even in the presence of ladies. As for dysentery—the "bloody flux" as the ladies delicately called it—it seemed to have spared no one from private to general. Four years of half-starvation, four years of rations which were coarse or green or half-putrefied, had done its work with them and every soldier who stopped at Tara was either just recovering or was actively suffering from it.

"Dey ain' a soun' set of bowels in de whole Confedrut ahmy," observed Mammy darkly as she sweated over the fire, brewing a bitter concoction of blackberry roots which had been Ellen's sovereign remedy for such afflictions. "It's mah notion dat 'twarn't de Yankees whut beat our gempmum.'Twuz dey own innards. Kain no gempmum fight wid his bowels tuhnin' ter water."

One and all, Mammy dosed them, never waiting to ask foolish questions about the state of their organs, and, one and all, they drank her doses meekly and with wry faces, remembering, perhaps, other stern black faces in far-off places and other inexorable black hands holding medicine spoons.

In the matter of "comp'ny" Mammy was equally adamant. No lice-ridden soldier should come into Tara. She marched them behind a clump of thick bushes, relieved them of their uniforms, gave them a basin of water and strong lye soap to wash with and provided them with quilts and blankets to cover their nakedness, while she boiled their clothing in her huge washpot. It was useless for the girls to argue hotly that such conduct humiliated the soldiers. Mammy replied that the girls would be a sight more humiliated if they found lice upon themselves.

When the soldiers began arriving almost daily, Mammy protested against their being allowed to use the bedrooms. Always she feared lest some louse had escaped her. Rather than argue the matter, Scarlett turned the parlour with its deep velvet rug into a dormitory. Mammy cried out equally loudly at the sacrilege of soldiers being permitted to sleep on Miss Ellen's rug but Scarlett was firm. They had to sleep somewhere. And, in the months after the surrender, the deep soft nap began to show signs of wear and finally the heavy warp and woof showed through in spots where heels had worn it and spurs dug carelessly.

Of each soldier, they asked eagerly of Ashley. Suellen, bridling, always asked news of Mr. Kennedy. But none of the soldiers had ever heard of them nor were they inclined to talk about the missing. It was enough that they themselves were alive, and they did not care to think of the thousands in unmarked graves who would never come home.

The family tried to bolster Melanie's courage after each of these disappointments. Of course, Ashley hadn't died in prison. Some Yankee chaplain would have written if this were true. Of course, he was coming home but his prison was so far away. Why, goodness, it took days riding on a train to make the trip and if Ashley was walking, like these men . . . Why hadn't he written? Well, darling, you know what the mails are now—so uncertain and slipshod even where mail routes are re-established. But suppose— suppose he had died on the way home. Now, Melanie, some Yankee woman would have surely written us about it!. . . Yankee women! Bah! . . . Melly, there *are* some nice Yankee women. Oh, yes, there are! God couldn't make a whole nation without having some nice women in it! Scarlett, you remember we did meet a nice Yankee woman at Saratoga that time—Scarlett, tell Melly about her!

"Nice, my foot!" replied Scarlett. "She asked me how many bloodhounds we kept to chase our darkies with! I agree with Melly. I never saw a nice Yankee, male or female. But don't cry, Melly! Ashley'll come home. It's a long walk and maybe—maybe he hasn't got any boots."

Then at the thought of Ashley barefooted, Scarlett could have cried. Let other soldiers limp by in rags with their feet tied up in sacks and strips of carpet, but not Ashley. He should come home on a prancing horse, dressed in fine clothes and shining boots, a plume in his hat. It was the final degradation for her to think of Ashley reduced to the state of these other soldiers.

One afternoon in June when everyone at Tara was assembled on the back porch eagerly watching Pork cut the first half-ripe watermelon of the season, they heard hooves on the gravel of the front drive. Prissy started languidly toward the front door, while those left behind argued hotly as to whether they should hide the melon or keep it for supper, should the caller at the door prove to be a soldier.

Melly and Carreen whispered that the soldier guest should have a share and Scarlett, backed by Suellen and Mammy, hissed to Pork to hide it quickly.

"Don't be a goose, girls! There's not enough for us as it is and if there are two or three famished soldiers out there, none of us will even get a taste," said Scarlett.

While Pork stood with the little melon clutched to him, uncertain as to the final decision, they heard Prissy cry out.

"Gawdlmighty! Miss Scarlett! Miss Melly! Come quick!"

"Who is it?" cried Scarlett, leaping up from the steps and racing through the hall with Melly at her shoulder and the others streaming after her.

"Ashley!" she thought. "Oh, perhaps—"

"It's Uncle Peter! Miss Pittypat's Uncle Peter!"

They all ran out to the front porch and saw the tall grizzled old despot of Aunt Pitty's house climbing down from a rat-tailed nag on which a section of quilting had been strapped. On his wide black face, accustomed dignity strove with delight at seeing old friends, with the result that his brow was furrowed in a frown but his mouth was hanging open like a happy toothless old hound's.

Everyone ran down the steps to greet him, black and white shaking his hand and asking questions, but Melly's voice rose above them all.

"Auntie isn't sick, is she?"

"No'm. She's po'ly, thank God," answered Peter, fastening a severe look first on Melly and then on Scarlett, so that they suddenly felt guilty but could think of no reason why. "She's po'ly but she is plum outdone wid you young Misses, an' ef it come right down to it, Ah is too!"

"Why, Uncle Peter! What on earth—"

"Y'all nee'n try ter 'scuse yo'seffs. Ain' Miss Pitty writ you an' writ you ter come home? Ain' Ah seed her write an' seed her a-cryin' w'en y'all writ her back dat you got too much ter do on disyere ole farm ter come home?"

"But, Uncle Peter—"

"Huccome you leave Miss Pitty by herseff lak dis w'en she so scary lak? You knows well's Ah do Miss Pitty ain' never live by herseff an' she been shakin' in her lil shoes ever since she come back frum Macom. She say fer me ter tell y'all plain as Ah knows how dat she jes' kain unnerstan' y'all desertin' her in her hour of need."

783

"Now, hesh!" said Mammy tartly, for it sat ill upon her to hear Tara referred to as an "ole farm". Trust an ignorant city-bred darky not to know the difference between a farm and a plantation. "Ain' us got no hours of need? Ain' us needin' Miss Scarlett an' Miss Melly right hyah an' needin' dem bad? Huccome Miss Pitty doan ast her brudder fer 'sistance, does she need any?"

Uncle Peter gave her a withering look.

"Us ain' had nuthin' ter do wid Mist' Henry fer y'ars, an' us is too ole ter start now." He turned back to the girls, who were trying to suppress their smiles. "You young Misses ought ter tek shame, leavin' po' Miss Pitty 'lone, wid half her frens daid an' de other half in Macom, an' 'Lanta full of Yankee sojers an' trashy free issue niggers."

The two girls had borne the castigation with straight faces as long as they could, but the thought of Aunt Pitty sending Peter to scold them and bring them back bodily to Atlanta was too much for their control. They burst into laughter and hung on each other's shoulders for support. Naturally, Pork and Dilcey and Mammy gave vent to loud guffaws at hearing the detractor of their beloved Tara set at naught. Suellen and Carreen giggled and even Gerald's face wore a vague smile. Everyone laughed except Peter, who shifted from one large splayed foot to the other in mounting indignation.

"Whut's wrong wid you, nigger?" inquired Mammy with a grin. "Is you gittin' too ole ter perteck yo' own Missus?"

Peter was outraged.

"Too ole! Me too ole? No, Ma'm! Ah kin perteck Miss Pitty lak Ah allus done. Ain' Ah perteck her down ter Macom when us refugeed? Ain' Ah perteck her w'en de Yankees come ter Macom an' she so sceered she faintin' all de time? An' ain' Ah 'quire disyere nag ter bring her back ter 'Lanta an' perteck her an' her pa's silver all de way?" Peter drew himself to his full height as he vindicated himself. "Ah ain' talkin' about perteckin'. Ah'm talkin' 'bout how it *look*."

"How who look?"

"Ah'm talkin 'bout how it look ter folks, seein' Miss Pitty livin' 'lone. Folks talks scan'lous 'bout maiden ladies dat lives by deyseff," continued Peter, and it was obvious to his listeners that Pittypat, in mind, was still a plump and charming miss of sixteen who must be sheltered against evil tongues. "An' Ah ain' figgerin' on havin' folks criticize her. No, Ma'm. . . . An' Ah ain' figgerin' on her takin' in no bo'ders, jes' fer comp'ny needer. Ah done tole her dat. 'Not w'ile you got yo' flesh an' blood dat belongs wid you,' Ah says. An' now her flesh an' blood denyin' her. Miss Pitty ain' nuthin' but a chile an'—"

At this, Scarlett and Melly whooped louder and sank down to the steps. Finally Melly wiped tears of mirth from her eyes.

"Poor Uncle Peter! I'm sorry I laughed. Really and truly. There! Do forgive me. Miss Scarlett and I just can't come home now. Maybe I'll come in September after the cotton is picked. Did Auntie send you all the way down here just to bring us back on that bag of bones?"

At this question, Peter's jaw suddenly dropped

and guilt and consternation swept over his wrinkled black face. His protruding underlip retreated to normal as swiftly as a turtle withdraws its head beneath its shell.

"Miss Melly, Ah is gittin' ole, Ah spec', 'cause Ah clean fergit fer de moment whut she sent me fer, an' it's important too. Ah got a letter fer you. Miss Pitty wouldn' trust de mails or nobody but me ter bring it an'—"

"A letter? For me? Who from?"

"Well'm, it's—Miss Pitty, she says ter me, 'You, Peter, you brek it gen'ly ter Miss Melly,' an' Ah say—"

Melly rose from the steps, her hand at her heart.

"Ashley! Ashley! He's dead!"

"No'm! No'm!" cried Peter, his voice rising to a shrill bawl, as he fumbled in the breast pocket of his ragged coat. "He's 'live! Disyere a letter frum him. He comin' home. He—Gawdlmighty! Ketch her, Mammy! Lemme—"

"Doan you tech her, you ole fool!" thundered Mammy, struggling to keep Melanie's sagging body from falling to the ground. "You pious black ape! Brek it gen'ly! You, Poke, tek her feet. Miss Carreen, steady her haid. Lessus lay her on de sofa in de parlour."

There was a tumult of sound as everyone but Scarlett swarmed about the fainting Melanie, everyone crying out in alarm, scurrying into the house for water and pillows, and in a moment Scarlett and Uncle Peter were left standing alone on the walk. She stood rooted, unable to move from the position to which she had leaped when she heard his words, staring at the old man who stood feebly waving a letter. His old black face was as pitiful as a child's under its mother's disapproval, his dignity collapsed.

For a moment she could not speak or move, and though her mind shouted: "He isn't dead! He's coming home!" the knowledge brought neither joy nor excitement, only a stunned immobility. Uncle Peter's voice came as from a far distance, plaintive, placating.

"Mist' Willie Burr from Macom whut is kin ter us, he brung it ter Miss Pitty. Mist' Willie he in de same jail house wid Mist' Ashley. Mist' Willie he got a hawse an' he got hyah soon. But Mist' Ashley he a-walkin' an'—"

Scarlett snatched the letter from his hand. It was addressed to Melly in Miss Pitty's writing but that did not make her hesitate a moment. She ripped it open and Miss Pitty's enclosed note fell to the ground. Within the envelope there was a piece of folded paper, grimy from the dirty pocket in which it had been carried, creased and ragged about the edges. It bore the inscription in Ashley's hand: Mrs. George Ashley Wilkes, Care Miss Sarah Jane Hamilton, Atlanta, or Twelve Oaks, Jonesboro, Ga."

With fingers that shook, she opened it and read:

"Beloved, I am coming home to you—"

Tears began to stream down her face so that she could not read and her heart swelled up until she felt she could not bear the joy of it. Clutching the letter to her, she raced up the porch steps and down the hall, past the parlour where all the inhabitants of Tara were getting in one another's way as they worked over the unconscious Melanie, and into Ellen's office. She shut the door and locked it and flung herself down on the sagging old sofa, crying, laughing, kissing the letter.

"Beloved," she whispered, "I am coming home to you."

Common sense told them that unless Ashley developed wings, it would be weeks or even months before he could travel from Illinois to Georgia, but hearts nevertheless beat wildly whenever a soldier turned into the avenue at Tara. Each bearded scarecrow might be Ashley. And if it were not Ashley, perhaps the soldier would have news of him or a letter from Aunt Pitty about him. Black and white, they rushed to the front porch every time they heard footsteps. The sight of a uniform was enough to bring everyone flying from the woodpile, the pasture and the cotton patch. For a month after the letter came, work was almost at a standstill. No one wanted to be out of the house when he arrived, Scarlett least of all. And she could not insist on the others attending to their duties when she so neglected hers.

But when the weeks crawled by and Ashley did not come or any news of him, Tara settled back into its old routine. Longing hearts could only stand so much of longing. An uneasy fear crept into Scarlett's mind that something had happened to him along the way. Rock Island was so far away and he might have been weak or sick when released from prison. And he had no money and was tramping through a country where Confederates were hated. If only she knew where he was, she would send money to him, send every penny she had and let the family go hungry, so he could come home swiftly on the train.

"Beloved, I am coming home to you."

In the first rush of joy when her eyes met those words, they had meant only that Ashley was coming home to her. Now, in the light of cooler reason, it was Melanie to whom he was returning, Melanie who went about the house these days singing with joy. Occasionally, Scarlett wondered bitterly why Melanie could not have died in childbirth in Atlanta. That would have made things perfect. Then she could have married Ashley after a decent interval and made little Beau a good stepmother too. When such thoughts came she did not pray hastily to God, telling Him she did not mean it. God did not frighten her any more.

Soldiers came singly and in pairs and dozens and they were always hungry. Scarlett thought despairingly that a plague of locusts would be more welcome. She cursed again the old custom of hospitality which had flowered in the era of plenty, the custom which would not permit any traveller, great or humble, to go on his journey without a night's lodging, food for himself and his horse and the utmost courtesy the house could give. She knew that era had passed forever, but the rest of the household did not, nor did the soldiers, and each soldier was welcomed as if he were a long-awaited guest.

As the never-ending line went by, her heart

hardened. They were eating the food meant for the mouths of Tara, vegetables over whose long rows she had wearied her back, food she had driven endless miles to buy. Food was so hard to get and the money in the Yankee's wallet would not last forever. Only a few greenbacks and the two gold pieces were left now. Why should she feed this horde of hungry men? The war was over. They would never again stand between her and danger. So she gave orders to Pork that when soldiers were in the house, the table should be set sparely. This order prevailed until she noticed that Melanie, who had never been strong since Beau was born, was inducing Pork to put only dabs of food on her plate and giving her share to the soldiers.

"You'll have to stop it, Melanie," she scolded. "You're half sick yourself and if you don't eat more, you'll be sick in bed and we'll have to nurse you. Let these men go hungry. They can stand it. They've stood it for four years and it won't hurt them to stand it a little while longer."

Melanie turned to her and on her face was the first expression of naked emotion Scarlett had ever seen in those serene eyes.

"Oh, Scarlett, don't scold me! Let me do it. You don't know how it helps me. Every time I give some poor man my share I think that maybe, somewhere on the road up north, some woman is giving my Ashley a share of her dinner and it's helping him to get home to me!"

"My Ashley."

"Beloved, I am coming home to you."

Scarlett turned away, wordless. After that,

Melanie noticed there was more food on the table when guests were present, even though Scarlett might grudge them every mouthful.

When the soldiers were too ill to go on, and there were many such, Scarlett put them to bed with none too good grace. Each sick man meant another mouth to feed. Someone had to nurse him and that meant one less worker at the business of fence building, hoeing, weeding and ploughing. One boy, on whose face a blond fuzz had just begun to sprout, was dumped on the front porch by a mounted soldier bound for Fayetteville. He had found him unconscious by the roadside and had brought him, across his saddle, to Tara, the nearest house. The girls thought he must be one of the little cadets who had been called out of military school when Sherman approached Milledgeville but they never knew, for he died without regaining consciousness and a search of his pockets yielded no information.

A nice-looking boy, obviously a gentleman, and somewhere to the south, some woman was watching the roads, wondering where he was and when he was coming home, just as she and Melanie, with a wild hope in their hearts, watched every bearded figure that came up their walk. They buried the cadet in the family burying-ground, next to the three little O'Hara boys, and Melanie cried sharply as Pork filled in the grave, wondering in her heart if strangers were doing this same thing to the tall body of Ashley.

Will Benteen was another soldier, like the nameless boy, who arrived unconscious across the saddle of a comrade. Will was acutely ill with pneumonia, and when the girls put him to bed, they feared he would soon join the boy in the burying-ground.

He had the sallow malarial face of the south Georgia Cracker, pale pinkish hair and washed-out blue eyes which even in delirium were patient and mild. One of his legs was gone at the knee and to the stump was fitted a roughly whittled wooden peg. He was obviously a Cracker, just as the boy they had buried so short a while ago was obviously a planter's son. Just how the girls knew this they could not say. Certainly Will was no dirtier, no more hairy, no more lice-infested than many fine gentlemen who came to Tara. Certainly the language he used in his delirium was no less grammatical than that of the Tarleton twins. But they knew instinctively, as they knew thorough-bred horses from scrubs, that he was not of their class. But this knowledge did not keep them from labouring to save him.

Emaciated from a year in a Yankee prison, exhausted by his long tramp on his ill-fitting wooden peg, he had little strength to combat pneumonia and for days he lay in the bed moaning, trying to get up, fighting battles over again. Never once did he call for mother, wife, sister or sweetheart and this omission worried Carreen.

"A man ought to have some folks," she said. "And he sounds like he didn't have a soul in the world."

For all his lankiness he was tough, and good nursing pulled him through. The day came when his pale-blue eyes, perfectly cognizant of his surroundings, fell upon Carreen sitting beside him, telling her rosary beads, the morning sun shining through her fair hair.

"Then you warn't a dream, after all," he said, in his flat toneless voice. "I hope I ain't troubled you too much, Ma'm."

His convalescence was a long one and he lay quietly looking out of the window at the magnolias and causing very little trouble to anyone. Carreen liked him because of his placid and unembarrassed silences. She would sit beside him through the long hot afternoons, fanning him and saying nothing.

Carreen had very little to say these days as she moved, delicate and wraithlike, about the tasks which were within her strength. She prayed a good deal, for when Scarlett came into her room without knocking, she always found her on her knees by her bed. The sight never failed to annoy her, for Scarlett felt that the time for prayer had passed. If God had seen fit to punish them so, then God could very well do without prayers. Religion had always been a bargaining process with Scarlett. She promised God good behaviour in exchange for favours. God had broken the bargain time and again, to her way of thinking, and she felt that she owed Him nothing at all now. And whenever she found Carreen on her knees when she should have been taking an afternoon nap or doing the mending, she felt that Carreen was shirking her share of the burdens.

She said as much to Will Benteen one afternoon when he was able to sit up in a chair and was startled when he said in his flat voice: "Let her be, Miss Scarlett. It comforts her."

"Comforts her?"

"Yes, she's prayin' for your ma and him."

"Who is 'him'?"

His faded blue eyes looked at her from under sandy lashes without surprise. Nothing seemed to surprise or excite him. Perhaps he had seen too much of the unexpected ever to be startled again. That Scarlett did not know what was in her sister's heart did not seem odd to him. He took it as naturally as he did the fact that Carreen had found comfort in talking to him, a stranger.

"Her beau, that boy Brent something-or-other who was killed at Gettysburg."

"Her beau?" said Scarlett shortly. "Her beau, nothing! He and his brother were my beaux."

"Yes, so she told me. Looks like most of the County was your beaux. But, all the same, he was her beau after you turned him down, because when he come home on his last furlough they got engaged. She said he was the only boy she'd ever cared about and so it kind of comforts her to pray for him."

"Well, fiddle-dee-dee!" said Scarlett, a very small dart of jealousy entering her.

She looked curiously at this lanky man with his bony stooped shoulders, his pinkish hair and calm unwavering eyes. So he knew things about her own family which she had not troubled to discover. So that was why Carreen mooned about, praying all the time. Well, she'd get over it. Lots of girls got over dead sweethearts, yes, dead husbands, too. She'd certainly gotten over

Charles. And she knew one girl in Atlanta who had been widowed three times by the war and was still able to take notice of men. She said as much to Will but he shook his head.

"Not Miss Carreen," he said with finality.

Will was pleasant to talk to because he had so little to say and yet was so understanding a listener. She told him about her problems of weeding and hoeing and planting, of fattening the hogs and breeding the cow, and he gave good advice for he had owned a small farm in south Georgia and two negroes. He knew his slaves were free now and the farm gone to weeds and seedling pines. His sister, his only relative, had moved to Texas with her husband years ago and he was alone in the world. Yet, none of these things seemed to bother him any more than the leg he had left in Virginia.

Yes, Will was a comfort to Scarlett after hard days when the negroes muttered and Suellen nagged and cried and Gerald asked too frequently where Ellen was. She could tell Will anything. She even told him of killing the Yankee and glowed with pride when he commented briefly: "Good work!"

Eventually all the family found their way to Will's room to air their troubles—even Mammy, who had at first been distant with him because he was not quality and had owned only two slaves.

When he was able to totter about the house, he turned his hands to weaving baskets of split oak and mending the furniture ruined by the Yankees. He was clever at whittling and Wade was constantly by his side, for he whittled out toys for him, the only toys the little boy had. With Will in the house, everyone felt safe in leaving Wade and the two babies while they went about their tasks, for he could care for them as deftly as Mammy and only Melly surpassed him at soothing the screaming black and white babies.

"You've been mighty good to me, Miss Scarlett," he said, "and me a stranger and nothin' to you all. I've caused you a heap of trouble and worry and if it's all the same to you, I'm goin' to stay here and help you all with the work till I've paid you back some for your trouble. I can't ever pay it all, 'cause there ain't no payment a man can give for his life."

So he stayed and, gradually, unobtrusively, a large part of the burden of Tara shifted from Scarlett's shoulders to the bony shoulders of Will Benteen.

It was September and time to pick the cotton. Will Benteen sat on the front steps at Scarlett's feet in the pleasant sunshine of the early autumn afternoon, and his flat voice went on and on languidly about the exorbitant costs of ginning the cotton at the new gin near Fayetteville. However, he had learned that day in Fayetteville that he could cut this expense a fourth by lending the horse and wagon for two weeks to the gin owner. He had delayed closing the bargain until he discussed it with Scarlett.

She looked at the lank figure leaning against the porch column, chewing a straw. Undoubtedly, as Mammy frequently declared, Will was something the Lord had provided and Scarlett often wondered how Tara could have lived through the last few months without him. He never had much to say, never displayed any energy, never seemed to take much interest in anything that went on about him, but he knew everything about everybody at Tara. And he did things. He did them silently, patiently and competently. Though he had only one leg, he could work faster than Pork. And he could get work out of Pork, which was, to Scarlett, a marvellous thing. When the cow had the colic and the horse fell ill with a mysterious ailment which threatened to remove him permanently from them, Will sat up nights with them and saved them. That he was a shrewd trader brought him Scarlett's respect, for he could ride out in the mornings with a bushel or two of apples, sweet potatoes and other vegetables and return with seeds, lengths of cloth, flour and other necessities which she knew she could never have acquired, good trader though she was.

He had gradually slipped into the status of a member of the family and slept on a cot in the little dressing-room off Gerald's room. He said nothing of leaving Tara, and Scarlett was careful not to question him, fearful that he might leave them. Sometimes, she thought that if he were anybody and had any gumption he would go home, even if he no longer had a home. But even with this thought, she would pray fervently that he would remain indefinitely. It was so convenient to have a man about the house.

She thought, too, that if Carreen had the sense of a mouse she would see that Will cared for her.

Scarlett would have been eternally grateful to Will, had he asked her for Carreen's hand. Of course, before the war, Will would certainly not have been an eligible suitor. He was not of the planter class at all, though he was not poor white. He was just plain Cracker, a small farmer, half-educated, prone to grammatical errors and ignorant of some of the finer manners the O'Haras were accustomed to in gentlemen. In fact, Scarlett wondered if he could be called a gentleman at all and decided that he couldn't. Melanie hotly defended him, saying that anyone who had Will's kind heart and thoughtfulness of others was of gentle birth. Scarlett knew that Ellen would have fainted at the thought of a daughter of hers marrying such a man, but now Scarlett had been by necessity forced too far away from Ellen's teachings to let that worry her. Men were scarce, girls had to marry someone and Tara had to have a man. But Carreen, deeper and deeper immersed in her prayer-book and every day losing more of her touch with the world of realities, treated Will as gently as a brother and took him as much for granted as she did Pork.

"If Carreen had any sense of gratitude to me for what I've done for her, she'd marry him and not let him get away from here," Scarlett thought indignantly. "But no, she must spend her time mooning about a silly boy who probably never gave her a serious thought."

So Will remained at Tara, for what reason she did not know, and she found his businesslike man-to-man attitude with her both pleasant and helpful. He was gravely deferential to the vague Gerald but it was to Scarlett that he turned as the real head of the house.

She gave her approval to the plan of hiring out the horse even though it meant the family would be without any means of transportation temporarily. Suellen would be especially grieved at this. Her greatest joy lay in going to Jonesboro or Fayetteville with Will when he drove over on business. Adorned in the assembled best of the family, she called on old friends, heard all the gossip of the County and felt herself again Miss O'Hara of Tara. Suellen never missed the opportunity to leave the plantation and give herself airs among people who did not know she weeded the garden and made beds.

"Miss Fine Airs will just have to do without gadding for two weeks," thought Scarlett, "and we'll have to put up with her nagging and her bawling."

Melanie joined them on the veranda, the baby in her arms, and spreading an old blanket on the floor, set little Beau down to crawl. Since Ashley's letter Melanie had divided her time between glowing, singing happiness and anxious longing. But happy or depressed, she was too thin, too white. She did her share of the work uncomplainingly but she was always ailing. Old Dr. Fontaine diagnosed her trouble as female complaint and concurred with Dr. Meade in saying she should never have had Beau. And he said frankly that another baby would kill her.

"When I was over to Fayetteville to-day," said Will, "I found somethin' right cute that I thought would interest you ladies and I brought it home." He fumbled in his back pants pocket and brought out the wallet of calico, stiffened with bark, which Carreen had made him. From it he drew a Confederate bill.

"If you think Confederate money is cute, Will, I certainly don't," said Scarlett shortly, for the very sight of Confederate money made her mad. "We've got three thousand dollars of it in Pa's trunk this minute, and Mammy's after me to let her paste it over the holes in the attic walls so the draught won't get her. And I think I'll do it. Then it'll be good for something."

"'Imperious Caesar, dead and turned to clay,'" said Melanie with a sad smile. "Don't do that, Scarlett. Keep it for Wade. He'll be proud of it some day."

"Well, I don't know nothin' about imperious Caesar," said Will patiently, "but what I've got is in line with what you've just said about Wade, Miss Melly. It's a poem, pasted on the back of this bill. I know Miss Scarlett ain't much on poems but I thought this might interest her."

He turned the bill over. On its back was pasted a strip of coarse brown wrapping paper, inscribed in pale home-made ink. Will cleared his throat and read slowly and with difficulty.

"The name is 'Lines on the Back of a Confederate Note'," he said.

"Representing nothing on God's earth now
  And naught in the waters below it—
As the pledge of a nation that's passed away

Keep it, dear friend, and show it.

"Show it to those who will lend an ear
  To the tale this trifle will tell
Of Liberty, born of patriots' dream,
  Of a storm-cradled nation that fell."

"Oh, how beautiful! How touching!" cried Melanie. "Scarlett, you mustn't give the money to Mammy to paste in the attic. It's more than paper—just like this poem said: 'The pledge of a nation that's passed away!'"

"Oh, Melly, don't be sentimental! Paper is paper and we've got little enough of it and I'm tired of hearing Mammy grumble about the cracks in the attic. I hope when Wade grows up I'll have plenty of greenbacks to give him instead of Confederate trash."

Will, who had been enticing little Beau across the blanket with the bill during this argument, looked up and, shading his eyes, glanced down the driveway.

"More company," he said, squinting in the sun. "Another soldier."

Scarlett followed his gaze and saw a familiar sight, a bearded man coming slowly up the avenue under the cedars, a man clad in a ragged mixture of blue and grey uniforms, head bowed tiredly, feet dragging slowly.

"I thought we were about through with soldiers," she said. "I hope this one isn't very hungry."

"He'll be hungry," said Will briefly.

Melanie rose.

801

"I'd better tell Dilcey to set an extra plate," she said, "and warn Mammy not to get the poor thing's clothes off his back too abruptly and—"

She stopped so suddenly that Scarlett turned to look at her. Melanie's thin hand was at her throat, clutching it as if it was torn with pain, and Scarlett could see the veins beneath the white skin throbbing swiftly. Her face went whiter and her brown eyes dilated enormously.

"She's going to faint," thought Scarlett, leaping to her feet and catching her arm.

But, in an instant, Melanie threw off her hand and was down the steps. Down the gravelled path she flew, skimming lightly as a bird, her faded skirts streaming behind her, her arms outstretched. Then Scarlett knew the truth, with the impact of a blow. She reeled back against an upright of the porch as the man lifted a face covered with a dirty blond beard and stopped still, looking toward the house as if he was too weary to take another step. Her heart leaped and stopped and then began racing, as Melly with incoherent cries threw herself into the dirty soldier's arms and his head bent down toward hers. With rapture, Scarlett took two running steps forward but was checked when Will's hand closed upon her skirt.

"Don't spoil it," he said quietly.

"Turn me loose, you fool! Turn me loose! It's Ashley!"

He did not relax his grip.

"After all, he's *her* husband, ain't he?" Will asked calmly and, looking down at him in a confusion of joy and impotent fury, Scarlett saw in the quiet depth of his eyes understanding and pity.

Other titles in the
Charnwood Library Series:

THE SILVER FOUNTAIN
by Michael Legat
Jean-Paul Fontaine came to London in 1870 with a burning ambition to be the proprietor of an exclusive restaurant.

THE CRUEL SEA
by Nicholas Monsarrat
A classic record of the heroic struggle to keep the Atlantic sea lanes open against the German U-boat menace.

BETWEEN TWO WORLDS
by Maisie Mosco
Alison Plantaine was born to the theatre. As a child she knew only the backstage world of provincial theatres. Then as a young girl she discovers with the shock of the unexpected, her Jewish heritage.

ANIMAL FARM
by George Orwell
The world famous satire upon dictatorship. The history of a revolution that went wrong.

THE FAMILY OF WOMEN
by Richard Peck
A panoramic story of women whose indomitable spirit brings them through the turbulent, events of the 1850's Gold Rush to the Europe of 1939.

SNAP SHOT
by A.J. Quinnell
On Sunday, 7th June 1981 an Israeli F.16 jet aircraft bombed and destroyed the Iraqi nuclear installation at Tammuz. This is the subject of this thriller.

THE BETSY
by Harold Robbins
Loren Hardeman rose to become the driving force behind Bethlehem Motors. At 91, still dynamic but confined to a wheelchair, he makes a last desperate gamble to head the entire industry.

SPELLBINDER
by Harold Robbins
Takes the reader into the world of the newest and most disturbing phenomenon in contemporary American life—the rise of religious leaders.

THE SEA CAVE
by Alan Scholefield
The naked body of a woman is found washed up on a wild stretch of African coastline. A young immigrant is drawn inexorably into the resulting murder enquiry.

HARRY'S GAME
by Gerald Seymour
The Prime Minister himself was ordering a special agent to be sent into the dangerous world of the I.R.A. gunman. And Harry was the choice.

IN HONOUR BOUND
by Gerald Seymour
A thriller about the forgotten war of the 1980s in Afghanistan.

RED FOX
by Gerald Seymour
Two unconnected events make headlines. A British businessman is kidnapped and Italy's most wanted woman terrorist is captured.

ACCEPTABLE LOSSES
by Irwin Shaw
A strange voice in the dead of night full of menace and loathing shatters the confidence of Roger Damon, a respected literary agent.

CROSSINGS
by Danielle Steel

Armand de Villiers, the French Ambassador, was crossing the Atlantic, with his American wife, Liane, when they meet Nick and Hilary Burnham, The spark between Nick and Liane is instantaneous . . .

GOING HOME
by Danielle Steel

Gillian and Chris pledged their love for always, their happiness seemed complete. Until a moment's infidelity broke the bond they shared . . .

ONCE IN A LIFETIME
by Danielle Steel

To the doctors the woman in the ambulance was just another casualty—more beautiful than most . . .

THURSTON HOUSE
by Danielle Steel

At forty four, Jeremiah, a mining baron was marrying for the first time. Camille was a captivating eighteen-year-old girl. But can money buy happiness, a family . . . or love?